"You Stupid, Bacon-Headed Boor!"

Catherine said furiously. "Do you really believe I'll become your mistress, just because it pleases you?"

A slow smile began to curve his mouth as Jason folded his arms across his chest and let his eyes roam lazily over her body, lingering on the heaving breasts that pressed proudly against the thin material of the blouse. Then sliding his gaze disturbingly down the curved length of her body, he realized she wore little or nothing underneath her outer clothes.

Abruptly he abandoned his lazy pose and with the ease of a striking panther dragged her roughly into his arms. She knew a momentary thrill of half fright, half excitement, before his mouth fastened on her. . . .

* * *

"One of the best romantic writers of our time."

—*Affaire de Coeur*

"Lets out all the stops. . . . A hero larger than life. . . . A heroine with glamour."

—*Publishers Weekly*

Also by Shirlee Busbee

A Heart for the Taking
Lovers Forever
Love Be Mine

Published by
Warner Books

Gypsy Lady

Shirlee Busbee

WARNER BOOKS

A Time Warner Company

WARNER BOOKS EDITION

Cover design by Diane Luger
Cover illustration by Franco Accornero
Hand Lettering by David Gatti

This Warner Book edition is published by arrangement with Avon Books.

Warner Books, Inc.
1271 Avenue of the Americas
New York, NY 10020

Visit out Web site at
www.warnerbooks.com

A Time Warner Company

Printed in the United States of America

First Warner Books Printing: June, 1999

10 9 8 7 6 5 4 3 2 1

Dedicated with affection and fervent thanks to my three great "helpers."

ROSEMARY ROGERS, who gave the incentive and who nagged and encouraged me every step of the way.

My husband, HOWARD, without whose understanding and confidence in me, not one word would have been written.

My father, J. G. EGAN, who volunteered, bless him, for the unrewarding task of making sense of my punctuation and who helped me so much during the final typing.

Gypsy Lady

PROLOGUE ONE

THE GOLDEN ARM BAND

September 1791

The day was hot, and after weeks in the saddle under the blazing sun, Jason Savage was glad their destination was in sight. They—Jason; his boyhood companion, a full-blooded Cherokee Indian named Blood Drinker; and Phillip Nolan, the actual leader of the trio—had been following the Red River, so named for the muddy red color it gained as it flowed across the rolling reddish clay plains of Texas. Now, deep in the Palo Duro Canyon, Jason heaved a sigh of relief as the first tepee of the Kwerha-rehnuh or Antelope Comanches came into view.

Frequently called Kwah-huher Kehuh by others of "The People," they were the most aloof and fierce of all the bands that held sway over the vast area known as Comancheria. The Kwerha-rehnuh rode the windswept ranges of the Llano Estacado and because of their very fierceness commanded the richest hunting grounds of all. They made their camps in the Palo Duro Canyon, and while actually being the smallest of the bands of Comanches, they went unmolested.

Like eagles, they would swoop down from the north, raiding as far south as Chihliahlia in Mexico and as far west as Santa Fe in the New Mexico territory, leaving a trail of burned-out ranches in their wake. There was no force in all of New Spain to control them—they were the great lords of the high plains, arrogant in their power and merciless in their dominion.

Like all of the bands of "The People," they owned immense herds of horses—a single warrior often owned two hundred and fifty horses, while a war chief might have up to fifteen hundred animals in his herd. The Comanches were the most skillful at horse stealing and more notably, of all the Plains Indians, were the only successful horse breeders. Consequently most other tribes traded actively with them for their horses.

The huge horse herds of the Kwerha-rehnuh were what had brought the three men so far into Comancheria. They had done it before. Once Nolan had lived with this particular band for two years, so they knew him well. Still they approached cautiously, Nolan in the lead making signs that they came to trade.

A bit uneasily, Jason kept his hand tight on the rifle carried handily across his saddlebow. The time for trouble was now, for once the Comanches agreed to talk trades, they would not break the truce with their visitors. Nolan and one of the warriors conversed in sign language, and a moment later, Jason relaxed a little when Nolan murmured out of the side of his mouth, "They're willing!"

The Indian camp was scattered along the river, and their tepees could be clearly seen through the breaks in the cottonwoods and willows that lined the river's sandy banks. The three visitors were given a tepee in the middle of this encampment. Jason never failed to marvel at the completely careless attitude of the Comanches towards fortification. The camp was strung out all along the river; if attacked, it would have been impossible to defend—but then, who in their right minds would *dare* such a thing!

Smiling at his thoughts, Jason helped Blood Drinker unload their pack horses and store, inside the huge buffalo-hide tepee, the goods they had brought to trade.

The women eyed these tall strangers curiously, and looking at the short, squat women with their cropped, uncombed hair, Jason was glad "The People" did not share their women with white men! He would have hated to insult some war chief by refusing his extremely odorous wife; except for certain purification ceremonies, the Comanches never washed.

Phillip Nolan had gone immediately to reopen acquaintances with those who knew him, and he looked decidedly cheerful when he returned. He was a big man with black hair and blue eyes. Standing six feet, four inches, he possessed the shoulders to go with his height. Five years or so older than Jason, he had lived a hard, exciting life, and the outrageous stories and scandalous tales that surrounded him were legion. Jason, barely eighteen and full of the quest for adventure, had a case of hero worship that he would never outgrow—there was nothing that Nolan could do that wasn't perfectly magnificent to Jason.

Blood Drinker, even in those days, had taken it upon himself to be Jason's shadow, and with certain reservations, he had watched aloofly the ripening friendship between the white men. But Jason by his very nature had that magical power to bind men to him, so the bond between Jason and Phillip Nolan was as strong as the one between Jason and Blood Drinker. And because the same wildness that drove Jason was in his veins too, Blood Drinker had become the third member of this trio that came to trade with the Comanches.

Inside the relative privacy of the tepee, Nolan said, "We should have no trouble striking a good bargain, and they are very eager to trade. A word of warning, though. Don't wager on any horse races. They're very clever at having horses that look like nothing and run like the winds—fleecing strangers is a favorite pastime."

They followed Nolan's advice, and the visit passed without incident until the morning they were preparing to leave.

They had traded all their steel knives, and axes, as well as some guns and quite a few mirrors—the warriors were fascinated by them—for fifty carefully selected horses.

The problem arose when Quanah, a warrior from a returning hunting party, demanded payment for a spotted pony he claimed was his. Nolan explained patiently that he had bought the animal from Nokoni, one of the war chiefs. Dissatisfied with Nolan's answer, Quanah became belligerent, so Nolan tactfully suggested that together they should go see Nokoni and resolve the question of ownership. Unfortunately both Comanches continued to claim the ownership of the disputed horse. Diplomatically Nolan asserted that he had no further interest in the horse. He returned the animal and said, in effect, that the two angry warriors could settle it themselves.

From a distance, Jason and Blood Drinker had closely watched the exchange, and Nolan's expression as he returned told them things were not well. "We'd better get out of here, quick! I don't like the looks of what's happening, and the sooner we're out of sight the better!"

The three men mounted their horses, and herding the newly purchased horses before them, they rode out of the camp.

Nolan was worried. If the loser of the unexpected argument decided to vent his spleen on the departed white men, all he had to do was cry for volunteers, and there would be a pack of murderous Comanches right on their heels. It could come to nothing, but they had better be prepared.

There was no need to speak his uneasy thoughts, for Jason and Blood Drinker were well versed in sensing danger, and instinctively, all three men scanned the barren canyon walls that rose a thousand feet or more in the air. With practiced eyes, they searched the incredible spires and pinnacles for some place of concealment or a niche that would offer them some protection, hopefully one which could be defended. The horses, regretfully would have to be conceded to the Comanches unless they were tremendously lucky—there would be no way to escape with their lives and the horses. It was against his nature to give in so tamely, and giving a shout, Jason pointed out a widening crack in the seemingly endless walls.

The crack branched off to their left, and leaving Nolan and Blood Drinker in control of the horses, Jason guided his own animal into the space in the canyon walls. It was barely wide enough for two horses. As he rode down this split in the walls, the sky above him was only a thin strip of blue, and he felt a thump of excitement when he discovered it led to another canyon, a considerably smaller canyon. With rising optimism, he turned his horse and quickly rejoined the others.

Minutes later, the Indian ponies were herded ruthlessly down the narrow passageway, and once again the area was given a lightning assessment. The pass was defensible, but this small canyon with its yellow, sandy floor littered only with gray-green sagebrush and mesquite, could become a deathtrap. So they continued to zigzag their way through what seemed like a maze of endless canyons that widened and then narrowed to almost nothing, as they steadily pushed their way southeastward, always with a wary eye thrown over their shoulders.

By late afternoon, they were fairly certain that whatever the outcome of the disputed horse, the loser would not be expressing his dissatisfaction by raiding the white men who had inadvertently been the cause of the argument. Unfortunately, in their desire to leave a trail as confusing and hard to track as possible, the three men had managed to lose themselves. The situation wasn't desperate yet, for all three were veterans of the trackless expanses through which they traveled, and at present they had plenty of food and water for themselves. But water for their horses was definitely a pressing need.

It was the search for that precious commodity that led Jason to check out a tiny passage. It was very narrow; his legs brushed the sides of the rock and limestone walls when he spurred his horse down the opening that was barely noticeable behind huge, fallen boulders. It was cool and dark between the canyon walls as he explored this queer, blade-thin slice in the unending sea of rocks and canyons, and with a sense of satisfaction, he noticed the dampness that seemed to permeate the area. The crevice appeared to snake its way between the majestic canyons for miles, and lured on by the increasing signs of moisture—little beads of wetness on the walls—he continued. Eventually reaching a place where water oozed out of the encroaching walls, he knew there must be a spring hidden within the rocky barrier that encased him.

Abruptly, the passage ended, and Jason found himself overlooking a small doll-like valley, the floor covered with lush buffalo grass and dotted with small blue lakes where willows and cottonwoods grew greenly upwards. Astonished at such an oasis hidden deep within this dry desertlike tract of canyons and cliffs, he stared, unable to believe his eyes. But even more startling sights awaited him as his bemused gaze scanned the incredible scene before him, and he stiffened suddenly in amazement. He saw row upon row of pueblos carved out of the rock walls and huddled under the overhanging cliffs. The dwellings appeared to cling lovingly next to the perpendicular walls of the encircling canyon. His disbelief growing, Jason's gaze was drawn irresistibly to the huge, soaring pyramid that rose loftily high above the canyon floor.

His eyes fastened on the endless steps leading upwards to the massive platform that must command a breathtaking view from its towering height. After a dumbstruck moment, he dazedly guided his horse down the steeply sloping wall from which he had emerged and cautiously approached the canyon floor.

That he was being extremely foolish never occurred to him. Mesmerized, he slowly rode towards the houses that effortlessly roosted like eagles against the vertical orange and yellow walls that towered hundreds of feet above them.

There was a narrow, winding track that led upwards to the first row of houses, and Jason's gaze swept the empty-eyed dwellings for any sign of life. They appeared deserted.

Belatedly aware of the risk he was running, he explored no further. Making a hasty appraisal of the box canyon, he spurred his horse back towards the barely discernible opening through which he had come. He returned to the outer world, as it seemed to him just then, and shared his discovery with Nolan and Blood Drinker.

It would be dark in less than three hours, and after a hurried discussion they decided to camp in Jason's newly discovered canyon. There was some trouble forcing the horses into the narrow channel, but finally, with Jason in the lead pulling one of the Indian ponies behind him, they were able to herd the recalcitrant horses in single file through the twisting passage.

Once again back in the canyon, Jason dismounted and watched the horses spill from the opening and race down to the deeply grassed floor. Expectantly he waited for Blood Drinker and Nolan, and the expressions on their faces when they caught sight of the valley made him smile with real enjoyment.

"I told you it's unbelievable!" he said. "Have you ever seen the like?"

Nolan, his blue eyes riveted on the great pyramid, nodded absentmindedly. His voice blank, he said, "In Mexico, the Aztecs built such pyramids for temples."

"Do you think—?" Jason asked excitedly, unable to complete the sentence, his young face betraying the thrill he felt at Nolan's matter-of-fact words.

Nolan shot him an affectionate look. "I've never heard of any Aztecs this far north, but its not impossible. When the conquistadors conquered Tenochtitlán—Mexico City to you—many of the Aztecs fled. And there's nothing to prove that some of them didn't flee this far."

Blood Drinker eyed the pyramid uneasily. A feeling of brooding evil feathered across his skin, and almost as if he knew the purpose for the high platform that crowned the stone edifice, he muttered, "This is not a good place. It is cursed!"

But Nolan and Jason paid him no heed, and with lagging steps Blood Drinker followed them as they slid, leading their horses to the canyon floor. He was not afraid, but being sensitive to things beyond the ken of normal man, he disliked intensely the currents of evil that blew softly over his body.

It grew dark too quickly for them to explore very far that night. With Jason in the lead, the two white men had to content themselves with a hasty glance at the empty interiors of the first row of the rock-hewn dwellings. Blood Drinker refused to join them. "You will find nothing there," he stated cryptically. "The ones who carved in the rock are gone for countless moons."

On the following day, loath to leave without further exploration, Jason and Nolan, Blood Drinker following disdainfully behind, combed the multilevel dwellings, finding only broken pottery bowls and rotted woven mats that crumbled when touched. The Cherokee's words of the night before had proven true. Seated dispiritedly on the flat roof of the highest building and shaded by the overhanging cliffs, Jason said disgustedly, "What a disappointment! No clue as to where they came from nor why they left."

Reflectively, Nolan said, "Who knows, perhaps word of further Spanish penetration reached them, and they left for another place." He shrugged his shoulders. "Disease or a bad year with crops could have driven them in search of another haven. Or their high priests might have commanded they leave—who knows?"

Dissatisfied, Jason asked, "Are you certain they were Aztecs?"

"I'm by no means an expert, but"—Nolan nodded in the direction of the pyramid—"that leads me to believe they were. Shall we take a closer look?"

His waning enthusiasm fired anew, Jason nodded eagerly. Blood Drinker, disinclined to go with them, at first, remained where he was, leaning against the coolness of the solid rock wall behind him. But then watching the two figures grow smaller, he reluctantly made his way to the canyon floor, and with the hair on the back of his neck rising in warning, he unwillingly approached the awesome stone pyramid.

It was a long way to the top, and with every step Blood Drinker felt the sense of dark evil increase. Reaching the top, he discovered Jason and Nolan poking around inside a small stone structure that Nolan said was their temple for whatever god they worshiped. But Blood Drinker's gaze was captured by a stone altar, its surface marred with dark brownish stains, and a shudder of revulsion shook him.

Perhaps feeling some of the horror that affected his companion, Jason looked at him suddenly and asked sharply, "Blood Drinker?"

But the Indian was in the grip of some queer force, and the present faded—he was seeing not Jason and Nolan but the black-garbed high priests, their hair matted with sacrificial blood, their ears ragged from self-inflicted cuts for blood offerings to the gods, and their cruel faces painted with wide, black bands across their eyes and mouths. The stone altar was no longer bare, and as if from a distance, Blood Drinker stared at the scene before him, unable to look away: a tall, finely formed youth was stretched across the altar held by four grotesque priests; a fifth priest, dressed in red, his eyes gleaming with anticipation, plunged the high-held, sacrificial knife deep into the chest of the prostrate young man, and from the gaping hole, tore out the still warm and beating heart, offering it to the sun.

Blood Drinker's face was drained of all color, and shaking he stumbled blindly away, halted only by Jason's troubled voice.

"What is it?"

Taking a deep, shuddering breath, Blood Drinker spoke

so low that Jason could barely hear the words. "This is an evil place. To die in battle or combat is honorable. But to be slain like a pig for a god that loves only blood is unspeakable!"

He would say no more, and withdrawing into himself for the balance of the day, he remained aloof from the others. He slept badly that night, his dreams haunted by dreadful scenes of brutality and wretchedness. Sunrise found him standing alone staring broodingly across at the stone pyramid. He was again on the highest dwelling of the cliff houses and finding some solace there, when suddenly, as if drawn against his will, he walked with lagging steps over to the stone wall. Guided by a knowledge beyond him, his fingers unerringly probed the seemingly solid stone mass. Instantly, a portion of the wall seemed to fall away, and he was left staring at the black hole that led into the interior of the canyon wall. Fighting the malevolent influence that pulled at him, he remained rooted to the spot until Jason's voice behind him broke the spell that gripped him.

Relief obvious in his voice, he turned and pleaded, "Let us leave this place."

Jason, always sensitive to Blood Drinker's emotions, would have done so if Nolan, his eyes bright with adventure, hadn't said, "Nonsense! Now that you have discovered a way into the cliff, we'd be fools *not* to explore it!"

Drawn and yet repelled, Blood Drinker gave in to Nolan's adjurations. Torches held aloft, the three men stepped into the stone cavern. The cavern had a high, vaulted ceiling and appeared to be almost circular in shape. It was small in size. Through an arched, rockhewn doorway, they could see another cavern.

"An antechamber, perhaps?" mused Jason, and it was he who walked first through the doorway. He stopped so suddenly that Nolan, following closely on his heels, bumped into him. And after seeing what held Jason's gaze, he remained frozen also. Blood Drinker was the last, but he knew what they would find.

A long ledge was carved from the rock, and placed within it sat a massive, scowling, teeth-bared statue. The statue was hideous. A deer symbol was carved on its forehead, and in a queer contrast, two stone hummingbirds rested on its cuffs. The statue was lavishly decorated with ornaments of gold, silver, pearls, and turquoise. A long-unused incense burner sat nearby, as did several artifacts of gold and silver, neatly arranged. But after that first startled glance, what held their attention was the small stone altar in front of the statue, the bones of it's last victim undisturbed through the centuries.

Gingerly, the two white men drew closer, and without thinking, Jason reached down and picked up a jagged blade made of obsidian, its handle adorned with a turquoise mosaic. He flinched when he touched it, and as if its purpose communicated itself to him, he gave a muttered expletive and threw it violently in the corner.

The silence was eerie, and they were disinclined to disturb the statue or to touch any of the beaten gold and silver objects that lined the ledge. Jason backed away incautiously, and his retreating body brushed the arm of the skeleton. The bones fell apart, and Jason watched, almost hypnotized, as the gold and emerald band that had once encircled flesh and bones, fell and rolled across the floor, stopping practically at his feet. Unable to help himself, he picked it up and whispered, "This I shall take, but nothing else."

Not as affected as the two younger men, Nolan laughed and carelessly removed the gold band's matching twin from the other bony arm. "Well, I'll take one, too. If I had a way of taking it all, I have to confess I wouldn't hesitate."

Repulsed by the idea, Jason stared at him. "I'll not help you," he said thickly, and Nolan's face changed instantly.

"It bothers you two that much?" he asked incredulously.

Simultaneously, both heads nodded. Shrugging indifferently, Nolan said, "Well, as we have no way of transporting the stuff, the question doesn't arise—today." Quizzically he asked, "Do you mind if I come back for it someday? I'd be willing to split it evenly with you." But again, both heads shook a vehement denial.

"You can have it all," Jason stated positively. Then he grinned. "Except this!" and he held up the gold and emerald band.

Blood Drinker wanted nothing, his only wish being that they put as much distance between themselves and this place as possible. Taking a long, last look back, Blood Drinker strode out of the cavern into the sunlight, unable to endure the smothering closeness of the stone walls, and Jason followed barely two steps behind him.

Nolan remained a few minutes longer, slightly amused and amazed at their reactions. But then, he thought, they were very young yet, and Jason had a large fortune behind him—not a hard man like himself who lived by his wits and whose parentage was clothed in mystery. Ah well, he decided prosaically, they might change their minds. There was enough to split three ways and still make each man independently wealthy. If they persisted in their odd refusal—well, who knew?

PROLOGUE TWO

THE HOMECOMING

Cornwall, England, October 1796

The sky was overcast. It was a black, forbidding, starless night. A silver crescent moon remained hidden behind heavy racing clouds, and a cold, icy wind blew inland from the English Channel, snarling its fury against the rocky cliffs and coves of the Cornwall coast.

Hidden among the tumbled ruins of an old Norman castle that clung tenaciously to a clifftop lay a girl, her slender body straining forward. She was peering cautiously downward, watching with eager interest the activity on the beach below, where shadowy figures were hurriedly stowing wooden boxes and chests in a narrow cave almost directly under her perch. Behind her stood a man, small and wiry, whose dark hair and swarthy complexion betrayed his gypsy blood. From his protective stance and the way he regarded the girl, it was apparent they had come together—Tamara to watch the smugglers and Manuel to watch over Tamara.

A feeling of adventure was growing within her, and Tamara wiggled restlessly, trying to find a more comfortable position on the hard rocks. A wistful sigh escaped her—how she wished she was on the beach! Adam, her brother, was down there in the midst of it all, and it seemed grossly unfair to her that he should be having such an adventure while she was relegated to waiting calmly in the background. Glancing back at her companion, she coaxed, "Manuel, couldn't we go down? Just to see if they've brought anything besides brandy and silk? Please?"

Manuel shook his head a decisive no, and giving an exasperated snort, Tamara turned back to watch the smugglers. Adam and Manuel had been unfair, she decided mutinously, not to have agreed with her suggestion that she dress like a boy and participate—especially since tonight's mission had been her idea in the first place! The more she thought about it, the further her lip stuck out in a stubborn curve. Angrily she kicked one foot against a rock, and the movement dislodged a tiny shower of pebbles and stones. She ignored Manuel's curt whisper for silence. It wasn't fair, she thought. Just because she was only twelve to Adam's fifteen was no reason for him to have all the excitement.

Moodily Tamara stared out at the faint shape of the French packet *Marianne,* anchored just beyond the white crested breakers that pounded onto the beach. The ship rode higher and higher on the choppy waves as the contraband cargo was lifted from beneath her decks and loaded into the small fishing boats that rapidly ferried the smuggled goods to shore. Soon, in a matter of minutes, the ship would sail quietly out of this protected cove, and her crew, rich in English gold, would guide the ship across the channel back to France.

A gust of wind made Tamara clutch her ragged shawl tighter, and she sighed as the packet began moving slowly out towards the open sea. She *could* have passed for a boy, and drat the other two for preventing her. She spared a guilty thought for Reina's certain angry reaction if this evening's escapade was discovered. The old gypsy woman was the nearest thing to a mother that she and Adam had ever known, and if Reina found out that her son Manuel had helped them disobey her express command to refrain from contact with the smugglers, she would skin them alive!

Manuel, too, was thinking of Reina, and he grew restless and uneasy, knowing that his mother would be doubly furious if she learned that he had allowed Tamara, enthusiastically assisted by Adam, to talk him into tonight's prank. Now, seeing that the activity on the beach had slackened and prodded by the unpleasant thought of Reina's anger, he said firmly to Tamara, "Adam should be here any moment, and it's high time that we left. You wait for him while I go get the horses, and don't argue with me! If anyone finds out about tonight, there'll be the very devil to pay."

Tamara's face was decidedly regretful as she watched Manuel make his way to where the horses were tethered. After he vanished around the corner of the ruined castle, she switched her gaze back once more to the now deserted beach. The smugglers had completed tonight's run, and the empty cove seemed to reproach her for not having been more bold and for having lost her chance for real adventure.

Adam's sudden appearance around one of the black boulders startled her, and she gave a faint cry of surprise. His bright blue eyes lighting up with laughter, he grinned at her, waving two gold guineas under her nose. "Not a bad night's wage for helping to stow a few bits of cargo, wouldn't you say? But you would never have been able to keep up, little sister, and if you had screeched like you did just now, our ruse would have been discovered in a moment."

"I did not screech!" she retorted hotly. "You took me unawares, creeping up like that."

Adam hooted with disbelief, and they promptly fell into a good-natured wrangle that ended only when Manuel reappeared leading the three horses. For a second he regarded them, thinking that they were, indeed, as Reina had begun to harp lately, growing up. Tamara was still a child, but the slight budding of her slender body gave the hint that she was fast leaving her babyhood years behind. Adam, however, already stood nearly six feet tall, with a pair of nicely filled-out shoulders that made more than one Romany girl stare at him with admiration. His hair, gypsy black, was in almost direct contrast to the reckless blue of his eyes, and like his sister, he had a charming smile that blinded.

There existed little physical resemblance between the children, but as they had been fathered by different men and were actually only half brother and sister, it was not surprising that they bore little resemblance to each other. In fact, the only common feature they shared beyond their delightful smile was the color of their hair, and even then, Tamara's held a blue blackness that Adam's lacked. It was in the eyes, though, that the greatest difference lay—Tamara's were almost almond-shaped and an incredible clear shade of violet, fringed by the thickest, blackest lashes Manuel had ever seen. Little Tamara, he decided sagely, was certainly going to break some hearts one day.

Absently he shook his head, thinking of the changes the years would bring and wondering if the children's real history would ever be revealed. But that was up to Reina, he thought hastily. He wasn't about to dance on the air at the end of a rope by talking about events best forgotten—even if Reina had lately begun to mutter otherwise.

The dispute between Adam and Tamara ended as it usually did with Adam affectionately throwing his arms around his sister and laughing, "Now, now, Kate, stop it! You win—I did creep up behind you."

Manuel's lips thinned at the words. No matter how many times Adam had been scolded and punished and warned not to, he persisted in calling his sister, Kate. Even now, in memory, Manuel could see him, a bewildered five-year-old, his blue eyes cloudy with confusion crying, "She is *not* Tamara—she's *Kate!*"

Bless the devil that no one questioned that oddity! Manuel thought grimly and said, "Lower your voices, you two. There could be revenue agents about, and we don't need them finding us here."

Instantly Adam and Tamara fell silent and walked quickly

over to him. He handed them the reins to their horses, and with lithe grace they both swung up onto the bare backs of the animals. Manuel was a little in front of them, looking in their direction and preparing to mount his own horse, when the sudden, dismayed expression on Tamara's face made him whirl around.

His face blanched; there before them, her eyes snapping with fury, her thin shoulders covered with a crimson shawl as ragged as Tamara's, stood Reina. That she was angry was very apparent—it vibrated from her, and Manuel, who was forty years old, suddenly felt like a frightened child.

A deathly quiet descended, and Reina let them simmer in it as she surveyed the three guilty faces. "So," she said at last, "this is how you spend your evenings."

Manuel swallowed. "Now, Reina," he began, but she cut him off with a furious movement of her hand.

"You lumping maggot! Silence! You shall answer to me later. And you"—her eyes were hard and without the usual glimmer of affection in their depths as they swept over Adam and Tamara—"shall regret this evening's work for a long time to come."

Instinctively the two huddled together. They had seen Reina angry before and often at them, but never like this. There was something faintly ominous in her words, and a shiver of unease trickled down Tamara's spine. Adam made a halfhearted attempt to wheedle Reina out of her current fury, but it fell flat, and after she had given them the rough side of her tongue, she ordered them to return to the gypsy camp. Chastened and apprehensive, they threw Manuel a glance of commiseration and fled, leaving him to face the full brunt of his mother's wrath.

And face it he did. Reina gave him such a tongue-lashing that when at last she subsided, he was nearly limp. She glared at him and then spun on her heels and began marching the mile or so to where they were camped. Meekly, leading his horse, Manuel walked by his mother's side. He stole a glance at her set features. Seeing that the worst of her hot anger had abated, he asked somberly, "What do you intend to do? Beat them? Adam is no longer a child, he would not submit to it, nor will he allow you to do the same to Tamara. So how will you punish them?"

His words hung in the air, and Reina seemed to shrivel and grow older before his eyes. She gave a heavy sigh, and Manuel's conscience bothered him. He had been as much at fault tonight as the two young ones—more so, because he knew better. He should have known Reina would discover them—she always did. Looking at her worn features, he realized that Reina was growing old. Too old, he thought, to control a lively pair like Adam and Tamara. It was no use telling himself that he should take them in hand—no one knew better than he that he was like wax in their eager young hands, particularly Tamara's, the little minx.

They continued on in silence, and Manuel had come to the conclusion that Reina was ignoring his earlier question when she said suddenly. "I don't intend to punish them." And then she added grimly, "Although what I have decided upon may seem to them like the vilest possible punishment I could inflict."

Worried and slightly mystified, Manuel stared at her, but she would say no more. And after a moment, he shocked himself by blurting out, "We did wrong in stealing them, Reina. We should never have allowed ourselves to be tempted by that man's gold."

"Manuel, we've been over this a dozen times in the past ten years," she said tiredly. "Yes, we were wrong to take them, but at least we didn't murder them as ordered. What real harm have we done? Besides, if we hadn't agreed to do it, the money would only have been given to someone else—someone who wouldn't have hesitated to slit their throats and throw the bodies down a well. Maybe we were wrong—but we needed the gold badly, and Adam and Tamara have been happy. I doubt if they even remember."

"I don't know," Manuel mused. "Sometimes I think Adam does—especially since we've started coming back to this area these last few years. Tamara wouldn't, she was only a baby, barely two years old. I've always wondered why he wanted both children taken. Tamara was the only one who was a threat. Why, Adam, too?"

Reina shot him a derisive look. "He was taking no chances on the boy inheriting. A stepson would have done as well if there were no other heirs."

Manuel agreed but added stubbornly, "It still wasn't good what we did."

"Oh, hush!" she said angrily. "Don't drivel on about good or bad. There are no such things. It is merely in how you look at things. We took them, and we've cared for them. Now is not the time for you to turn squeamish."

Manuel subsided, and there was no more conversation between them. They reached the cluster of caravans and shabby tents that comprised the settlement and parted, Manuel going to take care of his horse and Reina entering a large tent near the center of the camp.

Tamara was curled on her pallet on the ground. Warily she watched Reina as the gypsy woman prepared for bed. It was only when Reina had laid herself down that Tamara was able to relax and try to sleep. But she slept badly and woke the next morning with a feeling of impending doom. Reina was withdrawn and aloof, as if her displeasure with them had not yet abated. Even Adam's persistent attempts to make the old woman smile met with no response other than a preoccupied stare. He made a rueful grimace at Tamara as they sat on the ground near one of the blazing fires eating their breakfast of warm broth and black bread.

"What do you think she means to do?" Tamara asked softly, her violet eyes wide and anxious, and her bottom lip showing a tendency to tremble. She did not like to cause Reina pain and she was, at the moment, feeling very guilty. Tomorrow she would laugh, but right now her spirit was unusually subdued. Adam gave her a quick hug, and it was thus that Reina found them. She stared at them a long second, then asked coldly, "Have you finished?"

As the two heads nodded their answer, she grunted and said, "Good! Come with me!"

Warily Tamara and Adam followed her away from the camp and down a narrow dirt road. It was well known that this winding path led to the earl of Mount's estate, but they wondered what Reina intended to do. Gypsies were not welcomed at the homes of the respectable, especially not at the elegant houses of the wealthy and aristocratic members of English society. And the house, appearing at the end of a tree-lined lane, was imposing enough to give most people pause.

Made of weathered gray stone, it was built on massive lines. Flanked as it was by two ivy-covered turrets, it was not surprising that Mountacre was frequently referred to as "the castle." It certainly appeared like one to Adam and Tamara as they followed timidly in Reina's wake, skirting the neatly kept lawns and meticulously tended flowers that bordered the house.

Expecting to be led around to the back of the house, they were nearly dumbfounded when Reina purposefully strode up the wide front steps and lifted the polished brass knocker.

A very correct, uniformed butler opened the door at Reina's imperious rap. For a moment he stared at them in lofty disdain. Then as the full import hit him—that these nasty, dirty creatures that camped brazenly in the meadow were actually demanding entrance—he took an involuntary step backwards. Outraged by such a shameless action, he was about to slam the door in their faces when by chance his gaze fell upon Tamara's interested face, and a gasp of astonishment escaped him.

Seeing his reaction and guessing its cause, Reina asked dryly, "Now will you take us to the earl?"

He still might have turned them away, but fate in the guise of the earl himself took a hand. It was his voice calling irritably, "Who is it, Bekins? For God's sake don't keep them standing in the doorway," that made the butler usher the three into the hall.

Adam and Tamara stood very close to one another, looking curiously about them at the sumptuous house. Golden framed mirrors lined the walls, a crystal chandelier hung overhead, and beneath their feet the white marble floor glistened like newly fallen snow. Standing at the base of a gracefully curving staircase was a very fashionably attired gentleman and lady. A younger man, with a sardonic face, was crossing the hall to join them, but at the sight of the gypsies, he stopped suddenly, a flash of what could have been fear flickering in his cold gray eyes. The two on the staircase remained motionless. The woman's hand was resting on the man's sleeve and it appeared that they had just descended and were on their way into one of the other rooms.

The older man, his face wrinkled attractively with age and his blue-black hair liberally sprinkled with silver could only be the earl of Mount, Lord Tremayne. The woman, looking delightful in a soft muslin gown of rosepink, although much younger than he, was obviously his wife, the Lady Tremayne. The younger man was apparently either a guest or a relative.

Tamara regarded them with only tepid interest, but as the earl's face took on a scowl of displeasure at the sight of the unkempt trio cluttering up his hallway, her own small features unconsciously mimicked his and she glowered back fiercely.

But Adam suffered a shock at the vision of the slender, blue-eyed woman at the earl's side. Prompted by a feeling of familiarity, he took a hesitant step forward, frowning in puzzlement. And Lady Tremayne, staring at him like one transfixed, whitened visibly, her hand clutching frantically at her husband's sleeve.

The earl glanced at her in surprise, but her gaze was swinging in agonizing disbelief from the tall youth in front of her to the tangled-haired girl standing next to him. His eyes followed the direction of his wife's, and his expression became one of frank incredulity when he looked fully at the two children.

"What the devil . . ." he exclaimed. Then his voice trailed off into silence as he scrutinized Tamara. His breath caught painfully in his throat as Tamara's violet eyes plunged into his, eyes as violet as his own. Like one in a daze he stared into those tilted eyes and dimly, as if from a great distance, he heard the old woman say, "Here is your daughter Catherine, m'lord, who we have named Tamara. And your stepson, Adam. They have grown annoying, and I am too old to fight with the tantrums of the young. Take them!"

PART ONE

BEAU SAVAGE

Winter 1802–1803

1

Oblivious to the woman who lay sleeping by his side, Jason Savage crossed his hands behind his head and stared up at the rough-hewn wooden beams above him, his thoughts far away from this, the best room the Inn of the White Horse had to offer.

Davalos. He said the name softly to himself, feeling again the shock of recognition he had felt earlier this evening when he had glanced up and there, just beyond the main room of the inn, he had seen his one-time boyhood friend. That Davalos had not expected to see Jason was obvious from the start he gave, his Spanish black eyes widening in dismayed surprise, and the haste with which he had plunged outside. Jason had risen to follow him, still not quite able to believe that it was indeed Blas Davalos. After all, Virginia was a long way from Spanish New Orleans, and Davalos was an officer in the Spanish army—that fact alone should have precluded his sudden appearance in American Virginia.

Frowning in the darkness of the room, Jason admitted it was an accident that he had decided to stay overnight at the inn instead of returning to Greenwood, his father's estate, this evening. His horse had thrown a shoe and Annie, the woman who lay at his side had proved to be as accommodating as he remembered. Dusk had been falling by the time the new shoe was in place and rather than face the fifteen mile journey in the cold and dark to his father's home, he had sent a message on to his father that he would be delayed and would not arrive until morning. And there was the knowledge that Annie was waiting for him. So, if things had been different, he would not have been at the inn and would not have seen Davalos.

Knowing sleep was impossible, Jason rose from the warm quilts of the bed and with that jungle-cat grace peculiarly his own, he stalked naked to the wooden-shuttered window. Undaunted by the chill of the night air, he threw open the shutters and leaned his arms on the sill, staring out at the landscape.

The moonlight filtering in made him an arresting study of silver and black. His black hair appeared silver in the deceiving rays of the moon; the green of his eyes was shuttered and dark; his nose, the high cheek bones and the frankly sensuous mouth were bathed in silver; his chin and the hollows of his cheeks were in stark black, making his face at once handsome and yet unyielding and harsh in the waning moonlight. The corded muscles of his arms stood out, the moonlight caressing the gold and emerald band that encircled one arm, and the fine black hair of his chest stirred lightly as a faint breeze blew in from outside.

Jason, lost in his thoughts, was unaware of the coolness that swept into the room. Still frowning, he wondered again of Davalos's presence. It could have been coincidence, he thought slowly, but somehow he doubted it. There was some sixth sense that warned him of danger, and he wondered suddenly, bleakly, if Nolan had experienced the same feeling of unease before he had left on that last fatal trip to the Palo Duro Canyon. For a moment Jason's finely cut mouth twisted in half-healed pain as he remembered that Nolan was dead—dead by Davalos's hand.

Oh, Jesus, he thought angrily, you fool, let it be. Nolan was a man, and he'd known the risks. But stubbornly, Jason's mind wouldn't let it rest, seeming to take perverse delight in reminding him of the ugly incident, almost enjoying the hurt it created.

Nolan was dead—as were all the men who had accompanied him on the journey, except one. And that one survivor had recently returned to tell a tale of betrayal and horror—a tale that was vehemently denied by the Spanish government in New Orleans. But Jason believed it—he knew Davalos and knew what Davalos was capable of.

Jason's fist clenched, and he cursed the fate that had arranged that he be gone from the country when Nolan had left New Orleans. But it did him little good—he was honest enough to admit that he and Blood Drinker would not have been part of Nolan's expedition under any circumstance. And even if he had been in New Orleans, he would not have known soon enough that Davalos had cleverly convinced the governor that Nolan was actually a spy, that Nolan meant trouble; nor would he have known when Davalos and his troop of hardened soldiers had departed to stop, at all cost, the American Nolan's further penetration into Spanish territory.

Davalos knew that Nolan was Jason's good friend—and that would have given Davalos reason enough to hate the man. Even so, Jason could not convince himself that it had been merely to get back at himself that Davalos had gone after Nolan. There had to be another reason. Unconsciously, his hand touched the gold and emerald band on his arm.

Nolan had worn the twin and though Nolan's body and personal effects had been returned, there had been no gold band. For a minute Jason considered that fact. Davalos was greedy, and the lone survivor had stated that Nolan had been alive when they had surrendered to the Spanish troop. The official report claimed that Nolan had been killed resisting, but Jason's informant had shaken his head violently at this, saying that no one had been killed in the exchange of shots and that Nolan had agreed to a surrender only after Davalos had offered them safe conduct to the border. Jason smiled grimly in the moonlight. Davalos had broken his word. The men had been taken and tortured, and the last time the lone survivor had seen Nolan he was heavily manacled and chained, being led away for further questioning by Davalos—Davalos alone.

Jason sighed, his face clearly unhappy. Upon his return to New Orleans, he learned that Davalos had been the one to go after Nolan and for that reason only, he had challenged Davalos to a duel. But, unfortunately, Jason remembered Davalos when they had been friends, and so when the moment came to thrust his sword deep into Davalos, he stayed his hand and instead scarred him for life—his blade slicing an ugly stroke across Davalos's forehead and eyebrow. Of course *then* he hadn't known all the facts.

Angry and sick with the thoughts that kept winding and twisting in his mind, Jason turned away from the window and walked quickly back to the bed. His body, cool from the night air, gave a sudden chill in the woman as he slid in beside her. Sleepily she turned in his direction and murmured, "Jason?"

Suddenly very wide awake and aware of other passions, Jason laughed low in his throat, more a growl than a laugh, and gently nuzzled her ear. "Annie, Annie, love, wake up."

Annie awoke slowly, only half conscious of the warm kisses being pressed to her throat and ear, but when Jason's mouth found hers, sleep fled, and eagerly her body pressed against his hard length. Jason gave a small groan of satisfaction as her hand found him, and with quickening passion, he explored her soft body. Gently he caressed Annie's silken flesh until she was moaning for him to take her. Then swiftly he covered her body with his and slid deep between her opening legs. Urgently he drove into her, forcing her to move with him as his body possessed hers, taking them both over the edge of physical satisfaction.

Replete, his body at rest, and his mind firmly turned away from unpleasant thoughts, Jason gathered Annie to him, and together they fell asleep.

When he awoke, the pale November sun was shining in through the open window. Annie stirred in his arms, and a moment later she awoke.

Jason was once again nibbling her ear, but almost angrily she pushed him aside. "You!" she muttered half teasingly, half angrily. "It's late, Jason, and I'll lose my work, if I lay here much longer with you."

Regretfully, Jason let her slip from the bed. She glanced back at him, thinking it was unfair that any one man should have such charm and be so handsome. With his black hair tousled, his green eyes gleaming between astonishingly long lashes, and a smile on his mouth that would turn a woman's heart right over, Annie admitted to herself that he was a man most women wanted and few could forget. Remembering the feel of that long, hard body on hers and thinking of his mouth tasting hers, Annie wished she could climb right back into bed. But below she could hear the owner of the inn bellowing her name, and he would only allow Jason, good customer or not, so much of her time. Almost sadly she dressed, then dropped a brief kiss on Jason's mouth before departing.

Jason wasted little time once Annie was gone. With quick, impatient movements, he dressed and, not waiting for breakfast, was on the road in a matter of minutes. He had almost forgotten Davalos, but riding towards Greenwood, his thoughts once again were taken up with the Spaniard. And for the first time, he wondered if there was a connection between his visits to Jefferson at Monticello and Davalos's unexpected appearance in Virginia.

Spain was very jumpy at the moment—it was possible that Davalos's presence was due to political matters and had nothing to do with personal affairs. Jason didn't quite believe it, but when he saw Jefferson this afternoon, he would acquaint him with the fact that Davalos was in the area. What Jefferson wanted done about it could be discussed then. And knowing he must change before traveling to Monticello, he kicked his horse into a smart trot, his thoughts already leaping ahead to the meeting that afternoon.

To Jason, Thomas Jefferson's library at Monticello was a pleasant place to be—especially on a cold blustery November afternoon. A fire burned merrily on the brick hearth, and deep claret-red drapes of fine velvet kept out the icy winds that blew around the house.

There was no mistaking the leonine head, the large precise features, nor the hazel eyes set deep under shaggy eyebrows of the third president of the United States. Jason Savage's raven black hair was in stark contrast to the whiteness of Jefferson's. They were both tall men, although Jefferson was more slender than the powerfully built young man who sat at his ease in the chair before the fire.

At the moment they were enjoying a snifter of brandy and appeared merely to be relaxing. Jason was the son of Jefferson's very good friend Guy Savage—Greenwood, Guy's plantation, was situated only a few miles from Monticello—and through the years Jefferson had seen Jason grow from a squalling red-faced brat into the loose-limbed, extremely handsome man that he was now. It was because of this close association that when Guy had mentioned casually Jason's impending trip to London, Jefferson had seized upon the opportune sailing as the perfect way in which to transport several messages that he did not care to send through the usual channels. From over the rim of his snifter, Jefferson regarded Savage thoughtfully. He knew more of Jason's ancestry and of Jason the child than he did of the actual man Jason had grown into. After Jason had returned unexpectedly from Harrow some ten years ago, he and Guy had fought angrily over Guy's disposal of a certain female slave—her name just now escaped Jefferson—and Jason had departed for his grandfather's estates near New Orleans. And apparently he had remained there except for a few hurried visits to Greenwood.

Jefferson had never met Guy's father-in-law, Armand Beauvais, but he sympathized wholeheartedly when Guy complained bitterly of Jason's preferring his French grandfather and Beauvais, the New Orleans plantation, to Greenwood. To Jefferson's mind, Jason's place was with his father.

Nasty situation, that marriage, Jefferson thought gloomily. He could have warned Guy before he married Angelique Beauvais that these half Spanish-half French, high-born Creole women were regular spitfires, but unfortunately, Guy had never asked, and the resulting marriage had been a disaster. Angelique could not and would not adapt to American ways, and shortly after Jason's birth—the only good thing to come of the marriage—she had departed for New Orleans, vowing with a spark of pure temper in her fine emerald eyes that she didn't care if she never saw either her husband or her son again.

Glancing over at Jason, he decided that his mother's careless abandonment certainly hadn't hurt—Jason had grown up to be a mocking, arrogant devil, a gleam of taunting laughter never far from his emerald eyes. Young Savage was very sure of himself. But then he had reason to be. The only child of a wealthy Creole mother and a rich, aristocratic Virginia planter, he'd grown up without questioning his right to do exactly as he pleased. A selfish man? Yes! Not because he was selfish by nature, but because of the time and environment that had bred him. To his credit, he was not impressed with his own power or possessions, nor was he content to waste his days lazily throwing away a fortune on a Sybaritic existence.

Yet to imply that Jason was a paragon of diligent virtue would be untrue. He was quite as capable as the next young man of gaming through the night, losing and winning vast sums of money in the gambling halls of New Orleans, then sauntering down the street to whore away the time, until bored and restless, he'd slip deep into Spanish territory, spending weeks hunting the wild mustangs or trading with the Comanches for their highly prized spotted ponies before finally returning to Beauvais.

Yes, Jason Savage was exactly the sort of man that Jefferson needed—young, intelligent, well-bred, tough, capable with a blade or pistol, and upon occasion quite, quite ruthless. There was one other reason that Jefferson needed him—Jason's uncle, Guy's half brother, was the very powerful and politically discreet duke of Roxbury.

For a moment Jefferson smiled to himself and blessed the whim that some fifty years ago had taken the old duke of Roxbury to Louisiana to inspect a tract of land he had won on the turn of a card. It was there that he had met and taken as his second wife the young Frenchwoman, Arabella St. Clair. Guy was the result of that marriage, and it was his older half brother who was now the present duke of Roxbury, and—most importantly to Jefferson—personal advisor to Prime Minister Addington. Roxbury had been advisor and confidant of more than one prime minister of England, but it was his current connection to Addington that interested Jefferson—that and the fact that young Savage would be staying with Roxbury for part of his time in London.

With that in mind, Jefferson asked, "Well, Jason, are you going to do it—carry my dispatches to Rufus King?"

Jason's lips quirked into a rueful smile. "Why not?" he replied in a slightly accented voice. "I don't care for the present situation in New Orleans. The Spanish closing the port last month to the Americans was a stupid thing to have done, and I definitely would not like to see Napoleon annex the territory. Are you certain of your facts?"

Jefferson bit his lip, his forehead wrinkled in a frown. Finally, he admitted, "No, I'm not certain—no one is. But there is no denying the fact that rumors from high places are currently circulating Europe that Spain by a secret treaty has turned the Louisiana Territory back to France. I have Livingston in Paris trying to discover if there is any basis in the rumor, but so far France has been excessively coy with her answers. Unfortunately, I must make plans for the possibility that France is the new owner of the territory. And it is for that reason you will carry orders to Rufus King in London for him to seek an alliance with England. A military alliance with England is repugnant to me, but it is the only hope we have except to pray that France and England will soon renew hostilities. And there is every sign that they will! No one expects this treaty of Amiens to last. But in the meantime, it is imperative that we negotiate with England, for I believe that she does not desire, any more than we do, a French empire in the new world."

Silently Jason concurred. No one wanted Napoleon in New Orleans—except perhaps Napoleon and the French population of Louisiana. Jason certainly didn't. And it was for that reason he had agreed to carry Jefferson's letters to Rufus King, currently the American minister in England, and to hold himself in readiness should Robert Livingston in Paris need him. That and to convince his uncle Roxbury to give a favorable nod to the proposed American-English alliance. Altogether, he decided with a grin, his trip to England should prove very, very interesting.

Catching sight of Jason's grin, Jefferson snapped testily, "You find this all amusing?"

His grin vanishing, Jason admitted, "No—not the situation in Louisiana. I was just thinking how my innocent trip to England to buy horses had become colored with overtones of political intrigue."

Jefferson grunted. "Speaking of political intrigue—are you positive it was Blas Davalos you saw yesterday?"

"I'm positive."

"But why would he avoid you? You two used to be quite good friends, weren't you? Whatever caused the break? Some woman? Or is it that he is a lieutenant in the Spanish army that makes you dislike him?"

A grim smile flitted across Jason's dark face. "His being in the Spanish army definitely makes me dislike him—and the fact that he apparently followed me from New Orleans, and doesn't want me to know it! But the break between us happened before this—and it wasn't over a woman."

Curious, Jefferson couldn't help asking, "Well, what was the real reason?"

Avoiding Jefferson's question, Jason said, "You met him once."

"Did I?" Jefferson asked surprised, his shaggy eyebrows raising.

"About five years ago he came with me on one of my dutiful-son visits to Greenwood. We were here for almost two months, and you met him a few times then."

"Oh yes, I recall now—slender, black-eyed fellow about your age and typically Spanish, swarthy skin and all."

"Blas *is* Spanish—which makes me wonder why he is here in Virginia and not in New Orleans."

"Hmmm, you have a point there. But you've also very cleverly not answered my question—what caused the trouble between you?"

Jason seemed to hesitate as if he would not talk of it. Finally he asked, "Do you also remember a meeting with Phillip Nolan?"

Jefferson looked startled but admitted, "Yes, he came to see me once a couple of years ago—seemed a very intelligent young man. Pity about his death."

Feeling the familiar tightening in his gut at the mention of Phillip's death, Jason said in a harsh tone, "Yes, it was a pity. And Davalos was the man who murdered him!"

Jefferson appeared shocked and cried, "Are you sure? The report only said that Nolan was killed trying to escape from the Spanish troop sent to stop his exploration."

Unable to just rudely change the conversation, Jason briefly and unemotionally reported to Jefferson the true facts of what had happened on that last journey of Nolan's. He ended by saying, "And, as you know, Nolan's body was later returned, so you see it was not an accident."

Deeply troubled, Jefferson replied, "No, obviously not."

Then as if struck by a new thought, he asked seriously, "Jason, do you really think that Davalos is following you?"

Jason shrugged. "Why else would he be here?"

"I don't like it at all! Perhaps it would be wise if we knew exactly why Davalos left New Orleans."

Relieved that Jefferson had expressed precisely his own thoughts, Jason said quietly, "If you will let me, I would prefer to have someone of my own choosing discover what Davalos is up to."

Jefferson looked at him steadily for a moment before asking, "Someone you trust? Implicitly? Remember, we want no undue attention connected to your trip to England. Livingston may never have need of the information I have given you, but if he should, he will send for you. And in view of that, we do not want every agent in Europe watching every move you make."

Nodding in agreement, Jason smiled reassuringly, "Trust me to be most circumspect." Beyond that he would say no more.

Rather grudgingly Jefferson said, "Very well. I shall leave the details to you, but I cannot stress strongly enough the need for the utmost secrecy. We positively cannot risk a war with Spain at this point—despite what that hothead Andrew Jackson claims!"

Jason grinned. It was well known that Jackson would be delighted to march immediately on New Orleans and throw Spain off the entire Mississippi River. Jefferson was not precisely opposed to the idea—merely the timing!

Still smiling, Jason asked, "Have you any further instructions?"

"No, no. You have the dispatches, and everything else is in your head. Don't, I might add, forget any of it!"

Jason laughed at that. "I assure you, I shall not! Well, then, if you have nothing else, I'll be off—we won't meet again until my return, for my ship sails on the evening tide tomorrow."

A few minutes later Jason was astride a lean chestnut stallion riding in the direction of Greenwood. Shortly, he approached the tree-lined drive that led to his father's house, but there was no feeling of returning home. Greenwood held too many unpleasant memories for him, and he and Guy, though they tried, could never be in each other's company very long without nearly coming to blows. It was, Jason decided without amusement, unfortunate that they both liked their own way and did not take kindly to interference. Add to that flash point tempers and their relationship was not surprising. For a moment Jason smiled. Arabella St. Clair had been noted for her quick temper, and it appeared she had passed it undiluted onto her son and grandson.

Smiling, Jason rode his horse to the large red brick stable that was directly behind the white columned house, but hidden from view by a gently sloping hill. Tossing the reins to the waiting stableboy, he slid to the ground. He started to walk away when a soft whistle to his left caused him to spin around. Seeing the tall, proud-faced Indian rising from his apparent resting place in a pile of sweet straw, Jason's face broke into a welcoming grin—a grin that was matched by the one on the Indian's face.

"Blood Drinker, you devil! How did you know I wanted to see you and in a damned big hurry at that?"

Blood Drinker, his black eyes reflecting an answering spark of laughter, murmured, "It seemed reasonable that you would."

Jason's grin faded as quickly as it had appeared, and without preamble he said, "Davalos is here in Virginia."

Betraying no surprise, Blood Drinker stated calmly, "It is unfortunate you did not kill him when you had the chance. In any other man you would not tolerate what he has done, and like the panther who lives in the swamps you would strike swiftly and without mercy. But because he was your friend you hold back."

Jason was silent, aware that there was more than just a little truth in what Blood Drinker said. The quiet spun out for several seconds, each man lost in his own thoughts, until finally Jason said, "I don't know what Blas is up to—it could be nothing, or it could create a hell of a lot of trouble, and not just for us! I want to know why he left New Orleans, and I want you to discover it for me—quietly. If you find that the Spanish government has sent him to spy on me, let Jefferson know that information the instant you can. If it turns out that he's merely pursuing a vendetta between us—*that* little matter I will see to on my return."

Blood Drinker nodded gravely. "It shall be done," he stated simply, and Jason knew that Davalos was a worry he could safely forget about for now.

They stared at one another for a moment; then, a grin lighting his features, Jason changed the subject. "I shall miss you," he said mildly. "What a devil of a time we could have together. London would never recover from you—especially the ladies!"

Answering amusement flitted across the handsome chiseled features, and Blood Drinker laughed. "My brother, it is you the ladies will never forget! It is not I who the fond mamas look at with suspicion, and it is not I who cause jealous husbands to guard their women so carefully!"

There was nothing more to say, and after shaking hands solemnly, they parted, Blood Drinker drifting away into the falling darkness and Jason striding towards his father's house.

Guy was seated in his den at the rear of the house, and when Jason entered a few minutes later, he looked up from the papers he had been studying and said, "Business all taken care of?"

Jason nodded, helping himself to some refreshment from an array of various liquors set on a cherry wood cabinet. "It went well. With this last meeting behind me, it takes care of all my business. From now until I leave tomorrow morning to join the ship, I'm a man of leisure."

Guy smiled, and for some seconds there was almost a friendly silence between them. Then Guy, his sea-gray eyes hiding the justifiable pride that he felt at the sight of his tall broad-shouldered son, asked idly, "Jason, other than the favor for Jefferson, is your only reason for visiting England to buy horses? I know you are taking advantage of the peace presently existing between France and England, but I would think you could have postponed your trip until this spring if you are planning on sending animals back to New Orleans."

Jason slowly walked over to the fireplace. Setting his drink on the mantel, he looked at his father, stretched out his hands to warm them from the fire, and said, "I thought I explained the position to you some months ago in my letter. You yourself know how bad the horse situation is in the Louisiana Territory. We need horses of any type, and Armand and I have decided to establish a breeding farm either at the home place, Beauvais, or on my own lands near the Red River, Terre du Coeur. The sooner I can reach England and buy the necessary stock to begin the stables, the sooner we can show some results. A breeding farm is not something one accomplishes overnight, and we have wasted enough time as it is. I don't wish to put off my departure any longer than I have—and now with the commitment to Jefferson I cannot. I've postponed it once already as it is."

Guy nodded. "I realize that. It was unfortunate that the Spanish decided to close the port. Was your grandfather very upset by it?"

Shrugging and picking up his drink, Jason answered, "The Spanish officials only closed New Orleans to you Americans. It made no difference to those of us in the territory. But because your countrymen were extremely, shall we say, loud and outspoken about it, I thought it best to wait until the situation had resolved itself."

"Come now," Guy said irritably, "you're as American as myself, Don't forget that you were born right here in Virginia. And even if you prefer your mother's family to mine and choose to live in Louisiana, that does not make you less of an American."

Jason grinned, his emerald eyes gleaming with mocking laughter. "It annoys you, does it not, that I am more French than American. But you have only yourself to blame—you should not have married a Creole."

"You don't have to tell *me* that. I should never have married your mother," Guy muttered. "It was a mistake from start to the present. I do not mean to offend you, but that woman would try the patience of a saint—and heaven knows that I am not!"

Jason nodded, his eyes holding sudden amused affection for his father, and at that moment he looked very like his father. Seen together, as they were now, it was apparent that there was a great but not marked physical similarity between them. Both were possessed of the same black curly hair except that Guy's was beginning to show traces of silver at the temples. Jason's face was harder, the bones more clearly defined, and there was a ruthlessness to the slant of his mouth that Guy's lacked. Yet both had the same heavy, hawklike brows, and even if the color of their eyes was different the shape was the same. Jason was taller than his father, standing over six feet tall. He had the wide powerful shoulders, the lean hips and the long, steel-muscled legs of the natural athlete. For a large man, he moved with the quick almost lethal grace of a panther—as more than one unsuspecting culprit had discovered to his dismay. Despite Jason's deceptive air of indolence and the lazy amusement seen gleaming frequently in his emerald eyes, there was an aura of carefully leashed power about him that made him definitely a man who people noticed—especially women. His crisp black hair, worn carelessly long, just brushing the collar of his coat, and his dark, hard, uncompromising features coupled with those green eyes that so often shimmered with slumberous passion had caused more than one woman, who should have known better, to go weak at the knees. At twenty-nine there wasn't a great deal that he had not seen or done except, his father thought waspishly, marry and provide him with a grandson. But Guy hastily pushed the thought from his mind. Now was not the time to speak of such things.

Guy waited until after dinner to bring up the subject, and it was one near to his heart. Unfortunately, whenever he had brought it up in the past, it had invariably led to a quarrel.

Jason was sprawled in a large chair before the roaring fire, once again in Guy's den. His long legs were stretched towards the warmth, and one lean hand held a goblet of strong rum punch. He was staring absentmindedly at the swirling amber liquid, his mind on this afternoon's meeting with Jefferson, when Guy broke into his thoughts.

"I hesitate to disrupt your mood, but I think it's time we have a serious talk."

Jason gave his father a lazy smile and answered lightly, "I've had one serious conversation today. Is another necessary?"

"Jason, I feel very strongly that this one is. We've discussed it several times in the past, and you usually manage to avoid answering me. This time, though, I'm determined that you listen to me and consider what I'm saying. I want you to look for a wife while you're in England."

"Oh, my God, not *that* again!" Jason said angrily. The last time the subject had arisen he had made it clear—he had no intention of marrying. With his parents as examples of the wedded state, he had no desire to saddle himself with a wife—not now, not ever.

Guy firmly ignored his son's less than encouraging outburst. "Don't you think it's time that you married?" he continued. "I'm approaching fifty, and in less than a year's time you'll be thirty. Between us we've large holdings and don't forget—you are Armand's only heir also. I certainly would like to be assured that all I've acquired will remain in the Savage name at least for one more generation."

A bleak silence greeted his words, and his son's face wore a cold, stony expression. Almost despairingly Guy cried, "It's your damned duty to marry and breed me grandsons! Good heavens, boy. You'll not find it hard if you'll just put aside the fancy pieces you keep and settle down with a nice young gentlewoman."

A grimace of distaste on his face, Jason asked sarcastically, "Do you expect me to study your marriage as an example of what to look forward to?"

Guy had the grace to look uncomfortable. "I've admitted my own particular marriage was a mistake but that doesn't mean that yours would be. I needed a nice quiet Englishwoman and what did I do but marry a hot-tempered Creole termagant!"

"So?"

"So, this trip of yours is a godsend. Find yourself a well-bred English miss and make her your bride. At least for my sake consider it. It would please me no end if you brought home an English bride."

Jason tossed down the remainder of his rum in one quick movement and snapped, "Very well, I'll look. And if there is one who is rich, beautiful *and* willing to overlook my—er—fancy pieces, I believe you called them, well then—who knows?"

"I wish you would take this seriously. You know, Jason, it's possible that you might fall in love," Guy commented quietly.

"As you did?" his son returned insolently.

Guy hesitated and for a moment, his thoughts went slipping down forbidden and painful avenues of memory. *Her* features, Rae's laughing face, danced in front of his eyes, and for a second all the aching pain of their parting came flooding back—not the least of it the knowledge that she was to have borne him a child and that he would be unable to even give it his name. He had done the next best thing though—while the child might not be entitled to the Savage name there was nothing to prevent him from bestowing on it his mother's name, St. Clair. His thoughts bleak and unhappy he admitted softly, "Once there was a woman I loved dearly. I would have given up everything for her—but it was not to be."

"*Mon Dieu!*" Jason said ungraciously. "Spare me! I've said I'll look. More I cannot promise." With that Jason slammed out of the room and, intent upon cooling his hot temper, left the house and stalked to the stables. At the moment he preferred the company of dumb animals.

Chewing on a wisp of straw, Jason decided reflectively that it was as well he only saw his father once every few years; if they saw one another often, the tenuous thread of filial affection might very well snap.

Jesus! he thought with disgust—the very last thing he wanted from London was a damned simpering miss of a bride.

2

Jason Savage, his valet Pierre, and his head groom Jacques, having survived the fury of the winter storms that swept across the Atlantic ocean, stepped thankfully ashore some six weeks later at London, England. The trip had been cold and uncomfortable, and Jason vowed grimly that never again would he attempt a winter crossing. *Nothing* could be worth the discomfort and inconvenience that he had suffered.

He arrived at his uncle's Berkeley Square residence that afternoon to find the duke eagerly awaiting his appearance.

Roxbury—his full name was Garret Ainsley Savage, Lord Satterliegh, Viscount Norwood, duke of Roxbury—had been a widower for well over twenty years and his sons fully grown when Jason, a scruffy schoolboy, had come to England to finish his schooling at Harrow. The duke was a tall slender man of sixty-five, as impressive looking as his string of titles, with seemingly sleepy gray eyes that were deep set beneath heavy black brows. In his youth, he had possessed as black and curly a head of hair as his nephew's. Although the years had silvered his hair, his manner and bearing were such that his presence still caused a flutter among the ladies. Viewing the world with a weary cynicism, he was seldom moved by the emotions that motivated other men—and this made his pride and affection for his only nephew all the more puzzling.

Jason, himself, was at a loss to explain the affection that was between them, but he was also wise enough to realize that the duke placed England and her sovereignty over mere mortals and that if it was necessary to use or sacrifice an individual in order to maintain that sovereignty, Roxbury would do so without too much searching of his conscience. And as Jason felt exactly the same way about the Louisiana Territory and the United States, there was, in spite of the affection that existed, a certain not unnatural wariness in their meetings with one another.

But for this, his first evening in England since a short and hurried trip some five years ago, they put aside politics and spoke mainly of the past, Jason's father, and Jason's plans. It was only as they were preparing to seek out their separate bedchambers that the duke mentioned anyone outside their family circle.

Standing at the foot of the stairs, his gray eyes warm with amusement, he said, "I suppose you know that those two raffish friends of yours, Barrymore and Harris, have been bombarding me for news of your arrival. They started asking after you in December, and I have had no letup since then, even while in the country. When last I spoke to Barrymore, I explained, rather patiently for me, that I did not expect you until after the New Year and certainly not before the fifteenth of January. I am thankful that you have not made a liar out of me and have so kindly managed to arrive on that precise date. Rest assured that those two will be at my door as soon as it is decently possible tomorrow morning. I wish you joy of them."

Jason grinned. "At least this time we won't be letting a monkey loose at the headmaster's farewell dinner."

The duke shuddered. "Please do not remind me. How could you have done such a thing? No, don't tell me. Let that memory die peacefully along with several more that I would prefer to forget. Good night, Jason, I shall see you in the morning."

As his uncle had anticipated, Barrymore and Harris arrived promptly at ten o'clock in the morning requesting to see Jason. Jason had already spent a busy few hours, making arrangements with his uncle's very efficient head groom for the temporary stabling and care of the horses he intended to buy and ship to New Orleans, as well as writing a note to be hand delivered within an hour to Rufus King, the American minister in England requesting to see him at the earliest possible moment. So he was quite ready to relax and enjoy himself. And nowhere could he have found two companions more eager and willing to assist him in this endeavor.

Frederick Barrymore, heir to a barony, was almost as tall as Jason but built on deceptively willowy lines, with blond wavy hair and bright blue eyes. Possessing an exuberant personality, he was like a happy, restless butterfly. Tom Harris, with sad brown eyes and the freckles that usually went with hair as carrot red as that which grew in abundance on his round head, was on the short side and inclined toward plumpness. Harris was quiet, amiably slow-witted, and followed happily wherever the volatile Barrymore led.

It was Barrymore, his blue eyes lighting with pleasure as he shook Jason's outthrust hand who enthusiastically cried, "By God, Savage, it is good to see you again! And except for that brief trip of yours here a few years back, it must be almost ten years since our harum scarum days at Harrow."

Grinning, Jason acknowledged that time did indeed have a way of slipping past one unnoticed.

Harris, less articulate than the restless Barrymore, merely beamed. Clasping Jason's hand he said simply, "Pleasure!"

The three spent an enjoyable few hours in Jason's room at his uncle's house renewing their friendship and reminiscing.

And when Jason disclosed that he was in England to buy horses, Barrymore and Harris instantly demanded the privilege of escorting him to Tattersalls, renowned for its horse sales. And of course, when business was behind him, well then. . . .

Relaxing and smiling ruefully to himself, Jason listened as his friends cheerfully filled every moment of the duration of his stay. Feeling they were getting too far away from his objective of buying horses, he skillfully brought the conversation from the charms to be seen of certain opera dancers at the theaters near Covent Garden back to Tattersalls.

Although Jason had arrived too late for the early January sales in which the best of the yearling thoroughbreds had been sold, he was not dismayed. He was after breeding stock, not racing animals. And as he intended to remain in England some four or five months, he was certain he would be able to find horses that would satisfy him.

Barrymore and Harris both bemoaned the fact that he had not arrived earlier, but then dismissed it. Feeling that enough time had been spent on business, Barrymore asked, "Will you accompany us this afternoon to a cockfight at Bartholomew Fair? There's a splendid red crossbreed that I predict will win every match. Come with us. You will enjoy seeing the creature in action."

With his note to Rufus King in mind, Jason demurred, much to Barrymore's disgust.

"Oh, come now, Jason, don't fob us off with such a sorry excuse as you've just arrived! I know you haven't seen your uncle in some time, but you're staying with him, ain't you? He'll see enough of you before you leave to become sick of the sight of your face."

Jason smiled and remarked, "True, *mon ami,* but I do not intend to remain under my uncle's roof for my entire stay. I shall only be at this address until I can find lodgings of my own. And as I am his guest at the moment, I cannot, I fear, arrive one night and then disappear the next day in the company of such rakish fellows as yourselves. Knowing you, after the cockfight we would adjourn to Cribb's Parlor or some other low place and drink blue ruin till the early hours." Shaking his head regretfully, Jason continued, "No, my friends, I'm afraid that I really cannot come staggering up the steps of my uncle's home my second night in London." A wicked glint in his green eyes, he added, "Wait a week or two, until I have found my own rooms, and then I shall be delighted to join you in your revels."

Barrymore grinned at Jason's words, but it was Tom, recalling past escapades who said tellingly, "Lead, not join!"

Jason laughingly acknowledged his statement, and the three parted on that note. Jason escorted the pair to the door and after closing it behind them, he turned and walked down the wide hall to his uncle's study.

The duke was on the point of leaving to stroll down to take a look in at White's Club for Gentlemen. Glancing over at Jason, he suggested, "Would you care to join me? If you do, this would be as good a time as any to offer your name for membership."

Shaking his dark head Jason replied, "I would appreciate it, but unfortunately I am waiting for an answer to a note that I sent off this morning. Could we make it later this week—say, Friday?"

The duke shrugged, his gray eyes thoughtful as they rested on his nephew. "So diligent, so soon," he mused. "You've changed, m'boy. And I wonder if I like it."

"Shall I do something outrageous to allay your fears? If I set my mind on it, I could think of a way to instantly set the cat among the pigeons," Jason offered promptly, his emerald eyes gleaming with mocking laughter.

Roxbury gave him a reproving look. "Please, do not, I beg you, exert yourself in such a manner for my sake. I'm sure we can deal together famously just as things are."

Left alone after his uncle's departure, Jason roamed around the room, impatient to be busy. But as things were, until he heard from the American minister he was not his own man. His thoughts went to the dispatches currently resting snugly in a cunningly devised leather pouch next to his skin. The sooner he was rid of them the better! And for just a tiny segment of time, he allowed himself to think of the message that he carried in his head. But those instructions had nothing to do with England, and he dismissed them from his mind. He was not going to be dragged into politics if he could help it. He was here to purchase horses and enjoy himself—but not necessarily in that order, he thought with a grin.

The arrival of an answer to his note to Rufus King interrupted Jason's thoughts, and taking the envelope from the uniformed servant, he read the message quickly, pleased that King would see him this afternoon at two o'clock.

Exactly at two P.M. Jason was ushered into Rufus King's office. It could have been an awkward meeting. Jason was very much aware of the fact that the plump and balding man before him was not a supporter of Jefferson and was in actuality a firm friend of Alexander Hamilton, the President's bitter and outspoken enemy. King, in turn, knew very little of the tall, broad-shouldered young man seated across from him other than that he was related to the duke of Roxbury, whose actual position, while powerful in governmental circles, was not quite known, and that Guy Savage, Jason's father, was deep in Jefferson's confidence. But Rufus King was an able diplomat, and none of his reservations showed in his greeting.

"Well, I must say, it is a pleasure to meet you at last. I have heard a great deal about you."

At Jason's look of surprise, Rufus's heavily jowled face creased into a smile. He chuckled. "I know your father slightly, and like all men he is eager to speak of his son. But truth to tell, it is your uncle, the duke, who has spoken so highly of you."

A sardonic grin twisting his lips, Jason murmured, "I see that my fame has preceded me. Do not, I request you most earnestly, base your opinion of me on what those two have said. They are, for reasons best known to themselves, prejudiced in my favor."

Rufus laughed politely. "Yes, I'm afraid that is how it is with most relatives. But now, tell me. What can I do for you?"

Glad not to have to waste time in exchanging further banalities, Jason stood up, and before King's astonished gaze began to remove his slim fitting coat of dark blue cloth. Grinning at King's expression, Jason said, "Do not be alarmed, I am not ready for Bedlam—yet! I have some dispatches for you from Jefferson, and nothing would do but the damned things be concealed under my clothing. I beg you bear with me."

Rufus relaxed slightly in his chair, although his brown eyes were definitely speculative as Jason handed him the leather pouch. Shrugging back into his shirt and coat, Jason remarked, "*That* is the entire reason behind my visit to you. For myself, I'm devilishly happy to be rid of it!"

A preoccupied grunt was his answer. Rapidly, King scanned the large, scrawling script and finishing it, he lifted his head and stared with open curiosity at Jason.

"Do you know what is in this?" he asked finally.

Jason nodded. "Some of it, but not all. I did not feel it was necessary for me to know anything beyond Jefferson's desire for a treaty between England and the United States. His instructions to you concerning the negotiations of such a treaty are beyond my interest or capabilities." With a disarming smile he added, "Monsieur King, I am merely a messenger. And the only reason I know something of Jefferson's desire is because I would not blindly agree to his request without first knowing precisely what it entailed." And that, Jason said to himself, is a bloody lie.

"I see," said Rufus slowly. And partially he did. The president had his own system for receiving information and delivering messages, and some of Jefferson's ways were decidedly unorthodox—the present situation, a splendid example. Yet as the young man had stated, he was merely a messenger. But was he?

A very clever and intelligent man, King could find no flaw in Jason's story or demeanor, but he was left with the feeling that there was more to Jason's involvement—if Jefferson had used him to carry these messages, might the president not have given him further instructions? Concealing his suspicions behind a bland smile, he said, "Well, then, if this is everything, there is nothing more to be said, is there? Let me thank you for your promptness in their delivery." Rising from his chair and extending his hand, he added, "I hope you enjoy your stay in England. And if there is anything I can do to help you, please do not hesitate to call upon me."

Jason grinned. "Are you knowledgeable in the buying of breeding stock? If so, I may call upon you sooner than you think."

"Breeding stock?"

"Yes. My grandfather, Armand Beauvais, and I are intending to experiment with the breeding of thoroughbred horses in Louisiana. I am here in England to buy what I hope will be the foundation of a stud farm."

"Ah yes, your uncle mentioned something of that nature. I would suggest that you start buying at Tattersalls."

And Jason did just that. With Barrymore and Harris in tow, he attended the February sales at Tattersalls, and, overall, was pleased with the results. It had been a mixed blessing having his two boon companions with him. In the first bidding of the afternoon, Barrymore instantly had become enraptured of a showy two-year-old filly of impeccable lineage. Unfortunately, upon closer inspection, Jason was not impressed. The animal's back was too short, and the hindquarters were not as perfectly formed as they should have been, and he said as much.

Highly affronted, Barrymore had cried, "Dammit, Jason, I've as good an eye as anyone when it comes to horseflesh. You're just being damned difficult to please."

"Always was," Harris had added simply. Barrymore had thrown him an angry blue stare, but remembering that Jason had earlier turned down an animal of Tom's choice, his anger evaporated, and he had grinned and admitted, "You never did pay any attention to us. And I don't know why I expected you to be any different now."

After that the sales had gone smoothly, and Jason had purchased a number of horses. Most would be stabled and taken care of by his uncle's head groom as previously arranged. Although Jason had brought his own stableman with him, Pierre's cousin Jacques, he intended Jacques to handle the horses he would buy for his own use in England. He was fortunate enough to find a likely looking, burly black stallion and a pair of matched bays as well as a few hunters for just that purpose and had them delivered into Jacques' capable hands without delay.

February also found him established in his own rooms on St. James's Street. The duke had frowned when Jason told him of his plans, but then Roxbury had shrugged carelessly and remarked, "Do as you please—only remember that you are to be here to dine on Wednesday with myself and Rufus King."

Having delivered Jefferson's dispatch to King, having purchased a number of horses for the nucleus of the breeding stock, and now settled in his bachelor quarters, Jason was fairly well satisfied with his progress. Consequently, he began to allow Barrymore and Harris to take up more of his time.

He awoke one morning with such a thick head from a night of drinking with Barrymore and Harris that he wondered if he would survive their reckless pace. Lying there in his bed with his aching head, he decided that he had run loose long enough and that this wild drinking, gaming, and wenching would have to cease, or he would return to New Orleans a ruined man—in health!

Pierre entered the room just then, his monkey face wearing a puzzled frown. "Monsieur, were you searching for something last night?"

Casting a somewhat bleary eye at him, Jason asked mockingly, "When? At four-thirty this morning when I returned? And for what?"

"I do not know, but the clothes in your wardrobe have definitely been disarrayed, and your footwear is not as I had left it."

Shrugging Jason replied lightly, "It was probably that serving wench who looks after the rooms, unable to resist her curiosity."

"If that is so, monsieur, she has also looked into the bureau drawers and even your desk in the other room," Pierre returned tartly.

"What the devil do you mean? And how do you know?"

Looking very superior, Pierre replied calmly, "When I noticed this morning, monsieur, the disarray of your garments and footwear, I took it upon myself to see how far this—this snooping had gone. She has obviously looked through everything. There was nothing very much greatly disturbed, you understand—just enough so that one could tell that objects were not in their proper places."

"Well, tell the chit that you've discovered her nasty little vice and that if it happens again, I shall discharge her." And with that Jason dismissed the incident from his mind.

Less than a week later, he attended a horse auction at Epsom Downs accompanied as usual by Barrymore and Harris. England was enjoying an unusually warm February. The weather was beautiful, although there were still patches of snow on the ground, and the auction had drawn quite a crowd. Aimlessly the three wandered among the stalls and crowded aisles viewing all manner of horses from the small, sturdy Welsh ponies to the looming, majestic shire horses. And, of course, it was the thoroughbreds that drew Jason.

Standing near the edge of a scarlet-roped ring where the animals were paraded and bids called for, he was admiring a particularly sleek chestnut filly when he had the uneasy feeling that someone was staring at him. He ignored the sensation at first, but it persisted and somewhat curiously he glanced over the shifting, colorful crowd for its source. But his searching gaze revealed no one who appeared to be unduly interested in him, and shrugging his shoulders, he was about to turn back to the animal in the ring when he spied a fashionably dressed young woman and gentleman making their way through the crowd towards him. At that same instant, Barrymore said out of the corner of his mouth, "Don't look now my friend, but here comes the Markham woman with Clive Pendleton in attendance."

A wary smile on his face, Jason watched their approach, wondering if it was coincidence or design that brought them here.

Elizabeth Markham was a handsome widow of some five-and-twenty years. Her figure was lush, and she was displaying it admirably today in a high-waisted gown of lavender-sprigged muslin. A chipped straw bonnet with an outrageously large green velvet ribbon tied in a bow under one ear and kid gloves of soft green completed the ensemble of this wealthy young woman of the aristocracy. Her father was the earl of Mount, Lord Tremayne, a title he had inherited less than a year before upon the death of his brother Robert. Jason had met Elizabeth and her parents when, with Roxbury, he had recently attended a dinner held at their home in London. Attracted to Elizabeth by the sparkling sherry brown eyes and hair that, while not red, shone as richly brilliant as the silken coat of the chestnut filly in the ring, he had enjoyed a polite flirtation with her and had made it a point to seek out her company discreetly. She was a damned handsome woman, he decided, and felt his senses stir, a flicker of desire racing through his veins as she smiled up at him just now.

"How nice to see you again, Jason! It seems we are forever meeting lately. Did you enjoy your ride in Hyde Park the other morning? I was desolate that I could not go with you, but as I said then, I was already committed to other plans." Placing her gloved hand on his arm and glancing at him through spiky, gold-tipped lashes she added flirtatiously, "I do hope that you will ask me again."

Jason murmured a polite rejoinder. She would have been extremely vexed if that had been his only action, but at the same time he also shot her a lazy-lidded glance, and seeing the sudden hint of more than just casual awareness in his eyes, she felt her heart beat faster in her breast. Jason Savage was certainly a handsome animal! she decided with satisfaction. Clive's request that she make herself agreeable to him wasn't going to be all that hard, she thought, liking the way his coat of deep claret emphasized the darkness of his skin and set off his broad shoulders. The manner in which the elegant fawn pantaloons displayed his long, well-turned legs found pleasure with her as well—it wasn't every man who had the body to wear them to advantage.

Just then she looked up and caught him staring at her, his eyes lingering deliberately for a moment on her bosom, as if knowing the excitement his very nearness aroused within her. And she admitted to herself that even without Clive's prompting she would have been attracted to him—he was that kind of man. Her own gaze was drawn irresistibly to his full, mobile mouth, and she wished suddenly that they were alone and that the muscled arm beneath her hand was crushing her to him and that his mouth was claiming hers. It was a heady thought, and one she suspected Jason guessed from the tantalizing smile he flashed her way. It said so much—and yet she was left uncertain.

An impatient cough behind her made her look over her shoulder at her escort and smiling prettily she said, "Forgive me! How rude you must think me. May I introduce Clive Pendleton to you." Then clapping a hand to her mouth, she laughed. "How silly of me! You met him at my father's party, did you not?"

Jason acknowledged Pendleton's bow with one of his own. He knew Pendleton had been a captain in the army before his return to civilian life and was thought of as a family relation of the Tremaynes. His godfather had been the present earl's late brother, Robert. Jason did not care for Pendleton, disliking the cold gray eyes and the thin, dark, sarcastic features. As Barrymore put it, "Pendleton's a damned dirty dish! Every family has 'em, and the Tremayne's are no different." And Jason was inclined to agree with that revealing statement. There was nothing one could put a finger on: Pendleton's clothes were impeccable, fitting his manly figure with grace, his manners were acceptable, and he appeared to live in the style and fashion of a member of the ton. But in spite of all that, Jason thought, there appeared to cling to him a faint odor of dark, rank alleys and less than honorable dealings with his fellow men and women.

Concealing his aversion, Jason smiled and offered his hand to Clive. "Will you both join us?"

It was Elizabeth who answered. Looking doubtful she said, "Oh, I don't think so. Truly we just came out for the ride. We cannot stay."

Barrymore and Harris, after murmuring a polite greeting, rather pointedly turned their backs and displayed a sudden, absorbed interest in the bidding. Jason would have liked to have done the same, for although he was perfectly agreeable to the idea of paying lazy court to Elizabeth, at the moment his mind was more on the action in the ring. But unlike his friends, he could not just turn away—especially when her hand was still on his arm. Smiling down at her, he said mendaciously, "How unfortunate that we cannot convince you to join us. But perhaps we shall meet at your mother's ball at the end of next week? I hope you will save a dance or two for me."

"Oh, yes, of course," Elizabeth replied, her fine eyes narrowing just a little at Barrymore's and Harris's actions. The fact that they were ignoring her was irritating, and determinedly she asked, "Freddy, are you and Tom coming to the ball?"

"Eh?" Tom said, startled that Elizabeth should address a

question to him, but it was Barrymore who answered smoothly, "Regretfully, no. Tom and I leave tomorrow for Leicestershire. I have a hunting box there, you know, and we hope to get in a fortnight or better of hunting before joining Brownleigh's house party in March."

"Oh, how pleasant!" Elizabeth replied untruthfully. "We shall see you then at Melton Mowbray, for my parents and I as well as Clive are also attending." Looking at Jason she asked, "Do you intend to be there?"

"Yes. Although I know the Brownleigh's only slightly, Tom and Freddy have managed to get an invitation for me. I've made arrangements to put up at an inn nearby, so I shall not be inconveniencing them any more than possible. Despite the fact that Letitia Brownleigh has assured me that it will be no trouble at all, I *am* a latecomer."

"Oh," Elizabeth said, the word plainly indicating her disappointment that he would not be as available as she would have preferred.

Laying his hand over her slim gloved one still resting on his arm, Jason said softly, "Never fear, *you* will still see a great deal of me." Then, his voice losing its intimate tone, he continued, "I would also like to purchase a few more horses—mostly with an eye to resale in New Orleans, and by lodging at the inn, I shall be able to combine business with pleasure." Smiling, he added, "I do not think that the Brownleighs would appreciate my taking advantage of their hospitality to transact personal business."

Barrymore, tearing his gaze away from the horses in the ring, tossed over his shoulder, "Damned horse trader, that's what he is!"

Clive Pendleton, who had been standing quietly at Elizabeth's side, apparently unmoved by the sight of her blatant interest in another man, said briskly, "Well, I'm certain you will find that there are several farms near Melton Mowbray where you should be able to buy whatever you desire in the way of horseflesh without any trouble."

Tom, as if struck by a startling thought, jerked around and

said to no one in particular, "Melton Mowbray!" Then looking at Elizabeth he added, "Your cousin lives near there, don't she? Lives very quietly with her mother?"

Elizabeth nodded and, disliking the question, said dryly, "Very. She and Rachael are still in the year's mourning for my uncle." She would have preferred to speak of something else only Harris, taking a sudden and unexpected interest in the subject, continued, "Fetching little thing, your cousin Catherine."

"Oh, and how do you know that, Harris?" Clive asked curiously.

"Went to school with my sister Amanda. Used to take them into town at Bath and buy them cream cakes."

"I see. How pleasant for you," Clive said, his tone implying jut the opposite. Apparently feeling enough had been said about the absent Catherine, he raised his voice to be heard above the noise of the crowd and asked, "Will I see you three at White's tonight?"

"No. We're spending a bachelor's evening at Freddy's, playing cards and cracking a bottle or more to send them properly off on their journey," Jason said. Politely he added, "Would you care to join us?"

And Clive surprised them all by saying, "Thank you. I should like to. Freddy, you will have to give me the time and directions."

Hiding his dismay, Freddy did so, replying in a voice pitched to be heard over the increasing babble of the many voices nearby. And a few minutes later after Clive and Elizabeth had drifted away, he turned on Jason and growled, "Why the devil did you do that? That sly boots will ruin the entire evening."

"What else could I do?" Jason replied, adding truthfully, "I certainly didn't expect him to accept."

"Well, damn it, he did! And now we're saddled with him," Freddy grumbled.

Jason shrugged and changing the subject asked Tom, "Shall I stop by for you this evening?"

Suspiciously, because Jason had a disconcerting habit of walking unnecessarily, Tom queried, "You walking—or riding?"

Smiling, Jason admitted, "Tom, Freddy lives a bare three blocks away, and if the weather today is anything to go by, it should be a lovely night, so I shall walk. Won't you keep me company?"

Decisively Tom shook his head no. And it was then that Jason again had that peculiar feeling that someone behind him in the crowd was either staring at him or listening closely to their conversation. He spun around quickly, but there appeared to be no one paying any attention to them.

"What the devil is the matter with you?" Barrymore asked irritably.

"Sorry," Jason apologized and added to cover his action, "I just thought of something I wanted to ask Elizabeth, but I don't see her anywhere."

"Good thing, too! I tell you, Jason, you had best travel light with that baggage. She sails close to the wind and so far hasn't been involved in outright scandal, but it's only a matter of time until she ruins herself. Stick to Covent Garden bawds for entertainment and let that little ladybird find someone else to gull," warned Barrymore.

Looking amused, Jason said, "My friend, I am not so green as all that! I have been handling my misalliances with ease for some years now."

"Thing is," Tom broke in earnestly, "she gambles!" he said in a voice of doom. "Went through her husband's estate in a twelvemonth. Her father had to settle her debts and demanded she return home. Common gossip is that she's after a rich husband."

Gravely, hiding a twinkle in his green eyes, Jason assured them, "Believe me, I will take due caution that I do not find myself in the parson's mousetrap with the likes of Elizabeth Markham."

Not content that with, Barrymore finished, "You had best

step lively, Jas, for it's obvious she's attracted to you—and your money."

At the same moment Clive was saying something of a similar nature to Elizabeth. They were seated comfortably in his tilbury traveling back to London, and Clive was making no effort to conceal his displeasure. "You were being a bit obvious, weren't you? All big eyes and pouting mouth," he sneered.

"And what else was I to do? You said to be agreeable to him," she returned hotly, her eyes snapping with temper. "If you want me to find out anything for you, you'll have to let me do it my own way. *He* certainly didn't mind my big eyes and pouting mouth. There was a time that you found them very appealing I might add, but it's his reaction I'm worried about—not yours!"

Clive's thin lips tightened, and he said grimly, "You had better worry about my reaction, m'dear—I'm paying your bills, remember. Speaking of which—how much did you drop the other night at Mrs. Everett's? Five hundred—a thousand?"

Sulkily Elizabeth answered, "Over a thousand."

"I thought as much. Is your father going to cover it?" he asked coolly.

"You know he won't. Clive, don't be mean! If I don't pay my debts, my father will send me to rusticate in the country at Mountacre. You know what a storm he created when he settled my debts the last time. I couldn't bear to go through it again, and I would die if I had to remain in the country away from all the excitement in London. God, how I *hate* Mountacre!" she spat venomously. Then she pleaded, "Please, don't be wicked. I've never failed you before, have I?"

"No. And see that you don't," he threatened. But then reaching into his side pocket, he handed her a sizable leather pouch that bulged with gold coins. "That should hold you for the present. But remember. I want to know what Savage is up to."

Frowning, Elizabeth asked, "What makes you think he's up to anything? He's done nothing but buy horses since he arrived."

Clive smiled tightly. "Not quite. He paid an extremely prompt visit to Rufus King, and since that time Roxbury, who is a clever old fox if there ever was one, has held at least one intimate dinner at which King and Savage were the only guests. I'd give much to know what they spoke of. My instincts tell me that there's something afoot that Napoleon would pay dearly to know. And as you well know, I live by my wits—which also enables me, I might add, to pay you handsomely for the snippets of conversation you pass my way. You might remember that and try just a little harder to capture Savage's interest—but not to the extent that everyone knows what you are doing."

"Oh, very well. But I think you're wrong. Savage can't know anything."

"As you say, I could be wrong, and it wouldn't be the first time. But it is never wise to overlook any source, and I would like to learn more of Savage before I dismiss him as harmless."

Conversation lapsed for a mile or two, and then it was Elizabeth who quizzed slyly, "You talk of my being obvious. Weren't *you* rather obvious in choking off Tom Harris when he mentioned Catherine?"

"Not at all. I wanted to know where he had met her—and I found out."

"Have you hopes in that direction, Clive?" Elizabeth asked archly. Not waiting for his answer, she added smugly, "They're doomed you know. Catherine, or Tamara, or whatever those beastly gypsies called her, can't abide the sight of you."

Clive's hands tightened on the reins he held, but that was the only sign he gave that Elizabeth's shaft had gone home. His voice was cool as he said, "Catherine's liking of me has nothing to do with marriage. Rachael finds me acceptable, and I'm quite certain I can bring Catherine round, one way or another. And if I can't, I'll see to it that no one else marries her, either. I won't be done out of a fortune a second time!"

His words seemed to engender in Elizabeth a feeling of being ill-used, for she cried angrily, "That infamous, infamous will! Who would have guessed that so little would come to my father. I never realized that the title and Mountacre were the only items entailed. And now that wretched, wretched gypsy brat has everything else—the estates in Leicestershire and a fortune to boot! Why couldn't Uncle Robert have willed something for me? God knows he was rich enough! And you, his godson, were also ignored. What I couldn't have done with even a small remembrance from him." She laughed bitterly. "We're a sorry pair, Clive, expecting all those years to inherit handsomely, and then that miserable old gypsy woman had to bring Catherine and Adam back. I'd like to wring her scrawny neck!"

Clive, his face impassive, said nothing to Elizabeth's outburst, and Elizabeth wondered exactly how deeply he had been hurt when Catherine Tremayne and her half brother had been returned to the family. Clive had been, until then, the unacknowledged heir to the fortune and to find himself suddenly usurped by a black-maned, violet-eyed gypsy brat, must have been a blow. Elizabeth too, had suffered, for she had been her uncle's darling, something she had worked very hard to be, until Catherine's return. It still angered her to think of the money that might have been hers if Catherine, or Adam for that matter, had remained with the gypsies.

Moodily she said, "Even Adam came off better than we did. At least Robert deeded him outright those lands near Natchez."

Looking at her, Clive said dryly, "A small fortune too, don't forget."

"That's what really bothers you, isn't it, Clive? That Robert saw to Adam's future and ignored yours. He could have left the Natchez land to you."

"My dear, what my late godfather did with his money is

none of my concern. I admit I was disappointed when Catherine suddenly reappeared after all those years. But from then until his death last year, I had plenty of time to grow used to the idea. And as I intend to marry her, there has only been a slight delay in my plans."

"And what about me?" Elizabeth asked angrily.

"I shall of course see that you are well taken care of—provided that you do as I tell you."

"Like whoring for you to find out information?" she inquired icily.

"Exactly, my dear. It's a role that you fill admirably."

After a cry of outrage from Elizabeth, there was no more conversation between them. In a foul mood when Clive parted from her at the Grosvenor Square residence of the earl of Mount, Elizabeth spent the evening planning and discarding several ugly methods for Clive's disposal. And while Elizabeth was doing that, Clive was spending the time playing cards with Jason, Freddy Barrymore and Tom Harris in Barrymore's rooms.

In spite of Freddy's fears, the evening passed tolerably well, although it would have been better if Clive had not been there. It was well after three A.M. when the little group broke up. Harris had become quite intoxicated and was remaining the night with Freddy. Clive, with a great deal of tact, departed first. After he had left, Freddy and Jason talked for a few minutes. Jason wished Freddy a pleasant trip on the morrow, offered hope that Harris's head wouldn't ache too badly, and left saying that he would see them at Brownleigh's in March.

It was a fine evening and Jason had, as planned, walked. The oil street lamps threw golden patches of light here and there down the empty, narrow streets as he strolled towards St. James's Street. He was perhaps halfway home when a slight flicker of movement near a dark alley angling off from the street caught his eye. He was but a few yards away from it, and his step slowed. Casually he glanced up and down the deserted street. He was unarmed and cursing under his breath; he wished now that he had continued to wear a knife hidden under his clothes. He was only carrying a cane, which would do him little good, if, as he suspected, an attacker lurked there in the shadows. He considered turning back, but the two figures slinking swiftly out from the alley anticipated his thought—one moving to cut off his retreat. Jason's hand went up to the catch of his cloak and unhooking it carefully, he smiled grimly to himself, thinking a cloak and a cane were not very adequate weapons against the cudgels the other two probably carried.

They circled him like wolves, his size giving them pause. And because it was his way, Jason struck first. Whipping off his cloak, he threw it accurately over the man in front of him. Then, closing swiftly, he brought his hand down in a chopping motion that nearly broke the man's neck. At the same time his knee came up and gouged deep into the man's groin. Leaving the one attacker doubled up on the cobblestone street, Jason spun like a panther, intercepting with his cane the upraised cudgel of the other man. The cane splintered, but it gave Jason a moment in which to snatch up his fallen adversary's cudgel, and then he faced the other man, armed and ready. But the other attacker had no stomach for continuing the fight and, after taking one astonished look at Jason, bolted down the street. Turning, Jason was not surprised to find that the other man too had fled, scuttling down the street like a wounded crab. For a minute he stood there breathing heavily, and then the feeling stole over him that he was not alone, that someone was still in the shadows of the alley. For several seconds he hesitated and then, after a piercing stare into the darkness, decided not to pursue matters. He was not *that* much of a fool! Picking up his cloak and keeping a steely hand wrapped around the cudgel, he continued his walk to his rooms.

Reaching his rooms, he entered and with a careless flick of his hand, dismissed Pierre for the night. Walking into his bedchamber, he stripped of his clothes and, leaving them in a heap for Pierre, threw himself down on the bed. Sleep did not come, nor did he expect it to.

He could discount the searching of his rooms earlier as merely the work of a snooping servant. This evening's incident, for that matter, could also be dismissed as one of the risks one ran in London at night—except that for some reason he doubted that both events could have been coincidences. Had Pendleton been behind it? That Pendleton was interested in his movements was fairly certain. But to attack him—for what? And therein lay the crux. Why tonight's attack? Except for the obvious reason—thieves after an easy catch. Perhaps.

Jason did not sleep well at all and woke the next morning in a surly mood. His temper was not improved by the arrival of his uncle before he had barely finished dressing. And as it was unusual for Roxbury to call on him, he eyed him across the breakfast table somewhat warily.

The duke was attired in a suit of fine blue broadcloth that fit his broad shoulders like a glove. His cravat was spotlessly white and tied in a rather intricate manner. All in all, he represented the picture of a gentleman of leisure.

As the duke made no effort to speak, but merely looked about in an interested way, Jason was forced to ask, "Is there some reason why you have come to call so early?"

"Why no, my dear boy. I was just in the neighborhood and thought I would stop by. How have you been, lately?"

"Fine."

"Oh? Nothing more than that? Tell me, now. How have you been entertaining yourself?" the duke asked, his gray eyes very wide and innocent.

Thoughtfully Jason regarded him. Did Roxbury know of last night? And if he did, how the devil had he learned of it so soon? Sipping a cup of coffee that Pierre had just finished pouring, Jason said flatly, "I have been entertaining myself just fine. Barrymore and Harris have kindly introduced me to every haunt of vice in London, and I have managed to discover a few they had never heard of. Last night, I must admit, though, was rather tame. I played cards at Barrymore's with him, Harris, and Clive Pendleton till early this morning. Is that what you wanted to know?"

The duke frowned. "Jason, is Pendleton an intimate of yours?"

Leaning back in his chair, Jason admitted, "No. I wouldn't say that. I would say that he and Elizabeth Markham seem to turn up when I least expect them. Clive appears to want to become an intimate—for what reason I cannot understand."

Roxbury hesitated. Then as if coming to a decision, he said, "At this point, I think it's important that you have a complete understanding of Clive Pendleton. He's more than just a society hanger-on who feeds on juicy scandals. He was a captain in the army until two years ago when he sold out or, should I say, was asked to sell out. It was during his time in the service that we first took an interest in him. The army was utilizing a unique ability of his; he can scan a document, or whatever, in seconds and then days or months later repeat it verbatim! He proved invaluable behind Napoleon's lines until, unfortunately, he began to sell the information he gathered to the highest bidder. Very unpatriotic. Nothing was ever proven, but he was asked to sell his commission and return to civilian life, which he did; but it hasn't stopped his other activities. So far, we, like the army, haven't been able to catch him. He's very wily, and you can't arrest a man merely because he's seen in the company of known French agents."

A soundless whistle escaped from Jason, his green eyes suddenly alert. "So," he said slowly, "you think that Pendleton is interested in me as a possible source of information to sell?"

The duke nodded. "I think it's extremely likely. And I would warn you to be careful. Pendleton is a very nasty customer, indeed." He added, "There's not much that I wouldn't do to catch him, either."

"I see. I shall take your warning to heart, uncle, but I do not think he will learn anything from me."

"I'm certain he won't—if you have no secrets."

Jason smiled but would not rise to the quizzical look in his uncle's gray eyes. They talked a few minutes longer, and then the duke departed.

With Barrymore and Harris gone to the country, Jason found that the week had a tendency to drag. And while normally the thought of a ball did not fill him with joy, he found himself looking forward to meeting Elizabeth again at her mother's party on Friday. It would be amusing to watch her work her wiles on him, and he was curious to see how Clive would attempt to glean information from him.

Friday morning came, and Jason accompanied his uncle for a ride in Hyde Park at the fashionable hour of eleven o'clock. It was there that they met Clive Pendleton, but Pendleton was acting very cool, and he merely tipped his hat and rode on. Jason exchanged a glance with his uncle, and the duke shrugged his shoulders. "Did you beat him badly the other night at Barrymore's?"

"No. I don't think it's that. He's probably just changing his tactics—and leaving me to Elizabeth's tender mercies. I wonder if that is where he was going?" Jason mused.

Clive *was* on his way to Elizabeth's. Despite their argument earlier in the week, they had made plans to meet on the morning of her mother's ball, and Clive arrived at the earl of Mount's home to find Elizabeth in a rage. She barely let him enter the morning room and the servant depart before she exploded, "That damned gypsy brat and her mother are here—they arrived last night."

3

At that moment, Catherine Tremayne, in a bedroom on the floor above the morning room, was staring gloomily out of a narrow window that overlooked Grosvernor Square. Almost resentfully she glared at the cobbled street below and the elegant town houses that lined the square, thinking longingly of the quiet green meadows of Leicestershire. In the respect that she still preferred country life to the bustle of the city, she had not changed too much in the passing of six years. Yet there was a great deal of difference between this young lady wearing a highwaisted gown of lavender muslin, her black unruly curls captured in a neat coronet of braids, and the wild unkempt child she had been. The changes, however, were mostly outwards—she dressed in the manner required of the daughter of an old and noble house, she could, when escape was impossible, converse intelligently and politely with a high-nosed dowager, and pour tea. And there was nothing in her bearing, speech, or deportment that betrayed her earlier history. But inside, Catherine was still very much the "gypsy brat" who evoked Elizabeth's invectives.

Even the terms she had been forced to spend at a very strict and proper school for young ladies had not been able to subdue her headstrong nature and longing for the careless freedom she had known in those gypsy years. Thinking just now about Mrs. Siddon's Seminary for Young Ladies, her soft mouth tightened, and a glint entered the long, almond-shaped violet eyes. God, how she had hated it! For an instant she felt again the rebellion that had surged through her body that shocking morning when Reina had thrust them under the haughty nose of the earl—the earl, her father. She experienced once again all the resentment and fury she had felt at being torn from the cheerfully adventurous life of a gypsy and being plunged immediately into the bosom of an aristocratic family. She and Adam had clung and comforted one another, united against these strange people who demanded they do the queerest things—that they wash, and wear shoes. Remembering all the old hurts and confusion, Catherine shook her head sadly, wishing for the hundredth time that she could have remained an unknown, unkempt gypsy brat. It was frequently almost impossible not to fight against the chains that bound her to the Tremaynes.

Thank goodness, she thought suddenly with affection, that their real mother, Rachael, Lady Tremayne, was a woman of great tact. Rachael had not done as her loving heart demanded and showered the children with an overdose of motherly love. She let them, like the wild forest creatures they resembled, make the first overtures of friendship. Catherine had been deeply suspicious of this sweet-smelling, youthful-looking woman who was now supposed to take Reina's place in her affections, and she had resented bitterly any sign of love her mother attempted to bestow upon her. But time had blunted her first aversions, and Catherine had discovered with much surprise that she dearly loved her mother. One couldn't help loving Rachael, Catherine thought with amusement; she was that kind of person.

Now a faint moan came from her mother, who was lying on the silk-draped bed behind her, and with soft, quick steps Catherine crossed the room to her side. Gazing down with concerned eyes at Rachael's swollen jaw, she asked quietly, "Is there anything that I can do? Would you like me to bathe your forehead with some rose water? Do you think that it would help?"

Rachael Tremayne was a slim woman with bright blue eyes and an exceptionally sweet face. She looked more like Catherine's sister than her mother, a circumstance due in part to her youthfully dark brown curls, which betrayed no trace of silver. She was at the moment recovering from the less gentle effects of having had an infected tooth drawn that morning.

Smiling wanly at her daughter, she said, "No love, just let me lie here and presently, perhaps, I'll be able to swallow some of that excellent broth Mrs. Barrows has prepared. You don't have to stay here by my side, you know. You should be out taking advantage of our impromptu visit. Why don't you pay a call on Amanda Harris? I'm sure she would be delighted to see you again."

Catherine shrugged. "I'd rather not. Amanda might have other plans, and besides our stay is going to be so short that I would just as soon not see anyone. After all, we didn't come here to enjoy ourselves."

Smiling ruefully, Rachael agreed with her. "Certainly not! But as we are here, we might as well make the best of it. Perhaps," she added with a twinkle, "you would like to have tea with your aunt this afternoon. At least *that* will get you out of this closed room."

A decidedly unladlylike snort greeted her words. "I'd far rather be here with you than listening to my aunt prattle on about tonight's ball. Especially since she'll manage, ever so cleverly, to convey to everyone how inconvenient our arrival is! Does she think you planned to have that dreadful toothache?" Catherine demanded indignantly.

Rachael looked at Catherine's stormy countenance and

gave a soft sigh of distress. Her inflamed and throbbing tooth had necessitated this hurried trip to London, and, although the relationship had been strained for some time, she had hoped that Ceci, her sister-in-law, now the countess of Mount, would be willing to overlook past differences. Unfortunately, they had arrived the day before Ceci's first ball of the year. Submerged in the preparations, she had been considerably displeased by their visit, despite the reason.

Over the years, Rachael had tried very hard to keep things pleasant with Ceci, but Ceci's nature, cold and selfish, made it an impossibility. And when Ceci had discovered the fact that little beyond the title and Mountacre had fallen to her husband, Edward, upon his succession to his brother's estates, the relationship had become further strained. It had come as a nasty shock to Ceci to find that the wealth she had long coveted was not an automatic part of the inheritance. And Elizabeth, Ceci's eldest child, had been furious!

The reading of the will had been a thoroughly unpleasant affair, and when the provision providing the gypsies with the right to camp in a large meadow near Hunter's Hill, the Leicestershire estate, had been read aloud, Elizabeth, unable to hide her chagrin any longer, had been bitterly outspoken. She had ignored her father's angry, embarrassed attempts to hush her ridiculous rantings, until Catherine, at first amazed by her cousin's reaction, had grown furious herself and told her explicitly what a foolish creature she was. Ceci could not allow this to pass and had angrily rebuked Catherine, while Clive, his gray eyes malicious, had halfheartedly defended Catherine. Rachael and Edward had vainly attempted to smooth over the whole miserable scene, but to no avail. It had been a distasteful episode that was not soon forgotten.

Needless to say, there now existed an uncomfortable relationship between them, and the passing months had done nothing to lessen it. Edward, who was Catherine's guardian, was genuinely fond of his niece, and saw her and her mother occasionally. But for the most part there was little communication between the families.

Fortunately, Rachael and Catherine preferred to live in quiet seclusion at Hunter's Hill, where the late earl had established a large stud farm. Some years before, when Catherine had expressed an interest in the breeding of thoroughbreds, her father had instantly forsaken Mountacre, and they had made their home in the graceful Tudor mansion at Hunter's Hill near Melton Mowbray. And after his death in a riding accident less than a year ago, neither Rachael nor Catherine had seen any reason not to continue living in the home they had grown to love. They seldom left the area, having no desire to mingle with the fashionable throng that was so important to Ceci and Elizabeth. And besides, it was unthinkable for them to attend any frivolous entertainment until their year of mourning was up. Lately though, it had occurred to Rachael that the time was approaching when Catherine should be presented and enjoy her first season.

It troubled Lady Tremayne that Catherine had no interest in any of the pursuits of a young lady of fashion. At eighteen she still preferred mucking out the stables, working with her beloved horses, or roaming familiarly through the gypsy camp to choosing new dresses and gowns. Even the possibility of a trip to London aroused no animation. As for young men, she had met a few and seemed perfectly happy with things the way they were.

Recently, Rachael had mentioned the idea of living in London for a season, and in tones of the blankest astonishment, Catherine had asked, "London? Whatever for?"

Disconcerted and at a loss for words, Rachael had been unable to proceed farther. But regardless of the setback, she had determinedly resolved that Catherine should leave behind her unladlylike interests, take her place in polite society—and find a husband. She couldn't stay buried in the country forever with stable boys and gypsies as her only companions.

Thinking of the gypsies, Rachael frowned. She had been

as surprised as anyone that Robert had put in that odd provision for the gypsies. Especially since his first reaction to Reina had been to have her thrown in the nearest dungeon. And it had only been after pleas and tears and stony silences from Catherine that he had relented. With a flash of insight, he had realized that by punishing Reina and the gypsies he would be creating a further barrier between himself and his only child. Grudgingly he had allowed there to be some visiting between the two children and the gypsies. He certainly did not like it, but at least his daughter did not glare at him as if he were her deadliest enemy! And that, thought Rachael sadly, was probably exactly why he had assured that even after his death, Catherine would not be torn from her gypsies. He had been a cold, aloof man, unable to show his true affections, and yet in many thoughtful acts he had attempted to show Catherine how much he adored her. If only he had tried as much with her, Rachael thought unhappily, their marriage would have been much more meaningful and loving.

Determinedly she shook off her melancholy thoughts and watched her daughter pace restlessly about the room. The girl was a vivid figure against the cream walls and soft green carpet, and her ceaseless tread reminded Rachael of a caged lioness. Catherine was a vibrant person, always busy with something, and prolonged inactivity always seemed to affect her that way. Rachael wondered if, perhaps, it had been unkind to subject her to the tender mercies of Mrs. Siddon's boarding school. Such places were often like prisons, and for the first time she realized fully what a traumatic experience Catherine must have gone through adjusting to a society completely different from the one in which she had spent all of her early years. But the girl had managed, she thought proudly, and Rachael was struck anew by the wonder that she, unexceptional and shy, should have produced such a self-willed, lovely creature.

Catherine, slender and finely boned, wasn't a conventional beauty. She was a study of contrasts that caught the eye and held the attention. Blue black hair, almost shocking against the gardenia whiteness of her skin, and a triangular-shaped face were first impressions. Then, those intriguing, slanted violet eyes that frequently sparkled with mischief impinged upon the senses, until her lips, full and curved with innocent, provocative invitation, riveted the gaze.

Just now, there was a set expression about Catherine's mouth that boded ill for the remainder of their short stay. Staring at Catherine's determined countenance, Rachael wished heartily that it was already tomorrow and they were on their way back to Hunter's Hill. Soothingly she said, "Don't mind Ceci, my dear. She can't help being the way she is. And I suppose it *is* terribly inconvenient for us to be here now."

"I don't see why," Catherine argued. "We are not going to attend her silly ball, and heaven knows the house has enough unused rooms." A militant gleam in her eyes, she added, "We don't upset her servants like she does ours!"

A sympathetic smile on her lips, Rachael murmured, "I know, love, but Cat, please promise me you won't antagonize your aunt. Promise?"

Catherine's promise was given too promptly, and the glint in her violet eyes made Lady Tremayne view her sudden meekness with suspicion. "Catherine, you're not up to anything are you?" she asked.

With a look of assumed innocence on her face, Catherine purred dulcetly, "Why, of course not, madame! Whatever makes you think otherwise? To please you, since you're not feeling quite well, I promise not to annoy *Ceci!*"

The faint stress on her aunt's name warned Rachael, but before she could utter another word, there was a soft tap on the door. At Rachael's command to enter, the door swung open, and Clive Pendleton walked in, a polite, attractive smile on his lips.

Rachael was delighted to see him, her warm smile welcoming, but Catherine eyed him warily as he seated himself comfortably on a chair near her mother's bedside. The reactions of the two women were characteristic; to Rachael, Clive presented his most charming manner, and she thought of him as the pleasant young man who had been her late husband's godson; but Catherine guessed that there was another side, a dark, skillfully hidden side, and she avoided him.

During the past few years, he had come to call several times at Hunter's Hill, when he had been visiting in Melton Mowbray. But Rachael had been the one to see him, for Catherine always remembered some errand that took her from the house on that day.

Clive suspected that she purposely evaded him, and as he covertly watched her move uneasily about the room, an unpleasant gleam flickered briefly in his eyes, gone so quickly that Rachael, chatting idly to him, never saw it.

Catherine had seen it though, for she had never taken her eyes off his face, and suspicious of his affability, she held herself stiffly aloof. Consequently, she was considerably surprised when after a few minutes of polite conversation he left. After the door closed behind him, her slim brows drew together in a black scowl.

Rachael, seeing her expression, couldn't help smiling to herself, although she was mystified as to why both her children viewed Clive with such violent antipathy. Curiosity got the better of her, and she asked, "Why do you dislike him so? He's a handsome enough young man, and I must say he looked very elegant this afternoon."

Moodily, Catherine stared at her before admitting coolly, "He's fairly handsome, if one prefers that type of looks."

Rachael, an amused twinkle in the blue eyes, asked, "Do you really know what kind of looks you like? You sound very certain of your views!"

"Well," Catherine began doubtfully, "I've never given it much thought, but I don't suppose that one's physical features are *that* important. Of course, one wouldn't want a truly ugly husband! But a man can be extremely handsome, yet be mean inside, and I'd rather have a man who had a kindness for me than one like Clive, who'd mistreat a woman."

"You don't know that, darling, and you judge him unfairly; Clive has always, to use your own words, had a kindness for you. The day you were kidnapped, he was almost as frantic and grief-stricken as your father and I. No one could have searched more diligently than he. You have, I'm afraid, always misjudged his every real affection for you."

Catherine avoided her mother's serious look and muttered, "That may be, but *nothing* will ever convince me that Clive cares for anyone other than himself."

Wisely, Rachael let the subject lapse, for opposition only made Catherine dig in her heels and cling more adamantly to her own ideas. Rachael once again encouraged Catherine not to stay by her side. This time Catherine gave in, guessing that her mother was in some discomfort and probably wished to be alone. But before Catherine left, Rachael, remembering their earlier conversation, asked, "You really won't do anything to upset your aunt, will you?"

Catherine sent her a saucy grin and walking out the room said over her shoulder, "I promised not to bother Aunt Ceci, but I didn't say a *word* about Elizabeth!"

Giving a small moan of vexation, Rachael fell back against the white satin pillows, knowing there was no stopping Cat. She was guiltily aware of how little control she really exercised over her spirited daughter.

Catherine, meanwhile, smiling and humming happily to herself, ran lightly down the stairs on her way to the small library that Cecil had grudgingly set aside for their use. Catherine had fallen in love at once with the library's quaint, comfortable air, for it was the only room that reminded her of Hunter's Hill. One wall was lined with fine leather-bound volumes, while opposite was an ornately carved marble fireplace. A desk sat at one end, and in front of the fireplace was an old-fashioned couch of brown mohair.

She had barely shut the door behind her and taken but a few steps into the room when she heard the door opening again. Expecting one of the servants she turned, the questioning smile on her lips dying abruptly when she saw that her intruder was none other than Clive Pendleton.

For a second they eyed one another, Catherine's hostility very obvious from the expression of disdain on her beautiful face. Clive was wearing his most urbane smile, but it aroused no welcoming response from Catherine.

"You followed me, didn't you?" she asked bluntly.

Clive, making a depreciatory gesture with his hands, replied smoothly, "Could I help it? You avoid me otherwise, and this seemed like too good an opportunity to pass by."

"For what? Do you think that a few moments alone with you will overcome my aversion?"

His smile thinned ever so slightly at her scornful words, and for a moment the ugly expression she had seen earlier flickered in his hard gray eyes. He took a step nearer, and Catherine barely restrained the urge to move backwards away from him. But she stood her ground, her chin raised defiantly, and demanded, "Well?"

Restraining the surge of anger that shook him, his cold smile only deepened, and deliberately he reached out and lightly touched her cheek. Catherine flinched as if he had slapped her, and she struck his hand aside.

Apparently undeterred by her actions, he murmured, "Who knows what may happen? I am considered quite eligible, you know, and if you would put aside your childish dislike of me, you might find that I have several desirable virtues to offer a woman. Certainly your mother would not object if I were to pay my addresses to you—and you, my dear, could discover that I know to a degree how to please a woman."

Sheer astonishment held Catherine rooted to the spot. She had always avoided him whenever she could and despite Rachael's liking of him, could never bring herself to really feel at ease in his company. There was something that she couldn't name that she disliked about him, and he always made her feel definitely wary whenever she found herself in his presence. It was an instinctive dislike based not so much on any one incident so much as a natural aversion to his cold and calculating personality. Added to that was Reina's and Manuel's definite hostility to him—a hostility that was tinged slightly with a queer wariness, as if they knew something to his discredit, something that they would not speak of.

Despite having nothing of substance on which to base her feelings, Catherine knew that she distrusted Clive. The thought that he meant to court her was one she had never considered—dishonor her, yes, he was quite capable of that, but marriage?

Shaken by the idea, she really looked at him, and her mother's earlier words came back. Yes, he was a handsome man, she thought, but his handsomeness did not arouse any emotion within her other than dislike. True he was elegantly dressed, his manly form all that a maiden could wish for, his height a little above the average, giving him a commanding air, but his gray eyes were too cold and hard, and his features too thinly aristocratic and inclined to sneer. Certainly he was not a man she wished to marry!

Clive was watching her expressive face closely, having a fair idea of her thoughts. It had been a calculated risk on his part, displaying so soon his ultimate goal, but he had decided that Catherine should begin to think of him in a different light. It was time she became aware of him as a man—and a suitor.

Coolly his eyes ran over her, and he felt again the sweet bitterness she aroused in his breast. Why did she have to have reappeared after all those years? And why did she have to have grown so lovely? She had been lovely even in tattered garments, her face dirty, and her tangled black hair falling across her sparkling, fury-filled violet eyes that day when Reina had thrust her before the earl.

Clive had been fascinated then against his will, and while her reappearance had doomed his own hopes, instantly another thought had struck him, and he had been pleased that he found her so tantalizing. If she had been desirable then, now he found her even more so, and muttering an oath, his coolness vanished, and he dragged her into a hungry embrace.

Her mouth was warm and soft in surprise as he gathered her closer, deepening his kiss, forcing her lips apart, his tongue plundering her mouth.

Catherine had half sensed he was going to kiss her, and unaware of the emotions a single kiss could arouse, she had been partly curious, having more than reached an age to wonder about what happened between men and women in the throes of passion. It had been only curiosity that had ruled her in letting Clive take her into his arms, but she discovered immediately that it had been a horrid mistake—she didn't like his tongue in her mouth, and when his hand touched her breast, a tremor of revulsion shook her slender body. Confused and not a little disgusted by the storm of emotion she had unwittingly caused, she pushed violently against his chest, but to no avail. Ignoring her attempts to escape and lost in desire, Clive only pulled her closer to him. Able to free one arm and sheer fury lending strength to her efforts, she boxed him smartly on the ear, and at the same time brought her sharp little heel down hard on his foot. Attacked with such painful force on two fronts, Clive's passion died as quickly as it had risen, and with more haste than grace, he released her.

Catherine spared him not a glance. Spying a thin silver letter opener lying on the desk, she snatched it up in her hand, holding it like a knife, and, her eyes blazing violet fire, she faced him.

Clive took an impatient step forward, but the sight of the letter opener held so confidently in Catherine's hand halted him.

In a voice filled with loathing she spat, "Stay where you are! Come any closer to me, and I shall show you how well I can use this pretty little thing."

Willing himself to relax, a taut smile crossed his handsome face. Forcing a lightness into his voice, he murmured, "My dear girl, you mistake my intentions. What is one small kiss between us? Why, we are practically related. I meant no harm."

Catherine's eyes were narrowed with disbelief, and she snorted contemptuously. "I am not a fool, Clive. You can keep your kisses for Elizabeth. She, I am certain, will enjoy them far more than I."

A queer silence greeted her words, and biting his lip in vexation, Clive wondered how she had come to learn of his liaison with Elizabeth. Shrugging his shoulders he replied lightly, "You cannot blame a man for his indiscretions, my dear. The sins committed in one's salad days cannot be held against one forever. And," he added deliberately, "with my wild oats behind me, you can be assured that I would be a faithful husband."

Catherine's lip curled scornfully. "Save your polite speeches for someone else, if you please. And I would appreciate it if you would leave me alone. I cannot think of any reason for prolonging this distasteful scene."

Knowing he could gain nothing further and warily eyeing the silver letter opener, Clive made as graceful an exit as possible under the circumstances. For several moments after he had departed, Catherine's thoughts were not happy, but then telling herself that Clive could do her no harm, she pushed aside the memory of this latest unpleasant episode and willed herself to relax and think only of pleasant things.

Crossing the room, she knelt down in front of the fire, her slim hands held out to the warmth of the blaze. After a few minutes, she sat down, leaning her head back against the couch, staring dreamily into the fire and wondering idly what Adam was doing and if he was as happy in America as his few letters indicated. She still missed him awfully, even after three years.

Catherine, for all her liveliness, was a lonely girl, though she would have been surprised to be told so. Uncomfortable and uncertain with her contemporaries, she'd ~~had~~ made only one friend at Mrs. Siddon's, shy and gentle Amanda Harris—and that had not lasted. For when they left the school, their paths parted, Amanda going to live with her grandmother, the formidable dowager duchess of Avon, and Catherine returning to the comparative peacefulness of Hunter's Hill. But Catherine was happy in her life and seldom thought beyond the boundaries of Hunter's Hill. Content to spend her days immersed in the activities of the farm, she was unawakened to the outside world.

Immensely satisfied with the present, she was content to gaze at the fire, thinking of her home, aware that from a distance she could hear the bustle of the preparations for tonight's ball. The last thing she remembered before drifting off to sleep was the ringing of the hour by the huge grandfather clock downstairs.

She awoke with a start some hours later. What awakened her she didn't know, but from the sounds permeating the room it was obvious that Ceci's ball was well underway, and she knew the hour must be late. Silently, like a cat, she stretched and blinked at the glowing embers on the hearth. For a moment she sat thus, still not quite awake. Then, starting to rise, she was held motionless by the faint sound of the rustle of paper.

Cautiously, she peered around the end of the couch and discovered, much to her surprise, an unknown man seated at the desk, a candle flickering at his elbow, his dark head bent as he read the letter in his hands, and he was unaware of Catherine's keen scrutiny.

She couldn't see his features clearly, but from his clothes she supposed he must be one of the guests, for he was fashionably attired in a green velvet jacket with an elaborately embroidered, yellow silk waistcoat. Suddenly, as if sensing someone watching him, he glanced up, the light from the candles falling full on his face, and Catherine was gripped by a strange, painful giddiness as she stared at the hard, dark face.

It was an intensely masculine face with a bold nose that

seemed to flare at the nostrils, as if he scented her hiding there; and she felt a queer, choking sensation as his eyes, glittering greenly in the candlelight, pierced the room, seeking the source of his slight uneasiness. Frozen, like some small, frightened animal hiding from a stalking panther, Catherine was unable to tear her gaze away until he gave a careless shrug of his broad shoulders and bent his dark head once more.

Slowly, she released her pent-up breath in a shuddering sigh and felt a blind, unreasoning panic. Driven by the knowledge that she must escape this man, she crept quickly to the door. Exactly why she was impelled to flee his disturbing presence, she didn't know; she only knew this strange man aroused a primitive and nameless fear.

Reaching the door, her hand on the handle, she was momentarily startled when a drawling, accented voice called out behind her, "*Arrêtez!* Stop!"

Compelled to look back, she saw he was rising from behind the desk, his eyes meeting her wide, violet ones with a shock she felt in her bones. Suddenly, she wasn't frightened any longer, just angry at her own silly emotions, and glaring at him she wrinkled her straight little nose and impudently stuck out her tongue! Then, his shout of laughter ringing in her ears, she bolted from the room and fled up the stairs as if all the demons in hell were after her.

Like a shy child before strangers, she ran to her mother's room, hating herself for giving in to almost sheer panic. Standing breathlessly outside the door, she waited a moment, forcing her thudding heart to calm itself. When she felt she was once more in command of herself, she knocked softly and upon hearing Rachael asking who it was, she opened the door and entered the room.

"Why, Catherine!" Rachael cried, surprised. "What are you still doing up, my love? It is very late, you know."

Smiling, Catherine dropped a light kiss on her cheek and replied, "Actually, I've been sleeping. I fell asleep in the library and just now woke up. Is there anything I can do for you before I go to bed?"

"No, my love. I feel much better, and knowing we are leaving in the morning is even more restoring to my spirits. I can hardly wait to return home."

Catherine agreed. If all went well and if they had an early start as planned, this time tomorrow night they would be safe at Hunter's Hill. Safe was an odd word to use, but just now to Catherine it fitted perfectly.

They conversed for a few minutes longer, and then Catherine bid her mother a fond good night and walked to her room a few doors down the hall. It was an attractive room, decorated in much the same style and color as her mother's, but Catherine took little notice of her surroundings as she prepared for bed.

She had dispensed with the services of her maid for the hasty trip to London, and quickly she stripped off her lavender dress and undergarments and slid naked between the linen sheets, enjoying the almost sinful pleasure of their smoothness against her bare skin. A small giggle escaped her as she thought of the shocking and disapproving expression her mother's face would wear if she knew. Then, suddenly, the lightheartedness left her, and her small cat-shaped face wore an anxious expression as a dark, arrogant countenance with glittering green eyes flashed into her mind.

She tried to forget the young man in the library, but it was as if his face and form were seared into her brain. Even now, a thrill of fright and something else, as yet unnamed, raced through her veins as she recalled his tall, broad-shouldered body, the careless elegance of his dress and the aura of recklessness, of leashed male passion, that had seemed to reach out and touch her, as she had crouched frozen, staring at his face.

Restlessly she tossed in the bed, bedeviled by odd thoughts and alien emotions that disturbed and infuriated her. Angrily she punched down the unoffending pillow and told herself vehemently that she was acting like a silly ninnyhammer, mooning over a man she would probably never see again. And, she added viciously to herself, he was more than likely a conceited, mincing fop, who would bore her to death if she did meet him!

But nothing, not even harsh thoughts, would banish him from her memory. With a small moan of defeat, she dwelt upon their brief meeting, alarming herself just before falling asleep by dreamily wondering what it would be like to have his hard mouth pressed sweetly against hers.

4

Jason Beauvais de Ulloa Savage, laughing to himself, sank slowly back in his chair, his green eyes shining with amusement. What a saucy little minx! She had given him a start when he had looked up and seen her creeping toward the door, and at his command to stop, he had certainly not expected the young lady to stick out her tongue! He frowned suddenly, his recollection of her unclear. He knew she wasn't a servant, for her gown had been stylish, yet she hadn't been dressed for the ball. Elizabeth's younger sisters were still in the nursery, so who the devil was the little creature with those angry eyes? He gave her some seconds more thought, then regretfully dismissed her, and turned his attention to Barrymore's execrable scrawl.

Jas,

When are you coming down? The hunting is poor, and Tom and I are about to drive one another mad! Can you not move up your travel arrangements? I know you are to escort Amanda and her grandmother down for

Brownleighs, but can't you convince them to come a few days earlier? Enough of that. Now to the real purpose of this letter.

I have found near here the horses you are looking for! They are owned by a band of gypsies camped on the estate of the dowager countess of Mount (the fair Elizabeth's aunt). Perhaps Tom can arrange an introduction, although I think it best if the gypsies are approached directly. In any event, the horses are most superior, just perfect for your plans of resale in New Orleans. As everyone knows that gypsies are never very long in one place, I expect it would be wise if you came as soon as possible.

I am dispatching this letter with my most persistent man, with instructions to find you at once! With luck he will interrupt an indiscretion.

Yours faithfully,
Frederick Barrymore

Jason had been interrupted in the middle of a dance and given the letter. At his request the earl had shown him to the library, where in relative quiet he had deciphered the message. As he read the contents, his amusement grew, for he had been expecting the direst news. Leave it to Freddie to treat the discovery of additional horseflesh as a major event, he thought wryly.

Smiling to himself, Jason threw the note on the coals and thoughtfully decided that some days in the country would not be unpleasant. Accustomed to an active, vigorous life, London had begun to bore him, especially the well-meaning but persistent attempts of several matrons to introduce him to fashionable families with marriageable young ladies.

Distracted by a slight sound, he turned quickly and was surprised at the disappointment he felt when he saw Elizabeth Markham entering the room and not the engaging creature who had disturbed him earlier.

Smiling invitingly, her hips gracefully swaying, Elizabeth

came to Jason's side. An appreciative glint in his eyes, he surveyed her bronze-green satin ball gown that was cut so shockingly low that it revealed more of her full, firm breasts than it concealed. She was certainly displaying her wares!

The scent of her perfume drifted pleasantly to his nostrils, and her voice was soft as she said, "So this is where you have vanished to! My father said you received an urgent message and wished to be private. Nothing serious, I hope?"

"No. But if I'd known an urgent message would bring you to my side, I would have arranged to receive one ages ago."

Playfully, she slapped his wrist with her small fan. "La! What an accomplished flirt you are. I was merely concerned that you might have received bad news." She glanced up at him, her wide brown eyes clearly curious, but he ignored the unspoken question in their depths and lazily pulled her next to him, lightly brushing her soft lips with his. "Was it only concern that brought you here?"

"Not exactly," she admitted coyly, dropping her eyes demurely.

The sensuous curve of his mouth more pronounced, he pulled her slowly against his warm body, his lips taking hers, in a demanding kiss that left no doubt of his growing desire. Elizabeth pressed closer, enjoying the way he explored her lips—her tongue darting into his mouth, her body on fire for more than just kisses. Yet, she slipped casually from his arms when he murmured against her mouth, "Will you meet me after the ball, at a place where we can be private?"

Fluttering her fan she laughed, "My, sir, you've a bold way about you, but I'm afraid you've mistaken my character. It wouldn't be proper for me to meet you alone." Then unable to help herself and not wishing to discourage him too harshly, she added slyly, "I must be careful of my reputation. London is filled with scandalmongers, and someone might see us."

His smile tightening, one black brow raised derisively, he asked curtly, "What do you suggest?"

Uncertainly, she nibbled her bottom lip, thrown into a quandary by his abrupt question and by a longing to be in his arms. Living as she did almost at Clive's mercy, she was desperate to make an advantageous match. It would be one way out of her problems. And Jason Savage was absolutely perfect for what she wanted.

Unfortunately, marriage was *not* what Mr. Savage had in mind, and with one disastrous alliance behind her, she couldn't afford to have an open affair with the gentleman from Louisiana; yet, if she became his mistress, intuitively she knew he would be a generous lover, bestowing upon her expensive gifts and trinkets that later could be converted into lovely gold coin. And besides, becoming his mistress could even give her a better chance at becoming Mrs. Savage—it wouldn't be the first time a man had been caught by his mistress. Silken bedsheets had led to the altar more than once. And with this in mind, she pouted prettily up at him and sighed, "You're so impatient. Let me think."

Guessing at the mercenary thoughts running through her head, Jason was unable to control the twitch of his lips, and he bowed mockingly, saying, "Madame, you enchant me. I shall wait eagerly for your message. And," he added smoothly, "since you're so concerned with your reputation, I think it best if we weren't discovered here, alone."

But perversely, Elizabeth was not ready to break the tête-à-tête, and provocatively she said, "Are you always so cautious? If you are, it's no wonder you're welcomed by Mr. King and the duke of Roxbury. Being so very prudent themselves, they must trust you a great deal to be as familiar with you as they are. You certainly seem to spend a lot of time with them."

At the mention of King and his uncle, Jason's eyes narrowed with instant suspicion. His uncle had warned him about Elizabeth's connection with Clive Pendleton, but he hadn't really taken it as seriously as he should have. And it appeared that Elizabeth was indeed probing for information.

Jason's face gave no hint of his thoughts, but his eyes

were hard as he said bluntly, "How do you know how familiar I am with them? Do you have little spies that watch me?"

Elizabeth's arch smile faded abruptly, and she answered sharply, "Don't be silly! I was only teasing. And if you're going to take me up like that on everything I say, I don't think I shall talk to you any more this evening." With a toss of her chestnut curls, she started to walk regally from the room. Jason, an unrepentant grin on his face, turned her around and unhesitatingly pulled her into his arms.

"I'm sorry that I was short with you," he said slowly, "but I have no desire to exchange gossip. You're much too beautiful for us to waste our time talking. Stay here with me, and I'll show you what I mean."

Elizabeth felt all her anger draining away at his touch, and as she gazed up into his dark face, a reckless feeling invaded her body. Why not stay?

Reading the answer in her eyes, Jason gave her no chance to speak, but kissed her long and thoroughly. Feeling her response as she melted against him, he released her lips briefly and whispered into her ear, "If we lock the door, no one will disturb us."

It was tempting, too tempting, Elizabeth thought with Jason's body so close to hers. She looked at the waning fire on the hearth and took in the quiet intimacy of the room. No one would disturb them, for no one except her father knew where they were, and the earl, taken up with entertaining his guests, would have long since forgotten.

Giving her little time to think more on it, Jason took two strides to the door and turned the key in the lock. His eyes dark with desire, he walked back to her, and Elizabeth knew she was going to let him make love to her—she couldn't help it, and the possibility of discovery made it even more exciting.

Gently Jason laid her on the couch, his mouth warm against her neck, and she went dizzy with desire when his hand slid up under her gown to caress her thigh. She made a halfhearted attempt to stop him, but he only pushed aside her hands and kissed her deeply, the weight of his hard body keeping her a willing prisoner beneath him.

Fire seemed to scald through her veins as his searching lips traveled down to her bosom, and she wished that they dared to remove their clothing—she wanted Jason naked next to her. Yet there was something so very depraved, she decided hazily, about making love with all their clothes on.

Jason loosened her breasts from the low-cut gown, his hand warm as his thumb brushed a nipple, his mouth hard and demanding on hers. With his other hand, he pushed up the satin gown, and his searching fingers found the softness between her thighs. Elizabeth couldn't help her moan of sheer animal pleasure as he fondled and explored her. She was so hungry for him, she thought she would scream if he didn't take her soon. Her whole body was on fire for him, and she wanted him like she had never wanted another man. Her hands clutched his velvet jacket, and she muttered crossly, "Take it off." But Jason only murmured thickly against her mouth, "Next time. And it's not my *jacket* that I need to be rid of."

He shifted his weight slightly and with a quick motion freed himself from the black satin breeches. The next instant, Elizabeth felt him slide deep within her outspread legs, and hungrily she pushed up against him. Feeling him filling her, his very size and hardness a caress in itself, she cried softly, "Oh, God! Jason, take me!"

His mouth came down on hers with almost brutal force, and his hands cupped her buttocks tightly as he thrust himself deeper and harder into her again and again until her whole body shook with the force of their passion. Some minutes later, replete and full, she lay back against the cushions knowing that she had never been so completely satisfied in her entire life. Then drifting back to sanity, she became aware of what had actually happened and where they were, and she sat up with a jerk.

"Oh, I don't know what you must think of me!" Elizabeth

began, but Jason, calmly arranging his breeches, shot her a quizzical look and then leaned over and hushed her with a gentle kiss. Deftly helping her straighten her gown, he said, "I think that you are a lovely woman, and I hope that you will allow me to see even more of you than I have."

It wasn't precisely what she wanted to hear, but it left her with hope. At least he wanted to see her again.

They agreed to enter the ballroom separately, and it was Jason who entered first, giving Elizabeth a chance to escape to her room to remove any signs of their recent meeting.

He paused at the entrance to the ballroom, surveying the scene, and when he noticed Amanda Harris seated next to her grandmother, he walked quickly over to their side. Augusta Dudley, the dowager duchess of Avon, was white-haired, had lively black eyes, and was approaching seventy. She was a formidable old woman, and Jason did not relish the task of asking her to move up their date of departure for Brownleigh's house party. But it was worth a chance, and so without too much polite conversation, he came immediately out with it. Surprisingly, Augusta agreed instantly to the change in plans. London was still a bit thin of company, and she, quite frankly, was bored.

"Shall we make it a week from tonight, then?" she inquired.

Jason bowed and replied, "That will be fine with me. I shall send some of my horses ahead tomorrow and will make all other arrangements for our traveling. And now, with that out of the way—Amanda, may I have this dance?"

Blushing, her brown eyes hidden beneath her lashes, Amanda very prettily accepted his offer. She bore little resemblance to her brother other than being rather short and having red hair. Only in Amanda, the hair was a rich, vibrant deep red, and petite better described her than short. She was an enchanting little lady, and Jason had some affection for her—the affection of a big brother for a small sister. She was already on the friendliest terms with him, and so as they danced she eagerly prattled on about the proposed trip to

Brownleigh's. Near the end of their dance, remembering his angry-eyed intruder, Jason asked curiously, "Is there a young lady about your age staying with Elizabeth?"

For a second Amanda looked puzzled. Then she said, "Oh, you must mean Catherine, but I didn't know she was visiting. The little wretch. I wonder why she never came to see me."

"Catherine?"

"Why, yes. She is Elizabeth's cousin."

"Oh," Jason said slightly disappointed. His involvement with Elizabeth precluded any attempt on his part to make the acquaintance of her cousin, and so regretfully he pushed her from his mind. Certainly he paid little attention to Amanda's excited recital of Catherine's history. Later there would come a time when he would wish that he had listened with much more attention to Amanda. As it was, his mind was already on other things, so what Amanda had to say passed over his head.

Elizabeth had entered the ballroom and, with narrowed eyes, Jason watched her make her way immediately to Clive Pendleton. So, she *had* been probing for information. Smiling mirthlessly, he wondered if she would report everything that had passed between them.

Elizabeth had no intention of telling Clive everything. Her relationship with Jason she meant to keep to herself. If Clive had any inkling that she was trying to marry Savage, he would find a way to put a stop to it. She was too valuable for him to lose to the respectable state of marriage.

Clive looked up as Elizabeth approached. Detaching himself from a companion, he took her arm and walked a little way with her. "Well?" he asked under the cover of the noise of the other guests. "Do you actually have something, or are you merely postponing bad news?"

Glancing nervously over her shoulder, she answered sullenly, "He wouldn't tell me anything. As soon as I mentioned King and his wretched uncle, he accused me of spying on him!"

"Aren't you exaggerating slightly?" Clive asked irritably, a spark of skepticism burning in his cold gray eyes.

"Perhaps, a little," she replied slowly. "I need more time though, before he'll trust me. You can't expect the man to blurt out everything to a woman he barely knows. He's not a fool."

"Then I would recommend that you insinuate yourself into his affections promptly. That is, if you wish me to continue reducing your more pressing debts," he snapped harshly.

Her lips thinning with anger, Elizabeth forced herself to answer civilly, "I've every intention of becoming vital to Jason Savage, and as soon as I learn anything, I'll let you know."

"Very well. But remember, my pet, who will be paying your bills once he's gone."

Silently Elizabeth acknowledged the wisdom of his remark, and minutes later she drifted off with an admirer. Clive, smiling cynically to himself, watched her proceed to flirt outrageously with the besotted young man. Yes, if anyone could discover the reason for Jason Savage's intimacy with the American minister, as well as whether or not there was more than filial affection behind his frequent visits to the duke of Roxbury, it would be Elizabeth. She was very adept at worming information from her lovers.

Clive was exceedingly thoughtful for the remainder of the evening. Elizabeth might not have told him all that had transpired between her and Jason, but he was clever at figuring out things himself. And having recognized from past experience the blurred look of satiated desire in Elizabeth's eyes, he could well imagine what had happened. That Jason had managed to mount her disturbed him little, but that she had not reported it was something else again. So, Elizabeth was playing games, was she? Clive's lips twisted into a nasty smile. We'll see who plays games, he thought viciously—and that included Catherine. His pride had still not quite recovered from her attack on it that afternoon. He had meant what he'd told Elizabeth that afternoon coming back from Epsom Downs—if he didn't marry Catherine, he'd see to it that no one else did; he'd ruin her first!

Clive's thoughts were still in that vein when he returned to his lodgings a short time later. And relaxing in his sitting room before a fire, he began to toy with various plans to bring the little gypsy bitch and her fortune under his control. She had in no uncertain terms spurned his suit, but if she were faced with ruin, would she still do so? Clive thought not. It might, he decided, even be better to ruin her first, then offer marriage as a means of escape. Yes, the very thing!

Frowning in concentration, he walked over to his safe, built into one wall. Opening it, he rifled through the papers until he came to a letter written in Rachael's neat handwriting. How fortunate that he had kept it!

The letter, a few years old, had been written by Rachael to a French cousin, Madame Poullin, when English sympathies were at their height during the war with Napoleon. Clive, spying behind French lines at the time, had found himself forced to hide at Madame Poullin's until safe transportation could be arranged. And being Clive, he had systematically searched madame's house for any bit of information that he thought might be useful later. He had found the letter in madame's desk and had carelessly shoved it into his coat. And until now he had had no reason to even remember its existence. Carefully he reread the letter. Yes. It just might be used as a weapon against the fair Catherine. Exactly how, he wasn't sure, but if he thought about it long enough, he was certain to hit upon a scheme.

He awoke the next morning feeling quite pleased with himself. Catherine's comeuppance was only a matter of time.

He had just finished breakfast and was preparing to have his horse brought round, intending to take a ride in Hyde Park, when his servant entered the room.

"There is a foreign gentleman to see you. He wouldn't give his name, but said this would give him entree."

This was a large roll of money. Extremely interested and curious, Clive agreed to see the gentleman.

The man who entered was clearly a Spaniard, his black eyes and hair and dark complexion plainly declaring his ancestry. A scar twisted one eyebrow, and when he spoke he had a definite accent.

"Be seated, Mister—?" Clive looked questioningly at the gentleman.

After a second's pause, the man said slowly, "Señor Davalos."

"Ah, yes, please be seated Señor Davalos and tell me what I can do for you."

Davalos did so, taking a spindle-legged chair directly across from Clive, his black eyes and hard, unblinking stare reminding Clive uncomfortably of a reptile.

Repeating himself, Clive asked, "Now, what can I do for you?"

Again Davalos seemed to hesitate as if weighing the wisdom of his actions. Finally he said, "Your name has been given to me as a gentleman capable of supplying me with something I want rather badly. Something I would prefer others not to know of—you understand?"

Clive understood very well. More than one gentleman had sat across from him thus, wanting his services for activities they wouldn't wish to have see the light of day. Somewhat dryly he replied, "I understand perfectly. You want no connection between us, but you would like certain services from me, services that are best accomplished in secret *and* outside the law."

Davalos nodded his head in agreement, a slight, thin smile crossing his features.

Briskly Clive asked, "Now that we are in agreement, what is it you want of me?"

But Davalos answered with a question of his own. "You

are acquainted with one Jason Savage, currently visiting England for the supposed purpose of buying horses?"

Clive inclined his head in Davalos's direction, his eyes narrowing with interest. "Yes, I've met Savage. Do you want him killed or merely discomforted? I can arrange either."

Davalos shrugged. "I care not his eventual fate. But before he is removed from this earth, I would have in my possession a map he has. If you have to kill him in order to get it—so be it."

"A map? Of what?"

Picking his words with apparent caution, Davalos said carefully, "Let us say a map to a treasure."

Sudden avarice gleamed briefly in Clive's eyes but was quickly hidden. He only said contemptuously, "Buried treasure? Sunken treasure?"

"No, none of those. I am not," Davalos admitted grudgingly, "certain there is such a map as I seek. It can be it is all in his head. I only know that Savage might have one. And if his reasons for being in England are as I guess, he certainly must have some sort of proof to offer his investors."

"Investors? In what? Land? Are you telling me that this map that may or may not exist is part of some land-buying scheme?"

"No. And I must warn you that it has no political overtones, either. If it exists, it will be a map showing a trail into Spanish Territory in America. The area I speak of has seldom been seen by white men, but assuredly it does hold a treasure, of that I am sure." Davalos fixed his eyes unwaveringly on Clive's intent face. "If it has occurred to you, I would warn you, it will do you little good to doublecross me. The map is useless to all but a very few men. I, myself, am one of the few. I doubt if you could find another buyer for it. Do we understand one another?"

Clive's eyebrow rose at the underlying menace in the other's tone, and he felt a trickle of unease slide down his spine. Hiding his reaction, he said in a bored voice, "It is not my nature to go chasing off after pots of gold at the end of rainbows. I buy and sell information. If you wish me to steal this map for you—I will. But don't," Clive's voice hardened, "threaten me, Señor Davalos."

Davalos relaxed slightly in his chair, his lips tightening in a semblance of a smile. "Very well. We each know how the other stands, *sí?* Now, shall we discuss money?"

Clive nodded, and they parted shortly thereafter having agreed upon a price. Clive drove a steep bargain and demanded half the money to be paid immediately and the rest upon completion of the task. Davalos was not happy. The price he had agreed to pay was high, and telling another person about the map disturbed him. Unfortunately his own two bungling attempts had led nowhere, and he was becoming desperate. Damn Phillip Nolan for dying too soon! Who would have thought such a strong bull of a man would have died so easily under torture?

Returning to his own small room in a considerably less desirable area than that inhabited by Jason or Clive, Davalos locked the door and seated himself in front of a rough wooden table and withdrew a carefully wrapped object from beneath his coat. With almost reverent hands, he undid the wrappings and set it in the middle of the table.

It was beautiful. A barbaric gold armband studded with emeralds. For a long time Davalos gazed at it, almost mesmerized by the gleaming gold and glittering emeralds. Then his lips curled into a wolfish smile. One day it would all be his, and one evening very soon Jason Savage was in for a surprise. An unpleasant one, he hoped.

5

The night before Jason was to leave for Brownleigh's started out like many other evenings he had spent since arriving in London. He and a friend enjoyed an excellent dinner served in the room Jason had taken on St. James's Street; afterwards, the two had strolled the short distance to White's Club for Gentlemen and joined other friends in a game of cards.

Jason had imbibed rather freely of the port served during the course of the evening and so was slightly drunk when in the early hours of the morning he walked home.

In a pleasantly amiable frame of mind, a sleepy smile on his lips, Jason climbed the carpeted, narrow staircase to his suite of rooms. But after he had unlocked the door, a faint frown of dissatisfaction marred his wide forehead and drove the smile from his mouth. With distaste he surveyed the inky blackness that greeted him. Damn Pierre! He could have sworn he had seen a light from beneath the door. He had given that rascally valet the night off, but surely the fool had enough sense to leave a candle or two lit.

He threaded his way through the darkness, cursing softly when he stumbled over a chair. Dulled with drink, he was caught unprepared when someone cannoned into him, the force of the propelled body driving him to the floor. He was momentarily pinned under the weight of his attacker, his breath knocked from his chest, his pleasant stupor vanished. But then with steel-boned fingers he found the throat of the unknown person. A grunt of surprise came from the intruder as Jason's fingers closed with killing force around his neck. With desperate strength the man tried frantically to break the deadly hold, twisting and rolling in the blackness as they fought.

The grim struggle continued in the darkness, their flailing bodies crashing into furniture, sending chairs and tables flying, as gradually Jason increased the pressure of his hands, and the intruder no longer fought only to escape but for his very life as well. Jason's grip was merciless. Without compunction, with his bare hands, he strangled the unknown assailant to death. Then, when the body under him was still, he rose, breathing heavily, and with unerring steps crossed to the sideboard against the wall and struck a flint to light the nearby candle.

Holding the light high over the body, Jason viewed dispassionately his handiwork. The slain man was no one he knew and from his dress appeared to be a member of the lower class. Probably a wharf rat, he thought as he noticed the rough seaman's jersey the dead man wore.

He turned from his searching appraisal of the body and bellowed for Pierre, but an ominous silence met his call. Concern sharpening his features, he tore open the door to the valet's room and breathed a silent sigh of thankfulness when the flickering light revealed Pierre, bound and gagged, his black eyes flashing with apprehensive anger. As he recognized his master, the anger and fear changed to overwhelming relief.

Jason had barely removed the gag when he was greeted by a stream of excited French as Pierre jabbered and chattered volubly, his arms waving about wildly, while explaining in graphic terms what had happened. It took Jason a few minutes to quiet him down and put together the pieces.

Pierre had returned early from a friendly meeting with Jacques, at a pub just a few blocks over on Jermyn Street. He had just unlocked the door when suddenly he was attacked from behind, overpowered, then bound and gagged. It was all done very easily, for Pierre, in spite of having the heart of a lion, was slight and small.

Jason, his expression thoughtful, slowly made his way back into the other room, Pierre at his heels, still babbling. His string of rapid French came to an abrupt halt when he spied the body lying on the floor. And at his questioning look, Jason gave a curt nod in answer, pouring both himself and the now very silent Pierre, a generous brandy.

Both men were quiet as they sipped their drinks, until Jason, staring ruminatively at the corpse, said regretfully, "Pierre, I feel perhaps my uncle is going to be extremely unhappy with me."

"But yes, monsieur! These English, they are barbarians except," Pierre said, "your uncle. *He* will know what we should do!"

"True, but there's nothing to be done now, for I'm certain the duke would object strenuously to being roused from his bed at this hour of the morning. He's going to be very sour as it is, when he discovers why I want to see him. So for the present, we might as well retire and get what sleep we can. I have the disquieting feeling that tomorrow is going to be extremely wearing on my nerves!"

"But, monsieur, this mess! It must be cleared!" cried Pierre, his tidy soul revolted by the condition of the room; and it was then that Jason noticed the ruthless disarray, only some of which would have occurred during the fight.

The drawers of his desk had been dragged open, papers scattered over the floor, and the books on the shelves had been shoved aside, some joining the clutter from the desk on the floor. Even the massive oak sideboard hadn't escaped, its doors gaping open, the contents showing signs of having been impatiently thrust aside.

After gazing speculatively for some minutes at the havoc Jason cast a faintly apologetic glance at the dead man and remarked to no one in particular, "It seems I was wrong, and murder wasn't what he had in mind."

He strode over to the body and, kneeling, searched the corpse. He discovered nothing other than a few oddments obviously belonging to the dead man, and a puzzled frown creased his forehead. Rising in one lithe movement and after fastidiously wiping his hands, he walked with long, easy strides to his bedchamber. As he expected, the same relentless signs of a hurried search existed there.

His clothes were strewn about, drawers were thrown on the floor, the pillows on his bed had been ripped open, and from the slashed mattress, goose feathers drifted in little clouds over the whole unsightly mess. Yet, the puzzling fact remained that the man had ignored—beyond dumping them on the floor—a small fortune in rings, stickpins, and jewels that winked in the candlelight.

Pierre's outraged gasp as he entered the room broke into Jason's thoughts, but pursuing his own investigation, he said quietly, almost to himself, "Why would a thief not steal such a tempting pile of wealth?" He swung round and bending his bright green gaze on Pierre's bewildered face asked, "What time did you return?"

"Before midnight, monsieur."

Pulling out his gold pocket watch, Jason checked the time. "It's after four now, so I must have entered a little after three. Why was that fool still here? He had plenty of time to escape, and if he wasn't a thief, what the hell was he looking for?"

Knowing Jason expected no answer, Pierre paid him no heed, but began to pick up the pieces of clothing, clucking to himself that anyone, even an Englishman, should treat such exquisite garments so shamefully.

A sardonic smile twisting his lips, Jason watched him

while he sought a satisfactory solution to the riddle. Nothing made sense! He had been prepared for a possible search when he had first arrived two months ago. But now? Unless—unless, somehow, his other mission for Jefferson had been uncovered! No, it couldn't be! Tonight's happening had to be only a case of sheer vandalism. But the uncomfortable thought lingered.

"Bah!" he suddenly said. "Who cares why the stupid fellow was here? He's dead, and that's that!" Yet Jason had a shrewd idea the duke wasn't going to dismiss it so easily, especially since he would have the unlovely task of disposing of the body and would have to handle any awkward questions that might arise.

In answer to Jason's urgent deliberately worded message, delivered by Pierre, the duke of Roxbury arrived the next morning before noon, nattily attired in a suit of palest dove gray, a Malacca cane swinging negligently from one long-fingered hand. As Jason had suspected, he did not treat the news of the discovery of a corpse in his nephew's rooms as a shocking, horrifying circumstance. It was merely *inconvenient!* But the duke, for all his worldly ways, was not quite so blasé about the reality of violent death, and he was considerably put out to find his nephew enjoying a hearty breakfast of rare roast beef and washing large mouthfuls of the meat down with ale, while the body of the man he had slain the night before lay just a few feet away.

Jason grinned at his uncle's affronted look and waved him to a chair, offering him some refreshment as he did so, but the duke, with a theatrical shudder, replied, "My dear boy, I assure you I wouldn't be able to swallow a morsel!" Then, he cast those deceivingly sleepy eyes, which missed not the smallest detail, around the disordered room and remarked, "I presume this is the reason behind the clever little note I received this morning?"

His expression was grave as he listened to Jason's unemotional, succinct report of the night's happenings. He offered no comment, but merely sat relaxed on one of the few chairs to escape damage, his gray eyes never leaving his nephew's dark face until Jason had finished. Then, he drawled, "You had a busy evening, young man. I'd hoped that since your days at Harrow you'd outgrown such precipitate action, but I see my hopes were groundless." He gave a languid sigh and added, "And as you usually managed to extricate yourself from past indiscretions, I'm aware that if I don't dispose of that distasteful object, you're quite capable of doing so. I'm surprised you bothered with me at all—or could it be that you've at last learned a certain amount of caution and take your duties as courier seriously?"

Jason nodded without smiling, his face hard and unrevealing, and Roxbury sighed again. Frequently, his nephew reminded him vividly of the country that bred him; like America itself, he was young, brash, brawling, and inclined to flex his muscles without thought of the consequences. Slowly, Roxbury shook his head and looking over at the covered body murmured, "Jason, Jason, you're so reckless and imprudent! The poor fellow is obviously only a thief; was it necessary to kill him?"

"At the time, I didn't *know* he was a thief. I didn't know what he was. I was attacked in the dark, and when I believe my life is threatened, I act first and analyze later whether my actions were wise or not!" Jason snapped.

Roxbury, a pained look on his face, said testily, "Now, don't come the ugly with me, nevvy! That scowling glare might give others pause, but I've known you since you were in short coats!"

Instantly, Jason's expression changed, a wide grin splitting his mouth, exposing even white teeth. "I wonder if you'll ever let me forget it," he laughed ruefully.

"Not bloody likely!" shot back the duke. "It's the only way to handle you wild cubs. You need reminding occasionally that there are older and wiser heads around."

"That may be, but in this case, I think you're wrong to label him"—a jerk of Jason's head indicated the corpse—

"only a thief. I purposely didn't tell you everything. Walk into my bedchamber and let me show you something."

Slightly mystified, Roxbury followed him into the room, and gesturing towards the pile of jewels, Jason said, "My first reaction was the same as yours, that I'd inadvertently killed a thief; but, if that were true, why did he leave these lying on the floor? Why didn't he stuff them in his pockets and leave?"

The duke stared at the pile, absently running the fingers of one hand along his jaw. Abruptly, he ceased gazing at the jewels and thoughtfully made a detailed inventory of the room before saying slowly, "You might have surprised him in the act, you know."

A negative shake from Jason greeted his words. "The time element precluded that. He had adequate time to find my valuables and depart, if it was only money he was after. I've a hunch he was searching for something else."

Roxbury raised one black brow. "I sincerely hope you're not suspecting him of having any interest in the dispatches from Jefferson?"

"Oh, I agree, the poor devil in the other room wasn't after the dispatches for himself, but someone could have hired him. Figure it out yourself. He ignored money, clothes, and jewels."

"There's more than just *this* incident that makes you think that! And don't try to tell me there's not!" remarked Roxbury, his gray eyes narrowed and watchful.

Jason smiled grimly at his uncle's words, his own eyes as intent as the other's. Used to conducting his own affairs, he played his cards very close to his chest and didn't take kindly to interference; but knowing the duke was up to every rig and row in town and that very little slipped by those discerning eyes he said, "There are two incidents I haven't mentioned before, because taken by themselves they amount to nothing—and quite frankly, I didn't feel they were any of your business."

As he paused, Roxbury responded tartly, "If you're alluding to an earlier attempt to search your rooms and the time you had the altercation with that footpad, I'm already aware of the incidents. And being as well acquainted with me as you are, you should have known I'd know about them!"

Stung by his uncle's scathing tone of voice and feeling very much like an erring schoolboy, Jason, his mouth tight with rising anger, snarled, "As a rule I don't associate with such cunning men as yourself, so you'll forgive me if I occasionally forget the devious principles that you take such delight in following." Then fighting to control his blazing temper, he added in a calmer tone, "I gather you've had someone dogging my footsteps ever since I arrived in London. And if that's the case, why the hell did he let me walk into that fool last night?"

Outwardly unruffled by Jason's angry outburst, the duke said gently, "May I say first that I've set no one to spy on you? That it's of a recent date that a man was assigned to watch your residence? I might add it was by accident I learned of the first attempt to examine your rooms and the footpad's attack." If Roxbury had hoped to soften Jason's anger, he was doomed to disappointment, for his nephew's face remained coldly hostile, and Roxbury experienced a faint stab of regret that the openness that had existed between them was gone. Jason never trusted lightly, and the duke had always been secretly pleased that his wild, headstrong nephew preferred him to his own father; the duke returned the feeling by favoring Jason above his own sons.

It had been a mistake on his part—the duke admitted it heavily to himself—not to have taken Jason into his confidence. He knew he could trust Jason with his very life, and it had only been his innate cautiousness that had caused him to withhold the information. Unfortunately, it was too late now to explain that to the very distrustful young man before him, and as he sought for words that would at least establish a semblance of the old intimacy, Jason interrupted his distressed thoughts by saying icily, "All of what you've said, if true, is extremely enlightening, but I'm still waiting for an answer as to why your spy made no effort to stop me from entering what very well could have been a murder attempt on my life?"

Tiredly, the duke answered, "For the simple reason that your intruder had already slit my man's throat!"

An arrested expression in his green eyes, Jason stared thoughtfully at his uncle. He, as much as Roxbury, was unhappy with the sudden estrangement that lay like a sword between them. And, while it might be disillusioning to discover his uncle hadn't trusted him and had set a spy outside his very door, at the moment the knowledge that someone had wanted to search his belongings badly enough to kill someone unsettled him more. Realizing also that he had been giving in to a deplorable tendency to act like a sulky youth, he asked in a much more reasonable tone of voice, "Why was someone watching me in the first place?"

Unconsciously Roxbury relaxed. "A number of reasons brought me to that decision. Unlike you, I connected immediately those first two events. You might remember it's my job to do so; and due to the nature of my work, I'm afraid that over the years I've become very suspicious of even the most innocent-appearing actions. So, when Clive Pendleton engineered another meeting between you and that doxy of his, I became even more suspicious. From my limited observations, it appeared their interest was not so much in you, but in your dealings with myself and the American minister, Rufus King, which not unnaturally led me to believe your minor role in delivering the Jefferson dispatches had become known. And knowing Pendleton's past activities, it seemed logical that being unable to learn more from you, eventually he would have your rooms searched for any bit of information he could find."

The duke paused and glanced at Jason. Jason was partially dressed in a pair of yellow nankeen trousers and a white linen shirt, open almost to the waist. He was at the moment lounging casually against one of the huge bedposts, his long legs crossed at the ankles and his arms folded lightly over his chest. He was regarding his uncle intently, and Roxbury cursed himself silently for not having enlisted his assistance the minute Pendleton had appeared on the scene.

Jason had followed his uncle's words intently and as the duke paused, he broke in saying, "You don't have to tell me more. I can guess the rest. You hoped to trap Clive in an embarrassing situation that he wouldn't be able to explain away."

Roxbury nodded, an exasperated cast to his mouth, and he said disgustedly, "And all we gain from our attempt is two corpses!"

A lopsided grin crossed Jason's face, and seeing the laughter lurking in the green eyes, Roxbury was moved to remark stiffly, "It's not amusing! This was the first time that I'd even a hope Clive would make a mistake. I must admit, though, I'm surprised he's just now becoming interested in your activities." Then, as if struck by another thought, he asked suddenly, "Jason, are you absolutely positive there isn't something else the intruder could have been after?"

Frowning, Jason said slowly, "I have no information that would interest a spy, and the only other item of any value that wasn't in the room is this!" As he spoke, he walked over to Roxbury and, undoing his shirt, shook his right arm free of the garment. The limb he held out for his uncle's inspection was as sun-darkened as his face, and from the supple muscles that rippled under the brown skin, it was obvious that he was no city fop. But Roxbury's gaze was riveted by the wide band of gold, set with emeralds, that encircled Jason's upper arm.

The duke picked up the quizzing glass that hung from a black silk ribbon around his neck and closely examined the piece. It was a beautiful item, barbaric in design, and on further perusal, he discerned the faint signs that at one time there had been engravings upon the band. He stared at it bemused, realizing it must be centuries old, and was instantly struck by how appropriate it looked on Jason as he stood there, black hair falling across his forehead, dark lean-muscled chest bare, and his eyes as green as the emeralds in the gold band. He appeared the embodiment of a wild, savage prince, and the duke felt a slash of almost paternal pride in the young animal before him. But his voice held no hint of it as he drawled, "Very pretty."

Grinning at his uncle's prosaic remark, Jason shrugged on his shirt and laughed, "You old devil. You're curious as hell about the Aztec band."

"Aztec?" asked Roxbury, interestedly.

Nodding his head, Jason added carelessly, "I found it years ago in Spanish territory and can only surmise how it got there. I was enchanted with it, from the moment I spotted it, and I've never taken it off since then. You might say it's my talisman."

"Do you think last night's intruder was after *that?*"

Sarcastically, Jason drawled, "I doubt it. I assure you, I don't go around removing my clothing to display it."

"Well, why the deuce did you bring it up then?" shot back the duke, now in a bad temper.

In dulcet tones, Jason answered, "*You* were the one who asked if there was anything else."

His uncle viewed his grinning nephew from under those heavy black brows and was not diverted. "Very amusing, Jason. Now, if you're prepared to be serious, we can get on with it! I haven't all day. The prime minister, Addington, is expecting me at one."

Jason shrugged his wide shoulders. "What else is there? I have no information, except what's in my extremely hard head, which you refer to often enough. And aware of Clive's interest, it isn't likely I'll betray my knowledge. So, if we follow the assumption that last night's contretemps was at his instigation, there's nothing else to do but wait until—*if*—he makes another attempt."

"Well! I'm glad you acknowledge the fact that he might still find you an absorbing item!"

A bark of laughter greeted Roxbury's sharp words.

"Uncle, uncle, when will you admit that you're not the only one who can foresee probable events?"

"Jason, this is not a frivolous new pastime! Clive, and those like him, must not learn of the possible treaty between Britain and America. This uneasy peace will not last, but we in England must spin it out for as long as possible. If Napoleon was to learn of the terms of the proposed treaty, it would give him the very excuse he wants to invade New Orleans, or he could use it as a reason to break the Treaty of Amiens."

Sobered by Roxbury's grave words, the teasing glint died abruptly in his green eyes, and Jason said, "I don't treat it as lightly as you imagine. I assure you, I shall tread very warily around Clive and the delectable Elizabeth."

His uncle sighed and muttered darkly, "Just make positive you do!" Changing the subject, he asked, "Did you receive an invitation to Brownleigh's houseparty?"

Slightly startled at the change of conversation, Jason raised one brow but answered willingly enough, "Yes, I'm looking forward to it. I elected not to stay at Brownleigh's house, though, and have made arrangements to stay at an inn nearby. I'm meeting Harris and Barrymore there."

"When do you join the party?"

Becoming impatient with the questions, Jason demanded, "Is there a reason for this excessive interest in Brownleigh's soirée?"

"Yes, Jason, there is a reason. Don't be obstructive, answer the question!" snapped the duke.

Nettled, Jason was of a mind to show his uncle exactly how obstructive he could be, but a particularly piercing look from his uncle stilled the notion. "I am escorting Harris's sister and grandmother. And because I had planned to look at some horses near Melton Mowbray, we were going to leave this afternoon. Considering what's happening here, I'll wait a few days."

"Would you have any objections to adhering to the original plan?"

"None, if you would like, but what about the body?"

A faint smile curved the duke's mouth. "You'd already planned on my disposing of that for you, so there's no reason not to join Harris. I would prefer it, as a matter of fact, I think it best you leave London for a while. Last night didn't change things, it only confirmed what we suspected. You're still visiting here for the purpose of buying horses, and you'll continue to act as if nothing has happened. Have Pierre pack your things, but don't bother straightening up this chaos. I'll have someone take care of everything."

A twisted grin on his lips, Jason said, "You know, you're making me feel like a ninny. I've ordered my own affairs for a number of years, and I don't appreciate being wrapped in cotton wool."

A sympathetic twinkle in his gray eyes, Roxbury murmured, "I know I'm treating you as if you're still under my protection and attending Harrow, but forgive me. Old habits die hard, and at this point you can do me more good by going to Brownleigh's and allowing yourself to be enamored of the beautiful widow than remaining in London. Have no fear. If I need you, I shall be in touch."

Jason was inclined to argue the point, but common sense pointed out the justice of the duke's words. So, moments after Roxbury had departed, Pierre was busily employed packing his master's valises, while Jason, filled with a reckless energy, paced through the rooms, wishing briefly he had never agreed to Jefferson's request.

But then, he reflected fairly, beyond the meetings with the American minister and the few disturbances he'd had recently, it really hadn't cost anything to deliver those dispatches. He wasn't overjoyed with the implications of last night's events, but admitted honestly that it certainly livened up what could have become a dull trip. The prospect of crossing verbal swords with Clive Pendleton added spice to what already planned to be an enjoyable stay in the country!

6

Jason adhered to the original plan and drove his curricle down to Melton Mowbray, following sedately behind Augusta's lumbering old traveling coach. Amanda had taken one look at Jason's smartly turned-out curricle pulled by two very high-spirited chestnuts and had instantly pleaded to ride with him. Augusta had shot her a thoughtful glance but had given in. Consequently Amanda, her brown eyes sparkling with pleasure, had enjoyed the pale March sunshine and the smooth ride given by a really well-sprung vehicle.

Due to their late start and the pace set by Augusta's traveling coach, they had to spend one night on the road, and it was late the next evening before they finally arrived at Brownleigh's home. A noisy party was already under way, and Augusta, tired and inclined towards snappishness, had insisted that she and Amanda be shown to their beds at once!

With Amanda and her grandmother safely delivered, Jason sought out his host, a jovial, rotund little man, and inquired after Barrymore and Harris. Somewhat apologetically he was informed that Barrymore, Harris, and some of the younger gentlemen were dining at the home of the local squire. Hiding his disappointment at the news, Jason chatted idly while taking note of his fellow guests. He was quick to spot Clive Pendleton and Elizabeth Markham, but although Elizabeth tried several times to catch his eye, at the moment Jason was not in the mood for dalliance, and so her attempts were met with a bland, unrevealing smile. Eventually taking his leave from his host, Jason promised to return on the morrow for the fox hunt that was planned.

His quarters at the inn known as The Fox were a pleasant surprise, for nearly the entire second floor had been set aside for his use. He had obviously been given the best suite of rooms that the inn had to offer—two large bedrooms with their own dressing chambers, private sitting room and dining room as well as servants' quarters just down the hall. He had no use for the second bedroom, but it came with the suite, and Jason was thoroughly satisfied with the arrangements.

Slowly sipping a goblet of wine, he wandered through the rooms, animallike, acquainting himself with all the exits and entrances. Loosening his cravat, he sauntered into the second bedroom. Idly he flipped open the door of a cherrywood wardrobe, and staring at its gaping emptiness imagined it filled with laces, muslins, and bits of silk so necessary to the feminine sex. And he was startled when the faintly blurred memory of the girl in the library flashed in his mind. Damn! He wished he could remember what she really looked like. Too bad she hadn't been a serving girl—he might have tried his luck with her.

Then hearing Pierre moving about in the next room, he walked to the door and entered his own bedchamber. Pierre was putting away the last articles of clothing. Throwing down his crumpled cravat, Jason remarked, "I hope the landlord's lady is a good washerwoman. I won't put up with dingy linen."

An affronted look on his face, his button black eyes flashing, Pierre answered stiffly, "As if I would entrust your linen to these provincials!"

Jason, hiding a smile, refilled his goblet from the wine decanter on the highly polished table near a rough stone fireplace. Having braved the Atlantic Ocean to set foot in the old world, Pierre—who had rarely ventured farther than New Orleans—now felt himself to be a traveler of the world.

Years ago, Jason had been against his grandfather's desire that he hire a valet; but Monsieur Beauvais had insisted, and to keep peace, he had hired the monkey-faced Pierre. However, in spite of Pierre's determination to trick him out in the latest fashion, they managed to rub along together tolerably well. The only time they had fallen foul had been the time Pierre hadn't been able to resist the impulse to order a pair of lilac pantaloons for his master.

Jason had taken one look at the offending garment, and his shout of laughter had resounded through the hall. Greatly amused and doing little to hide it, he had thrown the garment at his startled valet and had said in no uncertain terms that he'd put up with a great deal from him but he'd be damned if he'd be seen in that bilious color. What pangs Pierre suffered, no one knew, and Pierre never said. Thereafter he contented himself with becoming a necessary adjunct to young Savage's comfort and now, except for Jason's mysterious journeys into the wilds of New Spain, traveled everywhere with him.

Not even Pierre, though, could fault Jason's dress as he left the inn the next morning. A well-cut jacket of bottle-green wool fit his arms and shoulders superbly; buff-colored breeches revealed the hard strength in his long legs, while shining black boots displayed Pierre's skill in keeping Jason's footwear in meticulous order. He carried a small black riding whip, more for looks than usefulness, and seated astride his newest acquisition, a splendid black hunter, he created a stir among the female contingent when his horse cantered up to join the laughing, expectant group gathered on the broad sweeping drive before Brownleigh's home. Elizabeth Markham particularly was unable to keep from shooting little side-glances in his direction.

It was a fine morning for the hunt; the air was clean and crisp, with small patches of fog floating ghostlike over the rolling hills and little valleys. The horses were restless as they started off, their breath clearly seen in the frosty air, and the hounds gave a series of sharp, excited barks that carried over the still countryside.

Jason looked forward to the morning. It was a chance to do some real riding, and there was the possibility for another meeting with the charming widow.

Elizabeth's glances hadn't gone unnoticed, and Jason made some attempt to reach her side before the hounds found the scent and the real chase began. But the pack struck a trail almost immediately, and the whole group, as a body, went thundering after the baying dogs, and Jason lost sight of Elizabeth. It wasn't until some time later that she appeared suddenly, out of nowhere, close to his side, throwing him a challenging look as she raced by on her neat gray mare.

An intrepid rider himself, he admired her skill in the saddle as she took a stone wall most riders would have avoided. He avoided it himself, not from a lack of courage but from a desire to spare his horse. The black horse had knocked a foreleg going over a wooden fence some miles back. A gate lay open nearby, and there was no need to push his horse unnecessarily. Even so, it wasn't much longer before there was a decided limp to his mount's gait.

Breaking from the group, Jason urged his horse over to a lane that led back to the inn. He hadn't traveled far when he heard the unmistakable sounds of another rider behind him, and it was with no surprise that he turned and discovered Elizabeth not far behind.

Wearing a green velvet riding habit cut in the military style, an absurd little hat perched on her glossy curls, she smiled pleasantly and reined her horse to fall into step with his. "It's a shame your horse has lamed himself. You'll miss the kill," she remarked.

Returning her smile, he replied, "There will be other days, and I'm afraid I haven't the Englishman's love of watching a pack of hounds rip a fox to pieces."

"Oh, come now. Don't tell me you're one of those milk and water people who shudder at the sight of a little blood," she said scornfully.

His eyebrow rose at her comment, but he merely nodded politely, saying in a mild tone, "As you say, madame."

Disconcerted at his brief answer, she said prettily. "Forgive me. That wasn't polite. My mother is forever telling me I'm too forward, even for a widow. I must learn to mind my tongue."

"Just as you say, madame," was the unencouraging response.

A pout on her full red lips, she snapped, "I wish you'd say something more interesting than 'As you say, madame'!"

He slanted an appraising glance that took in her full breasts, slim waist, and rounded hips. Slowly, deliberately undressing her with his eyes, he admired the blush that was beginning to mount on her angry face for the work of art it was. Then meeting her indignant look, he held her gaze and asked, "What would you like me to say? You followed me, and you started this conversation."

Uncertain how to cope with his mood, she answered stiffly, "I see you obviously prefer your own company. I'm sorry I intruded. Excuse me if I go back and join the others." She started to turn her horse, but his lean, brown hand quickly reached over and took the reins. The next moment she was roughly dragged from the saddle, crushed against his chest, and ruthlessly kissed. His mouth was warm on hers, and sheer surprise kept her still as he deepened the kiss, while his hand sought the softness of her breast. Elizabeth was achingly aware of the hard male body that held her close, and it was only the fact that they were in the middle of a country lane that caused her to struggle halfheartedly away from him.

Jason ignored her struggles and murmured against her lips, "Gently, gently, sweet. I know this isn't the place, but you're such a tempting armful." He bent his dark head and nibbled one little ear. "I want more than a stolen kiss on a country lane. When and where can we be private again?"

Furious with him for taking such blatant advantage and furious with herself for the flood of longing that shook her, she opened her mouth to say something particularly scathing, but he placed a finger against her lips and shook his head. "If you say it, I'll put you down and ride on. You can join your friends, and anything between us will end here and now. We're not in London this time."

Elizabeth stared at him. Remembering the feel of his hard body against hers in the library in London and knowing she wanted this man like no other, she said meekly, "The landlord at The Fox—I am told he is very discreet." At her words Jason flashed her a smile and without another word swung her effortlessly back on her horse, and together they rode to the inn.

Jason's sitting room was pleasantly decorated with thick mustard-colored carpets, pale yellow curtains at the two windows, and two red leather chairs that were drawn up before a cheerful fire. A Queen Anne table stood at one side of the fireplace and a blue mohair couch under one of the windows. But too aware of the dark, hard-faced man at her side, Elizabeth didn't spare as much as a glance around the room when she seated herself gingerly on the blue couch. Pouring out some mulled wine, which was waiting conveniently on the fire, he silently offered a cup of the warm brew with a smile so slow and intimate that it caused her pulse to race with anticipation.

There was no sound in the room but the crackle of the fire. Jason sat lazily in one of the leather chairs, his lean legs stretched towards the fire. As she watched him, the silence began to tear on Elizabeth's nerves.

Glancing at her, Jason smiled to himself. Women! Why did they have to be wooed all the way to the bed? Suddenly impatient with games, he set his wine down and rose in one silent motion. Crossing the room and standing before her, he removed the glass from her nerveless fingers and drew her slowly into his arms. Smiling languorously, the deep dimple in his left cheek appearing, his eyes were openingly caressing as they moved over her body. Then his mouth covered hers in a long, demanding kiss, and with a sigh of satisfaction, she strained against him—on fire for what was inevitable.

He wanted her, and she could feel his hardness as he molded his body next to hers, his hands now openly searching her body; and she sensed his rising passion as he gently pushed her onto the couch. Somehow, her jacket had been discarded, and her blouse opened to bare her nipples to his touch. As he continued to explore her eager body, his demanding hands urgently pushed up her skirt, and she arched her body up to his, moaning with pleasure at his touch. Swiftly, he covered her body with his, entering her with such violence that she gave a gasp of surprise. But then, caught up in her own desire, she met each hard thrust of his lean body as he took her up and over the edge of completeness with an expertise that left her weak and satiated.

There was a stillness in the room afterwards, until Jason broke it by sitting up and grinning down into her face. His voice was mocking as he said, "Wasn't that more exciting than watching a pack of hounds destroy one small fox?"

Later, he ruefully admitted to himself that he *had* been a crude barbarian and probably all the other names Elizabeth had hurled angrily at his head. But his teasing had accomplished two things for which he was grateful. It had stilled instantly any questions that she might have put forth in probing for information, and it had caused her to leave his rooms rather precipitously. Furious that he should treat their lovemaking so lightly, she had sprung up, barely straightened her clothing, and swept from the room. Jason, watching her movements, had been almost unable to control the laughter that bubbled in his throat. Smiling to himself after she had stormed from the room, he shook his head. It had been an enjoyable interlude, but he'd be damned if he was going to apologize to her or any woman for taking what was offered. Elizabeth took herself too seriously by half!

Barrymore indirectly echoed much the same thought that evening as he, Jason, and Harris relaxed after dinner in Jason's rooms. Barrymore, his blue eyes dancing with merriment, had breezed into Jason's rooms unannounced a few hours after Elizabeth had left, to report that he had innocently asked Elizabeth if she had seen Jason that morning and had had his head snapped off for his efforts. He had teased Jason for his supposedly clumsy handling of her. Jason took Barrymore's lively quips in good stead, returning noncommittal answers, and after a few minutes deftly turned the conversation to the horses they were to see at the gypsy camp.

Instantly diverted, Freddy plunged into a colorful account of his activities on Jason's behalf. He had made arrangements for them to ride out to the gypsy camp the following morning.

Before more was said, Harris arrived and Jason viewed his two boon companions with amused affection. And, Jason mused, as they settled themselves down for a long evening of cards and drink, he couldn't have found two more loyal and companionable men if he had searched all of England. He only wished Barrymore would stop twitting him on Elizabeth Markham.

But Freddy couldn't resist and blinking owlishly over the rim of his wine glass, he warned again, "You'd better watch yourself with the widow. If you're not careful, you'll find yourself returning home leg-shackled to that fancy piece! She means to have you."

Freddy was nearer to the mark than he realized. Elizabeth, after some hard thinking, had indeed decided that Jason Savage would be a perfect husband for herself. He was handsome, the possessor of a large fortune—a definite factor in Elizabeth's cold-blooded appraisal—and in spite of his peculiar habit of teasing at inopportune moments, an exciting lover. Mentally, she reviewed the possible competition, and smugly observing her own bountiful charms in the mirror, dismissed all other young ladies as negligible. And this morning had proven he wasn't indifferent to her charms. Consequently, Elizabeth was pleased and expectant as she drifted down the stairs that evening to join the other guests. But a discontented pout curved her mouth as the evening progressed and she discovered Jason had chosen not to attend the entertainment planned by Brownleigh. She had worn a shockingly low-cut gown of green silk in which she had planned to dazzle him.

Clive didn't help matters when he murmured, "I see your quarry has deserted you this evening. And, I offer a word of advice, my dear: be careful not to rush your fences; Savage may find more pleasure in hunting than being hunted!"

She shot him an angry glance and said coolly, "Are you telling me how to seduce a man? I think that in order to set your fears at rest I should tell you we spent the morning in his rooms, and he couldn't keep his hands off me! There's not a woman here who can say that!"

"True, but then most of them wouldn't spread their legs so eagerly, either!" returned Clive cruelly. He watched with satisfaction the flush of rage that crossed her face. Then, smiling sweetly, he wandered out of the room.

A few minutes later, he was frowning as he thought about Elizabeth. She was becoming too sure of herself since Savage's arrival, and he wasn't certain she could be trusted any longer. As long as she was desperate for money, she would do as he commanded. But if Savage was willing to set her up as his mistress, he doubted she would look in the future to the time when Savage was no longer in England. And, he reflected grimly, she was stupid enough to think Jason would offer marriage to one of her kind. But then, one thing about Elizabeth that had always fascinated him was her colossal conceit. Still, she might be able to glean something about Jason's connection with the duke of Roxbury and his visit to Rufus King, although it appeared that for the moment his curiosity would have to remain unsatisfied—so far, Elizabeth had come up with nothing but excuses.

Dismissing for a time Jason's possible political involvement, Clive turned his mind to the more profitable direction of the mysterious map that Davalos desired.

Not trusting Elizabeth, he had refrained from acquainting her with the details of his meeting with the gentleman from Louisiana. His bargain with Davalos would remain a secret. He frowned for a second, recalling with displeasure the failure of the other night's attempt to search Savage's rooms. Damn the man for returning so soon. And he wondered grimly how Savage had disposed of the intruder.

But he wasted little thought on past events.

He had found a way to combine his business with Davalos with his desire to have—or ruin—Catherine. The need to find this map, that Davalos was willing to pay a very high price for, coupled with the old letter of Rachael's, would give him the opportunity to make Catherine dance to the tune of his piping.

Catherine would do anything for Rachael—even, if compelled, search a stranger's room for a mysterious map. She wouldn't know that Rachael's old letter was relatively harmless—he would make certain Catherine believed that Rachael was in great danger from possible exposure. Besides, he thought with malicious enjoyment, there would be considerable gratification gained in bending Catherine to his will, in forcing her to do his thieving. It was time, he decided, an unpleasant smile on his lips, to have an intimate conversation with Catherine. She was about to learn that it was not wise to spurn him—that one way or another he always got what he wanted.

7

It was early the next morning when Clive sought out the gypsy camp. The camp was situated a few miles from Melton Mowbray, and he found the motley collection of gaudily painted caravans and tattered tents with little difficulty. Surrounded by encroaching woods, the dwellings nestled in a small hollow. A horse, one of many tethered at the far end of the hollow, snorted and stamped in the cold morning air, and the sound floated, muffled and indistinct, to Clive's ears as he reined in his own mount.

At first glance, it appeared all the inhabitants were still asleep, for the area had a forlorn and forgotten appearance; even the mongrels that infested the camp were curled and sleeping underneath the wagons. Then an old woman, her black hair streaked with gray, walked out of one of the tents and threw some small sticks of wood on one of the smoldering campfires. Her clothes were faded and worn but still bore traces of a once bright green and yellow design; gold hoops hung from her ears, and a scarlet shawl covered her bony shoulders. Watching her, Clive wondered with ill-concealed disgust what possessed Catherine to seek out these people.

He must have made some sound, for suddenly the old woman whirled to stare in his direction, and her black eyes widened as he came forward. He recognized Reina at the same moment she recognized him, and the welcoming smile that had begun to curve her mouth froze. Her lustrous black eyes narrowed, and rudely she spat in the direction of the fire. Annoyance sharpened his voice and wasting no time, he snapped, "Where is Catherine or, as you insist on calling her, Tamara?"

"Tamara is still sleeping, my fine buck. You'll have to amuse yourself until she arises and is ready to see you." She stopped and added slyly, "You should enjoy visiting with Manuel while you wait. He stays in the wagon over there." She gave a jerk of her head indicating the direction and then deliberately turned her back on him.

Clive's teeth clamped together fiercely at her tone and actions, and watching her coldly, he said to himself, "Insolent old bitch! I should have slit her throat long ago." Seeing Reina was not going to tell him anything else, he turned angrily on his heel and strode over to the wagon indicated.

The wagon was actually a house on wheels, as were all of the gypsy caravans. Manuel's was larger than most, as befitted his position as leader of the tribe, and it was painted a bright red and gold. Just as Clive reached the caravan, the gay red door was thrown open, and Manuel descended.

Manuel's skin was swarthy, and his eyes bright black, like two sparkling jewels gleaming in his merry face. He had been smiling as he came from the wagon, his teeth very white against his brown face, but the smile disappeared, and an unwelcoming frown replaced it as he saw Clive. "What do *you* want?" he growled.

Clive gave a pained grimace and shrugged. "The welcome you and your mother give me never fails to astound one."

Manuel ignored this sally and continued to stare with hostility at Clive. Clive, impatient and disliking every moment he had to spend among the gypsies, said in a voice cold with scorn, "Where's Catherine?" Manuel made no move or any sign that he recognized the name, and Clive angrily said, "Oh, very well, damn it—Tamara, as you insist upon calling her. Where is she? I know she's here, so find her for me—immediately!"

"I'm right behind you, Clive, and I would appreciate it, in the future, when speaking to people on my land, that you use a little common courtesy—if you're capable of it." Catherine's tone was very dry with a hint of sarcasm in it and Clive, turning slowly to face her, almost didn't realize that the slim girl in front of him was actually Catherine.

There was little resemblance between the young woman who confronted him now and the demure miss he had seen recently in London. Now, her hair, released from its confining braids, was a curling, wavy mass of black silk that hung nearly to the small waist, and it changed the whole character of her face, making her features take on a wild, sultry cast that hadn't been apparent before. She was no longer fashionably dressed, but wore the garb of a gypsy wench—a simple skirt of bright scarlet and a thin yellow muslin blouse. And at the moment, her violet eyes wary and unfriendly, she reminded Clive of a small cat uncertain whether to scamper away and hide or spring and claw.

Forcing his features into a semblance of a smile, Clive said, "I apologize. But I have to see you on a matter of some urgency, and Manuel was being rather—er—obstructive."

At his words, Catherine's face took on an expression of concern. Fear apparent in her voice, she asked quickly, "What about? My mother? Has something happened to Rachael?"

For Clive, Catherine's reactions couldn't have been better, and smoothly he murmured, "No, nothing has happened to Rachael—yet!"

"What do you mean—yet?"

"Well, it all depends on you, m'dear. Come, let us talk privately. This is a personal matter, not one to be bandied about a gypsy camp."

Frowning, she gazed at him, distrust written on her face. Manuel moved to her side speaking angrily in the Romany tongue.

The camp had gradually awakened and there could be heard the clank of the cooking pots; the smell of wood smoke and of frying bacon drifted in the air. From somewhere behind the wagons, the low voices of the men could be heard as they moved about feeding the livestock. But as far as the three by the red caravan were concerned, they could have been miles away. And abruptly, Catherine silenced Manuel with a sharp movement of her hand and replied apparently resignedly in Romany. Manuel must have been satisfied with her reply, for, after throwing Clive a look filled with dislike, he walked away.

Catherine eyed Clive a minute, obviously distrusting him, yet compelled by the threatening quality of his words into agreeing to his request. "Very well," she said. "We will move father away where we cannot be overheard."

"Why not go to your caravan? I understand that the earl had one built especially for you."

Catherine glanced at him and said quietly, "Is it likely that I would go anywhere with you that Manuel or the others couldn't see what you were doing? I haven't forgotten what happened the last time you found me alone. Besides," she added coolly, "I promised Manuel that I wouldn't. That's the only reason he agreed to leave us."

Clive lost some of his pleased air, and his eyes grew icy; but his thoughts were hidden as Catherine led the way to a small clearing just beyond the camp. Most of the trees were still bare, but there was a degree of privacy even though they were in sight of the camp.

Stopping in the center of the clearing, Catherine turned and asked sharply, "Now, what about my mother?"

"Actually," he began smoothly, "Rachael plays a very small part, and if you do as I ask, she will not be harmed at all. What I want is for you to extract a document for me from an American gentleman who is staying at The Fox."

Extremely puzzled, Catherine asked, "Why should I run such a risk, and why would I want to steal for you? I don't understand you. How is my mother involved?"

Clive drew a piece of paper from an inside pocket of his vest, a cold look in his eyes and an unpleasant smile curving his lips. "I'll let you read this if you like, but it'll be more to the point if I tell you that it's a copy of a letter Rachel wrote to a cousin in France during the war with Napoleon. Most of the letter is filled with feminine chatter, but at the end of it Rachael mentioned a Lieutenant Starmer who had been visiting with some friends near here."

He paused; Catherine was watching him intently, her slim eyebrows knitting into a frown of concentration. His unpleasant smile growing, he continued, "Rachael was unwise enough to mention the place of departure of Lieutenant Starmer and the name of his ship. Unfortunately, the ship was sunk by enemy fire a short way out from port."

A feeling of dismay growing inside her, Catherine asked with apparent indifference, "So?"

"So my dear Catherine, someone *could* say that Rachael was spying for Napoleon and telling the French about troop movements. We both know otherwise and that it was just a tragic coincidence—but I wonder if my friend Major White who is attached to the Horse guards would view it in the same light?"

If Catherine had ever had any doubts that she had treated Clive unfairly, they vanished in that instant. "You devil!" she spat and leaped for the letter, but Clive stepped nimbly out of her reach. Even as she leaped, reason overcame the blind fury that had engulfed her, and she made no further attempt to gain the letter but stood glaring at Clive, hating him for daring to threaten Rachael. And she had to admit to a feeling of, if not fear, something approaching it. She had no choice but to obey him—she couldn't run the risk that Clive would actually turn that letter over to the military. Even if

Rachael was proven innocent of any crime, she would have to suffer the gossip and speculation that the letter would bring. And Catherine felt sick at the thought of shy, quiet Rachael at the mercy of some bristling army officer. Clive had guessed correctly that Catherine would do anything to spare her mother—even if it meant putting herself in danger.

Frustrated and furious, Catherine glared at his smiling countenance. And Clive, staring at her expressive little face, couldn't control the naked look of hunger that leaped into his eyes. Sophisticated enough to recognize the undisguised lust that burned in his gray eyes, Catherine was disgusted by him. Determinedly, she stifled the feeling of nausea that rose in her throat and stared back at him.

"You sicken me! How can you do this to us? I thought you were fond of Rachael. And do you think this will make me like you any better?"

Clive shrugged. "If I say I will throw away this bit of damaging paper, will you marry me?"

"Of course not!" Catherine cried, outraged. "I wouldn't marry you if you were the last man on earth!"

"You see," Clive said reasonably, "I have nothing to lose. I've never made it any secret that I want you and would have you willingly or not. You will not come into my arms, so I shall have to take my pleasure in making you do whatever I can—and you will search that room for me."

Catherine knew she was beaten—for the moment—and grimly she said, "Very well. You leave me no choice."

Smiling, Clive thrust a piece of paper into her hand. "Here is a plan of the floor of the inn where Jason Savage is staying. You can gain entrance from the rose lattice near one of the windows." He pointed to the plan and continued briskly, "His valet sleeps somewhere else so if you're careful you'll be able to search his rooms without being discovered. A week from tonight, Savage and the rest of Brownleigh's house party have been invited to attend a ball at the count of Waterford's. As Waterford's home is some miles away, it will be late before Savage returns, so you'll have all evening to gain his rooms and search." Clive paused and added, "It isn't necessary that you actually search his rooms. If you would prefer that Manuel do it—fine."

Catherine shot him a sharp look. "I wouldn't want to put anyone else in danger. I'll do it myself. What is it that you want stolen?"

"I have reason to believe that somewhere within his belongings, Savage has a map or a chart that might interest me. I want you to find that map and bring it to me."

Sighing, Catherine asked, "A map of what?"

Clive frowned and at first seemed disinclined to answer her question, but then after a moment, he said slowly, "I'm not certain. I'm not even positive that there is a map. But I have good cause to believe there may be, and if it exists, I can sell it for a nice tidy sum."

Thoughtfully, still not completely committed to the plan, Catherine asked, "What's to stop me from not doing it and saying I couldn't find your map? You've just told me that you don't even know it exists for certain."

"You're not a fool, my dear. If you lie to me, I'll know it! I have ways of finding out. And I promise you that if you lie to me, then nothing would stop me from ruining your mother—have no doubts that I can do it if I chose. I could, if it suited me, compile a large amount of evidence against Rachael. I know so many clever people—some even capable of forging additional letters that Rachael could have written. You might think about that—and while you're doing it, perhaps you won't find my suit so distasteful."

"You really are a devil!" she said through gritted teeth.

"And I grow weary of your childish name calling! If you persist in it, I may expose Rachael just to teach you that it doesn't pay to annoy me."

Catherine's eyes blazed with hate, but she bit back the angry words that nearly came tumbling out. Clive was perfectly capable of doing exactly as he said, and stealing a map from a stranger seemed a small price to pay if it kept him from harming Rachael. But merciful heavens—it galled her!

Unperturbed by the look in her eyes, Clive continued smoothly, "If you do not find the map, make certain you leave no signs that his rooms have been searched. I don't want him to become suspicious. It's possible that what I want is still in his London lodgings."

There was nothing further for them to say to each other except to set up their next meeting and Catherine asked quietly, "How do I let you know the outcome?"

Before he could answer, a laughing male voice cut through the soft morning air, and Catherine spun around to regard the tall gentleman crossing the clearing, and her heart leaped inexplicably. She recognized him instantly and knew a momentary thrill of sheer fright that he might remember her. But then her eyes collided with his openly assessing gaze, and she was only aware of the increased beating of her heart and a crazy stab of excitement.

Jason was staring at her, making no effort to hide the fact that he found her very attractive indeed. He had noted the air of intimacy between Clive and Catherine as he approached, and he carelessly assumed that she was Clive's mistress—for the moment. There was no doubt in his own mind that before too long she would be under his protection, for suddenly, surprising himself in its intensity, he was hungry for a woman—*this* woman! She was much too beautiful to be wasted on a bounder like Clive.

Catherine was almost unbearably conscious of him standing there looking at her, and she wished for one wild mad moment that they were alone. But almost as soon as she thought it, she banished the idea from her mind—was she really that drawn to a man she hadn't ever met? So drawn that all she could think of was that they be private and she be at the mercy of all the exciting things his eyes and mouth promised? No! Never!

And she was extremely thankful, just then, that at Jason's prompting Clive referred to her merely as Tamara. For some reason, as yet unknown to herself, she didn't want this disturbing man to know that she was Lady Catherine.

After Clive's brief introduction, Jason, his gaze locked with Catherine's, said slowly, "Now, I'm especially glad Freddy made arrangements for us to ride out here today. Otherwise, I might have missed meeting your beautiful friend." And no one was in any doubt that he'd meant something considerably more intimate than friend!

Clive was coldly furious. The fact that this man was so coolly exploring Catherine's body with his eyes infuriated him and made him aware of a shocking flash of jealousy. How dare he look at her so—she was to be his and his alone. That Jason also had a strange effect on Catherine did not pass him by. Even if she wasn't aware of it, Clive could read the signs that Jason held more than just a passing interest for her. An ugly emotion coiled around his gut almost making him forget where they were. Pulling himself together with an effort, he vowed grimly that Jason would regret making his desire so obvious. Hiding his emotions, he inquired in a voice as bland as milk, "What has brought you to the camp, Jason?"

Jason, his eyes still insolently exploring the slim figure at Clive's side, answered carelessly, "I've come to examine the horses. I've been told this band of gypsies has some very fine animals." He gave a nod of his head in the direction of the camp. "I left Barrymore and Harris back there admiring some—er—animals of a different nature. Barrymore seemed so enchanted by a black-eyed charmer that he couldn't tear himself away."

It was obvious that Jason's thoughts ran along the same lines, for he was singularly disinclined to stop staring at Catherine. And Clive, driven by jealousy and spite found himself saying, "I must be leaving, but Tamara can show you the horses—if it's horses that you're really interested in!" Throwing Catherine a baleful look, he added, "And if not, perhaps she can help you otherwise, also."

Catherine, her thoughts jostling one another about, felt

her face burn with embarrassment at the meaning in Clive's words. She was angry with Clive and just now didn't want to examine her emotions concerning the American. There was something about him that fascinated her and yet at the same time warned her of danger. At the moment she only wished that he would stop staring at her so—it was certainly extremely rude and ill-bred of him! She was confused and uncertain as to what to do about Jason's very definite appraisal. Clive's sudden and abrupt departure a second later did nothing to solve her dilemma. She was left alone with Jason, and she wasn't so certain that it was what she wanted—despite having only minutes ago wished for that very thing. She bit her lip in vexation at her own wayward emotions and slanted a curious look at him. Her gaze met those hard green eyes, and the speculation in his glance caused her heart to thump painfully in her chest.

His eyes, deep-set under black brows that soared like wings, mesmerized her, and she forgot she was staring as her gaze traveled slowly over his face. Once again she was caught by the harsh arrogance of his features, the slightly flaring nostrils and high cheekbones. Unable to tear her eyes away, she stared, her gaze captured by his mouth. It was curved now in a impudent smile, but looking at the full, sensuous lower lip, she could imagine it hard with passion and was stunned by the sudden knowledge that she wanted him to kiss her as Clive had done. The sound of his laughter jerked her back to the present with an almost guilty start. "Satisfied?" he said lightly. "I'm sure you'll recognize me again."

Peeping up at him, she said demurely, "I'm sorry for staring, sir, but you see I've never seen an American before."

Jason glanced at her sharply, but those violet eyes gazed back innocently. Too innocently, he thought as he said, "Well, now you've seen one. And I suggest you take me to the horses or at least to someone who can answer some questions for me." Then, reaching out a long-fingered brown hand, he gently lifted her chin and continued, "I'll have time to further our acquaintance later, *chérie*, but just now I'm more interested in the merits of the horses than in your obvious charms." Grasping her shoulders, he turned her swiftly in the direction of the camp and gave her curving buttocks a playful slap, saying cheerfully, "March!"

Catherine's emotions were so confused, she dumbly did exactly as he commanded. But she hadn't walked far before anger rose up. Her temper was never very calm, and she almost turned on him like the spitting little cat she could be.

He was an arrogant, overbearing man who needed to be taught a lesson, she decided. Perhaps, she thought with sudden amusement, Manuel could trick him into buying the showy hack he'd won in a card game. The horse was beautiful to behold, but had no staying power—a real slug. What a fool Savage would look if they could get him to buy the animal. That would teach him not to treat her so familiarly!

Almost pleasantly she introduced him to Manuel and said gleefully in Romany, "Manuel, try to sell him the new one. You know, the gorgeous chestnut with no bottom. And stick him for a good price!"

Then casting a limpid smile at the lean dark man beside her, she started away only to be brought up short when Jason said thoughtfully, "I've always understood it was considered impolite to converse in a language others present can't understand. Of course"—he threw her a hard look—"I've done it when I've had something unpleasant planned for the other person."

His hard gaze and enigmatic smile pinning her to the spot, she fumbled for words as he said, "But I'm certain you'd never do a thing like that! Especially not to one who has so much to offer you." Idly, he picked up one glossy black curl that lay on her breast, and the hair, as if with a will of its own, curled lovingly around his hand. Still with that strange smile on his mouth, he said, "Believe me, little one, I have a great deal to give you. I wouldn't have chosen to discuss it now, but I can offer you more than Clive Pendleton and am more than willing to do so. You're an enchanting creature. As my mistress you'll want for nothing, nor will I share you as Clive seems to do. If you're mine, you only have to please me! So, don't play any silly games with me."

Catherine had gone completely scarlet at his words, and the calm assumption that she was for sale left her dazed. She couldn't help but know of the night visits made by dashing young bloods to the willing gypsy women, but that this stranger should state so coolly that he was prepared to buy her company and more left her silent and bewildered. Her mouth suddenly dry at the thought of precisely what he wanted, she was quite literally left speechless. For what seemed like hours, she stood rooted to the ground, staring at him; then, with a baffled cry of rage, she spun around and stalked off, determinedly resisting the urge to turn and slap his mocking face. He was a vain, conceited, dictatorial, high-handed, bold-faced commoner! *Ooooh,* but she'd like to tell him what she thought of him—and with relish she silently rolled the words off her tongue. She was still listing Jason Savage's faults when she entered her own caravan.

8

Catherine's caravan looked like the others from the outside, but inside there was a wealth of difference. A snug little bed was built into one wall, and a patterned quilt covered the feather-filled mattress. An oak chest shared the back wall with a squat potbellied stove, and a small wooden table with two matching chairs sat under the tiny window across from the bed. Catherine didn't pay any attention to its cosy appearance, but threw herself down on the bed and lay staring with unseeing eyes at the dark wooden ceiling.

It had been a disturbing morning, and she was a mass of conflicting, seething emotions. There was nothing she could do about Clive, he had her firmly within his power—at present, she qualified the thought. But with the American she had a choice, and it was this rather than Clive's threats that disturbed her thoughts.

She could take the sane, sensible way out, mount her horse, and ride swiftly to Hunter's Hill. There she would be safe; she could slip quietly into being Lady Catherine Tremayne, and Jason Savage would be left wondering what happened to Clive's gypsy girl. Intuitively, she sensed he wouldn't wonder long but would find some willing light skirt who would suit him as well. Perversely, it was the thought that he hadn't remembered her and would forget her again as easily that annoyed her most. She rolled over onto her stomach and absent-mindedly played with one black lock of hair, twisting it about her fingers. She gave a deep sigh. She'd like to do something that would make this insolent American remember her for a long time. Then an impish grin crossed her vivid face, and she decided *not* anything, after all! There were limits one would go for revenge. But it would be pleasant to bring that arrogant man to his knees.

She knew little of passion or of the hungers that drove men, but this morning she had come face to face with the fact that men could lust after her body. Clive made her feel dirty and soiled when he had looked at her, but when Jason's eyes had wandered openly over her, she had experienced conflicting emotions. Part of her had been elated at the look in his eyes; part had warned her to run and hide safely from that probing gaze. Even now, she felt again the power of those emerald eyes as they had moved over her slim form, and for the first time she perceived that there might be justice in Rachel's warnings and constant disapproval of her singularly wild and hoydenish behavior. It was forcibly being shown to her that while her mother might understand her actions there were others who would neither understand nor care and would be quick to take advantage. In one way, she didn't blame Savage for his reaction; he saw her only as a gypsy wench, and it would be inconceivable to him that a young lady of good birth and breeding would do something so ill-advised and fraught with danger as to actually roam through a gypsy camp. Catherine was becoming aware that her actions were outrageous and that if she had listened to Rachael or even Reina, neither Clive nor Jason would have treated her as they had done.

She gave an exasperated snort. Enough of this! She

wasn't riding back to Hunter's Hill like some frightened ninny, nor was she going to hide in here all day. She would pretend that this morning hadn't happened and that Jason Savage had not made his very improper proposal, but . . . !

An irritated tap on the door broke into her musings, and before she could move, the door was thrust open to reveal the lined face of Reina. "Well, well, and what are you plotting, my pretty?" Reina asked sharply, noting the strange look on Catherine's face.

Catherine smiled ruefully, helping the older woman inside. "You know me too well, Reina. I can hide very little from you."

"You forget, it was I who raised you and that wretched half brother of yours."

Catherine teased, "You old fraud, you know Adam is the apple of your wicked eye. As far as you're concerned, he can do no wrong."

Reina grumbled and lowered her bony frame to the edge of the bed. Catherine watched the old woman affectionately. Reina presented a cold exterior, and it was true that she could be as hard and unyielding as granite; but she had a soft spot for the two brats, as she frequently called them, and had raised them as well as sheltered them from the more unpleasant facts of life in the gypsy camp. She had for reasons best known to herself seen to it that Catherine remained a virgin and that Adam hadn't become entangled with one of the gypsy girls.

Just why Reina protected them, even she herself didn't know. Perhaps they had in her mind, really become her children, or perhaps she never forgot who they really were. And the two children couldn't have had a better protectress; she was, for all her rags, the matriarch of the tribe. Her word was law, and not even Manuel, her son, argued once she had spoken.

Now settled comfortably on the bed, she fixed her eyes on the girl before her, and a wave of something akin to envy swept through her frail, old body. Once she had been as beautiful and vibrant as the figure before her. But at Catherine's age, she had had a score of lovers, leaving a trail of broken hearts beneath her small feet. Coolly allowing her lovers to possess her body, she had never felt the least affection for any of the men who had known her so intimately. She used them and when they were of no further use, discarded them without a backward glance of her fine eyes. Even her son Manuel, she looked upon as a mere nuisance. Only for this child Catherine and her brother Adam had she felt anything resembling that tender emotion, love. And just now she was worried about what the future would hold for Catherine.

Catherine, sensing that Reina was uneasy, knelt before the old woman and smiled tenderly up at the worn face. "What is troubling you, old one? Is it Clive?"

Reina snorted disgustedly, "That fool! Huh!" Then she narrowed her eyes questioningly. "What did he want?"

Catherine sat back on her heels, extremely thoughtful. She couldn't tell Reina the truth, for nothing would stop the old woman from seeing Clive punished. And Reina hated Rachael, seeing that innocent lady as a stealer of the affection of the two children. The fact that Rachael was their real mother made no difference to Reina. Reina never shared anything and couldn't understand that Adam and Catherine could love Rachael without lessening any of the love they had for her. If in punishing Clive, Rachael was ruined, so much the better! So Catherine, who disliked lying, was forced to do so.

"He came to see me—" she began slowly.

"I know that!" snapped Reina. "I want to know *why!*"

Swallowing nervously, Catherine began again. "He heard I was staying out here and was curious to see me," she finished lamely.

Reina, her eyes hard, like pieces of black coal, stared at the girl, searching the young face, taking in the downcast eyes and the faint flush of color that stained Catherine's cheeks as the silence grew. "Do you take me for a fool?" Reina finally asked angrily.

"Oh Reina, don't scold! Really, it was just curiosity. You know what Clive is like. He's always poking his nose in."

"Humph!" greeted Catherine's words.

"It's true! He always seems to know everything, and this isn't the first time he's shown up unexpectedly."

Undecided, Reina stared so long and hard at Catherine that the girl almost blurted out the truth. Those black, unswerving eyes still had the power to make her feel like a child caught being naughty.

Another snort from Reina signaled that she was displeased with Catherine's rather lame excuse but would let it lie. Anyway, she was really more interested in Catherine's reaction to the young blood who had arrived after Clive and growled, "What does the stranger with Manuel want?"

A decidedly angry sparkle came into Catherine's violet eyes. "That toad! He says he wants to see horses, but I think he and his friends just rode out for a lark."

Eyes still narrowed, Reina asked dryly, "And that's all he wants? Just horses?"

Rising in one graceful movement, Catherine walked to the window. Idly her hands played with the snowy curtains. "No, that's not all he wants. He wants me to become his mistress! He said he'd pay more for my favors than Clive did. Just like that and as bold as brass, he told me not to play silly games with him." Her voice was angry when she finished speaking, but Reina's crack of laughter caused her to spin around and look at her with wide, questioning eyes.

"What a man!" crowed Reina. "A fine buck, indeed! He rides into camp and immediately decides to mount you. You should be pleased he finds you to his taste."

Catherine, a frown marring her smooth forehead, said confusedly, "You think I should become his mistress?"

"Do you want to?" Reina asked, watching the girl closely.

"Of course not! I'd like to teach him a lesson, though.

What an arrogant creature he is to think that just at the snap of his fingers, I'll leap into his bed."

"If you were a gypsy girl, one of the true blood, you would not be so insulted—you would be thinking of the gold he could give you. If you were not Lady Catherine, think what his favor would mean to you."

"But I *am* Lady Catherine!" she cried, distressed.

"Then tell me. Why does he find you dressed in gypsy clothes and meeting strange men in the meadow like some easy slut?" Reina asked in a stony voice, her face a cold gray mask.

Catherine stared at her, aghast. Never had Reina spoke to her so harshly, and quick tears filled her eyes. If Reina had slapped her, it couldn't have been more painful—it was like a knife blade in her heart. Reina twisted the blade further by saying in an icy voice, "The time has come. You must choose. Either accept him and be one of us or leave us. You cannot continue both paths. And I want you gone from us."

"But why?" Catherine asked blankly.

Reina reached forward swiftly and grasping Catherine's wrist, twisted the girl to the floor in front of her. She thrust her face forward, and staring into the bewildered young face, she snarled, "Do you think this young American will be the only one to desire you? Do you think always you will be protected by the tribe? That I or Manuel will always be within call? What if that young buck decided to lay you in the meadow? Do not shake your head at me! His friends could hold us until he'd had his pleasure with you. Do you think it has not happened before?" Reina's voice rose with passion at Catherine's look of shocked disbelief, and almost shaking with emotion, Reina cried, "How do you think Amber's child was conceived? I'll tell you—a young lordling, very like the American out there, rode into camp one afternoon with some friends while the men were gone, and Amber caught his eye. After he raped her, in full view of us, he shared her with his friends. How would you like that to happen to you, my proud lady?" When she finished,

Reina was breathing heavily, an angry flush adding color to her swarthy face.

Gazing at her in horror, Catherine whispered, "I never knew."

"Huh! You never knew!" Reina sneered. "Why should you? You're the great Lady Tremayne, who plays at being a gypsy. No, you'll never know what it's like to be a gypsy. Those young bucks out there could kill us, steal our animals, and rape our young women—the constable would not even ride out from town to see that we are decently buried."

One tear, like a crystal drop, slid unchecked down Catherine's white face. In a voice shaking with hurt, she asked quietly, "Why did you hide these things from me? Why didn't you ever let me know how you really felt? I had a right to know!"

"You have no right but what I give you. And I repeat, I want you gone from camp," snapped Reina.

"If you feel this way, you should have told me," Catherine said, pain underlying the softness of her words. Her face like carved marble, she rose from the floor and fighting for composure continued, "I'll saddle Sheba and leave now. And—and—" Her control broke, and turning her head to hide the tears, falling in earnest now, she said in a voice thick with pain, "I wish you would have told me I wasn't wanted, that you didn't want me here. I would never have inflicted myself upon you, but—I thought you loved me—as I love you."

Reina stared at the straight, proud back and sighed heavily. Her voice was tired as she spoke. "Child, it is not that I don't want you. But you cannot continue to inhabit two such opposite worlds. What happened today is a foretaste of what will happen in the future. Next time, you might not be asked if you are willing to become a man's mistress. You cannot run the risk. Visit us, yes, but as Lady Catherine! *Not* as a young gypsy girl. Come, yes, and spend the day with us, but with your servants in attendance. I love you, child, and would not willingly see you hurt. For this reason I've said these harsh things."

Catherine, whirling about, threw her arms around the old woman's shoulders and, hugging her close, cried brokenly, "Oh Reina, I thought you no longer loved me!"

Feeling those strong, young arms about her frail body moved Reina deeply, and gently she soothed, "Nay, child, it was never that! I love you! But this game you play must cease. It is dangerous! You are too young and lovely to go unnoticed."

Deep inside, Catherine admitted Reina was right, but torn, she cried despairingly, "Must it be now, today?"

Sadly, Reina shrugged her shoulders. "It will not grow easier, and I dislike forcing you. Perhaps not today, but soon Tamara must cease and Lady Catherine take her place for all time."

The unhappiness Catherine felt was plain to see on her expressive face. "Why must I be torn both ways?" she cried.

"Is it so very hard, little one? As Lady Catherine, you can do as much for us. You can still come to see us. We would always welcome you. I would be wounded if you never came."

"But never to feel free, Reina, always to be hemmed in!"

"Child, none of us are free to do as we like. And you must make a choice—either become a gypsy and give up all that being Lady Catherine Tremayne means or stay in your rightful role."

For a few minutes, Catherine stood staring down into the concerned face raised to hers. Then she turned and walked to the door; not looking back, she said, "I'm going for a ride. I can't decide today. You must give me time, Reina!"

"Whatever you decide, you must do it soon."

Reina's words buzzed around in her brain as she ran to where the horses were tied. She tossed her head angrily as if to shake the unwelcome thoughts that continued to plague her. The thoughts were not dispelled as she groomed Sheba, tugging at Sheba's black mane as if the Arabian mare were the cause of her problem. Usually, grooming Sheba was a happy, relaxed time. But she felt tired and dispirited—crying always made her feel that way. Thank goodness, she wasn't given to tears often! Gradually though, as she brushed and combed Sheba's already satin black hide, a sense of acceptance came over her.

Reina was right! She would have to stop acting like a wild hoyden. Rachael said the same thing, and as for the rest of the family, if they even suspected how much of her time was spent with the gypsies, it would probably send them off in one combined swoon. A smile flickered as she thought wickedly of Aunt Ceci's reaction in particular.

Well, if she was going to stop living half the time at the camp, she might as well take advantage of every second left to her and not spend it mooning about feeling sorry for herself. With this thought in mind, she untied Sheba, leaped gracefully upon her back, and using only a halter rein cantered from the camp.

9

Out of sight of the camp, Catherine left the dirt lane and, urging Sheba to greater speed, broke through a small patch of woods. A large, open meadow lay on the other side. As soon as her hoofs touched the spongy ground, Sheba tossed her head and, as if shot from a cannon, burst into a wild and seemingly uncontrolled race across the wide meadow.

Catherine, a slim, bright figure on the racing mare, exercised no guidance but let herself become in spirit part of the running horse. She leaned forward, her cheek almost resting on Sheba's outstretched neck; her hair, a long, black, flowing flag, mingled with the mare's flying mane, until mane and hair were indistinguishable. She forgot herself in the feel of the moving body, while the wind against her face whipped roses into her cheeks. She was lost—a nameless thing that could only exist; her mind a peaceful blank; Reina, Lady Catherine, and all the others blown away.

Aware only of the pounding, sleek body under hers, she neither saw nor heard the rider who was fast overtaking them. Suddenly another horse was thundering alongside

Sheba. Catherine felt the brush of the rider's leg as his horse closed the gap between them, and an arm with muscles like steel snaked out and tightened about her small waist, effortlessly lifting her from the back of her horse. Then she was thrown like a sack of meal across the saddlebow of the other animal. Shock held her still, her mind unable to comprehend what was happening. She lay limp, feeling the blood rushing to her head. The bite of the saddle against her soft belly was painful.

The unknown rider gradually slowed his horse and rode for the edge of the woods, where a small creek flowed. Once there, he dismounted swiftly and again she felt that steel arm around her as she was lifted none to gently from the horse. Abruptly, the peaceful blankness left her, and the events of the morning came rushing back as she stared at the big man in front of her. Jason Savage! It would be him, she thought angrily.

"Are you all right?" he asked in a low voice.

"Why shouldn't I be?" she spat ungraciously.

The concern left his eyes, and he said dryly, "I see fright hasn't robbed you of your quick temper."

"Fright?" she questioned impatiently.

A frown crossed his face, and he said slowly, "Perhaps I'm mistaken, but it looked to me as if you had lost control of your horse. I thought I was saving you from a runaway."

"Playing the gentleman?" she sneered. "It must be an unusual role for you."

Jason slowly relaxed back against a tree, leaning his broad shoulders on the rough bark and crossing one booted foot over the other. "You know, it will be a pleasure to tame you, little one. Clive must have spoiled you rotten. Our relationship will be a stormy one, but I think the pleasures will outweigh your fiery temper."

Rage held her glued to the spot, and her eyes sparked purple fire as she glared at him. Nearly choking on the angry words that came spilling from her lips, she said furiously,

"You stupid, bacon-brained boor! Do you really believe I'll become your mistress, just because it pleases you?"

A slow smile began to curve his mouth as he folded his arms across his chest and let his eyes roam lazily over her body, lingering on the heaving breasts that pressed proudly against the thin material of the blouse. Then sliding his gaze disturbingly down the curved length of her body, he realized she wore little or nothing underneath her outer clothes.

Abruptly he abandoned his lazy pose and with the ease of a striking panther dragged her roughly into his arms. She knew a momentary thrill of half fright, half excitement, before his mouth fastened on hers in a long, demanding kiss that shattered forever her naive, romantic notions about love between men and women. His lips were hard and bruising, but the warmth and sensual pleasure as they moved knowingly on hers drove all coherent thought from her stunned brain. Almost compulsively she slid her trembling arms around his neck, her fingers unconsciously caressing the black hair that grew low on his neck, and a strange, treacherous melting feeling invaded her entire being until she clung to him, unable to think clearly.

Crushed next to his muscled length, she could feel his long legs pressed against hers, and as his kisses became more passionate, his hands moving possessively down her back, cupping her taut buttocks and pulling her unresisting body closer, she felt the hardness of his desire rubbing intimately against her belly. Trapped in a web of sensuous anticipation, they sank to the ground. Still locked in a tight embrace, his lips forcing hers apart and his tongue exploring her virgin mouth, she could do nothing to still the exquisite sensations that were racing through her body. Gently, he undid her blouse, and his touch, as his hand slid along her warm flesh, was like fire engulfing her. Then he reached and brushed her firm breast teasingly. It was as if she were powerless to stop him, and from somewhere deep within she knew she didn't want to stop him, that she wanted him to go on—and on! And he did: his big body laying half on hers, one leg thrown over her thighs; his mouth leaving a trail of fire as he lowered his head, kissing the soft hollow at the base of her throat; and finally, shockingly kissing her naked breasts, his tongue burning her nipples as they leaped to his lips. His mouth left her throbbing breast and possessed her willing lips once more. Unthinkingly, she moved her body closer to him, while his hand lay heavy on her belly, kneading the flesh gently before lifting her skirt and touching her, suddenly, between the legs. A tingling, searing flame exploded within her, driving her to thrust up her loins to press against his exploring hand. Her soft moan of pleasure was lost as he ground his mouth more hungrily on hers.

Somewhere from the hidden recesses of her brain, danger signals were gradually interfering with the almost paralyzing quality of his lovemaking, and Catherine began to push away from him. But he only laughed deep in his throat and again reached under her skirt, sliding one hand lingeringly up her smooth thigh—she was frighteningly aware of how this meeting would end!

What had been faint warning became pounding alarm. She struggled in earnest, desperate to break his hold. This had to stop before it was too late! But it was only when Jason, becoming aware of her attempt to escape, raised his head, and only then, when she saw the raw, unleashed desire flaring in his eyes, that she was able to galvanize herself into action. With a strength that caught both of them by surprise, she flung herself from his arms and stood up, her bosom heaving as she stared down at him. His face was tight with hungry passion as she faced him, her lips bruised ruby from his demanding mouth, her eyes wide with frightening awareness.

He lunged forward, and with a cry of terror she eluded his grasp. Rising in one easy, lithe movement from his prone position, and very conscious of the extremely noticeable bulge in his tight-fitting breeches, his eyes narrowed and contemptuous, he snarled, "How much? What price do you put on your favors? What will it cost me to have you back in my arms and willing? A carriage of your own? A trip to London? Paris?"

"Pa—Paris?" she stammered, aghast that he should be agreeable to such a thing merely to lay a wench he had just seen this morning. But Jason, taking her stuttered question as a statement and reaching out for her, muttered, "Done! I'll take you to Paris then."

Catherine danced nimbly away from his hand, her only thought that he mustn't touch her again. He mustn't be allowed to destroy her inhibitions, even if it angered him. She was rattled, more afraid of his kiss than any physical harm he could do her. Jason leaped for her again, and this time his reaching hand encountered naked steel. Cursing, he drew back sharply and looked unbelievingly at the blood welling out of the deep slash across his palm; then with suddenly cold eyes, he stared at the girl, a small knife clenched firmly in her hand.

Catherine, her heart pounding frantically in her breast, had only used a blade once before, but she was thankful that Manuel had taught her how to fight with one. It was her one defense against this violently angry man who circled her like a hungry wolf. Both were breathing heavily, and her apprehension grew with every movement he made, for now the conflict between them had taken a dangerous and deadly turn. Jason, his eyes green slits of icy rage, raked her slim body for a weakness, but she held the small razor-sharp blade like she knew what she was about. His strength was greater, yet that knife put her in the stronger position. But it was an unequal contest, and Catherine knew it. Her only chance was to run, and she took it. Spinning on her heels, she leapt and ran for her life, deeper into the woods, praying desperately as she ran that he would allow her to escape. But Jason had no intention of allowing her to escape so easily—he had a score to settle with this teasing little bitch!

He moved like summer lightning, and she hadn't run more than a few yards when his hands, like iron talons, grasped both her arms from behind, pinning them uselessly at her sides. She was lifted from the ground and held, kicking and twisting, helpless against his heaving chest. He partially released her after a second and with cruel ease twisted her arm behind her back, ignoring her scream of rage and pain as he took the knife from her nerveless hand. Throwing the shining blade violently into the dirt, he spun her around and ground out angrily, "You little hellcat! You could have killed me with that little toy! What the hell kind of game are you playing? I'm greatly tempted to treat you as you deserve and break your pretty little neck!"

Catherine's temper exploded, and the furious, boiling rage she now felt eclipsed the fear that had dominated her earlier; blindly, she swung her hand and connected it, open-palmed, hard against Jason's dark face. The sound of the slap was like the crack of a bullet, and it startled both antagonists.

Then deliberately, his eyes like green ice, he slowly raised his uninjured hand and intentionally, viciously, struck her across one cheek. In an icy voice he said, "Don't ever strike me again, my dear. I will put up with a great deal from you, but *that* I will not tolerate!"

Fierce tears of pain and humiliation sparkled like diamond drops in her eyes. The imprint of his hand was a scarlet scar on her white cheek, and she bent her head trying to hide the tears. But they fell down from her eyes onto one tightly clenched hand, which she held to her mouth in a vain attempt to stop the trembling of her bottom lip.

Abruptly, his anger drained away, leaving him with a strange desire to comfort her. Gently he pulled her unresisting body close to his, and an odd smile crossed his face as her soft hair tickled his chin. He cradled her next to him, and his voice, kind with a thread of something that could have been amusement running through it, said, "Tamara, Tamara, what am I to do with you, *petite?* You smile so enticingly at me, you let me kiss you, then you spring a knife on me! And now I find my arms filled with a soft warm *jeune fille.*"

Catherine, her head buried against his broad chest, her

nose pressed hard against his white shirt, raised a tear-streaked face to gaze at him puzzled. Surely now that she was helpless, he would continue his practiced lovemaking. But there was no passion in the arms that held her so securely, and his eyes showed only mocking amusement as they gazed down at her. He released her slowly, almost regretfully, and then with one arm slung carelessly over her shoulders, he aimlessly began to walk with her back to the meadow where their horses were peacefully grazing. He led her to the creek, dipping his fine linen handkerchief into the icy water and gently bathing the marks of tears from her face. He surprised her even further by determinedly fastening her blouse. His unexpected change of manner completely confused her, and she was intensely aware of a desire that he remain in this strangely soothing mood. What a changeable creature he was, she thought, conveniently forgetting her own rapid reverses of emotion.

A charming smile curving his mouth, he set out with practiced ease to deliberately disarm her and murmured softly, "Shall we start over, *chérie?*"

Before she could speak, he bowed sweepingly in front of her startled eyes and coaxed, "May I present myself, one Jason Savage from Louisiana, who finds your charms so heady they chase all rational thoughts from his brain." And as a shy, encouraging smile began to appear at the corner of her mouth, he was oddly aware of a queer jump in the region of his heart. Taking note of her uncertain acceptance of his playful speech, he gaily embroidered upon his theme. "I must apologize for rushing you; but we are an impatient people, and such beauty as yours drives a man to forget his manners. After seeing your lovely face, it is understandable that I lost my head." A mocking gleam in his eyes, he said soulfully, "We Americans are very deprived!"

At that, she burst out laughing and exclaimed, "What a bounder! I'm certain that there are many beautiful women in America."

Jason, staring almost bemused at the sunny countenance

turned laughingly up at him, was jolted slightly out of his coldblooded detachment. Now that her violet eyes no longer sparkled with rage, the enchanting tilt at their corners pronounced, he was suddenly struck by a resemblance to someone, but to whom eluded his memory. She distracted his thoughts by saying lightly, "I fear you greatly exaggerate. I've heard from my brother that the women in the new world are very lovely."

"Ah yes, perhaps, but I'm positive in Louisiana there is no one to compare with you!"

She glanced at him suspiciously, but his face was guileless. He might have been acting clever, but she wasn't going to challenge him; she had the feeling that she would come off the worst for it. Instead she asked brightly, "Is Louisiana so different from the rest of America?"

"But yes, *chérie!* We are as different as the exotic rose is to the common daisy."

"Louisiana being the rose, I presume?" she asked tartly.

"But, yes!" he grinned down at her, his teeth extremely white in his sun-browned face. She noticed, abstractedly, the fine lines that crinkled at the corners of his eyes and the deep dimple that appeared in one cheek when he smiled. It was a nice face, she decided; but then, just as she was relaxing her guard, he disconcerted her by grasping her hand and pulling her slowly into his arms.

Smiling into her suddenly wary face, he murmured, "But let us talk of other things, hmmmmm?" Brushing her forehead lightly with his lips, he asked, "How soon will you come to me, little one? When will you let me love you?"

"Wha—what do you mean?" she stammered, once again unable to think clearly as the heat from his body invaded hers, and his clean male scent drifted to her nostrils.

He gave a mocking sigh and gently blew on her ear. "I mean how long will it take you to tell Clive that you have found another protector? I am impatient to consummate our relationship."

Catherine ran her tongue over her suddenly dry lips and

searched frantically for an answer. As she stared dumbly at him, his smile faded, the teasing glint in his green eyes vanished, and his stare became as hard and ruthless as when they had fought earlier. And she swallowed nervously, fearful of doing anything that would jar him from this seemingly complacent mood.

Mistaking the apprehensive look in her eyes, Jason said softly, "I understand. It is too hard for you to do. So I will see to Clive myself. All you have to do is gather your things and meet me at The Fox."

"When?" she managed to say, because it seemed safe.

The glinting smile flashed again. "Tomorrow night. I'll have made all necessary arrangements by then."

And then, much to her alarm, Catherine discovered she didn't want to move—she wanted to stay here, to feel Jason's lips on her mouth again, to feel the painful delight of his arms as they tightened about her. Some of her thoughts must have shown, or Jason was thinking the same thing, because a second later his arms tightened around her, and his mouth closed over her half-opened lips as if he were starving for their touch, flooding her whole body with a fevered excitement and intoxicating her senses until willingly, she would have let him do anything he desired!

But this time it was Jason who pulled away, leaving her with an aching, unfulfilled emptiness. He smiled crookedly down at her flushed face and seeing the soft, parted lips, the drugged looked in her eyes, almost took her back in his arms; but for once, fighting his own instincts, he muttered harshly, "Tamara, if you don't want me to lay you now, don't tempt me! I'm not a man used to waiting, and right now I want you badly. So, I suggest that unless you're willing to let me make love to you here and now, stop teasing me!"

His words and the half-angry look in his eyes effectively blasted her dreamy, drifting state and plunged her instantly into awareness of how near she had come to surrendering to his passionate demands. Violently she wrenched away from him and not looking in his direction walked stiffly towards her horse. Shame, anger, and a queer frustration slashed through her body like a sword. She was a fool! And silently she berated herself for her stupid actions. God! It would have served her right if Savage had raped her! She had certainly asked for it! Whatever possessed her to encourage him, to make her yearn for his caress and worse, to let him see that she wanted him to kiss her?

Engrossed in her own unhappy thoughts, she was unaware that he had followed close behind her, and she nearly screamed with surprise when finally standing next to Sheba and preparing to mount, he unexpectedly reached out and swiftly threw her upon the horse's back. Then laying a possessive hand on her thigh, he said, "Don't worry little one. I'll see to everything, and soon we'll have many delightful hours together. Be at the inn tomorrow night. I'll tell the innkeeper to expect you." His green eyes roaming leisurely over her tense body, he remarked, "Don't bother about your clothes. I'll buy you some fine feathers." Then his mocking smile glinted, and he laughed. "But I doubt if during the first days of our association you'll need any."

An indignant gasp slipped from her lips, but before she could think of a retort, he smacked Sheba's shining flank, and as the horse bounded forward, Jason called after her, "Remember, tomorrow evening at The Fox."

Controlling her sudden spurt of anger, Catherine stifled the impulse to return and wither Jason with a few well-chosen words. She rode, instead, at a breakneck pace back to the camp. Minutes later, preoccupied with her inner thoughts, she absent-mindedly rubbed down a sweating Sheba and then slowly wandered to where Reina sat with her friend Ilone near Catherine's caravan.

Ilone was one of the oldest and ugliest women in camp. Never, not even in her youth, had she been a beauty, and life had trampled heavily across her features. She had lost her left eye in a knife fight years before, and a dirty black patch now covered the sightless socket. But nothing could hide the ugly, discolored scar that ran diagonally across her shrunken cheek and broad forehead and disappeared into her thin, gray hair. Ilone smiled a welcome at Catherine, exposing several gaps in her mouth where teeth had either rotted away or had been kicked out. Catherine liked Ilone, and throwing herself down on the ground between the two old women, she joined their conversation.

After a few minutes Ilone, perhaps sensing Catherine wished to speak alone with Reina, left them. And Catherine admitted ruefully to Reina, "You were right this morning when you said it was dangerous for me to wander around without my servants. Whether I like it or not, I will have to stop coming here and pretending that I'm just a gypsy girl named Tamara."

Reina threw her a startled glance, her eyes filled with unasked questions, and Catherine said slowly, "I think I shall do as you said. My mother will be overjoyed when she learns I don't intend to haunt this place any more except in the company of my servants." Her decision made, she continued briskly, "You might as well move your things into my caravan, as I'll have no further use of it. And once you're in possession, I wouldn't have the nerve to tell you that I'd changed my mind!"

She turned and smiled impishly at Reina's impassive features, and Reina, pleased but determined not to show it, snapped, "And what changed your mind so suddenly? When you left earlier, you were undecided."

How to tell her, Catherine thought painfully, that she feared she was a wanton, a slut, and no better than a paid whore? And all because a man, a virtual stranger, had aroused her to such aching desire that she would have allowed him to take her in that most intimate act between man and woman. Moodily she said, "Something happened to make me change my mind, that's all. I said you were right. You should be happy I'm following your advice—besides, it is dangerous living here! I'll just have to learn to be a proper lady."

Reina shot her a suspicious look and would have liked to know what had happened to bring about Catherine's sudden reversal, but she knew that if the girl had wanted her to know she would have told her. So, she asked quietly, "Have you forgotten about the wedding? Will Lady Catherine grace it with her presence, or will Tamara?"

Catherine gave a dismayed sigh. She hadn't thought about that. In two days, Sanchia and Zoltan would be married, and she had been looking forward to it. An almost frenzied delight invaded the camp on a wedding night. Even the fires seemed to burn more vividly as wild gypsy melodies drifted from the madly playing violins, and the wine flowed freely as toast after toast was drunk to the young couple. It was unfair! Lady Catherine with the attendant servants would put a blight on the happy celebration—the gypsies would feel uneasy with a grand lady watching. Most of them had forgotten she wasn't one of them, but attired and groomed in elegant clothes, she would be a constant reminder. Damn Reina! She had made her choice, and now the old woman was testing her resolution. Catherine grimaced. Well, her resolution wasn't very strong, and she said determinedly, "I'll come that night as Tamara."

"Huh! I didn't think you could stay away!" Reina snorted.

A mulish slant to her chin, Catherine answered, "That will absolutely be the last time, I promise!"

Reina searched her face intently, and what she saw must have satisfied her, for she relaxed and gently patted Catherine's hand. "It's hard, I know, my child—but in time you'll see I was right. I only wish you would come as Lady Catherine that night also."

Stubbornly, Catherine shook her head. "No! I want to take my turn dancing. It will be my last chance. Lady Catherine couldn't—Tamara can!"

"Very well, child, I will not argue with you if you promise me that after the wedding, Tamara will end."

Catherine made a face but answered willingly enough, "I

promise. I'm leaving for Hunter's Hill now, and the night of the wedding shall be the final appearance of Tamara."

Just as Catherine started to walk away, Ilone came wandering back. Looking at the older woman, Catherine was struck with a devilish idea. A wicked gleam in her eyes, she stopped and talked for some minutes to Ilone. When Catherine finally mounted Sheba, she was smiling—a smile that was full of mischief.

10

Although Catherine had spent the afternoon arriving at fateful decisions, Jason had not. He had ridden into Melton Mowbray and spent a very enjoyable time picking out clothes in which to deck his newest mistress. He had promised Tamara some new clothes—so new clothes she would have.

Arriving back at the inn, he found that Pierre had already laid out his clothes for the evening, and restless and bored, he wished he'd declined Brownleigh's dinner invitation. Sighing, he wondered briefly how he had allowed himself to be caught up in the whirl of social activity that his friends found so enjoyable. But later that evening, dressed in a beautifully tailored, green velvet jacket embellished with black satin trim, his long legs encased in black satin knee breeches, and his cravat impeccably tied, he looked so handsome and alert that no one guessed from his handsome face exactly how bored he was.

Dinner was pleasant, the company congenial, and the only disturbing note was Pendleton's odd behavior. That

Pendleton was spoiling for a fight was obvious, but the reason mystified Jason. It wasn't the gypsy wench, for Clive had practically thrown her at his head this morning, and when he'd informed him earlier that she would be under his protection from now on, Clive had merely shrugged his shoulders indifferently. Yet, all evening Clive had been drinking heavily, and whenever his gaze encountered Jason's, there had been a menacing look of suppressed violence in the gray depths of his eyes.

After dinner, the ladies removed themselves from the dining room, and now the snowy linen tablecloth was littered with port and brandy bottles, and the air was thick with smoke, as the gentleman sat back and enjoyed their after-dinner cigars and wine. The evening was altogether predictable, a repetition of so many other evenings, and Jason was wondering how soon after they joined the ladies he could politely take his leave when Clive, seated across from him, an ugly look in his eyes, said loudly, "Americans! Bah! They're barbarians born to dangle at the end of a rope or die of the French pox!"

An embarrassed quiet fell over the assembled gentlemen, the silence tightening as Jason, his eyes hooded, their expression hidden, picked up his wine glass and remarked smoothly, "That depends, I think, on whether we embrace your principles or your mistresses!"

Someone laughed, nervously, and Clive took a long drink of his brandy before saying, "You're very clever," adding insinuatingly,"—for one of your breed."

Coolly Jason replied, "It's not often people are as discerning as yourself and recognize how very clever I am!" His mocking smile lurking at the corner of his mouth, he added, "I'll take your statement as a compliment."

Before Pendleton could say anything else, Brownleigh rose hurriedly from his place at the head of the long table and said hastily, "I believe we should join the ladies." Then without waiting to see if his guests agreed, he signaled the butler to usher them into the blue salon where the ladies sat gossiping.

Deftly, Tom Harris hustled Jason up the stairs to his bedchamber where Barrymore, following close behind, exploded, "Upon my word, Savage, how could you swallow that?"

Jason's expression was bored as he stared at his friend. "What would you have me do? Create more talk for the scandalmongers by challenging a drunk man to a duel?"

"Drunk!" Barrymore snorted. "Pendleton has the hardest head I know!"

Jason shrugged his shoulders and said disinterestedly, "I saw no point in challenging him merely for his lack of manners."

"Wasn't bad manners!" Tom broke in. "Did it deliberately, tried to make you challenge him, felt it!"

"Of course he did it deliberately!" Barrymore burst out. "And you"—he cast a darkling glance in Jason's direction—"sat there and let him do it!"

Jason yawned in Barrymore's angry face and smiled sleepily. "*Mon ami,* you would have me kill a man I hardly know, merely because he expressed an opinion I found distasteful?"

"It isn't that, and you know it! From the moment you arrived, Clive was waiting for an opportunity to be insulting. A half a dozen times this evening he said things that were disgusting, and you ignored them."

Lazily, Jason surveyed his friend. Barrymore was definitely in a pet! His teeth were tightly clenched together, and his handsome countenance was marred by a scowling frown. His blue eyes, normally smiling, were hard and angry. Even his carefully brushed blond locks seemed to bristle with anger.

"Don't you realize he deliberately offered you an insult no gentleman would stomach?" Barrymore grated.

"True," Tom said, nodding his head wisely. "Said it so you'd have to challenge him."

Jason sighed, and clasping his hands behind his head as he lay comfortably on the couch, said in a bored tone, "But I didn't rise to the bait, I turned his childish insults away."

"I don't give a damn!" Barrymore cried. "You should have told the bounder to choose his seconds! Tom and I would have been honored to serve as yours."

As Jason remained silent, Barrymore asked, "Don't you care that everyone will think you're afraid of the fellow?"

Nailing him to the spot with an emerald stare, Jason asked quietly, "Do you?"

"Of course not!" he answered in shocked tones.

"Thing is," Tom said earnestly, "*we* know you ain't afraid of Pendleton, but does everyone else?"

"You're afraid of what people will say?" Jason inquired coldly. He sat up suddenly, the lazy, relaxed air gone, an icy gleam in his eyes, and Barrymore and Harris exchanged concerned glances. Jason in a rage was fine—provided he was in a rage with someone else. And as he continued to look at them with that cold, unblinking stare, Tom began to fidget nervously, and Barrymore said soothingly, "Now Jason, there's no reason to come the ugly with us!"

Jason snorted disgustedly and said with an edge, "At least Pendleton never questioned my courage! But you, my two friends, seem very worried about it!"

Barrymore, his former anger cooling rapidly, made a face and said quietly, "Look. Exchanging insults isn't getting us anywhere. Tom and I certainly didn't mean to question your courage. And I had no business nearly losing my temper like I did. Pendleton gets under my skin, and I'm inclined to be quick off the mark where he's concerned."

Jason remained silent as Barrymore finished speaking. Then the tight, angry look about his mouth faded, and he gave a rueful laugh. "I turn aside a deliberate insult from a stranger and nearly come to blows with my friends."

Curiously Barrymore asked, "You know it was done deliberately?"

"Yes, *mon ami,* I know it was done deliberately! I have

not managed to live this long without recognizing when I am being baited," Jason answered tartly.

Frowning, Barrymore probed, "Then why did you let him get by with it?"

Jason stood up and strode unhurriedly to the door. He turned and said tantalizingly, "Why? Because, *mes enfants,* I too would like to know why."

Confused, Barrymore blurted, "Why what?"

Watching Jason, Tom felt a chill pass through his body at the look that gleamed briefly in his green eyes. Then Jason, his voice like black silk, asked, "Why does Pendleton want to kill me?"

"He would never make such a trivial thing a killing matter! He was just being obnoxious. He merely wants to let some blood," Barrymore assured him.

"You think so? Then why did he press a second insult on me, when I was willing to play the fool and pass off the first? You, yourselves, a moment ago, were eager for me to understand just how deliberately I had been insulted."

"But—but we didn't mean a duel to the death!" stammered Tom.

Seeing the apprehensive look on both their faces, Jason's black mood lifted, and, his most charming smile flashing, he laughed. "Come, my friends, I will not discuss this further. Let us join the ladies and enjoy the remainder of the evening."

Gloomily, Tom sighed, "Won't be able to enjoy the evening. M'sister and grandmother will expect me to dance attendance on them when they're not hanging on your every word. Elizabeth Markham will be setting her cap for you, too!" Then he brightened, struck by a new thought. "Better if we stay here! Ring for the butler to bring a tray of wine."

But Jason was not to be dissuaded, and so, with much grumbling on Harris's part, they descended the great marble staircase and entered the salon where several ladies and gentlemen were gathered.

Mrs. Brownleigh, gowned in an alarming shade of pink,

and as plump and amiable as her husband, came bustling up. Tapping Jason on the arm with her fan, she exclaimed, "Naughty boy, where have you been? Elizabeth says you promised to turn the music for her. We're waiting for you in the music room."

After one horrified glance at the waiting dowagers close on his heels, Tom threw Jason an "I told you so" look, and beat a strategic retreat with Barrymore. Resigning himself to another hour of boredom, Jason smiled charmingly at his hostess, complimented her outrageously on her dress, and escorted her to the music room.

Elizabeth was already seated behind the piano, and from the look she shot him, it was apparent she was in a temper. But temper became her, adding a decided sparkle to her brown eyes, and dressed in an amber-colored gown, she was a sight to quicken a man's pulse. Unfortunately, Jason couldn't have cared less.

Several delicate, gilt chairs were drawn up in a semi-circle around the piano, and as everyone chose their seats and settled themselves comfortably, Jason sauntered up to where Elizabeth sat. Under the noise of everyone being seated, she hissed, "And where were you this afternoon?"

For a moment he was nonplused, having forgotten he had halfway promised to go riding with her. Eyeing her speculatively, it was obvious she was too angry to forgive an honest admission of forgetfulness. This seemed to be his evening for extracting himself from tiresome situations, and growing impatient with having to tread so carefully, he shrugged his shoulders and murmured, "Later, my love. I'll explain everything."

Her lips curling in a sneer, she snapped, "Don't bother! Clive has already told me of your taste for vulgar company."

His jaw tightened, and aware that others were becoming curious and restless at the delay, he said smoothly, "Then there's nothing to explain, is there? And I would suggest we drop the subject and you begin to play, or the gossips will have something new to chatter about."

Elizabeth bit her lip, knowing he was right, but she could have screamed with vexation. This was not how she had planned their next meeting. Swallowing her chagrin, she smiled brightly at the waiting guests, arranged her sheets of music, and began to play. She had an adequate knowledge of the piano, but her performance was not inspired, being merely a mechanical interpretation of the notes on the pages that Jason turned for her. And it was not surprising that shortly the guests began to become restless, and wisely she brought her stilted playing to an end. There was the usual polite applause, and then the group broke up. Several of the older gentlemen, their duty done, escaped to the card room. The younger segment of the group gathered around the piano, while at the other end of the room the older ladies were partaking of the refreshments being served by the butler and a young footman. Jason left the younger group and made his way to where Amanda sat with her grandmother. Knowing it was only shyness that kept her by her grandmother's side and seeing the longing looks she cast at the gay crowd around Elizabeth, he teased her gently for being so timid.

Augusta, hearing his drawling voice, broke off the conversation she had been having with Ceci Tremayne to demand, "Where's that scamp of a grandson of mine? He should be here to take his sister about!"

"I believe he's joined Barrymore and the others for some cards, madame."

"Humph! I don't suppose we'll see him again this evening! Especially if he knows I want to see him," she finished shrewdly.

Smiling, Jason silently acknowledged the truth of her statement. Tom's aversion to his sharp-tongued grandmother was well known and caused a great deal of amusement among his friends. And the dowager, knowing precisely what prompted Jason's smile snapped, "Chicken-hearted rattle! That I would live to see the day a grandson of mine was frightened of one old woman!"

He made a light rejoinder and changed the subject. He enjoyed the dowager, but—*sur ma foi!*—what a tartar she was! Tonight, though, she appeared to be in a good mood and asked him conversationally, "How much longer do you plan to stay in England?"

"I'm not certain, madame. I've purchased several animals, but so far I haven't been able to find the stud I want."

"And I suppose once you've bought what you came for, you'll show us the backs of your heels?"

"What other reason would I have for remaining?"

"You might," she answered tartly, "stay and look for a wife!"

Jason's crack of laughter caused several people to look in their direction. Elizabeth, hearing his laughter and seeing him seated next to the red-haired Amanda, frowned her displeasure. But Jason, tired of her pouts and moods, was indifferent, and his green eyes dancing with amusement, he said to Augusta, "Madame, you and my father think as one! Those were his very words."

"Well, then?"

"Perhaps! Do you have a suitable bride in mind for me?" he teased.

Ceci, having followed the conversation avidly, gushed, "I would think that a cultured gentleman, such as yourself, would insist on only a well-bred Englishwoman for a wife. Of course, I do not mean to insult the young women of America, but I'm certain you would prefer a nice young woman of good family—a good *English* family."

Irritated by the interruption, Augusta threw her a disgusted look. "Of course he would!" she said scornfully and then continued, "But I think you would want more than just good breeding in a wife."

"Oh, I agree. Most certainly, you'd want more. You'd want a bride of beauty and accomplishment," Ceci cooed smugly, and her maternal glance, resting proudly on Elizabeth, seemed to add, "Here is the perfect answer."

Jason, all laughter banished from his eyes, said coolly,

"As you seem to know exactly what I need, I'll leave you ladies to decide for me. Who knows," he added, "I may even approve of your choice!" With that he turned on his heel and left them.

Augusta watched him stride from the room, and turning an unkind eye upon Ceci, she said grimly, "Well, my lady, you certainly put a burr under his coat! You'll not see that young gentleman dangling after that bad-tempered daughter of yours anymore!"

"How dare you say such a thing! Elizabeth is not bad-tempered!" Ceci replied, deeply affronted; an angry flush mottled her face.

But ignoring her outburst, Augusta continued, "Not that her temper matters. Savage would want a woman with spirit."

Ceci began to smile smugly, saying, "Dear Elizabeth is the most spirited girl."

And Augusta cut in hastily, "He won't settle for second-hand goods. Pity about her husband."

"It's certainly not her fault that he killed himself!"

"Bah! Everyone knows she drove him to it with her extravagant ways and tantrums."

"That is not true!" Ceci cried shrilly, and her lips tightened ominously. She would put up with only so much from this old harridan, even if she was Edward's godmother and the dowager duchess of Avon! "You don't know what you're talking about!" she continued, her voice shaking with temper. "The young man was always unstable. It was unfortunate that Elizabeth married him!"

"Unfortunate for him, you mean!" snapped Augusta.

Suppressing a gasp of rage, Ceci rose and in icy tones bid her tormentor good night and stalked out of the room. Augusta gave a pleased cackle of laughter. Ninnyhammer! Ceci should have known better than to cross swords with *her!* And the woman was as foolish as her daughter if she thought Savage would even consider Elizabeth as a possible bride.

Jason was thinking much the same thing as he entered the

card room in search of Barrymore and Harris. Elizabeth made an enjoyable bedmate, but God help the man stupid enough to marry her.

He didn't see his friends and was turning to leave when the incident with Pendleton happened. Later, he was to question why he reacted as he did, but at that instant, he was only aware that Pendleton grated on his nerves. A second later, the act was done, and leaving a stunned silence behind him, he strolled from the room feeling eminently satisfied. He ordered his curricle sent round, and while he was waiting, Barrymore, Harris, and Brownleigh found him.

Brownleigh's interest was mainly in keeping the whole thing quiet, but Tom thought gloomily, it couldn't be kept quiet, not with a roomful of interested gentlemen to witness the insult and the following challenge. Damn! What had made Jason do it? Especially, since earlier he had seemed intent on avoiding a quarrel. Moodily Tom stared at Jason's dark face as if the flickering candlelight that danced across it would reveal the answer. But Jason's face wore a cold, indifferent expression that gave nothing away.

Brownleigh, intensely mortified and embarrassed that such a thing should happen under his roof and to a guest who was staying at his house, was uncertain with whom he was angrier—Pendleton for starting the disgraceful business or Savage for finishing it! Thank God, the ladies hadn't been present! Wistfully, he wondered if everyone would keep mum.

But Barrymore had no intention of keeping mum and said angrily, "Damn it, Jason, you can't just say the fellow irritated you! If he irritated you so much, why didn't you challenge him earlier?"

Jason, his eyes hooded, shrugged carelessly and moved towards his approaching curricle. "I prefer to attack, *mon ami,* rather than wait like a lamb for slaughter!"

Barrymore, nearly hopping with rage, exploded, "God damnit! What the hell do you mean?"

Jason, ignoring Barrymore's outburst, climbed into the

curricle and grasping the reins of his restless horses, dismissed the groom at their heads. Then he turned in the direction of the three standing on the steps and said, "You'll forgive me if I don't linger? There's a wind coming up, and I don't like to leave my horses standing. Please convey my compliments to your excellent wife, Brownleigh. I've enjoyed myself enormously and will see you again."

Barrymore made an attempt to interrupt, but Jason threw him a look that killed the words teetering on his lips. Holding Barrymore's eyes with his own, he said, "You and Tom will arrange everything?"

Barrymore nodded reluctantly, and Tom ran a nervous finger around his neck, as if his clothes were suddenly too tight.

"Very well then. I'll expect to hear from you prior to Waterford's ball next week." His mocking smile glinted briefly at their worried expressions. "Don't worry, *mes enfants,* everything will be all right." On that note, he slapped the reins, and his spirited horses leaped into action, pulling swiftly away from the mansion.

11

It was a clear, moonlit night, and even though there was a slight wind from the north and a chill in the night air, Jason enjoyed the journey back to the inn. He was almost sorry when he slowed the horses at the stables. Jacques, hearing the noise, came out to investigate and, seeing his master, called impatiently to the dozing stable boy. Smiling to himself, Jason watched as the two swiftly unharnessed the steaming pair and led them to their stalls.

Jason found himself strangely reluctant for his bed and followed them into the dim interior. The smell of animals and freshly laid hay and the scent of the leather harness and saddles mingled to make a pungent, not unpleasant smell, that assailed his nostrils. He passed the two men who were busily rubbing down the horses and wandered down between the rows of stalls. Idly he noticed that the horses he purchased that morning had arrived from the gypsy camp and were already settled in their stalls. One mare, a blood bay with black points, her face betraying her Arab blood, whickered softly as he approached. She moved restlessly in the stall as if she found it strange to be inside and not out in the moonlit night. Gently Jason caressed the velvet muzzle that pushed against his hand and murmured softly, "There, love. What a beauty you are! I wonder how you and your stablemates came to be part of a gypsy band?"

Leaving the mare with a pat on her gleaming neck, he strolled through the stable to the entrance, stopping to watch Jacques and the boy as they blanketed his pair. Jacques looked up from his task with a question in his black eyes, and Jason replied, "No, I don't need anything. I was just watching." He continued to do so for a few minutes longer, then bidding them good night he strode to the inn.

Upstairs in his room, he discarded his jacket and cloak. Glancing at his pocket watch, he was surprised to see it was not many minutes past midnight. He kicked the smoldering log in the fireplace and throwing his crumpled cravat on the floor, called to Pierre to help remove his shining boots. And Pierre, having done so, was dismissed with a careless flick of Jason's long fingers.

The room grew quiet as Jason, now alone, lay relaxed in a comfortable chair before the glowing orange coals of the fire. The measured tick of the clock on the polished wooden mantel was heard above the occasional crack of the fire. The few candles still burning created a pool of warm light that flickered over the still figure. A small, elegant marble-topped table was at his elbow; upon it stood a crystal decanter partially filled with brandy. Jason loosely clasped a half-emptied glass in his hand as he stared into the dying fire. Throwing his black head back against the chair, he impatiently drained the glass and slammed it down on the table, the sound breaking the soothing stillness of the room. Swiftly rising from the chair, he prowled the room like some caged jungle beast. Abruptly he left the sitting room, stalked into his bedchamber, and distastefully eyed his bed.

The bed, a huge monstrosity, was on a dais at the end of the large room. Its ruby velvet canopy and curtains gleamed like blood in the dim light from the single candle Pierre had left burning on the night stand. Jason yanked aside the ruby hangings that encased the bed and glanced at the interior. Pierre had pulled back the blanket to expose the snowy linen sheets. The bed looked inviting, but he was not sleepy.

Restlessly, he paced the room. Damn, he wished he had demanded that the gypsy wench come tonight. She would occupy his time! Grinning suddenly, he strode silently in his stocking feet to the wardrobe. That's what he needed! A woman. Having hit upon a happy solution, he stripped off the remainder of his finery, revealing a body as lean and dark as his face. And reaching deep into the back of the wooden wardrobe, his seeking hand touched the garments they sought.

Pierre had protested loudly when Jason had insisted on bringing his buckskins—especially the shirt with the fringe on the long sleeves. Pierre had snapped that only a savage would think it becoming! The unintentional pun had made Jason smile at the time, and the memory of it evoked the same response now. Along with the loosely cut shirt and pants, he had packed his moccasins. Arrayed in the buckskin garments, he stood before the full-length mirror, a twinkle leaping into his eyes. Certainly this inn had never beheld a figure dressed as he. His garb was more suited to the plains of Texas or the villages of the Indians that lived there; and with his black hair and dark face, he could have passed for an Indian himself.

He was silent as an Indian when he crept from the sleeping inn. Unbolting the catch, he slid the door open, listening intently for sounds from the normally busy tavern room, but only silence met his listening ear. A moment later he was outside in the frosty air. It took only another minute to reach the stable. And smiling to himself, he wondered if he was still a clever horse thief.

It appeared he had remembered well, for a short time later he and a burly black stallion were galloping down the road towards Brownleigh's residence. Jason rode with no saddle, guiding the spirited black like an Indian, his long legs wrapped about the racing horse. He had taken the time to bridle the animal, but if no bridle had been handy, a length of rope would have done him as well. The ride had disarrayed his hair, and one unruly black lock fell across his forehead. Blood Drinker would have recognized the reckless glitter in his green eyes. Catlike, Jason skirted the house searching for a particular window. Finding it, he pushed aside the ivy leaves to grasp the ropelike branches that clung like limpets to the side of the house. Rapidly he climbed to the window he sought, a whisper of rustled leaves being the only sound he made as his body slid upward. The window was unlocked and opened as he expected. Not because Elizabeth was waiting for him, but because he knew of her passion for fresh air. A wolfish smile on his mouth, Jason stealthily entered the room and melted into the brocade draperies.

Elizabeth, preparing for bed, was wearing a filmy, sea green negligee that revealed more of her body than it hid. Her hair was a shining chestnut mass about her creamy shoulders as she sat before a dressing table watching the maid in the mirror brush her hair. Growing bored with watching the girl, her gaze roamed idly about the room. Suddenly her eyes widened, and she nearly spoke out loud as she glimpsed Jason's mocking face. Holding her eyes for a moment, he winked audaciously; then as the maid, sensing something, looked up from her task, he faded into the gold folds of the draperies.

Elizabeth snapped at the girl, "Leave it! That's enough for tonight. You may go, and I don't want to be disturbed again this evening."

Startled at her mistress's sharp command, the girl nearly dropped the brush. But then, that was just Elizabeth Markham, never grateful for anything and tightfisted, too. Nasty bitch! the girl thought spitefully as she left the room. She stopped in the hall for a moment and was surprised to hear the key turn in the lock behind her.

Elizabeth pivoted slowly to face Jason, the skirt of her

negligee swirling like sea foam about her slender ankles. Her hand still on the lock, she leaned back against the mahogany door, her hair a bright, warm glow next to its darkness. There was a pleased smile on her red mouth as she watched Jason cross to her.

A smile, almost as satisfied as hers, curved his mouth. He hadn't been all that sure of his reception, but it seemed he had read her character correctly. He paused a few feet from her, taking in the body so enticingly displayed for him.

The sea green negligee had a low, square neck that lay bare the swell of her breast, and her coral-tipped nipples could be seen hazily through the filmy material. A growing flame dancing in their green depths, Jason's eyes wandered unhurriedly over her. Elizabeth's smile deepened as she watched his appreciative perusal of her charms, and her voice was low as she whispered teasingly, "Do you like what you see?"

His answer was to reach out and pull her unresisting body next to his, and through his clothing, she could feel him hard with desire. Then looking up into the lean face above her, she discovered the smile was gone, and there was a look on his face that caused a shiver of pleasure to course through her. Feeling that shiver, Jason bent his head and kissed her warm, waiting lips. Not breaking the deepening kiss, he lifted her slender form up into his arms and carried her to the bed. Laying her gently down, he slowly began to undress her, pushing aside the filmy gown to release her full breasts to his caressing hands. Releasing her lips, he lowered his head to lightly kiss and fondle her hardened nipples, and as his mouth found hers again, she was lost in a swimming sea of desire. Her gown lay in a discarded heap on the rug, his knowing hands roaming with increased demands over her satin flesh.

He stopped momentarily to rapidly strip off his clothing and then he was in bed with her, his long, hard length pressed tightly against hers. His hands and kisses aroused her as no other man's had, and she arched her back, pushing her body even closer to his, and began to moan with pleasure when he entered her. Leisurely he brought her sobbing to the peak of emotion, moving slowly within her and increasing the hot desire that already consumed her. Her body rose to meet his every stroke until he swept her to a throbbing completion.

Afterwards they lay in silence, languid in the aftermath of passion. Then she rubbed her tousled head on his shoulder and running her fingers lightly over his chest, murmured, "Mmmmm, it was bad of you to come climbing through my window." She stretched lazily like a contented cat and purred, "But I'm glad you're so bold."

Jason, a crooked smile on his face, eyed her with amusement. She was a delightful bed companion, being almost as experienced as he. And thank God, she hadn't tried any coy tricks on him—so far, he amended silently. He lay back next to her, one arm thrown carelessly over his eyes, and relaxed. Elizabeth propped herself up on one elbow and began, again, to run her fingers idly over his prone body. She noticed for the first time the gold band about his arm.

"What's that?" she asked.

Jason glanced down at the Aztec band and remarked, "It's merely a piece of jewelry that I happen to like. Why?"

She shrugged her shoulders and said, "No reason. I was just curious. It's unusual for a man to wear such a thing, and I wondered if it had some special meaning—perhaps a particular woman gave it to you?"

Jason shot her an amused grin and laughed, "That would be telling."

Not at all pleased with his answer, she changed the subject and asked in a determinedly teasing tone, "Do you think I'm better than Clive's wench?"

"As I've never bedded Clive's wench, as you call her, I can't tell you," he replied with an edge to his voice.

Dissatisfied with that answer, too, she pouted and with apparent idle curiosity asked, "What were you doing out there?"

He sighed. Damn women, anyway! Why did they always want to talk afterwards? He rolled over onto his belly and said abruptly, "I went to buy horses."

"Darling, what an odd place to buy horses! Do you really expect me to believe that?"

He moved impatiently, disliking her probing questions. "I really don't give a damn whether you do or not. It's the truth, and if it doesn't please you, that's too damn bad!"

Wisely, she dropped the subject and nestled down next to him, her body curving to mold itself to his. He startled her by asking, "What did Clive tell you happened out there?"

"Only that you seemed more than taken with Cath—er—Tamara's charms," she finished quickly, hoping he hadn't caught her near blunder.

He frowned. "Why was he discussing it with you?"

She laughed nervously and stated, "Clive is one of those people who likes to cause trouble, and he knew it would upset me." Effectively closing the subject, she kissed him lingeringly on the mouth and her eyes holding his, murmured, "I'm very jealous!"

His mouth quirked in a smile, and he laid her back against the scented pillows and nuzzled her ears and neck, leaving a tingling trail of anticipation as his lips moved slowly over her. She moved her warm flesh suggestively against his lean body, her mind beginning to float as the first swirlings of reawakened desire began to flow through her.

"Exactly how well do you know Pendleton?" The question, whispered in her ear, nearly caused her to jerk with alarm, and the cold look on his face did nothing to allay the feeling.

Then she gave a purr of pleasure. He was jealous! She laughed deep in her throat and linked her arms about his neck. "Darling, everyone knows Clive! You may meet him everywhere."

"Was he your lover?"

"What a ridiculous thing to ask!" Her voice was waspish as she answered. Hiding her nervousness, she said in a cooler tone, "He was my uncle's godson, and I've known him since childhood. There's no reason for you to believe he's my lover, unless—are you jealous?"

"Not jealous, *chérie,* just curious."

"Why?" she asked bluntly.

"He seems inordinately curious of my actions. And I wondered."

"Oh, who knows why Clive does anything! I'm sick of talking about him!" she said crossly. "He's always creating problems."

Jason gave a mirthless laugh. "How true, my pet, how true."

Her eyes sharpening with interest, she queried, "What do you mean by that?"

"This evening he was very intent on creating a situation from which I found it very difficult to escape without complications."

"But you didn't escape, you challenged him." She blurted out and could have bitten her foolish tongue. She never should have said that! And his next words confirmed her fears.

"Yes, so I did. But how did you know? Clive again?" he asked coldly. "It was decided that the ladies were not to be told."

Silently she cursed Clive and his intrigues. Smiling seductively she complained, "Jason, did you come here just to ask me stupid questions? If that's all you're interested in, you may leave."

"I think not!" he said smiling and very deliberately kissed her parted lips. This time there was no prolonged arousal; the passion flared into flame as soon as he touched her. She groaned and thrust her body hungrily up to his. Suddenly he took her brutally, as if her pleasure no longer mattered to him. But his very brutality excited her almost as much as his earlier caresses, and quickly she felt the familiar explosion of feeling. Afterwards, she watched him as he lay there next to her, she wondered how much of her involvement with

Clive he guessed. Damn Clive! If she intended to wring a proposal from Jason, she had to be very careful. But right now she felt more sure of him than she had in days. He *must* love her! Didn't he seek her out? Wasn't the fact that he was here in her room proof? Of course it was! Who knew, he might even ask her to marry him tonight! Then she would tell him about Clive and his inquisitiveness. Snuggling down beside him and resting her hand on his naked chest, she asked the question women always do. "Do you love me?"

Jason could have groaned out loud. *Mon Dieu,* why did they persist? He was in no mood to tell meaningless lies. Abruptly he rose from the bed, jerked on his buckskin pants, and thrust his feet into his moccasins. He looked for his shirt and after a moment spotted it on the other side of the bed. Elizabeth, puzzled by his actions but not certain of her claim on him, took the few steps needed to stand in front of him. She linked her soft, scented arms about his neck and said with a provocative smile, "You haven't answered my question. Don't you love me?"

Staring down into the beautiful face raised confidently to his, he answered harshly, "No!"

Startled, she dropped her arms and stared at him, her confusion clear to see. "I—I don't understand. What do you mean?" she stammered.

His eyes cold and inscrutable, he said, "Very simply, I wanted you. You were willing, and in taking you I gave as much pleasure as I received. It was enjoyable—but that doesn't mean I love you. I desired you! You are a very lovely woman, but you hold no more allure for me than a dozen others I could name."

"How can you say that after what has passed between us?" she questioned, unable to believe his brutal words.

"Desire, my dear, is frequently mistaken for love. Fortunately, I do not believe in what you call 'love' and can recognize it for what it is—simple animal hunger!"

Her lovely dreams crumbling about her feet, Elizabeth

felt a bitter anger began to burn in her breast. He wasn't going to get away with this! She'd create a scandal! She darted a glance at the locked door. All she had to do was open that door and scream. Her parents, the Brownleighs, and the other guests would tumble into the hallway in a matter of minutes! Jason Savage would be caught half naked in her room, and he'd have no choice but to marry her! What did she care about the ensuing scandal and gossip? She would be the rich Mrs. Jason Savage of Louisiana! Pasting a glittering smile on her face, she said coolly, "How clever of you to be able to distinguish one from the other."

Warily, he watched her as she moved about the room searching for her peignoir. She found the robe laying next to his shirt, and after wrapping the garment about her, a calculating gleam in her brown eyes, she held out his shirt tantalizingly, saying, "Do you need this?"

He reached for it slowly, and just as his hand brushed it, she jerked it from his fingers and danced playfully to the center of the room, clutching his shirt to her breast. A tight smile creased his face as he crossed the room. Stopping at the corner of the bed, he leaned back easily against one of the four posts, watching her with slitted green eyes. There was a suppressed look of power about him that gave the lie to his relaxed position. He was like a waiting panther, and his eyes held a look that almost frightened her.

Her smile was provocative as she watched him. It was a dangerous game she played, and the very danger of it caused her heart to beat with excitement. Surreptitiously, she glanced at the locked door, but he was closer to her than she was to the door. She'd have to get nearer to that door—and she must have time to throw the lock.

A pout on the lips, she teased, "Aren't you going to put on your shirt? It's awfully chilly outside." She waved the shirt daringly close to his still form, but he made no attempt to catch the waving garment.

He stood motionless with an air of leashed violence that should have given her pause, but she ignored the warning sign. Jason was furious with himself and vehemently cursed his own stupidity. Very aware of his precarious position, he studied the woman before him and had no illusions concerning Elizabeth. Almost reading her cunning mind, he knew he must silence her effectively if he was to leave here tonight without a scene.

Like a moth to the flame, she danced nearer and then retreated from his waiting body. And foolishly, like the moth, each time she came nearer the waiting flame. "Jason, love, you're not playing! Come now, don't you want your shirt?" she taunted, holding the garment just out of reach.

"Certainly I want my shirt, but I have no intention of chasing you around the room to get it," he answered unemotionally.

If she had been less confident of herself, she would have noticed the slight tightening of his muscles. But she grew careless and skipped nearer. Then like a striking snake, his arm shot out and violently ripped the buckskin shirt from her surprised grasp. Thrown off balance, she stumbled towards him as his other hand, a fist of clenched steel, struck her chin so forcefully her head jerked back, nearly snapping her neck. Without a whimper she crumpled in an unconscious heap on the floor. Kneeling beside her he gently checked for any sign of serious injury. Finding none, he lifted and laid her on the rumpled bed, arranging her body in a position of natural sleep.

Moving quickly now, he threw on his shirt and crossed to the locked door. Hearing no sound from beyond the door, he started to turn away when he noticed the lock and silently released it. At the open window, one leg thrown over the sill, he gave the room a sweeping glance, his gaze lingering on Elizabeth's body. If she had been able to accept that part of himself that he was willing to give, he might have taken her as his mistress and might have sent the gypsy girl away with a handful of gold. But Elizabeth, like others before her, wanted something that wasn't in him to give. Then he grinned. What a conceited coxcomb he was; they would have gladly settled for his name and money, and not cared one bit whether he loved them or not. His grin broadened as he took one last look at Elizabeth; tomorrow she would wake with a throbbing headache, an aching jaw, and a bruise that would be hard to explain. Perhaps, he thought, she'd be more selective of her lovers in the future.

Returning to the inn stables shortly thereafter, he wasn't surprised to find Jacques waiting for him. The little man, his short black hair ruffled by the wind, growled, "Up to your old tricks again, I see. You would have felt like an ass if I had roused the place screeching about a stolen horse!"

Jason grinned at the older man and slid from the sweating horse, saying as he did so, "But I rely on your judgment, and I knew you were not a fool."

Grumbling, Jacques snapped, "Off with you!" Then waving a bony finger under Jason's nose, "But be warned! These English are different from us; you may find yourself in a deeper river than you know."

Leaving the stallion in the capable hands of Jacques, Jason returned silently to his rooms. On edge and not certain why, he paced through the empty rooms, unconsciously seeking signs that would assure him no one had entered while he had been gone. Finding everything as it should be, he threw another log on the barely smoldering fire and kicked it into a yellow blaze of warmth. Elizabeth was right; it was chilly outside!

Splashing some brandy into a goblet, he drank it slowly, savoring the taste and feel of it as it burned a trail of fire to his belly. Then striding into the bedchamber, he stripped off the buckskins and gingerly approached the bed. Seated on the feather mattress he had to admit it was comfortable, if awe inspiring! And laying on his back, staring at the ruby canopy and thinking of the past evening, he cursed himself for being a fool and losing his temper with Pendleton. But it wasn't Pendleton that he'd lost his temper with; it was the whole damn business that annoyed him. And he couldn't help blaming it on Jefferson and those damn dispatches. He sure as hell wasn't cut out for the intrigues that surrounded playing politics.

Even now, he could hear Jefferson saying quietly, "I trust you will behave yourself while in England. I realize I have no real power over you, but word of your activities in your territory has reached my ears. Considering you are acting as my personal courier, I hope you will conduct yourself accordingly and not embroil yourself in such escapades while in England." Jefferson's voice becoming drier, he had continued, "Try not to cause any scandal with the ladies, and if possible control that hot temper of yours."

His father Guy had echoed Jefferson's measured words, but his advice had been more pithily put. "Stay away from those damn light skirts and don't go snaffling anyone's wife."

Both men had been left with the uneasy feeling they had spoken to a stone wall and now, smiling in the dark, Jason conceded belatedly the wisdom of their remarks. Both men would be furious when and if they heard of tonight's doings. Which brought him to the heart of the matter. Why had Pendleton been so bent on provoking him? It was obvious the man had been primed and had purposely set out to engineer a situation where Jason would have no choice but to challenge him. That he adroitly avoided it at the dining table didn't alleviate the fact that Pendleton had intentionally been offensive and had, in the end, been successful.

Unable to relax, he got up; naked he stalked into the sitting room and poured himself another brandy. Staring broodingly into the dancing yellow flames, he wished he hadn't allowed his own bad temper to goad him into irresponsible action. But Pendleton's earlier taunts and Barrymore's and Harris's questioning of his courage had combined to raise his temper to a dangerous degree. It had only needed Pendleton to sneeringly turn his back on him, as he prepared to leave the card room, to cause his already smoldering temper to burst into white hot flame. Without thinking, he had spun the startled Pendleton around, and taking the wine glass from his hand, had contemptuously thrown the contents in the man's face. Pendleton, nearly choking with rage, had shouted for Jason to name his seconds, and curtly, Jason bit out Barrymore's and Harris's names.

For the love of God! He'd been a fool to let Pendleton get under his skin. Particularly without knowing what was behind it. Roxbury would be deservedly displeased with his antics and reviewing the situation coolly, he couldn't blame him. *Juste ciel,* he'd acted like a virgin schoolboy!

Settled once more in bed, Jason tried to force his disturbing thoughts onto more pleasurable objects, but even dwelling on the charms of the little gypsy did nothing to halt more unwelcome ideas from creeping in, and restlessly he turned in the big bed, wondering if there was a connection between those dispatches he had delivered to King and the attempts to search his London rooms. Or was Pendleton's interest merely curiosity? And if it was Jefferson's instructions that intrigued Pendleton, why now? Why weeks after he had delivered them? Unless—unless—but Jesus! It couldn't be that! Only he and Jefferson knew about the other. Not even his father knew of those last private instructions; but, he thought suddenly, there could be a leak at Livingston's end, in Paris. Momentarily he had the uneasy feeling he had stepped off into one of the treacherous patches of quicksand that abounded in the mysterious swamps and bayous of Louisiana.

12

The next day passed uneventfully, and very slowly, for Jason was eagerly awaiting the evening and Tamara's arrival. Wisdom made him avoid Brownleigh's—he wondered how long it would take for Elizabeth to gain control of herself—and having no pressing errand or plans, he spent most of the day cooling his heels at the inn. It was mid-afternoon when Squire Hampton, a middle-aged widower, entered the common room of the inn. Jason had been introduced to Hampton some days before, and now bored by the inactivity, he was more than happy to have company for a glass of ale. When Hampton discovered that Jason was staying alone, he insisted that Jason join him for dinner that evening. Unable to excuse himself, Jason had cordially accepted the squire's impulsive invitation.

Jason had hoped Tamara would arrive before he left, but as she hadn't by the time he was dressed and his curricle brought round, he had left word with the innkeeper and had told Pierre to expect her.

It had been a pleasant evening at the squire's, made more

so by the discovery that several gentlemen he already knew were also there. He had been momentarily disconcerted to find Edward Tremayne, the earl of Mount, as one of the guests, but since that elegant gentleman had smiled and asked how he was settling in at The Fox, he drew a relieved sigh. He hadn't been sure Elizabeth would keep her mouth shut about last night. But it seemed she had—or at least she had not informed her father. As the hour grew late, he became impatient to be gone, and as soon as he could, he politely took his leave of the squire, his thoughts as he drove in the silver moonlight being on his bed. More precisely they dwelt upon the delightful wench he would find there, and remembering the feel of Tamara's soft lips crushed against his, he felt an instant response from his body. He couldn't remember when he had hungered after a wench like he did the little gypsy. And remembering Elizabeth and last night, his desire for the black-haired baggage had nothing to do with his having been celibate lately! He grinned to himself and urged his English thoroughbreds to greater speed.

It was only a short time later when his curricle swept into the stable yard of the inn. Throwing the reins to Jacques, he leaped from the vehicle and rapidly crossed to the inn. The innkeeper met him as he entered the narrow hall, and Jason asked, "Did the wench arrive?"

The innkeeper gave him a peculiar glance and nodded slowly. Whistling softly to himself, Jason was about to climb the flight that led to his rooms when Pierre stopped him and inquired politely if he would need his services this evening.

Jason, a devilish twinkle in his green eyes, laughed, "I think not! There are some things a man prefers to do for himself. And laying a wench is one of them!"

"She's certainly not in your usual style," Pierre said dryly.

Jason raised one black brow and teased, "Could it be Tamara has ruffled your dignity? She's definitely a spirited piece."

"Of course not!" Pierre replied stiffly. "She was so bundled up I couldn't see her, and your taste is your own business."

"I'm glad you see it that way. After all, it would be a terrible thing if I offended my valet's taste."

Slightly miffed, Pierre said a cool good night and retired, while Jason quickly mounted the stairs to his rooms. He went first into the spare bedchamber but finding no signs of occupancy, swiftly crossed through the darkened rooms to his own bedchamber, where one small candle near the bed was glowing fitfully. The pleasing scent of perfume drifted to his nostrils as he stood on the threshold, and there was a satisfied smile on his mouth as he noted the colorful pile of feminine clothing tossed on a chair near the huge bed. The ruby hangings were drawn, concealing the interior from his gaze, but he saw the curtains move slightly and heard the bed creak as the occupant shifted her position.

His smile grew, and he called softly, "Tamara, are you asleep?" He had to strain his ears before he heard a whispered reply.

Striding up to the curtained bed, he reached out for the concealing folds and she whispered, "Please, sir, douse the candle and join me. I have waited hours for you."

He attempted to pull the curtains aside, but she held them tightly shut from the other side and said in a low pleading voice, "Please, do not shame me; no one has ever seen me naked before! Please leave it shut and blow out the light. Grant me this small favor?"

Laughing under his breath, Jason stepped away from the bed and its tempting contents. In his mind's eye, he could see her crouched there, that glorious black hair tumbling almost to her alabaster hips, and impatiently he stripped off his clothes and tossed them in an untidy heap on the floor. Pierre would wring his hands and weep over such sacrilegious treatment, but at the moment, Jason's only concern with his clothes was that he be out of them! It took just a second longer to douse the candle, and the room was plunged into blackness. He thrust aside the curtain, but his reaching hands met only empty darkness.

"Tamara?" he questioned low.

"Here, sir." Her answer drifted to him from the far side of the bed.

A second later, he had her locked in his hungry embrace. Her mouth parted easily beneath his as she pressed against his muscled body, and urgently his hands roamed over her slim form. Suddenly, he stiffened with outraged surprise and, cursing, pushed her clinging body away.

"Who are you?" he growled uncertainly.

"Only Tamara, your little love who longs for your embrace," came the muffled reply as her arms reached out for him again. He escaped their clutching hold and leaping from the bed quickly struck a flint and lit the candle. Holding the light high, he tore back the ruby folds and stared with mingled disbelief and anger at the naked woman before him.

Ilone, a malicious smile revealing her blackened and rotting teeth, stared insolently back. Breasts, shriveled and wrinkled, hung nearly to her waist while coarse, gray hair stood out from her head, giving her the appearance of a witch. Naked, she sat unconcernedly before the angry young man, her good eye watching him spitefully.

Jason, frowning blackly in the gloom, decided after his first astonished glance that he had never seen such a hideous hag. But more important, he knew a raging anger that nearly choked him. With difficulty he suppressed the blind urge to wring this woman's scrawny neck, and his voice was thick as he snarled, "What the hell are you doing here? Where's Tamara?" Even as he asked he knew the answer. She had planned cleverly, the little bitch!

Ilone gave a cackle of ugly laughter and said, as she had been told, "Tamara was unable to come tonight, and because she knew you would be lonely, she sent me as a token of the high esteem in which she holds you!"

At Ilone's words his eyes narrowed, and his whole body stiffened tautly at the deliberate insult. "Get out!" he said icily. He wasn't going to exchange insults with this old hag. His argument was with Tamara!

Hastily, Ilone dragged on her clothes, furtively glancing at Jason's ominously still form. She could feel the waves of frustration and hot anger radiating from him and prayed he would control the obvious blazing temper that was burning through him at least until she had made her escape. Jason remained by the bed, frozen and silent as a statue until after Ilone had left; then cursing he violently slammed the candle down, nearly causing it to fall from the holder, and with quick angry strides crossed to the wardrobe. Viciously he yanked on the buckskins, a murderous look on his dark face.

Play him for a fool, would she? Well, that pale-skinned witch would discover it wasn't such a wise thing to do! Before this night was over she'd plead for his "high esteem," and she'd be lucky if he didn't strangle her! He'd enjoy the feel of that slim white neck between his crushing hands.

Jason let the big black stallion gallop unhampered at a hard, fast pace for a few miles and then as the worst of that first white-hot blaze of temper abated, he slowed the racing animal and brought him under control. His thoughts were unpleasant as they dwelt on Tamara. She had insulted him as he had never been insulted in his entire life. What's more, she had struck a vicious blow at his male pride, and for that, he was unable to laugh off the little comedy enacted in his room. It seemed all she did was tease and trick him. Well, this time she wasn't getting away with it!

Silently, he came upon the sleeping gypsy encampment. He left the horse tied some ways back and stealthily stalked the quiet camp. He knew exactly where the caravan he sought was located, for yesterday, as Tamara had walked away from him, his eyes had followed her slim form, and he had made a mental note of which caravan she had entered. It was set a little apart from the others, and now that fact caused a grim smile to cross his face.

He crept to the darkened caravan and silently entered.

Hesitating, he stood just inside the doorway as the moonlight, filtering in from the small window, cast a queer gray, murky light over the interior. Dimly he could make out the small table and chairs. His eyes narrowed when his questing gaze found the bed with its sleeping occupant. He crossed to the unsuspecting sleeper and stood staring down at her sleeping form. Her back was to him, and he couldn't see her features, but he was certain she was smiling in her sleep at her cleverness in dealing with him tonight. And as he stood staring, he felt a wave of icy anger course through his veins.

Moving swiftly, he pinned her down, the weight of his own body crushing her motionless, while one hand effectively stilled her frightened cry and his other held a knife at her throat. Exactly what he planned to do beyond this point was uncertain, even to him, but any plans he may have had disappeared abruptly when a shaft of silver moonlight revealed that the struggling woman beneath him wasn't Tamara! Shock caused him to momentarily loosen his iron grasp, and Reina nearly succeeded in escaping before his own quick reflexes reacted, and he clamped her prisoner.

Silently, they glared at one another in the dim light. Reina, recognizing Jason's hard face above her, relaxed beneath his muscled body. Thoughtfully she took in the black hair drooping across his forehead, the blazing green eyes and the wide, mobile mouth. Tamara was a fool, she decided. A clever woman would work hard to bind such a man as this one closely to her. Feeling his long, lithe body crushing her frail form, she wished she were forty years younger. Ah, how she would have loved him! Even now, she felt a faint, almost forgotten swirl of desire. Bah! she thought suddenly—Tamara was a silly virgin. She should thank the heavens that this man desired her.

Jason, staring angrily into the wrinkled old face before him, cursed under his breath, long and with feeling. This seemed to be his evening to find only wretched old women wherever he sought the warm, slim body that was beginning to haunt him.

Suppressed fury in every word, he growled, "If you so much as breathe heavily, I'll cut your throat. Do I make myself clear?"

Reina nodded, and cautiously Jason removed his hand from her mouth and sat up. Reina lay motionless, watching him warily.

Coldly, he asked, "Where is Tamara?"

Reina snorted and lied, "Clive has her. You didn't suppose he'd leave her unprotected knowing you were sniffing about her heels!" She watched with sly interest the muscle that jerked tightly near his mouth. Ho ho, my fine buck was in a rage, and maliciously, for her own enjoyment, she added fuel to the already smoldering fire by saying, "Tamara thought you too forward. She is a spirited young wench and prefers to do her own choosing."

Impatiently, he shrugged and with slitted eyes, questioned, "When will she return?"

"Why? What good will it do? She has made it clear she finds you not to her taste."

"I wish to see for myself that she finds me so! I think you lie, old woman. Tamara is only trying to drive up her price, for if she found me so distasteful, she would not have let me nearly lay her in the meadow yesterday."

Surprised but hiding it, Reina wondered why Tamara hadn't seen fit to tell her of that meeting in the meadow. Staring intently at the young man before her, she came to a decision and said slowly, "Tomorrow, in the evening, there is to be a gypsy wedding. Tamara will be here then."

She saw the flash of his teeth as he grinned in the darkness and heard the low rumble of laughter he gave. He relaxed slightly and, a speculative gleam in his eyes, questioned, "Old witch, tell me. Am I to leave here without you screaming the place down?"

Chuckling, Reina said drily, "Your argument is with Tamara. Leave me to sleep in peace." Then she surprised him by turning her back and saying, "Latch the door as you depart."

Smiling to himself, Jason made his way to the horse. He'd been effectively brought to a standstill by two old women and an impudent baggage. He was still furious but realized that Tamara had won this little skirmish. There was nothing more he could do tonight.

In no hurry to return to his empty rooms, he let his horse set an easy pace down the road. Occasionally the moon hid behind fast-moving clouds, and the narrow way would be blanketed in darkness. The trees grew close to the dirt lane and created long, black shadows in the intermittent moonlight.

Tamara had thrown him off stride and badly damaged his pride. Mulling it over, he was undecided which made him the angrier—that she hadn't come willingly to his bed, or that she'd seen fit to place a repulsive old crone there. Remembering pressing his mouth against those shrunk lips, his stomach gave a sickening lurch. That little viper Tamara. She'd stung him badly and how she must be laughing at him. For the first time in his life, a woman had gotten under his skin!

Suddenly Jason heard the faint, stealthy rustle of dead leaves behind him and to his left. He had been half conscious of furtive sounds for some time, but deep in thought, he hadn't heeded them. Now, his invisible tracker must have grown careless, and Jason was alerted to the hidden presence.

Swiftly, he scanned the road before him and swore silently. Engrossed with his angry thoughts, he hadn't noticed where his horse was traveling, and recognizing no familiar guidepost, he knew he was lost.

His hand slid down to the long-bladed knife that hung at his side, and as his fingers closed tightly over its familiar hilt, he breathed an unconscious sigh of relief. If his unseen companion moved in closer, he would wager his own skill with the blade against any weapon yielded by the other. Briefly it occurred to him that the old gypsy woman had roused the camp, but the gypsies would have given noisy chase, and whoever was silently pacing him didn't want his presence known.

Pretending ignorance of the hidden rider, he continued along the narrow lane. The hair on his neck prickled, and his nerves were taut, alive for any overt move on the other's part. And from the small sounds that drifted to his straining ears, he knew there was only one rider. At least, he thought grimly, it's one against one. In the mood he was in, he'd almost welcome a fight. With seeming indifference, he kicked his mount into a slow canter. He didn't want to alarm his follower, but neither did he care to dawdle along waiting for the other to make a move. It was possible his shy friend was only curious, but remembering his uncle's advice, he felt it was extremely unlikely.

Increasing his horse's pace, he heard the other rider's animal continue to keep step with his as they played a strange and menacing game beneath the stars. When Jason slowed his mount, the other did the same; if he increased his speed, his unseen companion stayed close behind him. The other rider was no longer making any attempt to hide his presence, and Jason knew it was only a matter of minutes until the other man broke from the woods and showed himself. As his own horse broke into a smooth gallop, he toyed with the idea of making a run for it but having no idea of his whereabouts and not entirely convinced the other was dangerous, dismissed it. Careening down dark, unexplored country lanes and fleeing from shadows didn't appeal to him.

Bah! he thought disgustedly. This was a stupid, childish situation! Intent upon ending it, he impatiently urged his big stallion to a faster pace. Then, as if he too was tired of the game, the hidden rider suddenly burst from the trees. Swiftly Jason glanced over his shoulder, but the moon was hidden behind clouds, and he could just barely discern the shape of a bulky figure seated upon a fast-moving horse.

The pursuer had left cover, but was making no attempt to overtake him, and Jason was momentarily puzzled. Then with a blinding flash of insight, he knew he was being deliberately driven in this direction for a definite and lethal purpose. The moon suddenly appeared from behind the clouds, and in that second Jason's searching eyes saw the brief glint of metal as the silver moonlight struck the upraised pistol of a second horseman, who suddenly appeared on the path riding towards him.

Instinctively, Jason tore at his horse's reins, causing the stallion to rear on steel-sprung haunches and scream with rage at the pain to his tender mouth. Fighting for control of his horse, Jason forced the animal sideways in the narrow road, and in that moment several things happened at once. There was the deadly crack of a shot, and he felt a burning, searing pain tear across his shoulders. The first horseman, desperately trying to avoid Jason's thrashing stallion, swerved to the edge of the road, unable to prevent his horse from sliding into the stallion's flank. The attacker in front, startled by Jason's sudden move, was powerless to stop his own galloping mount from slamming broadside into the already entangled horses. The powerful stallion nearly went down under the combined onslaught, and the next few seconds were bedlam.

Shaken and furious beyond belief, Jason completely forgot himself, a blood-chilling snarl of rage escaped his throat, and he became the attacker. Swiftly he disentangled his plunging horse, only to charge back into the melee. This time, however, he was a merciless, vicious nemesis, and his two would-be killers were caught by stunned surprise. Still fighting to control their frightened horses, they were unprepared for his sudden, violent attack.

The man who had fired the shot never saw his killer—as a flashing blade leaped in front of his startled eyes, and an unspoken cry of fear became a soft, surprised gurgle as the knife sliced deeply into his throat. He fell dying from his horse, his head nearly decapitated by the deadly slice of the blade.

Jason, the smell of blood in his flaring nostrils, a frightening glitter in his eyes, and the blood-stained knife clenched in his hand, spurred his horse in pursuit of the remaining horseman. Rapidly he overtook the retreating figure and leaped with a chilling, triumphant cry onto the back of the other's animal. The fleeing man felt the iron-muscled arm close around his neck, nearly choking him, and felt the sharp bite of the knife Jason pressed into his side. Terrified he twisted away, and both men fell from the racing horse.

They fell rolling and struggling onto the hard-packed earth. Jason, in no mood to prolong the fight, quickly overpowered the smaller man, and with his knees crushing into his assailant's arms, he stared down into his attacker's face. Nonplused, he realized he had never seen the man before!

Placing the knife almost gently against the man's exposed throat, he snarled, "*Mon ami,* you are a fool! And perhaps I will kill you for your foolishness!" With hard green eyes, he studied the man trapped beneath him.

The man's clothes were made of cheap materials and had been worn a long time, his brown coat showing greatly frayed cuffs. An unclean smell drifted to Jason's nostrils, and he viewed with distaste the bulging blue eyes and weak chin of his captive. Deliberately he pricked him with the knife, and the man broke into a frightened babble.

"Gor, let me go! We was only after a bit of the ready."

"And you thought I looked like an easy mark?" Jason queried softly.

Eagerly the man nodded. "That's the ticket! Man alone, lonely road, seemed a plum ripe for picking."

"You lie, my stupid friend! My clothes are not those of a wealthy man, and your late companion tried to shoot me. Who set you to watch me?"

"No one! I swear upon me mother's breast!"

A cold, set look on his face, Jason drew his knife lightly across the man's throat and watched the thin line of blood that appeared. The man gave a convulsive leap under him, and Jason smiled down into his frightened eyes. "Again, *mon ami,* who set you to watch me?"

"No one! It was chance, I tell you!" the man cried.

Idly Jason flicked the blade against the man's coat and

coarse shirt and exposed his prisoner's upper chest. Almost conversationally, he said, "I feel I should warn you that I am not an Englishman. You have heard of the wild savages that live in the New World? Well, my stubborn one, from them I have learned many ways to use my knife. I could skin you like a rabbit and listen unmoved to your screams for me to end your agony." Watching the sudden terror that flashed across the man's face, he snarled, "Tell me who sent you, or you will feel my skill with this blade!" And viciously he dug it into the hairy chest before him.

A scream broke from the man, and words came tumbling from dry lips. "I don't know. He was a stranger, never saw him before. Don't kill me! It's the truth, I'm telling you."

"Bah! Do you expect me to believe a complete stranger approached you to kill me? How did he know you wouldn't immediately run to the squire and report what he said?"

Sullenly, the answer came. "The innkeeper at The Fox knows we can be trusted. He's the one who sent the man to us. Ask him!"

Thoughtfully, Jason stared at the shifty face. It was possible the man had finally told the truth. The innkeeper was in a position to know the men of the area who wouldn't be adverse to obliging a stranger's request—whatever the request! Especially if some gold pieces were pressed into their outstretched palms. Later, he'd have to have a private talk with the innkeeper, but right now there was still this creature in front of him. "What did he look like?" he snapped.

"I dunno. He didn't see me." The man gave a jerk of his head in the direction of the dead man. "Buckley, he made the deal. Five hundred pounds now and another five hundred when you was dead."

A surprised whistle escaped from Jason's lips. Someone certainly didn't want him alive. That fat innkeeper had better have a good memory, he decided grimly.

Curious, he asked, "Did the man tell Buckley why I was to be killed?"

A shake of the head was his answer. Then the man volunteered, "Said we was to take care of you. Said he didn't care how, just so you was dead within the week."

The furious rage that had consumed him earlier had died away, leaving only an icy controlled anger. He was also in a quandary. What the hell was he to do with the man in front of him? But then, as Jason hesitated, the man himself answered the question and sealed his own fate. Grasping a handful of loose dirt, he threw it in Jason's eyes, and as Jason, blinded and trying to clear his sight, stumbled away, the man leaped for the knife, attempting to drive it deep into Jason's stomach. They fought for possession of the weapon, Jason at a disadvantage, his sight still unclear. Desperately trying to regain his vision, Jason rolled and tumbled on the dirt lane, the other man still reaching for the knife. Blindly Jason struck out, and luck was with him; the blade unerringly sliced into the man's jugular vein.

Standing beside the corpse, he absently wiped the knife on his buckskin-clad thigh. Unemotionally he stared at his handiwork and was suddenly aware of the pain throbbing across his shoulders. Grimacing, he walked to his waiting horse and swung up onto the animal's back. Then he turned the horse in the direction from which he'd ridden earlier and started back. It wouldn't take him too long to find his way—he hoped!

13

The return to the inn was accomplished easily enough once Jason discovered where his horse had wandered from the more heavily traveled road that led to The Fox onto the narrow lane that had nearly taken him to his doom. Quelling Pierre's searching questions concerning the nasty, bloodied furrow that angled across his shoulders and beginning to feel the effects of delayed shock and loss of blood, Jason thankfully turned himself over to the valet's skilled ministrations. This was not the first time Pierre had patched and tended him.

The wound was ugly but not serious, although it was painful, stabbing Jason into awareness of it every time he moved unwisely. He ignored Pierre's renewed attempts to question him about the injury and Pierre, from past experience, knew it was useless to persist. So after binding the wound lightly, he retired to his room in tightlipped, disapproving silence.

Jason watched his valet's stiff retreat from the room, and for a moment an amused smile chased the serious look from his face. But then, the door was shut, and he was alone with his unpleasant thoughts. Thoughts that didn't amuse him at all!

He wondered how deeply Jem Noakes, the innkeeper, was involved. He'd like to question Noakes about the stranger—if he was a stranger—who must have asked some peculiar questions for the innkeeper to direct him to those two would-be killers. But Noakes was undoubtedly clever, and he might instantly leap to conclusions Jason would find a trifle inconvenient. Especially once news of two men found with their throats slashed filtered through the countryside. It was possible the innkeeper would link him with the deaths, and he wanted no connection between himself and those two bodies. For the present it appeared his curiosity would have to be unsatisfied.

He spent the remainder of the night lounging in a leather chair before the fire, too restless to seek his bed. Broodingly, he stared at the orange and red flames while his mind seethed with unanswered questions and endless speculation. Intent upon his own thoughts, it was not until the early morning light gradually crept in through the window that he tiredly ran a hand over his face and made for his bed.

It was perhaps three in the afternoon when Jason was jerked from a deep sleep by the sudden feeling of icy wetness on his face and his uncle's voice saying calmly, "I think it's time you awoke. I have been awake and traveling since before sunrise, and I find the sight of you slumbering like a babe offensive."

Still shocked by the sudden wetness, Jason had a shrewd suspicion where the water had come from for Roxbury was standing next to the bed, an empty goblet in his hand.

Slowly Jason sat up, his black hair tousled from sleep, a lazy grin curving his mouth, but his green eyes were alert as they surveyed the sartorial elegance of the duke's attire. He was wearing a well-tailored suit of superfine, dove gray cloth, which spoke of the very best tailor in London. It wasn't surprising he was again wearing gray, for it was his favorite color and he wore it often.

The duke's smooth-shaven cheeks and precisely tied cravat made Jason aware of the stubble of his own chin. The fact that he was naked except for the dressing Pierre had used to bind the wound last night didn't add to his joy. Casting a dark glance at his uncle, he asked ungraciously, "What brings you here? I thought you never left London."

"Ah yes, true, but occasionally it does one good to see the country, don't you think?" Roxbury said languidly, settling himself comfortably in a large overstuffed chair near the bed.

Jason shot him a frankly disbelieving look, and twisting the bed sheet about his waist, he rose and stalked to the marble-topped washstand to tidy himself.

"What have you done to yourself?" the duke asked, gesturing at the linen bandage.

"*I* haven't done anything to myself!" snapped Jason, never his best immediately upon waking.

The duke raised his quizzing glass, and after a slow unnerving appraisal of his nephew's surly face, asked, "Are you in a bad mood, Jason?"

"Yes, I'm in a bad mood! You come barging into my room, wake me, and you still haven't answered my question. What are you doing in Leicestershire?"

"Perhaps after you've bathed and eaten you'll be in a more amenable frame of mind. I took the liberty of ordering us a meal, and Pierre is preparing your bath. Shall I wander around this delightful inn for a while, or do you mind if I remain here while you dress!"

"Please yourself—you always do!" retorted Jason as Pierre entered, followed closely by four of the inn servants carrying a huge brass tub.

Jason's bad mood had evaporated by the time he and the duke had seated themselves at the table in the dining room, and the meal passed in amiable silence. But once the table had been cleared and the servants had left the room, the duke asked seriously, "Do you mean to tell me how you came by that bullet wound? And don't deny it is one! I watched Pierre change the dressing, and I know a bullet wound when I see one!"

Briefly and precisely, Jason relayed what had happened the evening before, leaving out only his reasons for being in the area in the first place. Roxbury's face tightened with displeasure as he listened, but surprisingly his only remark when Jason finished was, "I suppose I should be thankful I don't have to remove those two bodies from your premises!"

Ignoring his comment, Jason asked impatiently, "Are you going to tell me why you're here, now? I'm quite certain it isn't to revel in the sight of the countryside in spring!"

"You wrong me! Come, let us take a ride, and you may show me the trees in bloom." At Jason's incredulous look the duke added, "And I'll not be nervous of being overheard!"

They left the inn shortly thereafter, Jason driving his curricle with practiced skill as they swept down the road. For some minutes there was silence. Then the duke broke it by saying, "I could have wished you were more forthright with me the last time we spoke. It would have saved me the embarrassment of discovering you are much more deeply involved in Livingston's mission in Paris than you would have had me believe." He waited for Jason to make some comment, but Jason, his face expressionless, appeared more intent upon his horses than Roxbury's conversation. As the silence continued, the duke said heavily, "Very well, I see I shall have to tell you that I know Livingston received verbal word from another courier that if he was to reach an impasse in negotiations for the use of the port of New Orleans, he was to contact you immediately! You obviously have instructions from President Jefferson that could be vital to Livingston. And I'm disappointed you gave me no hint when I asked if there was another reason for the interest in your belongings. You'll note," Roxbury added dryly, "I don't ask what message you are to deliver."

"Only because you probably have already discovered it!" came the sharp reply.

"Jason," the duke began earnestly, "we are on the same side! I say truthfully that at this time England has no designs on the Louisiana area. We have a volcano in the form of a small conceited Frenchman named Napoleon about to erupt on our very doorstep. I can assure you that if Jefferson plans to let Andrew Jackson invade New Orleans and forcibly take the port, we in England would be *delighted!* I might add, my government has been wondering why yours hasn't done so before now."

His face still expressionless, Jason turned his green gaze onto his uncle and said levelly, "But you don't *know* that's what Jefferson told me! Only *I* know what passed between us! And you still haven't answered my question. You didn't tear yourself away from London merely to tell me you had discovered I've been less than truthful in my dealings with you."

"Damn it, Jason, the only message that would be of use to Livingston with that damn little frog would be the threat of violence! And ever since the Spanish closed the port last year, Andrew Jackson and his volunteer army of fellow Tennesseans have been spoiling for an excuse to invade the territory. So don't try to tell me Jefferson gave you some other message!" the duke answered angrily. But as his nephew continued to ignore his outburst, he said slowly: "I see. You really don't trust me any longer."

And Jason, concentrating on feathering a particularly sharp curve, didn't see the momentary flash of very real pain in the gray eyes that scanned his face so closely. If he had, his voice might not have been so harsh as he ground out, "Don't give me that! You have your government, and I have mine. You wouldn't have told me what you have if it were of some further use to you. Now for the last time—have done with this nonsense and tell me why the hell you are here."

Angered by Jason's surly treatment, Roxbury snapped, "I'm overjoyed you're so loyal to the United States, as Livingston is negotiating for the entire Louisiana territory—not just the use of the port of New Orleans and free navigation rights to the Mississippi River!" And he had the satisfaction of watching the stupefied look that spread over his nephew's face. As the full import of his words sunk in, Jason pulled the horses over to the side of the road and halted the vehicle. He turned to Roxbury and asked, "The *whole* Louisiana territory?"

"Yes, all of it! James Monroe is expected any day, and I have no doubt he and Livingston will, together, push for the purchase of it all. Napoleon seems to be listening to them—if the idea didn't originate with him! The land is useless to him, and he needs money for his war with us. From my knowledge of him, Talleyrand would probably prefer to colonize the area, but Bonaparte holds the power, and he wants war!"

The possibility of that enormous tract of virgin wilderness passing to the hands of the fledgling United States had never occurred to Jason, and the idea left him stunned—not that he objected to it, although if he had expressed any view at all it would have been for the territory to become a nation in its own right. It was the shock of discovering that France might actually own the land—or else she was involved in one of the greatest swindles of all time—and was willing to sell that immense area with its great potential for growth and power, merely to finance a destructive war in Europe! *Mon Dieu!* They must have a mistaken assessment of the wealth in the New World if they thought the United States would be able to meet what must be a very high price. And thinking of that, he asked, "How much do they propose to sell it for—or don't you know?"

"We've had reports of over seventeen million dollars."

"But that's more money than is in the entire United

States! They'd never be able to raise that amount!" Jason said slowly, then twisted to view his uncle's smug expression with suspicion. "How do you know what Livingston is doing? No, don't tell me! Obviously, if you've learned of my part and now you know this, you must have a spy on Livingston's staff."

The duke shrugged noncommittally, and Jason had to grin. Nothing, but nothing ever shook the duke from his air of cynical detachment. And knowing they would sit here apparently enjoying the fading spring sunshine until his uncle was prepared to reveal his reasons for being in Leicestershire, he leaned casually into the leather backrest, folded his arms and propped one booted foot on the dash of the curricle. The duke noting these signs asked, "Are you ready to listen and cease viewing my every move as a possible hostile act?"

His eyes holding a mocking gleam, Jason admitted, "I'll listen, but as for the other, I can't promise!"

Satisfied if not pleased with the answer, Roxbury asked briskly, "Are you acquainted personally with either Livingston or Monroe?"

His eyebrow rose, but the answer came easily enough. "I've never met Robert Livingston, but James Monroe is a good friend of Guy's. I've met him several times. As a matter of fact, he dined with us one night before I left for England and was present at one of the meetings I had with Jefferson."

Roxbury nodded slowly, as if confirming what he already knew, and fixing his gray eyes on the haughty face so like his own, said, "So, if you were to carry a proposal to Monroe, he would accept it as true and authentic?"

"Yes. *But* my dearest, crafty uncle, if you wish me to play the courier for you, you must convince me the message I carry is true and authentic!"

"Well, of course," the duke said testily, "that goes without saying. And in view of that, you'll have to return with me to London tonight and prepare yourself to sail for France within the next few days!"

"No," came the flat answer, and Roxbury stared at Jason in surprise.

"What do you mean *no?*"

"Simply that I'm not returning to London tonight! And I can't cross the channel for France until after I settle a disagreement with Clive Pendleton."

"Disagreement?"

"Mmmm," Jason answered maddeningly. "I threw a glass of wine in his face, and he disagreed with my actions."

"Jason, have I ever told you that you try my patience excessively?" asked the duke scathingly.

"Frequently!" came the unrepentant answer, as Jason sat up abruptly and grasping the reins, turned the curricle in the direction of the inn. "I'll see Harris and Barrymore this evening and insist the meeting take place in the morning. They'll be understandably scandalized, but if I leave for Paris soon, I must settle the affair with Pendleton first. Will it suit you if I arrive in London the day after tomorrow, provided I can force Pendleton to meet me in the morning?"

"Why ask me? You've already decided, and while I might wish you hadn't antagonized him, I agree it should be settled before you leave for France."

Jason shot his uncle a teasing glance and, tongue in cheek, said, "I thought you would be pleased with the news of my coming duel with him. Just think. I may kill him, and then you won't have to worry about trapping him."

Sharply, the duke said, "Don't be a fool! He may kill *you,* and I want more than just Pendleton dead! I want the others, too—the ones who buy his information. Clive, by himself, is very small fish indeed!"

They conversed desultorily for the remainder of the ride back to the inn, and shortly after their return the duke left on the long trip back to London.

Immediately after Roxbury's departure, Jason drove to Brownleigh's and tracked down Harris and Barrymore, and then waited impatiently while Harris and Barrymore held an unfriendly meeting with Pendleton's seconds, Phillipe de

Courcey and a Mr. Anthony Newhope, a foppish young gentleman with more hair than wit. It was dark before arrangements for the duel were set, but in the end Jason has his way and left Brownleigh's, knowing he would meet Pendleton at dawn in a small clearing not far from the inn. Pendleton had chosen pistols for their meeting, and that disclosure brought a satisfied smile to Jason's face. Good! He wanted the duel over and done with, and rapiers took time; but a pistol—one quick, well-aimed shot and the deed was done! It was possible he could be in London tomorrow night. And the sooner he knew what the duke needed carried to Monroe, the better—besides, he was curious as hell!

At the inn, he paid his bill and informed Noakes of his morning departure. Briefly he toyed with the idea of questioning the innkeeper about his knowledge of the attempt on his life but then, all things considered, decided against it. If someone—besides Pendleton—wanted him dead, they would, no doubt, try again, and next time he'd be ready.

Once more in his rooms, he settled down in one of the leather chairs to wait a bit—the festivities would be barely underway at the gypsy camp. That was another little score to settle before leaving. Pierre was already packing, and he had notified Jacques of their imminent departure, so all he had to do was waste time until the duel at dawn. Relaxing for the first time since his uncle had so rudely woken him hours ago, he viewed the sudden, unexpected curtailment of his trip to England with something approaching satisfaction.

The trip had proved to be a success in regards to *his* plans. By now his first shipment of thoroughbred brood mares would have arrived in New Orleans. A second group, consisting of several hunters and pleasure horses destined for sale in the Louisiana area, would arrive a few weeks behind the brood mares. He had intended to sail with the last bunch that comprised the gypsy horses—a few mares in foal, some with colts still at their sides, and the young black stallion. His only real disappointment had been that he hadn't found precisely the stud he wanted. He had hoped to buy two stallions, but it seemed one would have to suffice.

The one thing he hadn't done was find a bride. Thank God for that! But deep inside he admitted there was some merit to his father's request. It really was his duty to marry and produce an heir. He smiled unpleasantly to himself. The only problem was—he had not found a woman he cared to mount and breed. Unfortunately, the ones like the little gypsy, who stirred his pulses and warmed his loins, were very likely to present him with another man's bastard!

As the hour grew late, Pierre brought in a wine tray and set it near his elbow. Jason poured himself a brandy and savored the bouquet before letting it slide smoothly down his throat. Ruminatively he viewed the possible choices for a bride. Several young, well-bred ladies had been brought to his notice, but they were all alike: correct, identically curled and dressed, and with not more than two thoughts rattling around in their empty heads. Amanda Harris was the only one who might remotely be considered in the running—Elizabeth would have been greatly chagrined to know he ignored her existence completely—and even as he thought of Amanda, another face, seen only once in a gloomy library in London, leapt to his mind's eye; those blurred features seen the night of the countess of Mount's ball seemed to haunt him, and lately he was plagued with the tantalizing feeling he'd seen them again. Suddenly, angry with himself for mooning over a barely remembered beautiful face, he downed the brandy and poured himself another.

Pierre, seeing the scowling look on his face and noting the gradual disappearance of the liquor, wondered what was in the wind. One thing was positive: if Jason kept drinking he'd be foxed before midnight!

Jason had no intention of getting drunk tonight. He needed a cool head for the evening in front of him. Restlessly he moved in the chair, ignoring the faint throb of his wound, then rose and wandered over to one of the small windows that overlooked the cobbled courtyard of the inn.

In the faint light from two or three lanterns hung about, he could see it was deserted except for a few farmer's nags and a smart, gentleman's carriage. He glanced at the moonlit sky and seeing the lowering black clouds that raced across it, idly wondered if the threatened rain would hold off until tomorrow. He'd hate to meet Pendleton in the rain.

Bored, he checked the time. It was after nine. Suddenly a cruel smile crossed his face. It was time to leave for the gypsy camp. There certainly was a surprise in store for one little, too clever by half, saucy bitch!

14

The threatened rain had blown over, leaving a clear, cool, starlit night that Catherine silently blessed as she slipped from the darkened house. Rain would have spoiled the wedding celebration. Catherine knew she had missed the actual ceremony, performed at sunset, but she had been unable to leave until the household was settled for the night. Now she was free to join the robust and lively festivities that would be sweeping the gypsy camp.

The huge bonfire flickered and danced in the black night, casting a soft yellow glow over the loosely circled wagons and tents, creating an intimate, yet excitingly unknown atmosphere. The heat from the leaping flames banished the faint chill of the spring night; potent red wine added its own spell and warmth as toast after toast was drunk to the blushing dark-eyed bride and her proud black-haired husband.

There were happy smiles on the swarthy faces, white teeth flashing and black eyes sparkling with enjoyment as Catherine wandered through the camp. Pausing to speak with various friends, she was filled with a warm feeling of affection for all of them. She belonged here as surely as if she had been born of them. They were her people!

Violins and guitars were playing softly, and the faintly flamenco sound invaded her body, her feet moving in rhythm and her slim hips swaying in answer to the primitive music that drifted through the camp. One girl, Juana, leaped near one of the fires and began to dance in graceful abandon, the vibrating tambourine in her hand adding to the symphony of sound permeating the entire area.

Some of the older gypsies gathered in small groups, idly watching the whirling figure as they laughed and talked, while the younger ones, Catherine among them, clapped in rhythm and with their feet kept time to the throbbing beat. She was caught up in the spell of the excitement as the fires leaped and wavered in tune with the passionate, wild melodies that flowed through the dark night. A group had unconsciously formed a loose circle around the dancing figure of Juana, and when she grew tired, Catherine was pushed with good-natured enthusiasm into the center of the scattered circle.

The wine and music were fire in her veins, and as the tempo increased, she swirled and danced in compulsive movement. Her black hair rippled with a life of its own as she threw back her head, raised slim, white arms high, and began to stamp in sensuous answer to the music of the violins. The scarlet gown she wore molded itself to her pliant form from breast to waist, then spilled out full and vibrant over her hips down to the wildly dancing feet. And as she danced the scarlet cloth spun out and swayed with her almost frenzied movements, giving tantalizing glimpses of long, beautifully formed legs.

A creature possessed, trapped by the enchantment of the night and the lure of the music, Catherine's dance spelled out a message as old as time. She lost awareness of the laughing, clapping crowd—there was only the night, the flickering fire, and this strange, untamed abandonment that was fed by the pulse-quickening sounds of the violins. Her violet, cat-shaped eyes were half closed as she stared unseeingly at the moving, colorful kaleidoscope that surrounded her, until gradually her faraway gaze focused on a stranger, a tall, dark gentleman who leaned casually against one of the ancient oaks at the fringe of the firelight.

His face was in shadow, but she could see the hard line of his jaw and the brooding curve of his full bottom lip. A long, black cloak obscured his attire, but faintly she could see the patches of white of his cravat and the cuffs of his shirt. He seemed unmoved by the emotion sweeping the camp, and unconsciously she began to dance for him—and him alone!

Her slender hips swayed in time with the music, her arms appeared to seek his embrace, and her breasts, barely concealed by the scarlet gown were thrust forward, almost taunting him to reach out and touch them. Suddenly, he moved into the circle of the light, and she was jolted unpleasantly back to reality by the searing glance of Jason's green eyes. There was no mistaking the fire that burned in their emerald depths.

His bright, unwavering gaze caused her to stumble, but she quickly recovered and whirled away from him, dancing her way to the outer reaches of the circle farthest from his frightening presence. She plunged into the milling, smiling crowd, and they ignored her as another girl took her place and the dancing continued.

Breathing heavily, Catherine fought her way through the friendly mass of gypsies, the warmth and excitement of the night gone as if she had been splashed with a bucket of icy water; fear widened her eyes and pinched her full mouth. She cast a look over one shoulder and felt a stab of terror like a savage blow. Jason had vanished! Frantically, she searched the shifting crowd for his tall form, but he had disappeared. Panic-stricken, she foolishly bolted from the safety of the crowd and ran towards her caravan. She was in the power of such unthinking, primitive fear that she wasn't even able to scream as suddenly he was before her, reaching out to lift her body from the ground.

Violently, she tore at the arms that held her prisoner and tried desperately to free herself from Jason's iron grasp. Shock loosened the stranglehold of fear from her throat, but as she opened her mouth to cry for help, his lips closed over hers in a deep, hungry kiss. His mouth hard on hers, confused and stunned by his flagrant attack, she felt jolt after jolt of burning lightning shiver through her body as his lips demanded surrender. He raised his head after what seemed like hours and, laughing deep in his throat, tossed her unceremoniously over his broad shoulder and carried her to his horse.

The breath had been knocked from her body by his rough handling, and it was a second or two before she could manage even one small croak of fearful rage. But the music was at its peak, and the laughing crowd around the fire was intent on the dancing in the circle, and no one except old Reina saw or took notice as the horse carrying the big man and the scarlet-gowned, struggling wench galloped away.

Reina was of two minds as she watched them disappear into the black night. Undecided, she hesitated, then shrugged her thin shoulders. Bah! Let them work out their differences. Tamara had courted danger too often; now let her reap the folly of her stubbornness.

But Reina herself came to a decision as she watched them ride away. As long as the gypsies continued to stay nearby, Tamara would never break free of the bonds that bound her to them. And so, Reina would sever those bonds for her and at once. Striding determinedly, she sought out Manuel. Taking him a little distance from the laughing crowd, she said, "It is time we leave England. I've a longing for my birthplace in Spain. Tell the others we leave at dawn."

"At dawn! Spain!" Manuel was incredulous. "What about Tamara? If we depart for Spain, it'll be who knows when that we return. It might be over a year."

The expression in her black eyes hidden, Reina snapped, "Precisely! And by that time, Tamara will have accepted the fact that she cannot be both Lady Catherine and Tamara!"

Reina turned on her heel, her thoughts for just a second more dwelling on Jason and Tamara. A mirthless smile twisted her lips. That young blood would be an end to Tamara's waywardness!

Once free of the camp, Jason shifted Catherine's squirming body until she sat sideways on the horse, her heaving chest pressed to his, his arm a steel band across her back. She strained away from his hard body, but it was useless. Giving a muttered laugh, he easily pulled her to him.

Anger replaced that first wild panic, and she threw up her head and in icy, controlled tones asked, "And where do you think you're taking me?"

A mocking smile curved his lips, but his eyes remained flintlike as he said, "I thought we'd have our night together after all. I regret your substitute wasn't quite adequate. I thought her a little too—ah—mature for my taste."

Catherine was in no teasing mood, and his lighthearted manner infuriated her almost as much as the sudden abduction. Without thinking, she raised her hand and slapped his smiling mouth with all the force of which she was capable. Instantly, the mocking smile was wiped from his face, and an ugly, tight look took its place. Yanking the horse to a standstill, he wrapped one hand in Catherine's tangled ebony hair and snapped her head backwards with such violence that she let out a cry of mingled rage and pain. Then his lips found hers with a bruising force that brought blood to her mouth as he crushed her lips beneath his in a long, brutal kiss.

Ineffectually she clawed at his face; but one hand was captured behind his back, and the other he struck aside before he ripped the gown to the waist, freeing her lovely bosom. Outraged and frightened, she fought to escape, and as her flailing hand touched his hair, she gave it a vicious tug, even while her small teeth bit into his tongue. Snarling a curse, he dumped her onto the cold ground, and as she fell in a sprawled heap, her scarlet dress was twisted up around her slim hips, and her long legs gleamed whitely in the moonlight. She was motionless for only a moment. Then she bounded to her feet, but before she could bolt, he leaped from the horse, grasped her arm, and spun her around.

They faced one another like two spitting cats, both disheveled and furious. Their heavy breathing was a harsh, unlovely sound in the quiet night, and the very air seemed to vibrate with the violence of their emotions. Fleetingly, Jason remembered the last time they'd faced one another like this. Last time, he'd been a fool not to have taken her, and *this* time he'd not make the same mistake. She had taunted, teased, and insulted his very pride—it was time she tasted a little of the gall that had been his!

He moved suddenly, pulling her next to him. She reacted instantly at his touch, her small fists beating against his muscled chest, but with a muttered grunt he ignored her frantic efforts and again captured her mouth with his. Her hands were useless, trapped between their bodies, and freely he caressed her. Her convulsive movements to escape only added to the flame of desire that was sweeping through him; her thighs strained against his, and her twisting softness brushed his groin.

Catherine, her virgin body prey to conflicting emotions, was very aware of the dangerousness of her position, yet again his very touch destroyed her reason and made her want to stay, to let him make love to her. Suddenly unable to control herself, she melted with a wantonness that startled him. But laughing low he swiftly threw his cloak onto the ground and reached for her once more. Yet as he closed the space between them, her momentary weakness fled, and she brought her knee up savagely between his legs in one last desperate attempt to escape.

The pain exploded in Jason's body. Grimly, despite the blow, he held onto her struggling form. "You little bitch! You'll pay for that!" he grated and flung her onto the cloak, pinning her to the ground with his own hard body.

His green eyes glinted in the moonlight as he looked long

and searchingly into the hauntingly beautiful face so close to his. Feeling her trembling beneath him, he smiled tightly down into her defiant eyes and, shifting slightly, ripped the dress the rest of the way open.

Catherine, in a state bordering on shock, lay watching him, her thoughts in a turmoil. Uppermost was a half-curious, half-apprehensive desire to discover finally what it would be like for this man to possess her. Even so, she was totally unprepared for the sheer delight that tore through her passive body as he bent his head, and his warm mouth closed over one firm young breast.

They lay together on his cloak, Jason with one leg thrown across her thighs, stilling her feeble attempts to avoid his hands as they explored her body. *Mon Dieu,* she was lovely, he thought, as his desire for revenge disappeared abruptly, leaving only a blind, hungry need. He left off teasing her breasts and nuzzled at the hollow of her throat, before reaching up and taking her unwilling lips in a demanding kiss. His mouth was sweet on hers, but stubbornly she tried to resist his advances until he lifted his head and, capturing her chin, said, "Stop fighting me! You've teased me long enough, and before we leave here tonight, I intend to satisfy myself with you. You'll find I can give you as much pleasure as Clive. So stop playing the silly young virgin!"

Catherine attempted to cry out that she *was* a silly virgin! But he bent his head and kissed her deeply, his tongue forcing its way into her mouth, and almost lazily he ran one hand over her still form. Deliberately he moved his hand down her flat belly to explore gently between her legs. The sudden tremor of fire she felt as his hand brushed the silken triangle caused her to involuntarily arch her hips against his invading fingers; and when he saw the unconsciously sensuous action of her slender hips, an intent, urgent look crossed his face. There was no stopping the increasing heat in his loins as he openly touched her soft, curved body wherever he pleased.

Suddenly, he moved again so that his body lay over hers.

She made another attempt to escape, but cruelly his fingers dug into her thrashing thighs as he held her to the ground. With insistent hands, he spread her legs, undeterred by her frantically beating hands as she frenziedly twisted and attempted to claw his dark face. For an instant he was poised above her trapped body, and then with a savage thrust he entered her, driving deep into her vitals.

Catherine's scream of agony, as he ruthlessly took her virginity, was lost when he crushed her mouth with his; but he had felt that slight obstruction, and astonishment momentarily held him motionless, buried within her. Stunned by the implication of that delicate membrane, he released her mouth and stared into her pain-clouded eyes. He hesitated, uncertain, but what was done was done. Slowly he made love to her, moving within her gently and whispering softly, "I'm sorry, *chérie*," before surrendering to the demands of his body and increasing his rapid movements, as the sweep of pleasure that heralded fulfillment coursed through his body.

To Catherine, the pain inflicted upon her unwilling body was meaningless compared to the humiliation and agony of mind she suffered. Her gaze was cloudy with inner torment as she lay sprawled like a broken doll, unmoving, making no attempt to gather the torn garments about her naked body. She was so lost in misery she never felt his withdrawal or noticed when he stood up and arranged his clothing.

A bitter twist to his lips, Jason looked at her lying there, and he tasted the acid bite of bile in his mouth. Anger, remorse, and rage all burned through him, and the knowledge that he'd allowed his own selfish desires to blind him to the fact that the little gypsy hadn't been playing a game, but in actuality was defending her honor, left him feeling disgusted with himself. He knelt beside her and gently began to pull the ripped gown about her nakedness, but at his touch she shied away like a frightened animal, and he cursed softly under his breath.

Catherine was almost numb with shock; but his touch

could instill fear, and she couldn't control a shiver of terror when he reached for her again. But he was kind, this time, cradling her limp form next to his and soothingly murmuring meaningless phrases as he carefully wrapped her in the concealing folds of his cloak.

The ride back to the inn was accomplished in silence, Catherine lying listlessly against his chest, unconsciously listening to the steady beat of his heart. After leaving the horse at the stables, he carried her to his room, shielding her from any curious glances that may have come their way. In his rooms, he laid her gently on the bed and called for Pierre to prepare a bath. Then pouring a goodly amount of brandy into a glass, he forced the liquor down her throat. Choking and spluttering, she managed to swallow some of the fiery liquid. As the burning warmth spread through her chilled body, she slowly began to recover some of her scattered wits and searched desperately for a means of escape. But Pierre came bustling into the room, supervising the setting up of the brass tub near a hastily lit fire, and Catherine clutched the cloak more tightly about her curled frame, hiding her torn and ripped gown from his intensely curious eyes. Jason disappeared into the other room, and while the servants were filling the tub, Pierre and Catherine covertly studied one another. The valet's face seemed kind, and perhaps he'd help her to escape, she thought hopefully. Pierre, at the same time, was deciding she was by far the loveliest wench yet to share his master's bed.

Catherine recognized none of the other servants, but she kept her face carefully averted, praying no one would recognize her. Silently she willed them to leave before Jason returned and every chance of escape was destroyed. She could have screamed with rage when they finally did leave, for as she cautiously began to edge to the side of the bed, Jason returned. Slung over his arm were several frothy pieces of feminine apparel, which he tossed in an untidy heap on a chair. He noted that the blind, unseeing stare that had disturbed him earlier was gone, although there was still a pinched look about her mouth that he didn't like.

He dismissed Pierre and began to walk towards the girl crouched on the huge bed. Catherine's eyes were wary, and as he neared her motionless form, the fires of defiance began to blaze in the violet depths. Jason, seeing the hate and furious anger burning in her tilted eyes, suddenly grinned. The unfamiliar remorse he had experienced earlier was uncomfortable, and he had been annoyed and bothered by the feelings of compassion she had aroused. But angry women he could understand and handle, and his grin widened. Mockingly, he bowed and said, "Your bath awaits you, m'lady."

Angrily, she glared at him and spat, "Leave me then! I'll not expose myself further to your lascivious gaze."

Jason laughed. And as Catherine scooted to the far side of the bed, he threw himself down next to her and drew her struggling body close to him. She was pushed effortlessly down into the enveloping softness of the feather mattress, and he lay with his body half covering hers, smiling down into her furious face. Gently smoothing the rumpled hair away from her forehead, he surprised her by saying seriously, "My love, I am truly sorry for the way I took you. If I had known, I would have chosen a better place and seen to it you had little pain. You should have trusted me."

"Trusted you?" she spluttered, rage choking her practically speechless.

He nodded, arrogantly sure of his charm and power. But then he frowned, his black brows nearly meeting his bold nose. Curiously he asked, "How is it Clive hadn't deflowered you long ago?" But before she could force her stumbling tongue to answer, his brow cleared, and he said knowingly, "Ah, I understand! Clive has a taste for boys and used you as he would them."

Catherine stared at him uncomprehendingly, but he didn't see her confused look, for the cloak had fallen open and he was distracted by the sight of her nearly naked body. Instinctively, she attempted to gather the folds together, but he knocked her hands aside and moved his own hands caressingly over her silken flesh; she stiffened with unwilling desire. He seemed unaware of her reaction saying musingly. "Clive must be a fool. You, *chérie,* are so beautifully made, *mon Dieu,* it is a sacrilege that he used you so!"

He bent his head, and she gasped aloud as his mouth teasingly nibbled one pink-tipped breast. His lips left a tingling trail of fire as he moved from one breast to the other, then suddenly, hungrily up to her mouth. Leisurely, lovingly, he kissed her until she relaxed. But then, just as she had begun to involuntarily respond, he startled her by stripping the tattered dress completely from her, scooping her up in his strong arms, and carrying her to the waiting bath. And seconds later, her hair loosely secured to the top of her head, she found herself in the warm, scented water. Then nothing, not even his disturbing presence, could dim the delight she felt as the liquid warmth seeped over her abused body.

Jason sprawled lazily on the bed and watched her with curious eyes. She was such a bewildering combination of sultry temptress and yet-unawakened maid that against his will he was intrigued. He could keep her a twelvemonth, yet not know what went on in her beautiful little head. Nor, he thought grinning, would she bore him! Her changing moods were like quicksilver, and while she might exasperate him occasionally, he knew that soft, lovely body would always give him great pleasure. But as he studied the enchanting profile, he was struck again by some elusive resemblance. Damn! Where had he seen that face before?

While Jason lay relaxed on the bed, puzzling over her familiarity, Catherine was carefully studying him from underneath her long lashes. There was no denying he was an attractive man. His white silk shirt was open to his waist, revealing his tanned, muscled chest with its mat of coarse black hair, and she felt a shiver of something—not quite desire, yet not quite fear—as she remembered the feel of that powerful body on hers. She too, was perplexed by a fleeting feeling of having seen his handsome face long before that night at her aunt's—but try as hard as she could, she couldn't put her finger on who he reminded her of. For the moment, she was resigned to her predicament. It was like a horrid nightmare, and silently she prayed she'd awake and discover herself safe in her own bed.

She scrubbed herself thoroughly, as if by so doing she could erase his touch, and when she finished, he rose smiling and handed her a large, soft towel that had been warming near the fire. He held it out, and she had no choice but to rise from the water and allow him to enfold her in its warmth. Resentfully, she glared at him, embarrassment causing red flags to fly in her cheeks.

Guessing the reason for her red cheeks, he increased her agitation by murmuring wickedly, "You forget I have done more than look at you, my little cat!"

At his unknowing use of her pet name, she nearly jumped out of her skin, and he frowned blackly at her sudden look of fear. *Mon Dieu,* what was wrong with the wench? She seemed positively petrified! Gently, he chided her, "*Chérie,* do not be frightened—the worst is behind you. I will take care of you and teach you how best to please a real man. Clive must be only a half a man."

Catherine closed her eyes in sudden anguish. If only she had listened . . . if only she hadn't been so headstrong and insisted upon dancing with the gypsies tonight . . . if only. . . . But it was too late for futile wishes now, and opening her eyes she saw that he was watching her closely. Unable to control herself, she begged, "Let me go! You've had your pleasure—please, *please* let me go!" It cost her an effort to plead, but she was willing to do anything if only he'd release her. The violet eyes swam with threatened tears, and she bit her swollen lip to still its betraying tremble.

"Ah, little one, do not distress yourself so. I will not hurt you. I have been a big, clumsy oaf tonight. Soon you will learn that I can be very gentle," he soothed, exerting his considerable charm to allay her fears.

Incredulously, Catherine stared at him. Didn't he realize

she wanted nothing from him? For a moment she was almost overcome by the desire to scream her identity at him, but prudence held her tongue. She wanted no scandal, and she clung to the hope that somehow she would soon be able to escape back to gypsies with no one the wiser. And the unpleasant thought occurred to her—she had no guarantee that Jason would believe her. Abruptly she turned away from his mocking face, unwilling for him to see how completely confused and yes, she had to admit it, almost frightened she was.

She stood uncertainly in the middle of the room with only the towel hiding her nakedness and was thankful when Jason handed her a black velvet robe from the pile of clothing on the chair. He had just seated her near the fire when Pierre knocked and entered bearing a tray with covered dishes. The appetizing smells that drifted to Catherine's nose made her realize how very hungry she was.

It could not be said that the meal that followed was enjoyable, but it was an interlude from the night's violence. Jason set out to be his most polite, charming self; Catherine, relaxed by the warm bath, enveloped in the luxurious softness of the velvet robe, and her tormentor in a disarming mood, felt almost safe and shortly was astonished to find herself smiling at one of his amusing tales. As they ate that odd, strangely intimate dinner, Jason found himself more and more puzzled by the gypsy wench. No gypsy had features so finely cast, nor skin as clear and white as hers. He finally decided she must be a by-blow of one of the local lords. Yet gentlemen did not usually educate their bastards, and her manners as she ate were as correct as those of any lady of his society. Her speech also was not that of the uneducated: she spoke as clearly and precisely as he did, and he had been educated at Harrow! Perhaps, the unwelcome thought occurred to him, Clive used her to spy, and it would be useful for her to pass for a lady.

As they conversed, each probing the other, he was surprised at the intelligence she displayed and particularly her avid curiosity about Louisiana. A smile lifting the corner of his mouth, he asked, "How is it you are so interested in my country?"

And without thinking, she replied, "My brother is there. He inherited an estate, near Natchez, from my father."

She could have bitten off her tongue for those impulsive words, but he appeared unaware of the slip, although one black brow rose in surprise, and he asked dryly, "An estate?"

Moistening her suddenly dry lips, she returned brightly, "What else would you call land inherited?"

"It would depend on the size. Most of our land is measured in square miles, and we call them plantations. Did your brother fall heir to a plantation?" he teased.

Her eyes very big and innocent, and not all in pretense, she said in an awed tone, "Square miles? You mean thousands of acres?"

"*Mais oui!*" he laughed. "I myself have never ridden to my north boundary, although my grandfather has frequently. He enjoys surveying his domain."

She regarded him curiously. He was obviously a young man blessed by a kind fate. He possessed a handsome face, wealth, a charming manner, and was so carelessly sure of his possessions that he couldn't be bothered to ascertain the extent of the land he owned. What arrogance!

Jason had been diverted by her artless questions, but now his gaze rested for a moment on her face, before wandering leisurely over the exquisitely formed body barely hidden by the black robe. A slow, lazy smile widened his mouth; he knew how easily that robe could be discarded, for hadn't he given it to her with just that in mind? The memory of her smooth, satin flesh caused a tingle of anticipation between his legs, and through suddenly heavy-lidded eyes, he judged the extent of her disarmament.

Catherine, unaware of his change of mood, leaned languidly back into her chair. She was warm, fed, and Jason had seen to it that she had drunk freely of the potent rum punch he had served after dinner. Right now she was sleepy, and the memory of the shocking events of the night were hazy in her mind. Filled with a sense of well-being brought on by the strong liquor, she wanted nothing more than her bed—which was precisely where Jason wanted her, too!

She was drifting on a cloud of numbness when he unhurriedly lifted her and gently deposited her relaxed body on the huge bed. With sleepy eyes she noted the flickering fire and tried to remember if her bed had always been this big. Too bemused to ponder it further, she gave a sigh and burrowed down into the welcoming softness.

Jason, watching her movements as he swiftly stripped, smiled to himself. She would have plenty of time to sleep in the morning, while he met her late protector. Right now, he meant to relieve the ache between his legs!

She noted the movement the bed gave as he lay beside her, but still in her pleasant, hazy state, she viewed his intrusion into her bedchamber as part of the dreamlike trance. It was only when he began to slowly remove the robe that her euphoria vanished. Remembrance was instantaneous, and she made a convulsive dive away from him.

Laughing deep in his throat, he easily held her prisoner, whispering, "Easy, easy, little cat. You'll find it's useless to fight me when my mind is made up."

Catherine stared up at the green eyes and the full mouth that hovered near hers and resignedly accepted her fate, knowing it didn't matter how hard she fought—Jason would win in the end. Besides, what did it matter, now? She had nothing else to lose. He'd seen to that, she thought bitterly.

Leisurely, he explored her body, seeming to take immense gratification from the feel and taste of her silken skin as his hands and mouth moved knowingly over the hollows and curves that so intrigued him. Vainly, Catherine fought the insidious waves of pleasure that rippled through her, but his mouth was warm and demanding, his touches tender and experienced as they caressed her flesh; and with a shuddering sigh, she blindly turned her face up for his kiss and almost compulsively put her arms about his neck. Eagerly he took her mouth and pressed her lengthwise next to his hard, sunbrowned body, his hands skimming lovingly over her back and curved buttocks, pulling her closer against him. She felt the faint prickle of the black hair on his chest rub on her nipples, and when he pressed nearer, she was shocked to feel the heat and hardness of his desire push insistently into her belly.

He felt her move involuntarily against him, and said in a thickened voice, "Touch me, little one. Feel it."

Deftly, he guided her hesitating hand and gave a deep groan of pleasure as her small palm closed around him. Her touch seemed to inflame him, and hungrily he kissed her, his tongue searching the sweetness of her mouth, his hands moving with increasing urgency down to her thighs; and Catherine was gripped by an intense desire to feel his body take hers once again. She arched her hips, as if seeking his entry, and he, sensing her readiness, covered her slender body with his and gently penetrated her.

He moved on her slowly, savoring the feel and sensations of her beautiful body, and unconsciously Catherine began to move with him, a low moan escaping from her as he continued to kiss her ears, neck, and mouth, while his body thrust deeply into hers, making them truly one. Unable to think clearly, she twisted wildly beneath him, her hands running frenziedly up and down his back as her body met his, time and time again, until a huge burst of feeling seemed to explode within her, and she felt his big body shudder with the intensity of his release.

Catherine was stunned by the abandonment with which she had responded to his touch. In spite of everything, he had aroused her, made her aware of the enjoyment a man could give a woman, and gave her an inkling of the power of her own body. And now, he seemed curiously reluctant to leave her, as if he would never tire of her, and his lips gently brushed her forehead and nose, traveling lazily down to her mouth, kissing her thoroughly.

It was then, as they lay together, that Catherine first noticed the gold and emerald band on Jason's arm. But it, like the events of the night, seemed like something out of a dream, and she didn't question its oddity any more than she questioned Jason's finding her at the gypsy encampment. To her, at the moment, it appeared logical that the strange young man who had literally spirited her away from safety and taken her virginity would wear such a savage and barbaric piece of adornment—it was part of him and as such she never gave it another thought. And with Jason's insistent mouth wandering over her body, she was not in any state to think clearly.

Finally, regretfully, he slid from her and gathered her close to his warm body, her head against his gently heaving chest, her hair tickling his nose. One hand possessively caressing her hip, he dropped a kiss on her head saying, "Hmmm, *petite,* I can see I will get little done with you around. It is a good thing, I think, that we did not meet earlier."

Catherine, her eyes heavy with sleep, her brain drugged by the rum and a multitude of new emotions, only snuggled deeper into his embrace. She felt his chest rumble with soft laughter, and she moved resentfully away. She was exhausted and only wanted to sleep. Later, she'd worry. Much later!

15

Jason woke suddenly. The room was in darkness, but instinctively he knew dawn wasn't far. For a moment he lay there, the faint smell of burnt candle wax in his nostrils, uncertain what had awakened him. A second later, he discovered that not only was the little gypsy no longer nestled warm against him, but she wasn't even in the bed! Then, hearing a small noise, as if someone unfamiliar with the room had stumbled in the inky blackness, a frown creased his forehead. What the devil was the wench up to now?

"Tamara, get back here!" he commanded. Silence greeted his words. The minutes passed like years, and both remained motionless; Catherine, frozen as she stood near the door, felt her heart pounding with thick, painful strokes. Abruptly the silence was broken as giving a muffled curse, Jason swung out of bed and lit a nearby candle, while Catherine, knowing the chance to escape was disappearing rapidly, gave a cry of dismay and whirling about raced for the door that led to the stairs and safety.

But she hadn't reckoned with Jason's distrust of the

innkeeper, and she had been too drowsy last night to notice when Jason locked the door and for good measure placed a stout chair against it. With frantic hands she tugged the chair far enough away to allow her slim body to squeeze behind it, casting an apprehensive glance over her shoulder as she did so. Fear made her unusually clumsy, and even as her fingers closed on the key, Jason, stark naked, the gold band on his arm gleaming dully, hurtled through the bedroom doorway. In her haste, the key slipped from her fingers, falling with a clatter onto the wooden floor. Aware she had lost her chance for flight, she turned and faced him defiantly, her head held high, her violet eyes staring unflinchingly into his.

Seeing her predicament, Jason slowed his step and completely unconcerned with his own nakedness, took in Catherine's attire with amusement. She was wearing a pair of his yellow nankeen trousers, turned up several times; a white, linen shirt, many sizes too large; and a brown satin jacket that hung nearly to her knees. Barefooted, the black curls in artless disarray framing her white face, she stood like a wild creature at bay against the door.

Setting the candle down after that first amused appraisal, he ignored her and threw some wood on the coals that glowed dimly on the hearth. Then he casually sat down and turned to stare at her once more.

Catherine, keeping her eyes carefully averted from his body, was very conscious of his nakedness. His narrowed stare was unsettling, and she gave a nervous start when he asked in a harsh voice, "And where do you think you're going?"

Righteous indignation brought her simmering temper blazingly to the fore, and angrily, hands on her hips, she advanced upon his relaxed body. "You have no right to question me! I'm leaving, and where I'm going is none of your business. You can't keep me here, and if you don't unlock the door instantly, I shall scream this inn down!" She didn't dare do such a thing, but told herself consolingly, *he* didn't know that!

For a moment, they glared at one another; then, just as Catherine began to fear he had called her bluff, he shrugged his shoulders indifferently and rose from his seat. Arrogance in every movement, he kicked the chair from the door and after unlocking it, stepped aside, a sardonic look on his face as he motioned for her to leave.

Puzzled by his easy compliance, she threw him a wary glance before turning stiffly towards the unlocked door. She had barely turned her back on him when he moved like a hunting panther, one hand striking out to crush the startled cry she gave as his other arm closed around her waist. Holding her tightly against his chest, he lifted her from the floor, and as her kicking heels drummed against his shins, her hands clawing to break his hold, he calmly carried her back into the bedroom and threw her face-down on the bed.

She managed a muffled scream of pure rage before he brutally shoved her face deeper into the soft feather mattress. Then tearing loose the silk rope pull from the canopy, he captured her wildly striking arms and tied them tightly behind her back. Catherine tried to free herself from the suffocating pressure of the mattress against her face as Jason held one knee painfully on the nape of her neck, and she fought for air; from somewhere above her, he snarled, "I'll keep you as long as I please and where I please. When I no longer desire you, I'll let you know! Until then, you'll stay where I want you!"

When her arms were tied, he suddenly flipped her over onto her back. Then holding her prisoner between his legs, one hand held over her mouth, he reached up and shook the pillowcase free and gagged her with it. Her violet eyes burned almost purple with rage at his savage, coldblooded action. His chest was heaving slightly when he finally rose from the bed. Then grasping the long-bladed knife, which was never far from his side, he approached the bed once more, and for the first time Catherine actually feared for her life. His face hard, his green eyes narrowed, he cut another length from the mangled bed pull. Then glancing at Catherine's rigid form, he methodically slashed away every scrap of clothing she wore, as she waited icily calm and certain that any moment she would feel that cold blade slide fatally into her body.

But murder wasn't on his mind, for when he had her naked, he quickly roped her ankles together and tied them securely to the end of the bed. Satisfied, he sat back on his heels and grinning down into her blazing eyes, said ruefully, "I shouldn't have tied your legs together, *chérie!* But then, I suppose it's best, for if I started to make love to you this morning, I would be late for the duel with Clive."

Shock at his words drove the anger from her eyes, but Jason, yawning hugely and intent upon getting dressed, never noticed. And in silent, confused fury, she watched him as he moved about the room.

Jason was almost completely dressed when the sound of voices coming up the stairs caused him to carelessly throw the blankets over her, leaving only her tangled black hair and violet eyes showing. Then he walked without a backwards glance from the room. Laying helpless, she heard him open the door and speak to someone. Then, the sound of rattling crockery assailed her ears, and she guessed rightly that Pierre, acting as butler, must have entered with breakfast. Pierre wasn't alone, for she heard a different male voice complain, "I say, Jas, this is a devilish hour to be up. Why are these blasted things always held at dawn! Someone should make it the fashion to meet at a more civilized hour—say an hour before afternoon tea."

Jason laughed. "Mmmm, the next time I issue a challenge, I shall insist upon it, my friend. Have you and Harris eaten?"

Harris spoke up hastily, "Nothing for me. Afterwards!"

But Barrymore, his blue eyes filled with excitement said, "I'll have some of that excellent ham, if you don't mind. Ignore Tom, he's always a glum fellow until a duel is over. Never knew such a fusspot!"

Catherine, listening to their lighthearted conversation, felt sick with apprehension. Oh God, what if Tom saw her! But maybe, she thought hopefully, not expecting her, he wouldn't recognize her, and it had been more than a year since last they had met. She should be grateful Jason hadn't had her join them for breakfast, and she thought wryly that the only good thing to come from her abortive attempt to flee this morning was the fact that he wasn't at this moment showing her off as his latest mistress! She moved uncomfortably under the blankets, the silk rope cutting into her tender wrists and ankles, while the gag nearly choked her. How long before he freed her? How long did it take to fight a duel? she wondered despairingly. She might be here for hours before Jason returned, unless, she thought hopefully, he'd leave instructions for his valet to release her. But then, she decided, she didn't like the idea of another man seeing her so helpless. Jason was bad enough!

Her thoughts were extremely unhappy as she lay there, honesty compelling her to admit that the present situation was her own fault. Unfortunately, it was cold comfort, and she wondered wretchedly if Rachael already missed her from the house. How long did Jason intend to keep her? If only he'd release her soon, there was a chance she could return home and smooth Rachael's anxious questions. Her thoughts shied away from the memory of Jason's rape and his later lovemaking; just now she wasn't ready to peer too deeply into her own emotions concerning him. At the moment all she wanted was escape and a chance to recover herself and view objectively the entire incident.

She realized it was quiet in the other room, and correctly assuming the three men had left for the meeting with Clive, she wondered for the first time the reason behind the duel. It wasn't like Clive to expose himself to possible danger, and he must have been hard pressed not to have avoided the coming confrontation.

Pierre's entry into the room scattered her restless thoughts, and warily she watched him as he walked across the room. He cast her an extremely curious look but then began to pick up the torn and ripped clothing, muttering to himself as he did so. That he was eaten up with speculation was obvious, but it was equally apparent Jason must have given him explicit instructions concerning her, for while he glanced frequently at her still form, he addressed no conversation her way and for the most part seemed to ignore her.

Idly watching Pierre as he opened the wardrobe and began to remove Jason's remaining clothes, Catherine wished she had known earlier of the coming duel. To escape from the valet, she decided, would have been an easy task. But when she had wakened this morning and seen that Jason still slept heavily, it had seemed such an excellent chance to escape. If only she hadn't had to light that blasted candle and root through his clothes to find something to wear! Balefully she glared at the pile of feminine clothes Jason had tossed on the chair last night. Why couldn't she have remembered them? Probably, she told herself viciously, because she was too busy feeling sorry for herself to notice much of anything. So, instead of snatching up one of the dresses almost under her fingertips, she had lost costly minutes putting on his clothing. And even then, she hadn't followed her instincts and fled from the inn, but with Clive's blackmail threat in mind, had proceeded to search feverishly through Jason's belongings for the map Clive wanted so badly. She only took a few minutes, but it was long enough for Jason to grumble in his sleep; and even though she had hastily blown out the light and made to escape, she had unfortunately stumbled over a chair in the darkness, and its noisy scraping along the floor had alerted Jason to her position.

If only she hadn't wasted that precious time searching for something Clive wasn't even positive existed, she thought bitterly. But it had seemed so logical; Jason was sleeping soundly, and she was already here, in his room, so why not? How stupid she had been not to think that he'd wake and catch her! The unpalatable knowledge that she owed this present situation to her own stubborn foolishness made her squirm under the covers, and she fought against a sudden, childish desire to cry. Her arms were beginning to ache, and determinedly she turned her reproachful thoughts away from herself and focused on Pierre once more. Numbly she watched as he folded and packed Jason's clothes and personal objects in a large leather-bound trunk, and abruptly, the purpose behind the valet's precise movements leaped through her startled brain.

In her rapid search through the two packed trunks in the room, she hadn't grasped their significance. But now it was obvious that Jason was in the process of preparing to leave, and surprisingly, her first emotion was curiosity about his destination, before the ominous thought occurred to her that he might be planning for her to go with him. Almost ill with anxiety, she told herself staunchly not to be a goose! Jason would release her when he returned. He had only acted as he had to teach her a lesson, to satisfy his bruised male pride. Not, pray God, because he intended to keep her indefinitely.

Pierre's next actions seemed to belie her frail prayer, for he unconcernedly began to gather from the jumble of silks on the chair an assortment of clothing only a woman would wear. And after that, he disappeared into the other room, only to return with more feminine oddments from which he carefully selected a pair of pale pink kid half boots and a pelisse of fine dark blue wool, before packing the remainder in a smaller trunk.

Now, with an increasingly hollow sensation in the region of her stomach, Catherine eyed the deep rose dress of soft muslin and the lacy chemise that Pierre placed on a chair. And suddenly it struck her forcibly that it was odd that a gentleman should possess women's clothing. Malevolently she decided Jason kept them available to pay off his little amusements. She would have been astonished to learn that these particular silks and laces had been bought with her in mind—that after their stormy meeting in the meadow he had ridden into Melton Mowbray and had spent several enjoyable hours choosing these garments for her to wear.

Determined not to dwell upon Jason's reasons for having a variety of feminine apparel in his possession, she watched listlessly as Pierre finished his tasks, repeatedly encouraging herself not to give in to the bleak despair that was beginning to creep through her entire body. Pierre's horrified exclamation, as he took a last check of the other two trunks and discovered the havoc she had created in her lightning search, caused her to give a guilty start, and her eyes slid away from the look of hostile speculation he gave her.

Dawn was only seconds away, and a gray, patchy fog lent a sinister air to the small clearing chosen as the dueling place. The trees encircling the spot were bare of leaves, the pale green nubs along their limbs just ready to burst forth in greeting to spring, and the dark branches reached like beseeching arms heavenward as if praying for the sun to appear; but the sun was being sulky, almost as if she objected to starting the day in such a violent fashion. The grass was damp with dew, and there was the faint sound of dripping water as the heavy moisture collected on the naked branches and then fell to the ground with a soft, dismal, plopping noise.

Thoughtfully, Jason watched Clive dismount from his carriage and noted the odd fact that Pendleton's seconds, Phillipe de Courcey and Anthony Newhope, had traveled in their own vehicle. His eyes swung back to Clive's coach, and he viewed with sudden suspicion the baggage that was strapped to the top and back of the coach. From all appearances, it looked as if Mr. Pendleton was prepared for flight.

The same thought must have occurred to Barrymore because he hissed in Jason's ear, "I don't like the looks of this! If Pendleton's determined to make this a killing matter and is lucky enough to succeed, he'd have to leave the country in a hurry, and his coach looks as if it's packed for a damned long journey. You better be careful, Jas. I'm glad I insisted upon the sawbones being here!"

Jason grunted a reply, while his bored gaze wandered

briefly over the doctor, standing a little apart from the others, his small black leather bag resting near his feet.

There were only curt nods of greeting as the six men met, and solemnly the pistols were chosen. They had already agreed upon the twenty paces, so the two duelists were quickly, silently divested of their outer coats, both wearing dark clothing devoid of any shining object that would give the other a target for better aim. Coolly, Jason surveyed Clive, wondering again at the man's unexpected animosity, before mentally shrugging his shoulders. If the reason for the burning hate that gleamed in the gray eyes was important, he'd find it out some day, and if it wasn't, who cared what devils drove the man?

Harris was chosen to call out the paces, and nervously the first steps were called from his dry mouth, while Barrymore, his concern for Jason increasing with every step the two men took, stared gloomily at the widening distance between them before pinning his bright blue gaze on Pendleton's back as the count neared twenty. It was Barrymore's shocked gasp of horror that warned Jason, and instinctively he hurled himself to the damp ground, rolling swiftly onto his back as he did so. A bullet snarled past in the empty air, where only a second ago his head had been, and the quiet morning air was shattered by the crack of a pistol. Icily, he surveyed Pendleton's smoking pistol and as he took careful, deliberate aim, heard Barrymore cry savagely, "You swine, Pendleton! You jumped the count! That was intentional murder! You'll not leave this ground alive, I can tell you, for I shall kill you myself!"

But even as Barrymore started forward, Jason fired, the startling sound of his belated shot nearly rocking the others on their heels, and with great satisfaction he saw Pendleton, surprise on his face, sway and crumple. A grim smile on his lips, Jason leaped to his feet and ignoring Barrymore's and Harris's astonished expressions, asked politely, "My coat, Barrymore, if you please? It's devilishly cold out here, and that damn grass was wet."

Stunned relief made Barrymore almost stumble in his haste

to comply, and he babbled, "That was the sweetest piece of shooting I've ever seen, upon my word it was! But what a ghastly thing to have happened. I was certain you were dead. Thank God, Pendleton is a terrible shot and missed you!"

"He didn't miss me, my friend. I merely took advantage of your theatrical gasp of surprise and threw myself away from his line of fire."

"Theatrical! Well, I like that! I save your life, and you're damned ungrateful."

Jason avoided the accusing blue eyes. Clapping his friend on the shoulder, he prodded him in the direction of the fallen man. The doctor was kneeling beside Pendleton, effectively stopping the blood that welled from a high shoulder wound.

As the three men approached, Newhope, his young face red with mortification, blurted, "I must offer you my apologies. I'm greatly shocked by what has happened!"

"Apologies!" Barrymore broke in heatedly. "How can you stomach the fellow? When today's events are learned, he'll be lucky if he's not hounded from England!"

With his uncle's conversation in mind, Jason interrupted smoothly, "What happened this morning would be best forgotten. Let it suffice that we met, and I wounded my man."

Harris, his red hair nearly standing on end, turned to stare with disbelieving brown eyes at Jason. "You aren't going to do anything about it?" he asked incredulously, while Barrymore was for once dumbstruck.

Jason laughed. "*Mon ami,* I've already *shot* the man! What more do you want me to do? Let someone else create the latest scandal."

Reluctantly, like a terrier with a bone, Harris allowed himself to be persuaded from crying Pendleton's infamy from the rooftops of fashionable London, and as they walked to the carriage, Barrymore muttered dire threats of what he'd do if the choice was up to him!

The first warning Catherine had of Jason's return was his laughing voice, a thread of steel running through it as he said, "Enough, my friends, let it lie. I will not change my mind! I might add that I'm greatly shocked to discover what bloodthirsty savages you've turned out to be! I never would have suspected it."

Unaccountably pleased that he was alive and apparently unhurt, she lay there listening as the three made themselves comfortable. But then, the knowledge that soon she would have to face that mocking green gaze, caused all her nebulous fears to come rushing back, and her heart gave a leap of fright when Jason, followed closely by Pierre, suddenly appeared in the doorway.

It was patently obvious that Pierre hadn't wasted a moment before acquainting Jason with the fact that his trunks had been searched. It was equally obvious that Pierre had also stated whom he thought had gone through them, and Catherine held her breath as Jason crossed the room and after viewing the tumbled contents curtly commanded Pierre to repack them. That Jason was furious was very apparent, and from the angry thinning of his lips and the black look he threw her before striding from the room, Catherine knew that when he returned she had better have some answers for the extremely pointed questions he was bound to ask.

Resentment, warring with pride, stiffened her backbone as silently she vowed never to tell him why she had gone through his belongings. After the way he had treated her—why should she? Truculently she awaited his return, straining to hear what was being said in the other room. She couldn't overhear what he said to Barrymore and Harris to make them leave, but she did hear the heavy door shut and Barrymore's grumbling farewell.

Surprisingly, Jason did not immediately turn to her when he entered the room but instead stood watching broodingly as Pierre finished repacking the trunks and removed them from the room. It was then, when they were alone, that he walked determinedly to her side, a cold, implacable look on his face. He stripped back the concealing blankets with one angry jerk, and Catherine willed herself to meet his gaze.

Her violet eyes never wavered from his as challengingly she stared back at him. Insolently, his eyes traveled over her rigid body, his only sign of emotion the slight jump of a muscle in one lean cheek. The ensuing silence clawed at Catherine's nerves, and she couldn't control a shiver of alarm when suddenly he reached out and almost gently enclosed one small breast with his warm hand.

A mirthless smile curved his lips, and instinctively she sensed love-making wasn't on his mind as he casually fondled her breast. Her throat felt tight as if she had downed a glass of sand, and nervously she tried to swallow, bracing herself for whatever was coming. But she was unable to still a small moan of pure agony as cruelly he dug his fingers into her soft flesh, deliberately inflicting excruciating pain. His eyes, like frozen emeralds, stared down into her pain-contorted face and unemotionally he said, "That's just a sample, my little white-skinned witch, of what I can do to you. When I ungag you, you'd better tell me exactly what I want to know, or I'll really hurt you. Understand?"

Catherine nodded, a ragged sigh of relief escaping from her white lips as he quickly released his grip on her breast. With sharp, decisive strokes, he cut her ankles loose, and cautiously she sat up, unbelieving that the man who had made such tender love to her last night could be this grim-faced stranger who hurt her so painfully. Then glancing down at her breast, her eyes widened as she saw the imprint of his fingers still vividly red against the paleness of her skin. And bitterly she reminded herself of his rape and the brutal way he had treated her this morning.

Outwardly docile, she waited for his next move, and with every passing second her earlier resolution not to tell him what he wanted to know hardened. Coolly her eyes met the grim determination in his as he slowly undid the pillowcase from her mouth. It was such blessedness to be free of it that for a minute she did nothing but savor the pleasant fact that the gag no longer bit into her mouth.

His voice jerked her nastily back to the present as he said

harshly, "Before you try it, I should warn you that if you scream, it will be the last sound you'll ever make. Now, what were you searching for?"

"Money!" she answered, her chin thrust belligerently forward.

He appeared startled for a moment, as if that idea had never occurred to him, but then his mouth tightened. "Money, my dear?" he asked silkily. "I think not!" His hand closed threateningly around her slender neck, and he shook his head slowly. "You weren't searching for money. My gold watch and money were lying out in plain sight, but you ignored them. Or are you going to tell me you overlooked them?" he asked mockingly.

Her soft mouth hardened, and stubbornly she spat, "I'm not telling you anything! Why should I? You've kidnapped me, raped me, and made life intolerable for me." Breathing heavily, her eyes flashing purple fire, and an exhilarating turmoil raging through her, she gave full rein to her temper and taunted, "Go ahead, hit me! My arms are bound, and I can't stop you. What are you waiting for? But whatever you do, I'll never, never tell you why I went through those trunks. I'd rather die than tell you!"

Thoughtfully he regarded her, his gaze disconcertingly dwelling on the willful set of her mouth before their eyes locked in a silent battle of wills. Then he completely astounded her by grinning and saying, "Pax, little witch! You're too pretty to mark up, and I'll find out eventually what you were looking for."

Then he added to her confusion by abruptly reaching behind her and freeing her arms. Warily she stared at him as she thankfully rubbed the circulation back into her numb arms. Snatching up the rose-colored dress and the lacy chemise, he tossed them to her saying, "We'll continue this interesting conversation later, but for now, you'd better get dressed. We have a long journey before us."

An embarrassed cough caused both of them to turn and stare at Tom Harris, who hesitated in the doorway, his face nearly as red as his hair. He mumbled, "Am, um, excuse me, Savage, didn't know you had um—a lady with you!"

Unperturbed to be found with a naked young woman seated upon his bed, Jason merely asked, "What is it, Tom? Did you forget something?"

Catherine, clutching the dress, looked with horror at Amanda's brother. Oh, God, please don't let him recognize me, she prayed.

Unfortunately, Tom, who seldom remembered anything, remembered her from the few times he had taken pity on his little sister and visited with her when she had been attending Mrs. Siddon's Seminary for Young Ladies. And though he thought he recognized her as Amanda's friend, he was slow-witted enough and enough of a true gentleman not to believe the evidence of his eyes and looked, after that first stunned glance, everywhere but at the black-haired girl on Jason's bed.

Instantly aware that something wasn't right, Jason frowned, staring first at Catherine's plainly horrified face and then at Harris's carefully blank expression. Finally he asked quietly, "You know each other?" And his eyes narrowed with speculation when both burst out simultaneously, emphatically, "No!"

Harris babbled further, "Never saw the girl before! Talk to you later!" and bolted from the room.

"Now, what the hell was that all about?" Jason demanded, and Catherine was momentarily saved from answering by Pierre's entrance into the room.

"Monsieur, everything is packed. Will you need me to attend to anything else?"

After a quick lightning glance around the room, Jason replied, "I believe that will be all, Pierre. You may go now. I'll meet you in London."

16

Worn out and more confused than she could ever remember being, Catherine was thankful when they finally arrived at Jason's lodgings on St. James's Street in London. Too much had happened in the past twenty-four hours for her to do much more than view with dull eyes the small attic room in which, after he had fed her a late supper and once again stripped her naked, Jason had locked her in and departed.

The four walls of the room were bare. A straw pallet and some blankets were on the floor in one corner. A rickety chest, upon which sat a pitcher filled with water and a small bowl, constituted the remaining furnishings. Bewildered, she stood in the shadowed room, a shaft of silver moonlight coming from a tiny window above her head breaking the blackness. Eventually the chill of the room drove her to huddle on the pallet, the blankets warming her naked form as she stared unseeingly about the room.

Shock, regret, disbelief, and anxiety chained her to that room as surely as iron manacles, and tiredly she leaned her head back against the wall. Why had she taken the time to search for that map? she asked herself mournfully. If—but what was the use of futile longings? She was caught, and until an opportunity for escape presented itself, she must remain wherever Jason wanted her.

Tom Harris's incredulous recognition had sickenly clarified the whole unsavory wretchedness of the situation, and she could only pray that he would hold his tongue. Bitterly, she admitted she should have thrown herself at Tom's feet and begged him to save her, but false pride, the hope that somehow she could escape and be able to pretend that last night had never happened, sealed the plea before it was spoken. As it was, she faced certain ruin, for Rachael would surely institute a frantic search for her missing daughter, and in view of the much earlier scandal, it was unlikely a second disappearance of Lady Catherine would go unnoticed!

No trace of her would be found in Leicestershire, for barely had she swallowed a mouthful of breakfast when Jason had almost literally dragged her from the inn to his waiting curricle. She had thought of throwing herself from the fast-moving vehicle, but Jason must have sensed her half-formed intention, for a few miles from the inn, he halted the horses. Then, quickly he bound her arms beneath the blue pelisse, effectively killing any notion she may have had of escape. He warned her, in cold tones, that if she attempted to beg for interference, he would state she was his mad sister, that he was returning her to Bedlam and to pay her no mind.

All through the nightmarish events, she had cherished the faint hope that scandal could be averted if she could only escape, but now, locked miles away in London in a small attic room, there seemed little likelihood she would ever escape, much less return home again. With a despairing sob, she buried her face in her hands, moaning, "Reina, Reina, oh, why didn't I listen? Why was I so certain I could dance with fire and remain unburned?"

Traitorous tears suddenly flooded her eyes, and her slender body was shaken with great tearing sobs that painfully ripped through her chest. How long she sat crying, sunk in misery, she didn't know; but gradually the tears lessened and from somewhere deep within an unquenchable flame of ruthless determination to somehow surmount her difficulties began to burn brightly. A militant sparkle in her violet eyes, she lifted her head proudly and vowed fiercely that not only would she overcome her disastrous plight, but that one day Jason Savage's cold-blooded behavior would be punished! He must be compelled to suffer the humiliating anguish he had dealt her. She would see his insolent pride shattered if it took her entire life. Viciously, she promised herself she would destroy him.

Strangely comforted by her grim vows of vengeance, the tight ball of fear and misery that had lodged in her chest slowly disappeared, leaving her feeling drained and depleted. Calmer now, almost content, she settled down for the night, curling like a small child on the pallet to sleep the dreamless sleep of the young.

It was late in the afternoon when she woke, feeling surprisingly refreshed—the vindictive resolutions of the night before still clear and firm in her mind. Escape was the first step. She wrapped one of the blankets like a sarong around her naked body, splashed some of the water from the pitcher on her face, and attempted to restore some order to her tangled mass of hair. Then she surveyed the room, unconsciously hoping that last night in her dispirited mood she had overlooked some way out.

Unfortunately, she hadn't. The only exits remained the door and the small window high above her head. The stout oak door was firmly locked from the other side. Childishly she gave in to a wave of black temper and swung a vicious kick at the door, received a bruise for her pains, then removed the bowl and pitcher from the chest and dragged it across the floor, positioning it beneath the tiny window.

So intent was her effort that the sudden opening of the door made her gasp with surprise, and she nearly toppled from the chest on which she had climbed. Recovering herself quickly, she watched Jason saunter in, carrying a large silver tray. At the sight of the plates filled with ham, yellow cheese, and thick slices of generously buttered bread, her earlier resolutions nearly evaporated. She grimly ignored the low growl of hunger that her stomach gave and gazed disdainfully at him.

Slamming the door shut with a well-aimed kick of one booted foot, Jason set the tray down on the pallet and, grinning, viewed her position. Cocking an eyebrow, his voice teasing, he asked, "Was it a mouse that led you up there, or are you expecting a flood?"

At his tone, Catherine's lips tightened with displeasure. Already feeling foolish, she glared resentfully at him and bit back the scathing words that crowded her throat.

Amused rather than angered by her actions, he crossed the room and almost laughing out loud at her ruffled expression, swung her down easily from the chest. Then, his hands tightening their hold around her slender waist, he pulled her against him and leisurely kissed her.

"Mmmmm, *petite,* I missed you last night," he murmured against her soft throat, when at last he released her unwilling mouth. "If you persist in this unnatural desire to flee from me, I shall have Pierre lock us in together every night!"

Catherine, breathless and feeling as if she had been flung into a whirlpool, stepped determinedly away from him, fighting the spinning emotions he aroused so effortlessly. Fiercely reminding herself of his past treacheries and his brutal disregard of her feelings, she quelled the warm, throbbing ache that flared at his disturbing touch. Holding herself stiffly erect, she pushed past him and with quickened steps walked to the pallet. Sitting on her haunches, she almost gave in to a primitive desire to wolf down the food, but exercising great self-control, she compelled herself to eat slowly, lingering over each mouthful as if it were her last.

Jason lounged casually against one wall, his arms crossed over his chest, a speculative gleam in his green eyes.

Chewing a morsel of the delicious ham, she regarded him

thoughtfully. As usual he was tastefully dressed, wearing a slim-fitting pair of buff nankeen trousers and an embroidered, yellow piqué vest, which in spite of its conventional style gave him a flamboyant air. She distrusted his outward appearance of lazy calm and thought he was in one of those misleadingly charming moods, but she was uncertain, knowing he could change instantly and for no apparent reason into a harsh-faced stranger. But if he was in a charming mood, wouldn't this be the time to confess who she was? She played with the idea, but fear, fear of so many things held her silent. If he believed her—that she was truly Lady Catherine Tremayne—who knew what havoc the resulting furor would create? The thought of the reactions of her relatives was enough to cause her blood to run cold—she could hear all the malicious gossip right now. And there was Rachael—she just couldn't bear to shame Rachael further. Far better if she kept a still tongue between her teeth and took the first chance of escape. And again the unnerving thought occurred to her—Jason Savage was perfectly capable of brushing aside her explanations as if they didn't exist. She stared at him wondering bitterly what he *would* do if he knew the true story. She finally decided that, if he didn't throttle her on the spot, she would be lucky to escape with her life. He did not strike her as a man who would take kindly to being duped—even if it was his own folly that had led to the mistake. Catherine continued looking at him, and he moved somewhat restlessly under her unblinking stare.

He had expected tears, recriminations, or threats, but this silent, seemingly meek acceptance aroused his suspicions, and the teasing glint in his eyes vanished, leaving them hard and watchful.

Swallowing a last bite of cheese, she asked coldly, "How much longer do you intend to keep me?"

A black, thick brow flew up at her tone. "Until you learn better manners, my dear," he said.

Clenching her fist tightly, she fought the urge to fly clawing at him and asked instead, "Doesn't it bother you that I hate you? That I have no wish to be your mistress?"

Her lips thinned when he laughed, "I'm afraid not! You see, little baggage, you've begun to intrigue me. You don't follow the usual pattern of your kind." At her blank look he added, "You drove a hard bargain in the meadow, yet sent that old witch to my bed. You're supposed to be Clive Pendleton's mistress, but I discover you were very definitely a virgin. You search my luggage, tell me you were after money, but ignore the gold lying on the table. Your inconsistencies would fascinate me even if I didn't already find you extremely desirable."

Unable to continue staring at his mocking face without losing her temper, she dropped her gaze and watched her fingers intently for a moment as they aimlessly pleated the blanket. Then she asked carefully, "If I told you what I was searching for—would you let me go?"

There was a long, tense pause. It was on the tip of Jason's tongue to lie; but he bit back the affirmative answer she so obviously wanted and snapped harshly, "No!"

Abruptly, he left off his lazy stance and snatched her up from the pallet, dragging her roughly into his arms, his mouth closing ruthlessly over hers. Unsuccessfully, she battled against a queer flash of pleasure that washed over her as his kiss deepened, his tongue seeking, then probing the honey of her mouth. With one easy movement he swept away the blanket between them. Forcing herself to strain away from him, Catherine willed her body not to respond, not to give in to the wild urge to meet his hungry demand with one of her own.

Jason, furiously aware that she was deliberately holding herself aloof from the scalding desire that was sweeping through him, muttered savagely, "Don't enjoy it, then!" And he threw her on the pallet. Tearing her legs apart, he took her brutally, not caring if he hurt her or if he gave pleasure, intent only on his own satisfaction.

His big body slamming into her was like a fiery blade in

her belly, and frenziedly she fought to escape the burning, stabbing pain between her legs. But he held her fast, staring indifferently down into her face, uncaring that she clawed an ugly, bloody gash down one cheek or that he received little pleasure from the soft body thrashing beneath his. Finished, he rolled off and snarled, "Resign yourself to the fact that until I find you less of a puzzle, I intend to keep you."

Standing up in one lithe movement, he watched unmoved as she sat up painfully. Glaring at him through tear-filled eyes, she spat, "I hate you, Jason Savage! Someday, if it takes me a hundred years, I'll get even with you!"

A tight smile on his mouth, he said, "Hate me, my dear, all you want. I couldn't care less. I never said I wanted you to love me. Anything I want from you I can take any time I please."

Speechless with the rage that twisted her tongue, she haughtily gathered the blanket about her as if it were made of silk. She stood up, and stony-faced, she asked, "Will you leave now? You've taken what you came for, so there's obviously no reason for you to remain with me any longer."

"Ah, but there is! And I really had no intention of raping you again when I entered the room."

"I suppose you merely came to see that I was comfortable in my elegant surroundings?"

Thoughtfully touching the bloody groove on his cheek, he said slowly, "I'm inclined to believe that in addition to learning some manners, someone should teach you to hold that ready tongue of yours."

"Are *your* manners so wonderful?" she asked through gritted teeth.

He grinned suddenly. "No! Mine are terrible!" Then he added wickedly, "But you see, *I'm* not an impudent baggage, so people overlook mine, but yours. . . ." His voice trailed off suggestively.

The frustrated fury that had been smoldering inside her for hours exploded, and giving a scream of sheer rage, she flew at him, her fingers outstretched, intent on clawing his mocking face to shreds. He met her furious charge with a laugh, easily trapping her arms at her sides, and caught her up next to his hard body. Thrashing like a wild thing, she threw up her head and accidentally cracked him a painful blow on the chin. A surprised grunt escaped him, and in spite of the shower of sparks before her eyes, she managed to deliberately repeat the process. But it wasn't quite as effective, for he merely lifted his chin out of the way. Goaded beyond reason, she bit him savagely on his breast, her sharp little teeth cutting through the piqué waistcoat and even the linen shirt beneath it. With intense satisfaction she heard him yell and felt his fingers purposefully tangle in her long hair. It was worth even the pain of his jerking her away from him, breaking her vicious bite, to know that she had hurt him.

His breast smarting, Jason stared grimly down into her upturned face. Jesus Christ! What a little firebrand! He ought to toss her out in the gutter and have done with her. But even as he thought it, his gaze lingered on the willful mouth, and he was conscious of a sense of displeasure. Most women found him attractive, so why did this slip of a girl keep fighting him? His mouth tightened as she twisted in his grasp, still apparently determined to do battle.

Catherine's head hurt from the crack she had given him on the chin, and his fingers, pulling her back by the long hair only added to the throbbing pain that was pounding in her temples. But resolved not to retreat, she glowered so fiercely at him that he was suddenly reminded of a thwarted kitten and couldn't control an amused twitch at the corner of his mouth. Incredulously, she stared as he began to smile, and slowly he released the painful grip on her hair.

Holding her firmly away from him, he asked, "Shall we cry quits again? You've managed to scar my face, and I shall probably wear your teeth marks for some days to come. All things considered, I think you are the decided victor—this time."

Catherine gave a small, wary nod. His abrupt reversals were confusing, and she wished desperately he would either remain the hard-faced man who sometimes frightened her or stay the beguiling, fascinating stranger. One man she could hate, but the other! . . . When he smiled crookedly at her as he was doing now, one black lock of hair falling carelessly across his brow, she fell prey to a treacherous, trembling sense of excitement, a feeling that at any moment something wonderful was going to happen. Dear God! He twisted her emotions in such knots she couldn't think clearly!

It suddenly dawned on her that she was very close to smiling back at him, and with a shock she discovered the blanket had fallen to the floor. Wiggling from his relaxed hold, she bolted for the protection of the blanket. Wrapped safely in its concealing folds, she turned, surprised to discover he was watching her with a curious expression.

"Are you really that modest? You shouldn't be—you have a lovely body," he said, laughing out loud as a blush burned brightly in her cheeks.

Very much in a good humor, he said, "I can see that in Paris it is going to cost me a fortune to clothe you. I can't have my beautiful mistress garbed in an old blanket. I'm positive you must be longing to be rid of it."

Her eyes grew wide at his mention of Paris, and she whispered, "Paris? Are you really taking me to Paris?"

Smiling broadly, unaware of the icy chill creeping through her body, he replied, "*Mais oui!* And *that,* my cross little kitten, is actually what I came to tell you. I have been busy since last night making arrangements and saying goodbyes. Pierre has prepared a bath for you, and your clothes are ready. As soon as you're dressed, we leave."

Mistaking the sudden stricken look, he tipped her head gently back with one long finger and said, "I know you must be weary of these mad dashes across England. Once we reach Paris, I can assure you we'll be there for some time. I'm thinking of renting a château outside the city, and in Paris, I'll buy you all the feminine finery your heart desires."

The icy numbness increased its grip, and stupidly she

stared at him. Growing annoyed with her lack of enthusiasm, he chided, "Come now. I promised you a trip to Paris originally. I would think you would be happy that I'm honoring our bargain."

A stiff-lipped smile was his only answer, and impatiently he hastened her down the stairs to his own bedchamber. There he continued to prod her until she was bathed and dressed, and at last they were once again in the carriage, this time heading for Dover.

It was a beautiful spring day, with several hours remaining before dark, and as the shining black horses sped down the road, Catherine found herself forgetting the circumstances surrounding this journey and enjoying the fading yellow sunlight. She could almost pretend that Jason was her suitor and they were on their way for a pleasant afternoon outing. As the hours passed and the night closed over them, she pushed away the now familiar worries and arguments that began to buzz in her head and let a queer tranquil feeling of acceptance, of a waiting for the right opportunity, invade her body and still the barren thoughts.

It was only in the gray dawn when they stepped on the boat that would take her from England that the strange tranquility left her. She knew a wild feeling of panic, a feeling that if she didn't escape now she would never be free again. But Jason, watchful and curiously comforting, halted her involuntary movement to flee by simply sweeping her up in his arms and carrying her to their cabin. He left her almost immediately, locking the door behind him. Catherine, resembling a trapped, dumb animal, gazed about the small cabin, thinking wildly that at least, this time, he had left her clothed.

PART TWO

BITTERSWEET SPRING

France, Spring 1803

17

The ride from the ferry to Paris was nearing its end. They had left behind the pale green, rolling hills and quaint white farmhouses that sat back from the road. They would soon be in the city. Catherine had not acquired Jason's knack for sleeping in the lumbering coach, and she was looking forward to the journey's end.

They had stopped at posting inns along the way only long enough for a change of horses and a hurried meal, which often consisted of Jason ordering a basket of sandwiches so they would not have to linger at the next stop. Once they were held up for several hours while a broken spokc in one of the wheels was repaired. Watching Jason pace the floor of the private sitting room of the provincial inn, Catherine was conscious of the fact that Jason's impatience to reach Paris had little to do with her. Her fears that she would spend the journey fighting off his attempts at lovemaking had proven groundless. He was barely aware that she was in the coach with him and seemed to have dismissed her from his mind.

She was annoyed to find that his lack of attention bewildered her.

The coach wheel hit a particularly deep rut in the road—France's roads were even worse than England's and England's were ghastly—and though the whole vehicle shook from the impact, Jason who had been asleep for some time continued to sleep, his loose-limbed body swaying in unison with the jolting carriage.

Quietly she studied him, noting how in sleep his face still had an exciting aliveness to it, the harsh lines disappearing, making him look younger—not at all like a man who would kidnap and rape an unwilling woman! But Catherine knew from bitter experience how quickly his expression and intent could change. Frowning, she wondered uneasily exactly what he had planned for her and if eventually he would see that she was returned to England. She knew too little about him to even hazard a guess. Briefly she explored the possibility of throwing herself on his mercy and confessing the truth, but discarded it almost as soon as she thought it. The time for revelations of that nature was long since past, and angrily she berated herself for the stubborn fool she had been.

Lost in her brooding thoughts, Catherine stared moodily out the window. Then, turning her head, she suddenly met Jason's emerald gaze head-on. He had awakened and, with narrowed eyes, had been studying her averted profile. The look in his eyes was so coldly calculating that for one instant she feared he had read her mind. But grimly determined to give him no cause to extract his own humiliating form of punishment, she asked primly, "Did you rest well? You must have been exhausted to have slept so long."

Jason gave her a lazy, amused smile, his green eyes glinting wickedly as he drawled, "How very proper you sound—exactly like some convent-bred schoolgirl." He paused, watching her with open mockery before adding softly, "But we know differently, don't we?"

Catherine swallowed the harsh words that fought to pour

out, and her eyes burning with resentment, she answered tartly, "You may think you know whatever you like. I have no intention of losing my temper, so if you plan to amuse yourself by baiting me, I assure you—you're bound to fail!"

His left eyebrow flew up in surprise at her cool reply, but he completely disconcerted her by asking sharply, "What were you thinking about just now?"

Startled, her violet eyes wide, she countered, "Why? What difference does it make to you what I think?"

He shot her a sparkling look and murmured, "Ordinarily I wouldn't give a damn what any woman was thinking, but I have the uneasy feeling there's something you haven't told me—something I should know!"

Unable to help herself, she blurted, "How do you know that?"

"You have a very expressive face, my little *sorcière infernale,* and I'm afraid your thoughts are rather transparent."

Deeply mortified, she retorted, "If I'm so transparent, why did you ask? Why didn't you just read the answer on my face?"

Grinning at her apparent discomfort, he said, "Ah, but I wanted to be positive!"

She almost rose to the provocation, but guessing he was deliberately goading her into losing her temper, she glared at him venomously and subsided in dignified silence.

For some minutes, there was absolute quiet in the coach until Jason began to point out places of interest on the outskirts of Paris.

Dusk was falling when Jason ushered her across the marble-tiled foyer of the Hotel Crillon and guided her to the long polished counter where the stiffly correct concierge, wearing a somber black and white uniform, awaited them. Catherine stood to one side as arrangements were made for their rooms. Her gown was mussed, and she was hungry and wanted a bath, and she didn't care what the hotel staff thought. But she jerked as one stuck with a pin when the concierge murmured, "If Madame and Monsieur Savage will follow me?" and escorted them to a magnificent suite of rooms on the third floor.

After giving them a tour of the two bedrooms, each with separate dressing rooms and sitting rooms, he turned to Jason apologetically. "Our instructions did not reveal that Madame Savage would be with you. We shall make certain that an extra room is prepared for madame's maid near your valet's quarters. May I add that if Madame or Monsieur needs the services of the Hotel Crillon's staff until your own servants arrive, please inform me, and I shall see to it at once!" Then with a low bow, he strode from the room, leaving an ominous silence behind him.

"Madame Savage?" Catherine burst out angrily. Jason turned to her, a mocking smile tugging at the corners of his lips. One heavy black brow rose quizzically at her outraged tone of voice.

"Would you prefer I blazoned the fact that I have brought my mistress with me?" he asked dryly. "The Crillon is a conservative and highly respectable hotel. When my uncle sent word ahead of my arrival, he didn't know you were traveling with me. He still doesn't for that matter. If he had known, I'm certain he would have made more discreet arrangements."

A decidedly nasty gleam in her violet eyes, Catherine marveled with false innocence, "Could it be you actually care what people think of your actions? I never would have guessed it from your past performance. But then, perhaps this uncle of yours is someone you admire. I wonder—would he condone rape and abduction?"

Ignoring her obvious sarcasm, Jason shrugged his broad shoulders indifferently. "My uncle's views of my morals are already well known to me, and you might be surprised how often his opinion of me agrees with yours."

He walked over to the heavy carved door that opened onto the carpeted main hallway. "I will order a bath prepared for you and see that a maid is sent to unpack your things, meager though they be. As tired as you must be, I suggest that you eat dinner in your rooms and retire early." Not waiting for an answer and without another word, he left.

For a moment, Catherine stared at the closed door with disbelief. He wouldn't just leave her here like this! But as the seconds passed and Jason did not return, it appeared he not only would, but had! Her exhaustion falling away like a veil, she flew across the room and threw open the door. Hesitating in the doorway she glanced quickly in either direction down the wide white and gold hallway, but the corridor was empty, not even one of the black-and-white-clad servants in sight. Standing there she nibbled her full bottom lip, understandably uncertain as to her next move.

Thoughtfully, she stepped back into the room shutting the door firmly behind her. She had no money and nowhere to go. For the present her best line of action would be to accept Jason's highhanded actions. It went against her grain to so docilely submit, but she had not slept well for days, and a definitely vulgar growl of hunger from her empty stomach settled the point—she would wait at least until she had eaten and washed some of the grime of the journey from her body before embarking upon further strategic moves. Almost resigned, she wandered through the elegant apartments, unable to stop herself from exploring curiously.

The suite of rooms was spacious and beautifully appointed. Cream walls and high ceilings with crystal chandeliers blended tastefully with the soft gold of the rugs that clothed the polished wooden floors. Heavy drapes in dark gold velvet hung at the long windows, and Catherine was enchanted to discover a pair of glass-paned doors that opened onto a small balcony.

A tap on the door to the suite interrupted her wanderings, and at her cautious command to enter, the door opened, and a tiny brunette maid with lively brown eyes walked into the room. She gave Catherine a shy smile and dropped a curtsy, murmuring as she did so that she had been sent to help madame and that her name was Jeanne.

The maid's black uniform, with its lacy white apron and matching cap did nothing to detract from Jeanne's youthful freshness. She was undoubtedly pretty, with rosy cheeks that bespoke a country background. She couldn't have been more than sixteen. Watching the girl as she unpacked her few belongings and arranged them in the armoire in the bedchamber, Catherine wondered spitefully if Jason had chosen Jeanne himself—and for other reasons than lady's maid to his so-called *wife!* Instantly ashamed of herself and her suspicious thoughts, she left Jeanne to the unpacking and drifted aimlessly through the empty rooms ignoring the view of Paris at night that was unfolding beneath her windows.

The lamps that lined the cobblestone streets below had been lit, and the glowing yellow light fell in pools of brightness that interspersed the inky blackness of the night. Stylish carriages, pulled by spirited horses whose hooves beat out a soft tattoo of sound, swept by as they carried their fashionable occupants to many dissimilar places of entertainment. Some, no doubt, were on their way to one of the theaters, perhaps the Theater Francais, affectionately known to the Parisians as the House of Molière, or for the gentlemen there were the gambling halls that provided a variety of amusement—not all of it on the dicing tables.

Almost directly across from Catherine's windows was the Place de la Concorde, where a decade before, the unfortunate Louis XVI had lost his throne and his head to the guillotine. Beyond it, the slow-moving Seine River rolled peacefully on its way throughout the sprawling city.

But Catherine, her previous tiredness returning, had no eyes for the intriguing sights, and was delighted when Jeanne announced that her bath was ready.

Hurriedly stripping off her gown, Catherine slipped into the hot, rose-scented water, relishing the silken feel as it flowed over her aching body. A bar of fine rose-smelling soap was floating on the water, and she scrubbed herself from the crown of her black head to the soles of her feet.

Jeanne assisted by keeping the water hot, entering periodically with a copper kettle filled with additional hot water. By the time Catherine had been bathed and her hair rinsed to the satisfaction of both of them, the brass tub was filled to overflowing.

Stepping from the tub, Catherine submitted somewhat gingerly to Jeanne's brisk attention, but the maid was so efficient and impersonal that in no time at all Catherine had been thoroughly dried, dusted lavishly with powder, and helped into a soft white sleeping garment that was positively indecent! She had no time to object, for Jeanne held out a robe of black velvet barely a moment before another knock on the door signaled the arrival of the food Jason had ordered sent up.

Later, drowsily replete from the excellent meal she had eaten and the unaccustomed amount of wine, Catherine lay on the blue sofa sleepily blinking eyes that refused to remain open. Dreamy-eyed, she stared around the room. She felt such a strong sense of physical well-being that it was impossible to think clearly, and it wasn't too many minutes longer before her long-lashed eyes closed, and she slept.

It was very late when Jason returned to the hotel. His message to Livingston asking for an early audience with Monroe had been sent, he had had his meeting with François de Barbé-Marbois, the French minister of finance, and because he and his uncle had decided that it would not come amiss to have family reasons for being in France—not all of the Beauvais family had gone to the New World—Jason had sent notes to relatives who had remained in Paris. After eating dinner in the private dining room at the hotel, he was pleasantly surprised to discover that a cousin was requesting his company in the foyer.

Michel Beauvais was a slim, well-favored young man who had been on the point of leaving for an evening's entertainment at one of the better known gambling spots when Jason's hand-delivered note had arrived. An exceedingly amiable fellow, Michel had instantly decided to stroll over and greet his American cousin. The two young men took to one another instantly, Jason promptly fell in with Michel's offer to show him the night life of the city. And as the evening progressed, Michel proceeded to acquaint Jason with brief, often amusing, accounts of his various relatives—definitely stressing the ones to avoid.

Jason was in a decidedly good mood when he quietly entered the rooms that Catherine had wandered through so aimlessly earlier. He automatically entered the larger bedchamber and after tossing his cravat over one of the high-backed chairs and divesting himself of his boots, he walked through the hushed rooms searching for Tamara.

He hadn't expected to find her in his bed, but had assumed she would certainly be in hers. Staring at the empty bed in her room, he frowned, and thoughtfully rubbing a lean hand across the black stubble that was forming on his chin, he strode impatiently to the smaller of the two salons, stopping abruptly in the middle of the room when he spied Tamara's sleeping form on the sofa.

She lay on her side, the black, silky hair now dry and curling like a glossy cloud about her shoulders. One hand was underneath her cheek, the other lying limply on the floor. Gazing at the delightful picture she presented, Jason's frown vanished, only to be replaced by a curious smile—a smile that was not the usual mocking one nor yet a gentle one, but somewhere between the two. For a minute he stood watching the soft rise and fall of her breasts beneath the black velvet. Then disturbed and distrustful of the sudden wave of tenderness he felt, he determinedly crossed to the sofa and scooping her up in his arms carried her into the bedchamber.

When he discarded her robe and slipped her almost roughly between the warmed sheets of the big bed, she stirred lightly and blinked sleepily like a kitten. Barely awake, she stared up at him through half-shuttered lids, her violet eyes cloudy with sleep. Unable to help himself, Jason's lips found her soft mouth in a long, searing, searching kiss that left Catherine bewilderingly wide awake and Jason angrily confused.

He hadn't meant to kiss her *that* way! He had meant only to drop a light kiss on her mouth. But the moment his lips touched hers, something queer fused between them, her mouth had been warm and seemingly eager for his, her lips parting easily and her tongue answering the probing of his.

Fighting the urge to sink down into the softness of the bed with her and see just how far this sudden acquiescent mood went, Jason looked intently into Catherine's now wide-open eyes. Seconds passed as they stared silently at one another, each as if frozen and unable to break the odd spell—then, muttering an expletive, he turned abruptly on his heels and left.

With unhappy, mixed emotions, Catherine watched his tall form stride from the room. What was happening to her? She hated him! He had dishonored her, treated her brutally, and yet all it took was a full belly and a moment of gentleness for her to melt into his arms like a woman of the streets. Closing her eyes, she swallowed painfully as the memory of what had just passed between them returned. How could she have responded so willingly? And more shocking than that—she had felt unexpected disappointment when he had not continued further. Grimly she reminded herself that she was supposed to take revenge on him, not encourage him to do the very things that had created this situation in the first place. Remember *that,* you silly little fool, she told herself, the next time you feel like returning his embrace!

More equally unpleasant thoughts kept her awake for some minutes longer, but finally, unable to solve any of the immediate problems and the pure, blissful sensation of lying in a bed for the first time in days overriding everything else, she fell asleep for the second time that evening.

Not so Jason, who restlessly paced the floor of his own bedchamber for over an hour before finally succumbing to the need for sleep. Catherine would have been pleased to know that most of that hour was spent by his attempting to explain away the peculiar, unfamiliar emotions that she had made him feel. The harder he sought an explanation, the more confused he became. He fell asleep with a sense of injustice nagging him like a toothache, wishing he had never laid eyes on that damned little gypsy. How dare she trouble his mind!

18

The day was well advanced before either of them awoke, and Catherine, dressed this morning in a white sheath with an overtunic of rose colored silk that belted under her small, firm bosom, was leaning out over the balcony basking in the bright sunlight and straining for a glimpse of the Tuileries Gardens to her left, when Jason behind her spoke. Engrossed in her view, she hadn't heard him enter and gave a startled gasp of surprise when he drawled, "Well, I'm glad to see you're up and dressed. Before I took my bath I looked in on you, and you were still sleeping. Looking, I might add, extremely delectable."

Ignoring as best she could the blatant provocation in his voice, she faced him somewhat warily, glad she wasn't in that indecent garment of the night before. Flashing him a quick glance, her eyes sparkled with resentment at the implied slight. Coolly, pretending her heart was not thumping madly in her breast, she asked, "Was I supposed to be up? I thought you said this would be a holiday for me. Or am I to act as your valet and help you dress?"

The sudden gleam in the green eyes gave her pause. Allowing her to say no more, Jason pulled her into his arms and nibbling her ear whispered, "You arouse no thoughts of dressing, my sweet. Ah, but of undressing—anytime you prefer to offer your services, I would be more than willing to comply with your wishes!"

Torn between a foolish desire to giggle and rage at where her heedless barb had carried her, she was inordinately grateful when a soft tap at the door distracted Jason's attention.

The uniformed servant who entered at Jason's crisp order was not one of the hotel staff, yet Catherine sensed Jason had been expecting him. And it was apparent that the message delivered required no answer, for after handing a sealed note to Jason and pocketing the gold coin passed to him, the messenger inclined his head politely and departed.

Very conscious of Jason's arm still casually around her waist, she watched him covertly as he read, his head slightly bent and a more serious expression than she had ever seen on his face. It only took him a moment to scan the note, and glancing up quickly he caught her staring at him. An embarrassed blush pinkened her cheeks, and she slipped from his arm.

Smiling, Jason mocked, "Playing shy, little one? If you enjoy looking at me, please continue to do so. After all, I enjoy gazing at you!"

Not to be provoked, Catherine stifled the impulse to slap the expectant grin from his handsome face. Presenting him with an excellent view of the back of her head, she seemed absorbed in watching the nervous movements of her hands as they tightened around the balcony rail. Jason studied her straight, stiff back for a minute, then said slowly, "I have to leave you for a while. I'm sorry, but you will have to amuse yourself here while I am gone."

Whirling to face him, she asked in a hard little voice, "Aren't you afraid I will run away?"

"No. If I thought there was the remotest possibility of

that, I would not have left you alone last night. I am not a fool, and you are not as anxious to escape me as you pretend, my little love—and you have no money."

Goaded by his words she almost struck him, but he caught her upraised fist easily and twisting it behind her, pulled her hard against him. Imprisoned next to his muscled length, she glared up at him more furious with herself than him. He had been baiting her deliberately—deliberately trying to make her act as she had. Fuming, she realized it now that it was too late. Lifting her chin pugnaciously, she spat, "Now what? This is what you wanted in the first place, isn't it?"

"No, not really. But you rise so easily to the bait, my little fire-eater, that I can't resist seeing how often you'll leap for the same fly," Jason teased, his mouth hovering just above hers. He tightened his grasp, putting both arms about her slender body and holding her so closely that they merged into one. His mouth slowly wandered from her forehead to the tip of her nose, and then with his lips barely touching hers, he said softly, "I really do have to leave you for a while. Just in case you *do* have any ideas of running away—you can forget them! I think you should know that before I left the hotel last night, I had an illuminating conversation with the concierge and Jeanne. It grieved me greatly, as you can imagine, but I was forced to explain to them that although we are newly married and I am deeply in love with you, you are given to harmless fits of madness, during which you think you are someone else and that I have abducted you." Almost kindly he added, "You can see, *ma petite chou,* it will do you no good to try to escape. The servants would only lock you in these rooms. And as I said earlier, you have no money. Without money you cannot go very far. So amuse yourself this afternoon. Tonight, if I have the time, we can perhaps plan something more exciting." Then coherent thought fled as his warm mouth settled on hers, and she knew again the hungry, inexplicable yearning his kisses aroused.

The big rooms were unusually silent after he had departed, and angrily Catherine flounced down on her bed. Damn him! He treated her like a doll—a plaything! He would plan something amusing for them if he had the time, would he? Just once, she thought viciously, she would like to beat him at the cat and mouse game they played.

Jason was grinning to himself as he entered the American legation on the Rue de Tournon and presented his card to the man at the door. A moment later he was ushered into a small office that had been hurriedly prepared for James Monroe, President Jefferson's envoy extraordinaire to Paris.

Monroe had arrived only two days before, and as his task was to assist Robert Livingston, the American Minister to France, he was engrossed in reading Livingston's latest reports on the progress of the negotiations for the use of the Mississippi River and the all important Port of New Orleans.

He was seated behind a massive, black oak desk which dominated the entire room, apparently absorbed in his reading. But when Jason entered the room, he rose with a wry smile and, tossing down the lengthy document he had been studying, remarked, "Paper work!" he said. "Someday someone should invent a way to compress all these multitude of pages into one neat, concise paragraph."

Smiling sympathetically, Jason shook the hand Monroe extended and said, "So far it has not been my misfortune to be burdened with such as that. Do you actually read all of it?"

A twinkle in his blue-gray eyes, Monroe admitted sheepishly, "If I read every third sentence I feel I have exerted myself! But tell me, young man, what brings you to France? I thought Jefferson wanted you in England—unless Livingston sent for you. *That* I know Robert hasn't done. So tell me. What is the meaning behind that rather demanding note I received from you last night? Are you in trouble with the French government already?"

In spite of the teasing quality of Monroe's voice, Jason sensed the underlying thread of seriousness in the question, and Jason's own smile disappeared as he said quietly, "I apologize if my message was abrupt, but events have made it imperative that I talk with you before Livingston's negotiations proceed further."

Monroe, easing his tall angular form more comfortably against the padded softness of his chair, gave Jason a searching look before saying slowly, "I know that you are in Jefferson's confidence regarding a number of things in connection with New Orleans, but precisely what your role is I'm afraid I never understood completely. Would you care to enlighten me?"

A rueful gleam in his green eyes, Jason confessed, "I'm very much afraid I don't fully understand it, either! And if I do not understand it, I cannot discuss it very well with you, can I?"

Monroe did not smile at Jason's evasive answer. "I see," he said dryly. "I understand you, Savage—you will not tell me. I suppose I should be pleased that the president has such closemouthed individuals serving him—and of course you will not allow the close ties of personal friendship between us to interfere with your tasks?"

An affirmative nod answered Monroe's gently probing question, and respecting Jason's silence, although not liking it, he asked, "Well? What did you wish to see me about?"

Relaxing slightly at Monroe's tone of voice, Jason said carefully, "I'm about to lay before you a proposal—a proposal that will have great bearing on the task you and Livingston have in front of you. Before I do so, though, there are certain points I must make clear to you. First, I cannot explain where or how I learned what I did. You will have to trust me and take what I say as true. Second, I will not answer any questions, for in my fashion I am loyal, and I have given my word that I shall not divulge my sources." He looked Monroe straight in the eyes, then added, "If you are not willing to do as I request, I cannot proceed farther."

Perturbed and intrigued, as Jason knew he would be, Monroe stared steadily back, rapidly reviewing what he knew of this sometimes exceedingly arrogant young man. Jefferson had entrusted certain vital secrets to him concerning foreign policy, and it seemed Jefferson had chosen his tool wisely. He, himself, was on intimate terms with Guy Savage, and while he was not as familiar with the son as he would have preferred to be under the circumstances, what he did know he liked—in spite of the fact that young Savage had a reputation of looking out for himself and being hard-headed and ruthless about gaining his own way. Occasionally such characteristics had their advantages.

Monroe was a liberal Republican—many thought too liberal—and he was willing to wager that even if Jason might be motived by self-interest in this instance, whatever his reasons, Jason's interest could be used to benefit the United States. Consequently, he nodded his silver-flecked head in consent and said, "Continue. You have aroused my curiosity—and I shall try not to ask too many embarrassing questions."

Hunching forward in the chair, his face clear of all trace of its usual mocking amusement, Jason disclosed, "I'm in possession of knowledge that Barbé-Marbois called upon you and Livingston the other night. While that is public, what you spoke of is not. Barbé-Marbois's main reason for meeting with you, even before you have been presented formally to the French government, was to begin talks for the sale of the entire Louisiana territory."

Unable to control the look of startled amazement that momentarily lightened his chiseled features, Monroe gave a click of annoyance, wondering vexedly where Savage had come by his information. It was true. Barbé-Marbois was well-known to both Livingston and himself because for a time the Frenchman had lived in Philadelphia after escaping from the Reign of Terror. Now he was the French minister of finance, and he *had* called and *had* imparted the stunning news that Napoleon was seriously considering selling the whole vast tract of land that comprised Louisiana to the Americans. He wondered if Jason was aware that in addition to the question of money, there were two major obstacles that had to be surmounted before real discussion could begin—it was imperative to determine if France actually owned the land, and equally important, neither he nor Livingston were empowered to buy land! Navigation rights, riparian rights—yes! But land? . . .

Shrewdly, Monroe did not ask a question, but said, "You know the Constitution has no provisions for a situation such as this!" His irritation apparent, he added, "Who could have surmised when I sailed for France that Napoleon would even countenance so fantastic an idea, much less suggest it?"

Callously indifferent to the intrinsic legal questions the purchase would arouse, Jason said bluntly, "I am here today as an agent, if you will, for the British banking firm of Hope and Baring. They have authorized me to inform you that they are willing to loan you, as representative of the United States, whatever amount of money is required to secure Louisiana from the French."

For a moment, Monroe was speechless. This was beyond anything they could have hoped for! Eagerly, unable to hide it, he asked, "Exactly how far are your principals willing to go?"

For the first time since he had entered the room, Jason relaxed, and his mocking smile leaped into being. Pithily he said, "Ten million at six per cent."

At Jason's words a sigh of sheer pleasure escaped Monroe. Later he and Livingston would question how Hope and Baring had learned of the proposed sale, and more importantly, how they had known exactly the amount the Americans had been willing to pay. For the moment, however, Monroe was dazzled by the vistas this unexpected offer opened.

Jason, his part over for the time being, expertly fended Monroe's searching questions, admitting finally that he knew no more and that now it was up to the American diplomats. Realizing his unforeseen visitor would say no more, Monroe was forced to let him leave; before he did however, he extracted a wary promise that Jason would return in a few days and that he would keep the American legation abreast of his movements.

Walking briskly away from the meeting with Monroe, Jason knew he had escaped easily from the diplomat's probing questions, but the uncomfortable feeling persisted that when next they met he would not have things all his own way as he had today. Disgusted, he thought this whole question could be solved so easily if only everyone would lay their cards on the table. Then he grinned. No, not quite so easily after all—Spain, if she knew how effortlessly France was selling the country out from underneath her, would be bound to object loudly!

His mission to Monroe temporarily accomplished, his thoughts turned naturally to Tamara and plans for the remainder of his stay in France. His promise to Monroe meant discarding his original notion of hiring a house in the country, but that was no hardship. He was certainly satisfied with the lodgings at the Crillon.

On a whim, he stopped at one of the many flower stalls that lined the streets and purchased two enormous bouquets of red carnations. His arms filled with the spicy blossoms, he felt a bit ridiculous as he walked through the foyer of the hotel. The quickly hid grin of the concierge did nothing to improve his feeling, and he was certain within minutes the entire staff would know that Monsieur and Madame Savage had either had a disagreement or must be madly in love! To be the object of the hotel's gossip did not please him, and a slight frown furrowed his forehead as he entered his own apartments.

The enjoyment of the carnations somewhat abated, he dumped them down on the green brocade sofa in his room and tossed his narrow-brimmed beaver hat on a small table nearby. It was then he discovered that the giggles and voices he had carelessly assumed were coming from one of the other rooms down the hall were in fact originating from Tamara's apartments. Annoyed and not a little mystified, he crossed the room with swift strides and flung open the door that divided their suite of rooms.

Surprise halted his impatient entry into the room, and he stared almost numbly at the array of feminine garments, glorious materials, and fashion plates that were strewn about the room. Silks, muslins, and brocades were draped over the sofa, and every other available piece of furniture had some object of feminine apparel upon it. Two young women—from their dress it was obvious they were shop assistants—were busy unrolling lengths of even more exquisitely woven materials. They looked up startled at his sudden entrance, and his black frown wiped their happy smiles away. In a voice laced with steel, Jason thundered, "Tamara! What the hell is going on?"

The quiet murmurings coming from the other bedchamber ceased instantly, and a moment later Tamara, a vision in some gauzy material, drifted into the room followed closely by a stout gray-haired woman and the wide-eyed Jeanne. A provocatively innocent smile curving her lips, Catherine purred, "Why darling, you're back early. I didn't expect you for hours yet." Walking up to his frozen form, she stood on tiptoe and pressed a brief kiss at the corner of his mouth. Before he could recover from his shock, she pouted, "Darling, darling Jason, you left me alone all afternoon, and I was so bored. You can't imagine how ghastly it was having no money with me and knowing no one." Soulfully she looked up at him, and his eyes narrowed with appreciation. But Catherine, not done with him, said sadly, "It was positively unbearable until I spoke with the concierge, and he directed me to Madame Elouise"—a languid wave indicated the gray-haired woman—"and after the concierge was so kind to write to her for me, she came immediately. She's a very famous modiste, you know," Catherine added innocently.

Jason, having once paid for some gowns imported from France and made by the renowned Madame Elouise for a little ladybird of his in New Orleans, groaned silently. *Si fait*, this was going to cost him a small fortune!

Unaware of his precise thoughts but knowing he was displeased and glad that he was, Catherine prattled on. "Wasn't it obliging of her to bring all these wonderful things just for me to see? I've told her I intend to buy several dresses and gowns. After all, you *did* promise me a new wardrobe." A glint of unholy mischief in her violet eyes, Catherine leaned into him and mourned, "Just think how dreadful it would be if your wife had nothing to wear! You know we left England so suddenly that I didn't have a chance to pack a *thing!*"

Unreasonably disappointed and angry, and not certain why, Jason was extremely conscious of the soft, pliant body pressing into his. A glint of revenge flickering in his eyes, he pulled her closer, and in full view of the four waiting women kissed Catherine's unprepared mouth fully, deeply, and with intentional brutality. Completely ignoring the slightly startled silence that greeted his actions, he insolently caressed her slender hips, holding her prisoner against him as he deliberately allowed his desire to build until Catherine felt him hard with passion.

Chagrined at how easily he turned the tables on her, she broke away from him and flashed a furious glance in his direction. Shielding his very obvious state of emotion with her own body, she turned with a flushed face to the silent women and stammered, "Will—will you leave us for a few minutes? I believe Jeanne has prepared some refreshments for you down the hall. We can continue the fittings after you have renewed yourselves. Jeanne will show you the way."

A thunderous silence filled the room after the openly curious women had left, and angrily Catherine whirled on him. "How could you do such a thing? Have you no decency?"

His mouth tight with fury and the green eyes blazing with anger as hot as her own, he snapped, "You forget these are *my* rooms and I'll do as I please! Who the hell do you think you are bringing these women here?" Not waiting for an answer he bit out, "I was going to buy you more clothing. Couldn't you wait? Afraid I might escape your greedy little claws before you could really milk me?"

Her tone matching the scorn in his, her body almost rigid with rage, although inwardly shrinking, Catherine gritted, "If you will remember, when you left this afternoon you told me to amuse myself. Well, I have!" Defiantly she glared up at him, silently daring him to disagree.

Controlling his temper with an effort, Jason said levelly, "I can see that! And it's just as well I have learned early in our association that you are exactly like all of your kind." Casting her a look bordering on dislike, a sneering smile on his face, he asked, "Considering what it is going to cost me before Madame Elouise is finished, do I take it that the next time I seek out your bed I'll find you more accommodating than I have in the past?"

Once Catherine would have struck the sneer from his face, but she was learning painfully there were other ways to fight. Very coolly she said, "You never paid me for my virginity. Surely the cost of a wardrobe is little enough to pay for something that was given unwillingly and was irreplaceable."

Jason stiffened as if she had stung him, and this time the icy dislike was very obvious in his eyes and voice. "Well, well," he drawled. "You may have been a novice at your trade when first we met, but you certainly seem to be learning all the tricks fast."

"But of course," she answered sweetly. "I have such an expert teacher."

A harsh laugh acknowledged her retort, and after another sweeping glance at the room, he said more calmly, "You may call your women back. I promised you a Parisian wardrobe, so buy whatever you wish. Have madame see me before she leaves today."

"Why?"

"Don't raise your fur up, my little cat. I won't countermand your orders, I merely wish to discuss the more vulgar aspects of the transaction—for instance how much all this is going to cost me." Looking at her with brooding intentness, he added, "I had an idea you were going to cost me a great deal, but I never thought I'd get so little enjoyment for my money!"

He waited expectantly, but Catherine did not rise to the bait. She raised one slim brow in mocking imitation of him and questioned innocently, "Isn't there a saying, a Latin one, that translates something to the effect, 'Let the buyer beware'?"

The crashing smack of their connecting door was her answer, for after throwing her a murderous look Jason had turned and stormed out the door and into his own rooms.

A queer, unhappy smile on her lips, Catherine sank weakly down onto the blue sofa, her hands shaking. She had won this round with Jason, and only she knew how much willpower it had taken—how much it had cost her to act as she had. Curiously, instead of a happy feeling of elation, she was left feeling empty and uneasy. The look in Jason's eyes had been so icy, so disdainful, that even now she felt a quiver of remorse. He had stared at her as if she were something loathsome that he had found in the gutter. Bolstering her flagging spirits, she told herself he deserved what she did.

When the women returned, Catherine found it tiring to take an interest in the proceedings that had given her such joy a short while ago. She was almost relieved when the fitting was over. After the women had departed, she walked into the bedroom and listlessly threw herself on the bed. At the moment, she should be filled with glee. In the morning Madame Elouise would be back and had promised that at least two of the gowns would be ready by then. She had gotten even with Jason and soon would be the possessor of a gorgeous and dazzling array of garments any young woman of fashion would be overjoyed to own—so why did Jason's dark face, his eyes filled with disillusionment and his mouth thinned with disgust, keep appearing before her?

Gloomily, she decided it must be that she was still tired and confused from the shocking events of the past days. Tomorrow she would be able to take the proper enjoyment of her victory. Briefly, she wondered at herself—at her concern that Jason not think vile thoughts of her—at her sudden interest in feminine apparel. There had been a time, not too distant, when buying new clothes had been a bore, but today the exquisite materials and drawings of stylish gowns had excited and thrilled her—she who moaned and complained loudly whenever Rachael had even suggested a trip to the dressmaker's!

19

Catherine was quiet and rather subdued during the next few days and Jason's actions did nothing to restore her flagging spirits—or even enrage her. Many evenings and afternoons he left her alone, and she wondered where he went. He didn't appear to care one way or another what she did with her time, except that he saw that she never had any money, and from the curious looks thrown her way occasionally, she knew he kept alive the story of her apparent madness.

He seemed to want her and yet not want her, treating her with careful politeness, never entering her apartments without knocking and when speaking to her always addressing a spot somewhere above her head. In public, he acted very much in the manner of a loving husband showing a somewhat dimwitted little bride the sights, and Catherine could have screamed with vexation. They toured the Tuileries gardens, and they picnicked on several fine days in the Champ de Mars, a large and exceedingly pleasant park.

If it was at all possible to enjoy herself at those times, she did, for Jason appeared to put aside their differences and showed her his most charming manner. When he smiled at her kindly and exerted himself to please her, she knew again the desire to confess her real identity. But once again, she decided against it, clinging to the forlorn hope that somehow she would manage to return to England without anyone ever guessing of this terrible escapade. And as long as Jason made no attempt to reestablish an intimate relationship, she was lulled by his appeasing, yet perplexing, attitude.

There were nights that he returned to their rooms barely before dawn, having left her alone all evening, and sometimes she knew he was probably drunk because the faint fumes of liquor drifted to her own rooms, but he did not force his attentions upon her.

Jason did return to the Crillon many nights in a deplorable condition, but he was acting in a manner no different from any other young man of his birth and breeding visiting Paris. With his cousin Michel, a willing and eager guide, they explored nearly every den of sin in the city. It was in one of the more popular whore houses that Jason met the Chevalier D'Arcy. Michel had been forced to make the introduction, and instinctively Jason had not cared for D'Arcy. He was a man with a squat body; his blue eyes were hard and bloodshot. Later, Michel divulged that D'Arcy was barely tolerated by polite society due to his suspected activities during the terrible years of the terror.

In an undertone Michel had stated, "It was never proven, but there are many who believe he was instrumental in the drownings at Nantes!" At Jason's look of incomprehension, Michel had explained that the drownings had been grisly events during which "enemies of the state"—men, women, and in some cases children—had been locked below the decks of huge rafts and taken to the middle of the river where the rafts were deliberately sunk with their live cargo.

Jason had a nasty taste in his mouth when Michel finished relating the despicable details, and he had been hard pressed to remain civil to D'Arcy when, a few days later, the man accosted him as he walked with Tamara and a few

English acquaintances at Bal Dourlons. Jason had introduced him to his group and Tamara as his wife. Much to Jason's later fury, that one small incident was to have far-reaching effects.

Nights that he was not otherwise engaged, Jason and Catherine dined out in the most expensive and exclusive clubs of the city. But for the pleasure she derived from it, Catherine might as well have been marooned in the middle of some hostile desert. She almost wished he would rape her again. At least then she had had his attention, and she was beginning to think anything was better than the cool, indifferent manner in which he treated her.

Gradually, a raging feeling of injustice and resentment began to build inside her. She hadn't done anything wrong, quite the contrary, so why should she feel guilty? He was the villain, and if her company displeased him so, why did he keep her? She would gladly go back to England!

Pierre had arrived and with him Jason's curricle and horses, so they no longer depended upon the hired coaches with their sluggish horses. Prior to Pierre's arrival, though, Jason had bought two excellent saddle horses for pleasure riding. He had chosen a gleaming, Roman-nosed chestnut for himself and a sleek, long-legged gray mare for Tamara. The servants and residents at the Crillon grew used to the sight of Monsieur and Madame Savage leaving for their early morning ride.

Catherine truly enjoyed those rides. She fell in love with the gray mare, and it was a delight to feel the wind tearing through her hair and the fluid motion of a racing horse beneath her once more. During their rides together, some of Jason's aloofness fled, and more than once with an added thump to her heart she had caught his glance lingering on her flushed cheeks and rosy lips.

As time progressed, Catherine discovered to her horror that she was enjoying Jason's company a great deal more than she should have. Jason, once he had set out to charm, was almost irresistible, and she fought a losing battle against the powerful tug of attraction between them, as well as the pull of Jason's forceful personality.

There were times—mostly at night, as she lay alone unable to sleep—that all the hideous ramifications of her predicament haunted and revolted her. In those moments, she hated Jason and wished with all her young heart that she had never laid eyes on him or that she had never returned to the gypsy camp that fateful night. But except for those agonizing hours alone in the dark, she threw herself grimly into the charade that she was forced to play.

There were other British residents staying at the Crillon, for Paris since the Peace of Amiens and in spite of the imminent threat of war, was filled with the English aristocracy. Some came out of curiosity to view this new rabble government, others because it was *le dernier cri*—the fashionable place to be—and a few simply because there was no place like Paris in the spring. With the continued influx of her fellow countrymen, Catherine lived in dread that sooner or later someone was bound to recognize her. For Jason, without a qualm and with a good deal of sardonic amusement, coolly introduced her as his wife to their fellow guests and whichever of his acquaintances they met, although he took great pains to avoid Monroe when he had Tamara with him.

If it was a foregone conclusion that the chaste state that existed between them could not last—Jason was a demanding lover, and he certainly had not brought her along merely to show her the sights—it was equally evident that their charade would not go undetected for very long. Surprisingly, the first crack in the shell of deceit that encompassed them would come from an unexpected quarter.

Jason called again at the American legation as he had promised, and as he had foreseen, he had to contend with both Livingston and Monroe. It proved to be an excessively sensitive meeting. He delicately threaded his way between willingness to divulge whatever was necessary to calm their fears without revealing his source of information and outright refusal to answer their questions.

Robert Livingston was an older man, a large man with a receding hairline; unkind gossip said he was stone deaf. But deafness does not make a man stupid, and Jason felt decidedly wary when Livingston leveled a long assessing look in his direction. The sharp gray eyes seemed to peer into his inner thoughts, and he moved uneasily in the leather chair, wondering if Livingston guessed how adroitly the Americans were being maneuvered.

Astonishingly, in view of his dubious role in the proceedings, the Americans were oddly willing to keep him informed of their progress. And that they were somewhat confused was also apparent, for Monroe muttered angrily, "Damn it! What does Barbé-Marbois mean they will not discuss the Floridas? I understand one of the points we were to decide upon was our jurisdiction there! And now Barbé-Marbois states flatly that the *only* thing the French government is willing to negotiate with us is the sale of the entire Louisiana area! That and nothing else! I tell you I don't know if I'm on my heels or my head!"

Jason sympathized with the American position, but as long as Napoleon's government made no attempt to swindle them, he was unprepared to enlighten the diplomats further. His role so far had been a minor one, and he intended to see that it remained so!

He also noticed that Livingston allowed Monroe to do all the talking, but he was left with the feeling that of the two, Livingston was more likely to pull off the coup of the century than the voluble Mr. Monroe. Not that he doubted Monroe's abilities, but he sensed Livingston was coolly aware of the way they were being led at a smooth gallop to the negotiating table and that once there, the French would discover that Livingston was not as sleepy as he looked!

Jason was on the point of leaving when Monroe stopped him by asking, "Will I see you tonight at the reception? I hope you will not decline!"

Unable to refuse without appearing churlish, Jason nodded his head affirmatively, and after adding a few polite words regarding the evening, he took his leave. He was not looking forward to the reception; because of Monroe's friendship with Guy and because he suspected the Americans wanted him under their watchful eyes, he found himself invited to most of the social gatherings hosted by the Americans. He could not refuse every invitation, nor did he wish to, but neither did he intend to be drawn deeper into the diplomatic circles than was necessary.

And Tamara presented a problem. He did not want to introduce her in diplomatic circles as his wife—it was one thing to hoax chance-met acquaintances and another to hoax people who knew one's family well—but he had been leaving her alone too many evenings. His reason for this reluctance was not a feeling of guilt at the thought of her dining alone in their apartments while he enjoyed himself with the cream of Parisian society, but the uneasy worry that she still might attempt to escape.

Exactly why he was determined she stay in his possession was unclear even to himself. It certainly wasn't because she warmed his empty bed, for he hadn't touched her since they had been in France. Nor was it because of the enormous sum of money she had cost him in clothing and the jewels he had lately showered upon her. If she had displeased or bored him, he would have discarded her without compunction! So, why did he keep her in his sole possession like a princess in an ivory tower? Grudgingly, he admitted he still found her intriguing—she fascinated him like no other woman he had ever met. Not that he was blinded to the charms of other women. Certainly not! Indeed, his spirits rose when he thought about the lovely Clarissa, a small blond who had caught his eyes at the last two functions he had attended at the American legation. She had made it clear she looked favorably upon his amorous advances, and if she was at the party he planned to arrange a rendezvous.

Clarissa represented the type of woman who usually appealed to him, a bored society beauty married to a much older husband, a woman who enjoyed flirting outrageously with the younger, dashing blades—and if their flirtations led to an affair, who was the wiser?

The soirée was being held at Livingston's grand apartments overlooking the Seine River, and Jason felt good about it, now that he viewed the evening as a necessary prelude to his soon-to-be liaison with Clarissa. The fact that it would be carried on right under her husband's nose added a touch of excitement to it. Before the evening was half over, Jason had manipulated Clarissa into a darkened room, and her ardent response to his embrace confirmed that she was more than willing for a more private tête-à-tête. Between kisses that left Clarissa breathless, Jason had extracted a promise that she would meet him near the Pont-Neuf the next afternoon.

Distinctly pleased with his success, Jason left her to discreetly follow him back into the main salon while he nonchalantly strolled up to a small group of men talking near the wide flung, dark-paneled doors that led to a large balcony overhanging the Seine River. The group included Monroe, as well as Clarissa's paunchy husband who acted as an assistant to Marbois. Two of the other gentlemen he was not familiar with although hazily he remembered being introduced to them earlier in the evening. The fifth man, though, needed no introduction. Jason's mouth tightened as his eyes fell upon the heavy body of the Chevalier D'Arcy.

D'Arcy, because it was his nature to do so, had noticed the flirtation between Jason and Clarissa, and slyly he asked, "Monsieur Savage, where is your lovely wife tonight? I have not seen her all evening. Surely, she is not ill! She looked so very charming when we met the other day."

Monroe threw Jason an astonished glance and exclaimed, "Wife? Jason, you never said a thing! How thoughtless of you not to have told me! I would have been extremely happy to welcome your wife."

His face expressionless, Jason said coolly, "Being newly wedded, I wanted to keep her to myself, and Tamara is rather shy."

Monroe, once over the initial shock, was positively beaming, knowing as he did how fervently Guy wished Jason to marry. Clapping Jason on the back, he offered his sincerest congratulations. "My dear fellow, this is a delightful surprise! Have you written your father yet? He must be overjoyed that at last you have married!" The word spread rapidly through the assembled guests that young Savage was actually in Paris with his new bride, and resigned, Jason accepted with good grace the wishes that now came his way. The only person who appeared unmoved by the news was Clarissa; reproachfully she gazed at him, her large brown eyes saying more than words, and Jason knew with regret that there would be no meeting tomorrow. D'Arcy having no idea of the real facts surrounding the "marriage" watched the whole scene with malicious satisfaction, his only disappointment being Jason's calm acceptance of the situation. And he made the very bad mistake of taking Jason's reactions at face value, for although outwardly Jason smiled and laughingly accepted the good-natured teasing, inwardly he was in a flaming temper.

Knowing he had only himself to blame, Jason grimly hung on to a semblance of control. Even Monroe's excited questions about his "bride" did not disturb Jason's icy facade, although when Monroe insisted that he bring Tamara to the legation ball being held the following week, he very nearly swore out loud but gave, instead a noncommittal answer. He should have known that Monroe was going to leave him no way out.

Catherine and Jason were partaking breakfast outside on the balcony before their morning ride when the note arrived. It had become a habit with them to have breakfast here on fine days, and today was no exception. And curiously this was the one time of the day they seemed to drop hostilities and nearly forgot the true situation between them.

Catherine was looking particularly fetching in a filmy robe of a violet shade that exactly matched her eyes. Jeanne had not yet dressed her hair, and it had been merely brushed and tied back loosely with a green velvet ribbon. Opposite her on the other side of the small breakfast table, Jason lazed on a high-backed chair of straw-colored silk. He had taken the time to shave before joining her, but like Catherine he had not yet dressed. His robe was a deep rich maroon brocade that made him look exceedingly handsome. His green eyes veiled as he watched her read the message.

Catherine's slim brows drew together in a frown as she read, and after a minute she glanced up and with a silent question in her violet eyes handed him the note. He already had an idea of the contents, and so the message came as no surprise. Monroe had invited them for lunch. After scanning it quickly and tossing the note down, he stood up and flexed his shoulders briefly before saying carelessly, "I trust your good manners will hold up through the afternoon. So far you have not embarrassed me by betraying your gypsy background, and I presume you will continue to act the lady. Monroe will expect a quiet little miss, so if you keep your tongue from rattling in your head, we should be able to come about without incident."

Infuriated by the sneering content of his words if not their tone, Catherine's small jaw tightened, and she burst out, "You mean to hoax your own countryman? He writes as a personal friend. Surely you will not parade me before *him* as your wife?"

Jason gave a mirthless smile. "I really have no choice. Naturally I would prefer not to, but circumstances are such that at this late stage *not* to present you would cause more trouble than to continue to pass you off as my bride. Believe me," he added bitterly, "I wish I had never set eyes on you, much less said you were my wife!"

"Why you lop-eared jackass! Don't you *dare* lay the blame for this ridiculous situation at my door! If you hadn't been puffed up with such overweening conceit, none of this would have happened. You have only yourself to blame!"

Catherine spat the words out and, after throwing him a murderous glare, stormed into the salon.

Jason, his face like a thundercloud, grasped her arm in an iron grip and hauled her up next to him. His eyes glittering with suppressed emotion he grated, "Overweening conceit, eh! Who encouraged me in the meadow, my haughty love, and who agreed to a trip to Paris for her favors? I think it's time I tasted what I've bought—don't you?"

Not waiting for an answer, his mouth found her parted lips with punishing force, and his arms tightened about her, crushing her against him. Startled by the sudden eruption of violence, Catherine made no attempt to free herself until her own temper exploded, and then she fought like the hellcat he so often called her.

She managed one well-aimed blow that caught him painfully across the cheek before he captured her hands between their locked bodies and muttered against her lips, "Oh, no you don't! You're not going to claw me this time, my little wildcat. Not this time!" and then swinging her up in his arms, he carried her struggling in his hold into his bedchamber, kicking the door shut behind him.

Throwing her down into the silken softness of his bed, he tossed his robe on the floor and slid down beside her, the warmth of his nude body burning through the flimsy clothes she wore. Catherine strove vigorously to elude his embrace, but as her flaring hands met his hair-roughed chest, a queer thing happened. Suddenly she didn't want to fight him—she wanted—she *wanted* him to take her—but not in anger, not like the other times. The slim fingers that had been curved to claw suddenly spread out and gently caressed his warm skin; without volition, her hands slowly traveled from chest to his sun-browned, smooth shoulders. All desire to fight left her.

Unaware or uncaring of her changed emotions, Jason's mouth buried itself on hers, and with impatient hands he freed her firm, captivating body from the concealing folds of the robe and nightdress. Then when she was naked, he rolled half on her, capturing her body between himself and the bed. His lips left her bruised mouth and moved with increasing ardor down her throat, across one shoulder tasting the sweetness of her skin, and then hungrily back to the honey of her mouth.

Catherine was caught in a cauldron of seething emotion: her body, unable to control its response to his demanding lovemaking, opened itself to him, while in a haze her brain fought against a wanton desire to give in completely. But when Jason touched her silken triangle, all thought ceased—there was only the feel of his big body as he moved within her, his swollen rigidness creating such scalding sensations that a low moan of anguished pleasure escaped her parted lips just before his hard mouth settled once more on hers.

This time there was no physical pain, only pleasure. But in spite of the overpowering furor rippling through her body, her mind was on shameful fire at her own actions. With a soft animallike cry of torment, just as Jason attained the ultimate sensation, she wrenched from beneath him. Unable to control the tremor that shook him, he spent his seed on the silken sheets. His eyes like green ice, he snarled an ugly name and breathing heavily rolled over onto his back throwing an arm over his eyes.

Confused and uncertain at the abrupt end, Catherine hastily gathered her clothes against her body and slid to the edge of the bed. Feeling the bed move, she whirled swiftly to face Jason.

His face was like carved stone, and in an unemotional tone of voice, all the more frightening for its very tonelessness, he said, "Get out! Get out of my sight! And, little *slut,*"—he said the word deliberately—"after you appear as my wife at the embassy ball, I personally shall see you are on your way back to England! Don't worry about your virtue any longer—I'd have to be screaming for a woman before I'd touch you!"

Shaken by the undisguised venom in his eyes, she fled and seconds later was violently and disgustingly sick.

Jeanne discovered her crouched over the chamber pot, and after she had gently helped Catherine into a warm, scented bath she murmured, "Madame must be careful—it would be dreadful if you were to lose your *bébé!*"

Catherine froze as the new and horrifying thought uncurled like a serpent in her brain. This morning's sickness was reaction—it *had* to be! she told herself fiercely. Once more in her room, she stood before the mirror and gazed anxiously at her slim body while Jeanne calmly laid out the clothes she would wear to Monroe's. Her stomach was as flat as ever, almost concave, and her small upthrust breasts surely were not fuller? Sickly she realized that even as she stared Jason's child could be forming itself in her belly.

"Oh, my God! What am I going to do?" she cried silently. And the question was still jumping like a hideous spider in her brain when she met Jason in the salon shortly thereafter.

Jason noticed she was distracted and unusually pale, but he put it down to the fact that she realized she had pushed him too far and was now suitably repentant. Catherine was the one who had been pushed too far though, and she was numb, incapable of thinking beyond the alarming possible catastrophe that had befallen her. Even Monroe's recently leased, very elegant house on the Quai Malaquais made no impression on her, and throughout the ensuing afternoon she smiled, conversed, and acted generally like one in a daze. She was silent unless spoken to and then answered in dull monosyllables. "Yes," she answered to Monroe's question, did she like Paris? "No," she replied to his query, were they staying long?

There was an "other world" look about her, as if she had trouble focusing on what was happening. Any fears Jason may have had that she would embarrass him vanished, to be replaced by the irritable suspicion that she was overdoing the shy bride act. Damn her! She was deliberately creating the wrong impression! He could almost see Monroe thinking, "Lovely girl—but very definitely a moonling! A beautiful moonling, but *still . . . !*"

From Catherine's actions it would appear obvious that he had married merely to stop his father's nagging and had carefully chosen a young woman who wouldn't interfere with his other pursuits. It annoyed him intensely that anyone should think so! Why it should rankle when that had been his original intention was something he preferred not to answer. Watching Catherine's vague interest, his expression grew bleaker as the afternoon progressed. He could damn near strangle the little bitch!

Silence filled their carriage as it sedately carried them back to the Crillon, but once they were in their rooms all the frustration that had been burning inside him erupted, and Jason said nastily, "What an actress! If you had studied for the part of a dim-witted bride, you could not have portrayed it better!"

He might have said more, but for the first time since the unpleasant scene in his bedchamber this morning, he really stared at her and absorbed the impact of the stricken look deep in her violet eyes. No wonder Monroe had been so kind to her, he thought foolishly.

Angered at the sudden tenderness he felt, his mouth thinned with disgust at his own emotions. She had humiliated him the most destructive, degrading way possible to a man, and here he was tottering on the verge of sweeping her into his arms and whispering words of comfort! Ah, *diable!* He nauseated himself. He gave a disgusted exclamation and snapped, "For the love of God! Wipe that theatrical look off your face! We're private now—the act's over!"

Some of the iciness that encased her was blasted away by his fiery words. Sensing that for some unknown reason her actions of this morning and her cool aloofness of the afternoon irritated him more than any other thing she had done in the past, she stated calmly, "I'm tired. If you have nothing further to say, I would like to lie down."

Dumbfounded, Jason stared at her, and Catherine realized she had for once struck him speechless. Very much in the manner of a grande dame speaking to an underling, she said,

"Please send Jeanne to me. I think I shall eat a quiet dinner by myself tonight, so I shall say good evening to you now." And with that, her head held high, she walked regally out of the room leaving a stunned, baffled silence behind her.

20

Jason and Catherine were back to treating one another with frigid politeness and Jason took to staying out late gambling and drinking heavily, returning only when the darkness of night fled the golden dawn. Driven to erase the debasing scene with Tamara from his mind, he promptly bedded a buxom brunette who had been ogling him since he had first started gambling at the dice tables of the Club Royal.

It had been a welcome relief to find solace between soft white thighs and to himself and the satiated brunette, he proved his expert sexual prowess. More than one dawn he returned to the Hotel Crillon smelling of her cheap perfume, a relaxed, satisfied grin on his face. Sleeping most of the day away and spending his nights elsewhere, he saw little of the gypsy. Deliberately he kept it so.

Tamara shredded his usually ordered emotions to ribbons; she had tricked him and had committed the maximum crime—made him doubt his own masculinity! The sooner he was rid of her the better, and he vowed that as soon as the embassy ball was behind them he would put her on the next packet to England. That the sight of her still caused a sudden, inexplicable ache and a queer desire for the situation to have been different, he determinedly ignored, violently shoving the unwelcome emotions to the back of his brain where they lurked waiting to haunt him when he least expected it.

The last nights, his excesses with the brunette, and the excellent French brandy added a certain exciting rakishness to his lean, dark features, and Catherine felt her heart tighten painfully whenever they did meet. A sudden glance from those hard green eyes could cause her to feel precarious yearnings. Her newest worry disappeared when her body answered her fears of pregnancy two mornings after the disastrous afternoon at Monroe's—she did not carry Jason's child. The knowledge should have comforted her—and it did, in a way.

Left to her own devices, Catherine wandered through Paris with Jeanne as her companion, and a warm friendship sprang up between maid and mistress. Jeanne sensed that things were not right in the marriage of Madame and Monsieur Savage, and while not knowing the cause of the estrangement, all her loyalties were with her mistress.

Pierre, his sense of fitness outraged by Jason's behavior, occasionally accompanied them on their ramblings. It horrified him that Jason should allow the woman posing as his wife to wander about the streets of Paris without money and unattended except for one very young maid. Pierre disapproved of Jeanne violently, thinking her too young and flighty to be a proper lady's maid. Lady's maids and dressers were middle-aged and prune-faced, not apple cheeked slips of things with dancing dark eyes. If Pierre disapproved of Jeanne, she returned the favor by deciding he was too stiff and proper!

On the occasions when Pierre escorted the two young women, Catherine was often amused by the frequent polite battles that raged between maid and valet. If madame wished to visit a particular section of Paris that Pierre thought improper, he would delicately steer her away from the notion, only to be brought up short by Jeanne laughing at his stuffy attitude. His eyebrows raised haughtily in a manner reminiscent of his master, and ignoring the scoldings pelted upon him by Jeanne, he would guide Catherine away. A second later Jeanne would be sunnily trailing behind them, her eyes dancing with laughter at his pompousness.

Still, Pierre did manage to entertain them. It was with Pierre that Catherine discovered the delightfully scented shop of Jean-François Houbigant named appropriately, A Basket of Flowers. And it was here, their eyes wide with excitement, that Jeanne and Catherine watched Napoleon's empress, Josephine de Beauharnais, purchase some of her favorite Crème de Rose. Wistfully Catherine had wandered around the small shop inhaling the fragrancies of scents, soaps, and candles as well as the many perfumes for which Houbigant was famous.

Catherine's wistful face led Pierre to deferentially request that Jason entrust an amount to himself so that he could buy the little objects that enchanted madame.

It was a strange little trio they made—the beautiful young aristocratic woman, the very lively lady's maid, and the exceedingly prim gentleman's gentleman. Jason viewed the resulting friendliness with a jaundiced eye, but beyond sarcastically asking Pierre if he was thinking of leaving his service, he left it at that.

As the date of the embassy ball drew near, Catherine and Jason both perceived that their tempers were growing drastically short. Jason took to wandering unexpectedly into her bedchamber and more than once lounged indolently on her bed like a lazy panther, silently daring her to object as he watched Jeanne dress her. And when they were alone, it was as if he intentionally set out to provoke her into losing her temper.

After one particularly dreadful exchange of sharp words, Catherine didn't think she could stand the torment any longer. The suspicion had begun to nag her that she was falling in love with this harsh-faced man who taunted and mocked and thought her a cheat, a slut and worse! In a deep fit of despair, she considered selling the jewels he had given her and attempting to find her way back to England and home. But she had no idea where the moneylenders were situated, and Jason had promised to send her back to England after the ball. And so, grimly she fought against the feeling of love that struggled to be born. She would not love him! She could not love him! One didn't love a man who acted as he had. And yet—she would recollect the days and times when he had been so charming, wooing her into forgetfulness. Then with something approaching anguish, she would feverishly tear the memory from her mind.

The night of the ball finally arrived. There had been no appreciable change in their behavior towards one another. It was only when Catherine, wearing a gown of stark black velvet, walked into the salon where Jason stood impatiently waiting, that he wondered rawly how he was going to let her go. He stared at the achingly lovely picture she made, her breasts rising like alabaster from the ebony darkness of the gown and her blue black hair waving softly around her shoulders.

He too was bedeviled with memories—memories of her sudden smiles that could dazzle him blind, memories of her clear laughter when something pleased her, and most of all the memory of the softness of her mouth and her slim body. Baldly he acknowledged that he had never possessed that slender body completely—always she fought him, and except for the one time at the inn after he had raped her of her virginity, he had never taken her with the care and tenderness of which he was capable. He'd meant to, he had meant this time in Paris to be different. But always she infuriated him to the point that he became an animal and used his body as a weapon of punishment.

Jason stood so long staring at her in silence that Catherine cleared her throat nervously and felt a betraying blush of hot color stain her cheeks. Then he bowed mockingly and, a glint in the emerald eyes, he complimented, "You look enchanting, Madame Savage. Shall we agree, for tonight, to a truce between us?"

An answering hopeful sparkle in her violet eyes, Catherine murmured, "Please—yes!"

And so, it was a vastly different young woman Monroe met that evening, and he was promptly intrigued by the change—in both Savages. For tonight Jason's eyes continually strayed to the vivacious creature he called his wife, and more than once Monroe caught the impish smile she flashed at Jason. It was also now obvious why young Savage had not mentioned her earlier. The gentlemen flocked to her, and more than one young man exclaimed himself enraptured by her beauty.

Catherine was much in demand when the dancing began. Jason stayed on the sidelines, dancing with no other women, and though he talked with various male acquaintances, his possessive gaze never lost sight of the slim figure in black velvet as she was whirled around the ballroom.

Monroe took the opportunity afforded by Catherine's absence to have a private word with Jason. Under the cover of the music of a waltz, he said casually, "You know, Jason, Livingston is a little worried about the negotiations."

Jason shot him a questioning glance, but the two men were momentarily isolated at the back of the room. Monroe continued, "Robert is afraid that France is attempting to defraud us. Barbé-Marbois still has not admitted that Spain has ceded Louisiana back to France. For all we know we are about to commit the United States to paying many millions of dollars for a piece of land that does not belong to the seller."

Jason growled noncommittally, noting angrily that D'Arcy was soliciting Catherine for the next dance, and he strode away to sweep his wife from the chevalier's grasp. His dark head was seen to incline itself towards Catherine's upturned face several times during the ensuing waltz, and

Catherine's eyes were gleaming amethysts by the time the dance ended. No one was in any doubt that Jason found her irresistible!

It was a glittering crowd attending this ball to officially introduce James Monroe to French society, although he had been the American minister to France some years before. The women were arrayed in fantastic ball gowns of every hue, and their bright jewels sparkled in the candlelight. The men too were gorgeous to behold in their velvet and satin clothes; like peacocks displaying their feathers, they strutted about the huge ballroom. It was a mixed gathering of nationalities—the French, the Americans and several Englishmen, their wives, and in some cases eligible sons and daughters.

Catherine was enjoying herself hugely; it was her first ball, and Jason was again at his disarming best. During a late supper, he had secured a secluded table and proceeded to flirt shockingly with her, as if they had just met and she was a young woman he would like to know better—much better! Shyly, she returned his banter, frequently causing him to laugh out loud as she capped one of his more ridiculous compliments. There was a disturbing expression deep in his eyes as they rested on her flushed countenance, and as she encountered that look again, her heart beat so painfully fast she was certain he must see her pulse racing.

It was late, well after midnight, and Catherine and Jason were conversing with Monroe when the blow fell. They were standing near the doorway that led to a large tiled foyer where uniformed servants were helping departing guests into their cloaks and wraps. The crowd had thinned somewhat, but there was still a large company left. Perhaps if they would have been standing anywhere else, the meeting would not have taken place.

Jason had just thrown Catherine a particularly warm smile, and she was gazing off into space, her thoughts jostling one another about. Giddily she tried to still the happiness that was flooding her body, when a startled gasp made her glance casually at the party just passing. A woman's scandalized voice uttered, *"Catherine!* What are you doing here?" Ashen-faced, Catherine stared into her cousin Elizabeth's eyes. Dumbly she noted Aunt Ceci and Uncle Edward just beyond, staring in horrid fascination.

At Elizabeth's words, Jason broke off his conversation with Monroe, and in one lightning glance took in the scene before him. Tamara was standing in frozen horror, gazing at Elizabeth Markham and her parents, the earl and countess of Mount. A sudden frown between his brows, he questioned quietly, "Catherine?"

But Catherine, all her nightmares cumulating in this one appalling moment, didn't even hear him. She couldn't move, couldn't swallow, couldn't think—she was unable to do a thing but stare with haunted eyes at her relatives.

Ceci broke the growing silence by crying, "Catherine, you dreadful girl! What are you doing here? Does your mother know you are here? Poor Rachael has been frantic about you. I knew you would cause a scandal! I just knew it! Oh, I feel faint—Edward, my smelling salts!"

No one paid any attention to this last, for it was apparent from the malicious gleam in her eyes that Ceci was enjoying her big scene too much to end it by fainting.

Jason, his voice cold, snapped, "Would you please explain yourself, madame?"

Ceci was gathering herself to answer him when Edward Tremayne, his eyes icy, said grimly, "I believe, Savage, *you* owe *us* an explanation! What is my niece doing with you in Paris? Her mother is very nearly in a state of nervous collapse, having no idea what has happened to her daughter!"

Tremayne turned reproachfully to his strickened niece and asked, "How could you treat Rachael this way, to run off and leave her no word? Have you no shame?"

Jason stiffened as if turned to granite. A muscle bunched in his jaw. But otherwise his face was closed and unrevealing. Evenly he said, "I think we should discuss this somewhere more private."

Facing a bewildered Monroe, he asked quietly if they could borrow one of the small rooms, and Monroe quickly ushered the silent group into a little antechamber. After closing the door to any curious stares, Monroe said soothingly, "I'm sure there must be some misunderstanding. Tamara here is Jason's wife!"

"His *wife!*" hissed Elizabeth through clenched teeth, and she cast a venomous glance at the silent girl in black.

Tremayne, his face clearing, asked in a greatly relieved tone, "Your wife?"

Jason hesitated only a moment before he gave a curt nod. Monroe, an indulgent smile creasing his chiseled features, said, "I see that my young friend has again done the unusual. Do I take it this is a runaway match?" Again Jason nodded curtly.

Disappointed at such a tame explanation, Ceci muttered, "It may be an elopement, but why hasn't Catherine had the decency to at least write her mother?" Casting her niece a spiteful look, she added, "You could have left a note. At least that would have saved Rachael from rousing the entire neighborhood and would have prevented her from calling in the Bow Street Runners. I was never so embarrassed in my life. This disappearance raised all the talk about the time the gypsies abducted you. Everyone is talking about you! My goodness, girl, why don't you behave normally? No one else in the family causes any scandals. I'm just thankful that your poor father never lived to see this day," she ended piously.

Monroe, attempting to diplomatically avert a full-blown scene, said smoothly, "I'm certain Tamara—er—Catherine has already written her mother. After all, it is some days since you left England, and by now all her mother's fears have been allayed. As a matter of fact, she's probably delighted Tamara has made such an excellent match," he ended.

Tight-lipped, Elizabeth gritted, "Her name is not Tamara, it's *Catherine! Lady Catherine Tremayne!*"

Somewhat shaken by the naked hatred in Elizabeth's

eyes, Monroe was for the moment silent. The earl, knowing of the hostility borne by his female relatives for Catherine, was quick to allow them no chance to unburden themselves further. Very aware of the fact that Elizabeth and Ceci had cherished hopes of bringing Jason to the altar—Ceci had nagged Edward to take them to France once word of Jason's trip to Paris had become common knowledge—the earl wanted this unpleasant scene over with as soon as possible. Looking at the still silent Catherine, Edward said sternly, "I think enough has been said tonight. If you have not apprised Rachael of your whereabouts and marriage, do so immediately!" Glancing at Jason, he added, "If you will give me the direction of your lodgings, I shall call upon you tomorrow, and we can discuss settlements at that time."

Stony-faced, Jason asked coldly, and only Catherine could guess at the fury behind that coldness, "Settlements?"

The earl nodded. "Lady Catherine is a wealthy young woman in her own right, and as her guardian it behooves me to see that you intend to do all that is proper."

For a moment, Jason's icy green eyes swung in Catherine's direction. He noted the pale cheeks and the white look around her mouth, but he was not softened. What a fool she had played him for! And Catherine read in that comprehensive glance the death of any hope that she would be able to excuse or explain anything to him.

Steeling herself to speak she stared beseechingly at her uncle, swallowed convulsively and blurted, "Uncle, that really isn't necessary! We are already m—m—married," she stumbled over the word before rushing on, "and—and settlements are decided upon before marriage. Please let it be! I will explain everything when you come tomorrow."

Jason's arm tightened cruelly about her waist as he said silkily. "But my little love, you must let me put your uncle's mind at ease. Surely you knew I would do all that is *proper!*" He nearly spat the last word, but playing the scene he smiled tenderly into her upturned face, and only she saw how icy and remote his eyes were.

Elizabeth, unable to control herself, snarled, "How touching! Tell me, Catherine, did you and Rachael plan for him to meet you so opportunely at the gypsy camp, or was it an accident? I suspect your mother schemed wisely—for how else would she get you a husband? After all," she drawled hatefully, "fashionable London would have thought twice about allowing a chit like you in their midst. You're fortunate Jason was a stranger and didn't know your history—gypsy brat!"

A shocked silence greeted Elizabeth's outburst, and Jason's words of anger fell like splinters of ice in the frozen stillness. "Oh, but you're wrong, Elizabeth. I did know her history!"

Stunned, Catherine's eyes widened, and lips parted in surprise, but Jason, holding Elizabeth's furious brown eyes with his own, continued coolly, "Some time ago, Amanda Harris regaled me with," he hesitated, "er—Catherine's story. You might say it was her unusual background that first attracted me to my bride. And I should warn you that I do not take kindly to anyone lashing at my wife as you have. It is a pleasure I reserve solely for myself. I trust in the future you will learn to control your rashness."

Tremayne, deeply embarrassed by his daughter's vitriolic attack, said hurriedly, "Well, that seems to have settled any question of Jason having been misled. As the hour is late I would again suggest we leave any further discussion until tomorrow. I'm certain that tomorrow Savage and I can come to agreement privately between ourselves."

Monroe, having taken a violent dislike to Elizabeth and Ceci, murmured to Tremayne, "I will see your ladies to the foyer where they can await you until Jason has given you his address and answered any other questions you may have."

Elizabeth opened her mouth to object, but Monroe, at his most diplomatic self, firmly guided the two women from the room.

Edward relaxed somewhat after their departure. He had always been especially fond of his niece, and he smiled ruefully at her, asking, "Catherine, my dear, must you always do the outrageous? I will not scold you longer because I can see this has been a strain. What is done is done. But I do not understand why you and Savage decided on a runaway match. Surely Rachael would not have objected, and I certainly would not have. Couldn't you have asked us?"

At the hurt in his words, Catherine fought the treacherous tears that ached in her throat and brimmed in her violet eyes. Only by biting her bottom lip until it nearly bled was she able to control the desire to fling herself in his arms and pour out the whole ugly story. Tremayne waited vainly for her reply, and seeing that despite her distress she had no answer, he gave a tired sigh and turned to the tall man at her side. "Where are you staying? I shall be over in the afternoon if that is convenient."

Flatly, Jason gave him the name of the Hotel Crillon, and together the two men decided upon the hour of two o'clock for the meeting. After bestowing a polite kiss upon Catherine's pale cheek, Tremayne departed.

The accusing angry silence in the small room was almost a tangible thing, and knowing she would have to break it sometime, Catherine, staring unhappily at the carpet, said in a muffled tone, "You would not have believed me—if I had told you the truth."

"You could have tried me!" Jason shot back. "Instead of letting me continue to think you were only some gypsy slut out for a rich protector! *Mon Dieu!* What a coil we're in now, and all because you couldn't use your damn tongue!"

Stung, Catherine began to protest, but he forestalled her by snarling tightly, "Don't say a word! Right now I could very easily throttle you! Just let it be!"

Monroe entered the room before more could be said, and Jason stiffly thanked him for his help in averting what could have been a very nasty scene. The following minutes of conversation were strained, and Monroe, while exceedingly mystified and burning with curiosity, was almost thankful when Jason and Catherine departed.

At the hotel, Catherine slipped silently into her bedchamber, praying Jason would postpone the blazing row that threatened until she had had a chance to gather her scattered wits. For a short while it appeared he would wait until morning before attacking, but just as Catherine, looking like a pale ghost of herself, was sliding gratefully between the silken sheets, the bedroom door crashed open and Jason stood steely-eyed in the doorway.

He had discarded the green, velvet jacket and satin waistcoat he had worn earlier to the ball. The white silk shirt with its frilled cuffs was open almost to his waist, and he held a glass half-filled with amber-colored liquid in one hand. A lock of night black hair fell across his forehead, and there was a glitter in his green eyes that caused Catherine to feel a tremor of primitive animal fear. That he had spent the intervening time drinking heavily was obvious, but he was not yet drunk. Mockingly, he raised his glass high, and while the words were slurred, Catherine heard them clearly—too clearly.

"A toast to my lovely bride. I never realized when I made little Tamara my mistress I would find myself acquiring a noble-born bride. Tell me, *Lady* Catherine—just to assuage my own curiosity—did your mother plan it or was it an accursed accident that we met?"

Knowing he was in no mood to listen to excuses or reason and tired to death of scenes, Catherine said coolly, "You're drunk, Jason! We can discuss it in the morning."

It was precisely the wrong thing to have said, for the spiteful mockery died, and in a flaming temper Jason crossed the room with angry, stiff-legged strides. "And when will we discuss it, *Lady* Catherine? After your uncle has bled me further?"

Grasping her slim shoulders, he shook her ruthlessly. Twisting free, she spat, "All right, Jason! I'll tell you! No, my mother never planned it! I never planned it! You can blame your own blind lust for what has happened! I didn't rape myself—nor did I bring myself to France. *You* did it all, my dear *husband!*"

Her furious words hit him like a bucket of icy water, and for a seemingly endless time they stared at one another. Then he surprised her by throwing himself full-length on the bed beside her. Lying on his back and staring unseeingly at the ruffled canopy he said bleakly, "I may have been guilty of mistaking the situation, but you should never have continued to be at the gypsy camp once you knew of my interest—and you knew of my desire for you that first day! Why the hell didn't you say something?"

Her earlier anger draining away, she asked dully, "Would you have believed me?"

"Probably not!" he answered baldly. His very lack of compunction was insolence itself, and tightly she asked, "Doesn't it bother you, what you've done?"

"Not particularly! What have I done besides making a runaway match with, I discover tonight, a very eligible young woman? And as I am considered very eligible myself, what is the harm?"

Frowning, Catherine stared back at him. "But we're not married!"

Turning his head slowly, he gazed back at her, and the cold glitter in his green eyes made her suddenly, sickeningly aware that he was in an extremely dangerous mood—that underneath his relaxed exterior he was furious! Paralyzed she stared back at him, and he smiled deliberately, nastily. "That's true, my lovely little cat, but by this time tomorrow evening, we will be!"

Catherine's eyes grew wide with horror, and all trace of color left her face. "You can't be serious—you don't want to marry me!"

Grimly, "How true, *Lady* Catherine. Unfortunately, this evening has left me no other alternative. And marry you, I will!"

Aghast, she stuttered, "But—but we don't love each

other! We don't even *like* each other! I will not marry you! I couldn't bear it—not like this!"

Pushing her down into the soft pillows, Jason loomed above her, his face hard, his full, mobile lips thinned with anger, and snarled, "Love has nothing to do with anything! Marry we must, and marry we will! You may enjoy creating scandals, as your aunt implies, but I dislike being labeled a blackguard and a bounder who seduces young ladies of quality!" Bitterly, he added, "Why in God's name couldn't you be the gypsy wench you appeared to be? Then we'd have no problem. Now I'll—God help me—have a bride!"

Her face stormy, Catherine burst out, "I will not marry you!"

A mirthless smile on his mouth, Jason said grimly, "You haven't any choice either—we're stuck with one another. If we don't marry—immediately and secretly—how long do you think Elizabeth or her mother will keep this juicy tidbit silent?"

His argument was irrefutable, and to Catherine it was like a death sentence. She was to be forever tied to a man who hated and despised her, and her heart felt like a leaden weight in her chest. Wretchedly she wondered how an evening that had started out with such promise could end so disastrously. In her more optimistic moments, she had cherished the hope that perhaps given time and the right circumstances she and Jason could resolve their difficulties. Now he would never forgive her for having placed him in such an intolerable position. Reminding herself it was his fault did no good—it was patently obvious that Jason didn't or wouldn't recognize that his own actions had led them to this point.

She stared up at the hard, dark face before her, and the ache of unshed tears in her throat became almost unendurable. She was very much afraid she had fallen in love with this man, while he, although occasionally desiring her body, thought her a damned nuisance and a thorn in his side!

And now, she was on the brink of being compelled to spend the remainder of her life as his unloved, unwanted wife!

Catherine's face was a mirror of her emotions, and though Jason couldn't guess precisely what she was thinking, the bleak despair that filled her was overwhelmingly evident. He hadn't expected her to be happy with his decision, but he certainly hadn't anticipated she would view it with such obvious distaste! Damn her! *He* was the one that was going to be saddled with a viper-tongued wench whose body promised so much, yet never fulfilled any of its unspoken allure. She had no right to look so unhappy. She was getting a rich husband out of the blasted affair while he—he was going to live his remaining years bound to a woman who probably hated him! Heavily, he said, "You haven't answered my question. Do you think your aunt and cousin will be able to contain themselves with what has happened?"

"You don't need an answer," she replied in a small voice. "You know as well as I do that Elizabeth and Ceci will delight in telling the whole world."

"Well, then? You agree that as soon as I can make the arrangements—we'll marry?"

Catherine gave a sad little nod of her head, her eyes very large and appealing, and Jason felt a queer tautness in his chest. She was so lovely lying there, her hair like a black silken cloud against the white pillows, and instantly he became vividly conscious of the soft body beneath his. But even as the familiar desire spread through him, his mouth twisted bitterly. She was capricious, deceitful, and treacherous. She had tricked him, misled him, and with wanton carelessness created a living hell for him. Disgusted with his own body's betrayal at her warm nearness, he moved abruptly away from her and said in a cold voice, "I should be able to have us safely married by tomorrow night. In the meantime, we will continue as we are." He stood up and turned to leave but Catherine's voice halted him.

"Jason, will we be *really* married? I—I—mean, will it be a legal marriage?"

His eyes like furious green flames, he spun around and spat, "Don't worry, *Lady* Catherine,—you've managed to hook me! You can rest assured the marriage will be legal and binding. I do not intend to go through a phony ceremony and deceive you!"

"Oh, stop it!" she cried, becoming angry herself. "I didn't mean it that way! I just wanted to know. It's my life too, don't forget! You're not the only one who is being forced to marry against his will. Remember, I'm the other half of the injured party! Remember if you can," she sneered, "that *I* was the one raped and abducted. Not you!"

"Point taken, my love," he said nastily. "But you're not entirely innocent yourself. And," his eyes narrowed, "that reminds me—now that we're on the threshold of wedded oneness and should have no secrets between us—what were you searching for that morning at the inn? Did you think I'd forgotten that little incident? Or your relationship with Pendleton?"

21

The question was hurled at her like a knife, and almost physically Catherine felt it strike. Clive's interest in Jason's ownership of a nebulous map and his blackmail threat against Rachael had all faded from her mind in the past weeks. Since that morning at Jason's lodgings in London when she had bargained for her freedom with that knowledge and Jason had refused, she had completely forgotten it. Now when she least expected it and was already jangling with nerves, he sprang it on her. Dumbfounded by the sudden and unrelated questions, she missed the slight hint of jealousy that colored his last question.

It was late, she was tired, and she owed Clive no loyalty—quite the reverse in fact. Consequently, in halting words, she told Jason the truth—even Clive's threat to harm her mother. She did not clarify her relationship to Clive because to her mind there was nothing to explain—Clive had merely been her father's godson.

She told Jason how Clive had wanted her to search for a map, and at the first mention of the map, Jason's brows had gathered in a frown. Catherine, concentrating on her story, her eyes downcast as she stared at the nervous movements of her fingers, didn't see the ugly gleam that lit Jason's eyes when she elaborated upon Clive's method of forcing her to do his bidding. When she had finished she glanced up at him defiantly and said, "That's all I know—that's all I ever knew! You can believe it or not!"

Mildly he drawled, "Calm down, my little scowling kitten. I didn't say I didn't believe you. I'm just puzzled. Clive's not stupid nor is he likely to chase off after fairy tales—and either he's confusing me with someone else, or he's fallen for a Banbury tale. Are you certain he wanted just a map?"

She frowned. "He said a map—no, wait! he said there *might* be a map. And that if I didn't find it, he would have to search your London lodgings."

An arrested expression in his eyes, he asked slowly, "*Would* have to search—or *had* searched?"

Bewildered by his curious intentness, she stared at him for a minute. "I can't remember exactly, but I'm more than certain he said he hadn't searched in London—but that if I couldn't find anything, he would have to have someone trace it in London."

Her words didn't seem to be the answer he sought, and after a sudden and abstracted good night, he left the room.

For a moment Jason had thought the solution for the man in his London apartment had been solved. But if Catherine—it seemed peculiar to think of her by that name—was to be believed, and he *did* believe her, Pendleton couldn't have had any connection with that event. Still, he knew more than he had, and while he possessed no map, it opened up a whole new avenue of possibilities.

If Catherine had said Pendleton had been after official documents, that would have been another matter. Spain, England, and France all had reason to be curious about Jefferson's plans with regards to Louisiana. But unless this mysterious map was of some military significance, he couldn't connect it with the interest it had caused—and that was assuming the prowler in London had been after the same thing as Pendleton!

It was an interesting puzzle, and with pantherlike curiosity he pursued the thought as he lay in bed, his big body relaxed and supine while his brain worked with furious energy. After awhile, he grew impatient with himself for not discovering the answer. He had the disquieting feeling the answer was there, just out of reach, and that he *should* know the solution.

Sleep was elusive for both Jason and Catherine that night. Catherine, emotionally exhausted by the sudden discovery of her identity and the abhorrent scene at Monroe's that had followed, lay the entire night like a mortally wounded animal waiting patiently for the death-blow. Even as she meekly accepted Jason's pronouncement that they would marry, a part of her was in open revolt against the apathetic state into which she had fallen. Again and again, like a vixen in a trap, she sought feverishly for a way to escape. None seemed to exist, and the soft light of dawn was gradually dispelling the blackness of night before she fell into a restless doze.

Jason, regardless of having little sleep, was up and gone by early dawn. For him it was a fruitful morning. Rather than run the risk of discovery of their exact marriage date, he rode out of Paris to one of the smaller hamlets that lay some miles from the capital city. There he was able to find a willing and hopefully closemouthed justice of the peace to perform the marriage. By leaving an extremely generous fee, he was assured that a special license would be secured and that all legal papers would be duly processed. In view of the circumstances Jason was relieved that since the French Revolution there were only civil marriages performed, and those were done in a forthright manner.

He arrived back at the hotel with just enough time to wash the smell of horses and dust from his body and change his riding clothes for something more formal before his meeting with Lord Tremayne.

Catherine was very quiet during the encounter with her uncle, and her uncle put down the purple shadows under her eyes and her spiritless attitude to the lateness of the evening before—and perhaps remorse at the way she had treated her mother.

The meeting went off well; the earl found the settlements Jason offered excessively generous and Jason, once his mind had been made up, went about the business with cool efficiency. Only Catherine was displeased—not with the money that Jason was settling upon her, but with the ease with which she was sold! And *sold* was the only way she could view it!

Her uncle, for all his affections for her, appeared more concerned with the money transactions—even though it was for her benefit—than with her feelings. Not once did he ask after her welfare, or if she was happy.

She firmly brought her self-pitying thoughts to a halt by reminding herself that her uncle was under the false impression that she had run away with the man she loved. Naturally, he would assume she was happy. And as he was under the illusion that she had callously left Rachael in ignorance as to her plans, he would have little sympathy for her even if she were unhappy and regretting her rash marriage. It rankled, though, that he could so carelessly dispose of her without first assuring himself that she was truly happy and content. Some of her resentment was apparent in the mutinous tilt to her mouth, but the earl, vastly relieved that the possible scandal had ended so well, didn't see the obvious signs that all was not well. A moment later he was gone.

Returning from seeing the earl out, Jason noticed her expression and with a lazy smile curling his mouth drawled, "What's biting you, kitten? Don't you think I've been generous enough?"

"It's not that," she flashed angrily. "It's the very idea. I feel like I've just been bought! You've just purchased me like one of your horses!"

His smile deepening, he murmured teasingly, "I must admit you have been an expensive little filly!"

Catherine nearly strangled on the fury that choked her, but beyond tightening her lips and throwing him a fulminating glance, she said nothing. A second passed, and then in a hard little voice she asked, "Have you made the arrangements?"

He nodded slowly, the smile disappearing as he did so. "We have an appointment in Saint-Denis this evening. The official there is willing to overlook our sudden desire to marry and will see to it that all the necessary papers are filed. Have no worries, my dear Lady Catherine, in just a few hours you really will be Madame Savage!"

She hated the slight taunting quality his voice took on as he said the last words, but grimly she held on to her simmering temper. "How soon will it be before we have to leave?"

"Why? Don't tell me we're waiting for Madame Elouise to whip up a bridal gown for you?" he questioned sarcastically.

Levelly she said, "I merely wished to know at what time you wanted me ready. But I can see you're in an unreasonable mood. Whenever you are ready, let me know."

She started to leave, but his hand on her wrist halted her steps. Tiredly he said, "I'm sorry. I shouldn't let my dislike of the situation push me into making things worse between us. Saint-Denis is some miles from here, so unless you wish to change your clothes, we should leave within the hour to make our appointment. Whenever you're ready, I can have the carriage brought round."

Astonished at his unexpected apology, Catherine stared a moment before gathering her scattered wits about her. She was wearing a grayish-purple silk dress that made her skin glow milky white and intensified the amethyst shade of her eyes. It wasn't what she would have chosen for a wedding dress, but she couldn't see any reason for changing. It would do as well as any other gown, she thought unhappily. It was in this mood that they set out for Saint-Denis.

Dusk was falling as they left the small village, the deed done. They were legally, irreversibly *married.* Dully, Catherine stared at the heavy gold band that now encircled her slim finger. It didn't seem possible that those few words spoken by the dour-faced official in a dry-as-dust voice could have wed her to Jason Savage. But so it was, and blankly she gazed ahead. She had never thought of her wedding day, but knew she would not have wished for fanfare and fuss—orange blossoms and yards and yards of white lace were definitely not for her! Yet she knew she would have wanted more than that quick, impersonal ceremony she had just experienced. Bleakly she wondered at the fact that Jason had even purchased a ring—for beyond that there had been nothing except the bald, unvarnished reciting of the vows to remind one that it was a wedding.

Jason too was strangely silent. And as the night fell and the darkness increased, the silence between them became an almost tangible thing. Each was extremely conscious of the other and, each fought against the enveloping intimacy of the darkened carriage. The moon had risen, and in the dim light Catherine could barely discern Jason's features as he sat directly across from her. The shadowy light hid his eyes and fell on the straight, proud nose and full, mobile mouth.

He was her husband, and now he had the legal right to do whatever he pleased with her. Not only her fortune, but even her life now passed into those lean hands that could fill her with such delight and terror. A tiny sigh escaped her, and at the sound Jason leaned forward, his warm hands covering the fingers that she held tightly clasped in her lap.

"Is it so very awful being married to me?" he asked softly.

Catherine, her eyes almost purple in the diffused light, said in a little voice, "We really don't know each other very well, and it seems we're always fighting and at loggerheads with one another. I don't see how either of us can ever be happy."

His voice hardened slightly. "We'll just have to try harder. We're married, and nothing will ever change that! Perhaps in time we can, both of us, gather a measure of satisfaction, if not happiness, from our relationship."

Dumbly she nodded, not trusting her voice. In the murky darkness of the coach, Jason couldn't see the small movement and queried sharply, "Well? Don't you agree?"

The threat of tears was very evident in her halting words. "Yes. I know you're right. Years from now we'll look at all this differently. I—I just wish that—that—" Her voice was suspended as she vainly fought back the scalding tears that crowded her throat, but a miserably tiny sob slipped out. The sound of it tore through Jason's gut like a bullet, and moving instinctively he reached across the space between them and gently gathered her onto his lap and into his arms.

His unexpected kindness was her undoing, and Catherine's slender body was racked by the tears that had been held in for what seemed like weeks. Dimly she was aware that Jason, his lips softly caressing her hair, was murmuring against her hair. Eventually, the storm of tears passed, and she sat quietly in his arms, the silence broken only occasionally by a small hiccuping sob.

Like a father comforting a hurt child, Jason gently wiped the tear stains from her cheeks with his handkerchief, and she was reminded vividly of the time in the meadow. The same thought must have occurred to him because he murmured, "I seem to always cause you tears. This is not the first time we've been thus."

Misty-eyed, she stared up at him, and his breath caught sharply in his throat. God! She is so lovely, he thought gazing at her long lashes, spiky from the recent tears, and her soft lips that were still inclined to tremble. Blindly his mouth closed over hers in an urgent kiss that left Catherine breathless and hungry for another, and Jason, as if compelled, muttered, "Oh, kitten, listen to me! Things are all wrong between us, but this *is* our wedding night. We'll never have another, and others have found themselves married to strangers! Can't we for once put the bitterness and reproaches behind us and—and—" He hesitated as his lips moved caressingly over her upturned face. "Oh, hell! I don't know what I mean! At least for tonight don't fight me. Between us we *must* make this unfortunate marriage work!"

More than willing to agree, Catherine melted against him, her raised mouth an irresistible invitation. Jason gave a low groan, and his lips found hers once more. Engrossed in one another, it came as a shock when the carriage finally stopped before the Hotel Crillon. Jason, though, was extremely thankful—another few miles of Catherine's unhoped for surrender, and he wouldn't have been able to control himself from consummating their marriage on the carriage floor!

Endeavoring not to behave like a rutting boar, he was uncomfortably careful once they had reached the privacy of their rooms. Maintaining a tight rein on his desire, he forced himself to order a light meal to be sent to their rooms and reluctantly left Catherine to freshen herself.

Catherine, very much aware of what the evening would hold, was nearly quivering with trepidation and tremulous joy. Deliberately she ignored the unwelcome thought that kept persisting—that while he made his hunger of her very evident and the desire that they reach a workable agreement very evident—not once had Jason mentioned or even hinted that he loved her or that she meant more to him than any other woman! Fiercely she dashed the unpleasant thoughts away and in a fever of anticipation hurriedly ordered Jeanne to prepare her bath.

For the first time in her life she consciously wanted to make a man want her, and as she rifled almost frenziedly through the overflowing armoire for a gown, she wished she knew more of what a man would find irresistible. Finally, her gaze alighted on a negligee set Jason had given her shortly after their arrival in Paris. She had never thought to wear it, partly from sheer perversity and partly from an inborn knowledge that those garments had been designed with one thought in mind.

The gown and robe were of purple silk, a purple so rich and dark that it appeared almost black, and against Catherine's alabaster skin it was evocatively sensual. The gown clung to her soft breasts like a second skin before swirling with its yards of material like a purple cloud to her feet. Two minute ribbons on each shoulder were all that held it up, and with a curl in the pit of her stomach, Catherine knew that in a matter of minutes, with one small tug, the ribbons would be undone by Jason.

The robe had long, full sleeves so transparent that her arms gleamed whitely through its folds. The long train floated seductively behind her as she entered the room where Jason awaited her.

He had his back to her, staring out the balcony windows. For a moment she remained in the doorway, noting the small table set for two, the soft candlelight creating its own special spell, and then her eyes swung to the tall man, as yet unaware of her presence. He had changed into a silken robe and his hair shining with dampness bespoke the fact that he too had taken the time to bathe.

Hesitating, suddenly uncertain, she knew now was the moment to turn and run—now before he sensed she was there. She could slip back into her room and send Jeanne to him with the message that she was ill and would not see him tonight. Intuitively she knew he would not force himself on her this evening. But even as she hovered uncertainly, he divined her presence and slowly rotated to face her.

The quick fire that leaped to his eyes almost sent her whirling from the room, but ignoring the frightened thump of her heart, she smiled shyly and allowed him to seat her at the table. She was so conscious of him, his green eyes dark with that quick flame of possessive desire and his full mouth frankly sensual, that the following meal was forever a blur in her memory. What they ate and drank she never remembered, but his face, dark and unrevealing except for the flicker in his eyes, was burned into her mind for all time. Watching his long fingers curl carelessly around a Baccarat crystal glass, she was unable to stop a shiver of excitement from sliding over her body. Soon those long fingers and lean hands would have her body at their mercy, and the thought made a coil deep in her loins tighten almost painfully.

Incapable of standing the suspense building in the quiet room, Catherine suddenly jumped to her feet and stammered, "It—it—it's terribly hot in here! I think I'd like a breath of air."

Lazily, Jason watched her cross to the French doors and throw them wide, allowing the cool night air, lightly scented from the blooming acacia trees, to drift into the room. Her body becoming tenser by the moment, she stared blankly down at the avenue below. She felt, rather than saw, Jason come up behind her. His hands were warm and gentle when they closed over her shoulders, but she still couldn't control the slight stiffening of fear that coursed through her.

Firmly Jason pulled her body back against him, but for several seconds he did nothing more alarming than slowly caress her arms and shoulders while his lips traveled lightly over her hair and brushed the sensitive spot where her neck joined her smooth shoulders. It wasn't until he felt her relax completely against him that he gently turned her to face him. Catherine's heart caught in her throat at the expression on his face.

In the moonlight they solemnly studied one another, and then Jason kissed her. It was a gentle, questioning kiss as well as a demanding one, suddenly hardening into passion, and eagerly Catherine opened her lips under the onslaught of desire. Her blood was pounding in her temples when Jason at last raised his head, and she knew a hungry, throbbing pain deep in her loins. His eyes searched her face, and then without a word he swung her up into his arms and carried her into the bedchamber.

With quick, deliberate movements, he threw the gown and robe on the floor, and as he laid her on the bed, he gave a low, husky laugh. "I hope you're not planning on sliding out from underneath me at the crucial moment again?" he teased, his white teeth flashing in the darkness.

Too aware of the hard, warm body above her, she could only stare dumbly, and when he joined her on the bed and pulled her to him, it was as if she had been thrust into a hot second skin, her body molding itself next to his until they were so close that not even a shadow could come between them. His mouth was firm and knowing as it closed over hers, and at first he was satisfied with her untaught answering of his hunger. But then with desire driving him, his lips opened hers, and he drank fiercely of the sweetness of her mouth as his hands tantalizingly explored her body.

He was gentle with her, taking his time, his mouth following his hands as they moved over her shoulders and breasts. Catherine's emotions were spinning wildly. Instinctively her own untried hands hesitatingly began to travel over his body, moving slowly down over his muscled strength, down his broad back and firm buttocks, gathering courage to touch him as she had done the one time at the inn. But there was no need to bolster her courage because Jason gently but surely guided her hand to him, and when her palm closed around him, a low growl of pleasure burst from his lips.

"Kitten—*mon petit coeur*—ah—not that way—this way!" Expertly he taught her how to please a man, his hand over hers deftly showing her the way, encouraging her onward with soft words when she faltered. Soon he gave a breathless little laugh and said, "Slowly, slowly my pet, or this will be over before we've even started!" And then he moved his body slightly away from her while his hands still caressingly discovered her and slowly moved over her flat belly down to her trembling thighs. She couldn't help the involuntary impulse to tighten her legs against him, and his hands instantly stopped their search. Against her mouth, he questioned, "Kitten?" and then kissed her deeply. She was lost, her thighs falling apart to let him explore her very being.

His touch was like a flame shooting up through her body, and as his lips and hands continued to arouse her beyond anything she had ever known, unconsciously she moaned, her hands reaching for him hungrily. And this time she needed no guidance as she practiced what he had taught her. She was nearly shaking from the force of the emotion that held her enthralled, and then when she thought she could cry aloud for the pleasure he gave her, gently and slowly, he entered her. It was such blessed relief to at last be possessed that a satisfied sigh broke from her lips, and Jason laughed low. "It's not over yet, my sweet. You're just learning."

Then he began to move deep inside her, and the strong, deep emotions he had aroused seemed to build and combine themselves into one hard, aching feeling between her thighs. Her hands beating frantically against his back, unconsciously drove him on, and his body answered the urgings of hers as he plunged deeper and harder into her. Her body taut as a bowstring, Catherine felt the huge bubble of ecstasy that was swelling inside her burst, and she was left floating and dazed on a languid cloud of pure, sensuous pleasure.

She was so stunned by her own response that she missed Jason's eruption following quickly on her own, and she came back to reality cradled in his arms, his lips and hands still caressing her body.

Throughout the night that followed, again and again Jason aroused her to the point of near madness before taking her, and each time she experienced those exquisite emotions that heralded fulfillment. He couldn't seem to let her alone, allowing her to doze only lightly before again his body drove him to possess her. Catherine was as eager as he for that possession, and she responded to the fire in him with a blaze of her own. She stopped him only once—his dark head was traveling lovingly over her belly, and his lips were on the point of following his fingers between her thighs when a shocked gasp broke from her, and she stiffened, thrusting her body away from him, and stuttered, "No—no—I don't—*no!*"

A queer smile on his lips, he murmured, "Never mind. Some other time I'll teach you everything there is to know between a man and a woman. You're such an apt pupil, my love, that I forget you're still nearly a virgin." And then his lips took hers, and she forgot everything as his hands and body played with hers, drawing her deeper into the well of pleasure.

Dawn was spilling into the room before sleep finally captured her, and she woke hours later to discover that she was in her own room. Puzzled, she stared at the familiar hangings, and as full memory of the past night returned, a hot blush stained her cheeks, and childlike she snuggled deeper into the covers. Vividly now, she remembered Jason scooping her up in his arms and carrying her into her own bedchamber. After he had placed her under the warm quilt he had kissed her love-bruised mouth lingeringly and had buried his face against her throat muttering, "If I keep you with me, I'll make love to you all day, as well as all night! You're like a fire in my blood and I can't seem to have enough of you." He made to leave her, but Catherine with new-found confidence reached out and touched him deliberately. And with a groan of sudden, renewed hunger, he sank down beside her, and once more the magic was between them.

But now memory of her boldness made her blush all the more hotly, and she wondered how, after last night, she was ever going to face him. All the nasty, unwelcome thoughts she had pushed aside yesterday returned to devil her unmercifully.

Not once during the past night, even when their passion had been at its height, had he mentioned love. True, he had spoken love words and had called her his little love, but never had he given her any other indication that he wanted more than a responding body in his arms.

Catherine could fool herself once, but the thought of other nights of being possessed by him—knowing he didn't love her—was unbearable! Now, after last night, how was she to repulse him when he came, as surely he would, to claim his husbandly rights? If only he had said he loved her—if only he *did* love her!

The disturbingly unhappy thoughts continued to nibble and snap at the edge of her mind as she automatically bathed and allowed Jeanne to dress her. Staring at herself in the mirror as Jeanne brushed and arranged her shining locks, she searched her face intently for signs that now she was different. The face that gazed back at her was the same, yet she *was* different—there was no use denying it.

Until last night, until she had given herself to him so wantonly and acknowledged in her deepest being that she loved him, she had felt she was still herself: still the same Catherine who had so gaily planned his downfall with old Ilone, still the same Catherine who had vowed so fiercely in London to bring him to his knees. But that was before he had married her and before last night. Now she was lost on a sea of uncertainty. Without that burning sense of injustice to uphold and sustain her, she felt curiously bereft—as if somehow she had lost herself.

It was in this delicate, wavering mood of confusion that she made her way into the smaller sitting room, determined to avoid a meeting with Jason until she could compose herself. She was planning on ordering her horse brought round, hoping that once away from the scene of their recent intimacy she could find some solution, when her cousin Elizabeth's impassioned voice froze her in her steps. The door between their apartments was open, and Elizabeth's penetrating tones came clearly to Catherine.

"How *could* you? Didn't those times you made love to me mean anything? How could you make love to me one night and run off with her the next?"

"*Juste Ciel!* Elizabeth, we've been through all this before. I don't love you, I never have! I enjoyed your body—what man wouldn't? I never made any bones about it! But I love *no* woman!"

His voice was cold, and Catherine was unable to move,

shivering as each word destroyed any faint illusions that his feelings for her went deeper than common animal lust. Elizabeth's next words only drove the icy pain deeper into her heart.

"Do you love *her?*"

"Don't be silly! I just said I love no woman." Jason snapped, a thread of anger underlying the words and saying anything to get rid of her.

But Elizabeth chose to ignore the warning and cried, "Then why did you marry her?"

"Because," he ground out crudely, "it's time I had a wife and eventually, a son, to inherit my estates. Your cousin is young, and strong enough to give me as many children as I wish!"

"I could have done the same!" Elizabeth exclaimed stubbornly.

"No, you couldn't have," he said brutally. "With Catherine, I can be certain my sons will be *my* sons and not the offspring of the last man you opened your thighs to."

There was an outraged gasp and the sound of a stinging slap. Then Jason said in a level tone, "I deserved that. But you shouldn't have come here uninvited and thrown our past association in my face. And you have no right to question my motives for marrying your cousin. I think you had better leave. You've said enough, and I have nothing more to add to our distasteful conversation."

"We'll see about that!" Elizabeth spat nastily. "I wonder what your bride will think of your coldblooded reasons for marrying her. I wonder too, if she would like to know she's nothing but a brood mare for a host of little Savages?"

"The question doesn't arise. You will leave here, and you will *not,* if you value your life, have anything to do with *my wife!*" The threat was very apparent in his voice, and Elizabeth nearly choked on her rage. There was a moment of silence, and then Catherine heard the outer door slam angrily.

Numbed by what she had overheard, her thoughts in shambles, Catherine stood enveloped in icy despair, incapable of moving. The very idea of Jason sharing those intimate moments like the ones he had given her just last night with another woman made her distinctly ill, and the knowledge that the woman had been Elizabeth, her own cousin, made the thought even more nauseating.

She put a shaking hand to her mouth, fighting the overwhelming urge to be sick, and giving a small moan, fled to her bedchamber. Her whole body was trembling with reaction, and every word she had overheard was branded on her brain. She sank slowly down to the floor near her bed, and the memory of Jason's lovemaking on this very bed, this very morning, nearly made her gag. She had to get away! Knowing what she did now, she would go mad if he touched her again. She couldn't possibly bear it! Feverishly she gazed around the room, and her desperate eyes fell on the jewel box on her dresser, still open from this morning when Jeanne had placed a string of pearls about her neck.

22

It had been an ugly scene with Elizabeth, and Jason was heartily glad to see the last of her. *Sacrebleu!* What a shrewish woman! What a termagant! She should have known better than to face him like an avenging angel. No one had any right to question his affairs or his reasons for taking a wife, least of all Elizabeth. He rang for Pierre and ordered a light luncheon served on the balcony. He half expected Catherine to join him, and when she didn't, he was conscious of a faint disappointment.

La petite was probably still sleeping soundly, he thought tenderly. A picture of her as she slept, her lips rosy red and her cheeks flushed from their lovemaking, leaped to his mind, and he nearly left the table and sought her out. But, no, last night had been all and more than he had ever dreamed for, and just now it would be intolerable if she had changed back into the fighting, volatile creature who had haunted his dreams for so long. She was like some spirited, half-broken filly who shied away and fought the saddle so violently that each time they had to begin anew. Bemused by thoughts of her, he leaned back in the chair, visions of Catherine filling his brain. Eventually he shook himself free of his nearly tender mood. If he wasn't careful, he'd be mooning over his own wife like some lovesick boy!

But in spite of his resolutions, he couldn't help the smile that lurked at the corners of his mouth or the pleased sparkle that gleamed in the green eyes as he left a note for his sleeping bride and went off gaily to call upon Monroe.

The meeting with Monroe lasted well into the evening. The negotiations were proceeding at an alarming rate for Monroe. He didn't like rushing into things and was a little put out at the way Livingston was handling things. Some of his peevishness spilled over onto Jason, who spent most of the time listening to Monroe argue with himself.

"Jason, I tell you there's something suspicious about the way Napoleon is so eager to sell. Tell me, why does he expect us to buy the whole territory when he won't admit France even owns it?" Not waiting for an answer or expecting one, Monroe rambled on, "As I mentioned the night of the ball, Livingston is uneasy about the question of ownership, too. He feels we should push ahead and worry about the title afterwards—but I don't know. It would be ghastly if we committed the United States to pay France for the land and then discovered France didn't own it! My God—it doesn't bear thinking about!"

Jason was sprawled lazily on the couch in Monroe's office and reflectively studied the brilliantly colored Aubusson rug beneath his feet. "Hasn't France admitted yet that Spain has ceded the land back to her?"

"No! Yet France must own the land—even Napoleon couldn't countenance a land swindle of this size!"

"Well then?"

"Well then—nothing! If only Livingston would wait until we can hear from Jefferson. The president should be consulted before we take such a drastic step."

For a moment there was silence. Then with a note of wonder underlying his words, Monroe said, "Think of it,

Jason—by this one act, we'll double the size of the country!" And so it went, one minute uncertainty, the next excitement and awe at the prospect of what their work would mean to the United States.

Jason, at Monroe's insistence, remained for supper, and it was with a light step that he returned to the Crillon. The first inkling he had of something amiss was the darkened rooms of Catherine's apartments. Frowning he carried his lighted candle into her room where a bleak emptiness greeted him. The armoire gaped open revealing a barren state, not one scrap of clothing in it, and as his gaze roamed around the room he noted that all signs of her occupancy had vanished. No longer did her brushes and perfumes lay scattered over the dresser. Idly, the full impact not yet hitting him, he opened one drawer of the rosewood chest, and as he half expected, it also had been cleared of the filmy garments that only last night had been there.

Outwardly calm, although the frown had deepened and there was an unpleasant twist to his mouth, he prowled the empty room like a hungry wolf casting about for the scent of the hiding rabbit. And he found it in an innocent-looking note folded on the mantel. His name was scrawled on the front of it. With a hand that almost shook, as if he already knew its contents, he reached for it. It was a solemn little epistle that gave away none of the despair that had consumed Catherine as she had written it.

Dear Jason,

I'm leaving you. I should not have waited this long, and I'm sorry you had to marry me. Don't look for me—you won't find me. I'm going to someone who will take care of me.

I don't understand exactly how divorce is done, but I should think that after awhile you could divorce a wife who had deserted you.

I took all the things you gave me. Someday I will repay you—someday, a long time from now, perhaps when we have both remarried and look back on this episode as a time when we both went a little mad.

Catherine Tremayne

His bleakness increasing with every line he read, Jason sat down abruptly on the sofa studying the childish handwriting, his eyes finally riveted to the signature. An angry pain shot through him. He had grown used to thinking of her as his, and only yesterday, practically at this very hour, he had bestowed his name on her. How dare she sign her name Tremayne! She was his wife! Catherine *Savage.*

That his thinking was illogical never entered his head. He must find her—she was his wife! His woman! How could she leave him after last night? He would have sworn that she had willingly responded to his passionate lovemaking and had enjoyed it as much as he. How dare she desert him like this! He gave a bitter laugh. And to think he had begun to grow fond of the idea of marriage to Catherine, to believe that perhaps there was something to this love thing that seemed to possess even the most intelligent of men.

Well, his little gypsy lady had cured him of that foolish notion. Deliberately, to soothe the savage hurt, all the more painful because it was so unfamiliar and unexpected, he remembered every single time she had annoyed and infuriated him, from the episode of the hideous hag in his bed to the fact that she had hidden her real identity from him. Crime upon crime he heaped on her absent head until he had determinedly strangled any love he might have felt for her. He would never admit, even to himself, that she had meant more to him than any other woman he had taken to his bed—except this one was his wife!

It was unthinkable that she be allowed to do this to him. He would find her, and if he didn't wring her lovely neck the minute he spied her, she would learn that, like it or not, she would remain at his side and that there was no question of divorce. Not now—not ever!

Coldly he reviewed the possibilities open to her. The jewels and trinkets could be turned into gold, which would keep her for sometime. But she had to have a place to go, and there was no one in Paris she knew—except for her aunt and uncle!

It was in a black mood that he set out for the hotel where the earl and countess of Mount were staying. It was unfortunate, but when he was ushered into their apartments, he discovered Elizabeth seated on the satin couch next to her mother. The earl was standing, elegantly arrayed in evening wear, before an empty fireplace, and the welcoming smile he gave Jason instantly destroyed any idea that his wife had taken shelter with her relatives. The earl was a guileless man and if Jason's erring wife had come to Tremayne for help, the earl would not have greeted him so.

The Tremaynes were on the point of leaving for a soirée being held at the palace of the comte de l'Arotis and Jason, not wishing to give rise to more scandal, made a hasty apology and remarked, "I see I must have misread my wife's note. I thought she said she was visiting you, but as she is not here, I assume I have not yet learned to decipher her scrawl."

The earl smiled, very real amusement gleaming in his blue eyes. "Catherine's writing has long been the despair of her family. But considering how old she was before she had any schooling at all, it's lucky she can write as she does! She is not here with us, though. I have not seen her since yesterday in your apartments." Edward turned to his wife and asked, "Catherine has not been here today, has she?"

Ceci, still intensely annoyed that her niece had managed to capture such an eligible connection, muttered peevishly, "Of course not! What reason would she have for calling here?"

"Just so!" Jason answered curtly, cutting off the soothing remark that hovered on the earl's lips. Bowing politely, he departed, his thoughts already so far removed from the Tremayne's that he missed the malicious smile Elizabeth flashed in his direction. And Elizabeth, with the memory of

Catherine's face as it had been this afternoon, filled with despair and unhappiness as she pleaded with her for help, smiled all the more viciously. If Jason hadn't been filled with cold fury, he might have questioned that smile, but as it was, Elizabeth's knowing smile never permeated his consciousness.

Returning immediately to the Crillon, he sent for Jeanne and received another nasty shock. From the apologetic concierge, who came to his suite, he learned that Jeanne had left the service of the Hotel Crillon just this afternoon, without notice, and as far as he knew was now in madame's service. Was something wrong? Had madame been displeased with Jeanne? Giving the man some sort of answer, Jason escorted him from the room.

Growing more coldly angry and furious by the minute, Jason started cursing the moment the man had left. Damn her! So now she had a maid with her, did she? In a way that made the search easier *and* harder. Two young women would be easier to find than one, but the fact that Jeanne spoke French gave Catherine an advantage he hadn't counted on. But would she stay in France? he questioned himself. No, of course not! And he was a fool not to have guessed that like all runaway wives she must have made for home and mother!

It was too late tonight to start for England, but he barked out orders for Pierre to have his curricle waiting at dawn and spent what remained of the night tossing on the bed. As the long hours passed he lay there alternately cursing his runaway wife and then—suddenly aware of the danger that could befall a beautiful young woman without a male protector—worrying that no harm would come to her—before he could get his hands around her slim throat!

By the time dawn arrived his first thunderous fury had abated, but it left in its wake a deep, icy anger that was all the more dangerous for its very coldness. His pride was in shreds, and it was lacerated, arrogant pride that drove him merciless across France and England to Leicestershire once more. No one had ever treated him as she had done, and by heaven she was going to suffer for it! He stopped at The Fox only long enough to learn the directions to Hunter's Hill, and minutes later he was turning his exhausted horses down the neat oak-lined drive leading to the Tudor mansion that was Catherine's home.

Hunter's Hill had been built of mellow red brick in the reign of Elizabeth the First, and if his reasons for being here had been less urgent, he might have taken the time to admire this very handsome example of Tudor architecture, but he had no interest in such things at the moment, and after throwing his reins to the startled gardener, he rushed up the steps and demanded entrance from the gray-haired butler who answered his impatient knock.

The butler, taken aback to be greeted by a tall, broad-shouldered, haggard-eyed stranger, was inclined to argue; but Jason, after a nearly nonstop dash across two countries and almost at the end of his reserves, was in no mood to be trifled with. In a voice like splintered ice he threatened softly, "My good man, if you don't take me immediately to your mistress, I shall be compelled to remove you from my path and seek her out—in her very bath if necessary!"

His mouth forming an amazed "oh" of shocked surprise, the butler ushered the grim-faced young man into a small parlor where Lady Tremayne sat idly embroidering the sleeve of a pink muslin gown.

Jason, so certain that he would find his wife, was for a moment numb when he discovered himself in the presence of only her mother. And in the following minutes it was forcibly borne upon him that not only was Catherine not here, but that until he had entered the room Lady Tremayne had had no knowledge of Catherine's whereabouts since the night Catherine had vanished from the gypsy encampment!

The next half hour was one of the most harrowing Jason had ever spent. Not only did he have to explain who he was to this white-faced woman who sat regarding him in stricken silence, but he had to tell her that he was directly responsible for Catherine's disappearance. And if that was not enough, it was also his unpleasant task to inform her that he had made amends for his mistake by marrying the girl, but—and the most galling of all for Jason to disclose—that somehow he had unfortunately lost her!

An appalled silence met his final words, and eventually Rachael said in a weak voice, "Won't you sit down, Mr.—er—Savage?"

At any other time the situation and Rachael's prosaic words would have struck him as ludicrous, but his sense of humor at the moment was badly impaired, and he saw nothing laughable in the present predicament. He was, though, devoutly thankful that so far the small woman across the room from him hadn't had hysterics. With a taut smile he asked, "Is that all you have to say?"

Rachael took a deep breath. "No, Mr. Savage, that is not all—but it seems you have answered my most pressing concern! I know my daughter is alive, which is more than I knew a moment ago, and I know that until she disappeared from you, she was—safe."

"And?"

"And if you made your journey in as much haste as it appears, it is very possible you have passed Catherine on her way here. I do not believe the coach service is as rapid as your horses."

Blankly, Jason surveyed her. He had been so intent in his determination to reach Catherine's home that he had overlooked the possibly of arriving ahead of her! The thought of Catherine's horror when she *did* arrive and found him already on her doorstep, caused an unpleasant smile to curve around his mouth.

Rachael was much more shaken than she revealed and not all of her frightened emotions had to do with her daughter. When Jason, looking much like his father, had burst so arrogantly through her doorway, for a second it was almost as if time had reversed itself and once again she would have to live through that last terrible interview with Guy—but this wasn't Guy, this was his son, and intently she searched his face, comparing it with her memories of a man she hadn't seen in over twenty years. Had Guy's nose been so bold? His face as dark? His expression so harsh? Certainly Jason had not inherited his father's cool, sea-gray eyes. Remembering how those sea-gray eyes could hold such loving warmth in their depths, a shudder of nearly forgotten pain swept through her.

Jason mistook the expression on her face, and his voice held a note of very real regret as he said, "I'm sorry, madame, that I'm the cause and bearer of such ill tidings. I hope in time you will forgive my less than gentlemanly actions and accept me as your son-in-law."

She fixed him with a peculiar stare for some seconds before saying dryly, "I don't appear to have any choice in the matter. You have already taken affairs into your own hands."

A small, quick bow acknowledged her words. "True. But you could make this deplorable situation worse if you wished—though what you would gain by it eludes me," he said bluntly.

A faint smile twitched at the corner of her lips. "You're not a very meek son-in-law, are you?"

One of his most charming smiles was her answer. To his surprise he found he liked his new mother-in-law. As a matter of fact he was enchanted by her. No hysterics, no tears, just calm acceptance of the facts.

Throughout the next four days, he saw nothing to cause him to reverse his first favorable opinion. Rachael, he discovered, was a quiet, reserved person who hid a warm loving nature behind the dignified exterior of the dowager countess of Mount. Outwardly she presented a calm, unruffled appearance, but Jason sensed her daughter's disappearance preyed heavily on her mind.

The smile that on occasion reminded him vividly of Catherine's was strained, and the blue eyes, so wide and trusting, held an increasingly worried expression that grew as each day passed and Catherine did not make the expected arrival. Finally, on the evening of the fourth day, it was obvious to both of them that either Catherine was not coming or that something had happened to prevent her. Seated before a dinner that neither of them made any attempt to eat, Jason played with his wine glass while Rachael aimlessly pushed a piece of excellently roasted lamb around her plate. Viewing with growing anger Rachael's lack of appetite, Jason added another to Catherine's list of crimes. How could she so carelessly worry such a gentle creature as her mother? Searching the drawn face across from him, he felt a spasm of remorse for his part in this whole affair, and in typical Jason fashion damned Catherine again.

The next morning he joined Rachael in the small parlor where he had first burst in upon her. After some minutes of quiet everyday conversation, he said bluntly, "If she was coming here, she would have arrived by now. She must still be in France. I dislike leaving you without word as to her whereabouts, but neither can I dangle here indefinitely."

His words only confirmed Rachael's own unhappy thoughts, and she was unable to stop a sudden rush of tears. Deeply embarrassed at her inability to control her emotions, she desperately mopped at the tears with a delicate scrap of cambric.

Jason, feeling more guilty than he could ever remember, knelt before her and clasping her trembling hands in his said, "Rachael, Rachael, she must be safe wherever she is! She *must* be! Do not cry so. I shall speak with Roxbury before leaving for France. My uncle is a powerful man. If she is in England, he will find her. I have no choice but to return to France and search for her there. Do not, I beg of you, worry unduly. Between Roxbury and myself, we shall find her."

Later in the day, as he drove towards London, Jason wished he felt as positive as he had sounded to Rachael. Most of his anger had cooled, and now there was only a fierce, frantic desire to know where Catherine was and that she was safe. He still wanted to throttle her—but only after he knew she hadn't come to harm. He held all his own fears at bay by telling himself that she must be somewhere near and was no doubt enjoying a laugh at his expense.

The next evening as he approached the outskirts of London, his thoughts turned gloomily to someone who wasn't going to be laughing at all. He wasn't looking forward to the coming meeting with the duke. That he would come in for some extremely scathing remarks about his manners and morals was a foregone conclusion. That he deserved most of it nearly made him gag with disgust at his own actions.

What the hell had gotten into him? His normally cool head had seemed to desert him from the moment he had laid eyes on that violet-eyed little witch. But now, he told himself coldly, he was in command of himself and never again would she or any other woman be able to tangle his emotions.

The duke evidenced no surprise when Jason presented himself. Beyond raising a black brow in acknowledgment of his presence and waving him languidly into one of the many leather chairs in his study, the duke did nothing but wait patiently, his gray eyes only faintly curious. In bald terms Jason gave him a grim, unexpurgated report of his problem. At the mention of the name of Tremayne, the duke stiffened, and as Jason paused, Roxbury urged softly, "Continue. You interest me."

In a clear, unemotional voice, Jason proceeded to do just that. When he had finished his uncle murmured, "You married the chit, did you? Well, well, it seems that is a poetic justice after all."

A black scowl marring his handsome features, Jason snapped, "And what do you mean by that?"

Blandly the duke replied, "Hmmm, nothing. You must forgive me, my er—little quirks." Then apparently disinterested in Catherine or her whereabouts, he asked, "How do the negotiations proceed? I've been expecting hourly to hear that the bargain has been struck."

A disgusted snort from Jason caused Roxbury to level a

reproving look in that young man's direction. Jason, knowing that until he had appeased the duke's curiosity he would get no satisfaction himself, brought Roxbury up to date. As he finished his terse recital of the progress, Roxbury's lips curled into a pleased smile. "Good, good! It must be only a matter of days before the final papers are drawn. Can't you prod Monroe and Livingston into moving faster?"

"My dear uncle, Monroe is nervous enough as it is! And I don't really think a word from me would carry much force. Quite the contrary; You see, *I* have the dubious honor of being regarded as a double agent."

A quiet chuckle came from the duke. "Well, I suppose you could be called that—among other things."

There was no answering smile from his nephew, and covertly Roxbury surveyed him. Jason looked tired, and there were new creases and grooves in his lean face that hadn't been apparent the last time he had seen the young man. It would appear that so far his marriage had given him small joy. Ah well, thought the duke, it would do him good to suffer a little. Things had always come too easily to Jason—as had women. Who knew what might happen? Perhaps Catherine would be the making of him. It was time someone gave him a sound emotional trouncing. And apparently the little Tremayne girl stood as good a chance as anyone so far of slipping under his rigid guard. Thinking of some of Catherine's past actions, which Jason had told him about, he smiled, deciding he would like very much to meet the newest Madame Savage.

"Something amuses you?" Jason asked coldly.

"Mmmm, yes. But I seriously doubt if you would find it so!" he answered. Then with an abrupt change of subject, he asked, "Tell me. Aren't you interested to know if I have unearthed any further information on your unknown visitor?"

"Have you?" he asked waspishly. Jason was not finding his uncle's smiling mood amusing.

"Yes, as a matter of fact I have. Your intruder was an unsavory gentleman by the name of Henry Horace. He was a petty thief who had seen the inside of Newgate more than once. His—ah—wife, I believe she called herself, is a serving maid at one of the dockside taverns. It was she who identified the body."

The duke paused, and Jason asked impatiently, "Well?"

"She says on the night in question her husband was seen being very cosy—her words, not mine—with a black-haired individual. She served ale at their table, but the stranger remained in the shadows, so she claims she never saw him clearly." Disgustedly the duke added, "That doesn't do us much good though, because to her type anyone not from the vicinity of London is a foreigner. When I questioned her about their conversation, she grew rather coy until I helped her memory with a few pieces of gold." A grimace of distaste crossed the duke's face at the memory of the greedy look in the woman's eyes and the outstretched dirty hand. "From what I gathered, this man hired Horace to search your rooms. Why still remains a mystery, and who the man was, of course, we may never know. Unless"—he shot a penetrating glance at his nephew—"you have something to add?"

No longer particularly interested in an event weeks old, Jason shrugged. "Catherine confessed that Pendleton was after a map," he admitted. "I wonder if perhaps Horace was after the same thing."

"A map! What kind of map?"

"My dear uncle, if I knew I would have told you! I have no idea what kind of map, and I do not now have, nor have I ever had, a map. Quite frankly, I'm rather bored with the subject. I'm much more concerned about my *wife!*" Jason bit out the last word as if the admission was forced from him. His frustration bubbling to the surface, he said in a tight voice, "I have to return to France tomorrow. I cannot remain here cooling my heels until that little viper I married decides to show herself. It's very possible she never left France, and in between playing lap dog to Monroe, I can conduct my own search for her there. But," he eyed his uncle's relaxed form consideringly, "I need someone to look for her here in England."

His eyes very gray, Roxbury asked, "Are you asking a favor of me?"

"Damn it—yes! I can hire a Bow Street Runner if I have to, but you have so many more resources at your command, that if she's in England you'll find her before a Runner would even get a sniff."

"Such a gracious request overwhelms me," Roxbury murmured.

A sudden grin quirked at the corner of Jason's mouth, and some of the harshness left his face. "Are you roasting me, uncle?"

"Yes, to be sure! You're taking yourself much too seriously, and it pains me. Did you truthfully doubt that I wouldn't help you? Have I ever refused you?"

Jason had the grace to look uncomfortable, and he muttered, "No! And I apologize for my surliness. This marriage has me more rattled than I realized."

His nephew in an almost humble mood was very nearly Roxbury's undoing. A grave expression hiding the smile that twitched on his lips, he said. "We will say no more of this—other than, may I presume that with your usual arrogance you have already informed Lady Tremayne to write me if the girl arrives in Leicestershire."

Grinning suddenly, Jason nodded.

"Well, then," the duke said placidly, "I shall do whatever is within my power. As soon as I have any word, however small, I shall write you. You *will* let me know when you leave France for America, I trust?" he asked dryly.

A frown creased Jason's face. "If she hasn't been found by then—by the time the negotiations are finished—I may not return directly to the United States, but may pay you another visit."

Roxbury stiffened and sat up abruptly, staring hard at Jason. Choosing each word carefully he said slowly, "I would not! I should warn you that it is in your own best interest to leave France no later than the middle of May. It would not be wise to linger after that time, and you can do nothing here in England that will not already have been done. Do I make myself clear?"

Jason's green eyes, suddenly alert and hard, bored into equally hard gray eyes, and the silence that filled the room was tense and ugly. Very softly Jason asked, "Are you *ordering* me?"

The duke, torn in two by duty and affection, opted for affection, knowing that, like himself, if pressed too hard Jason would do exactly as he pleased. It was easier than worrying where or what his unruly nephew was up to. "No, Jason, I'm asking you." Then not willing to give in too tamely he tacked on, "You might say, I'm *telling* you for your own safety."

More relieved than he cared to admit by his uncle's capitulation, Jason forced a taut smile and proceeded to very nearly unnerve the duke by stating carelessly, "So o-o—you warn me that Britain is about to strike the first blow and reopen hostilities with Napoleon!" He needled the duke further by audaciously musing aloud, "I wonder which side I would choose to fight on. Having a French grandparent on both sides of the family tree and only one English strain running throughout makes it rather a difficult choice, don't you think?"

"Jason, don't try me too far." The words were spoken quietly, and recognizing—just as the duke had recognized—that the other could only be pushed so far, Jason cocked an eyebrow at his stony-faced uncle and grinned. "Very well! We will cry pax! You must forgive me for getting a little of my own back. You were enjoying yourself too much at my expense earlier for me to allow you to escape without some retaliation!"

23

Jason had a last score to settle before returning to France, and leaving Roxbury's town house, he drove promptly to Pendleton's lodgings hoping to find him there.

Luck was with him, for not yet completely recovered from the effects of the duel with Jason, Clive remained in seclusion in his rooms. Brushing past the manservant who answered his curt rap on the door, Jason strode into Clive's rooms like a brash north wind.

Clive, his arm in a black silk sling, was reclining languidly on a couch, a bottle of port near his elbow. He had been idly leafing through the latest racing gazette when Jason stormed into the room. At the sight of his visitor, he sat up quickly and throwing the gazette on the floor growled, "Who let you in? I have nothing to say to you."

Jason cast him a look filled with dislike and grasping the lapels of Clive's brocade lounging robe hauled him to his feet. "I have something to say to you. Take this as a friendly warning, *salaud*—do not *ever* threaten Catherine again! And if you cause Rachael one second of worry, I shall personally beat your brains out!"

Clive's eyes were like hard gray marbles, and twisting out of Jason's grasp he panted, "So, the little bitch told you! I should have known better than to use her. Just once, I wish a woman would do as she's told!"

Jason took a menacing step forward, his fists closing at his sides. "Clive, Catherine is now my *wife!* And if you so much as look at her the wrong way, it will go ill for you. Next time it won't be a shot in the shoulder I'll give you—it will be in the heart. My aim is very good, as you know. Remember that, if you ever think to force either one of them into a similar situation."

A queer glitter in his eyes, Clive exclaimed, "You *married* her!" Flinging himself down in a chair he sneered, "What a fitting combination—a gypsy lady and a Loiusiana savage! You deserve one another!"

"Thay may be," Jason said levelly. "But I warn you, I will take no insult about my wife, and you had better forget any past relationship you had with her."

"You mean I should forget she was my mistress?" Clive asked slyly.

Jason's glance was deadly. "That horse won't run, *gros lourdaud!* She was never your mistress—no matter how you and that old gypsy tried to mislead me. I've often wondered why you let me think it."

"It suited me," Clive said petulantly. Fixing Jason with a malevolent stare, he muttered bitterly, "I planned on marrying her. You and Catherine—my two failures."

At Jason's look of incomprehension, Clive's harsh laugh rang out. Having nothing to lose, he boasted, "Oh yes, I hired those two men who failed to kill you." He shot Jason a look brimming with hatred. "And I failed with Catherine, too. She should never have reappeared after I gave her and that damn brother of hers to the gypsies. But it was just my luck. Reina took a fancy to her and doublecrossed me. By rights the little slut should have been dead and in the bottom of the sea."

In an odd voice Jason asked, "Are you telling me you arranged for Catherine to be kidnapped? For God's sake, why?"

Clive gave him a derisive glance. "Money! What else? I was the earl's favorite until that noxious little bitch was born. God! How I hated and loathed her! He would have left me everything if he hadn't married that insipid Rachael, and she had to give him a child! I was to—"

Clive never finished the sentence because Jason snatched him up bodily and hurled him across the room.

Pendleton had no defense against the sledge-hammer fists that pounded into his body, and Jason, blind with rage and in the grip of a savage, frenzied urge to kill, struck him again and again, sanity returning just before he beat the man to death. Staring at the bloodied huddle on the floor, Jason said softly, "I should kill you, vermin that you are—and I will if you ever cross my path again." Then, sickened by Pendleton as well as himself, his face twisted with disgust, he stumbled from the room.

But Jason was not Clive's only unwelcome visitor that evening. Jason had barely departed, and Clive had just managed to have his many cuts and hurts tended when his servant entered announcing, "Another gentleman who will not give his name to me is here to see you!"

Davalos walked in a second later, halting with surprise at the sight of Clive's battered face. "*Dios!* What has happened to you?"

Clive threw him a smoldering glance. "I've just had a taste of a Savage, you might say."

"Jason? He is returned?" Davalos asked quickly.

"Of course, you fool! Who else?" Clive bit out angrily.

Davalos, looking very proud and aloof, said, "I know nothing of your friends, and it is possible that there are others who would do you harm."

Hunching an impatient shoulder, Clive turned away and

with a hand that still shook raised a glass of brandy to his lips.

Watching him with narrowed eyes, Davalos said softly, "So Jason has returned from wherever he had hidden himself. And the first thing that he does is see you. Why?"

"How the hell should I know?"

"I find that rather hard to believe, *amigo*. I have paid you a large sum of money to accomplish a certain task, and as yet you have not done so. *You* say that Jason disappeared suddenly from Melton Mowbray and that you could not find him. I have learned from other sources that he held a meeting with a prominent banking firm shortly thereafter. And now as suddenly he reappears and proceeds for apparently no reason to give you a sound thrashing." His eyes glittering and a dangerous cast to his thin mouth, Davalos continued silkily, "Have you tried to double-cross me—and perhaps Jason as well?"

Clive was in no mood to stomach Davalos's comments, and he made a fatal mistake in not realizing the nature of the man standing so near him. Angry and bitter and looking for someone on whom to vent his frustration, he sneered, "Wouldn't you just like to know?"

Davalos's features darkened, and an expression that should have warned Clive crossed his face. He was standing near a window in Clive's room, and almost idly his hand played with a silken cord tied around the drapes. Slowly, with apparent abstraction, he unhooked the cord, letting the drape swing free. Holding the length of silk in his hand he said, "*Sí*. I would like to know. And I would like to know where Jason has been and now where he has gone."

Clive, paying little attention to Davalos's actions, gave a twisted grimace of a smile. "That, my friend, you didn't pay for. So you'll just have to wonder."

"True," Davalos agreed calmly as almost caressingly he drew the silk cord through his hands. "But I did pay you to deliver a map into my hands."

Nastily Clive snapped, "Prove it!"

His voice very quiet, Davalos inquired tightly, "Are you telling me that I shall get nothing for my money?"

Clive threw him a derisive smile and turning his back on him said curtly, "That's exactly what I'm saying. Get out of here. I think—"

Clive never finished his sentence for, like the reptile he resembled, Davalos struck. He slipped the thin cord of silk around Clive's throat and tightened. Vainly Clive's fingers clutched at the band biting into his neck. Davalos, a smile on his face, only increased the pressure bending the other man almost backwards with his strength. "See, *amigo,* it is not wise to thwart me," Davalos hissed in his ear.

Clive, fighting off the blackness closing in before his eyes, barely heard the words. He fought desperately, but it was no use and a few minutes later his body slid to the floor.

Davalos stared at him a moment. Then quickly he left the room. There was no one in the small hallway, and if luck was with him the corpse would not be discovered for hours—perhaps not even until morning. It all depended on how long Clive's servant would wait before checking the room.

Reaching the street Davalos hurried away into the night. Now there was no choice—he would have to leave England immediately, before a hue and cry was raised. But that suited his purpose. Jason must even now be preparing to leave for New Orleans—and he, Davalos would be right behind him.

But there Davalos miscalculated. Jason was not on his way to New Orleans. There was nothing to hold him in England now, and Jason left that night for France. His return to Paris was accomplished almost as quickly as the dash to England. And as his curricle covered the now familiar roads leading to the capital city, his eyes were unceasing in their search for a slim, violet-eyed figure. His curt questions at the posting inns along the way elicited no new information.

As each day passed and he still heard no word of his vanished wife, his face grew harder, and his green eyes took on an icy expression that gave more than one person pause.

In private conversation with Monroe, he intimated that the situation in Europe was such that he had felt it necessary to send his bride home to Louisiana. To those who asked after his missing bride, he told the same story.

Unable to bear the empty rooms at the Hotel Crillon, he moved his lodgings to a less splendid address and proceeded to commit such wild excesses that he soon earned the title of "The Mad Man from Louisiana." No wager or dare was too reckless or dangerous for him. He fought two duels, one of them with the Chevalier D'Arcy, killing the man outright with a shot between the eyes. Only the fact that D'Arcy was universally disliked saved Jason from a very nasty state of affairs. Napoleon frowned upon dueling, but as D'Arcy was no loss and Jason was connected, however slightly, with the very delicate question of the purchase of Louisiana, it was good politics to look the other way.

Bent upon his own path to destruction, the gambling halls and cockpits became his haunts, and a different beautiful woman hung on his arm each night. Pride that had at first driven him after a runaway wife now forbade him to search for her. She wanted none of him, did she? Well then, the devil with her! He wouldn't waste his time languishing like a lovesick fool over a woman who didn't want him—not when there so many who were eager and more than willing to share his bed. And share it they did! It was as if by possessing as many women as possible he could tear Catherine's lovely face from his memories.

A note from Monroe abruptly interrupted his rakish pursuits, and he managed to arrive at the American legation showing few signs of his latest indulgences. But Monroe, seated behind his desk, studied the tall, slim-hipped figure, as Jason restlessly prowled the room, and observed the faint air of dissipation that clung to the young man before him.

His green eyes held a reckless glitter that hadn't been obvious earlier, and his full bottom lip definitely had a cynical twist to it. Disturbed by Jason's unceasing pacing, Monroe brought a halt to it by remarking testily, "Jason, *will* you sit down and stop moving about so! How can I concentrate with you stalking around the room like a lion in a cage?"

Throwing Monroe an impatient glance, Jason forced himself to settle in a large overstuffed chair next to the desk. His long legs, encased in a pair of tight-fitting buckskin breeches, were stretched out in front of him, and after shoving his hands into the front pockets, he slouched back against the fabric and rested his dark head on the top of the chair. His voice expressionless, he asked, "Satisfied?"

Monroe eyed him warily. This was a side of young Savage he hadn't encountered before, and he wasn't sure he liked it. At the moment Jason reminded him ever so much of a banked fire; behind his exterior a blazing flame roared, and it would take very little to release the inferno that Savage barely held in check. Deciding against polite conversation Monroe said bluntly, "We have agreed to pay France sixty million francs for the Louisiana territory."

Jason raised an eyebrow and murmured, "So, you and Livingston finally overcame your differences. Do you know exactly what you have bought? The extent of the territory has always been obscure—did the French make it clear precisely where the boundary lines run? And did Barbé-Marbois offer proof of ownership?"

Monroe squirmed uncomfortably and uneasily bit his lip. Trust Savage to put his finger unerringly on the two points he and Livingston preferred not to think about. War with Spain over the territory was implicit in the contract, and neither he nor Livingston had any positive idea of what they were committing the United States to pay fifteen million dollars for.

Jason, reading Monroe's thoughts fairly accurately, questioned softly, "Do you even know where the western boundary of the territory is?"

Almost curtly, Monroe answered, "Robert was dissatisfied with Barbé-Marbois's answers on that subject and has discussed that very point with Talleyrand."

"And what did the astute minister of foreign affairs have to say?"

Disliking to disclose to this increasingly insolent young man how little they did know, Monroe hesitated. But recalling Jefferson's latest letter and the president's admonition that Savage was to be trusted implicitly, he said dryly, "We are to construe it whichever way we wish!"

Jason smiled to himself. Clever, clever Talleyrand! Trust him to give an ambiguous answer.

"Does the thought of United States ownership please you?" Monroe asked, breaking into his thoughts.

Jason shrugged. "At the moment I can see little that the change of ownership will bring. Besides," he added, "Congress may not approve of what you have done—or has that thought not yet occurred to you?"

It had, and he and Livingston between themselves had already discussed the question of whether the Constitution even allowed the Federal government the right to buy foreign lands. And both were certain the Federalists would question it, as well as several Republican congressmen.

Yet the purchase of the territory, whether legal or not, would solve so many problems that had plagued the United States lately: Spain would no longer control the Mississippi River; there would be peace with France and not war, although war with Spain was not resolved; and most importantly, the Americans would no longer be bound east of the Mississippi River. Hopefully, Congress and Jefferson would take the same point of view. Whatever the outcome, he and Livingston had signed a bargain, and now all they could do was inform Jefferson and their own nation of what they had done.

Looking at Jason, Monroe asked, "Now that our negotiations are done, is there any reason for you to remain in France?"

Pausing only a second, Jason said in an odd tone, "None."

"Then perhaps you will continue to serve Jefferson as you have in the past and carry these dispatches explaining the treaty to him?" It was really more of a statement than a question and both men knew the answer.

Two days later Jason stood on the deck of a sleek American ship and idly watched the coastline of Europe disappear. He was on his way home and in a small leather pouch around his waist rested the documents from Paris.

Gazing at the widening expanse of blue-green water, his face was expressionless. Somewhere across the ever-increasing distance, he had left a wife—a wife who could be caught up in the holocaust of war that was ready to erupt between England and France! For a minute a flash of something approaching anguish cut through him as the memory of a pair of dancing violet eyes leaped to his mind. Then the icy facade was back, and after one last glance he turned with a shrug of indifference and made his way below deck.

PART THREE

AMERICA

Summer 1803

24

After over five weeks at sea, Jason was glad to have the feel of solid mother earth beneath his feet. *Mon Dieu,* it was good to be back, he thought, smiling with pleasure as his gaze rested upon the gently rolling green hills of Virginia. But his pleasure was mixed; he had the dispatches to deliver to Jefferson, and the long overland journey through the treacherous Natchez Trace to face before he would find himself once more on home ground.

He had lost a whole day in Norfolk cooling his heels while waiting impatiently for his belongings to be unloaded. Then, deciding at the last moment to take Pierre with him, he made arrangements for the transportation of his belongings to New Orleans by a ship that was sailing on the evening tide; he did not wish to risk their loss on the overland trail. If he hadn't had to deliver the dispatches, he and Pierre also would have been on that ship for the final phase of their journey.

As it was, he hired what he hoped were two decent mounts for the trip to Federal City, already beginning to be called Washington, and on the morning of July 15, 1803, Jason Savage handed over to President Thomas Jefferson the papers regarding the Louisiana Purchase.

It was a hot, bright morning and Jason, immaculate in breeches of buff nankeen and a superbly cut jacket of tobacco brown cloth, could have thought of other ways to spend such a delightful morning. But he had undertaken to play courier and play courier he would!

He gazed about the president's office, noting with satisfaction that the large windows were thrown wide to allow a breath of fresh air to drift through the room, while Jefferson eagerly devoured the dispatches.

Finishing the last page, the president slowly laid it down and glanced with a pleased smile at Jason. An equally pleased grin broke the serious expression on Jason's face, and for a minute both men regarded one another with almost idiotically smug expressions. Then Jefferson broke the silence with, "So—it is done."

A slow nod from Jason greeted his words, and Jason, his grin fading, added, "Except for Congress."

Jefferson's blue eyes narrowed, and his jaw hardened. "It will be a fight, but by God, they *will* ratify this treaty!"

"Perhaps! The Federalists will certainly create opposition, and I don't envy you once the newspapers learn of it. You're in for a hot summer in more ways than one, sir."

But Jefferson, his eyes filled with visions, only nodded vaguely. Bringing himself back to the present with an effort, he asked, "And you? What are your plans now?"

Jason shrugged. "I leave this afternoon for Greenwood to see my father, and then I shall be for home. That is," he said quietly, "if you have no further use of me."

"Jason, such amicability alarms me!" teased Jefferson, his wide smile creating deep creases in his craggy face. Seeing Savage was serious, he added, "I depend upon your help in New Orleans once the treaty is ratified. And I will need you to keep me informed of the reactions of the populace until that time. But I have at this time no special task for you. Go home and enjoy the summer. When I have a use for you—I know where to find you."

Leaving Jefferson, Jason rode directly to Greenwood. He had sent Pierre ahead to warn Guy of his imminent arrival.

The meeting with his father was not something that Jason was looking forward to with pleasure. Guy would be full of enthusiasm for the marriage and then, Jason guessed, highly offended and furious when he learned that his son's bride was not accompanying her husband—had in fact deserted him. It was a galling enough thought for Jason to stomach, and he didn't relish the telling of it to his father. And, he thought grimly, if Monroe had minded his own business and hadn't been so eager to write to Guy about it, there would be nothing to explain.

Jason arrived at Greenwood late in the evening on Wednesday to find that Guy was not at home. A long-standing dinner engagement was the reason. Jason, seeking out his bed, was almost guiltily thankful that he did not have to talk of his missing bride at once. Unfortunately the unpleasant news could only be postponed so long, and the morning would come soon enough.

Entering the breakfast room the next day, Jason was met by a jubilant if very curious Guy. They exchanged greetings, and Jason took a seat across the table from his father, wishing that Guy would have managed to sire a few more sons before that last break with his wife. At least then, the onus of continuing the family line would not be on his shoulders alone and the whole subject of marriage would never have arisen. Sprawled in his chair, Jason eyed his father speculatively. Guy certainly looked capable of fathering a good-sized brood even now. At fifty years of age, Guy Savage was still a handsome and virile man. His dark face was only faintly lined, and his unruly black hair was sprinkled lightly and, women agreed, very attractively with silver. His shoulders were as straight and as powerful as those of his son—if not quite as broad. Jason topped him by an inch or two in height, but Guy had a lean whipcord strength about him that even his son respected. And looking at him, Jason hoped the day would not end with them coming to blows. Although just now Guy appeared very relaxed and expectant, Jason knew how quickly that mood could evaporate. And considering how disappointed Guy was going to be, Jason was not liking the task in front of him.

Guy had learned that his son had arrived late the night before, and with it the puzzling news that he was alone. So Guy's first action was to ask eagerly after Jason's absent bride.

His pleased excitement turned to anger when Jason snapped, "The marriage was a mistake from start to finish! My *bride,*" his voice grated on the word, "and I are not living together. She prefers Europe, and I left her there!"

"You did *what?*" bellowed Guy, his sea-gray eyes blazing.

Jason, glancing over his shoulder with undisguised venom, snarled, "I left her there. And, father, if you are wise you will not plague me further!"

Guy, his eyes bright with frustration, stared for some seconds at his son. Guy was a hot-tempered, volatile man and was at the moment controlling his wrath with difficulty. And Jason was doing nothing to avert the storm that was obviously brewing. It was almost as if he suddenly welcomed the opportunity to release some of his own hurt and dull rage at what had overtaken him.

A full-blown argument erupted, and they parted in tight-lipped anger. It was understandable—Jason would not answer any questions, would volunteer no information, and Guy was totally thwarted and frustrated.

They did not see one another for several hours, each in his own way somewhat regretful of the harsh words hurled at one another. They finally met again in the late afternoon. A shaky truce existing, they were seated outside under a honeysuckle-draped arbor enjoying what coolness could be found. Guy tried not to bring up the subject of their earlier altercation, but he just couldn't let it lie. Almost peevishly he complained, "You could at least explain a little. Dash it—at least tell me about the girl! Does she come from a good family? Monroe only wrote that you had married an uncommonly pretty girl."

Jason, lounging in a cane chair, threw his father a resigned look, "I notice you don't ask if we love one another. I seem to remember you thinking that more important than anything."

"Obviously you don't, or you wouldn't now be separated. I saw no reason to question what I can see with my own eyes. And if it wasn't a love match, you must have married well. An heiress, perhaps?"

"As a matter of fact—yes, she is. And she does come from a good family. Her father, deceased incidentally, was an earl. You might have met him—the earl of Mount, Lord Tremayne. His brother Edward has the title now. And her mother, Rachael, with whom I spent a few days, is a delightful woman—you'd like her."

Guy made a queer choking sound, and Jason glanced curiously at him. His father's face was drained of all color and Jason, his eyes suddenly narrowed, asked sharply, "Something wrong?"

"No! I—er—was just startled. Tremayne, you say, eh?" Guy's voice was shaking, and Jason, his eyes narrowing further, watched him closely.

Casually, Guy asked, "Your wife, Catherine, is the youngest child?"

"Yes, now that you ask it, she is. Her mother was married before, and I believe there was a child by that marriage. Does it matter?"

"No, no," came the hasty reply. "Just curious."

Surprisingly, Guy seemed disinclined to discuss the matter further after that, and Jason, delighted to drop the subject, volunteered nothing more. But the relationship was strained, and Jason saw no reason for prolonging his visit. Consequently, he set about preparing to leave at dawn on Friday. There was little to be done, as he was traveling exceedingly light, and beyond choosing horses and seeing that adequate food was packed, there was nothing more to be taken care of.

He was extremely careful in his selection of the horses though; he needed good animals with stamina and speed and yet not of such breeding and appearance as to incite envy or greed among the inhabitants of the Natchez Trace. Men had been murdered and their bodies left to rot on the Trace for nothing less than a high-spirited horse.

As planned, he and Pierre left just before dawn. The air was cool now but already with a hint of the heat that would follow. The journey ahead was hazardous—more than once Pierre hinted that perhaps they should travel back to Norfolk and wait for another ship—but with the familiar long-bladed knife resting comfortably against his buckskin clad thigh and a rifle strapped over his bedroll, Jason was prepared to face any danger on The Trace.

The *Trace!* Pierre gave a shudder and glared resentfully at his master's broad back. *Mon Dieu!* Monsieur was crazy, he decided. Look at him, he thought disgustedly, dressed like some backwoods lout, his coarse, black hair no longer fashionable but growing long, so long it covered the back of his neck.

Jason, elegantly clad, was the kind of man he would have followed willingly to hell, but monsieur, wearing those deplorable buckskins and so carelessly groomed that at a quick glance he might be mistaken for some half-breed trapper, revolted Pierre's very proper sense of what was fitting.

The area known as the Natchez Trace was old. The first trail had been made by the wild animals, the deer and the buffalo, on their way to the open grasslands. Next came the Indians, following the tracks left by their prey. The white man did little to change the Trace, which twisted like a snake from Nashville to Natchez—five hundred miles of treacherous trail that wound around impassable swamps and through virgin timberlands. Travel normally was from Natchez north, for most people took the Mississippi River for the southward journey, but after all those weeks at sea watching the waves of the ocean, Jason was disinclined to travel on water.

He wanted the feel of a good horse under him and the tiredness that comes from a long day on the trail. And he was halfway spoiling for a fight. Pierre prayed fervently every night that they would attract no attention from the unsavory population of the Trace, but Jason was almost disappointed when they arrived at The King's Tavern without incident. The King's Tavern marked the end of the Trace and the most harrowing part of their journey. Now there was just a long ride down the Mississippi River to Beauvais.

As the huge flatboat pulled away from Natchez, Pierre prayed that the pilot was experienced and knew every sandbar and current in that mighty river and that the river pirates were busy elsewhere. The barge was loaded with lumber from the north and a variety of goods headed for New Orleans. The very richness of its cargo would make it irresistible to the many river gangs that preyed on just such flatboats.

In spite of Pierre's unspoken fears, the journey was uneventful, but the little valet couldn't help making a loud sigh of relief after they disembarked at the docks of Beauvais and had mounted their horses. Jason, hearing the sigh, turned in the saddle and grinned back at him. "Happy to be home?"

"But yes, monsieur!" The words were heartfelt, and Jason shared them, his eyes eagerly scanning the familiar and beloved land. Urging his horse into a gallop, he raced down the broad oak-lined road that led to the plantation house. The hot Louisiana sunlight filtered through the huge old trees and the gray-green Spanish moss hung ghostly and motionless from their massive limbs. Abruptly the trees ended, and Beauvais, stately and white, was before them, the tall pillars gleaming brightly in the sunlight and the emerald lawn beckoning like a soft velvet cloak.

Slowing his horse to a trot, Jason guided the animal past the sweeping circular driveway that curved in front of the house and made his way to one of several whitewashed, low buildings that were nearly hidden by a grove of thick trees. Beyond them stretched acres and acres of tall sugar cane.

The sound of his approaching horse brought several people from one of the buildings and recognizing Jacques among them, Jason halted his horse beside him. Dismounting, he had barely enough time to exchange greetings, when Jacques said dryly, "Well, you're back. Have you seen the old master?"

Grinning, Jason handed the reins to a waiting servant and answered, "No. I haven't been up to the big house yet. Is he well?"

"Yes, but he's been expecting you for days. You had better to make your peace with him."

Smiling, Jason walked away in the direction of the house, his moccasined feet making no sound on the manicured path that led past the cookhouse and skirted a lush rose garden, the smell of blossoms heavy in the still air. Armand, his grandfather, already alerted to Jason's arrival, was hurrying down the broad steps to the house to meet him, his dark eyes full of affection he had for this, his only grandchild.

For a second they eyed each other, Jason noting with fondness that the old man appeared as lively and cheerful as he remembered. Jason's grandfather was not by any stretch of the imagination a large man. He barely reached Jason's shoulder and had always been slender to the point of thinness. He had the graceful, supple movements of a man half his age and the olive coloring of the true Frenchman. Armand was also very vain about his seventy-one years and he was proud of the fact that while his fine almost delicately featured face revealed a certain amount of natural grooves and creases, his skin was as smooth and soft as a woman's.

Jason grinned at him a moment before nearly engulfing him in a quick bearlike hug. Together the two men mounted the steps and entered the coolness of the house.

Armand was, of course, like Guy, impatient to hear news of Jason's bride. And unlike the unrevealing information he had given his father, Jason found himself telling his grandfather the entire story. It helped, Jason discovered, to talk of the incident as if it had happened to someone else. Certainly from Jason's measured, impersonal tone, Armand, who knew him well, could not guess of the pain and regret that twisted like a knife inside him. Bleakly Jason finished the tale, and there was little Armand had to say—what could he say?

Armand hesitated, wishing to offer some word of comfort, but seeing the forbidding expression in the green eyes, he let the subject drop.

They enjoyed a leisurely dinner together, and as the peace and tranquility of Beauvais stole over him, Jason felt himself relaxing for the first time in weeks. *Mon Dieu,* he thought, it's good to be back. And later that night, talking to his grandfather as they sat on the broad front gallery of the house, he said as much.

His grandfather, not a gray strand in his full black head of hair, and a twinkle in his merry brown eyes, teased, "You always say so, *mon fils.* Yet in another month you will begin to pace the floor like a trapped swamp panther, and then you and that Blood Drinker will be off to run wild. *N'est-ce pas?*"

Grinning, his face burnt very dark from the hot sun, Jason acknowledged the truth of this statement. "That is so—in the past." His voice took on a serious note. "I intend this time to settle down. I think chasing after wild adventure just over the next hill has lost its charm for me."

His bright eyes quizzical, Beauvais asked, "This wife that deserts you—she is the reason you decide this?"

Jason, his own eyes bleak, a puzzled look on his face, replied haltingly, "I don't know. But I suppose she's tied up in it somewhere. I've never been confronted with anything like her before, and I've never felt so damned helpless and frustrated in my entire life!"

Nodding his head wisely, Beauvais murmured, "And so now, you try to lose yourself—and perhaps find yourself in hard work. Very well, it is done. I have long wished to turn over the plantation to you, but always I feared you were not ready for it. Too often you are like the wind—one minute here, the next, miles away. But I think you are ready now, for you need Beauvais more than it needs you!"

It was many hours before they parted for the night, but Jason, climbing slowly up the stairs to his room, knew it would be a sleepless night for him. His mind was busy with what he and his grandfather had discussed, and he hoped he would not disappoint the old man. He entered his room, and momentary surprise halted him in the doorway as his eyes fell upon the tall figure who leaned with animallike grace against the bedpost. A smile of genuine affection crossing his face, he quickly shut the door and eagerly shook the outstretched hand. "By God, it's good to see you! How did you know I had returned?"

Blood Drinker smiled slowly, his dark eyes evaluating Jason's face. A faint frown wrinkled his forehead at what he saw. Something had happened to his friend in the months since they had parted, and whether this thing was good or bad he could not yet tell.

Jason's face was thinner, the tiny lines near his eyes more pronounced, and the grooves in his cheeks when he smiled were deeper. His green eyes had a shadowed look, unlike their usual bright, clear sparkle, which disturbed Blood Drinker. Bluntly he stated, "This trip to England has transformed you. Tell me what has happened to bring about the signs I read on your face."

Quickly and concisely Jason related all that had occurred in London and France, leaving Catherine and the events leading to his marriage until last. Blood Drinker guessed more of what had happened by what Jason left unsaid than from what was spoken, but he probed no deeper. There were some things a man had to overcome alone. He offered no words of comfort or sympathy, knowing Jason would reject them with loathing. Instead he asked, "And now? Will you become your grandfather's shadow?"

Jason grinned. "Hardly! But I shall take over the reins of Beauvais—at least for the time being. We talked long tonight, my grandfather and I, and at first I did think I could follow in his footsteps—he was willing for me to do so. But as we talked more seriously about it, we both decided to give it a trial first. He knows me better than I know myself, and so I shall remain here for the present. When and if events change my mind, we shall discuss it then."

When Jason finished speaking Blood Drinker said slowly, "It is good you have decided thus. You would never be content to tread the path another has cleared of all stones."

Jason shrugged a shoulder and changed the subject. "What did you discover about our friend Davalos? I take it he was on his own business in Virginia?"

Blood Drinker nodded. "It took me awhile to find it out. But he apparently requested leave, claiming a family crisis, and his captain gave him permission to be gone from duty. I had to check deeper to ascertain if that was the true story and not just a tale presented for our edification. It appears it *is* true."

"Where is he now?"

A smile crept across Blood Drinker's features. "He is at present in Mexico. I do not know what he is planning, but I can tell you that I have had a busy time keeping track of him while you have been gone. Did you know that he followed you to England?"

Considerably surprised, Jason had the sudden, queer conviction that Davalos had been behind part of his troubles in England. He did not say the thought aloud—it was not necessary; Blood Drinker would have already come to the same conclusion. His companion confirmed this by saying. "Perhaps he is the man who hired the one to search your rooms."

"Mmmm, it could be. You say he left immediately behind me?"

"Not immediately, but within the month. After I discovered all I could in New Orleans, I returned to Virginia and picked up his trail there. It was then I learned of his departure for England." A sheepish look gleamed briefly in the black eyes. "I was angry to think that perhaps I had overlooked some clue in New Orleans, and I feared that he was truly under orders from Spain. I found myself in a dilemma and resolved it by writing to Jefferson about what I had learned, and then I returned to New Orleans."

"Had you overlooked anything?"

Blood Drinker shook his head. "No. And after I had wasted many weeks running to and fro like a rabbit pursued by a wolf and had gone over all I knew of Davalos's activities, what happens? Our friend appears in New Orleans suddenly and as suddenly disappears into Mexico. I could have saved myself much time if I had merely waited in New Orleans as we had originally planned," he finished disgustedly.

Jason agreed absentmindedly, his thoughts on Blas Davalos's erratic behavior. Davalos had to be the interested party behind the mysterious map Catherine had alluded to. But *what* map? And what was Blas up to in Mexico?

He sighed, wishing again his disordered emotions concerning Davalos had allowed him to kill the man when the chance had presented itself. He could swear to kill him now, and yet always some silly half-forgotten memory of another time would deflect the death-dealing blow. Jason took a deep breath, longing for the clarity of feeling that Blood Drinker possessed.

Sensing some of Jason's thoughts, Blood Drinker asked, "You still cannot bring yourself to slay him, can you?"

Shamefully, Jason admitted it. "I know he deserved killing—*needs* killing—and I yearn to do it. But I cannot coldbloodedly plan his death. In a rage I could kill him—easily—and if he was to offer me violence or to threaten any of my own, I would not hesitate. For Phillip, I *should* kill him, but I remember that Phillip was a man who knew the risks he was running and who perhaps only suffered the consequences of his own actions. I owe it to Phillip to kill him, but—" Jason's painful words halted. He was angry at his own indecision.

The question of Davalos was something that ate at him like some foul gangrene. Only one other person had ever caused him such heart-rending vacillation as did this man who had been his friend. And as if to stop one pain by suffering another more terrible one, his mind was suddenly filled with thoughts of Catherine, and wretchedly he said, "What a fool I am! I cannot keep a wife, and I cannot kill an enemy. Truly, I have indeed sunk very low."

Blood Drinker said nothing. Jason's pain was his pain, and he was helpless to alleviate any of it. Jason glanced at him and seeing his own tortures reflected in Blood Drinker's black eyes, laughed harshly. "This will never do! Soon I shall be crying like a babe because the world has stepped on my toe! Bah! We have other things to do. I am to become a gentleman planter and you—?"

Blood Drinker hesitated before saying quietly, "I have spent many months following your orders, and it is time now for me to tend to my own affairs. There is much I must see to."

Jason nodded in agreement. "Will you remain here tonight?"

Shaking his head no, a glimmer of amusement in his eyes, Blood Drinker murmured, "Your grandfather does not know of my arrival, and there is no need to make him uneasy. If he discovers me here in the morning, he will be certain that I mean to tempt you away. It is better if I leave the way I came."

He clasped Jason's outflung hand tightly. "When you have need of me. . . ." He left the sentence unfinished. A moment later Jason was alone in the room.

Jason was pensive for some minutes after Blood Drinker departed through the open window, but then he determinedly shook himself free of the melancholy mood that threatened to overpower him and turned his thoughts to the plans he and his grandfather had discussed this evening. He was looking forward to the coming months and hoped that the plantation would offer some relief from the thoughts that racked him so often lately. He *did* need Beauvais more than it needed him; his grandfather had said it was so, and he was wise enough to realize it himself. When he finally fell asleep, his mind, for the first time since Catherine had disappeared was filled with enthusiasm for the coming day.

Beauvais ran itself smoothly, as Jason discovered in the following months. The crops—cane, a little indigo, and rice—grew easily in the rich, dark soil and ripened rapidly under the bright sun. His grandfather's competent overseer saw that the slaves harvested and loaded the crops for the trip down the Mississippi River to New Orleans. At New Orleans the Beauvais business agent saw to all of the necessary storing and selling as well as the accompanying paperwork.

It would appear at first glance that Jason would have little to do. But capricious or unconcerned masters make for capricious or slovenly servants, and so Jason worked as hard and as unceasingly as his lowest slave. There were decisions to be made concerning next year's planting, trips to New Orleans for the selection of the finest seeds and grains, and a multitude of other problems to be solved. Even Beauvais with its greased-wheels operations was not above such catastrophes as a levee bursting and flooding a newly planted field or grain growing moldy in the humid heat; and as with all thriving businesses, there were sharks and charlatans ready to move in and snatch what they could for themselves. And so Jason's careful glance traveled over every detail, small or large, that affected Beauvais in any way, from the buying of a new slave to the selling of the harvest in New Orleans in the fall.

Armand stayed in the background and watched with affection, satisfaction, and sometimes a faint prickle of uneasiness, his tall grandson's progress. It is not good for the boy to drive himself so hard. Such hard-working diligence could only be followed by an attack of revulsion from the harness in which he had placed himself. One does not take a newly broken mule—Armand smiled to himself at the comparison—and plow an entire field, *non!* One gradually accustoms the animal to it! So Armand gently suggested that Jason travel up the Mississippi River to the Red River Valley and observe the condition of Terre du Coeur, the lands his mother had ceded to him on his twenty-first birthday.

Jason agreed with alacrity, but not for the reasons Armand thought. In assuming that his grandson would tire of his responsibilities, he did Jason an injustice. Jason had changed, and he took his duties very seriously; but Beauvais was his grandfather's, and even the knowledge that someday it would be his couldn't change the fact that it was not his now, and that it was already a working plantation.

Terre du Coeur was a different story. There was a house nearly as grand as Beauvais and several attendant outbuildings, but the land itself was wild and untamed—acres and acres of grassland where cattle grazed, as well as stands of pine trees, thickets of wild blackberries, and woods that provided hiding places for game and fowl. When the lands had come to Jason years before, he had installed a manager, and washed his hands of the matter. But now, the need was on him to make for himself his own Beauvais—and to create his own future.

The hot summer months were a thing of the past by this time. As October approached, Jefferson had not written, and Spain still outwardly owned the Louisiana Territory. It worried Jason slightly that the United States had not yet ratified the discreetly worded secret treaty. News took so long to travel from one place to another that it was possible that a letter from Jefferson was already on its uncertain way to him. And for this reason alone, he debated the wisdom of leaving Beauvais, but then, he decided, if a message arrived, his grandfather could pass it on. Before leaving, he did write to Jefferson explaining that he would be at the northern plantation.

As it was, his letter must have passed Jefferson's, for he

had barely unpacked and begun to organize at Terre du Coeur when a rider arrived from Beauvais with the expected summons. Thoughtfully, he read Jefferson's large, untidy handwriting and then ordered a thoroughly scandalized Pierre to pack up—they were headed for New Orleans!

25

New Orleans was humming with the news of Spain's cession of the Louisiana Territory to France. Jubilant Creoles accosted one another on the streets with the amazing news.

"Isn't it *merveilleux,* Alphonse? Now we are truly Frenchmen again!"

"It is amazing, to be a French colony! *Vive la France!*"

Listening idly to the buzz of speculation, Jason wondered what their reaction was going to be when they discovered that the French rule was to be short—very short, indeed!—and that soon France, who had solemnly agreed to return the colony to Spain if she no longer wished to keep it, was to relinquish it to the United States, very neatly selling it out from underneath its rightful owners. A grin slashed across his face as he visualized the baffled fury of Spain and the thunderstruck wonder of the Creole population when the brash Americans arrived and took over.

Jason's first act on reaching New Orleans had been to open the Beauvais town house. He did not wish to live with his mother, and indeed, that coldly sophisticated woman would have been horrified if he had suggested it. Angelique Beauvais Savage preferred to ignore her marriage and her son. She had her own elegant house and her own circle of friends; and she adamantly refused to speak of Guy or Jason, much to the hidden amusement of the New Orleans Creole aristocrats.

Despite his mother's attitude, Jason was welcomed back with open arms by everyone else. The women were especially delighted to see his broad-shouldered, lean-hipped figure moving about the town, and the men enjoyed his engaging and charming company at the many places of masculine amusement that made New Orleans famous.

"Young Savage is a magnificent fellow, isn't he?" one of the men remarked. "So droll and amusing, so proficient with the pistol or sword!"

Without effort Jason slipped easily into New Orleans society once more. It was an attractive, frivolous existence: arising late, strolling around to one of the many coffee houses to join his friends; attending a horse race or a cockfight in the afternoon; and then, after dinner, gambling, drinking, or seeing what new delight madame had imported to her house. But Jason found himself exceedingly bored by such activities and felt chained to New Orleans by Jefferson's letter and his own knowledge of what the coming months would hold. He would have preferred to be at Terre du Coeur.

Jason took to remaining home many evenings, preferring his own company to an evening spent out on the town. He was this evening wandering restlessly around the library, not quite able to bring himself to choose a book and settle down like an old man by the small fire, when his butler entered and announced that a Señor Davalos wished to see him. On the point of ordering Williams to tell Davalos to go to hell, he changed his mind. Why not? He might discover answers to some questions—and fencing words with Blas was preferable to wearing a path in the fine woolen rug of the book-lined room.

It was nearly a year since they had met near his father's home in Virginia, but Jason felt the familiar sweep of dislike as Davalos bowed formally and composed himself comfortably on the high-backed couch placed before the fireplace. Jason offered him a brandy, and at Davalos's uncertain look he said sarcastically, "It isn't poisoned. When I kill you, I'll do it with my own two hands. I would not choose the coward's way of disposing of you. You should know that!"

Davalos flashed him a tight-lipped smile, his cold black eyes glittering with emotion. "So, you begin again the argument, *sí?*"

"Why not? Did you expect me to kiss your cheeks affectionately?"

"No. But I remember a time when we were *amigos.* A time when you would have been happy to see me, *amigo.*" There was a softly accusing tone to the words, but Jason, his green eyes veiled, murmured quietly, "Ah, yes. But that was before you murdered one of our mutual friends."

"*Diablo!* Will you always bring up Nolan's death between us? He was a spy, I tell you! My orders were to stop him. It was an accident that he was shot," Davalos cried passionately.

Jason was unmoved by the words. For a long, unnerving minute Jason stared coldly at his uninvited guest before shrugging and saying indifferently, "So you say. Is that why you came? To protest your innocence once more?" Before Blas could answer, he added ruminatively, "It makes little difference, you know. I, too, have my spies, and I know it was you who incited Gayoso against Nolan and you who urged the sending of troops after him. Would you care to tell me why?"

A muscle twitched in Davalos's cheek. Guessing Jason would remain unconvinced no matter what he put forth, he said resentfully, "I think you know."

A black eyebrow lifted lazily. "You're not telling me it was because of Fannie, are you? I know you were paying her a good deal of attention before Phillip appeared in

Natchez, but no one ever stood a chance with her once she had laid eyes on him. And if you thought she would accept the man who killed her first husband as her second, you greatly misunderstood the lady! She's much more likely to slit your throat!"

"*Dios!* You think I would kill over a woman? Puf! They are less than nothing!"

Grimly Jason demanded, "Then why?"

Suddenly, a slight smile curved Davalos's thin lips, and crossing one leg casually over the other, he said, "For the same reason you had such a highly secret meeting with the banking firm in England."

Jason stiffened and carefully put down his crystal goblet. "And what do you know of *that, mon ami?*" he asked softly.

Davalos seemed to study the design of Jason's waistcoat a second before his eyes met the narrowed stare of the man across from him. "Did you think I wouldn't learn of it?" Davalos asked sarcastically. "Did you think that after the only other man who knew its location was accidentally killed—and it was an accident, believe me. Nolan was no good to me dead!—I would let you arrange for an expedition to steal it from underneath my very nose?" Giving a harsh bark of laughter he added, "Oh no, *amigo!* I am not stupid! But you, I think, were stupid enough to try to borrow enough money to go after it. Didn't the conservative bankers trust your map?"

His face carefully blank, Jason asked, "My map?"

"*Sí!* You have to have some way of finding your trail back. And you must have it—Nolan did not!"

"And, of course," Jason said conversationally, "*you* hired Horace to search my lodgings. Might I know how soon you followed me to England?"

"What for? It matters not! All that is important is that I *did* follow you and that I know of your meeting with Hope and Baring. I have been extremely curious of your movements since then. You disappeared so quickly from England that I assumed the bankers were willing to invest the money. Believe me," Davalos went on coolly, apparently unaware of the dangerous stillness of Jason's form, "I was so certain you had slipped my net and were already on the way to New Orleans that I took the next ship to Louisiana. You can imagine my confusion when I discovered you had not arrived. You have led me a sad chase, *amigo.* I have been searching for you all over Mexico, and what do I discover when I return empty-handed but that you are here in New Orleans, obviously enjoying yourself."

"Where else would I be? And why would I go to Mexico?" Jason replied carelessly, slowly picking up his brandy glass.

Frowning, Davalos watched the casual movement suspiciously, and as Jason continued to do nothing, Davalos gave an angry laugh. "You do not fool me! I know what you and Nolan discovered."

"And what did we discover?" came the silky question.

Intensely annoyed by the continued fencing, Davalos snarled, "Cibola, the seven cities of gold!"

Rigid control was the only thing that prevented Jason's jaw from dropping open in stunned surprise. And then when the full impact hit him, he nearly burst out laughing. Here he had been as nervous as a cat with kittens that Davalos was on the point of somehow upsetting the entire treaty, only to discover that the fool was chasing after some legendary nonsense! He sobered quickly enough, realizing that the Spaniard actually believed in the story of the seven cities of gold.

A bitter taste in his mouth, Jason stared unblinkingly at the angry man across from him. Davalos had murdered one of the two people who had been like another half of his being, and the knowledge that it had been for greed nearly made him tremble with the desire to slowly crush Davalos into nothingness. Hiding his rage behind a taut, white smile, Jason said softly, "Leave, Davalos! Leave now if you wish to live another minute!"

Blas didn't think he had heard the words correctly. Then,

looking into the glittering green eyes, he *knew*. Without a word he rose swiftly and walked to the door. His hand on the crystal doorknob he turned and bit out, "Always, it will not be thus! Someday, *amigo,* you will go after the gold, and I shall be not far behind you. You cannot escape me forever, and be warned—you shall not cross the Sabine River without my knowing it. Don't make Nolan's mistake!"

Jason rose in one lithe, menacing movement, but Blas, his moment of bravura over, hastily fled the room and as hastily hurried out the front door past the startled Williams.

Thoughtfully, Jason gave the library door a slight shove to close it. He was in control of himself again, but, toward the end, if Blas hadn't ceased his threats and left, he would have torn him limb from limb.

So. The knowledge he had gained brought him little satisfaction. Tonight's conversation only confirmed that the map mentioned must have been the same one Catherine had spoken of.

Finishing off his brandy in one gulp, he poured another and prowled about the quiet room. The seven cities of gold! Cibola! My God! He almost couldn't believe it. That Blas could be so foolish and blinded by greed to believe there was such a place and that he and Nolan had discovered it!

Jason knew the old story well enough. Everyone did. The rumors about the cities with their gold and turquoise had led the first conquistadors north from Mexico City in search of it. In spite of the fact that in the middle 1500s, Coronado's expedition had discovered the rumors to be untrue, stories and tales of Cibola's unfound wealth persisted.

Biting his bottom lip, he absently lifted a leather-bound volume from the shelf and vacantly flicked the pages, his mind still stunned by Davalos's words.

The cities could exist—it was possible. Didn't scholars and men of knowledge claim there was a mountain of pure white salt hidden somewhere in the unexplored regions of the Louisiana territory itself? Didn't they also state that there was a tribe of white Indians who spoke Welsh? Jefferson, attempting to fire up enthusiasm for the territory, had even said as much to the newspapers. And it was true that there were miles and miles of Spanish territory where no white man had ever walked. Who really knew what was out there? Maybe the cities did exist.

Unconsciously, his hand slid up his arm to touch the gold and emerald band hidden beneath his velvet jacket. The band was one of two; the other Nolan had possessed. If Blas had found Nolan's, it would only confirm his wild suspicions that they had indeed discovered the legendary cities. Convincing Blas otherwise would be an impossible task, a task Jason had no thought of attempting.

A grim smile curved his mouth—now he wouldn't bet on Davalos having a cat's chance in hell of escaping him! Throwing his head back against the chair, he pushed Davalos to the back of his mind and slowly drank another brandy, his gaze riveted to the flickering yellow flames, his thoughts slipping unrestrainedly from his control and drifting down dangerous paths. He appeared fascinated by the fire, but it wasn't the flames that held his attention—it was the memory of a pair of violet eyes and a bewitchingly curved mouth that danced before his intent stare.

Where was she, he wondered? England had reopened hostilities with Napoleon in the middle of May, and Europe was again at war. He had heard nothing from either the duke or Rachael that gave any clue to Catherine's whereabouts. He hadn't even the comfort of knowing she was safe in England. She could even be dead—but his mind shied away violently, as if from a leper, at the thought.

No, she wasn't dead. She was too clever and scheming for anything to have happened to her, he thought contemptuously. Oh, no! His little kitten was probably somewhere very secure, laughing delightedly up her sleeve at how extremely clever she had been to have trapped such a very desirable man into marriage and then clever enough to have charmed him nearly besotted.

Examining his own emotions closely for the first time, he

admitted grudgingly to himself that he had been almost bewitched by Catherine. If she hadn't disappeared, he might have committed the unspeakable folly of actually falling in love with her! A harsh laugh broke from him. Hell! He'd been halfway in love with the chit ages before the marriage—only he had been too blind to realize it! And even under the circumstances, no one could have compelled him to marry her if he hadn't wanted to. And he had wanted to—he admitted.

A mirthless smile curved his mouth. Jesus! What an admission. His grandfather would have stared at him incredulously if he had spoken it out loud.

Armand had a very French outlook about wives. Wives were a necessary evil. One had to marry to insure that the line continued. If a bride brought wealth with her, so much the better, and certainly no Beauvais would marry a *poor* girl. And if not for a son, what did a man need a wife for? On the plantation there were obliging negresses, and in New Orleans if one wanted more than just a willing body found in the whorehouses, there were the delightful quadroon balls where the gentlemen could choose at will a young woman who had been trained from earliest childhood in the methods and manners necessary to please the most discriminating man. And they were so beautiful with their dusky to cream complexions, their glorious dark hair, and their eyes—ah, the eyes Armand had once sighed expressively, the eyes from midnight black to bewitching hazel green. With such a magnificent display of young womanhood so readily available, what was the use of a wife—except to breed sons? It was the way of life, *n'est ce pas?*

This was the creed under which Jason had been raised, and his own parents' stormy marriage certainly had not engendered any taste for connubial bliss. *Au contraire.* Nor had his opinions of marriage been helped by the fact that his grandfather and father had encouraged him from an early age to support a string of mistresses. Armand went so far as to give him a handsome young negress for his thirteenth birthday. Jason was often thankful in later years for his grandfather's choice of the present—and of the woman. For the woman, Juno, a tall long-limbed beauty almost ten years older then Jason, had initiated her young master expertly in the manner of physical love. She had taught her eager pupil how to slowly and lovingly please a woman, as well as receiving satisfaction himself.

He had become very fond of Juno. His dealings with women had been few. His grandmother was dead, and his mother had other things to worry about besides a son who reminded her of her detested husband. It had been only natural that he should become enamored of the one woman who had shown him love of a kind—the only kind he understood. Unfortunately, Guy had viewed his attachment for Juno with deep misgivings, and Jason had returned from Harrow to discover that during his absence his father had sold Juno to a trapper heading west.

He had been furious, but as the heartache eased, it taught him a lesson he had never forgotten. Women were delightful—but never allow them to mean too much. And that was how he had always viewed them; he looked upon women in much the manner he would the pleasing antics of a small dog or with the admiration he might give a particularly clean-limbed thoroughbred filly. Until Catherine—until she had stuck out her tongue so impudently, stung his pride badly by eluding his lures, and had made him painfully aware that she was a person, a person in her own right and not just a toy for his amusement.

But, he reflected bitterly, what good did the knowledge do him? He had no way of convincing her she was more than just a warm body to him if he couldn't even discover where she was! Staring broodingly at his long legs stretched towards the dying fire, his jaw hardened. What the hell difference did it make? She wanted none of him, and he'd be damned and cursed to hell if he would nurse painful thoughts of what might have been. No, he would do as her note had suggested and see his lawyer next week. The divorce could be handled discreetly. Few beyond Guy and Armand knew of his marriage, and no one in Louisiana had ever heard of Catherine Tremayne. There would be little food for gossip.

In those minutes, Jason's heart, which had perhaps begun to love a slim slip of a girl, enveloped the stabbing hurt of her rejection in marble. Not once in the following weeks did Catherine's face haunt his unwilling dreams. But even if he had surrounded his emotions in stone, it is interesting to note, that he never managed to find the time to visit his lawyer.

The news that Spain had ceded the colony to France was old news, and on the cool day of November 23, 1803, Jason was part of the crowd of laughing, excited French and Spanish Creoles that lined the streets and watched as the Spanish flag was officially lowered and once again, after more than fifty years of indifferent Spanish rule, the fleur-de-lis of France flew over New Orleans. Jason's smile was sardonic; his feelings untouched. He knew, as the others did not, that in less than a month France would relinquish forever her claim and the colony would pass into the eager, outstretched hands of the Americans! The Americans that the French population viewed with such disdain and uneasiness.

Another letter from Jefferson sent Jason upriver to Natchez where he met William Claiborne, soon to be the first American governor of the territory, and Brigadier General James Wilkinson, who would be in charge of the military branch of the government in New Orleans—Wilkinson, who had treated Nolan as a son and who had spied for Spain!

Wilkinson needed no introduction; Jason knew him well, and he viewed him with mistrust. Even the fact that Nolan had been Wilkinson's protégé did not overcome Jason's dislike of the man—Wilkinson had been involved in too many shady and near-scandalous operations for Jason's liking. Claiborne was a Virginian like Jefferson and had been governor of Mississippi, but beyond that Jason knew nothing of the man.

At first he was not impressed by Claiborne, and he wondered how the volatile, pleasure loving Creoles would take to this sandy-haired, serious-faced, almost prosaic young man. After a long briefing at Claiborne's hotel, Jason felt more confident of Claiborne's abilities. The man was no fool. Jason offered his services, and Claiborne had promptly accepted; in the future Jason would be part of the governor's staff, acting as a liaison officer between the American and the French. Claiborne knew it would be wise if he gathered more Creoles to his personal staff, for if the new government was to attempt to ride roughshod over the Creoles and cram American ways down their Gallic throats, it could be disastrous.

As Jason has suspected, the French and Spanish residents of New Orleans were not happy when on December 20, he, Claiborne and a troop of thirty or more American army men arrived, and the territory passed very quietly from France to the United States. It was a gray day, almost damp, and there were no smiles on the faces of the men who watched with dismay as the fleur-de-lis, raised so joyfully just barely a month before, was replaced by the American stars and stripes.

Jason, watching the unhappy expressions on his companions faces, knew the coming days were not going to be easy. His thoughts were introspective as he idly surveyed the group that was assembled once more in front of the Spanish government house to observe the brief ceremony. His gaze drifted incuriously over a tall, black-haired young man, not too many years past twenty, who was laughing down at his entrancing companion, her face lifted smiling up at his. They were directly across from Jason in the cobbled courthouse, and if they hadn't been the only ones smiling in the sea of gloomy faces, he might not have really noticed them. His gaze had already passed them over when suddenly he tensed, and like steel to magnet his eyes swung back, riveted by the girl.

A feeling of fierce, incredulous joy surged through him, and almost hungrily his eyes devoured the unforgettable features. It *was* Catherine! There was no mistaking her blue black hair or the gardenia creaminess of her skin or her enchanting red mouth. A thousand impatient questions hurtled through his mind in the split second it took him to recognize her, and he had already taken an impetuous step forward when he noticed three things that drove all emotion from his body and left him frozen.

One, she was gazing up at her companion with undisguised affection. Two, her escort was returning the look. And three, and most damning of all, as the crowd parted slightly, he was afforded an excellent view of her cumbersome and pregnant body!

Coldly, assessingly, Jason studied the pair as they stood talking casually at the fringe of the crowd. They were as yet unaware of how closely they were watched or how dangerous the watcher. Catherine's companion's features were darkly handsome, his clothes obviously expensive, and Catherine, her expanding belly aside, was even more beautiful than Jason's memory of her.

A grim, unamused smile crossed his face. Well, he had known she would land on her feet, and there, across the courtyard, merely a few yards separating them, was proof. He wondered what tale she had woven to entrap her apparently dazzled escort and if with careless indifference to the fact that she already had one husband she had taken another!

Suddenly, as if aware of the hard gaze traveling over her body, Catherine looked inquiringly across the space between them, and her violet eyes locked with Jason's icy green stare. For timeless minutes they stood frozen—Catherine's eyes widening with shocked disbelief, and Jason's ugly smile beginning to distort his mouth.

A small, anguished whimper came from Catherine's white lips, and involuntarily her hold tightened painfully on her companion's arm. Jason watched with derision the look of concern the young man flashed down at her. But the look of concern vanished as her companion sought the source of her obvious distress, and his narrowed blue-eyed stare clashed with Jason's contemptuous gaze.

Silently, an unspoken challenge was hurled between the two men, but before Jason could do more than take a determined step forward, the crowd shifted, and he watched powerless as Catherine, words tumbling from her lips, argued passionately with her escort. Abruptly she broke off the spate of words and pushed her way angrily through the crowd away from the scene of confrontation. Her companion stood undecided for a minute longer. Then, throwing a harrassed look at Jason, he plunged into the crowd after Catherine.

26

Her heart beating frantically, Catherine fought her way to the edge of the crowd and glanced back defiantly, almost expecting Jason to loom up behind her like some avenging god. But the dark-haired, sun-browned man who reached her side was not her furious husband but her equally angry brother, Adam.

"Damn it, Kate! Why did you run off like that? You've got to meet him eventually, and you've nothing to fear because if he lays a hand on you, I'll kill him!"

Still intent on putting as much space as possible between herself and Jason, Catherine only compressed her lips stubbornly and walked as fast as she could in the direction of their hotel. Her unseemly haste and her physical condition made her awkward, and after the second time she nearly stumbled, Adam disgustedly thrust his arm beneath hers and muttered, "I knew I never should have let you talk me into bringing you with me! If you'd have stayed in Natchez where you belong, this wouldn't have happened!"

"No!" Catherine spat back. "You would have just had a

nice little meeting with Jason and said, 'Sorry, old man, to bother you, but wouldn't you like your wife back? She's about to make you a father, and I really feel she belongs with you,' " she finished sarcastically.

Stung, Adam retorted, "Kate that's a mean untruth, and you know it! I might have looked the chap up and seen how the land lay, but you know I'd never just turn you over to him like that!"

Ashamed at her outburst, Catherine silently acknowledged the truth of Adam's statement. He would never force her to leave Belle Vista, his home near Natchez. Although he had been understandably appalled when she and Jeanne had arrived, exhausted and bedraggled after the long sea journey to New Orleans and the uncomfortable trek by land to Natchez, he had quickly risen nobly to the occasion. In no time at all the women were settled within his bachelor household as if they had been there for years.

It was only by bits and pieces that he had learned the full distasteful story. Catherine had been reluctant to discuss her reasons for fleeing halfway across the world, and Adam had trouble enough merely adjusting to the few bald truths she had told him the night of her arrival. Gradually the whole sordid tale had come out, and Catherine had held nothing back—nothing from the first time she had laid eyes on Jason Savage to the humiliating conversation she had overheard between Elizabeth and Jason that fateful morning.

She had been completely honest except for one point—she could not bring herself to admit that she loved her indifferent husband. Pride demanded that not even her loving brother know she had fallen in love with Jason or that it was injured pride that had driven her away.

Adam had been justly angered at her revelations, and being as hot-tempered as Jason, if he could have laid hands on his new brother-in-law on the day Catherine arrived, he no doubt could have killed him. But by the time his first flush of anger had died, being a fair-minded youth, he admitted to himself that all of the blame could not be laid solely at Jason's door. The fellow was wealthy and respectable, wasn't he? He wasn't mean with his money, and he didn't beat her, did he? He had married her, hadn't he?

Stubbornly, sister and brother had argued hotly. Adam took the stand that while he violently disapproved of Jason's methods, the man had attempted to rectify his mistake, and if she hadn't acted like loose baggage in the first place, none of it would have happened.

Catherine grew more and more tight-lipped and mulish until finally, after one long and blistering discussion, she burst out despairingly, "Oh, Adam, I thought if anyone would understand you would!"

Staring down into her unhappy face, he had felt all resistence ebb. He did understand! And there wasn't in him one ounce of real disapproval for any of her behavior. How well he knew the wildness that drove her—wasn't he plagued with the same emotions? Only he was a man, and no one questioned his actions.

But Kate was different, and he had to admit he hadn't yet recovered from the change in her. When he had left England she had been a bright-eyed little minx with shining braids hanging to her waist, and it was hard to reconcile that image with the woman she had become.

While Adam was trying to fit the violet-eyed, lovely creature who had invaded his home into Kate, his saucy little sister, Catherine was trying to discover the brother she had known in England.

Adam St. Clair, Catherine's half brother, had always been a quick-tempered scamp, as fiery and explosive as his sister. It had been partly because of Adam's unruliness that his stepfather had sent him to Natchez—that and the fact that Robert couldn't abide the boy. Young St. Clair was a constant reminder of things he wished forgotten and of his own lack of a son. And so at eighteen, more than three years ago, the earl had packed Adam off to Belle Vista, the estate he owned in America. Robert had done nothing with the land since it had first come into his hands twenty-two years previously. He had merely held the title. Sneering, he had told Adam, "It'll be the making of you. It should give you a challenge to bring it into a paying proposition. And perhaps keep you too busy to cause any scandals—at least I sincerely hope it does!"

St. Clair appeared to have outgrown much of his earlier recklessness, but there was still an air of suppressed vitality about his whipcord, slim body. His eyes, their sapphire blueness startling in the bronzed face, could still burn almost incandescently when he was deeply moved. He had grown up in many ways, but, being a man and much more worldly for all his youth than his younger sister, he held fast to the argument that the only possible solution to her predicament was to arrange for a reconciliation with her husband. People of their sort did not divorce!

But Catherine was firm in her vow to have no more to do with her husband, and eventually Adam unhappily agreed that things were probably best as they were. And no matter how distasteful, in time Savage would no doubt put aside a natural reluctance to undertake anything as repugnant as divorce, and dissolve the marriage.

But when Catherine had discovered to her horror that she was pregnant, nothing could change Adam's mind. There was a child to think of and more to bind her to her husband than that brief, hurried ceremony, and she and Jason *must* lay down their differences and come to some kind of agreement.

"Damn it! At least let the man know he's going to be a father!" Adam had shouted, and Catherine, stubborn and confused, could only shake her head adamantly *no!*

They avoided discussing it after the first months, but occasionally Adam would bring up the subject, still not resigned to Catherine's decision. "Look, Kate—let me visit the man. He must be back from France by now, and from what you've told me, I should be able to find him without a great deal of trouble. I don't even have to admit you're here—just introduce myself and see how the land lies." His plea had merit, and at least this time she considered it.

They were sitting quietly after dinner one evening in Adam's library when he had brought it up again. Catherine was attempting to embellish a tiny nightshirt, her pregnancy already obvious under the soft woolen dress, her expression distracted, and Adam sensed that her thoughts were less than happy. Without thinking, he had blurted out the words and had been satisfied when she seemed to turn it over in her mind. But then she laid the mangled shirt down and gave a small negative shake of her head.

"Adam, it's no use! Please don't plague me with it. I know all of your arguments—do you think I haven't argued within myself the same things? Would you have me just a brood mare like one of your horses?" Looking down ruefully at her expanding midriff, she had laughed sadly, "Although, right now, I look very much like a brood mare."

Adam's face softened instantly. He adored her, and it was only because he knew that behind the outward smiles and light steps she was miserable that he even mentioned the matter. Part of her unhappiness he put down as the megrims of an expecting woman, but he knew the unsettled state of affairs between her and Jason weighed heavily on her mind.

"I'll tell you what," he said suddenly. "The crops are done for this year, and it'll be some time before we start the spring planting—let's go down the river to New Orleans for a while. You need something to cheer you up." Then glancing at her belly, a crestfallen look crossed his face and he muttered, "Kate, I'm sorry. I just didn't think. We'll go after the baby is born."

But Catherine, an unexpected sparkle in her eyes, said, "Why not? I'm not that big, and a ride down the river won't hurt me. I'd like to see New Orleans. When Jeanne and I landed, we were in such a hurry to reach Natchez we barely saw the place. Let's go, Adam!"

A doubtful curve to his lips, he hesitated. "I don't know,

Kate," he said at last. "It's not the trip down the river I worry about—it's the one back."

Catherine leaned forward, coaxing. "Please, Adam! The baby's not due for almost three months. As long as we're back by the middle of December, it should be perfectly fine."

Reluctantly he capitulated, and in the following days, seeing how much pleasure it gave her, he convinced himself he had done the right thing. Both of them thoroughly enjoyed New Orleans, Catherine marveling at the soft shades of pink, blue, and purple of the houses with their delicate ironwork and the fascinating habit the residents had of building their homes right to the edge of the wooden sidewalks, called banquettes in New Orleans. At the French Market, although Adam had been there before, both of them wandered about equally wide-eyed, staring at the rows and rows of vegetables, fruits, materials, trinkets for the ladies, leather goods for the gentlemen, and lastly, the slave block set in the very center. Tall Indians wandered at will through the narrow aisles, some with feathers adorning their heads, others with only a strip of black hair running down the center of their scalps and colored blankets draped over their half-naked bodies, and squaws following humbly behind their haughty husbands. And above all, there was the babble of a half-dozen different languages, as Spanish matrons haggled with Cajun vendors, French planters considered the goods of an Indian trader, or an American argued over the price that a freed slave wished for his wares.

Because of the port, which made it famous, the city also had much to offer, and walking through the well-stocked stores, Catherine spent a good portion of this year's crop money on items for Belle Vista—a velvet chair that would look lovely in the main salon, a gilt-edged mirror, just the very thing she needed for her room, and—wasn't that cage of song birds delightful? It was fortunate Adam was a wealthy young man as well as an indulgent one.

They would have been gone long before December 20th

if Catherine hadn't developed a bad case of congestion in her lungs. She was in bed for a week and then had to spend another week resting before Adam would let her step foot from her hotel suite. He wanted her completely recovered before they began the journey to Natchez, and while the extended stay brought the baby's birth nearer, he decided they would stay an additional week before leaving.

It was an accident that they had attended the ceremony this morning. Adam had been providing Catherine with a tour of the points of interest in the city, and after seeing the Ursuline convent on Chartres Street, he had taken her to the *cabildo*—and so it happened that they were part of the crowd that momentous morning.

When Adam had said they would remain a week longer, Catherine had been secretly delighted at their unexpected extension in the city. But now, still trembling from the shock of seeing Jason and looking at her brother's grim face, she wished with all her heart that she was halfway home to Natchez.

Adam said nothing until they reached their rooms in the hotel. Then not even giving her a chance to take off her cloak, he snapped, "Now what, Kate? What good did that little exhibition do?"

Tiredly, Catherine pleaded, "Adam, don't start in on me! Please!"

Throwing her an angry look, he stalked over to one of the long windows that overlooked Canal Street. Watching him—his dark hair brushing the collar of the smart blue jacket he wore; his long legs, slightly spread, encased in a pair of buckskin breeches; his hands crossed behind his back—he reminded her vividly of Jason. So might *he* have stood before erupting with anger.

Steeling herself for the argument that was to come, she laid her cloak carefully on the bed and turned to stare at Adam's uncompromising, stiff back. Quietly she asked, "What do you suggest we do?"

Suspiciously, he glanced over his shoulder. "Will you listen to reason?" he queried gruffly.

A tiny smile quivered at one corner of her mouth. "Yes. I'll listen to reason—but I can't promise I'll obey you."

She seated herself on the edge of the bed like a good child about to receive a lecture, and her air of forlornness pulled at Adam's heart. Crossing swiftly to her, he knelt and grasping her hands in his said earnestly, "Kate, you must believe me when I say I would never force you to leave my home. I can't tell you what a difference it has made having you to run the house for me and how much I look forward to arriving home knowing you are there. I didn't realize how much I missed you. But"—he paused deliberately—"you are married to Savage, and I doubt if there is anything you can do to change that. You have no reason to divorce him! And you are carrying his child. You can't pretend or ignore the fact that what happened, happened. Nor can you deny the child his birthright."

"You're certain it will be a boy?" she asked lightly, and Adam frowned.

"Don't try to change the subject—you know what I meant."

She nibbled at her bottom lip uncertainly and asked curiously, "Adam—you saw him. Does he look like the type of man who would take back an erring wife without question?"

Adam, his memory of the harsh-faced, flinty-eyed stranger vivid in his mind, was compelled to answer truthfully, "I don't think it will be easy—but we should try to mend things between you."

"How?" she cried despairingly. "You saw how furious he looked. I mean less to him than an unnecessary slave! It's only pride that motivates him. How can you wish me to spend the rest of my life with him?"

Gazing into her distress-filled eyes, Adam sighed heavily. "Very well, Kate, we'll let it be—for now. But this state of affairs cannot continue indefinitely. And," he added quietly, "today we were lucky. Have you considered that we may have mutual friends and that it is extremely possible our paths could cross when we least expect it? That, God forbid—some unsuspecting hostess might try to introduce you to your husband? What a lovely surprise that would be!"

Catherine nodded unhappily. "Adam, please, I know all your arguments. Don't let's talk about it now. Let's go home and let me think. After the baby is born, perhaps then we can settle the problem."

"Kate, the problem is not going to evaporate! The longer you wait, the harder it's going to be."

Adam left it there. He knew his sister rather well. If he leaned too hard she would dig in her small heels and mulishly refuse to budge. Little donkey, he thought affectionately.

They left early the next morning for Natchez, and Catherine did not take a normal breath until New Orleans was several miles behind them. Any moment she expected Jason's thunderous voice to freeze her in her tracks, and she was never so thankful to see Adam's home than she was on the night they returned. It was truly like returning home, for she loved Belle Vista. The property had been given this name because it was situated on a high bluff overlooking the Mississippi River and the lowlands of Louisiana. Most of his property lay in Louisiana, but like the majority of the Natchez plantations, the home was on the east side of the Mississippi—being at a higher elevation, it was healthier. The swampy lowlands were the source of much of Adam's wealth but were also excellent breeding grounds for mosquitoes, and malaria was a common illness during the summer.

Catherine was attracted to the house, though it was smaller and less pretentious than some in the area. It had been in a predictable bachelor state when she arrived, but with Adam's uncertain support—"Damnit, Kate, I think this room looks nice as it is! What do you want to change it for?"—she had made Belle Vista as elegant and comfortable as any of the other magnificent homes that looked down on the muddy Mississippi River below.

That night, glancing fondly around her large bedroom at the pale green walls, the soft champagne-colored rug and the airy curtains hanging at the wide windows, she gave a sigh of satisfaction. Adam might have objected at first, she thought, as she drowsily snuggled down between lavender-scented sheets, but even he must admit the house was more becoming since she had taken it in hand.

Catherine was exhausted after the long trip, and a low, nagging backache wouldn't let her sleep. She had noticed the ache off and on all day but had put it down to the strain of the trip. After moving about uncomfortably for what seemed like hours, she decided she might as well arise. Wrapping a robe about her cumbersome bulk, she padded barefooted down the wide staircase to Adam's study. It wasn't too late, not much past midnight, but Adam had retired early. She lit a candle and poked hopefully at the smoldering embers on the hearth. Reviving a spark she tossed on a few small pieces of wood and knelt awkwardly in front of the fire.

Almost hypnotized by the wavering glow of the fire, she stayed there motionless in front of it for some time, her mind blank. But gradually, insidiously, the thought of Jason began to curl around the edges of her mind until without warning the memory of his cold stare leaped to the front of her consciousness.

How angry he had looked, she thought tiredly. But hadn't she expected him to be angry? Well yes, she admitted silently. A woman doesn't leave her husband of one day without being aware that his first reaction would be anger.

Moving uncomfortably, the pain in her back increasing with every moment, she forced herself to try to look at the estrangement between them objectively. Maybe Adam was right. Perhaps she should let him see Jason and if possible effect a solution. Logically she knew Adam was right, that she was being stubborn and foolish not to set aside pride and in essence forget she had ever overheard that ugly conversation.

If only, she thought painfully—if only she didn't love him! If only her emotions were as uninvolved as his obviously were, then perhaps they could manage a life together. She would have her friends and lovers discreetly on the side, the same as her husband. They would become polite strangers to one another, polite strangers who just happened to share a name and a house. Probably not even a house, she decided cynically. Jason would more than likely bury her somewhere in the country while he continued his rakish existence. Dismally she came to the conclusion that except for necessary visits to produce heirs, he would prefer to forget he had a wife.

She might have been able to accept such an arrangement—it was a common one among many of her station—if she hadn't foolishly fallen in love with her unwilling husband. And loving him as she did, she wouldn't have been able to hide her feelings from him for long.

By nature Catherine was a warm, generous creature, and sooner or later her love would have been obvious for everyone to see. She couldn't have borne Jason's amused contempt for a woman who was so unsophisticated and naive as to wear her heart on her sleeve. Oh, he would be kind to her, she sensed. But that very kindness would shrivel something inside her. Perhaps in time she would have become as hard and brittle as those brazen, sophisticated women who seemed to enjoy their many adulterous liaisons conducted under their husband's bored and often indifferent eyes.

No! Never! she cried silently. Better to do as she had. Better to cut him completely from her life than to year by year watch her love destroyed and her pride trampled upon.

A sharp, tearing pain deep in her bowels jerked Catherine from her unhappy thoughts, and before she had time to catch her breath, another one, harder and longer than the first, struck her again. Not the baby, she thought helplessly. The baby wasn't due for almost another month. Surely her time wasn't yet. But then another stab of pain tore through her body, and she knew that due or not her child was coming.

Suddenly she remembered how she had resented her unborn baby and had guiltily half-hoped she would miscarry. Now, a fervent, silent plea crossed her mind. Please, God, let the child be well—*please*!

Struggling to her feet, panting a moment from her exertions, she braced herself while another spasm racked her body. She gave a small cry of protest. The contraction over, she leaned weakly against the chair wondering how she would rouse the house. Suddenly the door opened, and Adam, his black hair ruffled, a pistol in one hand, stood staring at her.

"My God, Kate, what are you doing down here? I thought I heard someone moving about and came to investigate. You're damned lucky I didn't shoot you!"

Unable to speak, in the grip of another contraction, she stared speechlessly. Then, the pain gone for the moment, she gasped, "I'm having my baby!"

"My God!" cried Adam, horrified. Crossing the room in two strides, he scooped her up and flew up the stairs, taking the steps three at a time, all the while bellowing at the top of his voice for the servants.

"Damnit, where is everybody?" he muttered distractedly as he laid Catherine on the bed.

The next hours were chaotic, but Nicholas St. Clair Savage, impatient to be born, thrust himself into the world barely three hours after Adam had laid Catherine on the bed. It was a fast, hard birth, and Catherine, agonizing over the well-being of the child, fainted from sheer relief when the tiny, perfectly formed, squalling bit of male humanity was placed in her arms.

Nicholas was born tiny, but in the next months he grew and gained in size and weight until by the time he was four months old he had overcome any ill effects of his premature birth. With an adoring mother, a doting uncle, and the entire staff of Belle Vista at his small command, there was little reason for him not to enjoy this new world in which he found himself.

After his birth, Catherine seemed to find the world an enjoyable place in which to be. She blossomed, her smiles more gentle and her movements more assured and confident. Her figure regained its slim shape, almost unchanged, but her face revealed the biggest transformation—the bones seemed more finely drawn, her eyes had an added depth.

She was a woman now, and as she and her son lazed away the spring months, sitting under the huge magnolia trees that clustered near Belle Vista or relaxing quietly on the cool, wide gallery at the front of the house, her beauty intensified.

Even Adam was startled by the dazzling creature who now inhabited his home. Watching her laughing down at her green-eyed son, her long, curly hair as lustrous as a raven's wing, her complexion tinted apricot by the warm sun, her lips like ripe cherries and eyes that gleamed like shining amethysts, he was a little bemused.

After much argument, Catherine had finally convinced him that her decision was the right one, and brother and sister had settled down as if the tenor of their lives would remain unchanged. Together they had written Rachael of her grandson's birth, and both had expressed the desire that she join them in Natchez.

Catherine especially wanted her mother nearby, if not at Belle Vista, at least established in a town house in Natchez. It was as if the birth of her own child gave her an insight into what Rachael must have suffered when Reina had stolen her and Adam, and she knew the urge to renew and seal the bond of blood that linked them. There was no reason for Rachael to remain in England alone, not when both her children made their lives in America and wanted her to join them. Catherine wrote as much.

It was her third letter to her mother since the night she had disappeared, and in both of her earlier missives she had pleaded with Rachael not to divulge her whereabouts if Jason sought her out. Rachael had done as Catherine requested, returning vague replies to the duke of Roxbury's letters inquiring after his nephew's missing wife. But reading Catherine's last letter, her tender heart twisted for both Jason and Catherine—so young, so proud, and so *stupid!*

This last letter made no reference to Jason, but Rachael's mind was filled with his image as she read of his son's birth; and she was extremely thoughtful for many days after the letter's arrival.

As Catherine had written, there was nothing to hold her in England, and because she was relatively affluent, she need have no fears of being or becoming a drain on her children's resources. She was able to take care of herself, thank you! And while the idea of living with Adam and Catherine sounded like heaven, she was wise enough to know that it would be best if, before the novelty of the three of them together under the same roof wore off, she found herself a neat, tidy little house in the nearest town.

So it was with a sparkle of adventure in her blue eyes that Rachael placed her affairs in the hands of a respectable agent and an equally conservative banking firm. Ignoring Edward's comments that she was mad and foolish, she continued to make preparations for joining her children. And before she sailed, her mind finally made up after many sleepless nights, she paid a visit to London and sought out the duke of Roxbury.

The duke, his gray eyes quizzical, showed no surprise when she laid Catherine's letter before him and said a trifle defiantly, "I've known where Catherine was for a number of months. I never would have told you where she was, except for the birth of the boy. I don't intend this child to be denied his birthright!"

Imperturbably, Roxbury picked up the letter and read it slowly. "So, Jason is the father of a son—and isn't aware of it," he said finally. "Do I take it you wish me to apprise him of the fact?"

Rachael hesitated, and the duke, staring at her still youthful face, her soft curling locks and bright blue eyes, wondered idly if the child born to her so many years ago resembled her or his father.

Roxbury's straying thoughts were quickly brought to order when Rachael said, "I'm going to join Catherine and my son in Natchez, and I intend to attempt to unravel this tangle. I would suggest that you write to Jason and explain that he is to do nothing until I see him. I would do it myself, but *you*"—she shot him a challenging look—"are adept at smoothing over affairs of this nature and would no doubt do a better job!"

"No doubt," he answered dryly. Then he asked casually, "Do you still hold it against me, m'dear? It was for the best you know."

Rachael blushed painfully, as she hadn't in years, and stammered, "Of—of course not!"

His eyes narrowed, Roxbury stared at her discomfiture for a minute. Finally he asked, "Do you think your decision to go to Natchez is wise?"

Rachael didn't pretend to misunderstand him. "It may not be wise, but I see no reason why I should remain a lonely old woman in England when I can live near my children. I'm not, you know, a possessive woman."

The duke nodded slowly, suddenly feeling very tired. Quietly he said, "If your mind is made up, I will not try to change it. I'll write Jason this evening. Shall I tell him you will meet him in New Orleans?"

"No! I must talk with Catherine first. I feel I'm betraying her as it is. She is adamant that nothing will reconcile her to being Jason's wife."

"Then what in heaven do you possibly hope to accomplish?" he snapped.

Unanswering, her eyes locked with his, and her soft mouth set. "I intend that at least Jason and Catherine agree to share their son between them. It's not right that a boy should grow up without knowing his father. And if they cannot live together, they can at least meet politely."

Rachael left the duke's home unsettled by the meeting and was extremely thankful to reach her rooms at the hotel where she was staying. Composing herself with an effort, she sat down at a small spindle-legged desk and began to write Catherine. As she wrote, her agitation lessened, and, a small smile of anticipation hovering about her mouth, she finished the letter. *They* were not to have all the adventures and fun. Soon, very soon, she would join them, and then they would have a tremendous time together.

If Rachael had any inkling of the contents of the letter the duke was sending to Jason, her smile would not have been happy, and she would have been justly incensed and equally horrified at his complete disregard of her request. Jason could have told her *never* to trust Roxbury, he always did precisely as he saw fit—and Rachael should have remembered that fact herself!

27

May was a lovely month. The humid heat of summer hadn't yet begun, so Catherine took full advantage of the delightfully warm days. The month before, her milk had dried unexpectedly, and an indignant Nicholas had been regretfully turned over to a wet nurse. Since she no longer had to nurse him and since there was a staff of black servants ready to leap at his slightest cry, Catherine found herself with more and more time on her hands.

She had met several of Adam's companions, but as these for the most part consisted of young bachelors like himself, she had little social life. Her pregnancy had naturally curtailed the acceptance of the invitations that had been extended when she had first arrived. Now, however, she made a determined effort to widen the scope of her acquaintances; after all, she was going to make Natchez her home.

One of Adam's more respectable friends was Stephen Minor, a former governor. His wife, Katherine, and Catherine took to each other instantly. Katherine Lintot Minor, a cool, long-faced blond, admired Catherine's aloofness, unaware it was brought on by shyness and the fear of meeting someone who knew Jason. The "Yellow Duchess," as Katherine Minor was known, gave Adam's sister her smiling nod of approval, and so Catherine found herself at the hub of Natchez society. And never having known the delights of the balls and soirées that were commonplace to the planters' wives and daughters, she delighted in them as well as reveled in being the latest rage.

Her horizon, though, was not without its black cloud, and there were a few eyebrows raised that so lovely a creature's husband never seemed to put in an appearance. Of course, no one was quite forward enough to ask outright where her husband was, but nonetheless it created a good deal of feminine speculation.

To those who were inclined to probe deeper than good manners dictated, Catherine was usually able to return an airy answer, but she had felt a chill of fear when one old woman, resplendent in diamonds, had murmured, "Savage, you say? Any relation to the Beauvais Savages?" Catherine had pretended not to hear, swiftly offering a new topic of conversation.

But there was one who would not take a hint that the subject of her absent husband was one she did not care to discuss, and she grew to dread the sight of the slim, smiling Spanish lieutenant, Blas Davalos.

The lieutenant appeared to be an ardent admirer, but Catherine disliked the flicker of conjecture that had leaped to his black eyes at the mention of her married name. He paid her determined court, always managing to gracefully cut ahead of her other admirers, and she had no choice but to suffer his compliments and advances. Despite Catherine's repeated reminders that she was a married woman, Davalos openly pursued her, much to the disapproval of the older matrons.

One night when Davalos whisked her out of the bright ballroom at Concord, Minor's grand home built in the Spanish style, for a walk in the warm night air, Catherine was compelled to mention his actions.

"This is not seemly. I am a married woman, and you should not place me in such a compromising position. Take me back inside at once!"

Blas only smiled lazily and, ignoring her command, urged a step-dragging Catherine down a brick path that wandered between tall, sweet-smelling roses. He added to her growing disquiet by asking silkily, "But are you, my dear?"

Warily, Catherine glanced at him in the light from gay lanterns that were strung overhead. "Am I what?"

"Married?"

Angry yet frightened, she snapped, "Of course I am! How dare you question me so intimately!"

"I notice you don't threaten me with your husband's wrath. Could it be your husband is unaware that you are living in Natchez—or that you even exist?"

Catherine had no answer. Pulling her arm away from Blas's light clasp, she turned on her heel and walked determinedly back in the direction of the ballroom, her topaz silk gown billowing out behind her. Blas halted her retreat by musing aloud, "I wonder—did Jason marry you? Or did he only dishonor you? Your son certainly reminds me of Jason, and I cannot blame you if you invented a marriage to hide your disgrace."

Aghast, the color draining from her face, Catherine brazened it out. "I can see little reason for me to discuss my husband with you! And if you think this J—J—Jason is my husband, why don't you ask *him?*"

"I might do that! But I would prefer that, instead of my asking him, *you* behave much nicer to me than you have!"

Sick inside at the implied threat, she threw him a look filled with loathing. "You are despicable! Go ask Jason whatever you wish, but I would rather die than stay one minute longer in your company!"

Her head held high, she marched back towards the ballroom, and whatever else Davalos would have said was stilled when Godfrey Anderson, another of her admirers, came walking down the path obviously in search of her. Smiling blindingly up at the besotted youth, she let him escort her back into the house and flirted with him for the rest of the evening, effectively allowing Davalos no chance for further conversation.

The conversation scared her, and for days she lived in fear that Blas would carry out his threat. When she heard by accident that he had been recalled for duty in Louisiana, her alarm increased. But then a note from Blas, delivered the following week in which he stated his sorrow at their unpleasant parting, made her hopeful that he would say nothing to Jason—if he really knew Jason Savage.

The sly curiosity about her absent husband continued, but with the former governor and his wife obviously finding her very pleasant company, Catherine was universally accepted into even the most high-stomached planters' homes. The air of mystery that hung about her only added to her charm as far as the young gentlemen were concerned, and there were few gatherings that she attended, in which Adam didn't find himself shouldered out of the way by a bevy of gallants eager for her company.

Catherine strove very hard to act the part of a young matron with a growing son, but it was very hard to sit and converse quietly with the older women when her feet were unconsciously tapping in time with the latest waltz. It was especially hard when there were so many delightful gentlemen who were more than willing to whirl her around the gleaming, polished dance floors.

"You had better watch it, m'lady," Adam warned her one night as they rode home from another pleasant evening at Concord. "There are a few who think that your husband is merely an invention to explain away Nick's birth. If you're not careful, someone is going to take the time to discover if there really is a Mr. Savage! It's too bad we didn't give out another name besides your true one. But more to the point, I don't like the calf looks young Anderson is throwing you.

His father is a stiff-rumped old Tory, and you can wager that if he thinks his only son is about to propose marriage to a woman with a questionable past, he'll have your pedigree run clear back to Eden!"

A sleepy smile curving her mouth, Catherine teased, "Adam, you sound rather stiff-rumped yourself! And," a gurgle of laughter spilled out, "at least fifty years old!"

An answering gleam of amusement lit his vivid blue eyes. "You're absolutely right, Kate! I'm taking my duties much too seriously, and I'm damned if I can see how you wind the most hardened flirt around your little finger. I can tell you that lately I live in the greatest dread that I'm going to have to play the heavy father and turn down several offers for your hand."

Her laughter gone, Catherine asked anxiously, "You don't really mean that, do you? I've been very discreet, and I haven't encouraged anyone. I know I'm married, and I've tried to behave properly."

"That you have, my love, and that's part of the fascination. You look so inviting, and there's that hint of a mysterious past that is so conflicting with the polite, demure young lady you appear to be. You've got them all knocked in a teacup."

The slight awe in Adam's voice caused another laugh to peal out, and laying her head affectionately on his shoulder, she inquired lightly, "Shall I attend the next outing with my hair pulled back into a neat little bun and dressed in sackcloth and ashes?"

His own eyes dancing with enjoyment at the thought, he muttered, "By God! I'd like to see their faces if you did!"

Both were smiling as the carriage pulled up in front of Belle Vista, and Catherine still experienced a happy bubble of amusement as she undressed for bed. A slight sound from the opened doorway caused her to cross quickly into Nicholas's room. Nicholas, sound asleep, jammed his fist into his mouth and with a satisfied sound began to suck quietly as his mother fondly watched.

How like his father he is, she thought gazing down at him. An unruly mop of black hair already topped a broad forehead that someday would be exactly like Jason's, and to Catherine's discerning eyes Nicholas's nose jutted in small imitation of his father's arrogant one. But it was his eyes that reminded her most of Jason; closed, the long, silky lashes nearly brushed his cheeks, and when opened their color was a deep, startling emerald green that was a constant stabbing reminder of another pair of eyes.

Her smile went a little wry. Every day Nicholas reminded her more and more vividly of Jason, and soon his resemblance to his father would be too marked not to arouse comment; Blas's remark on that same subject came back to her uncomfortably. Even Adam, with only one sighting of Jason Savage, admitted that Nicholas looked like his sire.

Well, she decided, curling up in her own bed, she would take one day at a time. It was fruitless to argue and fight situations that hadn't arisen. She fell asleep on that thought.

The morning heralded another bright, sunny day, and by ten o'clock Nicholas was happily rutting on a wide, white blanket laid on the soft green lawn, while a black maid sat in attendance. Catherine, her hair unbound and curling becomingly around her face, was sitting on a high-backed rattan chair on the veranda drinking a cup of the strong black coffee so dear to American hearts. They were at the side of the house, half under the sprawling, shady branches of a huge magnolia tree, where Adam and Catherine both frequently began their day. Often they sat here eating breakfast watching delightedly the antics of young Nick.

Adam seemed to be running later than usual, and Catherine correctly assumed it had something to do with the harassed-looking rider who had arrived shortly after she had wandered outside. Her guess was confirmed a few minutes later when Adam, his forehead creased in a frown, came out of the French doors at the side of the house and walked over to her.

"Kate, it's the damnedest thing! I'll have to leave for a few days. Harris here"—a jerk of his head indicated the waiting rider—"has brought some bad news. The levee broke on that new area we're clearing, and I'd best go and oversee the mopping up. I shan't be gone for more than a week or so."

A half-hour later, Adam mounted his horse and disappeared out of sight down the long, sweeping driveway. Feeling a bit flat after his sudden departure, Catherine wandered restlessly through the big house. Finally sheer boredom drove her to order a horse saddled, and she rode off in the direction Adam had taken.

She was on her way back from a singularly carefree gallop along the red-colored bluffs overlooking the Mississippi when Godfrey Anderson joined her. He met her just as she was guiding her horse into the driveway that led to Belle Vista. Viewing his blond fairness and his blue-eyed, cherubic handsomeness, she wondered why he aroused nothing more than amusement in her.

She should have been flattered that one of the richest, most eligible bachelors in the district had been undeniably smitten with her. It was patently apparent from the languishing glances he cast her and the stammering earnestness of his speech. Although he wasn't much older than herself, she viewed him as so very much less mature than herself that Adam's teasing worry of a proposal hadn't made a very deep impression on her.

But it appeared that the young man was on the point of declaring himself, and frantically Catherine tried to turn his thoughts in another direction. The news that Adam was not at Belle Vista seemed to plunge Godfrey into gloom, and Catherine, feeling rather gloomy herself, quickly realized that Godfrey had ridden forth this morning with every intention of requesting Adam's permission to pay his addresses to Catherine.

His young face clouded with disappointment at the news of Adam's unexpected departure, and Catherine, feeling sorry for him, cautiously invited him for some refreshments.

She chose the long, cool veranda for their tête-à-tête and after they had seated themselves quietly ordered the butler to serve something tall and refreshing.

James, his black face contrasting darkly above the white linen uniform whispered softly, "Madame, there is another gentleman to see you. I have put him in the blue sitting room. Do you wish to see him now?"

Frowning, Catherine asked, "Who is it? Didn't he give his name?"

Looking slightly uneasy, James admitted, "He wouldn't give his name, but he is obviously a gentleman and," he added honestly, "was insistent about waiting for you."

A thoughtful expression on her face, she watched James walk through the open French doors that led to the interior of the house. Uneasy, she suspected that her unasked visitor was Davalos. If so, he could wait a moment or two.

Turning and smiling, she attempted to maintain a polite conversation with Godfrey. She was searching rather desperately for something to say to break the tense, uncomfortable silence when Godfrey, taking his courage in both hands, unnerved her by suddenly kneeling before her, grasping her hand, and stammering out a fervent proposal of marriage.

Dismayed and at a momentary loss for words, she stared down into his earnest face. Then determinedly disengaging her hand she said quietly, "Mr. Anderson, you presume too much. I'm afraid you've forgotten that I'm a married woman. And"—he opened his mouth to protest but she added quellingly—"you should have discussed this with Adam before approaching me."

The sound of clapping and a lazy voice drawling, "Well done, my love! You did that beautifully," caused Catherine to freeze in her chair while Godfrey, angry embarrassment flushing his features, rose in one furious motion to face the tall man who lounged casually in the opened doorway.

Clenching his fists at his side, Godfrey burst out, "How dare you! What right have you to mock me?"

An insolent smile lurking at the corner of his mouth, Jason said coolly, "I am merely the lady's husband!"

The high color vanished instantly from Godfrey's cheeks leaving him looking ashen. Questioningly he stared at Catherine, her own complexion as white as his.

"Is this true? Is he truly your husband?" Godfrey asked disbelievingly.

Unable to speak or even turn to look at her husband, Catherine nodded her head miserably. Godfrey, after swallowing painfully, said manfully to Jason, "You must forgive me, but as you never put in an appearance and—and—Madame Savage seemed unwilling to speak of you, I—I—assumed you were—ah—dead! If you wish to call me out, I shall be happy to name my seconds."

There was a nerve-tingling silence as Jason's bright gaze flickered over the shaken young man. Then with an exasperated snort he said, "I see no reason for you to die merely because my wife was overly reticent in talking of me. You just forget about her and get on your horse and leave. The next time you decide to propose—make certain the lady is *free!*"

The scorn in his voice nearly precipitated a challenge from Godfrey, but realizing that under the circumstances he was escaping lightly, Godfrey gave a stiff bow, stepped down from the veranda, and disappeared rapidly in the direction of the stables.

The silence he left was deafening, and for a moment both figures remained motionless. Then Jason's voice, still with almost indulgent amusement uppermost, curled around Catherine.

"Do you intend to present me with the back of your head all day? It's a very lovely head, but I would prefer to see your face. After all, it has been over a year since last I looked upon you—*love!*"

"Nothing is stopping you," she answered tightly.

With a lithe movement, he abandoned his casual stance and moved to stand directly behind her chair. "What a delightful invitation! Do I take it you're requesting me to join you?"

A lean hand reached down and captured Catherine's chin, tipping her face up to him. Slowly, leisurely his eyes roamed over her features, noting the smoldering fires in her violet eyes and the determined slant to her lips. Then his gaze dropped disturbingly to the pulse that pounded madly at the base of her throat. Unable to stand his almost insolent appraisal, she jerked her chin from his hand and leaped out of the chair knocking it over in her haste.

"What do you want?" She spat the words at him.

He raised a mockingly astonished eyebrow at her question. "Why, my love, what do you think I want? Is this any way to greet your long-lost husband?" he reproached.

Gazing at him much in the manner she would a coiled rattlesnake, Catherine bit her lip doubtfully. The lazy, teasing mood was stunning. If ever she had pictured a reunion with Jason, it certainly wouldn't have been with Jason acting in this cool, bantering manner.

He ignored her for the moment and straightened the chair she had knocked over. Then with a smile on his lips that did not reach his cold green eyes he seated himself. And, as if he did it every day, he waved her to a seat opposite him. "Do sit down, my love. We have a great deal to discuss, don't we? Ah, very good—er—James, I believe the name is?" he asked as the butler made his reappearance bearing a large silver tray with a frosted pitcher of wine punch. "Just set it there, will you?" Jason commanded.

James threw a startled look at his mistress and at Catherine's curt nod did as ordered. After pouring the silent couple two slim glasses of the sparkling liquid, he left silently, a faintly worried frown marring his features. Ummhmmm, he sure wished the master was here. He didn't like the looks of that strange gentleman at all!

Catherine wasn't too happy with the looks of that strange gentleman either, but there was little she could do about it. He seemed to be making himself very comfortable, and gingerly she sat down across from him, watching warily as he pushed his long legs out in front of him and took up one of the glasses. Forcing herself to remain calm, she asked cautiously, "What do you want to discuss?"

Jason left off his contemplation of the sprig of mint that adorned his glass, and his eyes, hard and oblique, swept over her. "That rather depends on you, doesn't it?"

Relaxing slightly at his apparent lack of temper, she gazed back steadily at him, almost mesmerized by his green eyes. The sight of his firmly shaped mouth that could reduce her to a state of sobbing acquiescence made a shiver of remembered joy run through her body. Forcing herself to remain as cool and unruffled as he appeared, she asked, "How did you find me?"

"Mmmmm, it wasn't too hard after your mother was so obliging as to tell my uncle where you were," he answered carelessly.

"My *mother* told you?" she gasped incredulously.

"Not your mother, little one—my uncle!"

Stunned by his words, she could only stare at him wordlessly. Finally, she stammered, "Ra—Rachael would never have betrayed me!"

His expression sardonic, Jason contradicted, "Don't wager too much on it! I don't know what her reasons were, but she did tell my uncle, and my uncle wrote that I could find you at a plantation named Belle Vista near Natchez."

Her thoughts jumbled, Catherine asked carefully, "Was that all? He didn't write about anything else that Rachael had said?"

His green eyes narrowed, and silkily Jason said, "He didn't write that you were about to present me with a *bastard!*"

Her eyes sparkling with fury, she stood up. "You said what we had to discuss depended upon me. Well, my opinions haven't changed since I left you in Paris, and I see no reason for continuing this distasteful conversation."

She had meant to sweep regally by him, but his hand shot

out, and forcefully he jerked her down onto his lap. Every fiber in her body tingling, and too aware of the hard thighs beneath her, she glared up at him, her mouth tightening angrily.

"Jason, let me go!"

He ignored her command, holding her prisoner against him, and his lips began their remembered magic as they caressed her neck where the pulse beat frantically, then slowly traveled up towards her mouth. Alternately loving and hating him, she was powerless to stop the surge of desire his touch ignited. Dear heavens! she thought despairingly. It's been so long since he's held me, and I love him so very much—damn him!

She fought to elude his questing lips, but it was a useless struggle. When his mouth finally captured hers, she gave up to the shudder of longing that shook her, and against her will she felt her swimming senses responding to the demands of his mouth; with a tiny sigh of defeat, her lips opened under his, letting him explore deeply. Then when her brain was pounding in tempo with her thudding heartbeat, he raised his head suddenly, and instead of the familiar fires of desire she saw only contempt in his green eyes.

He stood up, unceremoniously dumping her on the floor, and in clipped tones snapped, "Slut! Still the same teasing little tart, I see! No wonder that young fool was ready to lay his heart and lands at your greedy little feet!"

Too stunned for words, Catherine picked herself up from the ground and with a shaking hand arranged her skirts. He had been as aroused as she—she knew it. His desire had been urgent against her soft body. But as in the past, he was now prepared to blame her, she thought bitterly. Raising her head, she looked steadily across at him. "Now that you've proven to yourself that I am a slut, I don't think there's any more for us to say to one another, and certainly no reason for you to remain, don't you agree?"

His eyes glittering dangerously, he studied her with insolence. "No, and I have no intention of remaining! But neither do I have any intention of leaving you behind."

Aghast, she stared. "You—you can't mean to take me with you?"

"Why not? You're my wife, and I think I've lent you to St. Clair long enough! I hate to take you without leaving him a reminder of my thanks for his tender care of my wife, but perhaps it's for the best. While I may have the mother, he will at least have his child!"

Uncomprehendingly, Catherine shook her head. And coldly Jason's eyes drifted over her slender body. "At least it appears childbearing hasn't damaged your value. Tell me," he went on in a cool tone, "did you present him with a son or a daughter?"

Catherine blinked, her eyes huge in disbelief at his words and at his sneering tone. He couldn't be saying these terrible things! Didn't he realize the child was his son? The thoughts buzzed in her brain like angry wasps.

Jason snarled impatiently, "Well, what was the little bastard?"

"A boy. I had a boy," she answered tonelessly.

His mouth twisted as if in pain, but it was gone quickly—gone so swiftly she thought she imagined it. And his voice gave no hint of emotion as he said, "Just as well. A boy needs a father more than a mother, so he won't miss you."

"What do you mean, won't miss me?" Catherine asked sharply.

An ugly gleam lit his eyes. "I've come to take back an erring wife, but I'm damn sure I have no intention of having your bastard tied to my shirttails. When we leave, which will be as soon as it takes you to pack a change of clothes, I'm not taking your son along with us!"

He stood facing her, his face strong and proud, and her heart squeezed with anguish. How could they have created Nicholas between them, yet be so distrustful and ready to believe the worst of the other? Why wasn't there some way in which to resolve their differences? Why did these ridiculous misunderstandings arise every time they met? And how, she asked herself angrily, *how* can I love a man who thinks I'm the kind of woman who would defile her marriage vows and flaunt the fruits of an adulterous association? Disgusted with herself at her own weak emotions, Catherine fought a raging battle between the desire to fling the truth at Jason's arrogant head and stubborn pride that commanded, "He thinks the worse—so let him!"

A militant gleam springing into her violet eyes she muttered to herself, "If he thinks I'm leaving *my* son, he's in for a decidedly nasty shock!" Throwing up her head much in the manner of a wild, spirited filly, she placed her hands on her slim hips and arms akimbo defied him.

"I let you bully me once into a compromising situation, but I'm *damned*"—she smiled to herself at his look of surprise when the curse fell so easily from her lips and deliberately, almost enjoying it, repeated it—"I'm damned, if I'll let you do it again! I'm not leaving here with you, today or ever!"

His unexpected shout of disbelieving laughter annoyed her intensely, and frowning fiercely at his amusement, she gritted, "I mean it, Jason! I'm not leaving!"

The laughter died from his eyes instantly, and very softly he threatened, "You'll come with me all right! It's either that or I stay and face St. Clair. Will you enjoy seeing your lover shot down?" he taunted. "Because I'll do it, I promise you. I've been promising myself that pleasure ever since I saw him with you in New Orleans. The only thing that's stopping me is his infant son! So don't tell *me* what you're going to do!"

The words fell like deadly drops of poison into a pool of silence, and the fight drained out of Catherine. Faced with this cold-eyed stranger, Adam would pick up the thrown gauntlet with alacrity. She couldn't allow that to happen. How could she bear it if either her husband or her brother were killed? But how could she leave her son? No, she thought stubbornly, she wouldn't! She would have to tell Jason the truth—if it came to that.

Impatient with her silence, Jason grated, "Well?"

Meekly, hating herself for the meekness, she said in a low voice, "I'll pack."

At the moment that seemed the easiest way out. In the mood he was in, any explanation she offered would be angrily repudiated, and she could visualize his look of incredulity if she told him Adam was merely her brother!

She started to walk past him, but he grasped her arm and smiling tightly, drawled nastily, "You don't mind if I watch—you have a disconcerting habit of disappearing."

She shrugged, and together they entered the house.

James, his brown eyes straying constantly to the lean hand that gripped his mistress's arm, listened impassively as in a low voice she ordered him to have one of the servants pack a trunk for her and Nicholas. At the last command Jason threw her an icy stare.

Waiting only long enough for James to begin his way up the staircase, he growled, "Nicholas?"

Appearing much more calm than she felt, she said quietly, "Yes, Nicholas—my son." Steadily her eyes fought with his. "I'm not leaving him, Jason. You can threaten St. Clair, you can break every bone in my body, but I will *not* leave my son!"

There was no fear in the eyes that gazed into his, only grim determination, and finally with a harsh laugh, he barked, "Take the brat then—but don't expect him to keep you from your wifely duties!"

Flushing at the implication, she twisted away and ran up the stairs. Jason followed immediately behind her and watched every movement she made. An hour later she was seated in Adam's coach with Nicholas on the seat beside her and Jeanne, her eyes wide with fright, across from her.

After a quick look inside, Jason slammed the door and mounted his own horse. As the coach pulled away from Belle Vista, a soft, gusty sigh of relief left her. She had her son safe beside her, and surprisingly, considering the circumstances, Jason had allowed her to write a brief note to Adam. Granted, he had read it before tossing it carelessly down on the table, but she had been thankful that Adam would not return home and hear just from the troubled servants of Jason's arrival and her subsequent departure.

Her note had said only that her husband had come and was taking her and Nicholas away. Fervently Catherine hoped that Adam would accept her letter at face value and would take no sudden action—at least that he would do nothing until she had had time to acquaint Jason with the true facts. She had enough to cope with without Adam's volatile presence complicating matters.

28

The sun was hot, and looking resentfully at Jason, his dark head covered by a crisp white linen hat, Catherine wondered how he could appear so cool and vital. She felt like a limp rag. Brushing back a heavy lock of hair, she grimaced at the feel of the perspiration on her temple. Her dress clung wetly to the middle of her back, and for the hundredth time she wondered where he was taking them.

It was five days since they had boarded the flatboat at Natchez and begun the trip down the Mississippi River. She had assumed their destination was New Orleans, but on the morning of the second day they had disembarked at one of the landings along the river and had continued towards their unknown destination by horse and wagon—Jason by horse and the women and child by wagon.

Loaded wagons, men, and horses had been waiting for Jason's arrival. Definitely uneasy, Catherine had eyed the boxes of provisions that filled four of the wagons. A fifth wagon apparently was used as a cookhouse, and looking at the glum-faced individual who was in charge, she hoped the food would not be an extension of his personality.

She had been inordinately relieved to discover that a sixth wagon, a covered wagon, had been set aside for her use. It offered privacy from the curious stares of the men and a certain amount of respite from the blistering sun, but it also became very stuffy and close by late afternoon, a disagreeable facet—and Nicholas often let everyone know how very disagreeable he found it.

She and Jeanne were the only women except for a small, dusky-skinned young girl who Jason had thrust at her, saying curtly, "If I'd known I was to be saddled with a nursery I would have brought you more servants, but as I didn't, madame, between Jeanne and Sally here, you'll have to manage!"

That Jason had planned for this trek well and that these hard-eyed men, mostly bearded, worked for him was apparent from the start. And that he knew them more than just casually was also obvious from the scraps of conversation Catherine overhead when at night the men gathered around the chuck wagon. There were several blacks included in the group, but they appeared to prefer their own company and always formed a smaller group a short distance away. Whether they were slaves or free men she was uncertain, and when she had idly questioned Jason on one of the few occasions he stopped to speak with her, he had snapped, "Does it matter?"

Bewildered at the hostility in his voice, she shook her head and was thankful when after a cool, faintly contemptuous glance, he had urged his big bay gelding away from the wagon and had ridden ahead to converse with a wizened little man who went by the misnomer of Goliath.

One evening when Jason appeared to be in a more approachable mood, she braved herself to ask about Indians. They were obviously traveling deeper into uncivilized places, and Catherine, her head filled with grisly tales of what the savages were capable of doing, was worried that her life might end by the blow of a tomahawk.

Jason had laughed at her worry. "Listen, little kitten, the Natchez were the most powerful tribe in the area, but after they nearly destroyed the old town of Natchez, the Spanish, with the help of the Natchitoches broke their power forever. And over the years the Natchitoches have been decimated by disease and what have you. We never had anything approaching the Iroquois coalition in this region. That doesn't mean that in the early days there wasn't bitter, bloody fighting with the settlers, but only that our Indian problem never reached the magnitude of, say, the settlers in the eastern part of the United States."

"Aren't there any Indians left?" she asked wide-eyed.

Smiling indulgently, he replied, "Of course there are. But now our Indians seldom attack. There are occasional outbreaks of violence, but it's usually a handful of braves who get liquored up and go on a rampage. They certainly wouldn't attack us. We are too many and too excellently armed—and I do post guards, just in case."

Catherine hadn't been entirely satisfied with Jason's answer, but took heart from the sight of the rifles and pistols that every man carried. Gradually, she came to recognize the men and was able to place names with faces. She knew, of course, that the gold-toothed, bald-headed Negro who drove her wagon was named Sam and that the cook was called Henry, and that the only Indian in the party, a tall, strikingly handsome Cherokee who rode his horse as if he had grown out of the saddle, had the chilling name of Blood Drinker. It had been Blood Drinker who had prompted Catherine's earlier fear of Indians. She had caught his steady black-eyed stare on her more than once and was positive he had designs on her long hair.

The rest of the men remained strangers, and aware of the watchful eye Jason kept on her, they would continue to remain so. The distance between the master's wife and the rough-mannered men he employed was wide and deep, almost feudal. Even Jeanne, in her capacity as Catherine's maid, was safe from their advances merely because she was madame's personal servant.

Ordinarily, a well-born Southern lady did not consort with the men her husband hired to work on his lands. In the normal course of events Catherine, and Jeanne for that matter, would probably never have met these individuals, much less spoken to them. The men had their place and the women of the master's household another.

There was one thing that puzzled her. Adam, except for a few trained white men, ran his plantation entirely with black slave labor. Judging from the mixed group that looked to Jason for command, it seemed he employed an equal amount of white men. But there was more than just idle conjecture about the men that puzzled Catherine. There was Jason himself—and where he was taking her.

It was a peculiar thing, though, that with her son safely asleep in the swaying wagon behind her and her tall, if distant husband riding not too far ahead, Catherine felt a queer contentment even though their destination was as yet unknown to her. Eagerly she scanned the passing countryside, her eyes wide and fascinated, as every day revealed a new and totally different landscape.

They were moving slowly in a northwesterly direction, and as they left the swampy lowlands created by the huge flood plain of the Mississippi River, the ground began a slight, gradual rise; there were fewer and fewer signs of the murky, nearly opaque, almost motionless bayous that crisscrossed the arca. And as the ground began its infinitesimal slope to the north, so did the vegetation change.

Gone were the gray, moss-hung cypress trees, their gnarled roots like great knobby knees rising out of the brackish water of the bayous, gone were the swamp oaks with their wide-spreading branches. Gone too were the stands of the tall, stiff, razor-bladed palmettos. In their places now stood mile upon mile of long-needled pine trees and gray-barked beech and shady ash trees, virgin stands of timber as yet untouched by the hand of the white man.

In spite of its terrifying beauty, Catherine had been happy to leave the swampy lowlands behind. During the day it was a visual treat, but at night—there was a different feeling, a feeling of danger and menace that couldn't be hidden underneath the soft, low murmurs of the frogs and crickets or the haunting cry of the owl. After darkness the roar of a bull alligator would cause her to shudder with a primitive fear, and the scream of the hunting cougar or the sudden ear-piercing cry of some hunted creature dying beneath the claws or fangs of the hunter jerked her upright from a sound sleep on more than one night. The swamps were a primeval place, and the further the swamps were behind them, the better she liked it!

She lost track of time, one day drifting smoothly into the next as they continued on their journey, always pushing steadily northwest. This journey reminded her vividly of the days of growing up with the gypsies as they roamed from place to place in their gaily colored caravans. The small cook fires at night brought the memories back even more strongly as she sat, her knees drawn up under her chin, watching the leaping reddish yellow flames. So had she done as a child, Adam at her side, watching Reina prepare the evening meal. There was even music—not the stirring blood-tingling sob of the gypsy violins, but the livelier and occasionally sadder music of the blacks; the sound would carry and wind through the quiet night broken only by the cry of the night animals.

After the first few days Jason had ordered Catherine and Jeanne to stay near their own wagon except for those necessary trips into the woods. They did not even join the men for meals—Sally cooked for them at their own small fire. After tasting the revolting fare prepared by Henry, Catherine was delighted with the arrangement. Jason's surprise at her ready agreement had been evident, and instead of relieving some of the tenseness between them, in some odd way it had only added to it.

The air fairly crackled with unspoken fiery emotion whenever they were near one another. It grew with every passing mile, though consciously neither did anything to add to it. Even Jason, beyond those few comments he had made at Belle Vista, did not bring up the estrangement between them.

Nor did he mention Nicholas—he ignored him. And Catherine, giving into a wave of feminine spite, would manage to flaunt her son very nearly right under Jason's disapproving nose on thc occasions when he sought her company. That he never looked at the child was evident—for if he had, he might have wondered about those clear green eyes so like his own. But he never so much as glanced at the black-haired imp who so resembled him, and eventually Catherine's desire to thrust the baby to his attention died, to be replaced by an empty feeling of defeat. What was the use, she thought wearily? Jason had decided the child was not his, and injured pride, she admitted grudgingly, kept her from telling him the truth. Eventually, she reversed her actions and made certain Jason had as few opportunities as possible to observe Nicholas.

Catherine also spent more than one sleepless night trying to figure out Jason's attitude towards her. What precisely did he have planned for her? His manner was cool to the point of indifference. Beyond seeing that she had everything she needed and slowing his horse to walk by the side of her wagon and asked politely how she did, he treated her much in the manner he did Nicholas—he ignored her!

Why? she asked herself silently, night after night. Why this remoteness? If he wanted none of her, why take the trouble to find her and compel her to come with him?

Granted, there was little privacy, but still, she told herself doggedly, there were moments when they could have talked—if he had wished. Even just making everyday conversation would have been better than his habit of gazing right through her. It reminded her painfully of those days in Paris. Yet—and yet—more than once she had been surprised to see some spark of emotion in his eyes, but it was so quickly shuttered and gone that she couldn't identify it. Desire? Hate?

His silence on what their future would be nagged at her unmercifully. Always, no matter what she did, there was wonder and worry about what he planned for her. One night, in the depths of despair, she decided he must have some subtle revenge in mind and didn't want to alarm her unduly until it was too late. With the unwelcome thoughts driving any hope of sleep from her brain, she crawled carefully out of the wagon. Sitting on the hard wooden seat, she stared perplexedly out into the black night.

The darkness was broken by the soft silver rays of the waning moon. Except for the men who had the night watch, the camp slept quietly. Here and there in the faint light from the coals of the dying fire, she could discern the shapes of the men as they lay on the ground asleep. Idly she wondered what they thought of the odd situation that existed between her and Jason. And as always, her wonderings shifted to her husband. Where was he? Asleep out there before her? Making the rounds to see if the guards were alert and watchful?

Suddenly, as if her straying thoughts had conjured him there, he loomed beside her and asked harshly, "What the hell do you think you're doing?"

Startled, she twisted in the direction of his voice and would have fallen off the edge of the wagon if his arm, a steel band of muscle, hadn't snaked out and prevented her fall. It also crushed her against his body, and for a moment she hung there, half lying against his chest, her face upturned to his and her legs still within the wagon. But only for a second. Then muttering a curse, he lifted her to the ground, holding her tightly to him, his mouth hungrily seeking hers.

Remembering his reactions to her unguarded response at Belle Vista, she fought the wild surge of dizzy desire that swept through her. He wasn't going to place the blame for his own unleashed emotions on her this time! Stiffly, she held her body as far away as his arms would allow, and her mouth, usually so warm and yielding, was pressed tightly closed against her teeth. Instantly aware of what she was doing, if not the reasons behind it, his hold slackened, and he raised his head, his eyes glittering in the faint light.

"Playing the tease again?" he asked in a black velvet tone. His hand was lightly running up and down her bare arm, and she was unbearably conscious of the sheerness and flimsiness of the chemise she wore for sleeping. It barely covered her breast, and a tremble of hunger—hunger for his body to take hers—sped through her veins as his eyes dropped and almost caressingly rested on the faint outline of her nipples against the material.

But if she felt desire, she also felt anger—anger at her uncontrollable weakness for him and anger that no matter what she did it was wrong! Her eyes searched his closed face, noting the ominous tightening of his jaw and the faint muscle that jerked in his cheek. In a low voice that was shaking with sudden, fierce anger, she spat, "What is it you want, Jason? When I respond, I'm a slut. When I do not, I'm a tease. Just tell me what role I should play to suit you!" she finished nastily.

Jason's mouth thinned in anger as fierce as hers, and his hand tightened painfully around her arm. "Look," he said levelly and with effort, "we have got to have a talk. And right here is not the place or the time. And whether intentional or not, sitting outside your wagon clad as you are at this time of night was an open invitation to any man. I'm sorry," he added sarcastically, "if I misread your actions."

"Why are you sorry?" she shot back just as sarcastically as he. "You never have been in the past."

She tore her arm from his grasp and turned around to climb back inside the wagon, but his hands, closing around her shoulders like vises, whirled her back to face him. "Damn you! You're the most obstinate, hot-tempered shrew I've ever met. There seems to be just *one* way that we can communicate," he said grimly. Then before she understood his meaning, he reached down and picked up a blanket that had been lying near the front wagon wheel. Stupidly, she stared at it and puzzled, she asked, "Is that where you've been sleeping?"

His voice hard, he snapped, "Yes! Every night, rather like the faithful dog protecting his mistress!" He gave a harsh laugh at his words and jerked her along with him as with fast, long-legged strides he dragged her away from the sleeping camp.

Suddenly aware of what he intended, she said breathlessly, "Jason, let me go! Let me go back!"

He gave her an angry look. "Hardly! We have only one way of talking and—I feel like *talking*."

Hidden from the wagons by the trees and the underbrush, he stopped abruptly and threw the blanket down on a soft carpet of pine needles. Making one last effort, Catherine threatened ridiculously, "I'll scream!"

"No, you won't!" he said tautly. "Your mouth will be much too busy!" And pulling her to him, his lips closed down purposefully over hers. This time he wasn't taking no for an answer!

Weak with a sense of inevitability, Catherine let his lovemaking drug her into passion—she wanted him, so why pretend otherwise? No longer did she fight against the aching swirl of hunger that bit into her loins, almost like a pain, and when Jason pulled her down onto the blanket and removed her chemise, she offered no resistance. Dimly in one small part of her brain she knew that afterwards she would hate herself as well as Jason, but then desire exploded in her veins, and she could no more have denied him than she could control the spasm of sheer animal need that spread like fire into every fiber of her being. Blindly her mouth sought Jason's, and her hands were as bold and brazen in their caresses as his.

Tantalizingly, she ran her fingers down his chest, each finger leaving a trail of flame and slowly, slowly, she reached lower across his flat stomach to his groin. Jason stiffened at her first light touch, and as her hand hovered teasingly he groaned, "For God's sake, kitten!" Roughly he pulled her hand down where he wanted it. Then, as if to punish her effrontery at teasing him, he played with her nearly driving her wild as his mouth and hands followed remembered hollows and curves until at last he slipped a knee between her thighs, spreading her legs. His hands and fingers probed deeply, creating such a sweetly agonizing ache that Catherine thought she would die of wanting if he didn't take her soon. Feverishly, her body straining, she let him know what she wanted, and then when her lips were opening to plead, he took her, his mouth on hers cutting off the small purr of catlike satisfaction she gave as at last he slid into her body, his bigness almost hurting her. As he moved within her, the exquisite sensation of his body on hers, the coarse hair of his chest crushed into the softness of her breast, his hands beneath her tight buttocks controlling the tremors that shook her, his mouth hard against hers, Catherine was conscious of nothing, only Jason, and he took her into a world of intense, blazing contentment, his name reverberated through her entire body like a quivering bowstring—Jason, Jason, *Jason!*

Then as she drifted back into this world, his hands still gently caressing and his lips nibbling teasingly at the hollow of her throat, as if from a great distance she heard him say with an undercurrent of laughter, "You little wildcat! Did you have to claw up my back?" Then nuzzling her smooth shoulders, he murmured, "Hmmmm, kitten, I've missed you so. You're in my blood like a fire. But," he added regretfully, "I'd better get you back before one of the guards stumbles over us—or worse, someone unfriendly to lovers decides to decorate his scalp belt with our hair. And," he continued grimly as he pulled on his pants with swift, controlled movements, "the guard who has this section had better have a good reason for not discovering us."

A slight sound behind them made Jason whirl, automatically crouching, the knife Catherine hadn't noticed appearing as if by magic in his hand. Her eyes wide, she rolled swiftly and instinctively out of his way, taking the blanket with her. A sudden low laugh from Jason caused her to look up sharply, and there—not more than two feet away, his face expressionless—stood Blood Drinker!

For a moment the tall Indian stared eloquently at Jason and then like a shadow was gone. Her cheeks crimson in the moonlight, Catherine asked mortified, "Was he there the whole time?"

A wide smile slashing his face Jason shrugged. "Probably! Blood Drinker is the best man I've got, and no one can make a move without him knowing it. But don't worry, kitten," he teased audaciously. "He's very discreet, and his sense of what is seemly is very nice. Knowing him as I do, more than likely he averted his eyes, ignored your ladylike cries of pleasure, and made certain no one interrupted us—no one, friend or foe."

Embarrassment flooded her body, and furious at Jason's unconcerned lightheartedness, she fumbled around in the darkness searching for her discarded chemise. Finding the garment she pulled it on hurriedly. Ignoring Jason's broad-shouldered body she walked stiffly towards the wagon, outrage apparent with every step she took. Jason's low laughter taunted in her ears as she climbed inside, and it did nothing to cool her temper. Lying down in the soothing darkness of the interior of the wagon, she felt her cheeks burn with remembered shame. And the thought of having to face the Cherokee tomorrow made her wish fervently that the ground would open up and swallow her. How could Jason treat it so casually?

The next morning Catherine was unduly subdued, so quiet and withdrawn that Jeanne was moved to ask solicitously, "Is madame not feeling well?"

Blood Drinker happened to walk by just then, and Catherine, her face suddenly flaming bright red at the suspicion of a smile that twitched at the corners of his chiseled lips, snapped in a tight little voice, "No! And mind your own business!"

Considerably startled, for madame was notoriously sunny tempered, Jeanne immediately withdrew into reproachful silence, deciding that this long journey must be beginning to wear on her mistress's nerves. A happy gurgle from Nicholas distracted Jeanne's attention, and she forgot about Catherine and her queer mood entirely.

But Catherine couldn't dismiss the events of the last night so lightly, and grimly she climbed up on the seat, her mind filled with a hundred pictures of Jason and Blood Drinker suffering the most hideous excruciating tortures her fertile imagination could devise. But as the morning progressed and she had to face Blood Drinker time and time again, her embarrassment faded, if not her resentment. After Blood Drinker had ridden by her wagon several times, slowing each time to ask Sam a trivial question supposedly at Jason's request, her eyes narrowed in suspicion, and when the wagons halted at noon for a brief rest, determinedly Catherine sought Jason out.

She found him shortly, seated astride a rangy chestnut. One long leg was hooked casually over the saddle horn, his white shirt was opened nearly to the waist, and his hat was pushed rakishly towards the back of his head. He was busy rolling a long, slim cigar and diverted for a moment, she watched, fascinated by the motions of his long fingers. His task finished to his satisfaction, Jason lit the cigar. Then with the smoke curling fragrantly in his nostrils, he slanted an eyebrow upwards in question at her presence, and Catherine felt her heart swell foolishly with love. What a silly goose you are, she scolded silently, and in a stern voice said, "I want to talk to you."

His expression quizzical, Jason replied, "So talk. I'm not stopping you."

Her violet eyes smoldering, she gritted, "Is there any special reason why Blood Drinker should be asking Sam a multitude of needless questions? Barely a mile goes by that he isn't riding up to ask some silly question!"

A twinkle in his green eyes, a grin turning up the corners of his mouth, Jason stared down, his eyes traveling leisurely over her, noting with undisguised amusement the rapid rise and fall of her bosom as she waited for his answer. Finally, when she was on the point of stamping her foot with rage, he took the cigar from between his teeth and studying it intently said slowly, "After last night, I figured you'd be a little uncomfortable around Blood Drinker, and I decided the quickest way for you to get over it was to have to face him—frequently!"

"Thank you very much! Your kindness and thoughtfulness is overwhelming," she said with stiff politeness.

All trace of laughter gone from his eyes, they locked with hers for a minute before he added, "You might not appreciate my methods, kitten, but I do what I think is best. He's important to me, and I don't like there to be strained relationships between people who are necessary to me. Understand?" There was no hiding the thread of steel that ran through his quietly spoken words, and Catherine glared impotently at him a minute longer before turning on her heels and stalking back to her wagon.

Blood Drinker did not pay any more visits to Sam, but that gave Catherine little satisfaction. Jason had proven his point, and she acknowledged fairly that he was not one to belabor it. Unfortunately, she was in no mood to find pleasure in his virtues—*if* he had any, she tacked on mentally.

The remainder of the day passed swiftly for Catherine. Not because there was any particular change in the usual daily routine and not because of any noticeable change in the terrain, but because she had a great deal to think about. Memory of Jason's lovemaking last night caused a blush to stain her cheeks more than once during the day, but it was those murmured words he had spoken afterwards that troubled her thoughts. With all her heart she wanted desperately to read more into what he had said and done. But afraid—

almost terrified—of making a mistake or misreading the motives behind his actions, she finally put down his words as those any man would say to any woman in the aftermath of passion.

As for his hungry assault on her body—well, she told herself bitterly, he hadn't loved her the first time he'd taken her, so what made the difference this time? It was a long journey and he'd been without a woman—that was all there was to it! Firmly she held on to that thought and promised herself silently that, no matter what, she wasn't putting herself in any situation that would allow another confrontation with him! Her body betrayed her mind every time, answering the passion of his touch too swiftly for her to control it. Even now, viewing last night from a distance, she knew he had only to reach for her and the hard-won restraint she put on her emotions would crumble like ancient parchment.

But as if that night had somehow lifted a barrier between them, Jason began to seek her out and to display that charm of his that twisted her heart, and tenaciously she fought against it. Her face stony and for the most part averted, she ignored the flashing smile that was often directed at her. She pretended not to hear him when he spoke to her and exasperated him with her icy composure. His snapped questions received only monosyllabic answers.

He took to joining her for the evening meal. Afterwards, lying sprawled on the ground with his back resting against the wagon wheel, he attempted to draw her out of the cool shell she had retreated into, but found her maddeningly elusive. Physically she was there, so close he could reach out and touch her, and Catherine would have been shocked if she had known how often he *ached* to take her in his arms and hold her near.

But suspicious of every overture he made and grimly determined to quell any weakening of the protective shield she had erected, she froze inside whenever he was near. She was polite when he spoke and interested in what he said, but only if he kept to impersonal topics. And Jason, viewing the calm stranger's smile she reserved solely for him, would have liked to have shaken her until her teeth rattled—or kissed her until she melted against him.

Yet, in spite of everything that lay unresolved between them, they were slowly learning about one another. There was a silent, tacit understanding that they did not discuss their past. Nor did they discuss their future. Incidents that had occurred prior to their meeting at the gypsy encampment and things that happened on this journey were perfectly acceptable.

Frequently, unable to help herself, Catherine's rippling laughter pealed out at some particularly amusing tale he told. Jason was totally unaware that even his lazy, slanting smile could cause Catherine's heart to thump painfully fast. Nor was he aware of the very attractive, virile picture he presented leaning comfortably against the wheel of her wagon, his green eyes glinting with enjoyment. But Catherine, watching him from beneath lowered lids, a soft light in her violet eyes was almost overwhelmingly conscious of it.

One night as they sat talking—or politely fencing—Jason said casually, "Well, this time tomorrow I hope we'll have reached our destination. You'll be glad to see the last of this wagon."

Catherine's head jerked up and with natural curiosity, asked, "Where are we going? You never did tell me."

His eyebrow rising, he said coolly, "You also never asked."

Swallowing the desire to snap a sarcastic retort, she asked sweetly instead, "Well, I'm asking now. Where are we going?"

An unusual smile hovered about his mouth, a faraway look in his eyes, and his voice held a softness to it that made Catherine look at him closely when he said, "It's called *Terre du Coeur,* Land of the Heart, and it's acres and acres of land that lies almost halfway between Natchitoches, or Fort St. Jean Baptiste as some of the older people call it, and Alexandria on the Red River." His voice almost dreamy, he continued, "I inherited it on my majority from my mother and she from her mother. It's wild, untamed, and more beautiful than one can imagine." He shot her a wicked glance and murmured, "Rather like you." But as her smile froze, he added hastily, "There are a house and outbuildings that were built in my mother's youth, but very little has been done to bring the land into production. Mostly the land has been used to fatten cattle, although some acres have been cleared for cotton. The women of my family have always married well, and they had no practical use for it. Probably if there had been more children, it wouldn't have come to me, but being an only child has its advantages as well as its curses!"

A slight frown crossing her forehead, Catherine stared at him and asked very carefully, "Why haven't you done anything with it before now?"

Pointedly, he retorted, "I never had a wife before."

Nearly stuttering in her hurry, Catherine changed the subject. Being his wife was one thing she didn't want to talk about, and her haste was such that she missed the faint gleam of amused disappointment that flickered in his green eyes.

PART FOUR

TERRE DU COEUR

Summer 1804

29

If Catherine lived to be a hundred, she would never forget her first sight of the massive wood and brick house at Terre du Coeur that was to become her home.

The house crowned a small rise, ascending like a shimmering yellow jewel, a topaz set on a lush expanse of green velvet lawn. Many years ago the tall, wooden columns of the first story had been tinted a pale yellow but now, faded by the hot sun, they gleamed creamy white in the late afternoon sun. The brick, once bright ochre, was bleached flaxen by the weather and the burning rays of the sun. Built when Jason's Spanish grandmother had been a mere child, Terre du Coeur betrayed its Spanish origin by the wide bow-shaped staircase on the outside of the house, forming a graceful, sweeping arch that led to the cool, vine-draped upper story. Recessed French doors opened onto the shaded verandas that encompassed three sides of the house, and the hipped roof with its deeply protective slant jutted beyond the verandas making them cool retreats from the moist heat of the day. Delicately carved railings were covered with honeysuckle and trumpet creeper, the leaves shining darkly green against the paleness of the wooden railings. Yellow and orange trumpet flowers blazed vividly in the mass of greenery, and the sweet scent of honeysuckle drifted through the air.

Catherine had been unprepared for a house in the middle of this apparent wilderness, especially one appearing as it did, flanked by encroaching, pungent-smelling pine trees and huge oaks. She blinked with surprise when the trail they had been following opened onto the large clearing where the house sat. At their approach, the house—which had at first seemed deserted—leaped to life, and in a matter of seconds the weary travelers were engulfed by a crowd of smiling and excited men, women, and children who unexpectedly appeared to greet the new arrivals.

Later, Catherine learned that Terre du Coeur was more like a settlement than merely a plantation; that behind the main house, hidden by a belt of tall pine trees, were smaller houses where many of the men who had traveled this particular trip with Jason lived with their families. But today, sick to death of the swaying wagon, she was just thankful for the smiling black servants who made those first hours in her new home heavenly.

Jason came back to her wagon and grasping her firmly about the waist, lifted her down, holding her against him as he did so. Surrounded by his arms and under the interested view of the entire tiny community, he bent his head and kissed her long and searchingly, then raising his mouth from hers said softly, "Welcome to Terre du Coeur, my little fire-eater."

Unable to think clearly and stunned by the caressing quality of his voice, Catherine allowed herself to be led meekly upstairs by a bustling little woman he called Susan. Susan showed Catherine into a bright, cool room and then, muttering she had to see that the other servants were doing their jobs properly, vanished.

For a moment Catherine stood staring blankly at the bare,

wooden-planked floors, the stark white walls that were naked of any ornament, and the sparse furnishings. There was a massive four-poster mahogany bed, that gleamed darkly against the pristine whiteness of the walls, an equally massive but delightfully and ornately carved wardrobe, and in the same heavy Spanish style a dressing table with a red velvet-covered stool. These were the only objects in the appallingly large room. Even the huge brick fireplace in one corner couldn't detract from the room's size.

Not certain what she was to do next, Catherine walked back outside and stood on the veranda staring down at the hive of activity that was taking place beneath her window as the wagons were unpacked and put away. She felt a pang of regret when her wagon was driven off around the side of the house; it was in that moment dearly familiar to her, even the bruising hardness of the wooden seat, and she almost wished they were still traveling.

She wandered back inside, thankful for the coolness of the interior and immediately noticed another set of carved double doors. Upon opening them she discovered herself in another room. It was, if possible, larger than the one she had just left, and it was empty. Not one object marred its echoing hollowness. Frowning she walked slowly back into her room and froze at the sight of Jason lying indolently on the bed, a lazy grin creasing his face.

"Well, what do you think of it?"

Truthfully, Catherine answered, "It's awfully large, isn't it?"

"Hmmm, perhaps. But by the time all the furnishings and geegaws you will no doubt fill it with are added, I'll probably have trouble winding my way through the house without stumbling over some object."

"You don't know that! And where," she asked sarcastically, "am I to find all these furnishings and geegaws you mention here in the middle of nowhere?"

His grin widening, he casually kicked off his boots, and they fell with a loud clump to the floor. "Soon, *petite,* I'll show you the storerooms. My grandmother once thought she'd like to live here and consequently brought an excessive amount of God knows what with her. Some of the stuff will be useless or ruined, I'm certain, after this many years, but there'll be enough for you to start doing something with. And those wagons we brought with us, love, weren't exactly empty! Whether you'll approve of the cloth goods and materials I selected is another story."

Arms akimbo, she glared at him, resentment building in her breast. Levelly she asked, "Is that why you brought me with you? To arrange your house and run it for you?"

Lying on his side, propped up on one arm and lazily taking his time, his eyes swept meaningfully over her slim body. "No, that's not the only reason you're with me."

Ignoring the teasing light in his green eyes as well as the unspoken challenge, she asked stiffly, "Where are you putting my son? I want him near me. I shall want him to sleep in the same room."

Jason's smile vanished, and his jaw tightened. "I'm afraid you'll be too busy sharing a room with me to worry about *him!* But allay your mother's fears. I haven't sent him to the servant's quarters. He's across the hall and down a few doors, being fussed over by Jeanne and Sally. For now, they can tend to him as well as you, and there are enough servants around so that he won't be neglected!"

The sneer in his voice was very obvious, and for an instant she was almost overcome by the desire to hurl Nicholas's parentage into his insolent face. But in her own way as proud and stubborn as Jason, she bit back the words and instead asked pointedly, "Do I *have* to share a room with you?"

"Where would you suggest I stay? At the moment this is the only room with a bed in it. Unless," he drawled, "you expect me to sleep in the quarters with the men or the servants."

Rising suddenly from the bed, he walked over to where she stood her eyes bright with frustration and anger. Reaching, he gently pushed a stray curl behind her ear. Catherine was unbearably conscious of the warmth of his fingers as they lightly brushed her cheek and of the hard, lean body that stood only inches from her.

She wouldn't meet his eyes and stared at the floor as if hypnotized, fighting the traitorous urge to fling herself into his arms and cry that it didn't matter where he slept as long as he took her with him! His voice, husky with emotion, as he cajoled softly, "Will it be so bad sharing a bed with me?" did nothing to slow the rapid racing of her pulse.

As she continued to stare at the floor, his hand slid down her cheek and capturing her chin, turned her face upwards to his. His eyes searching hers, he said slowly, "You did it once, kitten. And I seem to remember we made a bargain to try to make something of our ill-starred marriage. Did you find me so distasteful after only one night that you had to put an ocean between us and present me with another man's son?"

Silently her heart cried out, "Oh, God, Jason it was never *that!* But how could our marriage be anything when all you ever wanted was a brood mare?" But the words were said only in her heart, and hurt again by his determination to invest her character with such vile traits, she willed a steely note in her voice and taunted, "Does it bother you to think of me in another man's arms, his lips kissing me as you do and our bodies creating a separate life?"

His grip on her chin tightened so hard that her eyes were misty with sudden tears of pain. And as if to still her lips from saying more, his mouth descended on hers with a bruising strength. There was no joy, no passion in that kiss; it was meant to punish and hurt and, at last releasing her mouth he snarled against her tremulous lips, *"Mon Dieu!* You ask *that!* Yes, it bothers me! After I saw you in New Orleans, there were nights I woke dreaming I had your soft, white throat in my hands, and if my dreams—" he laughed harshly, "nightmares would be more likely—were true, I'd have strangled the life out of your bewitching, betraying body!"

His hand had unconsciously encircled her slim throat and raising her head, she stared up fearlessly into the dark, lean face above hers. Jason's gaze was locked on her mouth, and a white line of anger near his lips revealed more clearly than words the fury that must have racked him. Driven by a force beyond her she jeered, "What's stopping you?"

She felt a slight tenseness leave his body at her challenge and as the white look faded, his lips curved slowly, incredulously, into a deeply sensuous smile. His hands left her neck and pulled her tightly to him. "No, oh no, little love, if I was to kill you, you'd haunt my dreams until the day I died. *This* way, I have you where I want you, when I want you, and you can no more deny the attraction between us than I can!"

Then his mouth took hers and he lifted her up and carried her to the bed. Her senses swimming and her blood clamoring with desire, Catherine resolutely ignored the cry of outraged pride that demanded she resist what every bone in her willing body yearned for, and hungrily she responded to the passionate urgency of Jason's lovemaking.

It was quick taking, with few preliminaries, his body merging swiftly with hers as if there were some compelling force that drove them together. Even so it was, as always, eminently satisfying, and afterwards as they lay naked on the rumpled bed, their bodies still locked together, Jason muttered against her throat, "Why is it like this between us?" There was a note of dull anguish in his voice and Catherine, her eyes luminous from remembered passion, could only stare dumbly at the ceiling, groping for an answer that did not come to her.

Gently, Jason's lips traced her jaw line, his hands now softly caressing where before they had been painfully demanding. "Why do we tear each other apart with words? Yet, I have only to touch you and nothing else matters—I could in this moment forgive you anything, but I know, and you do too, that an hour from now we'll be clawing at each other, each trying to be the first to draw blood!"

Jason's words were spoken low, more to himself than her,

and at the underlying tone of wondering sadness Catherine felt her whole being melt with love. Tentatively her fingers stirred tenderly across his dark head, delighting in the feel of his black hair. For the first time, driven not by passion but by love, she voluntarily caressed him, but neither one of them noticed it.

As if ashamed of admitting the pull between them, Jason suddenly jerked away, and leaving the bed he began to dress; and any trace of the mood of seconds before vanished. His face fell into it's familiar sardonic cast, killing the hesitant words that hovered on Catherine's lips.

Silently she slid from the bed and, as quickly as he, put on her clothing. Whatever the meaning behind it, that little interlude of queer introspection was over, and their habitual state of cool hostility was in force again.

Catherine's first week at Terre du Coeur flew by in a kaleidoscope of shifting scenes as Jason, in a surprisingly amiable mood, acquainted her with the estate. The first few days she suffered dreadfully from the heat, having only the elegant riding habits made in France to wear when riding over the estate. One morning, looking thoughtfully at her face, damp with perspiration, Jason had a trunk unearthed and sent up to her room. Catherine was delighted to discover it was filled with garments that a much younger Jason had outgrown. Many of the masculine clothes were of no use to her, but the trunk also contained several pairs of practically new breeches that didn't hang too badly on her slender frame and a number of snowy white linen and silk shirts. With the help of Jeanne and one of the other women, the clothes were altered to fit, and thereafter, Catherine never went riding in anything but Jason's cutdown breeches and shirts.

Once the question of comfortable clothes was settled, she was able to take enjoyment from Jason's guided tours of the plantation. Malelike, he took her first to those places he thought were important. Consequently, she saw the entire workings of the plantation before she was able to rummage through the fascinating objects that were to be found in the storeroom.

But she wasn't so far removed from the Catherine who had ridden Sheba so wildly over the hills of Leicestershire not to appreciate the stables and barns with their sleek-spirited occupants. Entranced by the large, brick barn with its clean-smelling hayloft and the new gleaming white buildings that housed several of the horses bought in England, she nearly had to be dragged away by Jason. Every now and then she would stop and stare at a horse that looked familiar, but then decided it must be her imagination. She was like a child promised the biggest sweet she could find, and happily she ambled throughout the complex of barns, stables, and paddocks. She stopped often to speak knowledgeably with the men who were busy about the area, and gleefully she offered an apple to a haughty-nosed stallion. An indulgent smile on his face, Jason allowed her to wander freely. Frequently he was amused at the searching questions she asked the stablemen and was often surprised at her grasp of the intricacies of breeding the spirited thoroughbreds. Secretly Jason hoped that someday these thoroughbreds would make Terre du Coeur famous amongst the breeders in the United States.

This particular morning, they were walking slowly towards the last of the new buildings, and Jason had explained he had planned it for the mares in foal or newly foaled. It was set some distance away from the other buildings at the edge of a large meadow, where already a few graceful mares with spindle-legged foals at their sides grazed peacefully.

Catherine, her arm linked companionably in his, her face shaded from the hot sun by a delightfully feminine broad-brimmed hat, gave a sigh of sheer happiness. "Oh, Jason, it's all so lovely. It's even more beautiful than Hunter's Hill, and I never thought there could be any place I'd like better."

"It's as well," he answered dryly. "Remember, this is your home from now on."

For a minute, a shadow crossed her vivid face. Wistfully she asked, "Will we never go back?" Suddenly struck by another thought she inquired bluntly, "What will happen to my lands? I hope to convince Rachael to stay in America, and there will be no one in England to manage the estates."

His expression thoughtful, Jason replied carefully, "We can put your property in the hands of a good estate agent, and I have relatives in England who will be willing to keep a friendly eye overall. You won't get cheated, I'll see to that! I imagine we will go back to England occasionally, so we can do our own checking every now and then. Who knows," he finished flippantly, "we may have a child who prefers England to America."

She searched his face for a long moment before asking quietly, "Would it annoy you if he did? After all, your roots are here."

Grinning down into Catherine's serious face, he lightly ran a finger down her straight little nose and teased, "My dear woman, I intend fathering so many children on you that having several clamoring for England would still leave enough for Terre du Coeur!"

Torn between the desire to laugh at his outrageous statement and pain that he should so openly state his use for her, she managed an uncertain smile and said briskly, "Never mind that! Show me this race course you said you were having built."

The course lay just beyond a small wooded area, and it was an incongruous sight in the middle of the wilderness. At present only the track itself had been cleared, and a rough wooden fence stood in place of the smooth white railings that would eventually line it. Viewing it uncertainly, Catherine asked, "Do you really intend to raise thoroughbreds and race them here?"

"Hmmm, why not? All things have to start somewhere. Besides, my disapproving madame, the horses are only my hobby. Don't worry. Your bread and butter don't hinge on them!"

"I wasn't worried about the financial end of things, and you know it! Why do you twist everything I say?"

Staring down into her stormy face, he laughed softly. "Because, my dear, it's so seldom our thoughts run on the same course, I just automatically assumed you would view it that way. I apologize."

At a loss for words and not at all in the mood to start another useless argument, she let her mouth relax in a smile and began to make her way back in the direction of the brood mare barn.

The woods were shaded and cool, and Catherine liked the sharp pungency of the pines as she walked the narrow little path that led back towards the barns. The path was edged with clumps of delicate wild star grass and scattered throughout the forest were carpets of wild flowers, phlox, asters, and mint. A few splashes still remained of the yellow jasmine that blooms in the spring, and Catherine, her face framed by the floppy-brimmed straw hat and wearing a high-waisted gown of lavender muslin, looked not unlike a wild flower herself.

Reaching the building, Jason strolled on ahead, leaving her to walk the length of this, the last stable, alone. She stopped occasionally to peer inside, noting the roomy stalls. Jason was waiting for her near the last stall, leaning casually against a post, his hands in his pockets and one booted foot crossed over the other. In spite of his careless attitude Catherine thought she detected a slight tenseness about him, but then the movement of the horse in the nearby stall distracted her attention.

At Catherine's approach, the mare abruptly left off nuzzling the ungainly heap of long-legged horseflesh that was her son and stuck her shining black head over the bottom half of the door. Frozen, Catherine stared at the familiar silken muzzle.

"Sheba!" she whispered. As one in a daze, she drifted nearer to the horse. Almost unbelievingly she ran one hand down the warm, black satin neck and after a minute turned

to face Jason. There were dozens of questions she wanted to ask, but her tongue couldn't sort out which words to say first.

Taking pity on her obvious astonishment, Jason sauntered up and said dryly, "When I visited your mother after you first were missing, while I waited for you to appear, I spent a great deal of time acquainting myself with your stables. And as there was never any doubt in my mind that I would eventually—ah— recover you and bring you to Louisiana, I saw no reason to leave behind your extremely commendable stock of animals. Especially, I couldn't bring myself to leave Sheba behind as she holds certain memories for me."

Vividly, as if it had happened yesterday, Catherine remembered that day in the meadow when he had first made her so vibrantly aware of his power over her body. The fact that Jason remembered it too gave her a queer breathless feeling, and suddenly shy of the emotion that his words created, she muttered, "I'm awfully glad you brought her."

A mocking glint of laughter in the green eyes, he teased, "Can't you do better than that?"

Flushing she sent him a resentful look and replied, primly, "Thank you *very* much for bringing her over here." His crack of laughter did little to soothe her ruffled feelings, but determinedly she asserted, "Really, *truly* I am grateful!"

Shaking his head, a tiny smile lingering about his lips, he guided her in the direction of the big house and placing her hand on his arm, led her away, saying, "You'll have to do better than *that*—but for now I'll let it be!"

He made no further reference to it, but every morning from then on when she ran down to offer Sheba some treat, she wondered anew at the motive that had been behind his actions. He was being so kind lately. Yet, *kind* wasn't the right word. Indulgent? Perhaps. Certainly, he had been considerate in familiarizing her with the plantation.

For several days she rode with him over the vast tract of land, and she looked attentively as he pointed out the shallow valleys where the cattle grew fat on the lush grass and where someday there might be cotton and sugar cane fields. Some areas were already cleared and planted and she stared curiously at the acres of bright green sugar cane planted near the river and the fields of cotton growing on the higher drier ground. One afternoon they stopped on a slight rise and looked back at the crops growing rapidly under the hot sun, and Catherine breathed, "It looks almost like velvet."

Jason smiled at the note of wonder in her voice. He had enjoyed these days with her and was hopeful that at last they were about to reach an understanding. The thought of Nicholas and the child's father could still fill his body with black, violent fury, but he had *her,* and it appeared she wasn't finding his attentions too distasteful.

Jason did not, as he had implied, share her room. Almost as if he knew how much she hated and dreaded those times her body would without volition answer the command of his, he refrained from forcing her to accept him in her bed. And Catherine was grateful for it even if puzzled and suspicious.

Sally, the young Negro girl Jason had thrust at her when they started the journey to Terre du Coeur, had become inordinately fond of Nicholas. So fond, in fact, she became exceedingly jealous of anyone, even Catherine, having anything to do with that young man, and so Jeanne was once more acting as lady's maid for Catherine. And as Jeanne and Catherine were extremely attached to each other, Jeanne's role was more companion than maid.

Having satisfied himself that his wife was fairly knowledgeable about her new home, Jason finally showed her the storerooms. What a wealth of treasure she found there! Any object through three generations that had not found favor with the Beauvais women or their husbands had been sent off to become moldy and gather dust at Terre du Coeur. Catherine could almost imagine one of Jason's relatives saying, "After all, one can't throw it away, but perhaps someone will find a use for it someday!" And as each succeeding generation had not bothered to inventory what was already stored, but had merely added to it, the result was chaos.

Catherine discovered in a carton perched precariously on the arm of an ugly, old-fashioned chair, a set of lovely Baccarat crystal that Angelique had detested. Jeanne stumbled over a gorgeous set of fine English bone china that had been a wedding present to Jason's parents, but Guy had never cared for the pattern of delicate green and gold leaves that adorned it.

Some things were badly damaged, including several paintings. Viewing them in the strong sunlight and recognizing drab colors and insipid themes, Catherine was happy to add them to the growing to-be-burned pile. But the sight of a really fine Spanish carpet, badly eaten by moths and rats, depressed her. It would have looked just right in the main salon.

Jason took such disasters indifferently, and when Catherine continued to mourn its loss, he said casually, "Make a list of the things you want, including the damned carpets, and I can send it back with Blood Drinker!"

Surprised, she asked, "Is he going back to Natchez?"

"Not Natchez, my love. New Orleans. There are certain things I need, and he and several of the men are leaving in a few days."

It was as yet early evening, but they had just finished dining and were still in the dining room. The room was large, and they were seated at opposite ends of the table separated by a snowy expanse of linen tablecloth. Catherine had found the tablecloth in an old trunk, as well as the matching pair of silver and crystal candelabras that decorated the table. Viewing Jason's face in the flickering light from the candles, she wondered if she would ever know him.

Even though things were much better between them, they were still at an impasse, neither willing to be the one to bring up any personal or explosive subject.

Within reason, Jason gave her anything she wished. She had a lovely home that he was perfectly agreeable to let her do with as she willed, she had servants to answer her smallest request, and certainly he made no demands on her.

She knew he was busy with the plantation; he had been working especially hard for several days now in the clearing of a new section that was to be planted in cotton next year. And before fall, the cattle that roamed in those open valleys had to be branded, and some were to be culled from the herd and sold in New Orleans. Jason was indeed a busy man, and Catherine wondered a bit wistfully if that was why he did not seek out her bed. Not that she wanted him there, she reminded herself hastily.

Viewing his relaxed position at the end of the long table, one hand curling languidly about the stem of a crystal goblet, she hated to be the one to break this companionable silence. But he had been the one who had brought up Blood Drinker's trip, and it opened the door to something that had been worrying her for weeks. Finally mustering up the nerve to say the words, she blurted, "May I send a letter with Blood Drinker?"

Stiffening only slightly, Jason stared at her thoughtfully before asking, "Who in New Orleans are you writing to?"

Determined to get it behind her, she rushed on, "No one in New Orleans. My mother will have arrived by now, and I would like to let her know where I am. Blood Drinker could carry the letter to New Orleans, and I'm sure he could find someone else to take it to Natchez. She'll be staying at Belle Vista."

His nostrils flaring with anger, he said nastily, "Your lover's home? How quaint!"

A bright spot of color flared into Catherine's cheeks, and she almost spat the truth at him. But swallowing the words she looked everywhere except at him, knowing the supercilious look his face would be wearing.

"May I send the letter?" she persevered.

Jerkily, he tossed off the remainder of his wine. "Why not?" he returned coolly. Then he completely astonished her by adding. "Better yet, why not invite Rachael to come here? There's nothing for her in Natchez while you are here."

Her eyes very wide, she breathed incredulously, "Really? You won't mind?"

A crooked smile leaped suddenly into being. "No, I won't mind. I enjoyed your mother's company, and I know you must get lonesome for feminine companionship."

Staring at him like one in a daze, Catherine hardly believed she was hearing correctly, but too happy at the battle so easily won, she broke into a dazzling smile of sheer happiness.

Watching her, apparently casually beneath half-closed lids, as that beautiful smile of hers spread across her face, the delight obvious in those violet eyes, Jason felt his heart give a queer, uncertain leap. Damn! How was he ever to get her to look at him that way without bribery?

30

Blood Drinker left two days later and with him, Catherine's letter. Her heart had given a fearful bound when, after she had handed the sealed missive to him, Jason had for a number of minutes turned it over in his hand and looked long and hard at her and then at the letter addressed simply to Rachael Tremayne, Belle Vista, Natchez, Mississippi.

Finally, with an odd smile, he handed it to the waiting Indian. Together, she and Jason had stood on the wide, brick steps and watched the half-dozen men ride away.

Their going left her feeling fairly flat. She had spent a long time writing that letter at the dark oak desk that now reposed in her room. And she had held little back. It was imperative Rachael know exactly how things stood between her and Jason.

Drained by the emotion it had taken to write the letter, she slipped away upstairs and lay in her room for several hours gathering strength for the next battle with her husband. Ruefully she smiled to herself—it seemed their life so far was a series of battles. Jason had won some, and she had a few to her credit, but as yet, neither had a decisive victory.

Gradually, the house was taking shape under Catherine's young hands. Rugs that were not damaged, and there were a few, found their way into a number of rooms, adding a needed note of beauty and warmth. Upholstered furniture that had appeared ruined by unsightly stains and rats' nests had been rejuvenated with the skill of one of the wives of Jason's men, who made use of the seemingly endless store of cloth Jason had brought with him.

Sara was an excellent seamstress, and with the aid of a young wench and Jeanne's somewhat inexpert help, she had replaced the soiled and faded cloth with bright, colorful satins and damasks. Curtains had been a problem until Catherine had discovered bolt upon bolt of soft champagne-colored silk, and now graceful, silken draperies lined the long windows and glass-paned doors.

Terre du Coeur was built high from the ground and with an optimum of openness in order to catch whatever breath of cool air was available. Nearly every room had a set of double glass doors that opened either onto the wide galleries or onto the courtyardlike patio at the rear of the house.

The patio was nearly encircled by the main body of the house and the two long, low wings that ran parallel to each other, and swept out from either side of the house. A brick fence with a lacy ironwork grill for a gate sealed off the open end of the patio from prying eyes.

Catherine spent many enjoyable hours there seated under a wisteria-hung arbor that was attached to the rear of the house, watching fondly while Nicholas, beginning to crawl and pull himself up, played in the early morning sun.

A large, tiered fountain was in the center of the buff-bricked patio, and wooden tubs of gardenias and various small plants were placed symmetrically about the area. It was a pleasant place, where the scent of wisteria and gardenia blended in the air, and the drone of the bees as they flew from blossom to blossom mingled with the tinkle of the water in the fountain.

This particular morning, Catherine, wearing a cool white gown of worked muslin, her hair captured into a queenly coronet on her small head, had been absorbed in watching Nicholas, his fat, little legs trembling with effort as he stood nearly alone, one tiny hand clutching the lowest rim of the fountain.

He stood swaying a second before his confidence vanished and with more haste than grace, sat down abruptly, wearing the face of one who had accomplished wonders. Catherine was beaming with motherly pride at his antics when Jeanne called to her from a small room that opened onto the patio.

The room had been pressed into service as a sewing and dressmaking area, and walking to the doorway, one eye still on Nicholas, Catherine gave her approval as Jeanne held up a length of soft green chiffon.

"Oh, that would do lovely for an underdrape in the bedrooms! Do you think there is enough?" Then casting another glance at Nicholas and seeing his attention riveted on his suddenly discovered toes, she took a few steps into the room.

At the same time that Catherine stepped into the sewing room, Jason was walking up the front steps of the house. He was hot, and he was exasperated. This morning's clearing should have gone well, but one of the mules had gone lame, and the untried youngster substituted in its place had created trouble. Even harnessing him to one of the other teams had done little but waste time. Finally, impatiently, Jason had sent the incomplete team back, and no sooner had they left than one of the ropes used to haul out the stumps had frayed and broken. It was just one of those mornings, and as the day was becoming increasingly muggy and there was no mistaking the signs of a coming thunderstorm, he had decided to let well enough alone and start everyone fresh in the morning.

Handing his hat to the waiting butler, he walked down the cool hallway towards the patio, knowing that at this time of the morning Catherine was usually to be found there.

The patio was vacant, although a pitcher and a half-filled glass of sangria sitting on the white cane table gave evidence that his wife had been there earlier. He was already turning to walk back into the house when Nicholas, having pulled himself up into his brave new stance, made the mistake of letting loose of his grip on the fountain, and he fell down hard on his round, little bottom.

More surprised than hurt, Nicholas's eyes filled with frustrated tears, and he let out a small, thwarted sob. Jason had as usual glanced through the child without seeing him, but the sound caught his attention. Knowing little of babies and thinking that the seemingly deserted child was hurt, he crossed swiftly to his side.

What aid Jason intended to lend was uncertain, but no sooner had he reached the baby than Nicholas, diverted by his approach, halted the angry bawl that threatened to erupt and instead stared open-mouthed at the tall stranger. And Jason, staring incredulously down into the small babyish replica of his own lean features, froze. A ragged breath caught in his throat, and like a man in a trance he sank slowly to his haunches, his searching gaze devouring young Nicholas.

Nicholas, perfectly happy to be the center of adult attention, sent him a blinding smile that was so like Catherine's that Jason felt a quiver of something approaching delight spear his body. The smile may have been Catherine's, but the gleaming green eyes were undeniably his! The child was *theirs!*

Hungrily, Jason's eyes ran over the baby noting the unruly black mop of hair that either parent could have passed on, but what gave him that trembling-in-the-gut feeling was the fact that the child had his eyes. The child had to be *his!* How else would he have inherited those emerald eyes and the miniature copy of his own bold nose?

With a surprisingly gentle hand, he reached out and almost timidly touched the small black head. *His son!* And he never knew it! Pain like an avalanche roared through his body. Did she hate him so much? So much, she would deny him his own son, his own flesh and blood? And anger, anger such as he had never experienced in his entire life, swept the pain away and left him frozen with fury at *this,* the final betrayal.

Staring at his son, Jason's dark face was nearly ashen with emotion, and a muscle jerked near his tightened lips. Reaching out he picked up Nicholas, and his body was suffused with a sudden, aching love for this small part of himself.

Always happy being held, Nicholas gave a gurgle of satisfaction as his father cradled him close, and Jason looked hard at his son as if trying to memorize those little features that gave proof of his parentage. That was how Catherine saw them as she stepped out of the room into the soft shade given by the low, overhanging roof. The two, man and child, bathed in the bright sunlight, were absorbed in each other—Nicholas, deciding his father's nose was a fascinating object, had one little hand busily exploring it, while Jason enfolded his son protectively against his own hard chest, his eyes never leaving the child's face.

Catherine's lighthearted step died, and as one turned to stone, every vestige of color fleeing her face, she stared almost frightened, yet filled with a swift, encompassing joy. Sensing her presence, Jason looked up, and the look that he speared Catherine's rigid body with would have slain her, had it been a sword. She felt the hate that blazed in those green eyes like a knife, and at her involuntary step forward and the small inarticulate cry of pain that escaped her white lips, Jason held the child closer as if he feared she would snatch him away.

For what seemed like an eternity, they stood frozen there, the man and child near the tinkling fountain, the drone of the insects soft in the warm air, and the woman looking like a small, white ghost in the shadows of the sloping roof. Then throwing her a glance that combined hate, contempt and—surely not pain?—Jason turned on his heel and stalked off into the house with his son still clasped in his arms.

Shaking with shock, her teeth chattering with the force of the emotion that tore through her body, Catherine watched the tall, stiff-backed figure disappear into the house. Like a broken old woman she stumbled across the patio, the pain inside her body like a live thing that threatened to tear her apart. She reached the table and sank down, drained, into the nearby chair. Blindly she stared out over the silent patio.

Could it have been less than an hour ago that she had sat here happily watching Nicholas, while weaving improbable dreams of one day Jason loving her and understanding the confused motives that had driven her to hide his son from him? Bitterly her mouth twisted with a new shock of pain.

What a fool she was! She should have told Jason the truth at the beginning. Never mind that he wouldn't have believed it from her lips, never mind that until he saw proof with his own eyes he would have thought her a liar and a cheat. Better *that* than the undisguised glare of hate—yes, hate—that had burned in his eyes!

Tiredly, she dropped her head into her hands, the desire to weep like a beaten child very strong. But no, she had put weeping behind her a long time ago—tears were for fools! And dully she remembered a stray line from one of the Greek plays that had been pounded into her head at Mrs. Siddon's: "I have wept for these things once already." Well, she wasn't going to weep—not today.

Coolly, her brain working furiously, she examined the paths open to her. She could go, despite an inward quaking, and face him *now.* Yet another part of her knew that she should not go yet—not while he was still laboring under the shock of it. Not now while they both were so upset that they would say ugly, hurtful words that later could not be forgotten, much less forgiven. Wait—wait like a coward, sneered another thought. But she wasn't a coward! No, it wasn't fear that stopped her from racing into the house after him. Common sense said wait—let him recover and have a chance to ponder the situation before they faced one another. But then she murmured to herself, "Yes, let him have a chance to arm himself against you. Let him guard his emotions, and he will annihilate you as he has done in the past. *Fool!* Do you think he will even *try* to delve into your possible motives, that he will even attempt to understand your side?"

The thoughts were like rattlesnakes in her brain causing her to stir uncomfortably, but eventually the wisdom of waiting until cooler counsel could prevail won out. She lay back in the chair, her eyes closed, willing a calmness into her body.

Any chance of happiness they had could very well depend on the next few days, and hot-tempered words would destroy everything. At all costs, she must remain cool and avoid the furious rampage that must surely follow today's discovery. That Jason had a certain amount of right on his side, she freely acknowledged.

Why did she let provoked pride push her dangerously into situations that could have been avoided? she wondered, depressed. "Aren't you ever going to learn?" she asked herself scathingly. And guiltily she answered, "It's not all my fault! If he wasn't so willing to believe the worst and wasn't so arrogantly sure of himself, I wouldn't act that way! It's his fault, too!"

Catherine finally succumbed to a very natural curiosity about Jason's whereabouts with Nicholas and discovered them in Jason's study, still enchanted with each other. Tiptoeing away unseen and intent upon avoiding him, she changed rapidly into a pair of breeches and a white silk shirt. Looking like a slender boy, she shoved on a wide-brimmed, masculine hat and slipped like a wraith out of the house.

Minutes later, she guided a long-legged, chestnut gelding through the quiet coolness of the pine forest, the horse's hoofbeats muffled by the carpet of pine needles. She was headed to a favorite spot of hers, located only a short distance from the house. It was a peaceful spot, a dappled, leafy glen where the slender beech and tall ash trees grew instead of the familiar long-needled pines. A wide creek ran sluggishly through the center of the area, and often she sat on one of the large stones that lay along its edge and dangled her bare feet in the sun-warmed waters.

Today though, she gained little peace, the mugginess of the day making her clothes stick uncomfortably and the sun too hot to tolerate for very long. Almost with relief, she watched the dark clouds gathering on the horizon knowing that the coming thunderstorm would cool the air temporarily, even if the moisture would add to the humidity.

Her thoughts still unresolved, but with a wary eye on the approaching clouds, she mounted her horse and rode at a fairly brisk pace back to the stables. It was fortunate that she hadn't followed her inclination and dawdled because she had barely reached the protection of the big brick barn when an ominous flash of lightning split the blackened sky, and the heavens opened up with a sudden deluge of rain.

Idly watching the rain from the safety of the doorway of the barn, she hoped her absence had gone unnoted. Usually she informed one of the servants of her whereabouts, but her mind had been taken up with Jason and their problems, and she had completely forgotten to tell anyone where she was going.

Once the rain slackened, she hurried towards the house, hoping that her absence had not been discovered. But, just as she put one foot on the first step, Jason's angry voice halted her.

"Where the hell have you been? Haven't you any better sense than to disappear when there's a storm coming?"

The contrite look in her wide-spaced eyes had no effect on him today. Coldly, he noted the sudden whitening of her lips, and his own mouth curled in a cruel, wolfish grin. Let the little bitch try her tricks on someone else. He wasn't *ever* being fooled again by a pair of bewitching violet eyes or a soft, vulnerable look that even now caused a tightness in his throat. Angered by the feeling, he snapped, "Well? Answer me!"

Unprepared for his attack, she stammered, "I—I—m-meant to tell someone, but I—I—forgot."

"Why?" The word was like a pistol shot, and it hung heavy in the air between them, both knowing suddenly that the question had nothing to do with the present situation.

Dumbly, Catherine shook her head wishing the ground would open up and swallow her. She wasn't ready for this—she might *never* be ready for this! Casting an apprehensive glance at her tall husband, it was evident that neither was he. He was still in the grip of that first white-hot fury. And sickly, she knew that in a minute all her cool resolutions would flee, and like a wild tigress she would snarl back—then the battle would be well and truly joined! She flashed a look around, seeking some way of averting the coming explosion, but nothing was going to prevent Jason from forcing the issue down her throat.

Seeing her apprehension, Jason mistook it and softly, menacingly he asked, "Are you frightened of me?" Then his control broke, and grasping her arm in a bruising hold, he thrust his face near hers and snarled, "By God, you have reason to be! I could damn near kill you for what you've done to me!"

Yanking her from the step, he dragged her down the hall. Struggling to free herself from his iron grip she resisted every step of the way, her fingers digging into the steel hand that propelled her so effortlessly into his study. Panting, she pleaded, "Let it be, Jason! You're in no mood to discuss anything now!"

He whirled on her like a striking snake, spitting the words out venomously, "And when *will* it be convenient? When my son is an adult? When I lie on my deathbed? How will you tell me, I wonder? I can see it now," his voice rose in imitation of a false simpering tone—" 'Oh, by the way, Jason, I forgot to mention, the boy Nicholas is not the issue of my sluttish association with another man, but your very own son. Fancy that!"

Catherine whispered, "I meant to tell you. I *would* have told you! But you were so positive that the child wasn't yours, I let you believe it. You must believe me—I *did* intend to tell you!"

"When?" The word was sharp, like a knife blade. Catherine flinched, but the sight of the violet eyes, wide with regret, evoked no softening in the harsh face. "Tomorrow?" he sneered as the silence grew. "Next year? The next?"

Catherine's mouth opened, but no sound came out, and viciously Jason regarded her. The slim form pressed against the door seemed to goad him into fury. And brutally, her shoulders crushed in his hands, he shook her violently. *"When?"* he thundered.

Remorse vanishing, her own temper broke, and twisting away, one long braid shaken loose and lying over her heaving breast, she spat, "When I damn well felt like it! And if I could have presented you with a bastard, believe me I would have! A dozen bastards!"

Blind with rage, nearly insane with pain, Jason struck her. The blow split Catherine's lip and smashed her head against the wall. The sickening crack as her head hit the wall brought him dreadfully back to reality. The taste of bile was in his mouth, and his soul was filled with horror.

The sight of the already darkening bruise on her white cheek and the bright red trickle of blood from the corner of her mouth instantly drained every ounce of anger from his body. Sick and shaken by the sight of his own violence, he put out a trembling hand, and in a voice raw with wondering pain whispered, "Why? Why do we do these things to each other?"

Caressingly, his shaking hand traveled like a butterfly's wing down Catherine's bruised cheek. There was a blank, vacant stare in her violet eyes, and at the shudder that shook her slender body, Jason's mouth thinned. "Kitten, kitten, I never meant to hurt you! Why are things so vile between us? We seem intent upon destroying each other."

In a state bordering on shock, Catherine unseeingly gazed at the stricken face so near her own. Her thoughts were jumbled, not making any sense. If only the buzzing in her head would stop—then she could concentrate, she thought befuddled.

Gently repulsing Jason's attempt to cradle her next to him and with her head held very high, she quietly slipped from the room. Ignoring the shocked glance of the butler she walked steadily down the hall, concentrating on one step at a time. Like a wounded animal she made her way upstairs to privacy.

In the cool sanctuary of her room, she realized the unpleasant taste in her mouth was blood, and she was aware that her cut lip was beginning to swell and sting. Solemnly, like a punished child, she stripped and climbed into the bed. Her one thought was to sleep—to sleep and not dream. Thankfully, mercifully, she fell into a deep, exhausted sleep.

Jason's study was silent like a tomb, and empty-eyed, he walked over to a table where a crystal decanter sat. Pouring himself a large glass of strong whiskey, he drank it in one long gulp. But not even the straight hard liquor could burn out the remorse and shame that ravaged his body.

What was wrong with them? he asked himself moodily. Were they forever destined to erupt in these ugly, soul-destroying arguments?

He poured another stiff drink and stared broodingly down into the amber-colored liquid. He hadn't meant to hit Catherine. God knows, he hadn't—she was the most important woman in his life!

Then furious at the damning admission, he wondered stony-faced how the hell he had let that little baggage get so embedded in his being. How had he allowed her such power over him that she drove him nearly mad with rage?

Jason swallowed some more of the liquor, slower this

time, tasting it this time. Calmer now, he began reluctantly to see some of Catherine's side of the hellish tangle, and a mirthless smile crossed his face. Who knows, he thought, if he had been a woman—God forbid!—and used whatever logic women did, he might have acted the same way.

Certainly, he could understand the pride that would seal her lips and let him think what he wanted. And how often, he probed, how often had he ever looked beyond the surface of his wife? Frequently he wondered why she acted as she did, but had he ever plumbed deeper for *her* reasons? Or even cared? He was becoming angrier with himself at each passing moment.

Oh, hell! What good does this do? he demanded of himself. Nothing, jeered a small voice in his brain, nothing, if you don't learn from it!

Rubbing one hand tiredly over his face, he felt bitterness clawing in his gut. He should be the happiest of men—he had a lovely wife and a healthy son. He was young, and he was rich. And yet what a mess they had made of things: she by being foolish and stubborn, and he, by believing he could reach out and snatch with impunity whatever took his fancy.

His harsh laugh broke the silence. *Juste ciel!* He would never make *that* particular mistake again!

After a long time, he wrenched his thoughts away from painful memories and deliberately compelled himself to think of their future. But the future stretched out, nearly as bleak as the past, and finally, unable to bear the accusing silence and his own torturing thoughts, he left the room and instinctively, as if compelled by a force stronger than himself, made his way to where Catherine lay asleep.

For some minutes, he stood staring down into her sleep-softened face, his mouth whitening at the sight of the angry bruise that discolored one flawless cheek and at the swollen, torn lip. How could he have done that to her? Why, instead of flaring into almost crazy rage, hadn't he listened to her and let it be?

Pride, he thought grimly—outraged pride at that! And

temper, he added, temper. No matter what he seemed to do, she alone seemed to have the ability to shake him out of his usual arrogant complacency and drive him to extraordinary lengths.

But it wasn't his sin alone, he argued wordlessly. She had been angry and had hurled infuriating words at him, tossing oil on a smoldering fire. Ah, *diable!* With her temper and his, they were liable to live like snarling wolves or spitting panthers.

Suddenly, smiling ruefully, his eyes were tender as they moved slowly over her features. If they ever learned to control their blazing tempers, they might just make this marriage work!

Lightly, he reached out and lingeringly ran his fingers over her face, as if by touching her he could erase those ugly reminders of their latest fiery conflict. At his touch, however, Catherine's eyes flew open, and for a few seconds Jason drowned in those clear amethyst pools.

Her sleep had been more in the manner of a coma, but even while consciousness had been mercifully deadened, her brain hadn't ceased to seek a solution for their latest impasse. From the multitude of thoughts, one thing had emerged, and that was the certainty they could not continue on this self-destructive path they stalked together. Memory of Jason's words the night of their marriage came back clearly to pound and whirl in her brain.

Once, he had wanted them to try and build something from the unfortunate events that had joined them together—if only to beget an heir—and even before Jason's fingers touched her, Catherine was struggling up from the deep waves of sleep with the thought uppermost in her mind that this time *she* would ask that they attempt to bridge the differences that were tearing their lives to pieces.

It was like a dream or a figment of her imagination to wake and find him bending over her, a sadly rueful smile on his mouth as his fingers gently caressed her face. Wonderingly she gazed up at him, stunned by the tenderness that blazed briefly in the green eyes then disappeared. That sudden, barely glimpsed emotion prompted her to say in a low voice, "Jason, once you asked me to help you make something of the situation in which we found ourselves. I'm asking you now to help *me!* I cannot bear to go on as we are. And if you cannot or are not willing to try, then at least let me go!"

A part of him snarled silently, "Go? Where? To your lover?" But with the memory of what had just happened vivid in his mind, he bit back his jealousy.

Seating himself on the bed beside her, he reached for her hands and lightly holding them, said thoughtfully, "I was willing then, and nothing has changed my mind since. Others in our position have found themselves married to complete strangers and have managed to survive and even obtain a measure of happiness. I see no reason why we can't manage the same."

A tremulous smile curved Catherine's lips. "I wonder if all those countless others had tempers such as ours?"

With a sudden grin mitigating his harsh features, he said lightly, "Probably not! But we both know how easily ours erupt, and perhaps knowing that we can be more understanding in the future." Honesty compelled him to add, "If I had listened to you earlier and waited at least until I had a semblance of sanity, we wouldn't have come to blows. This time, I must take the blame entirely—although the provocation was great!" For a moment, a teasing glint danced in his eyes but then it vanished, and he asked abruptly, "How *could* you keep our son's birth a secret from me?"

Catherine searched his face a long moment before saying painfully, "I never thought to see you again, and for all I knew you were divorcing me. I thought it best for all our sakes. But I would have told you at Belle Vista if you hadn't been so overbearingly positive that Nicholas wasn't yours." Watching the stoniness that crept into his face, she gave a tiny sigh and added doggedly, "Jason, I have as much pride as you do, and you accused me of unspeakable things! I could no more have told the truth then, than I can deny now that Nicholas is your son."

His mouth taut, Jason forced a smile and, releasing her hands, stood up. "I haven't yet thanked you, madame, for my son, and I do so now. Perhaps it's as well that events turned out as they have today. Certainly, I mean to become better acquainted with Nicholas and,"—his voice dropped intimately and the gaze that lingered on her lips was openly amorous,—"I have every intention of making myself *extremely* agreeable to his mother!"

31

With a growing sense of elation, Catherine watched Jason leave the room. He knew Nicholas was his son, and the secret burden of guilt she had carried at hiding that knowledge from him slid from her like a lead weight.

Feeling curiously lighthearted, she dressed for dinner that night, taking special care with her toilet. An application of rice powder helped to conceal the worst of the bruise on her cheek, and a series of cold compresses reduced swelling of her lip, if not the tenderness.

Carefully, she chose a low-necked gown of greenish bronze silk and watched critically as Jeanne dressed her hair in a cluster of tiny curls on the top of her head. A sprinkling of delicious scent from Houbigant's, and she was ready to face her husband.

Her heart thumping in galloping rhythm with the pounding of her blood, she descended the curving white staircase and walked to the large salon. As she opened the door and entered, her emotions vacillated between something approaching rapture and the quelling fear that she had dreamed that scene in the bedroom.

But she hadn't. Looking more relaxed and confident than she could ever remember him, Jason walked to her side eagerly as she stepped into the room. He was so heartbreakingly handsome in his scarlet jacket, his face rising darkly from the whiteness of his ruffled shirt, that Catherine felt her breath catch in her throat.

Throughout the ensuing evening, he treated her with a courtesy and gallantry that swept away every unpleasant remnant of every argument they had ever had. By the time they had eaten and he escorted her up the stairs, Catherine was certain he could feel the tremble of anticipation that raced through her body. But as they reached her door, he bowed politely and gently pushed her into the room—alone! For several stunned seconds, she stared at the closed door, and her bewilderment increased when a minute later the door to his room shut quietly.

Thoughtfully, she allowed the waiting Jeanne to undress her and brush the curls from her head. Jeanne's ministrations were soothing, and only when the long, shining locks were spread about her shoulders like a mantle of black satin, did Jeanne desist and ask permission to retire. A moment later, Catherine was alone, her slim body barely covered by a thin, clinging night gown of soft, flame-colored silk.

The room was lit by only a few candles, and, her heart pounding, Catherine waited for the twin doors that separated their rooms to open. Surely, now that he knew she was alone, he would come. But as the minutes passed, she reluctantly realized that Jason was not seeking her bed tonight. Feeling chastened and definitely frustrated, she climbed into bed, her thoughts busy with this, his latest incomprehensible deed.

Sleep came eventually, but no answer did she find for his actions. And it was with rampant curiosity lurking in her eyes that she joined him for breakfast. Remembering sickly how swiftly his mood could change, she almost expected to be met by the cold, haughty stranger who so infuriated her. But Jason's smile was warm and caressing as he seated her at the table, and as they ate, he kept a flow of pleasant conversation running. At the end of the meal, as if he had done it for years, he dropped a casual kiss on the tip of her nose before he left for the fields.

Greatly puzzled, she stared after his retreating back. What was he up to now? she wondered. The thought was to be repeated almost hourly in the following days, until suddenly it dawned on her that Jason was letting *her* set the pace of their ripening intimacy. The idea was intriguing in the extreme, and, at first hesitant, she tested the theory in little ways.

After a few more days, she was positive it was true. If she wanted for his company, all she had to do was murmur, "It's boring just staying here by myself all the long day."

Instantly a smile lurking at the corner of his mouth, Jason would reply, "Have the cook pack a basket and join me today. It's hot work, but you might enjoy watching us instead of Nicholas."

And so they spent many agreeable hours together, Jason stopping at noon for a long, private tête-à-tête with his wife in some secluded glen where they ate the excellent lunch prepared by the cook. Then, replete from the small feast, he would rest his dark head in her lap, and companionably they would talk of little things. So it went. Whatever she wished seemed to be Jason's chosen task for the day. She had only to hint she would like his help or advice with this or that, and without hesitation he would throw himself wholeheartedly into whatever was her whim.

It was Jason who when asked, pointed out that the heavy oak desk in her room would look better in his study, and Jason who found the feminine, delicate desk that took its place at the far end of her room. And it was Jason who unearthed the small well-sprung open carriage for her use, and Jason who, controlling his scathing retorts with admirable restraint, taught her to drive the spirited horses that pulled it.

The days were passing in an excited haze for Catherine,

and each day she grew bolder, going so far as to turn up her waiting lips for his kiss on those days she did not accompany him. The first time she offered her mouth, he hesitated only for a moment, then kissed her much more deeply than she had expected. When her eyes widened with surprise at the warmth of the kiss and she made to draw away, he kissed her again—a hard kiss that left her feeling as if her heart was lodged somewhere in her throat. From that morning on, without waiting for her to make the first move, he would kiss her a lingering goodbye, a curious smile breaking the harshness of his features. Sometimes she had the disquieting feeling he was secretly laughing at her, but with a defiant toss of her head, she continued to walk cautiously the path they were now traveling together.

Jason's undisguised delight at his son added to the growing bubble of happiness that was swelling inside Catherine. Those times when together they watched some particularly astonishing or amusing feat Nicholas accomplished, their eyes meeting each other's with warm enjoyment, Catherine thought her heart would burst with joy. The house seemed to radiate a growing happiness, and her light-hearted laughter, often followed by Jason's deeper rumble of amusement was heard frequently.

There were only two dark clouds on her horizon. First, she was still uncertain of his feelings for her—his words to Elizabeth often haunted her happy dreams as she slept alone in her bed. And sleeping alone was the second cloud of discontentment. She wanted her husband, and she wanted him in her bed! Sometimes she tortured herself with the thought that he no longer desired her that way. Miserably she tossed in the empty bed, her body on fire for his hard male form. How she wished he would kick open those doors that divided their rooms and with his breathtaking lovemaking overpower the last divider between them.

One night, before dressing for dinner, she glared at those closed twin doors and flounced down resentfully on her dressing stool. Suddenly, her eyes narrowed in thought. If he wouldn't come to her, than she would go to him!

She took a long time selecting a simple but provocatively fashioned gown of lavender silk to wear for dinner and an even longer time deciding on a negligee for bed. Finally, after she had nearly discarded every item of sleepwear she owned, she chose an intricately pleated gown of deepest rose.

A satisfied smile on her lips, she laid it reverently on the bed and had Jeanne do no more to her hair than thread a wide velvet ribbon of darkest fern green through it. She dismissed Jeanne for the evening and with determination in every step, she met Jason for dinner knowing she was looking her most enticing, for the lavender gown clung lovingly to her slender body and her breasts rose alluringly from the bodice. More than once she saw him glance at the slimness of her hips, and his gaze seemed to burn whenever it rested on the soft rise and fall of her bosom. She was at her most provocative, leaning into him seductively when he offered his arm as they walked to the dining room, and with a thrill she felt the slight tenseness that invaded his body at her nearness. He wanted her! She was certain of it, and with a gleam of mischief hidden in the violet depths, she proceeded all evening to tempt him.

As the evening progressed, she breathlessly watched the sensuous curve to his lip grow more pronounced and the fires that flickered in the hooded eyes burn stronger. A dozen times, she thought he would smash anything in his path and sweep her into his arms, and a dozen times, he checked the involuntary movement. Feeling rather like a kitten playing between the claws of a tiger, she teased him. But none of her shy, uncertain wiles seemed able to drive him beyond the rigid control which he placed on himself.

It was only when she was preparing to climb the stairs alone to her lonely room that he gave her any encouraging sign. Usually he escorted her to her door, but tonight he made no move to accompany her; uncertainly she waited, not wishing to leave him alone downstairs, but too embarrassed to ask him to take her to her room. Her uncertainty was apparent, and with a hard smile hovering around his full lips, Jason murmured, "I trust you can find your way tonight?"

Unable to hide her disappointment, she said, "Aren't you coming now, too?"

Impassively he answered, "For some reason, I find the thought of my bachelor bed unappealing, and not wishing to upset the harmony that currently exists between us, I think I had better stay here for a while."

"Oh!" she said blankly, but driven by the thought of the lovely rose negligee lying on her bed, she asked shyly, "Will you be long? I—I—" The words died in her throat, and unaware of the unspoken plea in her big eyes, she stared at him mutely.

He set his glass down very carefully and walked over to her, deliberation in every stride. Slowly, giving her every chance to escape, he drew her into his arms, his mouth finding hers as if he were starving for her. For endless seconds, they were locked together, Catherine nearly mindless with happiness, and then he thrust her from him and pushed her swiftly toward the stairs saying tightly, "I'm not a boy to be teased and then denied. If you stay one minute longer, I'm afraid—yes, very definitely afraid—I'll tip those skirts of yours up and take you right here on the stairs! *Good night!*"

He turned to stalk angrily back into the salon, and gathering every bit of boldness she possessed, she blurted, "I'm *not* teasing!"

Jason stiffened and spun to face her, a fire leaping into his green eyes. Suddenly her knees felt weak. They stared at one another, and then he said deliberately, "I'll be up in a few minutes. If you want me, I'll be in my room!" Then he strode away from her.

The blood racing in her veins, Catherine sprinted up the stairs and with trembling hands practically tore the dress from her body. Leaving it in a crumpled heap near the bed, she hastily slipped the rose negligee over her naked body. She stared at herself apprehensively in the mirror, and her eyes widened when she saw how transparent the gown was. Her small coral-tipped breasts were clearly defined, as was the dark, shadowy triangle between her legs. Suddenly unsure of herself, she nearly changed her mind. Then she heard the click of Jason's door as it shut, and, with a fluttering in the region of her stomach, she knew she would have to open those hateful doors that separated them. Nervously, she waited, changing her mind a dozen times.

Jason had made it clear that any move to change their relationship would have to be made by her. Wobbling slightly, Catherine walked toward the twin doors. For a second she hesitated. Then taking a deep breath, her head thrown up bravely, she flung open the doors.

The room was dark except for a wavering flame of soft light from one single candle near Jason's bed. Unaware of the increased transparency of her gown caused by the brighter light from her own room, she stood uncertainly in the doorway, her body appearing bathed in a rosy hue, her long black hair rippling like silk to her small waist.

A movement by the bed caught her attention. Peering into the shadowy blackness, she watched frozen, unable to move, as Jason rose up slowly from the bed. He had been lying there casually relaxed, his narrowed eyes revealing the only sign of tenseness. As Catherine made no further attempt to cross the intervening space, he walked leisurely up to her, his eyes lighting with gentle mockery.

"Hmmmm, and to what do I owe this honor?" he teased.

But Catherine's tongue was trapped to the roof of her mouth, and she was overwhelmingly conscious that beneath the green silk robe his lithe body was naked. His amused gaze traveled lazily over her still form, his eyes lingering on the darkness between her white thighs. Suddenly his amusement fled, replaced by a hard, urgent tautness.

Grasping her shoulders, he roughly pulled her to him and in a husky voice muttered, "You came to me this time, but if

I make love to you tonight, that damned door might as well not be there for the protection it will afford you in the future."

Mutely, she returned his searching stare, her senses swimming with delight at the feel of his hands on her. Her thoughts were dizzy with expectation. She wanted him so badly, so badly she was almost shaking with desire, and almost angrily she snapped, "Oh, shut up, Jason!" Then melting against him, she whispered, "Shut up and make love to me!"

A muffled laugh greeted her demand, and then she was caught up in his arms, his mouth capturing hers as he carried her eager body to the waiting bed. This time, it wasn't Jason's hands that tore the gown from her body but her own, and she needed no prompting to wind her soft, silken arms around his strong neck and to thrust her slim body close to the muscled hardness of his. She was hungry for him, and in every way she knew, she let him know it, her hands exploring him with growing confidence, even as his mouth and hands skimmed the alabaster smoothness of her body. Jason, as if to punish her for not coming to him sooner and for keeping the doors shut between them, played on her senses like a master on an exquisitely fashioned instrument, his caresses driving away her natural reticence.

His mouth like a trail of fire traveled slowly down her neck onto the firm, upthrust breasts that seemed to beg for his touch, and all the while those lean fingers were moving sensuously over her flat belly to the beckoning softness between her legs. A moan broke from her lips when at last he touched her there, and as his fingers entered and began to move in rhythm with her writhing body, Catherine was engulfed in pleasure. But she wanted more, and demandingly she beat out a tempo of desire on his broad back until with a smothered laugh he muttered, "All right, you little devil! All right!" He thrust himself deeply between her legs, his laughter gone, and his body nearly shaking from the fierce emotion that tore through him as Catherine's rising passion met his. Crushing her body next to his, his mouth burning against hers, he deliberately held back, deliberately intensifying the pleasure he gave, until Catherine was almost mindless with ecstasy. Only after he felt her body convulse with fulfillment, did he allow his own body to explode with pleasure.

Satiated and cradled in his arms, Catherine ran her hands lovingly over his face, exploring with soft finger tips the contours of his beloved features. His eyebrows felt coarse and her fingers slipped down his nose—ah, in her mind she could see the proud boldness of it. Then she touched his mouth—sensuous mouth! Almost compulsively her fingers traced its outline.

He was smiling, she could feel it in the darkness, and remembering how he could drive her into incoherent, blind passion, she blushed, glad there were no lights to reveal her embarrassment. There were no words between them, but as if sensing the constraint that so often sprang up afterwards, Jason pulled her closer, and her soft body molded itself unconsciously to the leanness of his. Capturing her wandering fingers in one hand, he kissed the tips lightly and murmured, "I never thought you were going to open that damned door! And I didn't know how much longer I could hold out. It's regrettable to admit, but if you hadn't come to me tonight, I'd have resorted to sheer male dominance and forced you to accept me." Laughing softly he said, "It was thoughtful of you to pander my ego."

Catherine stiffened, but Jason rolled over, trapping her beneath him, and nuzzling her ear whispered, "Kitten, kitten, don't fight me now. We've come such a long way, let's not ruin it merely because I can't resist teasing you." Since fighting him was the least thing in the world she wanted, her arms closed around him tightly, and both forgot everything but each other as the fires of desire began to roar once more.

From that night forward, their relationship took another bend, and there were few nights that didn't find them locked in each other's arms, their young bodies saying what words could not. And there in the darkness together, each night Jason taught her more and more ways to give pleasure and showed her all the ways a man can please a woman.

Nearly blind with joy, Catherine looked forward to each day with increasing happiness, laughter bubbling through her veins. Soon, soon, her blood seemed to sing, soon he'll admit he loves you, and you'll be the happiest woman in the world! Only occasionally did she let uncertainty creep into her thoughts, and she longed for the day she could ask him why he had said those hateful words to her cousin. Deliberately she blotted out any hint that Jason might have meant those words and that he was now only insuring that she produce another child. But then without warning, the increasing quiet happiness of their days was shattered.

It had been another hot morning, a muggy morning, and Catherine was feeling the heat more than a little. Even the coolness of the white linen gown did nothing to alleviate the stickiness that seemed to form in the steamy air. She could feel her hair curling damply at her temples, and she wished fervently for the black clouds that would herald a thunderstorm to appear on the horizon. It would be muggier afterwards, but a shower would cool things off momentarily.

She was seated on the downstairs veranda in a cane-backed chair, idly staring out over the green lawn at a series of white smoke puffs that drifted lazily over the darker green of the pine trees, when Jason and the crew that had been busy clearing a section of land near the north end of the plantation galloped up.

There was a grim cast to Jason's mouth, and after dismounting, he threw the reins to one of the men and barked, "Get those horses around back and yourselves as well. You know what to do."

Startled, Catherine watched as the men quickly rode towards the stables. With long, hurried strides, Jason mounted the steps, and seeing her sitting there, he snapped, "Catherine, get inside and stay there!"

Stung, she drew herself up stiffly and said haughtily, "Well! I beg your pardon!"

His features relaxed instantly, and he said softly, "Kitten, don't argue with me. This is important. Just do as I say."

Her anger evaporating, she obeyed him immediately. She had barely entered the house when the wives and children of the workers came streaming across the patio, and for a second, she stood staring, completely at a loss. One of the wives, Sara, explained, "We always come up to the big house when trouble is expected. It's easier to defend this one place and Mr. Savage always has plenty of supplies on hand for whatever emergency may arise."

Everyone but Catherine seemed to know exactly what was expected of them. Sudden, inexplicable fear drove her to see that Nicholas was safe, and after a distracted look at the women, she ran upstairs to check on him. Nicholas was sleeping soundly, and Sally, sitting by his crib, her eyes wide with alarm, was vowing to protect the sleeping child with her life if need be. Unable to remain still, Catherine ran back downstairs. Jason, a long rifle slung over his shoulder and a pistol shoved into his waistband, was pacing the hall as she came down the staircase, and she couldn't help asking nervously, "Is it Indians?"

"No. I damn well wish it were. Listen, kitten," he said seriously, "I don't expect there to be too much trouble, and the men are armed and in their places. But if there's any shooting you and Nicholas stay upstairs and away from the doors and windows. Promise?"

Her throat tight, Catherine nodded dumbly, but she knew if there was any danger she wanted to be at Jason's side—not locked upstairs with a group of weeping women and worrying about what was happening to him!

At the sound of approaching riders, Jason grabbed her and pressed a hard kiss on her mouth. Then pushing her urgently in the direction of the stairs, he stepped outside. Stupidly she stared after him and with a whimper of fear—for him, not herself—she flew across the hall and peeked outside.

A troop of about thirty Spaniards, their uniforms limp in the heat, were gathered at the front of the house, and at the head of the hard-bitten column sat Davalos. An unpleasant smile on his thin lips, he greeted Jason.

"So, *amigo,* we meet again."

Not by so much as the flicker of an eyelash did Jason acknowledge the words. He stood in the center of the wide veranda, partially concealed by the deep shadow of the overhanging roof. His voice expressionless, he inquired, "What do you want, Davalos?"

Davalos, his grin widening, started to swing from the saddle, but the ominous click of several hidden rifles, their hammers made ready to fire, caused him to sink slowly back into his seat, his black eyes searching to discover where the enemy lay concealed.

Softly, Jason said, "You ought to know better than to try to catch me by surprise. The borders of my land are wide, but I knew within minutes when you crossed onto Terre du Coeur. I expected you weeks ago. What took you so long? Gathering nerve to face me?" Jason taunted. "Afraid I would kill you on sight?"

Thinly, Davalos muttered, "Your hospitality is slender, I think."

"You think right, *mon ami!* I would suggest you continue on your way. There's nothing at Terre du Coeur for you—not even the courtesy one would ordinarily offer. I don't like snakes in my house!"

Davalos stiffened, his expression ugly, and unconsciously his hand dropped to the pistol at his side. The click of the hammer of Jason's rifle and the slow, steady swing as it followed Davalos's hand made Catherine blanch with sudden horror. Oh, God! she thought, don't let Jason get killed! And with grim determination she ran to Jason's study and snatched up a rifle from the glass case, her hand shaking as she loaded the powder and checked the flint. Then, she sped back to her observation post, noting that nothing had changed in the seconds she had been gone.

She took in the scene carefully, the only thought clear in her mind being that if Davalos shot her husband he wouldn't live long to enjoy his triumph. With her rifle aimed at Davalos's chest, she waited tensely for someone to break the nerve-stretching silence.

A sudden sharp laugh from Davalos made her fingers tighten painfully around the trigger, and she leaned forward to hear the Spaniard's low, furious words.

"Very well, *amigo!* You win again, but you cannot always be prepared, and who knows—the next time I appear, you might not be ready! You are lucky this time, but it will not always be so. Terre du Coeur is a long way from New Orleans, and you would be wise to remember it!"

Smiling tightly, Jason conceded the truth of his words. "You're absolutely correct, but don't threaten me too much, Blas, or I'll shoot you down like the damned dirty dog you are and take my chances with the authorities. It would make an interesting trial—my men testifying against yours. I wonder which the jury would believe? But it would make little difference to you because you would be dead, wouldn't you?" Jason mocked.

Blas's face grew darker with impotent fury. His teeth bared in a feral snarl, Blas growled, "You are lucky, my friend, *this* time. Don't let me catch you unawares in the future!"

Sick inside, Catherine knew intuitively that if Davalos had come upon the men as they labored in the fields or when she and Jason were at the house alone except for the servants, there would have been a very different ending to this meeting. They *were* lucky this time! And with a hard knot of premonition in her breast, she watched the column of Spaniards wheel and ride away. They would be back. She knew it!

Her foreboding thoughts came quickly to an end at Jason's swift entry into the house, and she threw the rifle down and flung herself into his arms. "Oh, Jason, I was so frightened for you. What does he want?"

Holding her tightly, he murmured into her hair, "It was nothing, little one. Davalos is a bully, and he thinks I have something he wants."

Gazing intently up into his face, she asked, "Do you?"

A slight smile driving the harshness from his features, he shook his head slowly. "No. But that won't stop him from trying. He's tenacious, and sooner or later, I'll have to kill him! God knows I would avoid it if possible, but a man can only stand so much—and Davalos has run his length."

Jason's words were spoken matter of factly, but Catherine sensed the icy purposefulness behind them. For a moment, his face was hard and implacable, and she clung to him tighter as if the warmth of her love could drive out this terrible half-guessed side of him.

Knowing instinctively that he had almost enjoyed that confrontation made her ask sharply, "If you're going to kill him anyway why didn't you do it today while you had the chance?"

"Because, my furious little love, you could have been hurt—not to mention a score of others. Davalos only wants me and he wants me alive! And so long as there are plenty of armed men around, Davalos will sulk about for a while and eventually give up and leave."

"How can you be certain? He might not give up so easily!"

Jason hesitated a moment, and then, as if having made up his mind to something, drew her down the tiled hall into his study. Throwing himself onto a wide leather couch, he pulled her onto his lap, cradling her body comfortably against his. Her expression troubled, Catherine looked up into his dark face, unable for once to derive any comfort from the close warmth of his body.

Not meeting her questioning eyes, Jason threaded the fingers of one hand through hers, all his attention seemingly absorbed in that simple task. For a second, they both stared down at her slim fingers intertwined with his browner, more powerful ones. Finally, Jason broke the stillness by saying slowly, "I have to go back a few years for you to understand what happened today and why Davalos's appearance doesn't alarm me."

His face serious, his mouth a little grim, he stared thoughtfully down into Catherine's upturned face. "You see," he began quietly, "Blas and I grew up together—off and on. I've always known him, and even though my childhood years were spent divided between Beauvais and Greenwood, my father's home in Virginia, we were always good friends. Even through the years I was in England at Harrow, we remained companions, and whenever I returned to Beauvais, we picked up the threads of our friendship just as easily as if we'd just parted only the day before. It was an easy, undemanding friendship, and Blas was with me through a lot of unhappiness." He threw her a slightly embarrassed look and confessed, "When I was much younger, the situation between my parents used to bother me a great deal, and Blas has a kind, understanding set of parents who are devoted to each other—I'm afraid I envied him, them."

He stopped speaking, a sudden frown marring his forehead, and Catherine longed to reach up and smooth it away. Uncertainty stopped her, and silently she waited for him to continue.

Picking his words with care, he went on, "I don't think that he would have changed—or I, either—if Blas's family hadn't lost their plantation and most of the family fortune when the indigo crops failed some years ago. I just don't know. At any rate, things were vastly different for them after the plantation was sold. Most of the money salvaged from the sale went to pay debts, and his father and mother returned to Spain. I think some of the younger children went with them. And I know Blas did have some relatives in Mexico because we visited with them one year." For a minute his face was blank, and Catherine knew he was seeing a different, younger Blas than the one she knew. His voice hardening, he continued, "Davalos had always been Army-mad, and it's fortunate in some ways that he obtained his commission before the family fortune was wiped out. But being a lieutenant in the Spanish army with a wealthy, influential family behind you is different from having to live solely on a lieutenant's pay, and I know it grated on him. Not only did the lack of money bother him, but he took it as a personal shame that the plantation failed."

Switching his faraway gaze back to her face, Jason smiled slightly, "I'm sorry I'm taking so long, but all this helps to explain him a little. You see, it was only after the money was gone that he started searching for other ways to recoup what had been lost. And not all the methods he chose were exactly right and honest. He took bribes and blackmailed more than one person. It was those activities that alienated all of his old friends—not the financial loss. But Blas never saw it that way, and he took particular delight in harassing those of us who had survived the disaster—almost as if he blamed us for his own misfortunes. And the fact is that we were lucky at Beauvais, for my grandfather had switched to sugar cane and cotton the year before the indigo crops were devastated by insects." He suddenly smiled down at her with a lazy grin that tightened her heart and teased, "We're very astute businessmen, we Beauvaises." His voice serious again, he continued, "Anyway, Blas and I began to meet head-on more and more, until finally there wasn't even a pretense of friendship between us. Blas likes to bring up the past, but he and I know it's over. At least he *should* know it!" Jason laughed harshly, adding, "I fought a duel with him over two years ago, and if I hadn't been crazy with rage, I would have killed him. He knows how I feel about him!"

Catherine could feel the tenseness building in his body, and sympathetically her hand tightened in his. He glanced down at her, his eyes hard with unpleasant memories. She waited for him to go on, and when he didn't, she asked carefully, "What prompted the duel?"

At her innocent question his whole body stiffened, and his jaw went taut. Caustically, he snarled, "Why we fought is none of your business! It's only sufficient for you to know that we did fight!"

He hadn't meant to snarl; but memory of Phillip's death always crazed him a little, and even now he couldn't bring himself to speak of it. Someday, perhaps, he could tell her of a boy's hero-worship of an older, adventuring godlike creature. But not yet—not while the wound of Phillip's death still lay open like a fresh-bloodied slash.

Hurt by his tone, Catherine bit her lip and, just a little resentful, snapped, "I only asked. You don't have to be nasty about it."

A sheepish smile crept across his face, and hugging her closer to him, he soothed, "Don't go all stiff on me! I didn't mean to be a bear, but sometimes—" the words trailed off.

Not completely mollified, she asked coldly, "Why did Davalos come here? Why now?"

"I can answer your second question easily. That troop, I'm willing to bet, has been ordered back to Mexico. And whether he likes it or not, Blas does have to obey orders. He just combined business with his own personal interest and took a detour. It's a considerable detour, but he can always cover it with some excuse—such as saying that he was merely surveying the extent of American encroachment. Spain is very jealous of her lands, and she views us with a suspicious eye."

Frowning, Catherine reasoned slowly, "If he's been ordered to Mexico, he can't linger *here* too long."

Smiling broadly, Jason answered lightly, "That's right, my love. His opportunities to catch me are few, and he took a chance today that he might be lucky and surprise me."

Not to be sidetracked, Catherine asked again, "Why does he want you so badly?"

Sighing a little, he questioned, "Remember that map Clive wanted?"

She nodded quickly, clearly puzzled.

"Well," Jason continued, "Davalos thinks I have found a legendary place called Cibola—the seven cities of gold—

and he's assuming that I have a map to lead me to and from it. He followed me to England because he was certain I went there to solicit investors into backing an expedition to retrieve the gold."

"Did you?"

"No! I went to England to buy horses. But Blas followed me, and Clive must have discovered enough from whatever unsavory characters he deals with, to make him interested in me. More precisely, any map I might have had."

"Jason, did you find such a place as Cibola?" Catherine couldn't help asking, her eyes wide with childlike excitement. He shook his head, smiling at her obvious disappointment at his answer. "Greedy puss! Aren't I rich enough for you?" he teased gently.

"Oh, no, it's not that! Only think how very exciting it would be if you *had!*" Her thoughts having been only momentarily diverted, she asked seriously, "Couldn't you explain to Blas that you haven't found Cibola?"

"No," he answered flatly, his amusement gone. "There's nothing on this green earth that would convince him I haven't found it and that I'm not hoarding the knowledge to myself!"

"But that's awful!" she cried. "If he believes you know where it is, he'll just keep after you!" A shudder shaking her body and fear flickering in her eyes, she whispered, "Oh, my God, Jason! What would you do if he did capture you?"

Gently to calm her fears, he soothed, "I know him well, and I think I'm clever enough to stay out of his clutches. Don't forget, Davalos is hampered by the army. He has to go where they send him. And as Spain has no more hold on Louisiana, he'll have to be stationed somewhere on Spanish territory. He might even be recalled to Spain."

"But you don't know that!" she argued. "You'll never know when he might show up again."

"Catherine, listen to me! I can handle Davalos. He's not particularly a brave man—if he were he'd cause me some sleepless nights. He's sly and cowardly. Today proved it.

Any other man would have shoved the insults I gave him down my throat. Don't worry about him! I have men in strategic places throughout Terre du Coeur just watching out for strangers of his type, and they will give us plenty of warning if he comes back."

At her disbelieving snort, he shook her slightly. "Davalos can only be dangerous if he finds me *alone*. I'm not a fool, and I intend to be on my guard. I can assure you, I have no desire to go wandering off by myself to make it easy for him! And you might remember that yourself. From now on don't go riding without an escort. I don't think you have anything to worry about, though—*I'm* his quarry!"

Unconvinced, she asked tightly, "How can you be so blind? Are you going to spend the rest of your life looking over your shoulder, wondering where he is and when he will strike?" Not waiting for an answer or expecting one, she spat viciously, "I wish you had killed him today!"

Flatly he returned, "I don't intend to spend the remainder of my life worrying about Davalos. And believe me, it would have given me great pleasure to shoot him from his horse." His eyes icy he added with cold amusement, "Killing a man is not just a matter of deciding to do it! Sometimes, my little firebrand, you have to wait for the right circumstances—or make them."

He left her then, striding purposefully out of the room. Catherine sank back down onto the sofa, all her fears still alive and unabated. She was filled with a queer premonition of disaster.

Men! she thought disgustedly. They had to do everything their own way, while their women could only stand back and watch and pray that everything came out all right. If she were a man, she wouldn't have been swayed today by such niceties as the fact that Davalos hadn't pulled a gun first! He was on Jason's land, and more importantly he was a threat—that's all the excuse *she* would have needed, and she would have shot him, dead!

Why did men, she wondered despairingly, with their incomprehensible code of honor, let the oddest things control their actions? The question was unanswerable. A cloud of gloom on her pretty face, she ran up the stairs, seeking the comfort derived from holding her son next to her body.

But later that evening, a set expression on her face, she sought out Jason's den at the rear of the house. Opening a drawer that she knew held several hunting knives, she eventually found a small delicately balanced blade that suited her purpose. Quickly and deftly she hid it gypsy fashion under her clothes. Feeling considerably safer she left the room—at least Davalos wouldn't catch *her* unarmed!

The next week was a great strain for her—the sound of an approaching rider would make her drop whatever she was doing, check that her knife was secure, and fly through the house, Jason's long rifle clutched menacingly in her slim hands. The second occasion when she met her husband thus, he cocked an eyebrow amusedly and murmured, "Do you know how to use that thing?"

Scarlet-faced, she admitted she wasn't *positive,* but she thought she grasped the idea! Hiding his laughter commendably, he proceeded to spend the afternoon showing her the finer points of priming the rifle and testing her marksmanship. She was an apt pupil, displaying a gratifying facility for learning quickly. It had been an agreeable afternoon, and Jason's expression, as they walked together towards the house, was content. Basking in the beam of his approval, Catherine was radiant. On the following morning when Jason returned unexpectedly, she was made even happier when he said, "Don't worry about Davalos anymore—as we guessed he's on his way to Mexico. He crossed the Sabine River three days ago, apparently heading for Nacogdoches."

"Are you certain? How do you know?"

He shot her a sardonic look. "You really should have more faith in me, my love. Did you think I just let him ride away to hide and wait for me like a coiled snake? Davalos has had two of my men on his trail ever since he made the mistake of showing up. You should know by now that very little escapes me!"

For a moment, anger at his insolence warred with relief in her breast, but relief won out, a delightful smile lighting up her entire face. Dazzled as always by that smile and unable to control himself, Jason snatched her into his arms and kissed her soundly.

The threat of Davalos still nibbled at the edges of her mind, but she was so taken up with the blossoming rapport between herself and her husband that she pushed thoughts of the Spaniard to the back of her mind. She was young, and she had a son and a husband, and while he had never said he loved her, her heart cried, he must—he *must!*

Oh, how she longed to admit out loud that she loved him and have him tell her the same! For in spite of their increasing closeness, she was never certain exactly how he felt about her. He was considerate with her, and there was hardly a night that his warm, hard body didn't possess hers. But then, she had never doubted his desire for her body. But was that all that drove him into her arms at night? Wasn't there something more? *Please,* dear God, let there be *more!*

32

The weeks following Davalos's departure were pleasantly tranquil. Catherine spent many of those days with Jason, accompanying him as he rode to and from the various tasks that needed his attention.

The "little missy," as she was called—dressed in slim-fitting breeches and a white linen shirt, her hair braided and hidden beneath a wide-brimmed hat and looking more like a slender boy than the wife of the master—became a familiar sight to the men in the fields, as well as to their wives and children. Catherine was everywhere, taking a keen interest in every facet of Terre du Coeur. The small lumber mill Jason had started fascinated her as much as the exciting and potentially dangerous work of branding and culling those fat cows that grazed in the sloping valleys. And yet, the news that Sam's wife was having her seventh child or that Horace's youngest was down with a fever would take her quickly to the houses of those who needed her help. Without being overbearing or appearing the haughty lady of the manor, she became very much the lady of the manor indeed.

Jason, an odd smile on his handsome face, watched all this with amused pleasure. More times than not, it was Catherine's presence that was wanted in time of domestic crisis. For both, the days were busy, and yet there was always time for Nicholas; and that young gentleman—with two loving parents to dote on him—grew exceedingly smug.

One morning, Jason commented on it, saying with an undertone of laughter, "If we don't want a real terror on our hands, we'd better get busy and provide him with several brothers and sisters to share his glory. After all, he might grow up to behave with my arrogance."

Catherine shot him an uncertain smile. She never knew exactly how to take those remarks of his. Any thought of more children made her achingly remember those ugly words he had thrown at Elizabeth. And yet there was the possibility that she might already be carrying another child.

After Jason left, she had another attack of the nausea that had appeared lately in the mornings. Quietly, she admitted to herself that she was definitely expecting. She couldn't be much more than two months pregnant and decided it must have happened that night Jason had made love to her in the woods and Blood Drinker had discovered them. Gloomily she wondered if, when Jason was apprised of her condition, he would cease making love to her until after the child was born, or until he felt it was time to breed her again. The thought was distasteful, and her heart shriveled a little. Well, she decided sturdily, if that's the case, my lady, you had better find it out right away. Tell him at once.

The opportunity came sooner than she expected—that very afternoon in fact. It was another one of those hot, muggy days, and the morning sickness had left her feeling apathetic and looking wan. At lunch she listlessly pushed her food around on her plate, and Jason, preoccupied with other thoughts but having noted her paleness, watched her intently for some minutes before asking, "Aren't you feeling well?"

Because the thought was paramount in her mind, she said

flatly, "I'm going to have another child!" Whatever she had expected his reaction to be, it hadn't been for him to stare at her blankly and say, "Oh," as if it didn't matter to him in the least.

But Catherine had chosen an unwise time to fling the news of her pregnancy at him. They were still groping towards one another, neither quite certain how the other felt, and while Jason welcomed the coming of a second child, if it was what Catherine wanted, it was an added complication. And there was Davalos. Jason was more worried and concerned about Davalos's unexpected arrival than he revealed—not for himself but because of the possibility of danger to Catherine and Nicholas—to everyone at Terre du Coeur.

Nettled at his lack of surprise or pleasure or any emotion at all, she glared at him and jumped up from the table. "Is that all you have to say?"

He eyed her consideringly as she stood at the end of table, her dawning anger apparent from the set of her lips. From her reactions he guessed she was not happy about the second child and that made his temper rise. What the hell was he to do about it now? Angry and a little hurt at her attitude, he said the worst possible thing he could.

His face expressionless and his eyes hooded, he answered coolly, "What should I say? You're young and healthy, and I've certainly done my share to insure you became pregnant. You were bound to breed sooner or later."

Fury and sick dismay tangled in her throat and throwing him a look filled with loathing, she fled. Throwing herself face down on the bed, her eyes aching with unshed tears, she bleakly admitted to herself that all her fears had been real. He only wanted a brood mare—all his acts of kindness had been merely to disarm her. Her hand clenching into a white fist, she thought about what a bloody fool she was! She actually believed he had changed. Thank heaven, she had not let him see how badly he had tricked her, nor, her breath caught in her throat, how much she loved him—still, in spite of everything.

The sounds of nearing hoofbeats drifting in through the opened doors that led to the veranda made her sit up suddenly. Her face tight with apprehension, she flew across the room and grasping the railing, she looked down at the two riders leisurely approaching the house.

It was not Davalos, but they were strangers to her. No—she recognized Pierre's slim form rising behind the tall, loose-limbed man who was in the lead. The man's face was hidden by the wide brim of his hat, but his clothes, as well as the fluid grace of the thoroughbred he rode, bespoke wealth.

Racing back inside, she took a quick glance in the mirror, straightening her lemon-colored gown automatically and nervously pushing a stray tendril of hair underneath the heavy coronet of braids. Her cheeks and mouth were pale, and hurriedly she bit color into her lips and pinched her white cheeks until they bloomed rose. Then with a haunted look in her violet eyes, she started downstairs.

Pierre, she knew, had stayed in New Orleans at Jason's request. Jason had told her that Pierre had grumbled and complained so at the constant moving around that Jason had felt a holiday would do the little man good. He had set no time for Pierre to return, but as Pierre was of the mind that Jason could not do without him, Jason had said with a grin, that when Pierre had decided that Jason had muddled through long enough without him he would suddenly appear at Terre du Coeur just as if nothing had happened. And it would seem Jason's estimation of his valet was correct. She knew one person who would be extremely glad of the little man's arrival—Jeanne. Despite words to the contrary, she had been greatly disappointed when she discovered that Pierre was not at the plantation, and Catherine had then wondered if perhaps Jeanne felt more for the stiff, very proper manservant than she would admit.

Smiling briefly at the thought, her hand on the dark oak

railing, she hesitated on the landing, and from the reassuring murmurs coming from the downstairs veranda, she gathered that these unexpected men were friends. Well, she told herself, if Pierre was with them they were bound to be.

She was halfway down the stairs when Jason, his face wearing a guarded smile, strode inside. The stranger, now hatless, followed him. Instantly, she noted the similarity between them. They both had tall, lithe bodies, even though Jason was taller and broader-shouldered. The man's hair was as Indian black as Jason's, but his temples were silvered.

Jason caught sight of her standing there, and she really didn't need his, "Ah, Catherine, come down and meet my father, Guy," to know the man was Jason's parent.

Guy's head snapped up at Jason's words, and for the first time she saw his face clearly. Yes, she could see a resemblance between them, but what reverberated through her startled brain was the strange awareness that Guy's thin, rakish features reminded her vividly of Adam. Before she could begin to gather her scattered wits, Guy was climbing the stairs, two at a time, smiling charmingly.

Grasping her hand he said, "My dear! You have no idea how happy I am to meet you. I hope you'll forgive me for intruding upon you this way, but I just couldn't possibly stay away. I have longed for Jason to marry, and I so wanted to welcome you to the family."

Responding to the undisguised warmth in his voice, like a flower to sunlight, she returned his smile, deciding instantly she was going to adore this handsome father-in-law of hers.

Together, they descended the stairs, watched by Jason. His sarcastic smile deepened when Catherine said, "I'm very happy to meet you, too! Jason has told me very little of his family, and I assure you that you are not intruding." Throwing her husband a defiant glance, she added, "It's definitely dull with just Jason and me here, and your company is most welcome."

A malicious gleam in his eyes, Jason broke into the obvious rapport between them by saying, "But things are not *dull!* You have yet to meet your grandson, Nicholas, and even more *exciting,* Catherine is expecting our second child. You see how eagerly I follow your advice."

Guy looked uncomfortable, and Catherine's eyes went dark with pain. With apparent relish Jason went on, "Yes, my little wife, I never told you but it was my father who so earnestly advised me to marry and er—ah—breed him some grandchildren was the phrase, I believe he used."

"Now, Jason—" began Guy in a troubled tone.

But Jason cut him off saying harshly, "You two seem so taken with one another, I'll leave you to become further acquainted. You will no doubt agree on my vices and have a pleasant time tearing my character to shreds. I'll leave you to it—I have work to do!"

Dismay breaking over Guy's face, he made an attempt to speak, but Catherine interrupted tightly. "Yes, I think that's an excellent idea. You've performed the introductions, so there's no reason for you to linger, is there? I'll enjoy visiting with your father and showing him his grandson. I hate to disappoint you, but I'm afraid we'll be much too busy to waste time discussing your lack of character."

Jason's mouth thinned, and an ugly gleam flickered in his green eyes. "Do that!" he snapped and flung himself out of the house.

Guy turned to Catherine, his consternation plain. "My dear, I am most sincerely sorry if I have chosen an inconvenient time!"

Smiling brightly, her eyes glassy with unshed tears, Catherine laughed, "Don't be silly! I can't tell you how much it means to me to have you here. Do you plan to stay long?"

Taking his cue from her, Guy answered lightly, "I shall stay until that bad-tempered son of mine throws me out!"

The following hours were some of the most enjoyable Catherine had spent at Terre du Coeur. Guy was plainly delighted with Nicholas, and almost shyly he commented on her condition. His being so sincerely happy that she was to bear another child touched her. And as the long afternoon passed, she found herself drawn more and more to this polite and thoughtful gentleman.

He flattered her gently on the changes she had wrought throughout the house saying, "What a difference you have made here! I especially like the feeling of coolness and serenity you have achieved with your choice of colors. Before the house always struck me as drab, but now! . . ."

By unspoken agreement, they did not mention Jason's behavior, and Guy with years of practice at his disposal made Catherine relax and feel she had known him forever. She had been dreading dinner, but now with Guy to act as a buffer between herself and Jason, she was able to face the meal with acceptance, if not tranquillity. Dinner went surprisingly well—Guy being urbane and Jason, his dark face closed and shuttered, at least making a pretense of politeness. Catherine was notably silent, smiling at Guy's witticisms but saying very little. Frequently she felt Jason's hard gaze on her face, and her heart shook as she thought of the hours ahead when they would be alone.

After dinner, the three of them settled down comfortably in the sitting room, the men with glasses of whiskey and brandy, Catherine with a fragile china cup filled with tea. The two men had been discussing the situation in New Orleans, and Catherine's thoughts wandered aimlessly until Guy's words attracted her attention.

"How much longer do you expect to remain at Terre du Coeur this year? I know Claiborne gave you a year's leave, but he wants you back in New Orleans somewhat desperately. He's coping admirably so far, but he needs all the support he can muster and not just politically."

Jason raised his eyebrow quizzically, and spurred by the glimmer of interest in Jason's green eyes, Guy continued, "The French and Spanish are intolerant of the Americans, and considering how some of the latest arrivals lord it over the city and look with scorn and contempt upon the Creoles, it's not unreasonable of them to do so."

Guy risked a glance at Jason, and almost indifferently Jason prompted, "So?"

"Well, you know how it is! Claiborne has had some sticky moments trying to bring together both elements of the city. I can give you, if you like, two examples of the luck he's had lately."

Jason grunted an assent, and making light of it, Guy said, "Claiborne attended a ball recently, and as usual the French guests began to dance a quadrille. Some of the Americans made a few snide remarks about it and a few requested, less than politely, that an American dance be done. No one was particularly offended, but there were quite a number of nasty glances exchanged. That might have been the end of it, except that an American surgeon angrily demanded that the musicians play another selection—an American selection. Naturally the Creoles were incensed. Claiborne stepped in hastily and calmed things down. But later, another American insisted peremptorily that they do away with the French dances and all the ladies, being French, naturally refused to dance and en masse swept out of the ballroom. It was very embarrassing for the governor, I can tell you!"

"I can imagine. But what did you expect? After all, New Orleans has been French at heart from the beginning. You can't expect them to take lightly to American ways," Jason retorted.

Guy ignored the interruption and went on, "That was only one incident. To make matters worse, when General Wilkinson attended another gathering shortly after that and when his staff began to sing 'Hail Columbia' the French were highly affronted, and one began to sing 'La Marseillaise.' Tempers got out of hand, and the fracas ended with each group trying to outshout the other."

Looking at his son levelly, Guy said, "It is amusing in some respects, but you can see why Claiborne needs someone like you—accepted by both sides and in a position to smooth over and help avert such contretemps. Claiborne is trying very hard, but it's not easy for him. The Creoles refuse to learn English, and it's chaos now in the courts because they're American. The French don't understand the Americans, the Americans don't understand the French, and when you throw in a Spaniard it adds to the confusion. It'll be years before just the language barrier is resolved, let alone the customs." Reflectively Guy added, "I didn't realize how very different we must appear to them—or they to us!"

"*We?*" Jason questioned sarcastically.

"Well, Americans at any rate. Fortunately, having been in and out of the area for years, I'm accustomed to New Orleans and wouldn't change it for the world. But some of the Americans can't understand the love of gambling, for instance, that predominates, and the way bets are placed on the waterfront and along the streets." Guy shook his head, smiling slightly. "The New Orleans people enjoy life, their liquor, their food, and their music, but the Americans look only to their businesses and are too busy making money to relax and enjoy the easygoing life of the Creoles. The Creoles can't understand that type of attitude, and to them, it's all very perplexing."

Rising to fix himself another drink, Jason remarked, "All you say is true, but my return isn't going to solve anything."

"I know that!" Guy returned waspishly, becoming angry with Jason's indifference. "But your presence would help. You know these people, you know how hot-tempered they are—you are yourself, so you *should* know! There are many ways you would be of use to Claiborne in helping him not to blunder in dealing with the Creoles—and you *did* promise Jefferson!"

Frowning, Jason stood staring into his drink. "True," he finally admitted. "I suppose, considering Catherine's condition and the news you bring, the sooner we return to New Orleans the better. She won't be able to travel in a few months, and it would be best if we arrived and settled in before—" he hesitated and finished lamely—"well before."

Both men turned to look at Catherine, who was sitting silently on a green damask couch. There was an unspoken question in the air, and Catherine said woodenly, "It makes little difference to me when we go. But then," she added bitterly, "my wishes have never been particularly important to Jason's scheme of things."

Jason's hand tightened on the glass, and his green eyes were snapping with anger as he snarled, "Well, that settles it then! As my wife's wishes are unimportant to me, I see no reason to discuss it with her. Come father, we can continue this conversation privately!"

Guy had no choice but to follow his son from the room, but he did take time to squeeze Catherine's hand reassuringly and throw her a commiserating look. She sat there a few minutes after they had left and then numbly made her way to the bedroom. But the numbness left her almost immediately, and appalled at her own silly thrust at Jason, she was trembling with reaction as she prepared for bed. How could she have been so stupid and rude to say such a thing in front of Guy? Especially after he had so painstakingly made the evening bearable, why did she have to let her unruly tongue spoil things? Damn, damn, damn! she thought viciously, at first angry with herself but then furious with Jason. Why the hell should she be careful of what she said—he certainly wasn't!

Guy intimated as much to Jason as they strolled outside in the direction of the stables. "You know," he commented quietly, "you shouldn't be too upset. After all, you were pretty brutal to her this afternoon."

Tautly, Jason retorted, "We'll leave my wife out of this, if you don't mind! Considering the state of your own marriage, I really don't think you should attempt to give me advice about mine!"

Guy smothered an angry answer and asked instead, "Were you serious about returning to New Orleans?"

"Yes. And not because of those little bits of tittle-tattle you dropped in front of Catherine! You were only laying groundwork for something else. Now tell me—what is the *real* reason behind your visit, and why does Claiborne really want me back?"

The night was quiet except for the low hum of the evening insects and the strangely soothing croak of the frogs, and Jason's words were clear in the night air. The two men stopped near one of the wooden-rail fences, and Jason, resting one foot on a bottom rail, laid his arm on the top and faced his father. Guy, leaning back against the fence, his hands in his pockets, his head bent, openly admitted, "I didn't want to say a great deal in front of Catherine, but there *is* a more serious reason that Claiborne needs you. The marquis de Casa Calvo is still in New Orleans!"

"The Spanish representative?" Jason asked surprised. "I thought Spain and France both were to leave once the Americans arrived."

"They were," Guy replied. "But Calvo seems to have discovered an undying love for Louisiana, and he can't bring himself to depart. Nor, I might add, have any of the French troops or their officers left either. As you know, they were to leave within three months after the exchange, and now within a short while of being a year, they still remain!"

Jason whistled softly to himself. "No wonder Claiborne is nervous. I knew they were overstaying the time limit because they were still there when I left—but there was talk that it was only a short delay."

A snort from his father made him smile. "A short delay, ha!" Guy snapped. "You're isolated up here, and you haven't kept abreast of things. Calvo keeps smiling and dropping little poison barbs that don't help the Spanish-American relations. And to make matters worse, Claiborne is constantly receiving less than encouraging reports that the Spanish forces are amassing and making mysterious marches to God knows where or for what reason. Beside which, the French are very openly admitting that as soon as

Napoleon trounces the English in Europe, he'll march right into the Place d'Armes in New Orleans!"

"And?" Jason prompted, knowing what was coming.

"Well, you're related to a lot of the French and, equally important, to several Spanish families. You can move freely among them without arousing suspicion."

A grim smile on his lips, Jason murmured, "I'm to spy on my relatives?"

Guy looked pained. "Don't be so vulgar! You won't be spying precisely—just keeping a watchful eye on events. Of course, if you hear of anything—"

"I'm to run like a lap dog to Claiborne," Jason finished sarcastically.

"Are you trying to be difficult, or are you doing it naturally?" Guy asked, exasperated.

"But naturally, *mon père!*"

Responding to the thread of laughter in Jason's voice, Guy smiled slightly and asked, "Are you going to do it?"

Jason shrugged. "Probably. Someone has to. And I don't want to see Louisiana torn up like a bone between starving dogs."

A companionable silence fell between the two men as they stood quietly in the darkness, their white shirts a pale blur in the night. Presently, Jason lit one of the long cigarillos made of fine Virginia tobacco that his father offered him, and the fragrant smoke floated in the air while the glowing tips were small dots of red in the blackness.

Finally, Guy remarked, "Well, I'm for bed. It's been a long several days for me. I'm getting too old to come running off into the wilderness like this."

"Why did you come? Besides the New Orleans situation."

Moodily, Guy replied, "Roxbury!" as if that said it all, and to Jason it did. Considering the letter he had received from his esteemed uncle, he could very well imagine the one Guy would have received.

Damn Roxbury, Jason thought, why couldn't he leave well enough alone? Yet, it made him smile to think of the malicious glee the duke must have felt as he penned those letters. Ah, well, Roxbury was Roxbury, and if he occasionally played God with a spiteful touch, who was to blame him.

Together, the two men made their way back indoors, parting at the head of the stairs, and with lagging steps Jason approached his own room. Stripping off his clothes, he put on the green silk robe. He hesitated a moment before the twin doors that led to Catherine's room; but then remembering how they had parted, his mouth twisted, and he went instead to his own lonely bed.

Catherine, lying awake and dry-eyed, heard his movements, and if she needed any further proof of his callous, coldblooded use of her, those retreating steps gave her the answer. Unable to sleep, she slipped from the linen sheets. Like a pale ghost in her green filmy nightdress, she wandered out onto the veranda. Leaning her head against the wooden support, she stared out over the dark expanse of lawn, her eyes lingering on the blacker, soaring shapes of the encroaching pine trees.

Her emotions were mixed as she stood there. She wasn't exactly happy about the second child, but neither was she unhappy. She wasn't even angry at Jason any longer. He had never hidden his reasons for marrying her, and if she had read more into his actions than was warranted—the more fool, she!

Disillusioned, perhaps, best described how she felt. She had been so full of hope these last days, and now like a fragile, crystal goblet smashed against stone, all her dreams lay shattered about her feet.

A shuddering sigh shook her slender body, and grimly she decided that one thing was for sure—this would be her *last* child by Jason. If he wanted more sons, he could father little bastards, but no more would come from her body.

She couldn't run away again, and deep inside she didn't want to. But within the narrow confines, she had to live. From now on, she would make a life of her own, and in time, involved with Nicholas and the unborn child, she could soothe the ache in the region of her heart.

In the future, Jason would have no cause to complain; she would run his home, be his hostess, and rear their two children; but she and her body would be closed to him. Beyond the times they would naturally have to be with one another, she wanted none of him—no more of those heartbreakingly dear rides together; no more quiet picnics in the pine-scented forests; and no more nights of exquisite passion when his touch made her flame with desire!

Cynically she decided, he could slake his male needs on another woman and leave her to find her own amusements. A derisive smile on her lips, she visualized what his reactions would be if she were to take a lover, and then her eyes narrowed as the idea expanded. What a laugh to cuckold Jason and present him with another man's child! Mirthlessly, she giggled to herself. What a fitting revenge, and the cream of the jest would be that he would know it, yet be forced to acknowledge the child as his own! Extremely thoughtful, she went back inside and climbed into bed, her mind busy with vengeful plans.

The next morning, she was pleasantly polite to both men as they ate breakfast on the sunny patio. Aware of the wary looks cast her way by Jason, she smiled sweetly in his direction whenever their glances met. But the smile didn't light her eyes, and by the time they were enjoying a last cup of chickory-flavored coffee, Jason was frowning blackly.

Guy was to spend the day with him inspecting the numerous changes being instituted throughout the plantation, and at the last minute Jason asked curtly, "Will you join us?"

Opening her eyes very wide, Catherine replied airily, "How kind of you to think of me! Unfortunately, considering my—er—delicate condition and the importance of producing another heir, I don't think I should."

His eyes hardening, Jason nodded brusquely and asked if Guy was ready. Guy was, and a moment later Catherine was alone, her eyes unseeingly on the tinkling fountain. Eventually, she roused herself from the lethargy that threatened to overcome her and went inside.

She managed to occupy herself, with Jeanne's help and the assistance of a black servant, cleaning out the last storeroom. There were several dusty trunks that yielded scraps of odds and ends, including some old-fashioned dresses that must have belonged to Jason's grandmother. The sight of those unused gowns made her remember that in a few months her own gowns would be useless. Thankfully she recalled the bolts of soft materials that at Jason's insistence had been ordered from New Orleans. As soon as Blood Drinker arrived, she would have several loose gowns made to accommodate her expanding shape. But then she remembered that they would be leaving for New Orleans soon, and she was sunk in gloom.

She had grown very fond of Terre du Coeur and would hate leaving it. Secretly she admitted that she wanted this second child to be born here—yes, in this house that had given her so much fleeting happiness!

That evening at dinner, remembering Blood Drinker's possible arrival, she asked, "Have you any idea when Blood Drinker will return?"

Jason looked at her curiously before saying, "He's due back any day now. Why?"

"Mmmmmm, I just wondered."

His glance rested on her a second longer. Then as if losing interest in her, he began once more to talk with his father. They were discussing the merits of raising cotton against Jason's plan of expanding his cattle herds. Growing bored, Catherine excused herself and went to bed.

After the troubled night before, she slept soundly and woke early. It was such a glorious, bright, shining morning that she gave in to the urge for a ride through the cool, pungent-scented woods, and quickly scrambling into breeches and shirt and clamping on her head the wide-brimmed hat that she habitually wore when out in the hot sun, she ran lightly to the stables.

A sedate ride wouldn't hurt her—not yet, anyway. And the fact that Jason would be furious after she had turned down his invitation yesterday added to her enjoyment and caused a spiteful smile to cross her usually sweet face.

It was early yet, the sun barely risen, and the plantation was just beginning to show signs of waking. Catherine laughed at the sleepy-eyed stableboy and said she'd saddle the horse herself. Quickly and efficiently she did so, remembering mornings at Hunter's Hill when she had done the same.

Without effort, she swung herself up into the saddle and was on the point of kicking the gray mare into a canter, when suddenly Jason loomed up out of nowhere and laid a firmly detaining hand on the bridle. "What the hell do you think you're doing? I thought riding was out for you," he snapped, his green eyes like chips of ice and his mouth tight with anger.

Impudently, Catherine smiled down at him. "That was yesterday—with *you!* This is today, and I feel like a ride by *myself.*" As she finished speaking, she noted a man standing by a foam-flecked horse and wondered vaguely if he was the reason for Jason's presence. Nodding the direction of the waiting man, she added, "I believe he's here to see you. Don't let me keep you."

A muscle bunched in Jason's cheek, and he ground out, "Yes, I know he's waiting. And the news he brings isn't good. Even if you weren't with child, I wouldn't want you riding alone. Now get down off that damn horse and wait for me at the house!"

Her impudent smile wavered, and nearly blind with swift rage, she jerked the reins from his grasp and spat, "You forget, I think, dearly beloved, that I am not a servant!"

Jason made a frantic lunge for the bridle, but the mare, restless and high-strung, reared up, her slender, steel-pistoned forelegs striking out and giving Jason barely enough time to leap out of the way of those thrashing hoofs. Catherine held her seat, easily controlling the mare as the animal danced nervously beneath her light weight, and as Jason approached again she shot him a mocking look and deliberately dug her heels into the horse's silken flanks. Like an arrow released from a bow, the mare shot forward nearly knocking Jason down as he made another fruitless grab for the bridle. But the horse swept by him, and Jason, his broad chest heaving, hands on his hips, green eyes narrowed, watched Catherine gallop away.

Then crossing to the waiting man he queried sharply, "How far away did you say they were?"

"Not more than an hour. I damn near killed my horse to get here as soon as I could! Packy is still following them, so even if they don't come here directly, we'll know where they are."

Biting his lip undecidedly, Jason, his eyes still staring in the direction that Catherine had disappeared, said, "Go rouse the rest of the men and get the women and children up to the big house."

Embarrassed at his own temerity but nonetheless determined, the man blurted out, "What about the missus?" At the icy look he received he wished he had torn out his tongue with white-hot pincers before asking.

Damn it! Jason thought angrily. What about her? Davalos only wanted him, but he couldn't take the risk that his stubborn, willful Catherine wouldn't meet up with the returning Spaniard and come to harm. He'd better let Guy know the situation and then take a few men and go after her.

Shouting for one of the boys to saddle up his favorite black stallion and a half-dozen other horses as well, he started off in the direction of the house. As luck would have it, he met Guy as he descended the staircase.

Guy was smiling, having just spent an enjoyable few minutes with his grandson, but at the expression on Jason's dark face, his smile faded and, concern sharpening his words, asked, "What is it?"

"Davalos is on his way back, and Catherine just rode out of here like a wild Valkyrie. I have to go after her." Pausing, he eyed his father levelly, then continued, "I haven't time to explain everything, but the men as well as their families know what to do. And right now, I want you to forget every kind memory you have of Davalos and remember only that I'd view an approaching band of marauding Comanches with a far more lenient eye than I do him!"

His own face matching the grimness of Jason's, Guy nodded with quick comprehension. A moment later Jason was on his way to the stables. He spotted most of his men armed and escorting the white-faced women and children up the slope to the house. Calling to several of them he briefly explained the situation again. Grim-faced, they all walked quickly to the stables, and swiftly mounting the waiting horses, they thundered off in the direction that Catherine had taken earlier.

Where the hell would she have gone? he wondered uneasily. And he cursed the luck that Blood Drinker wasn't back yet—that Cherokee could follow the trail of a feather across stone! His own tracking abilities were not to be slandered, but he wished like the devil the Indian was with him. But in spite of his misgivings, he discovered Catherine's tracks easily enough, and quickly the men followed them to one of the wide streams that crisscrossed the property.

Almost as if she had known Jason would be tracking her, Catherine had urged her horse to the center of the shallow creek, and Jason cursed again because precious minutes were wasted casting about for the clue that would show where her horse had left the water. After finding it about a mile downstream, Jason, with a growing sense of urgency, guided his horse from the creek into the pine forest.

Suddenly, the air shook with the sound of gunfire, and viciously Jason, his heart a lead stone in his breast, kicked the stallion into a dead run and raced in the direction of the shots, the others galloping close behind him. It took them almost fifteen minutes of wild riding, ducking low-limbed branches, and following the twisting path to reach the glen where Catherine had gone—but by then, it was too late.

The glen was empty except for a riderless horse standing over a still figure sprawled on the ground. His face white, Jason slid from the stallion and ran to the motionless form. It wasn't Catherine, but he instantly recognized Packy, the boy who had been following Davalos, and with a sick dread in his body, Jason knelt beside the wounded boy.

At his approach, Packy opened his blue eyes and muttered, "They got the missus, them dirty greasers! She fought like one of them panther she-cats, but there were too many of them." His eyes pleading, his voice weak from the loss of blood that seeped through his shirt from an ugly wound, Packy said laboriously, "I tried to stop them. I think I nicked one, but the missus was right in the middle, and I was scared I'd hit her!"

Hushing the boy, Jason praised, "You did fine. Don't worry—we'll get her back. Right now, we need to get you some medical aid." Forcing himself to grin confidently at the boy, he said, "Before I let you pass out, can you tell me how many there were?"

"Twenty or thirty—looked like the same bunch as last time."

Jason's face stony, his mind deliberately blank, he carried the wounded boy in his arms to Terre du Coeur. And only after he had removed the bullet and Packy was resting comfortably, did he answer his father's anxious questions. Betraying no outward emotion, his voice perfectly controlled, he explained briefly what had happened.

Guy was horrified. "You've got to go after her! At once!"

Jason stared with icy eyes and shook his head a decisive no.

"Why ever not?" cried Guy. "She's your wife, and even if it was her own fault, you can't abandon her to them!"

"It wasn't her own fault!" The words came low and passionately from Jason. "I didn't tell her Davalos was back in the area. If I had, no matter how angry she was with me, she wouldn't have disobeyed me!" Bitterly, he added, "I know her that well, at least."

"What do we do now?"

"We wait."

"I beg your pardon! Have you lost your wits?" Guy demanded angrily.

His outward calmness hiding his own fears, Jason met his father's furious stare and said quietly, "Davalos wants *me*. Capturing Catherine was nothing more than a lucky accident for him. And her life means little to him. If cornered, he'd kill her without question. Certainly, I could have left Packy and continued after them, but it's unlikely I would have overtaken them, and it's much more probable that if I had been able to get within shooting distance Davalos would have killed Catherine then and there. Do you think that would help the situation? Or have you considered that in an exchange of gunfire it might be my own bullet that kills her? I can't take the risk. And remember this—I know how Davalos's mind works. He'll use her as a lure. I know you don't like it, I don't like it myself, but knowing Davalos, very shortly he'll send me his terms. All we can do is wait—and pray."

Regarding his son with dislike, Guy wondered how he had ever sired such a coldblooded, unfeeling person. Unable to bear the sight of that blank, closed face, he stomped out of the room.

They waited tensely throughout the long day. Then, as Jason had predicted, Davalos sent word. A rider appearing out of nowhere in the deepening dusk and flashing past the guarded house hurled the message, tied about a stone, through the window. A volley of shots followed him, but the whole incident happened so swiftly that the rider galloped away unharmed.

A tremor shook his long fingers as Jason untied the scrap of paper from the rock. His voice unemotional, he read aloud, "I have your wife. You may find her in my keeping, west of the Sabine. I await you at Trader's Clearing."

"When do you leave?" Guy asked quietly, and blindly Jason looked in his direction. "At dawn," he said dully. "I would gain little by departing tonight, and there are things to be seen to first."

33

The threat of immediate danger over, the men and their families who had gathered in the big house slowly returned to their own homes. It was a silent group—even the children for once were quiet and subdued—and Catherine's fate was foremost in many minds.

A whiskey in his hand, Jason leaned against one of the massive posts of the downstairs veranda, staring at nothing, his mind completely blank. As long as he didn't think of Catherine and what might be happening to her right now, he could *appear* normal. And if he was to get her back safely and himself as well, he had to plan unemotionally. He had to think of her as merely something to be bartered! He didn't dare let fear or the sick dread that lurked in the back of his mind take hold.

A sound from the forest made him stiffen and peer through the gathering twilight. Now clearly he heard the sound of wagon wheels creaking, and a moment later he stepped down and grasped Blood Drinker's hand. "You're back!" he stated unnecessarily.

The Cherokee, searching his drawn face said simply, "It came to me that I should be here tonight."

No more words needed between them, silently they watched as the wagons rolled out of the woods. Jason's own people, drawn by the sound, drifted up from their homes to greet the new arrivals. Guy came to stand on the bottom step next to his son, his face pale and set.

Blood Drinker had leveled a piercing glance at Guy when he joined them, and then his black-eyed stare had gone to a wagon that was leaving the others as they made their way to the stables and unloading area. This wagon slowly approached the house, and Jason cocked an inquiring brow in Blood Drinker's direction. "Your mother-in-law," came the answer, and Jason sighed. Poor Rachael! He was forever being the messenger of bad news to her, and this time he had to make light of the abduction—there was no need to worry Rachael unduly, if it could be helped.

A strangled exclamation from his father disrupted his thoughts, and curiously he cast a look at Guy. Guy, his body braced as if for a blow, was staring unbelievingly at the small, dark-haired woman being helped down from the wagon by a tall young man. Jason's gaze swung back to the scene in front of him and his own body stiffened as he caught sight of Adam St. Clair!

He had seen him only once, but those hawkish features were burned on his brain with a white-hot, jealous brand, and angrily he strode forward to meet his rival. But first there was Rachael to be seen to, and hiding his emotions, he took her outstretched hands and raised them to his lips. "My dear Rachael," he said gently, "it gives me great pleasure to welcome you to my home. I regret I was not able to escort you myself, and I hope the journey was not too fatiguing."

The enchanting smile that so resembled her daughter's peeped into being. "Oh, heaven's no, although it's nothing like travel in England," she laughed. "Jason, it is *good* to see you again. I'm so delighted you and Catherine have finally found each other." Then looking around expectantly, she asked, "But tell me. Where is she?"

The innocent question hung in the air, and Jason's grip on her hands tightened painfully. A twisted smile on his lips, he said lightly, "It seems I've misplaced her again."

The tired, brilliantly blue eyes slowly searched his face. "Again?"

He nodded. Angrily aware of the quiet but intense interest of the man standing only two feet away, he shot a haughty glance in his direction.

Coolly, Adam returned the hard, green-eyed regard, the sapphire blueness of his own eyes increasing as silently he met and returned the hostile scrutiny of the other. Kate had definitely picked a black-tempered rogue for a husband, that was for certain! he thought, almost amused. And she still hadn't explained everything to her husband either, he guessed. There was a heavy feeling in the pit of his stomach. Sighing inwardly, Adam hoped Jason didn't kill him before finding out the truth. Pity he couldn't tell the man himself.

Adam needn't have worried, for Jason's gaze suddenly sharpened, and his swung from one pair of identical blue eyes to the other. His stare leveled at Adam, he said tightly, "And do I have the honor of meeting Catherine's *brother?*"

Rachael, her thoughts diverted, forced a strained laugh. "How silly of me! Of course, you two haven't met. Adam, as you've guessed, this is Jason Savage, Catherine's husband."

The two men shook hands warily, and Jason was torn between the desire to laugh at the sheer relief that flooded his body and bitter resentment that Catherine had let him be tortured by thoughts of this man being her lover. The gleam of sympathetic amusement in Adam's blue eyes decided it for him, and for the first time that day his smile was natural. Laughingly he admitted, "If you only knew what that minx of a sister of yours has put me through!"

"Don't tell me—I can guess. She's always been a willful, troublesome baggage."

Blood Drinker had watched the meeting carefully and now, satisfied at its outcome, melted away into the darkness leaving the trio standing there. Rachael's eyes were misty as she regarded the two tall, handsome young men standing so close to each other. Adam was within an inch of Jason's height, and his hair was as black, but being slimmer, he was the rapier to Jason's broadsword. Adam broke the silence by inquiring, "Did I hear you correctly when you said Kate was missing—again?"

Jason's momentary relief fled, and he admitted heavily, "Yes! But don't worry, I know exactly where she is this time, and I'll have her back very shortly." That the confident words were said for Rachael's benefit was obvious from the warning glance that Jason shot at Adam.

Smiling down at Rachael, Jason said quickly, "What a poor host you must think me, leaving you standing here! Come inside, and after you've been shown your rooms and rested a little, we can have refreshments and talk."

Rachael was indeed tired. It seemed she had been traveling for months, which truthfully she had. There had been the long trip from England to New Orleans, then from New Orleans to Natchez, and now from Natchez to this wilderness place. And to discover that she was still unable to see her daughter was a monstrous disappointment and a worry—and Jason's calm words did nothing to soothe the growing fear in her breast. Perhaps once she had rested things would not seem so gloomy, she thought, bravely hiding her uneasiness. Gently she clasped Jason's proffered arm and confessed, "Do you know that lately I have dreamed incessantly of literally wallowing in a bath and sleeping in a real bed? It will be a novelty to sleep inside a house after weeks of camping under the stars."

Slowly they walked up the broad brick steps to the veranda, and Jason ushered Rachael and Adam inside the house. Guy seemed to have vanished, and it occurred to Jason to wonder at his father's queer behavior. It wasn't like Guy to rush off and not wait to be introduced or to extend a welcome. Oh well, he was probably seeing that the rooms were being readied, and with no feeling of premonition, Jason saw Rachael safely in the hands of a waiting servant.

Adam declined to be shown to his rooms, and Jason, recognizing the expression on her brother's face as one Catherine sometimes wore when she was determined to have her say, opened the doors that led to the main salon and offered his brother-in-law a drink. Waving Adam to a comfortable, cushioned chair, he poured two whiskies and handed one to him. After settling his own long form in a large lounging chair, Jason asked abruptly, "You want more details, don't you?"

His glittering blue eyes never leaving Jason's harshly handsome face, Adam nodded. And Jason, his voice devoid of any betraying emotion, told him exactly what had happened.

"My God!" Adam exclaimed, his blue eyes blazing with youthful scorn. "Are you going to do nothing? *I* would have followed Davalos *immediately!*"

Weary and impatient, Jason snapped, "Trust me to know my enemy! And for God's sake take a look out there. It's nearly dark, my friend, and I have little taste for stumbling into a trap set by Davalos. What good would that do Catherine? Remember, he knows exactly where I am, but I have no idea where he may be hiding. I don't even have the satisfaction of knowing he will do as he has written and meet me at Trader's Clearing. Have you considered the possibility that his message might have been sent for the sole reason of sending me off on a wild goose chase? That while I'm riding furiously towards Trader's Clearing, he and his men are heading in another direction? Well, I have, believe me! And before I go haring off after Catherine, I have to know that they are actually going to Trader's Clearing, and the only way I can do that is to track them. Something," he spat out angrily, "that I can't do in the dark. My hands are tied, and at this moment there *is* nothing that I can do except wait for dawn and hope that Catherine is unharmed. I am as concerned for Catherine's safety as yourself, and I'm fully aware of what a blow this is to your mother." Bitterly he mused, "It escapes me how anyone as sweetly tempered and undemanding as Rachael could have been the mother of two such thoughtless firebrands as you and especially your sister!"

Deeply offended by Jason's words and mortified at his own uncalled for outburst, Adam answered stiffly, "I apologize. I spoke without thinking. It is inexcusable that I should tell you how to go about your business."

Adam looked suddenly very young and very proud to Jason, and smiling he asked, "How old are you?"

Startled, Adam blurted, "I am twenty-two."

Jason's smile deepened. "At your age and in the same circumstances, I would probably have said the same thing and worse—more than likely I would have started a brawl." Raising his drink in a silent toast, he added, "You are to be commended on your forbearance."

The doors were suddenly thrown open, and Guy entered, impetuously striding into the middle of the room. Both younger men, understandably on edge, had leaped to their feet at the unexpected intrusion, and Guy, preoccupied with his own private devils, didn't notice Adam standing near the door. His gaze fixed painfully on Jason, Guy exclaimed, "I must talk to you *immediately!* There is something you must know!"

Jason, his narrowed regard flashing from Adam's face to Guy's, frowned. And something that had been nagging at him leaped to the front of his mind. Very quietly and very slowly, he said, "I think I already know what you have to say."

Blankly, Guy repeated, "You know what I have to say?"

Nodding, Jason said in an odd tone, "Father, you must let me introduce you to Catherine's brother, Adam."

Guy turned absolutely white, his eyes now frozen on Adam. Puzzled and not a little uneasy at the strange currents he sensed in the room, Adam murmured politely, "Perhaps later would be more convenient for such niceties. Your father obviously wishes to be private with you. We can continue our discussion later."

Fighting to recover his lost poise, Guy mechanically extended his hand and in a hollow voice enunciated painstakingly, "How do you do?"

Adam felt the tremble in Guy's hand as it closed around his, and the almost convulsive clasp made him stare at the older man, perplexed. Uncertainly he smiled and said, "Jason neglected my last name. It's St. Clair."

"I know," Guy whispered, his eyes bright with some undefinable emotion.

The connection of the name suddenly hit Jason, and shooting his father a derisive look, he muttered, "St. Clair! I should have questioned that! Couldn't you have thought of something better than your mother's maiden name?"

"I beg your pardon?" Adam asked, clearly at sea.

On the point of speaking, Jason happened to glance at the opened doorway, and the words died on his lips. Rachael, her dark brown ringlets newly brushed and waving gently about her face, stood mesmerized on the threshold of the room, her eyes on Guy. She had changed her travel-stained gown for one of soft sky-blue with a white, lacy trim about the neck, but her taut features were much whiter than the narrow strip of lace encircling her throat.

An exclamation of concern on his lips, Jason started forward, as did Adam, but it was Guy who reached the still figure in the doorway first. With a hand that visibly shook, he guided her blind steps to a low couch. Oblivious to the stupified stares that followed them, Guy and Rachael had eyes for no one but each other, and Guy's words drifted with painful clarity throughout the room.

"Oh, Rae! I never—if I had only—I had no idea you were coming *here!* Oh, my little love, do you think I would have caused you one minute more of distress if it were in my power not to?"

Adam, a horrifying suspicion taking hold in his mind,

took a determined step towards them, but Jason's hand shot out and gripped his arm. Adam flicked him an angry glance, but Jason said softly, "I think not, *brother!* We are definitely *de trop,* and until they are both recovered, we shall have to stifle our rampant curiosity."

Swiftly he thrust the undecided young man from the room, and stepping into the hallway behind him, he shut the door quietly. Facing one another, they stared with new intensity at each other. Finally after a nerve-racking pause, Adam bit out, "I don't believe it! It's impossible! My father was killed before she married the earl!"

His eyes inscrutable, Jason shrugged his shoulders. "Perhaps. But you bear an uncommon likeness to Guy, and you have my grandmother's maiden name. Add to that their reactions to one another just now, and I should think it would give you pause."

Baffled, Adam clenched a fist and eyed him with smoldering blue eyes. Imperturbably Jason returned his stare and said gently, "If it's true, there's nothing you can do about it. And whatever the story, they took great pains to keep it hidden—remember that!" An uneasy peace between them, Jason steered the uncompromisingly rigid Adam to his study, and together they sat silently waiting. Tiredly Jason ran a hand across his forehead, his thoughts automatically planning tomorrow.

He had to see Blood Drinker tonight. The Cherokee would naturally go with him, but no others. He couldn't risk it—an out-and-out confrontation with Davalos was useless as long as the Spaniard had Catherine. If only, he thought wearily, he had said the few words it would have taken to stop her this morning. And he cursed again the hurt pride and blazing temper that had ruled him. A knife blade of fear in his guts, the terrifying thought burst on him that those hot, angry words they had hurled at one another might well have been the last Catherine would ever speak to him—that even now, she might be dead!

His face nearly gray from the agonizing thoughts that

wouldn't stop, Jason sprang to his feet and muttered, "There are things I must see to. You can wait here or come with me, but I warn you I won't have the time to act the polite host." It was an ungracious invitation but the need not to be alone was in both men, and without a word Adam accompanied Jason as he left the room.

Jason achieved a certain amount of relief from his torturous thoughts as he chose the horses to be readied and waiting at dawn and methodically saw to the packing of the supplies that would be needed. He had to plan for every contingency, and so in spite of the desire to ride as lightly as possible, the pile of goods to be taken gradually grew. Morosely, Adam watched the preparations. He had offered—indeed had almost demanded—to be allowed to accompany Jason, but a flat negative that brooked no further argument had been his answer. Feeling extremely young and useless, he informed his host punctiliously that he would await him in the study.

Thoughtfully, Jason watched him stalk off, the desire to call him back very strong. But, no—while Adam had spirit and determination, this was not a lark for untried youths. Blood Drinker, materializing out of the darkness, disrupted his thoughts and turning to him Jason asked, "You've heard?"

Gravely, Blood Drinker nodded, "I have heard, my brother."

No more was needed between them beyond Jason's curt, "We leave at first light."

The preparations complete, Jason returned to the study and found Adam idly flipping the pages of a leather-bound volume. Desultorily they made conversation for some minutes before the door opened and Guy, his expression revealing a variety of emotions, stuck his head inside the room. Certainly regret and not a little apprehension was displayed on his face but what struck both young men was the quiet joy that blazed in the sea-green eyes. "May we come in?" Guy asked.

Nodding, Jason watched curiously as his father, a possessive arm about her waist, led Rachael to the leather couch. Looking considerably revived, Rachel flashed Jason a faintly apologetic look, but she couldn't bring herself to glance at Adam, who was standing stiffly before the brick fireplace. Guy cleared his throat uneasily. Standing behind Rachael, his hands resting lightly on her shoulders, he said almost defiantly, "We have something to say to you both. You might not like it, but you're entitled to an explanation—especially Adam."

If the situation hadn't been so serious and the other three so intense, Jason would have burst out laughing. Calmly, not wishing to listen to the type of beating about the bush Guy would find necessary, he said, "I take it Adam *is* my brother?"

The color fled Rachael's face, but bravely looking at her son for the first time, she stared steadily at Adam and said baldly, "Yes."

Adam's face seemed to freeze, and Rachael cried distressfully, "It wasn't like you think! We *thought* the marriage was valid."

Jason, his eyes hard, locked glances with his father and ground out harshly, "Your marriage to my mother must have taken place some years before you met Rachael. How did you explain her away? And me?"

His hand tightening on Rachael's shoulders, Guy's gaze encompassed both waiting men, and bluntly he stated, "My marriage to Angelique was a terrible mistake. I stood it for as long as I could, and finally we *both* agreed to separate. We discussed it at length and decided that, while shocking and dreadful, a divorce was the only answer open to us."

Looking at Jason, Guy unconsciously pleaded, "You must believe me when I say that we were miserable with each other! Angelique agreed wholeheartedly with the idea of divorce—it was not solely at my instigation!"

Jason regarded him quietly and shrugged his shoulders.

"Your relations with Angelique are your business—you owe me no explanation about them!"

Controlling his temper, Guy remarked stiffly, "Why thank you. Your kindness nearly unmans me."

"Did you get a divorce?" Adam broke in abruptly, and Guy shook his head slowly, his eyes never leaving the features that were like a younger image of his own. "When I finally left for England, Angelique was in agreement with me. We had decided that in order to cause as little a scandal as possible, she would return to New Orleans, and I would see to the distasteful details in England. It was to be done quietly and discreetly." His voice growing bitter, he continued, "And if Angelique hadn't changed her mind, it would have been done and over with."

"And while the lawyers were busy with their incessant legal work you met Rachael?" Jason probed.

Guy's eyes softened miraculously as they looked down at her. "Yes. I was friends with the earl of Mount, and he invited me down to Cornwall for a while. It was there that I met Rachael, his youngest cousin."

Astonished at that disclosure, Jason's thick black eyebrows flew up. Guy, seeing his surprised expression added grimly, "Oh, yes, *that* relationship helped enormously when the time came to cover up the whole ugly situation."

Adam, his gaze riveted painfully on Guy, demanded, "Are you saying you *seduced* my mother?"

Unable to remain silent a moment longer, Rachael sprang up and ran to her son. "Listen to me Adam!" she begged. "The day before he left for Cornwall, Guy had received a note from the lawyer stating that the divorce was completed. It surprised him because everything had gone so quickly and smoothly. He meant to go round to see his lawyer the second he returned, just to make certain. But the important thing for you to remember is he *thought* he was a free man!"

Gently, Adam disengaged her clasp on his arm. His smile a little strained, he soothed, "There's a love now. Just sit down and don't look so worried. Whatever happened, I'm on your side!" Looking uncertain, Rachael sank back down, her hands clasped tightly in her lap.

Aware that he was being judged by *both* his sons, Guy said simply, "It's true. I did believe I was free. And before I offered my hand and heart to another woman, I would have checked further, even though there was no reason not to believe the lawyer's scribbled note—but I had fallen deeply in love with Rachael and her parents were on the verge of thrusting her into marriage with the vicar's son."

"You see," Rachael added painfully, "we were the poor cousins, and mama and papa were overjoyed at receiving a respectable offer for me. We never could have afforded a season in London or anything like that."

"When I learned what was happening," Guy said, "I instantly approached Rachael's parents, but they insisted that no daughter of theirs would marry a divorced man, no matter how much he had to offer. So—we eloped."

"To Gretna Green?" Jason inquired.

Guy nodded. "It had to be. Rachael was only seventeen."

"And?" prompted Jason when Guy showed a tendency to falter.

Taking a deep breath, Guy stated, "And we remained there. Scotland is beautiful, and we were in love. There was no reason to return." Guy moved closer to Rachael, and she encouraged him with a small, unhappy smile and reached for his hand. A bleak note in his speech, he continued, "Jason, I was happier then, than I have ever been in my entire life, before or since, and when Rachael told me she was to have our child my joy knew no bounds."

Guy paused and looked levelly at Adam's white face. "I loved you, boy, even though I could not acknowledge you."

"You see," Rachael whispered, "the lawyer had made a mistake. And when it was discovered, Guy was not in London, so the lawyer saw Roxbury."

Jason's eyes opened very wide, and he asked stupidly, "Roxbury? My uncle?"

"You forget, he's also my brother," Guy reminded him

testily. "The lawyer did what he thought best. Roxbury knew I'd gone to Cornwall for a month or so, and when I didn't return he merely assumed I had extended my stay. Certainly, he never suspected that I had met someone, fallen in love, and remarried. But even if he had acted immediately, it would have done no good because by that time Rachael and I were already married and living in Scotland."

A low whistle of dismay came from Jason, and Adam asked helplessly, "When you did find out the truth, why didn't you proceed with the divorce?"

"Because," Guy announced bleakly, "Angelique not only changed her mind, she came to England to stop the divorce!" He laughed harshly. "Oh, she didn't want me. She still wanted a separation. She had just decided it wouldn't be a good thing to be a divorced woman!"

Knowing his mother, Jason could well believe Guy's harsh opinion of her, and pityingly he looked at Rachael. What a ghastly situation it must have been.

Tiredly, Guy finished the tale. "When the mix-up was discovered, the earl and Roxbury decided between themselves to pack me off to America for good and for Rachael to have the baby in seclusion in Scotland—the story of a husband dying in the army was concocted to save her reputation. Before I left, I signed over the Natchez lands for the baby—whatever its sex—and made provisions through the earl for the lands and a sum of money to be inherited when the child reached eighteen. Beyond that, my hands were tied. Angelique would not reconsider the matter of a divorce even though she knew all the facts, and I pleaded with her—God, how I pleaded! I had no grounds—not to mention the *real* scandal that would have erupted if a hint of the true facts was to have been discovered."

There was a strained silence in the room when Guy stopped speaking. It was Adam who asked blankly, "What do we do now?"

"Nothing," Jason said decisively. Crossing to Rachael he said softly, "I think you have much to hold against the men of my family—not to mention my mother's selfishness. Forgive us?"

"You're not angry?" she asked almost timidly.

He shook his head. "You took nothing away from me. My parent's marriage was in shambles long before Guy met you—you were the innocent one harmed. And I certainly don't begrudge Adam the Natchez lands. Tell me one thing, though. Why did you marry the earl?"

Rachael risked a glance at Guy's suddenly impassive face. "He was kind to me, and after all the trouble he'd gone to—to save my reputation—I owed it to him. He didn't love me, but I never loved him either. Your father had all my love." She hesitated then added, "I would have tried to make our marriage work, but you see, he only wanted an heir, and I had proven that ability by having Adam. I think he always felt cheated when the only child we ever had was a girl, Catherine."

Smiling whimsically down at her, Jason said, "I'm thankful that you did have her."

Guy spoke up abruptly, his voice laced with gruff concern. "Rachael, you should retire for the night. It's been an emotional evening for all of us and especially you. We can discuss it more tomorrow if you wish."

Jason watched the way his father hovered over Rachael as he escorted her from the room, and his thoughts of his mother in that moment were not kind.

"What's going to happen to them now?" Adam asked as the door closed behind them. Jason shot him a sharp look. "That rather depends on them, don't you think? More importantly, how do *you* feel about it?"

Truthfully, Adam admitted, "Well, it's a bit of a facer to learn one's really a bastard!"

Jason grinned. "Don't let that bother you—people have been calling me one for years!" For a second Adam maintained a serious expression, but then he burst out laughing, saying, "Well, if *you* don't mind it, neither shall I!"

Lying in bed later that night, Jason found himself surprisingly disturbed. Oh, not about what was in the past—curiously he found the idea of having a brother pleasant—but it was the future for Guy and Rachael that disturbed him. That they still loved one another was obvious and that nothing had changed in the passing years was also apparent. Angelique had changed!

Musingly, he decided that he wouldn't blame his father if he discreetly set Rachael up as his mistress, but somehow, he couldn't see either one of them agreeing to such a thing. Oh well, he thought glumly, they'll have to work it out themselves—his life was full enough just keeping possession of his own prickly kitten.

34

The faint grayness of predawn lay over the land as Blood Drinker and Jason rode away the next morning. Ahead of them lay at least three days of hard riding to reach the Sabine River. They were hampered only slightly by the loaded pack horse and the extra mount that Jason had brought for Catherine. Both men would have preferred to travel with just the clothes on their backs and a bedroll strapped behind their saddles, but they had no idea in what condition Catherine would be found, nor precisely how long a journey they were taking nor in what direction their quarry would lead them. At the moment though, they were headed for a small clearing a few miles west of the Sabine River.

Several years ago, an attempt had been made to establish a trading post there, and the optimistically minded agent had cleared the forest land and had built a smallish log building and a few lean-to sheds that he probably hoped to later replace with barns and storehouses. The venture had failed mainly because most travelers to the west took the old Spanish trail that lay a considerable number of miles to the south.

Eventually, it was abandoned and ironically, while not profitable, it became a landmark and stopping place for the thin stream of humanity heading into Spanish territory for various and usually nefarious reasons. It was there at Trader's Clearing that Jason was to meet with Davalos, and late in the morning of the third day, Jason and Blood Drinker crossed the Sabine River some miles to the north of their destination. Taking great care not to betray their presence, they approached the clearing.

It was deserted, and for a moment the terrible thought occurred to Jason that somehow he had miscalculated. But the possibility of a trap couldn't be ignored, and it was only after they had circled and searched the outlaying forest for any sign of hiding Spaniards that they stealthily made any attempt to gain entrance to the building.

In their preliminary search of the forest, they had discovered signs that several riders had left very recently, and with a sinking heart, Jason stepped carefully into the log structure, entering from a back window while Blood Drinker remained secreted in the tall trees. The building was empty, but again there were signs that as late as last night someone—Davalos?—had been there. Able to draw no conclusions from the meager clues that remained, Jason opened the heavy door and slipped cautiously into the clearing. Dodging between what cover existed, his rifle clenched in his hands, he quickly searched the dilapidated sheds and found nothing until he entered the last one.

The gray thoroughbred that Catherine had ridden that fateful morning lay dead, its throat brutally cut, the ground near its head damp with blood. Still saddled and bridled, Jason judged the animal had not been dead too many hours, the soft hide barely cool to his experienced touch. A knife, its blade blackened by dried blood, rose up from the saddle and impaled a scrap of blood-spattered paper. With a dangerously steady hand, Jason wrenched the knife free, and slowly, his face betraying nothing, he read the message Davalos had left. Then without a backwards glance, he disappeared into the forest and rejoined Blood Drinker. The two men walked swiftly towards their concealed horses and in short terse sentences Jason relayed what he had found.

Blood Drinker had grunted disgustedly at the news of the wanton and needlessly vicious destruction of the horse, but Jason's news that Davalos was taking Catherine to Nacogdoches, a Spanish fort deeper into Spanish land, caused his black eyes to glitter with anger. Silently both men swung up on their horses and followed the trail that the departing Davalos had so arrogantly made no effort to hide. But then Davalos was in his own territory now, and he had Catherine, which must have pleased him enormously. Jason could almost see the satisfied smile that would quirk at the corners of the thin lips, and his own tightened angrily.

There was little conversation between the two men as the day passed, but then there was little need for words between them. Both knew the dangers that lay ahead, and both were aware that if Davalos was able to reach the comparative safety of the fort, they would be at his mercy. Their only hope was to overtake the Spaniards somewhere within the miles of wild forest land that lay between them and safety. By ambush or trap they would attack and somehow free Catherine. There had been no clear plan when they had ridden away from Terre du Coeur, but the driving thought uppermost in both minds had been to free Catherine—whatever way possible—even at the cost of Jason offering himself to Davalos!

Davalos needed him alive, and while the fact had to be faced that once Davalos had him, he would dispatch Catherine much in the same manner he had her horse, Jason had no choice but to give in to the Spaniard's demands. He realized that Davalos might kill Catherine, but he didn't really believe the Spaniard would—not from any compassion for her, but because his position would be infinitely stronger if he had both of them as hostages. Once that was accomplished, Davalos would be twice as safe from reprisal. And more importantly, Jason reasoned grimly, torture of Catherine would loosen his tongue considerably faster than anything Davalos could do to him, and Davalos would know that! Damn him!

Increasing fear for Catherine bit into Jason's vitals like a razor-toothed serpent, and unconsciously he goaded his horse to an even more dangerous burst of speed as they plunged through the tangled undergrowth of the tall trees and followed the trail.

From the signs left behind, Davalos could only be six or seven hours ahead of them at the most, and Jason had every intention of narrowing that time to nothing. Viciously he yanked at the lead rein of the pack horse that followed recklessly behind him. For a moment, he considered leaving the two extra horses; he and Blood Drinker could diminish the distance between themselves and their quarry faster if they had only their own mounts to worry about; but caution, the thought that they might need that extra horse for Catherine as well as every single item he had so carefully chosen to bring, stayed his hand. Yet with every passing minute, every hour, the need to close the gap and to at least gain sight of his enemy drove him onward. Even into the night they traveled, their path clearly seen by the beam of a friendly full moon, whose light silvered the trees and lit their way through the darkness.

Impelled by a feeling of imminent danger, the premonition that he must reach Catherine tonight took such violent possession of Jason that he was like some green-eyed vengeful zombie, controlled by, and bound to, his woman. Fleetingly, he let himself wonder if she was alive, and if alive, what terrible things Davalos had done to her during this time she had been captive. Was she unharmed? Had she been tortured? Raped? The thoughts flayed into him like diamond-tipped whips, his eyes growing opaque with iciness, and his mouth thinning until it was only a narrow slash across his hard face.

Onward they raced through the moonlit night until at last the need for caution and the desire not to stumble across the sleeping Spaniards as they camped slowed their breakneck speed and gave their foam-lathered horses a chance to regain some of the stamina needed to accomplish whatever lay before them. As it grew later, the quietness of the night was broken only by the hoot of an owl or the cough of the hunting cougar. More slowly now, the horses moved through the forest, their hoofbeats muffled by the deep, centuries-old piling of decayed leaves and pine needles.

Jason's uneasy thoughts were bedeviled by worry for Catherine. Would she be able to last through the punishing pace Davalos was now setting? The child she carried within her slim body—what of it? And most of all, what was she thinking? And how frightened was she? Too frightened to think clearly? To frightened to be of any help to himself and Blood Drinker?

Jason needn't have worried about Catherine being frightened, for even after four days of Davalos's brutal behavior, she was still almost livid with rage: rage at Jason for not stating why she shouldn't have gone riding that morning, rage at herself for once again blindly leaping into folly, and pure, murderous fury at Davalos! If ever she hated, she hated that slender, thin-lipped Spaniard! Her body ached from his abuse, but so filled was she with undiluted venom that she was indifferent, numb to whatever he did to her.

Fright was not one of the emotions that coursed through her body, not even in those first horrifying moments when Davalos and his troop had swooped down so purposefully on her in the glen. She had been too busy fighting like some untamed, wildly clawing animal to be frightened, and in spite of being overpowered—for she was just one slim woman against many men—she managed to nearly claw one man's eye out, while another lost a portion of his cheek to her neat, white teeth and still another would have pain for some days between his legs where the sharp tip of her riding boot had unerringly struck. And when Packy in a desperate attempt to save her had exploded from the woods, his gun blazing, she hadn't been frightened but only terrified that the boy would come to grief, as he had when Davalos leveled a careful shot in his direction. Her eyes wide with horror, Catherine had watched powerless as Packy slumped in the saddle and then slid slowly to the ground, the widening patch of blood very red against the faded blue of his shirt.

With Catherine clamped across his saddlebow, Davalos and his troop had wheeled and sought the safety of the woods, dragging her riderless horse behind them as they galloped away to hide and lie in ambush only a few miles from the violent scene of her abduction. A dirty gag hastily thrust between her lips effectively halted any warning she could have given, and the ropes that tightly bound her hands behind her back made escape impossible. But still, she thrashed furiously like a maddened, trapped animal until Davalos had struck her across the temple with his pistol, and mercifully the blackness of unconsciousness had burst in her head.

When she awoke, it was dark, and she discovered herself tied like a sack of grain across the back of a horse. Her head ached like thunder, and with every step the horse took, the throbbing pain in her brain seemed to reverberate through her entire body. Even then she wasn't frightened, only incredulous that such a thing had happened, and filled suddenly with sick worry about Jason and what he would do.

When the full enormity of her predicament blasted through the pain-washed waves of returning consciousness, she very nearly gave in to a feeling of defeat. What did it matter what happened to her? She had nothing to live for now, and certainly, if Jason was captured or killed because of her, the burden of guilt that his death would bring would crush her like an ant beneath a boulder. Dully, she stared at the passing ground, her body swaying in motion with the horse, but then, insidiously, like a snake sliding from beneath a rock, the thoughts came: Are you so weak to give in without a struggle? What of your son, Nicholas? Can you bear the knowledge that he will grow to manhood, raised by strangers and never knowing a mother's love? What of the child that grows within you now, will you let it die with you? Like the blade of a sword, the thoughts cut savagely through the uncaring lethargy that threatened to sap her will to fight, and unable to stop them, the thoughts slid on. And Jason, will you concede to him the final victory? Allow him to be so easily freed of a marriage that has irked him since its inception? The dullness vanished from the violet eyes, and the spark that made them glow almost incandescently would have given another man pause, as would the set jaw of the finely boned face.

Davalos had only a few meetings with Catherine on which to base his opinion of her, and on those occasions she had been trying to be a model of decorum; but like a fool, he had overlooked the signs that should have warned him that here was no frightened, whimpering, gently reared lady to be cowed by the shocking events of the day. She possessed a steely determination that Davalos had overlooked.

Also, he did not know her history and that she had learned things from gypsies that were never forgotten, nor more importantly, that she carried, hidden on her body, the small, razor-honed knife. It never occurred to him to search her for a concealed weapon. Yet, he did know that Jason's wife was unlike any woman of his acquaintance, and suspiciously he eyed her as they made camp that first evening.

Releasing the gag and expecting tears and possible hysterics, he was totally unprepared for Catherine's cool, almost contemptuous, "What a bloody fool you are! I hope you have enjoyed your life so far because no matter what you do to me Jason will kill you just as soon as he overtakes us."

Smiling almost kindly at his astonishment, she added, "If I were you, I'd leave me here and put as much distance between yourself and my husband as possible. He's very hot-tempered, you know, and I don't think he's going to think very kindly of what you have done. He'll kill you!"

The quick flash of surprise that shuttered in his black eyes before Davalos recovered himself caused a warm feeling of satisfaction in Catherine's veins. Bastard! Given the chance, she might kill him before Jason had the opportunity!

Aware that his men were watching them curiously, Davalos allowed his ugly temper full freedom and, taking delight in her helplessness, slapped Catherine viciously across the mouth and commanded, "Silence! I will do the talking! How dare you threaten me!"

The taste of blood on her tongue, her teeth stained faintly pink, Catherine created a slight ripple of surprise through the soldiers as she smiled with her bloodied lip and taunted, "How brave you are against a bound woman. Loosen my hands and let us see how really bold you can be!" Casting a look in the direction of the men who sat silently nearby, she jeered, "Afraid I shall mark you as I did them?" And Juan, whose face would forever wear the mark of her teeth, involuntarily made the sign of the cross—what manner of woman was this? Surely, she must be of the devil!

Nearly choking with fury and driven by the need to wipe the mocking smile from her face, Davalos swung his booted foot and caught her full in the chest and sent her sprawling at his feet. The breath being knocked from her body combined with the knowledge she must be cautious froze the derisive retort she would have flung in his face. There was no sense in getting kicked to death merely to prove Davalos was a cowardly bully—she already knew he was!

Davalos stood staring down at her as if he hoped she would dare him again, but she lay motionless, her eyes glittering defiance, her mouth remaining shut. Smiling at his sudden victory, he left her there and swaggered over to his men, satisfied he had proven to them that she was only a bothersome woman like any other. Show enough male strength and they were all the same, he thought contemptuously, mewling, clinging objects to be ground beneath a man's foot.

But Davalos miscalculated his men. They were *not* reassured by Catherine's capitulation, and uneasily their glances slid away from this strange female who smiled despite blows and whose eyes glowed so queerly violet. They were a brutish, uneducated lot, viewing with suspicion anything that did not fall within clearly defined lines. Catherine was obviously outside of anything they had come across, and she aroused a feeling of superstitious fear in several breasts, for unaware or uncaring of what they thought, she continued to taunt and jeer at Davalos like an angry wasp against a raiding bear, and when Davalos, driven beyond control, would strike her, she would smile—a mirthless, frightening smile.

By the time they reached Trader's Clearing, she was riding on her nerves alone. It was pride that kept her stiffly erect in the saddle and anger that gave her courage when she would have faltered. The sight of the log building aroused hope, but then its deserted air let her know that no help would be found here. Knowing that Davalos had no intention of freeing her and that he was using her as bait to draw Jason further into danger, she constantly racked her brain for a way to escape. The knife was a comfort to her, and she would have freed herself long ago, if only she would have been unobserved for a short time; however, she was watched closely. Several times she thought of attempting it despite the odds, but knowing she would have just one chance, she couldn't risk having her knife taken.

Fiercely concentrating on a method of escape, she missed the openly assessing glance Davalos gave her as they entered the empty building. Her eyes had lit with a hopeful gleam when he had shoved her into a small room and locked the door, and she was so busy planning on how best to use the privacy offered that the long, knowing look that swept her body went unnoticed. Left alone in the small room she listened intently to the sounds of the men as the horses were unsaddled and camp was made for the night. "Please," she prayed silently, "please let them leave me locked in here tonight." And already her fingers were defying the ropes that bound her hands behind her back and were itching towards the hidden knife. All she needed was for the Spaniards to bed down, and when she was certain they were asleep, like a flash she would be free and out the window. A second more and she would have a horse—then nothing would stop her. She would make damn sure they didn't recapture her, even if she had to drown herself in the river to stop them. A nervous giggle slipped out when she realized how foolish it would be to carry things *that* far!

She could smell the wood fire now burning in the long unused cook pit, and from the sounds of their movements, she decided the men must be settling down in the main room of the building. Briefly she wondered how long they would be staying here. Was this where Davalos planned to ambush Jason? And if so, what could she do to prevent it?

The sound of the door opening caused her to give a start of surprise, and hiding her emotions she faced Davalos. "Feeding time for the beasts?" she asked scathingly, one slim eyebrow raising disdainfully as she eyed the plate of food he held in his hand. But for some reason Davalos only smiled and putting down the full plate of greasy beans untied her hands.

She waited for him to leave, briskly rubbing the circulation back into her numb arms and hands. When he crossed to the door and dropped the wooden bar in place, she was vaguely uneasy, but determined to ignore him, she quickly ate the food. Finished she waited docilely for him to retie her hands as he had done every night, but with a strange glint in the black eyes he murmured, "You know I have always admired you. Even in Natchez you fascinated me. And," he added meaningfully, "I find the way you defy me stimulating!"

Frozen, the color draining from her cheeks, Catherine stared at him. Oh, God, she moaned silently, not *this!* Warily she backed away from him hoping she had misread the flicker of desire in his cold eyes. Her throat tight she muttered, "You have a queer way of showing your admiration."

An ugly smile crossed his thin lips. "You see, even now you fence with me. Another woman would have asked questions or shed tears but you—you resist me! It is intriguing."

Catherine regarded him steadily, much in the manner she would a ravaging wolf, and he surprised her by saying casually, "Your husband does not love you, and since you were obviously hiding from him in Natchez, I can safely assume you bear him no love. If, *amiga,* you throw in your lot with me, I can rid you of him and make you the richest woman in New Spain!"

Unable to believe what she was hearing, Catherine stood dumbstruck in the center of the room. She shook her head impatiently as if trying to clear her brain, and Davalos, still smiling, reached for her. Her stunned brain flashed a warning a second too late, but still she fought him like a young tigress intent on escape. Her struggles seemed to delight him, but when she very nearly escaped his clutches a third time, he grew angry and as the quiet, furious battle raged, he managed to capture her hands and bind them cruelly and tightly behind her back. Like a cornered animal, Catherine searched feverishly for a hiding place, a sanctuary, anywhere that would protect her from what she knew must come. But there were only four barren walls. Her eyes like violet fire, she spat, "You call yourself a man? What manner of *man* are you that the only way you can mount a woman is with her hands tied?"

But Davalos was in such a grip of lust that her words were brushed aside heedlessly, and he threw her onto the dirt floor, ripping open the linen shirt, his hands reaching brutally for her small, full breasts. Her arms pinned not only by the weight of her body but roped as well, Catherine was helpless as he dragged the breeches from her body, and with a cold feeling of fear she saw the little silver knife fall to the ground as he tossed the clothes in a heap in the corner. Grimly, she hung onto the thought that thankfully the knife had fallen beneath the breeches, and if he didn't notice it, there was a chance she could hide it again.

But that would be later, and this was hideously now, and she fought any way she could, twisting away, kicking at his body, and when that failed locking her legs together tightly.

Defenseless and having no way of protecting herself, she suffered his touch, her skin crawling with revulsion as his hands explored her body. But when he was unwise enough to try to kiss her, her teeth sunk deeply into his bottom lip, and she hung on viciously until a powerful, painful crack at the side of her head made her release his mangled lip. But nothing could stop him, her desperate fight seemed to inflame him even more, until finally exhausted and barely conscious she was powerless to prevent him from joining his body with hers.

Spasm after spasm of sheer murderous rage shook her body as he moved on her, and venomously she hissed, "Finish, damn you! Finish, so I may vomit! You sicken me!" Then at last it was over, the pain between her legs ceasing, and he rolled away from her.

Smiling with satisfaction, Davalos straightened his clothes and still breathing heavily said thickly, "Jason is to be congratulated on his good taste. But a few months of my tutelage and you will be truly without peer. Your husband should thank me for teaching you all that I intend to." He paused, a calculating spark leaping into his eyes as they moved over her body. "If I don't kill him, it would best please me if you were to bear my child. It would be worth letting Jason live to foster a bastard on him. His blasted pride is such that he would never recover from the blow."

Kneeling suddenly beside her, his eyes devoured the alabaster body, now dirt-stained and showing the bruises of his brutality, and Catherine prayed that he would not take her again. They stayed thus, his hands running over her shrinking flesh, and she knew from the flame that was growing in his eyes that he was becoming aroused again. Terror-stricken she fastened her gaze on the ceiling, as if by staring at the beams she could divorce her mind from what was happening to her body, but the sounds from the other room disrupted him and made him frown and look in that direction. He rose swiftly and unexpectedly released her bound hands.

Like a wide-clawed cat that seeks freedom, she sprang for

his face, but prepared for such a move, he avoided her lunge and with a vicious backhanded lash that connected with her chin, nearly broke her neck. She was flung across the room and landed on the floor near her breeches, the linen shirt she still wore barely covering her nakedness. Coldly he said, "I will leave you to dress. If you are not clothed when I return, I shall assume you enjoyed my lovemaking and shall give you another lesson in the joys you can find in my embrace. And if you resist me, I shall let the others have you to teach you that it is unwise to disobey me!"

Catherine grabbed her breeches and keeping the knife hidden scrambled to the far corner as he opened the door and walked out. She was dressed in seconds, and more importantly the knife was hidden once more. Bitterly she wished for the strength of will and courage to bury the knife deep in her own breast. But that was the coward's way out, she told herself grimly and cursed the lost chance she had had to sink the blade to the hilt in Davalos's retreating back. Common sense told her she would gain little with his death, for without Davalos to control them, she would be at the mercy of the soldiers. Still, even knowing that, the urge to kill him was almost overpowering.

When he returned, he methodically tied her hands again, and with his warning clear in her mind, she didn't offer any fight, although when his mouth sought hers and his hands roamed familiarly over her, she almost wasn't able to control the frantic desire to leap away from his sordid touch. But apparently he had no intention of forcing her to submit to his demands again tonight, for he tossed her a blanket and said, "You will sleep here undisturbed." Catherine glanced at him sharply, and he smiled nastily. "Oh, I haven't tired of you—yet. But there are grumblings among the men, and if I don't want to share you I shall have to deny myself until we are more private. Waiting will only increase my appetite, and when we reach Nacogdoches I intend to take my fill of you—then perhaps I will give you to the men!"

Balefully, Catherine glared at him, and the undisguised

hatred that burned in her eyes made him slightly uneasy. Threateningly he stated, "Don't try to escape! Remember that I have guards patrolling the outside, and if they capture you I'm quite certain before they would return you, they too would know you rather intimately."

He waited for her comment, and when she didn't say a word, he looked at her in suspicion. Catherine quickly dropped her eyes, hiding the loathing she felt. And after a moment, he gave a swift, encompassing glance around the room, and seeing no way she could free herself except out the window, he left, deciding it would be wise to have a guard posted at that particular spot.

When the door closed behind him, Catherine ran to the window and stood staring outside into the moonlit clearing. Her heart sank as she saw several soldiers making the rounds, and when one detached himself and stood solidly in front of her, grinning at her in the darkness, she stepped away, back into the concealing gloom of the room. Biting her lip undecidedly, she sank down on the blanket, one part of her recklessly wanting to risk an escape at any cost—even that of offering herself to the guard—while a cooler, saner part of her brain whispered, "Wait! You have no margin for error. There will be only *one* chance." And so, fitfully, her body aching and soiled, she spent the night tossing restlessly on the floor, unable to sleep, yet too exhausted to stay awake.

But again, fear was not an emotion she felt. On the contrary, the rape perpetrated on her unwilling body by Davalos filled her with cold fury—a kind of burning fury that she had never before experienced. Not even immediately after Jason's first brutal taking had she been so enraged. And she took grim enjoyment from the fact that by being already with child, she had thwarted Davalos before he'd had a chance to carry out his threat. Maliciously she smiled to herself—how she would like to throw that knowledge in his face! But caution and the need to protect the unborn child prevented her from making any outburst, and she was thankful her body as yet betrayed no signs of the life that grew within it. She was worried about the child though, and it was concern for the harm Davalos could do to it that made her less inclined to taunt him to violence. And while the last three days had been extremely unpleasant to say the least, she didn't think any damage had been done. But uneasiness for the future fed ravenously at the back of her mind, and she knew she had to escape.

She *must* escape! She faced the thought squarely and knew she must do it soon. Every mile, every day took her deeper into unfamiliar territory, and she could not delay much longer. There had been no opportunity so far, but she couldn't afford to wait. Getting up, she went to the window again. But even as she stood there undecided, she saw two of the soldiers meet near a shed and then separate, one checking the main building, stopping for a minute to talk with the guard that stood out of her range of sight by her window, and the other patrolling where the horses were stabled. Her roped hand clenched into a fist, and black frustration nearly drove her to smash it into the wall. But then controlling herself, she sought out the blanket. Leaning against one wall, she sat on the floor, the blanket spread over her lap.

So, she told herself, you cannot do it tonight. But tomorrow night, no matter what conditions exist, you *shall* free yourself. And she sent up a silent prayer that Davalos would not touch her again, for if he did, nothing would stop her from stabbing him with her knife!

Her flesh crawled when she remembered those disgusting moments of his possession, and she was unable to control the violent retching that shook her body at the memory. The spasm passed, and she spent the few hours until dawn sitting like a white statue staring blindly at the wooden door.

They were up and ready to leave by dawn, Catherine being compelled to watch as Davalos, taking vicious amusement in the task, deliberately killed the gray thoroughbred, the horse's dying scream of agony as the knife bit deep seeming to afford him a great deal of pleasure. Catherine was sickened again. Smiling into her stony face, Davalos murmured, "Just a little warning for your husband." And unable to prevent herself, she spat directly into his grinning face.

It cost her another bloody lip, but Davalos's smile was gone, his face dark with fury. Contemptuously she jeered, "Behold the brave killer of defenseless animals and see how valiant he is against a helpless woman."

Muttering a curse he tossed her up onto his horse and mounted swiftly behind her. As they rode off, she couldn't help taunting, "Your gesture will cost you dearly, Davalos. With the horse alive you could have traveled faster but now. . . ." She let the words trail off suggestively.

Enraged he hissed in her ear, "Silence, bitch! You will drive me to tear out your tongue."

But Catherine only laughed scornful and retorted, "I don't fear you! You gained nothing by the slaughter of the horse." Gleefully, she added, "We shall lose time today, I think."

Her words proved true, for they were not able to cover as many miles as before, and her hopes expanded when after they had settled for the night her hands were left tied in front of her. Davalos seemed to be growing more carelessly confident each mile they took, and that night he made a disastrous error by letting Catherine sleep just beyond the light of a small fire and partially concealed in the shadow of a large boulder. Her violet eyes gleaming, she watched the fire sink lower until her body was in complete, unrevealing blackness. Except for one dozing guard who sat propped against a tree, the others lay on the far side of the fire, asleep.

Quickly she found the knife and effortlessly sliced through the rawhide that bound her hands and feet. Then taking great care to make little noise, she bunched the blanket as best she could to resemble a sleeping body. A second glance would have shown it for what it was, but hopefully by the time anyone grew curious, she would be many miles away. The knife held tightly in her hand, she ducked behind the boulder, her heart thudding against her ribs with terrified excitement. Again, she surveyed the sleeping encampment, and her mouth grew dry as the guard blinked and cast a blurry eye around the quiet camp.

The unsaddled horses were tied in two rows to a length of rope stretched between the trees. Unfortunately, one of those trees was the one the guard had chosen to rest against. For the first time, the taste of fear was in her mouth as stealthily she stalked her unwary prey. To kill a man was an awesome thing, but to do it in cold blood, to noiselessly creep behind him and drive the knife lightning quick and deathly deep and deadly silent into the unprotected throat, was even more monstrous than she imagined—yet *she did it!*

The man gave only a startled grunt before he died, and her chin trembling with revulsion, she prevented the body from slumping to the ground, letting only the head slip forward as if he slept. Grimly she made certain that he stayed propped against the tree. In a manner reminiscent of her husband, she glanced distastefully at the corpse and wiped the blood-stained blade carefully on the dead man's clothes. For a long moment, her narrow-eyed gaze sought out Davalos's sleeping form, and the sudden feral light that blazed in her eyes was frightening in its intensity. But then she realized there was too much risk involved, and regretfully she slipped over to the horses.

The horses moved restlessly as she approached, perhaps smelling the blood, and swiftly she selected a deep-chested, clean limbed gelding from the second row. Carefully she unhitched the animal, and moving cautiously, her heart in her throat and her legs quivering like jelly, she led the horse away from the camp.

The need for haste was like a four-fanged devil on her back, but she willed herself to walk slowly, noiselessly guiding the animal in a wide arc out and away from the sleeping Spaniards. It was some minutes of nerve-racking cautious stepping before she felt safe enough to risk mounting the horse. Then with quicksilver grace and speed, she leaped upon the horse, her legs gripping tightly around the animal's middle. With Catherine's sudden weight upon its back, the gelding snorted and danced for an instant while Catherine's blood drummed through her tense body and she strained to hear if the camp had been awakened. But there was no sound from the direction of the camp, and now more confidently she urged the horse towards the trail that she knew lay directly to her left.

Once more, she was grateful for the gypsy years, for the knowledge she had of following signs, and most importantly for the self-reliance those years had taught her. She was now alone in a hostile wilderness, her only weapon a knife and her only advantage the gelding she rode, but she was unafraid.

She found the trail easily enough, but again the need for caution made her keep the horse at a slow, quiet walk. Finally, about a mile down the path, Catherine decided she was far enough away to risk kicking the horse into a run.

Any other time, she would have enjoyed this wild ride through the moonlit night as the horse flew down the trail that lay like a twisted silver ribbon between sweet smelling pines. But tonight, there was the knowledge that behind her lay degradation, danger, and possible death.

The shadows from the towering trees fell in black, eerie shapes across her path, and Catherine sent up a silent prayer of thankfulness for the bright moonlight that enabled her to urge the horse to an even faster pace. She had to put as many miles between herself and Davalos as possible, yet she had to conserve her own strength as well as her horse's energy. She couldn't afford to stop until she reached Terre du Coeur, and so she alternated the gelding's speed, holding him to a brisk walk, then urging the animal into a distance-eating gallop, and then slowing him to a walk again before he tired.

She had been traveling steadily for almost two hours, unerringly picking out the signs she had committed to memory to guide her back—there, the huge, dead pine snag rising blackly stark above the forest; and there, the small, winding creek that cut across the clearly discernible trail followed by the Spanish—when suddenly she became aware that she was not alone!

At first, she hadn't heard the sound of pursuit above her own horse's hoofbeats, but then slowing the gelding, she instantly became aware of the ominous tattoo of sound behind her. Throwing one frustrated glance of fury over her shoulder, her face illuminated by the moon, she dug her heels into the horse and compelled the animal into a neck-breaking burst of speed. Down the trail they sped, and by the tingle of awareness that shot along her spine, she knew the pursuers were gaining; but still she kicked her horse to an even more reckless pace. Suddenly, without warning, as they came around a bend in the trail, Catherine went flying from her horse as the animal ran full tilt into a half-rotted log that lay across the trail. Both woman and horse were thrown, the gelding skinning his knees and lower jaw on the rough ground, while Catherine landed with a sickening thud a few feet beyond the horse.

She had a moment of consciousness as a tearing pain ripped deep in her belly before the red light burst in her brain, and her last coherent thought was, "Oh, my God—I'm losing my baby!"

35

Waking was agony, and even as she swam up through layers of pain-filled awareness, she knew the unborn child was no more. Nearly defeated by that knowledge, she lay for several seconds of semi-wakefulness, her gaze unfocused, her mind uncomprehending of anything but her terrible sense of loss. Vaguely she realized someone was holding her in his arms, and like an animal alert to danger, she stiffened and blindly struck out at the arms that, if she only knew, held her so gently. But she was held powerless against a familiar, hard body, and at first the muffled words were unclear.

Then like a bolt of lightning Jason's words made sense. "Shush, kitten. Keep still, *amour.* You've hurt yourself, sweetheart. Don't struggle so, *please,* love!"

The unaccustomed endearments caused her to blink unbelievingly, and dumbly she stared up at the lean face inches from her own. *"Jason?"*

The blank astonishment in that one word made him smile crookedly at a time when he had never felt less like laughter. His lips brushing her forehead, he muttered, "Yes, little spitfire. It's your hateful husband, but you're safe now. I have you, and you have nothing to fear from Davalos."

"Not *hateful,*" she murmured, and like a tired child, one who has borne too much, she buried her head against his chest and quite effortlessly fainted.

Jason felt her slump, and for a terrifying second a fearful feeling of utter helplessness swept over him. But then the soft, even breathing relieved his mind of its greatest terror, and gently he laid her on the blanket Blood Drinker had hastily unpacked and thrown on the ground. Wrapping the slender form, Jason said dully, "She must have lost the baby, and she's losing blood. I have to get her somewhere fast where she can be safe and undisturbed. She can't be moved too far or she may hemorrhage to death." Bleakly he added the words that were obvious to both men, "She may, anyway."

Silently, Blood Drinker looked slowly from Catherine's white face to Jason's carefully unemotional one. On the point of speaking, he was halted as Jason said grimly, "There's a hunting cabin a few miles from here. It's not much, but it's shelter not easy to find. Davalos certainly won't find it, and I can make her fairly comfortable there. Once we're settled at the cabin, I want you to return to Terre du Coeur and as fast as possible bring back enough men to give Davalos a distaste for further intimacy with us."

Blood Drinker frowned, and Jason, anticipating the argument he knew would come, forestalled him by saying briskly, "Don't worry about Catherine and me. The cabin is hidden in a small valley well off any known trail. I built it one winter when I decided to try my hand at trapping, and it's not easily found even if Davalos is lucky enough to blunder up the valley. We'll be safe."

A noncommittal glance was Jason's answer, and without further words between them, they gathered their horses and mounted. With Catherine's body cradled next to his, Jason led the way through the forest. Blood Drinker followed more slowly, destroying all signs of their passage and covering their trail as they rode to the long-fingered, narrow valley Jason spoke of. It was truly a hidden valley, for even knowing where it was and in spite of the spreading light of dawn, Jason very nearly missed the opening himself. The sloping terrain and the thick forest blended so perfectly that there was no clue that the valley existed, and Blood Drinker grunted with satisfaction as his eyes swept assessingly over the area.

The place Jason had taken them looked like a tree-studded, shallow ravine with a small, clear stream running through the center of the secret valley. The stream itself originated from a crystal blue lake at the north end of the valley, and it was there, concealed among the trees, that Jason had built a one-room, rough-hewn cabin that overlooked the lake. Even if the cabin was crudely made, it was shelter; but while the days were still fairly warm, the nip and chill of autumn was in the air, and the nights were growing increasingly cooler.

It was broad daylight before they had finished unpacking. While Blood Drinker had seen to the unsaddling of the horses and then turning them loose into a small wooden-pole corral behind the cabin, Jason had quickly and efficiently put the cabin to rights. When Catherine regained consciousness a second time, she found herself comfortably ensconced in a neat, wooden bunk attached to one wall of the cabin.

She raised her head, and her gaze moved curiously around the room, noting the small stone fireplace, more a hole in the wall than a fireplace and, against the wall opposite her, the two sturdy pine chairs and a tiny table. At the moment, the window above the table was thrown open, the thick wooden shutters lashed back against the wall, but regardless of the bright beams of sunlight and the cool, fresh air that drifted through the room, there was still the unmistakable dampness and the faint, musty odor of a building long-unused.

Exhaustedly, Catherine let her head fall back against a rather lumpy pillow. Closing her eyes she weakly called Jason's name. He couldn't possibly have heard her low call, but as if sensing she was awake, an instant later he opened the stout door and walked swiftly over to her bed.

He wore the dress of a backwoodsman, the fringed buckskin pants and shirt. His moccasined feet made no sound as he approached Catherine's side. Her eyes had flown open at the sound of the opening door, and with a queer mixture of love and disillusionment, she stared up at Jason, never guessing that having hidden his emotions for so long, it was habit that made his face blank and his green eyes remote. Nonetheless, he couldn't disguise the faint note of concern in his voice when he asked casually, "Feeling better?"

She nodded slowly, her eyes clinging to his, not aware of how darkly purple they seemed against the whiteness of her skin nor how obvious were the signs of strain about the soft, pale lips.

"I lost the child, didn't I?" she asked unnecessarily, and Jason nodded, saying gently, "It doesn't matter, kitten. We'll have others, and all that really matters now is that you're all right."

"We won't, you know," she persisted, driven to make things clear.

Puzzled, he frowned slightly. "Won't what?"

"Have any more children."

He smiled reassuringly and soothed, "Don't worry about that. Time enough to cross that bridge when we come to it."

Depleted, she hadn't the will to continue, yet at the same time, illogical though it was, it seemed the most important thing in the world that he know she would not submit again to his body's demands; and doggedly she muttered, "I don't want you to give me another child."

Jason's indulgent, half-tender expression vanished, and his mouth tightened. Noncommittally he said, "We'll talk about it later. Right now, you just rest and get well."

Worn out and weakened by the loss of blood, she pathetically turned her face to the wall and shut her eyes, unable to continue the argument. Jason stared at the closed, weary face, his eyes dwelling on the mauve shadows beneath the lowered lids that told more clearly than words how very close to depletion of reserves she was. He had never felt so helpless in his life, and there was nothing he could do except hope that rest and his own inexperienced care would hasten the healing of her body. He was even denied the release of some of the cold, coiled hate that sat like a viper on his chest, for until Catherine was safe, taking revenge on Davalos had to be forgotten. But he promised himself silently that as soon as Catherine was out of danger and returned to Terre du Coeur, he and Blood Drinker would find Davalos and this time—this time—there would be no mercy, no second chance for Davalos!

Blood Drinker's entrance broke into his savage thoughts, and turning from Catherine, Jason joined him, both men sitting Indian fashion on the floor near the fireplace. Glancing from one lean, dark face to the other, in that moment it would have been difficult to choose which was the savage and which the gentleman. Both were dressed identically, their features similar. Both had the same high cheekbones and straight, slightly haughty noses, but there was no relation between them, unless one counted the summer years ago when they had solemnly cut their wrists and let their blood mingle, vowing to always remain blood brothers.

Green eyes stared into inscrutable black ones, and after a minute Jason said, "You're not going back to Terre du Coeur, are you?" It was more a statement than a question, and gravely Blood Drinker shook his head.

His voice full and melodious, he said, "It grieves me, brother, to disobey your wishes, but the Spaniard is a hidden snake armed with fangs of poison who must be destroyed. Even as we sit here, he is coiling and preparing to strike again."

"Goddamnit! I know that! I intend to go after him, but my wife must be safe first!" Jason's frustration was obvious in his low, angry words.

Blood Drinker nodded slowly. "What you say is true. And I would not deny you the vengeance your blood calls for—

yet you are hampered by the bond to the woman. While we wait, the snake can hide himself and to find him again will be no easy task."

Bleakly, Jason eyed him. "You intend to go after him—alone." Again it was a statement, not a question.

For the first time in days there was a glimmer of amusement in the Indian's black eyes.

"Would you, my brother, do less for me?" Blood Drinker asked quietly, and an unwilling glint of answering amusement entered Jason's green eyes.

No, Jason wouldn't do less. If their positions had been reversed, he would do exactly as Blood Drinker planned to do. His main objections to Blood Drinker's decision were that he, himself, badly, very badly, wanted to do the killing of Davalos, and the unvoiced anxiety that Davalos would somehow be able to harm Blood Drinker. The thought of his oldest friend being killed while doing something he, himself, should do and *ached* to do, left the bitter taste of acid in his mouth. He glanced at Catherine lying so still and pale in the bunk, and the compelling need to kill Davalos was so strong that for one tiny instant he actually considered leaving her here and going after Davalos with Blood Drinker. Yet, even as he thought it, he knew he could not and would not.

Realizing he could not sway Blood Drinker from his chosen scheme and resigned if not satisfied, Jason said, "I can't stop you, but it's going to be dangerous—very dangerous. He'll be expecting us to do something, and your task will be the harder because of it."

Shrugging carelessly, Blood Drinker retorted, "The danger only adds to the pleasure of success." Then suddenly the black eyes became fixed at a point behind Jason's left shoulder, and turning his head around in that direction, he discovered that Catherine had again awakened.

She was propped up on one elbow, her loosened, tangled black hair hanging over one shoulder, and her eyes were locked painfully with the Cherokee's. Jason, watching the pair of them closely, felt as if some silent message was being passed—as if Blood Drinker had guessed something that he had not.

Her eyes fever bright, Catherine stared mesmerized at Blood Drinker's impassive face, astonished by the sure knowledge—without a word being spoken, without one hint given—that the Indian *knew* exactly what had been done to her! An imperceptible nod confirmed her wild surmise, and through clenched teeth she hissed, "Kill Davalos, Blood Drinker! Kill him for *me!*"

Cast in the role of unwilling spectator, Jason, his eyes narrowed and hard, said dryly, "It appears I'm outvoted. At least we *all* agree. Davalos is to die."

Catherine shut her eyes and sank back weakly into the bunk, and quickly Jason stood up and strode to her side. Gently he brushed her hair from her white forehead and murmured teasingly, "What a bloodthirsty little wench you are. You should be resting and not eavesdropping on our conversation. Such things are not for your delicate ears."

The violet eyes flew open at his words, and with a touch of returning spirit she flashed, "If you don't want me to overhear you, pick another place—other than my bedroom."

After a caressing flick of one long finger against her cheek, Jason walked back to Blood Drinker, and together the men left the cabin. Watching the door shut behind them, Catherine muttered with a spurt of annoyance, "Well! They didn't have to take me literally."

Rapidly, Jason helped Blood Drinker saddle a horse and watched him as he efficiently packed all he would need in one slim bedroll, which was then strapped securely behind the saddle. Unemotionally, the two men shook hands. After looking long into Blood Drinker's face, Jason said finally, "Take care of yourself, my brother. On your return, if we are not here you know where to find us. I will wait two moons from now, and if you have not come back to Terre du Coeur by then, I shall come after you."

Soberly, Blood Drinker nodded, knowing full well that if

Davalos did not die by his hand, he surely would by Jason's. A second later Jason watched as horse and rider disappeared into the forest, and then with a curious reluctance he entered the cabin.

He glanced at Catherine, but she appeared to be sleeping; not wishing to wake her, he went back outside. There were a variety of tasks that had to be done, and in spite of no sleep the night before, Jason tackled the work with grim determination. By keeping busy he was able to hold back the tormenting thoughts that buzzed like enraged hornets at the edge of his mind. Proficiently, he double-checked the horses, frowning a moment at the skinned knees of the gelding Catherine had stolen, but the animal seemed well enough; and so he set about storing the saddles and other equipment in the tiny lean-to next to the side of the cabin. The water trough needed filling, and there had to be water for the cabin. Both tasks took a considerable amount of time, for they entailed several trips to the blue lake, and the sun was high overhead as he chopped down and dragged a few small trees to the back of the cabin and began to chop them into good-sized logs for the fireplace. He stacked some of the wood in the front of the lean-to and carried the remainder into the cabin. He would risk a fire at night.

Catherine was staring blankly at the ceiling when he came inside, his arms filled with wood, but she barely acknowledged his presence as he moved about the cabin, storing what food supplies he had brought with him in one of the two cupboards near the fireplace. She hadn't noticed them earlier, and as he continued to work, ignoring her, she began to watch him.

The stubble of black beard on his face gave him a decidedly raffish appearance, but Catherine judged that it did nothing to detract from his attractiveness. He looked tough and capable in his buckskins, and she was comforted by the knowledge that now she could indeed stop worrying—no matter what, Jason would see to it and would not allow anything else to harm her. Fair-minded, she didn't blame him solely for what had happened. The abduction could have happened without Jason having had any warning of Davalos's presence on his land. That it hadn't happened that way—that Jason had not seen fit to tell her *why* she wasn't to ride out that morning was what she held against him. Yet, she had already admitted to herself that she had been almost equally at fault. How much grief could have been spared them if only she had taken heed of his commands that morning! She gave a tiny sigh of deep regret, and hearing it Jason turned to look at her, his eyebrows rising quizzically.

"What was that all about?" he asked.

Twisting her head in his direction, she admitted truthfully, "Oh, I was just thinking that if I had stayed in the house that morning how differently things might have worked out."

He shot her a queer glance, one that seemed combined with anger as well as remorse, and his slowly spoken words caused her eyes to widen in surprise. "Don't blame yourself! I've cursed myself a thousand times a day since it happened for not telling you Davalos was in the area. I should have told you immediately. There is nothing I can ever do or say to make up for what you suffered because of my arrogant, misguided, overbearing actions."

Nearly speechless at such a handsome confession from him, Catherine faltered, "Are you—are you saying you're *sorry?*"

A crooked smile curving his mouth, he squatted down in front of her and taking one of her limp hands between his two warm ones murmured, "Is it so surprising for me to admit I made a terrible error in judgment? Or so shocking for me to apologize for the pain and discomfort you've had to bear because of my conceit?"

"Conceit?" Astonishment was plain in her tone.

He nodded. "It was exceedingly conceited of me to be so confident that I could foresee what Davalos would do."

Catherine stirred uncomfortably. This bearded stranger with the beguiling green eyes and soft voice confused her, and she was further dismayed by the warm, reckless surge of blood that raced through her body at his kindly impersonal touch. She had expected angry, violent recriminations and had been instinctively, mentally bracing herself for the fury she was certain would erupt. Jason, furious and enraged, she was halfway prepared for, but this quiet-spoken, almost gently apologetic man, threw her into confusion. Swallowing with difficulty, she stammered, "It—it—wasn't *all* your fault."

Jason bent his head and studied the finely shaped hand he held in his long brown fingers, unconsciously caressing the smooth skin. Suddenly he raised his head and stared into her shadowed eyes. The icy expression in the green eyes was uncomfortably familiar, as was the tight look about his mouth and, Catherine felt a pang of sorrow that she was infinitely more familiar with this cold look of anger than the almost tender expression of the moment before.

"No, it *wasn't* all my fault!" The words were spoken harshly, but at the stricken look that crossed Catherine's face, he sighed heavily and muttered, "This is no time for us to be arguing. Forget I just said that!" With a forced teasing glint in his eyes he added, "I prefer you to be up to lashing back at me when we fight! Right now, looking at you, I feel like I've just crushed a month-old kitten with my booted foot."

Pity was the last thing she wanted from him. Her badly bruised pride couldn't stand it, and she snapped, "Don't let *that* stop you!"

He grinned at her angry retort, his teeth very white in the black-stubbled face and almost tenderly crooned, *"Ma petite sorcière."*

She shot him a fulminating look, knowing he had called her a little witch, and then with a bewildering change of attitude she said plaintively, "I'm hungry."

His laughter rang out in the small room, and an instant later Catherine watched as with surprising efficiency he fixed a quick meal of thick chunks of bread, some dried meat, and a slice of hard, yellow cheese.

It was not perhaps the diet for an invalid, but Catherine ate it quickly despite finding it very dry. Having observed her determined attempt to get it down, silently Jason handed her a tin cup filled with clear, cool water, and thankfully she washed down the bread and meat with it. He was scowling when she finished, and taking the heavy white plate from her hand, he set it on the table and said, "I don't suppose that was the best meal for someone in your condition. Before it gets dark tonight I'd better set a few snares." Grinning down at her, he mocked, "I may not compare with the chef at Terre du Coeur, but I think I can manage to cook a fairly tasty stew or broth, provided we have fresh meat!"

Catherine was dependent upon him for everything, and she thought she would die of embarrassment that first night when despite her protests he gently sponged down her filthy and bruised body with warm water heated in a huge black kettle over the glowing coals of the fireplace. Her dirty, bloodstained garments were tossed in a pile in the corner, and as professionally as a nurse, he tore one of his clean linen shirts into rags for her more private use and gowned her in another one. The soft linen shirt felt blissfully gentle against her aching body, and, her face still flushed from his most intimate ministrations, she sank down gratefully once again on the bed.

Jason's face had been stony as he had tenderly washed the grime from her slender body. There had been no passion in his touch, and lovingly as a mother, he tucked the blanket of the freshly remade bed about her.

It was only after Jason had made Catherine as comfortable as he could that he asked her for details of her ordeal. But Catherine couldn't speak of it—not the rape, nor the man she had killed. At his gently probing question about her escape, she turned her head into the pillow and in a tight little voice said, "I don't want to talk of it."

Jason sighed and let her alone. Later would be soon enough to learn the exact extent of her calamity. All he wanted now was for her to rest and regain her health. He didn't want to think of the lost baby, and he was overwhelmingly thankful that at least they had Nicholas and that Nicholas was safe and loved at Terre du Coeur. For a moment he smiled—with a set of doting grandparents at his every beck and call, young Nicholas was going to be even more of a handful when they finally did return home.

True to his word, the next morning, having caught a young deer in one trap he had set the night before, he did fix a thick, tasty broth that Catherine found delicious. And like an eagle with only one newly hatched young in its nest, he watched her appetite closely, making sure she ate every mouthful put before her.

As much as it was possible under the circumstances, Jason cosseted Catherine greatly during the next few days. He scanned her face anxiously for any sign of fever or infection, and as none appeared, a little of the load of guilt and fear for her which he carried hidden inside, lightened.

He hardly ever left her alone. Those short times in which he absented himself were needed to replenish their water supply, to see to the welfare of the horses, and to check his traps for game. He would accomplish those tasks and return immediately to the cabin as if he feared some harm could come to her in his absence. And twice each day, once before dawn and again just at dusk, he left her long enough to carefully stalk the entrance of the valley to make certain there were no signs of Davalos. He was taking no chances on being surprised again. Most of his time, though, he spent lounging in the open doorway of the cabin, his gaze fixed unseeingly on the skyline where the tall, darkly green trees met the blueness of the clear skies. Whether he was bored or impatient, Catherine couldn't tell from his expressionless face. Definitely, he was not in the mood for any idle chatter, and kindly, if impersonally, he saw to her needs, but that was all. Despairingly, she longed for her son, for Terre du Coeur, and her mother, for Jason had told her she had arrived, but most of all for this enforced intimacy to be over.

They seldom spoke to one another, their conversation

consisting usually of Jason's curt questions of her wants and Catherine's tired, monosyllabic answers. Both knew there were subjects that needed desperately to be discussed between them, but like war-scarred veterans arming for one last terrible battle, they waited, Catherine gaining strength each day and Jason's face growing harder and bleaker as each night passed. On the third day, he let her get up from the bed awhile, but when she showed signs of becoming tired, he harshly ordered her back to the bunk. Inclined towards weepiness and not knowing why, she had immediately burst into tears, shocking both of them. Instantly, Jason's arms had closed around her shaking body, and seating himself on the bed, his broad shoulders propped against the wall, he had held her tenderly next to his own hard, warm body, his lips traveling urgently over her tear-stained face and his voice shaken and husky with emotion as he soothed, "There, my little love, don't cry so. I shouldn't have snapped at you, but you're such a stubborn, willful little cuss that sometimes you drive me mad. Hush now. I'm a brute, and when you are well you shall have any revenge you want."

Hiccuping back a sob, she had looked up into his face, catching such a look of tender remorse on his face that her mouth fell open with astonishment. It must be her illness, she finally decided. She was hallucinating, for surely Jason wasn't looking at her *lovingly?*

Dropping a light kiss on her enchanting nose, he murmured, "Better now?"

Suddenly, Catherine flashed him the wide, devastating smile that always left him feeling slightly lightheaded. Slowly, his mouth widened into an answering smile, as they both sat apparently entranced, staring at each other. Then after a quick, hard hug, he put her into the bed.

The next day, she was allowed up for a longer period of time, but it wasn't until the sixth day that he let her dress in the clean breeches and shirt he had packed for her. He still made her rest for part of the day, but that night after dinner, eaten for the first time together at the wooden table, he allowed her to join him as he stood in the doorway watching the setting sun. Instinctively, without conscious thought, his arm dropped around her slender shoulders, and he pulled her close to his side, lightly brushing a kiss across her forehead. Cuddled next to her husband's big body, she watched the red and then gold light fade from the sky, wishing with all her heart that somehow this moment of precious togetherness could last forever. But with the sun having gone down, the night grew chilly swiftly, and Jason, feeling the slight shiver of cold that shook her body, turned her gently back into the cabin.

With so many days spent in bed lately, she eyed the bunk with distaste, and pouring herself a cup of coffee from the pot that stayed warm at the edge of the leaping fire in the fireplace, she sat on one of the chairs and asked brightly, "It's too early for bed and as I'm much too awake to sleep—well, what shall we do?"

Jason sent her a mocking smile and realizing the implications of her innocent question, she blurted, "Oh, I didn't mean *that!* I—I just meant I wasn't sleepy, and I didn't want you to pack me off to bed like some tiresome child."

An unholy gleam of amusement in his green eyes, Jason teased, "I'd *never* put you to *bed* like a child."

She ignored the challenge and hastily swallowing a gulp of the hot coffee, promptly burned her tongue. Resentfully, as if it was his fault, she glared at him, and yet not really spoiling for a fight, she suddenly smiled and asked, "Tell me about this cabin. How did you know it was here?"

He poured himself a cup of coffee and took the chair opposite from her. Briefly, embellishing it slightly for her entertainment, he answered her question. They talked quietly for some minutes, then from out of nowhere, her elbows resting on the table, her chin propped in her hands, Catherine asked abruptly, "Jason, what did you find out there? I know it's not Cibola, but you did find something."

Startled in the act of raising his cup to his mouth, he

glanced at her sharply. Then with a curiously deliberate movement he set the cup on the table and parried, "How do you know that? I never said so."

An unladylike snort greeted his statement. "You found something. You must have! Davalos had to have some reason for deciding that you had the knowledge he wanted. And," she guessed shrewdly, "that gold and emerald band you wear holds some clue to what Davalos is after."

Slowly, Jason ran one hand along his bearded jaw and in a resigned tone of voice, said, "The band holds no clue. It was merely a trinket I desired." For no reason at all he added, "It's one of a pair or rather—it was." Ignoring Catherine's widened stare, he continued, "I had a friend once, named Phillip Nolan, and together we three, Nolan, Blood Drinker and myself, found a treasure—not a large one—and certainly not Cibola."

Like a child being promised an exciting bedtime story, Catherine breathed, "Go on."

A tired sigh escaped him, and leaning his head back against the wall Jason stared upwards, only he wasn't seeing the ceiling—he was seeing the hot, searing sun of the high plains of Comanche territory. And suddenly the memory of that time came back so strongly it was as if he were reliving it.

He could see again the tall, towering wall of the Palo Duro Canyon and feel again that shaft of amazement that had knifed through him when he had first laid eyes on that soaring pyramid that rose high above the canyon floor. He tried to convey the immensity of it all and instead lost himself in the telling of it—of his own emotions and Blood Drinker's; of Nolan's knowledge that it was indeed an Aztec temple they had found; and finally of the discovery of the hidden cavern and the taking of the twin gold bands.

He was so caught up in the tale that it was with reluctance that Jason came back to the present. And Catherine held spellbound by his words, probed, "Did you ever go back?"

Flatly, his face hard, Jason snarled, "No! Why, when I have a fortune of my own, should I loot for more?"

Dismayed at the tight anger that flared in his eyes, she stammered, "I—only asked! There's no need to bite off my head!"

"Forget it! It happened long ago, and whether or not Nolan ever went back I don't know—or care!" Cynically, he smiled at her rapt interest, reminding himself that she wasn't much older than he had been at the time they had stumbled across the canyon, and his expression softened.

Seeing that, Catherine asked cautiously, "Was it Nolan's gold band, do you think, that alerted Davalos?"

His eyes hard again, Jason retorted, "Probably. Davalos always was a avaricious creature. And Spain has never recovered from the shock of discovering that Texas is not another Mexico! I'm quite certain there are still a vast number who believe more Aztec cities of gold are out there, just waiting to be plundered!"

Catherine gave a deep sigh. "How I wish I were a man! It seems totally unfair for you to have all the adventures."

Jason grinned at the reproachful regret in her voice and gently teasing, asked, "Wasn't being abducted by me adventurous enough for you?"

Bitterly, unthinkingly the words burst from her. "It was horrible! How can you possibly compare something that ruined my whole life with the excitement of seeing what you have seen?"

Watching his face freeze, she could have wept with frustration at her own careless destruction of the fragile peace between them!

36

Time passed slowly after that night, and by the time they had been at the cabin nearly two weeks, Catherine was greatly recovered and growing more and more short-tempered at the enforced closeness. Determinedly she had brought up the subject of leaving, but Jason seemed in no hurry to return. Driven by exasperation she had demanded to know how much longer they would remain, and he had given her a lazy grin, inquiring lightly, "Why the apparent hurry? I won't eat you!"

Eyeing him suspiciously, she asked, "Won't everyone be worried about us?"

He hunched a shoulder indifferently. "A few days one way or the other won't make much difference to them."

"How cruel you are! I want my son, and Rachael must be mad with anxiety. If not for me at least for them—let us return soon!"

A curious glint in his green eyes, his lean cheeks and firm chin now covered by a short black beard, Jason pulled her down on him as he lay resting on the bunk. Pressed against his chest, her face inches from his, Catherine glared into the face of the man—the man, she knew with despair, whom she loved regardless of every cruel thing he had done to her. And anger, fed faithfully every day, was the only weapon she had against the powerful pull of attraction that existed between them. Some days though, she didn't have to deliberately whip up a fury against him—some days, like today, it was easy to hate him and his lazy arrogance.

"Let me go!" she spat, fruitlessly struggling against the iron-muscled hands that held her captive. He smiled indolently at her efforts and with studied insolence dragged her beneath him, his mouth moving with tantalizing confidence over her features.

"Why do you fight me so? I'm beginning to suspect you're fighting yourself as much as me, and I wonder why?"

Outraged and terrified at the closeness of his body, her frantic attempts to escape increased, but with ludicrous ease he stilled her thrashing body beneath his, certain that at any moment she would melt against him as she had done so many times in the past. Unfortunately, Catherine was finding it appallingly simple to resist him, for at his touch there was not the remembered thrill nor the wild uncontrollable heat of desire—only panic, sheer horrifying panic. Trapped in Jason's arms, he suddenly, in her mind, became Davalos—and all the debasement and wretchedness of that despicable rape came flooding back. Like an untamed savage animal, she fought, her eyes wide with terror, and in a voice filled with loathing and fear, she screamed, "Don't touch me! Oh God, please don't!"

Jason was at first skeptical of her attempt for freedom, but the undisguised look of fear in her wide, violet eyes and the tremor of sheer panic in her voice convinced him that something beyond her usual stubborn resistance was driving her to fight him. He let her go instantly and frowning watched as she scrambled away to nearly cower in the corner. She was shaking with delayed reaction, and clutching her arms across her breasts, she stared back at him. "I'm—I'm—

sorry," she stammered. "I—I—just don't want you to touch me that way."

Still frowning, a lock of black hair drooping rakishly over one eye, Jason glared at her, baffled. Heavily he said, "Catherine, this has got to stop! I have no intention of raping you every time I want you. Nor do I desire to live in a state of constant warfare! It's time you grew up and faced the fact that, like it or not, we're married—and I'll be damned if I'll live platonically with you! I don't know what maggot has got in your brain, but will you please tell me what I've done *this* time to arouse such antipathy? You've been in an odd state since before Davalos abducted you, and will you please, for the love of God, tell me why?"

Incoherently, she muttered, "The baby."

Sighing exasperatedly, he brushed back the unruly lock of hair and regarded her impatiently as she huddled like a beaten animal in the corner. Finally he asked, "The baby you lost?"

Dumbly, she nodded.

"What the hell does that have to do with the way you froze me out at Terre du Coeur?"

Angered at his obvious stupidity, she burst out, "I won't be your brood mare! Go find someone else to play that role! I heard what you said to Elizabeth that morning in Paris. You never wanted to marry me but, why in God's name, if all you really wanted was someone to present you with a string of brats, didn't you choose *her?*"

His eyebrows raising in haughty disdain, Jason replied with distaste, "Do you know what you're saying? I certainly do not, and I don't think you do, either!"

"I heard you, I tell you! You said I should do very well to bear your sons, but you had no further use for me beyond that."

Truthfully, for he had long since forgotten that scene with Elizabeth, he stated angrily, "I have no idea what you're talking about. *If* I ever said such a foolish and disgusting thing to your tart of a cousin, it was merely to discourage her from inflicting herself upon me!"

On her knees, her hands clenched into fists, her small breasts heaving with emotion, Catherine exclaimed, "I don't believe you! You were forced to marry me, and you, in your usually arrogant fashion, decided I would suit your purpose."

Jason's face was tight, and he growled thickly, "I think I should clear up one misapprehension you appear to be laboring under. *No one* could have forced me to marry you if I didn't *want* to. You could have been the daughter of the king of England, but if it hadn't been my own choice—my own free choice, I might add—nothing could have compelled me to marry you!" Jason was now as angry as Catherine, and breathing heavily, he bit out, "I would like to point out further that no one held a sword at my back. If you will remember, *I* suggested we marry! I could have spirited you back to England and made different arrangements just as easily."

At his words, a feeling of fierce joy swept through Catherine's body, but she had let the thought of that conversation with Elizabeth cloud her mind for so long that she could not easily release it. "You only wanted a brood mare. You said so to Elizabeth!"

A dangerous gleam in his green eyes, Jason spat, "Disabuse your mind of that notion!" Viciously he added, "If I had wanted a woman for that, I wouldn't have chosen a skinny-hipped slip of a flighty baggage! Elizabeth would have been much more fitted for that role—she has nice full hips if you will remember."

Hurt, Catherine taunted, "Then why, if I'm so unsuitable, did you marry me?"

His lips thinned with fury, Jason moved swiftly. Yanking Catherine to her feet and shaking her soundly, he shouted, "God knows! It certainly wasn't for your sweet temper!" Controlling his own temper with difficulty and responding as always to her nearness—to the desire to sweep her stubborn, slender body into his arms and to forget all the anguish and hurt they bedeviled each other with—he was suddenly aware of the real reason behind all his fury, and softly, with stupefaction, he said, "I love you, Catherine. I've loved you, I think, from that moment in France when we were in the coach traveling to Paris . . . I awoke, and there you were, staring out the window, planning God knows what, but I knew in that instant I wanted more from you than just your body—and I planned *then* to have more than just your body!"

Distrust fought with dawning, hopeful joy, and the bitter struggle was obvious in the confused, violet eyes that stared up at him. She had lived with the need to have him say those words for so long that just now they were nearly incomprehensible to her. Bewildered and uncertain, but wanting desperately to believe him, some of the tensions left her body, and she sagged against him. His next words, however, made her stiffen as he said slowly, wonderingly, "Maybe I didn't love you when I took your virginity, but I know before we left England that you were so deeply embedded in my bones that it was unthinkable that I leave you behind."

"Lust," she stated dully, convinced that that had been the only emotion that had driven him, but Jason shook his head. "I don't think so, my little love—but who knows what it is that first attracts a man to a certain woman? Maybe it was lust, I just don't know. But it didn't stay lust, not beyond that first time—no, I don't think even then that it was lust. If it had been, once I'd possessed you it would have been satisfied, and I would have had no further use for you—certainly I wouldn't have taken you to France!"

Jason was at a loss for further words, and finding himself in this queer situation, he was uncertain how best to proceed. The glib professions of love, used by him so frequently in the past to woo women into his arms and bed, dried up on him. Here, in this most important moment, he was as fumbling as a youth. Perhaps, because for the first time he meant those tender words of love, it made them hard to speak aloud, and Catherine's attitude was definitely not encouraging. She stood dumbly accusing in the circle of his arms, apparently unmoved by his revelations, and a bit impatiently he shook her. "Didn't you hear me? I love you, willful, stubborn brat that you are! *I love you!*"

It was his impatience that finally convinced her, for Jason would never be a humble lover, and with a great sigh of blissfulness, she leaned against him. Her throat tight with tears of happiness, she choked, "Oh, I love you, too! I thought I'd die sometimes if you didn't love me!"

A queer, tender smile on his face, he murmured, "Couldn't you tell, minx? A man doesn't act as I have if he doesn't love a woman. Why did I marry you? Why did I ship that damned horse Sheba to Terre du Coeur if it wasn't for you? And why was I eaten up with jealousy when I saw you with Adam? My God, kitten, if you only knew the torment you've put me through. Every time I thought that at last we were growing closer, you turned into a little wildcat and nearly clawed my eyes out!"

Catherine gave a watery chuckle and pressed closer as his mouth moved tenderly over the black curls until he found her ear and bit it gently. His breath warm on her neck, he muttered, "I can never think straight when you're in my arms. Didn't you know that every argument we ever had could have ended instantly, if all you would have done was melt in my arms as you are now?"

"That's not true! You were hateful to me at Belle Vista when I did," she accused reproachfully, a warm light in her violet eyes.

His muffled laugh, as he buried his head in her curls, made her shiver with anticipation. "Kitten, I was so wild with jealousy, I damned near strangled you then! You have to remember, I hadn't a clue where you were for over a year, and I was certain Adam was your lover."

"Adam?" Catherine questioned curiously, for while Jason had mentioned her mother's arrival, he had been reluctant to reveal Adam's arrival and the subsequent story of his parentage. Regretfully he pushed her away, but after seating himself on one of the chairs, he pulled her down onto his lap and gently explained that *her* brother was also his brother!

Astonishment made the smilingly slanted eyes go nearly round with wonder. But unable to brood in the face of her newly found happiness—and as it had happened long ago—she applied herself to the far more agreeable task of showing her extremely appreciative husband how much she loved him. Cradled in his strong arms, she found it easy to speak of her love and to tell why she had acted so outrageously those many times. It was a time of confession for both of them, but not every hurtful incident could be spoken of—Catherine couldn't bring herself to tell of Davalos. And so it was not a time of complete joy for her. Even as with greedy, eager hands she clutched these minutes in Jason's tender hold, she knew that as long as what had happened with Davalos lay unspoken between them, they would never know total, encompassing joy. Resting her head on Jason's broad chest, her hand played restlessly with the fringe of his buckskin shirt, and grimly she fought to say the words; but they were locked tightly in her chest, and no matter how hard she tried, they wouldn't come out.

Unaware of her struggle or of the reason behind it, Jason dropped a feather-light kiss on her bent head and murmured, "I do love you, Catherine. You are mine! You always have been—only you were too stubborn and willful to admit it. I knew it that night as I watched you dance before me in that red dress at the gypsy camp. I remember thinking at the time: little witch this is the last time you'll flaunt yourself before strangers. From now on, you'll dance only for me, and only I shall see those flawless charms you display so enticingly!" He added with an unwilling laugh, "I was jealous even then at the thought of your possible lovers."

A tremor went through her body and, a pathetic catch in her voice, she asked painfully, "Would it have mattered if I'd had other lovers?"

His arms tightened painfully, and thickly he muttered, "It

would have mattered like the devil! Once I possessed you, I never would have been able to stomach the thought of others having lain with you! How I suffered from the very idea of you and Adam being lovers! *Mon Dieu,* it doesn't bear thinking of!"

Pain spreading like a canker in her body, she lay in his arms savoring these minutes of bittersweet joy—they might be the last she would ever know with him. She attempted to tell Jason of Davalos's act, but the words refused to speak themselves. Then Jason's mouth sought hers, and for a second she responded with all the love and longing in her young, ardent body; but as happened before when Jason's kiss deepened and his hands began to caress her—shudderingly, horrifyingly it wasn't Jason any longer! The lips, so warm against hers, were Davalos's and the terror and loathing they evoked shook her body. Uncontrollably she began to shake, and with revulsion screaming in her every movement, she thrust herself violently out of Jason's embrace.

Startled, he stared at this white-faced, wild-eyed creature before him. "What's the matter?" he asked, puzzled, and made to reach for her.

Sick with dread, unable to control herself, she sobbed, "Oh, my God! Don't touch me! I can't bear it when you do!"

His face frozen with stunned disbelief, Jason demanded sharply, "What the hell are you talking about?"

A paralyzing iciness spreading with each passing instant, Catherine tried again to speak, but her tongue refused to obey. And patiently, like an adult with a particularly shy child, Jason asked, "What is it?"

Her lips trembled traitorously, but the words stuck until finally, bluntly, she said, "I can't tell you. Please don't ask me."

Narrowed eyes mercilessly raked her face. Softly, deliberately, he said, "Not good enough. You don't tell me you love me with one breath and the next push me away like I was going to rape you."

She flinched at the words, and suddenly impatient with her, Jason pulled her into his arms. It was hell for both of them when the sick loathing that again overcame her flashed damningly across her delicate features.

Tearing herself from his embrace, she flew to the door and like an animal at bay faced him, her violet eyes tortured. Driven to explain away the incredulous, dawning anger in his face she moaned, "Oh, Jason, it's not *you!* It's Davalos! He—he—" She was not able to say the words, but her meaning was unendurably clear.

All color fled Jason's face, leaving it shockingly white, his green eyes glittering in its paleness. Intent upon her own misery she didn't see the anguish in their depths—She only heard the iciness of his voice when he rasped, "He raped you?"

A tiny, tormented nod was her answer. She couldn't bear to look at his face, to see the disgust and censure that would be there. Braced against the door, she cried silently inside, unaware of the weary little monologue she muttered aloud.

"I fought him, but he tied my hands. It was like a nightmare, and I couldn't stop him. I wanted to die—he only did it once—thank God! I think I would have killed myself if he had touched me again."

She raised her head and stared into his eyes, flinching at what was revealed in their green depths. She saw the white-hot anger and fury in his face and completely and utterly misjudged the reasons for it. She couldn't know of the raw pain that clawed at his gut at the sudden sharp knowledge that she had been forced to endure such degradation because of him. Nor did she guess that at least some of the blazing anger was directed at himself for not having protected her better, for not having kept her safe from danger that morning at Terre du Coeur. He cursed his own stupidity for not suspecting what had happened and felt sick inside at the thought of what she had suffered—and all because he had lost control and snarled when he should have cajoled. His hands clenched into fists, thinking with painful clarity of

Davalos daring to take her against her will, and his mouth grew thin and ugly. Seeing it, Catherine could bear it no longer. "Oh, my God, Jason it wasn't my fault! I'm only a woman, and my hands were bound!" The words were flung at him angrily, and now weeping uncontrollably, she threw herself down on the bed.

At her actions, his own anger fled, and he was left with only a desire to comfort, to take her into his arms and reassure her of his love and to somehow erase the shame and pain of what had happened.

He reached out to touch her and Catherine, on the verge of hysteria, slapped his hand aside. Glaring at him, she spat, "Don't touch me! Don't ever touch me again! I hate you! Do you understand—*I hate you!*"

And at that moment Jason believed her, retreating instantly behind a cold exterior. It was an endless night for both of them. Catherine, lying dry-eyed after that first outburst of tears and staring at the wooden beams, wished the iciness that radiated from Jason would freeze her numb so she could no longer feel anything.

Wearily, she dragged herself from the bed the next morning and with dull eyes watched as Jason packed. "We're leaving for Terre du Coeur?" she asked flatly.

His own face stony, he said, "There is no reason for us to stay here now." And Catherine was certain her heart shriveled and died in that instant.

It didn't take Jason long to pack everything, and after saddling the horses they mounted silently and left the hidden valley, each mourning the loss of the bright happiness that had seemed theirs for that short while. There was no conversation between them, for they had nothing to say. And Jason, tortured by Catherine's expression, found relief of a sorts by dwelling upon Blood Drinker, his thoughts winging to the Cherokee as they made their way steadily towards Terre du Coeur.

Blood Drinker had no need of Jason's thoughts, for his own scheme for Davalos was rapidly approaching fruition.

He had found the Spaniard effortlessly, and his emotions hidden behind a blank façade, he had offered bluntly to guide Davalos to the gold the Spaniard coveted so desperately. Suspicious, Davalos had hesitated until Blood Drinker had said scornfully, "You will never learn of it from Jason. Nolan is dead, and I am the only one who can guide you to it."

His black eyes narrowed, Davalos asked, "Why will *you* show me?"

Blood Drinker raised one eyebrow and with apparent candor admitted, "You will plague Jason until you possess it. Jason does not desire thc gold, but if you will share it with me evenly, I will show you the way."

Hiding his elation and secretly laughing at Blood Drinker's stupidity, Davalos had agreed smoothly. The soldiers had never known the reasons behind their lieutenant's actions—they had merely followed orders assuming that Jason had committed some crime against Spain and that capturing his wife had been a stroke of luck that could be used to make him give himself up. They followed blindly wherever Davalos ordered them, but when he commanded them into Comanche territory, there were frightened mutters that grew with every mile they traveled—and their fears were not lessened by the fact that their guide was none other than an Indian himself!

Impassively, Blood Drinker led the way, never saying more than was necessary, until one night he motioned to Davalos that he wished to speak privately with him. Striding a little distance from the others, he asked, "Will you share it with them?" A vehement shake was his answer. "Absolutcly not! What would *they* do with it?" Davalos asked contemptuously.

Blood Drinker, his eyes curiously gentle, inquired, "How then do you propose to keep it from them if I lead you to it?"

"Is it near?"

A slow affirmative nod from Blood Drinker.

"Very near?" Again another nod. Davalos, his eyes gleaming with avarice demanded, "Show me!"

"The others?"

Davalos bit his lip. "If we leave while they're sleeping, you can show me, and then we can rejoin them before they become suspicious."

Blood Drinker nodded indifferently, and so while the others slept that night, they crept away. For two hours, they rode in silence until Davalos complained, "I thought you said it was near."

"It is," came the quiet reply. Another hour passed, and dawn was lurking just over the canyon's rim when Davalos snapped, "How much farther? We'll never make it back without the others knowing we've been away and up to something."

Appraisingly, Blood Drinker slowly looked up and down the canyon. In another hour the sun would be shining high overhead, and smiling faintly, he noted the dry, barren plain before them. They were miles from nowhere, deep in Comanche territory, and there was no doubt the sleeping Spanish soldiers left behind would find it impossible to track them through the canyons into which he had led Davalos. He stopped his horse suddenly and when Davalos drew abreast struck him with the butt of his rifle like a striking snake. The butt caught the unprepared man full on the chin, and like a crumpled sack of meal, he fell to the ground.

Smiling now, an ugly smile for such a handsome face, Blood Drinker worked swiftly, rapidly stripping Davalos of every vestige of clothing, and then methodically he laid the unconscious man, spread-eagled, on the sand and with ease bound his wrists and ankles with dampened rawhide. After driving four stakes, which he had carried concealed in his bedroll, deep into the canyon floor, he secured the rawhide to them. Satisfied, he watched the sun rise, blazing and hot over the canyon rim, and almost gently he nudged Davalos awake.

Davalos awoke, and fear widened his eyes as he stared up into the face of death—knowing it was death that stared back at him out of the Indian's eyes. Blood Drinker squatted down beside him, and almost lovingly he slowly cut away Davalos's eyelids, completely unmoved by the Spaniard's screams. The eyes, now unprotected, were left open to face the mercilessly burning sun, and from the shade of an overhanging cliff, Blood Drinker sat and waited patiently for Davalos to die. The man's pleas for mercy fell on deaf ears as stonily Blood Drinker waited silently for his self-imposed vigil to end.

The way he had chosen for the Spaniard to die was not pleasant, but then Davalos was not a pleasant person; and knowing the grief this man had caused, Blood Drinker was satisfied. This was the only way for him to die. By dawn on the third day, Davalos was barely alive, and Blood Drinker, his face revealing little, squatted once more by his side and said softly, "It is not good for a man to die without knowing why. I kill you this way not for Nolan's death, who Jason loved as a brother, but because you dared to strike at Jason, *my* brother. You see," he went on almost gently, "we cannot live knowing you are a blade at our backs, and I chose this way to punish you a little before death for the anguish you have caused my brother." The gentleness vanished, and if Davalos's eyes, long since eaten out by the desert creatures, could have seen, terror would have been reflected there as the Indian purposefully fingered the long, razor-sharp knife in his hand. His hand rested for an instant on Davalos's genitals, and then he said clearly, "For my brother's wife," and the blade slashed downwards, and Davalos's scream of agony echoed down the canyon. Without a backwards glance, Blood Drinker left the wreck of the dying man lying in a slowly widening pool of blood and mounted his horse and began the long trek home.

He arrived at the plantation well ahead of Jason's time limit of two months. Riding in just at dusk one evening, he stopped at the big house, meeting Jason on the steps—a Jason clean-shaven and once more dressed as a gentleman. They stared long and hard at each other, and Blood Drinker finally said quietly, "It is done."

Jason's hand tightened on his arm, and he asked after a moment, "Do you wish to tell Catherine yourself?"

The taste of what he had done strong in his mouth, Blood Drinker said, "No. Tell her only that he suffered for what he had done."

Thoughtfully, Jason watched the Indian ride off in the direction of the bunkhouse, and slowly he entered the house. The three men, Guy, Adam, and Jason, had been enjoying their after-dinner wine when word of Blood Drinker's return had been brought, but Jason did not rejoin them in the dining room; instead, he walked to the big salon where Catherine, dressed in a pretty gown of green silk, sat talking animatedly to her mother.

He appreciated the pleasing picture they made—Catherine, appearing to him more and more beautiful, and as untouchable as the moon, and Rachael, fairly blooming, her blue eyes sparkling with enjoyment. Smiling to himself he said as both women looked up at his entrance, "Nothing to alarm you. I merely wanted to say to Catherine that before you retire this evening, I'd like a word with you."

Mystified, Catherine inquired, "Is it important? Can you tell me now?"

He shook his head. "It'll keep," he said, and then left them. After his departure she found it hard to concentrate on her mother's light conversation, her thoughts constantly drifting to Jason. What could he have to say to her? Her enjoyment in the evening spoiled, she found herself on edge for no apparent reason, a frequent occurrence lately, and shortly she pleaded a headache and retired early.

After Jeanne had helped her undress, she dismissed the girl, and draping a soft, white, lacy robe over her nightdress, she sank down into a green velvet chair that was cozily placed before the fireplace and sat staring into the flames of the fire that now danced on the hearth. Outwardly all signs of her ordeal were healed and had vanished. But inside, Catherine was so deeply scarred that she thought she would never recover. The present situation between her and Jason was fraught with pain and disillusionment. They hid their hostility behind frigid politeness and acted out the roles of loving husband and wife so perfectly in front of their family that everyone was fooled—except Adam.

With dismay, he had noticed the imperceptible flinch Catherine gave at her husband's apparently devoted touch. And Jason couldn't disguise the flicker of bleakness in his eyes from Adam's discerning gaze. That something was very wrong between them, he was certain, and yet he was greatly puzzled, for if two people were ever deeply in love, it was these two.

Catherine could have told him that her husband's touch made her fearful and her flesh creep—not because he was Jason but because by some strange quirk in her nature he turned instantly into Davalos.

Her unhappy thought vanished as the connecting doors between their rooms flew open, and with a sudden feeling of dread she watched Jason walk to where she sat. He stared broodingly down at her and then threw himself into a chair. Bluntly he said, "Blood Drinker has returned. He says you're to know that Davalos suffered for his taking of you." Jason had to force himself to say those words, the bitterness they engendered like bile in his mouth.

She stared at him and was shocked to discover that the news of Davalos's death did not bring her the solace she thought it would. She was glad he was dead, but curiously it didn't move her the way she had assumed it would. There were too many obstacles between her and Jason, the living, to spare much time on the dead.

In the time since their return, she had determined that if she was to have any life at all, this aversion to Jason's touch had to be overcome—she had to put away what had happened and she had to somehow come to grips with herself over the betrayal she had felt at Jason's reactions when he had learned of the rape! But so far she had not been able to, and warily she glanced at him as he made no move to leave. The hard gleam in his eyes made her tighten up inside, and his next actions did nothing to relax the hard ball of fear that grew in her belly.

Casually, he removed his impeccably tied cravat and tossed it negligently on the floor. Next, his boots were thrown off, and all the while his gaze almost mockingly considered her reactions to his every movement. Like a lazy panther with a small rabbit, his green eyes glittered with savage enjoyment as Catherine fidgeted uneasily on the chair across from him. He was sprawled as he usually was in the chair. His long, muscular legs, encased this evening in buff-colored pantaloons, were stretched out towards the warmth of the fire, and his face rose darkly handsome above a white silk shirt. He was still wearing the emerald velvet jacket he had put on for dinner, and he was a vividly virile creature who made Catherine's heartbeat increase to such a degree of speed that she felt lightheaded with emotion.

Her nerves were like rawhide that had been tightened to the snapping point as Jason continued to stare at her in that coolly insolent fashion that belied the seething emotions hidden beneath the surface. His gaze shifted over her features, and his eyes with their brilliant shine suddenly shuttered as he looked down at the fire and hid whatever he was thinking. She didn't trust the small mirthless smile that quirked at the corners of his full mouth, and driven to break this silence that heralded the unpleasantness that was to come, Catherine, for something to say, blurted, "Do you think Rachael and Guy will ever find a solution? I feel so dreadful for them."

Jason glanced at her through lowered lids, silently applauding the unconsciously seductive picture she made. Her curling black hair formed a perfect foil for her as it lay shining on the virginal whiteness of the lacy robe that allowed tantalizing glimpses of the pale apricot flesh it covered. The deep green of the velvet chair provided a pleasing backdrop for her slender body, and Jason decided that, despite the faint mauve shadows beneath the clear violet eyes, she had never looked so adorable and lovely.

He let the silence spin out before he answered her question. Finally he said, "I don't think there is any easy solution for them. My mother is still very much alive and living in New Orleans. And divorce is still out of the question even at this late date. At least now, if they are circumspect, they can see one another, and *they* have the satisfaction of knowing their love is mutual."

She couldn't meet the accusation that flared in the green eyes, and following her own train of thought she asked impulsively, "Do you think that they're—they're—"

"Sleeping together?" he finished bluntly as the stammered words failed. Catherine nodded. Coolly her husband said, "I doubt it! They're not in their hot-blooded, passionate youth any longer. Don't misunderstand me. I'm certain there is nothing more Guy could wish for than to make Rachael his—in all ways that a man does possess his woman. But once, through a nasty set of circumstances, he very nearly brought her to the brink of disgrace, and I feel he loves her too much to risk another scandal. They are not," he added meaningfully, "beyond the age of producing another child. I know my father well enough to have a very good idea of how his mind works. Rachael will be adored for the rest of her life and given the utmost respect and courtesy he can bestow upon her outside of marriage. But for any physical union—I seriously doubt it."

Unable to stop the memory of remembered joy in Jason's embrace, Catherine said sadly, "How awful for them! It must be agony to love someone and yet be unable to do anything about it."

"Yes, isn't it?" Jason asked calmly.

Catherine's eyes flew to his, and the sudden unexpected tenderness that seemed to lurk in the emerald depths caused a quick flutter deep in her stomach. Swiftly dropping her gaze, she pleated her gown nervously, staring hard at her busy fingers while fear and delight rioted inside her.

Jason stood up abruptly and shrugged out of his jacket, draping it carelessly over the chair. Very deliberately he pulled his shirt free of his pantaloons and began to undo the pearl buttons. His eyes betraying a hard determination as well as tenderness, he said softly, "I think it's time we did something about the estrangement between us! I love you, and you are my wife. We cannot continue as we are. Call me vain if you wish, but I don't really believe those words that you hurled at me in the cabin. You don't hate me. Your eyes give you away every time you look at me—did you think I wouldn't notice?"

Catherine shot him a wary glance, but meeting his gaze and seeing the softened expression in his eyes, she looked quickly away.

"Catherine, I love you. Trust me and let me help. Together we can resolve any difficulties that lie in our path."

Compelled by the persuasive softness in his voice, she looked up again and uneasily eyed the masculine chest with the black mat of hair revealed by the open shirt, the sight of it recalling vividly memories she would rather forget. Unable to stand this cat-and-mouse game, she stood up suddenly and whipped around behind her chair. Facing him, her hands gripping the sides of the chair, she pleaded, "Jason, I'm not ready for this kind of confrontation. Please leave! I don't want to talk any more tonight."

He shook his head slowly, and the shirt joined the jacket. Smiling sadly he murmured, "No. You'll never be ready on your own. Every day that passes, you build what happened into something more terrible than the day before. Don't misunderstand me! I do not mean to belittle what occurred—but it did happen, and now it's over! Neither one of us can undo it, no matter how desperately we may wish. Davalos is dead. And now, I think we should bury what he did with him."

Her eyes huge, her mouth dry, nervously she avoided looking at the half-naked man before her. He stepped forward, and with a little inarticulate cry, she flew to the other side of the room; but Jason, only a step behind her, grasped her arms, and inexorably drew her against him. Stiff with fright and revulsion, she suffered his hold, but he did nothing more than keep her in his arms. His mouth brushing her sweet-smelling curls, he soothed, "Now see, there is nothing so awful about it. Just remember, my little darling, I love you, and you've led me down a stony path. At this stage I'm certainly not giving up!"

A tiny quiver of longing to believe those reassuring words trembled in her heart, and she asked anxiously, "Why were you so cold when I told you? You hated me then—I know it! You blamed me—and you'll never forget it!"

A warm finger slid down her cheek to her chin and raised her head until she was looking directly into his eyes. They were bleak, those emerald eyes, but there was anguish there too as Catherine's eyes locked with his.

"We *will* forget it!" Jason stated firmly. "And I'm growing weary of your habit of endowing me with the most despicable thoughts!" He shook her gently. "Catherine, I love you. My emotions when I realized what had been done to you were indescribable—but not *once* did I blame *you!* You must believe me! All I could feel just then was that *I* had failed you again. I wanted to murder Davalos for what he had done to you, and the only emotion you must have seen on my face was directed solely at him—*never you!*"

Gazing up at his pain-twisted face, she believed him. It was glaringly apparent he suffered as much as she. Instinctively, the need to comfort him drove her closer, her hand wandering gently over his face, and Jason caught it and pressed it to his lips. "Catherine, *never* think that I blamed you. I was sickened to think of your anguish and horror, for I know you, little love, and deep inside you're a wide-eyed innocent. I couldn't bear that you again had to suffer so much because of me." Bitterly he admitted, "It seems all I've ever done is cause you pain and misfortune."

Sighing with something bordering on joy, Catherine leaned her head onto his chest. "You've given me many happy moments, Jason. We have Nicholas," and with a catch in her throat she added, "and—and—we have each other—I think? If you truly mean what you say?"

His arms tightened painfully, and in a voice shaking with emotion he muttered, "Yes, I mean what I say! What happened doesn't matter. If you had been raped by the whole damned Spanish army, I couldn't love you less than I do. Forget Davalos!"

A tremor of uncertainty underlying her words, she said, "I want to. But something happens inside when—when you begin to make love to me. Suddenly all I can remember is Davalos."

His hands gently caressing, Jason murmured, "Trust me, little love."

She did trust him with all her heart, and so docilely she stood quietly in his embrace, torn between the hope that he could drive memory of Davalos away and the fear that he could not. Tenderly, like a woman with a hurt child, he laid her on the bed and slowly deliberately undressed her. When she lay naked and trembling before him, his pantaloons joined her gown on the floor, and his warm, powerful body slid onto the bed next to her.

Her body was stiff and unresponsive as he lay near her. She was certain she was damned always to feel this way, and wet tears slid from the corners of her eyes. Jason's mouth, as he gently kissed them away, was feather light, and every caress he made was filled with tenderness and restraint. His hands moved lightly over her body, demanding nothing, and his lips were soft as they kissed her face and nibbled at her ears and throat. Gradually, she felt the tightness in her limbs disappear, and with a will of their own, her arms fastened around his neck. Jason chuckled at their unexpected warmth around him and teased, "Are you making advances, my lady?"

Dimpling and feeling increasingly more confident, Catherine kissed him at the side of his mouth. "Yes, I am!" she admitted, surprising herself.

Jason smiled at her crookedly, and deliberately he kissed her full on the mouth. At first she lay passive, enjoying the feel of those firm warm lips, but as his ardor increased, the blind panic erupted, her overwhelming fear quickly communicating itself to him. Instantly, he ceased. Breathing heavily he lifted his head and nuzzled instead against her throat.

His voice muffled, he said, "Relax. Remember I'm not going to do anything you don't want. And most of all hold on to the thought that I'm your husband and I adore you!"

The panic subsided somewhat, but Catherine cried bleakly, "It'll never be the same. I can't help it."

For several seconds, Jason lay looking down into her tormented face. Then, as if he had made a decision, he moved deliberately, trapping her thighs beneath one bronzed leg. Grimly ignoring her start of uneasiness he kissed her deeply, hungrily. Sudden revulsion rising in her throat, she tried to escape but Jason, his face tightly drawn, would not release her but instead continued to explore her body, his hands lovingly moving over her satin skin and his lips forcing hers to open beneath his. That Catherine was filled with fear was apparent in her thrashing struggles, but he captured her flying hands and doggedly pretending that the woman in his arms wasn't stiff with fright, let his fierce desire for her thunder through his body. And then forgetful of the need for caution, his hands demanded she respond even as his mouth curved with passion, crushing her lips beneath his.

Exactly when it became obvious that all revulsion and loathing had vanished, leaving her body trembling not in fear but in hunger for him, she never remembered. There was only blind need, frightening in its intensity, to feel him deep within her. Her mouth blossomed under his, all her love and longing crying out as her body moved sensuously against his hard-muscled strength, and her hands sought to tell him without words of the fire that burned in her belly. A long shudder shook Jason's body at her touch, and with a groan of terrified relief mingling with his throbbing need of her, he slid gently between her thighs, his hands lifting her hips to crush her even closer to him as he drove deep into her welcoming flesh. Eagerly, all restraint and terror gone, she responded with every fiber of her being, and as they made love, filled with only the desire to please her beloved one, any lingering memories of Davalos were seared forever from her mind; and as before, there was only Jason—Jason arousing all those exquisite sensations as only he knew how; Jason, his big body molding her to him, making them as one, and Jason *loving* her!

Satiated and replete, she lay in his arms, her head upon his chest, and suddenly she hugged him tight, muttering fiercely, "Jason, I love you so much! Never stop loving me! I couldn't endure to go through everything again, all the torment and unhappiness."

Shifting his position slightly, he pushed her down into the silken pillows, and looming above her, he looked down at her tenderly, his fingers unconsciously twining themselves in the outspread black hair that tumbled carelessly over the pillows. "You are my life," he stated simply. "Without you, I have nothing. Catherine, my whole world is contained in your slender body and never fear I shall ever stop loving you." His emerald eyes swept over her with such a warm, melting flame of love in their depths that her very heart shook with love of this one man.

"I love you," he whispered against her mouth. "You're a willful, stubborn little minx that I can't live without!"

Bliss gleaming in her eyes, she teased, "Even if we fight!"

A thread of laughter in his voice, he retorted, "*If* we fight? My dearest love, it's a foregone conclusion we will fight! I'm still as overbearing and arrogant as I ever was, and *you,* my little hellcat, are still going to plague me unmercifully."

Suddenly, his face serious, he captured her head between his hands and staring intently into her eyes said quietly, "Whatever happens in the future, hold on to the thought that we are one—that we love each other. We're rather like two gladiators who have survived the arena. We both have scars hidden inside, but if we hold onto the knowledge that we *have* won, that by the grace of God we've found our love, then those scars will heal, and there will be only happiness ahead for us."

Her heart brimming with love, joy singing in her veins, Catherine's own arms tightened around him, knowing every word he spoke was true. They *had* won, and the love they had hidden and denied would now, like the bud of the magnolia tree, open and bloom under the hot Louisiana sun.

A Special Note

From

Shirlee Busbee

To You

Spring 1999

Dear Reader:

Well? How did you like GYPSY LADY? I sincerely hope that she gave you several hours of reading pleasure. Want to know how she came to be written?

GYPSY LADY was my first book. She was published over twenty years ago and was, undoubtedly, the hardest book for me to write. Why? Well, because I'd never really written anything before, much less a book, and quite frankly, I hadn't a clue about what I was doing!

I had, however, toyed with the idea of writing a book for a long time. "Toyed" being the operative word here. In fact, years before my writing career became a reality, Howard, my husband, had often teased me, saying that if I spent as much time writing as I did reading that our future would be made. Who knew he was such an oracle?

My love of reading came naturally—both sides of my family, even grandparents, were voracious readers. I mean we would read anything including the telephone book if nothing else was available. So what does all this have to do with GYPSY LADY? Everything. I firmly believe that you have to be a reader first; then, and only then, can you become a writer.

But I still probably wouldn't be a writer today and

GYPSY LADY never would have been written, if it hadn't been for Rosemary Rogers and a book she wrote entitled SWEET SAVAGE LOVE.

There is little doubt that SWEET SAVAGE LOVE was one of the books that launched the whole current Historical Romance genre and it was my fantastic luck that Rosemary just happened to work down the hall from me in the Solano County Parks Department. I was then working in the Solano County Assessor's Office as a draftsman and Rosie and I often crossed paths in the ladies' lounge. I would be in there sitting on the couch during my break, my nose buried in a book, an alarm clock nearby to let me know when my time was up, and she would come in to use the, ah, other facilities. She noticed what I was reading and we began to talk about books, what we liked, didn't like and the name of favorite authors. It turned out we liked several of the same authors and our long friendship began. Something as simple as making a friend in the ladies' lounge, was, you might say, the first step toward GYPSY LADY's presence in your hand right now.

Over the months the friendship between the two of us grew, but Rosie never breathed a word that she was writing, or even sending a manuscript to a publisher. I'll never forget the day she burst into the ladies' lounge, nearly quivering with excitement, and blurted out that she'd sold her first book, SWEET SAVAGE LOVE! I was as thrilled as she was. Well, maybe she was more thrilled, but I was sure excited for her.

Did I sit right down the next day and start GYPSY LADY? Nah. It was too much fun just watching what was happening to Rosie to even think about writing my own book. But the fact that someone I knew personally, a friend, had actually written a book and was going to have it published, made a big impression on me—and dropped the idea of writing, well, right in my lap.

My friend had written a book! And I could ask her anything about it that I wanted to. More importantly, she would answer my questions and share with me the joys and anguish that come with writing a book. In case you're wondering—GYPSY LADY was still a long way off from even being started. I hadn't even considered writing my own book yet.

By this time, Rosie was hard a work on her second novel, THE WILDEST HEART, the novel which led directly to my writing GYPSY LADY. And just as clearly as I remember the day she sold her first book, I can vividly recall the moment that my own writing career really began.

It was nearly twenty-five years ago and Rosie and I were on our coffee break. She was at her desk and I was seated across from her. We were talking about her problems with the second book when she said something like, "I've got them (the main characters) up on this damn mountain and I don't know how to get them off."

I looked at her in open-mouthed amazement. "What do you mean you don't know how to get them off—you're writing the book, aren't you?"

"Well, yeah, but I still don't know how to get them off the damn mountain."

My eyes narrowed. "Do you mean to tell me that you don't know where you're going with this story?"

"Not exactly," she said. "I know some of the things that ware going to happen, and I know it will have a happy ending . . ."

I sat back and stared at her. "Let me get this straight:

you don't know everything that's going to happen? You don't know exactly what's going to be in every chapter? You don't know the whole story?"

She made a face. "Something like that. I have an idea of the story; I know my characters; I know my setting and my history. I know how I want it to go and I know the general outline, but I don't know how to get them off the damn mountain!

"Uh, could we please forget about the damn mountain for a minute? I want to explore this idea of you not knowing every move, thought, word and action in the book," said I with lightbulbs going off in my brain.

"Okay, what do you want to know?" replied she.

"How do you write a book?"

She looked at me. I looked at her. Almost crossly she said, "I just told you: the characters, the setting, the history. Oh, and you start with an idea, like, what if there was this beautiful woman in search of the father she'd never known, and what if there was this handsome cowboy who did know her father and hated him, and what if . . ." She stopped and shrugged her shoulders. "And you go from there."

"And that's it? I asked incredulously, my voice rising.

"Yeah, in a nutshell, that's how you write a book."

I thought about it. Finally I said slowly, "You know, I think I could do that."

She fixed me with a stare. "Then do it!

And that, gentle reader, is how I came to write GYPSY LADY. Did I immediately sit down and diligently write twenty pages of wonderful, breathtaking prose a day? Nah. For one thing, I was lazy and writing was harder than I expected. For every word I wrote, I scribbled through ten. And if I read any passage aloud to Howard and he dared to criticize, I would snarl and sob and pout for hours. I mean who was he? For eighteen months I had four hand-written pages on a yellow legal pad. Speedy I was not, and am not to this day. Uh, I don't still sit for eighteen months with four pages—I have made progress in that department.

Every Monday when I would go in to work, the first words out of Rosie's mouth were, "How much did you get done this weekend?"

I would mumble some reply and slink away. I grew to dread Monday mornings. This went on for months. But gradually, I really did begin to write GYPSY LADY. And the pages in that yellow tablet began to add up, if a bit erratically. It was difficult work; remember, I was still working full time and I'd never seriously written anything before in my life. But I persevered. I had to. Rosie was nagging me to death, she never let up, and Howard was right behind her. I could never get away from those two who by turns encouraged, nagged and nipped at my heels until I finished the book.

The first draft of GYPSY LADY was entirely handwritten on yellow legal tablets. Part of the second draft was typewritten on a rented typewriter. (I didn't even have a typewriter in those days.) The third draft was also typewritten, but on a typewriter Rosie lent me. Wasn't she a great friend? Still is.

By this time, Rosie had quit her job and I was working out of her old office in the Solano County Parks Department. Rosie's former boss and now my boss, Dean Kastens, ("Daddy Dean" to Rosie and I) knew about my writing ambitions and he often joined the chorus with Rosie and Howard; how much had I gotten done? He was tickled to death by Rosie's success and he was delighted by the possi-

bility of lightning striking twice. It seemed like I was the only one who had doubts. A lot of them. There were days I loved Jason and Catherine; other times, I hated them.

When the third draft was about half done, Rosie literally ripped it out of the typewriter and sent it off to her editor at Avon Books, Nancy Coffee. I was terrified. I was elated. I was scared to death. A stranger was looking at my baby. Deciding on it . . .

While waiting for an answer from Avon, I worked half-heartedly on GYPSY LADY. Months went by. Nothing—either from New York or progress on my part. And then it happened. That magical Saturday that I went to the mailbox and there it was, a letter from Avon Books in New York.

I was all alone at home. Howard was visiting relatives; Rosie was off touring; Daddy Dean was away. No one else really knew about my so-called writing career.

For ages, I simply stared at the letter. Months and months of hard work, a lot dreams and a whole future were in that white envelope. Finally I opened it. AVON WANTED THE BOOK!

And I had no one to share the news with! I spent the rest of the afternoon just walking around the house, all by myself, a little half-hysterical giggle escaping from me every time I re-read the letter. I was going to be published!

Well, there you have it. That's how GYPSY LADY, Jason, Catherine, Davalos and Blood Drinker and all the others came into being.

Life's a funny thing, isn't it? Just think, what if Rosie and I hadn't both worked for Solano County at the same time and our offices hadn't been just down the hall from each other? What if I hadn't been a reader? What if Rosie hadn't noticed what I was reading and started talking to me about books? What if . . . well, you get the idea.

If you're interested in comparing how my writing has progressed over the years, then I would humbly suggest that you look for my next and fourteenth novel, FOR LOVE ALONE. It will be published by Warner Books in early 2000 and has as its hero and heroine, Lady Sophy Marlow and Viscount Ives Harrington.

When the main part of the book opens in London, 1809, Sophy is a widow, and having survived an ugly marriage to a wicked Marquis, has sworn that if she ever remarries, which is highly unlikely, that it will be FOR LOVE ALONE. Ives, of course, takes one look at her golden beauty and is immediately smitten. Sophy is not the least impressed by the tall gentleman with the devil-green eyes and brigand's smile.

Unlike Sophy, Ives is actively seeking the state of matrimony. Due to tragic circumstances, he is the last of his line and has newly come into the Harrington title. A wife—and more importantly, the heirs she will bear him—is of paramount importance. Having set his sights on Sophy, he is confident that half his goal is complete. Ha! He has underestimated the lady's aversion to wealthy, titled gentlemen.

Besides trying to seduce a spiritedly resistant Sophy into marriage, Ives, as charming a rascal as you are ever likely to meet, has the added burden of tracking down a dangerous spy known only as Le Renard, the Fox. Unbeknownst to them, Sophy and Ives both have more than a passing acquaintance with the deadly and dangerous Fox. And the Fox has plans for them . . .

If you'd like a romp through Regency era England, tag-

ging along as Sophy and Ives fall passionately in love, with the occasional murder thrown in, then I think you're going to thoroughly enjoy FOR LOVE ALONE. Look for it in early 2000.

In the meantime, happy reading and remember—you never know who you'll meet in the ladies' lounge!

All My Best—

Shirlee Busbee

More
Shirlee Busbee!

Please turn this page
for a
bonus excerpt from

For Love Alone

Coming February 2000
from Warner Books

The stealthy opening of Sophy's door brought Ives instantly awake and barely taking time to fling on a robe to cover his nakedness, he sprang across the room. The click of the closing of her door made him stiffen. Has someone entered her room?

The faint gleam of light peeping under his own door told him that such was not the case. Someone was standing in the hallway right outside her door. When the light receded, disappearing in the direction of the main staircase, a terrible fear struck him. Was he too late? Had someone already entered her room and ravished her while he had slept? Was it the *departure* of the villain which had roused him?

His face grim, Ives warily opened his door. The hall was in darkness except for the faint light drifting down the stairs. Concern for Sophy overrode his instinct to follow the predator and Ives slipped into Sophy's room, calling softly, "Sophy. Do not be fearful. It is Ives. I heard a sound. Is all well with you?"

Complete silence followed his words. He swiftly crossed

the room and discovered that Sophy's bed was empty. It had been *Sophy* descending the stairs?

Utterly perplexed and not a little worried, Ives stepped back into the hallway. What the devil was she up to? The unwelcome thought occurred to him that she might be meeting a lover. It did not seem likely and he banished the idea almost as quickly as it had occurred. So what was she doing?

The light from her candle had already vanished when he reached the top of the stairs. He hesitated a moment, debating the wisdom of his next actions. The lady already believed the worst of him and he doubted that if she discovered him creeping after her in the darkness that she would readily believe that he had only her best interests at heart.

Yet, he simply could not go back to bed and forget about her. There could be some innocent reason for her to be wandering about the house at this ungodly hour, although he could not imagine what it could be. But if this were the case, she could find herself in a rather vulnerable position if she were to stumble across one of the drunken revelers.

He grimaced. It seemed he had no choice but to follow her and make certain that she was unmolested. He suddenly grinned. Except, of course, by himself.

Ives had almost reached the bottom of the staircase, when the sound of a shot exploded throughout the house. Leaping down the remaining stairs, he hesitated, trying to get his bearings in the blackness and attempting to get a fix on the direction from which the shot had come.

As the seconds passed and he stood there indecisively, he heard the sounds of the first doors opening and the apprehensive exclamations from the floor above. He had to find Sophy.

After one false start, he caught a glimpse of the faint glow of light from beneath a door midway down one of the long halls which snaked through the house. Only moments ahead of the others, Ives plunged into the library to find a dazed

Sophy half-standing, half-leaning on a table . . . a very dead Edward nearby.

The ugly hole in the center of Edward's forehead and the pistol clasped in Sophy's hand told the story, but Ives could not credit his eyes. Sophy, a cold-blooded murderess? Even enraged, she would not shoot a defenseless man. He would stake his life on it.

He smiled grimly. It looked as if he were going to have to do just that.

The progress of the other inhabitants cautiously coming down the stairs could be heard and Ives knew he had only seconds in which to act. He snatched the pistol from Sophy's slack fingers and concealed it in the deep pocket of his brocade robe. Pulling Sophy into his arms, he shook her slightly and gave her a smart tap on the cheek.

"Look sharp, sweetheart! We haven't a moment to lose."

Sophy groaned and put a trembling hand to her head. She stared uncomprehendingly at Ives's dark, terse face. "My head," she muttered. "Someone struck me." She blinked. "Edward," she said weakly. "My uncle. He was here. Drunk."

"Well, he is dead now." Ives said coolly. "Very dead. And if we are to brush through the next few minutes without you ending up on the scaffold, you will have to trust me and hold your tongue. Let me do the talking."

"Dead!" Sophy gasped, horrified as she gazed up at him. "But he cannot be. He was alive, I tell you, only a moment ago. I spoke with him."

"Let me assure you, you will not be speaking with him again," he retorted bluntly, uneasily aware that they were on the point of being discovered. He swung her around and pointed to Edward's corpse. "As you can see, he is quite dead. And you were lying beside him with a pistol in your hand. Now keep your mouth shut and follow my lead."

At his words and the sight of her uncle's lifeless body, Sophy instinctively shrank back against Ives. "But what happened?" she asked, shocked and shaken by the scene. "Who shot him?" An urgent look on her lovely face, she said, "I swear to you that I did not!"

His features softened and he gripped her shoulders reassuringly. "I never doubted it, but I am afraid, dear Butterfly, that someone arranged it to look as though *you* had." It was the only explanation that fit the scene, Ives thought grimly. Sophy had a very bad enemy.

There was no time for further speech. The door to the library was slowly pushed wide and Allenton, followed by several of the other gentlemen garbed in hastily thrown on robes and carrying candles, came into the room.

"Good Gad!" exclaimed Allenton as he took in the scene before him. "Someone has shot poor Scoville. Murdered him."

All eyes went from Edward's body on the floor to Sophy firmly clasped in Ives's protective embrace. "It would appear so," Ives said levelly. "We heard the shot and found him like this."

"Together?" drawled Grimshaw, a decidedly unpleasant look on his saturnine features.

Ives nodded curtly.

"But how is it," inquired Lord Coleman, his eyes full of suspicion, "that you happened to arrive here ahead of all of us? Hmm?"

Ives grinned at him and dropped a kiss on the top of Sophy's head. "The lady," he said smoothly, "had a notion for a moonlit walk." His smile faded and his gaze boring into Coleman's, he added, "We were downstairs when we heard the shot."

"Now why," asked Grimshaw, "do I have trouble believing you? It is just a little *too* convenient."

Sophy felt Ives stiffen. "Are you implying that I am lying?" he asked very softly.

Realizing his danger, Grimshaw said hastily, "Ah, no. Not at all." He cleared his throat and muttered. "But what was Edward doing here? And who killed him? And why?"

"Do you think it might have been a robbery?" asked Allenton, glancing nervously around the room.

"It could have been," Ives answered slowly. "But we have no idea what occurred. We are as puzzled as the rest of you."

Etienne Marquette, who had entered the room a few minutes behind Henry Dewhurst, said bluntly, "*Mon Dieu!* But this is all very odd. Lady Marlowe's animosity toward Edward was well-known, *oui*? Recently many of us have heard her threaten to kill him. Even this very evening there was that scene between them in the saloon. If I had to choose someone who might have murdered Scoville, my first choice would be, I regret to say, Lady Marlowe." He bent a hard eye on Ives. "Are you saying that Lady Marlowe has been with you the *entire* evening? That she has never been out of your sight?"

Ives's clasp tightened around Sophy when he felt her stir in what he suspected was vehement denial. "Not only with me," he replied levelly, "but hardly out of my arms."

Still half-stunned from the blow to the head and the shock of finding her uncle dead, Sophy had been following the exchanges with difficulty, but she already realized precisely how precarious her position was. If Ives had not reached her first, the scene that would have greeted the others would have, without question, condemned her to the scaffold. She would have been found swaying over the body, a pistol clasped in her hand. All her protests of innocence, of being struck on the head would have been for naught. She would have hanged.

Gratitude for Ives's quick thinking flooded her, but as the minutes passed she perceived that in trying to shield her, he was digging a trap for both of them, a trap she greatly feared would be impossible to escape.

Henry Dewhurst approached them. A peculiar expression on his face, he demanded, "Are you telling us that you are *lovers*?"

Dewhurst's incredulity was obvious and Sophy felt a pang. In his fashion, Henry had been one of her most persistent suitors and she knew that Ives's words hurt him. But without placing herself in grave danger and publicly proving Ives a liar, she could not refute any of the tale. Miserably she stared back at Henry.

"Yes," she said in a low tone. "We are lovers."

She was aware that Ives relaxed slightly at her statement. Aware, too, that she had thoroughly ruined herself, she turned her head aside, unconsciously resting her cheek against Ives's broad chest. She supposed a ruined reputation was better than hanging, but at the moment that thought brought little comfort.

"Not only are we lovers," Ives added boldly, "but the lady and I intend to marry by special license, just as soon as I can arrange it."

Sophy gasped and stared up at him in horrified disbelief. Fierce protest hovered on her lips, but Ives silenced her by the simple expediency of kissing her, hard and possessively. Lifting his head a brief moment later, he surveyed the startled gentlemen and murmured, "Our walk in the moonlight was to celebrate our decision to marry."

"I see," said Dewhurst tightly, his hands clenched into fists at his side. "If that is the case, even under the sad circumstances, I suppose that congratulations are in order."

"Most unusual," murmured Lord Coleman, who looked unconvinced of Ives' story. "Man dead on the floor. No time to be thinking of congratulations."

Since Ives held firm to his story and no one could contradict his words, attention turned to Edward's corpse. Eyeing the body uncomfortably, Allenton said, "The authorities must be notified. Sir John Matthews is a neighbor and a Justice of the Peace. He will know what to do."

He looked around at the others and muttered, "It is difficult to believe, but someone murdered Scoville, perhaps even someone in this house. We are all going to be under suspicion and it is going to be damned unpleasant until the guilty party is discovered. In the meantime, I suggest that the library be locked and we retire to our rooms to dress. I shall wake the servants and have one of my men ride to Sir Matthews' place." He sighed. "There will be no more sleep tonight for any of us."

Everyone agreed and after watching him lock the door to the library, they all returned upstairs to their various rooms. Ives kept a firm hand on Sophy's arm and when she would have sought out her own room, he gently but inexorably guided her into his chamber.

The door had hardly shut behind him when Sophy freed herself from his grasp and swung round to face him. "I cannot marry you!" she said forcefully. "Whatever made you say such an outrageous thing?" She frowned. "I understand why you had to indicate that we were lovers, but to declare that we are to wed! Are you mad?"

Despite the lateness of the hour and the terrible events of the evening, Ives thought that she had never looked lovelier. It was true that there were purple smudges under her eyes and that her hair tumbled wildly in great golden masses around her shoulders, but those signs of her ordeal only increased her ethereal beauty. Her features were pale and strained, her eyes huge as she stared at him in the dancing candlelight, increasing her look of vulnerability, and Ives was suddenly aware that he would move heaven and earth to see that she never had to undergo a night like this one again. He would keep his little golden butterfly safe from harm, if she would allow it. And from the expression on her face, he thought ruefully, it appeared that he was going to have a fight on his hands.

Smiling faintly, he murmured, "It is true that I am mad, sweetheart. Quite mad. For you."

Sophy glared at him, her hands on her hips. "Will you cease? This is no time for frivolity. What are we going to do?"

"What we are going to do, dear heart," Ives said slowly and determinedly, "is precisely as I told the others. I will obtain a special license and we shall marry."

"I will not marry you!" Sophy said through gritted teeth, her earlier gratitude evaporating, the memory of his deplorable actions during the preceding several hours rushing to the fore.

The man had recently shown himself to be a drunken, hardened rake, every bit as bad as Simon had been. And he thought she would *marry* him?

It was common knowledge, too, that he was hanging out for a wife simply to sire an heir. She had been married once for that reason and she had no intention of finding herself in that deplorable position again.

Something else had been niggling at the back of her mind and scowling, she asked suddenly, "How was it that you arrived so timely to the library?"

Ives shrugged. "I heard you leave your room. I followed you."

"You followed me!" exclaimed Sophy, perplexed. "Why?"

"Because I was afraid that you might come to harm wandering about unprotected in a place filled with the wickedest sort of rascals I have ever seen in my life," he said simply.

Her confusion evident, Sophy stared back at him. "You were trying to guard me?" she asked incredulously.

A crooked smile curved his mouth and he bowed. "That was my intention."

Sophy put a hand to her head and turned away from him. "I do not understand you," she muttered. "I do not understand why you are here or why you act one way and then another, or why you came so readily to my defense this evening. I do not know why Edward was murdered, nor why someone tried to implicate me in his death. I do not understand any of it."

Gently Ives pulled her to him. His warm, broad body at her back, his arms wrapped around her and his chin resting on the top of her head, he murmured, "There is only one thing that you need to understand right now; I will never allow you to come to harm and I will never do anything to make you hate me." He hesitated and then asked, "Sophy, why were you in the library?"

Dully she returned, "Edward sent me a note requesting

that I meet him there." She frowned. "It was an odd sort of note, even for him. He threatened me and told me not to play any tricks, as if I would!"

"Was it signed?"

"Yes. I would recognize Edward's signature anywhere."

"Do you still have the note?" he asked sharply.

She nodded. "It is in my room, on my dressing table."

"When you go back to your room, I will go with you. I want that note."

She stiffened, and would have turned around except that Ives held her where she was. "Do you think the note is important?"

"Very. I suspect that the note was originally intended for the murderer and that he used it to lure you downstairs to the library."

Sophy shuddered. "Someone must hate me very much."

"I doubt it, sweetheart," Ives said softly. "I think our murderer was simply looking for a handy scapegoat and you were available. Your feelings about your uncle were well known. Do not worry about it. I have every intention of keeping you safe. And," he added in a hard voice, "finding out who put my future wife's very pretty neck in danger."

"*Must* we marry?" she asked in a small voice, the cold reality of her situation sinking in.

Ives sighed. "I am afraid so, sweetheart. Your reputation will be in shreds after tonight. You have a dangerous enemy, one I do not want you to fight alone. I can protect you far better as my wife than I can if you were merely a lady I am courting."

Sophy stirred in his embrace and turned around to stare up into his dark, brigand's face. "Have you been courting me?" she asked uncertainly.

He smiled gently. "To the best of my poor ability."

"I thought you wanted me to be your mistress," she returned honestly.

"That, too," he answered wryly. He looked at her, the expression in his devil-green eyes hard to define. "I was willing to take whatever you were willing to give me."

With trembling fingers she brushed the lapel of his robe. "Ives . . . my first marriage was . . . terrible . . . and when Simon died, I swore that no man would have me at his mercy again."

"You would rather hang than marry me?" he asked bluntly, his expression enigmatic.

Sophy hesitated. "I do not look forward to death any more eagerly than the next person, but there are some things that are *un*endurable."

"And you think that marriage to me will be unendurable?" he demanded.

She searched his craggy features, her heart aching. Just a few weeks ago she could have answered that question with a resounding no, but because of his actions lately, she was no longer certain. She had, after all, seen him half-drunk and ogling one of the housemaids just the other night.

When she remained silent, Ives's lips thinned and he said flatly, "You really do not have any choice. You *will* marry me, else you are ruined. And then there is the problem of Edward's death. And who murdered him. At the moment, my story has carried the day, but if you spurn me, if we do *not* marry, don't you think that suspicions are going to be roused? Don't you think that people are going to wonder why we did not marry?"

He shook her slightly. "You little fool! I am your only hope to brush through this ugly affair with a modicum of scandal. Marry me and I can protect you. Refuse me and you leave yourself vulnerable to the worst sort of ignominy."

Gently he added, "People might speculate that I lied and claimed you as my lover to protect you, but no one is going to believe that I married you for that reason."

Sophy looked away. Everything he said was true. Her reputation was in shreds, had already suffered simply by being in this very house, and there was no possibility that the inhabitants would keep their mouths shut about Ives's declaration that they were lovers. All of London would know. She shuddered.

It was not for herself that she dreaded the gossip and innuendo, but she knew her reputation would reflect on both Marcus and Phoebe. They had weathered the storm of Simon's death, but could they weather this one as well?

No matter what she did, marry Ives or not, there was going to be rampant speculation and gossip about Edward's death. But if she were to marry Ives, there was no denying that much of the scandal would be blunted. She would be the wife of an aristocrat with powerful connections, the bride of a man respected and liked by others of high rank and standing. Few people would be willing to risk offending Harrington and his family. As his wife, that mantle of protection would extend to her and also to Marcus and Phoebe. They would be safe from the majority of the stigma.

But if she and Ives parted, it would open the door for even more ugly gossip and scandal. And not just for herself. Marcus and Phoebe would share in the shame.

Indecision churning in her breast, she glanced up at him. "Why are you willing to marry me?" she asked quietly, her lovely eyes fixed intently on his face.

His mouth twisted. "Because I need a wife. An heir." He drew her nearer. "And quite frankly my dear, because I find you utterly irresistible."

He kissed her. A long, lingering kiss, his lips warm and compelling, his hunger kept fiercely leashed.

Sophy's mouth quivered beneath his. Uncertainty, fear and a stronger, more elemental emotion sprang cautiously to life within her. His embrace awakened all her old demons, Simon's brutal kisses never far from her mind. And yet with Ives, she was aware of a vast difference, a difference she could not explain nor understand, but it was there and it comforted her.

Conscious of the fragile ground on which she tread, Ives did not force the pace, but with great reluctance, eventually broke the embrace and set her slightly away from him. "Well?" he inquired coolly. "Are you going to marry me?"

Sophy stared blindly at the open V of his robe, trying to sort through all the contradictory emotions roiling within her. "Yes," she said finally. "I do not see that I have any choice in the matter."

"I could have wished for a trifle more enthusiasm," Ives said dryly, "but I see that I shall have to content myself with simply the knowledge that you have agreed to be my wife."

Turning away from her, he added briskly, "And now I suppose we should dress and see about meeting with the others."

In a daze, Sophy allowed Ives to escort her to her room and handed the note over to him. What had happened seemed almost incomprehensible to her and for several minutes after he had left, she stood in the center of the room unable to think clearly. Edward was dead. Murdered! And she was going to marry Ives Harrington!

His expression thoughtful, the Fox climbed the stairs with everyone else. His plan had not gone as he had envisioned and he was furious. Murderously so. The look he flashed Ives before he continued down the hall to his own room was *not* kind.

In the safety of his room, he shed the robe and quickly dressed, his mind on the events of the evening. Everything had gone just as he had planned until that bastard Harrington had shown up. Now, because of Harrington's unwarranted intervention, there was going to be a lot of speculation about who had murdered Edward. And why.

With Sophy out of the picture, he was still certain that there was nothing to point to him, but he was anxious—anxious and infuriated as he had not been since he had sent Harrington's relatives to the bottom of the sea. Though he had been scrupulously careful tonight, there was always the possibility that he had overlooked some tiny element, that someone had seen some trifling event, remembered something that would tie him to Edward's murder. His face darkened. Damn Harrington to hell!

Even now he experienced a thrill of fright as he remembered his shock at the sight of Ives's broad form appearing so unexpectedly out of the darkness. A few seconds earlier and he might have been caught. As it was, he had barely stepped out of the room and into the concealing shadows when Ives had come striding down the hall. He frowned. The fellow was proving to be quite meddlesome.

In the meantime, however, he had other things to think about. Such as providing another convenient scapegoat, even if only temporarily. Frowning, he paced his room, seeking some way to find an additional measure of safety from tonight's debacle. Recalling that someone mentioned robbery, a glimmer of an idea occurred to him. A robbery. He smiled. Of course. But his satisfaction vanished almost immediately and his smile faded as another thought came to him. A robbery would solve one difficulty, he admitted sourly, but there was still the infuriating problem of Harrington.

Harrington's advent onto the scene troubled him in many ways. He was suspicious of the men already and for him to have thwarted a perfect solution to a vexing problem . . .

Did the man know something? Suspect something? Had it just been luck that Harrington had followed Sophy? From his concealment in the shadows, it was obvious that Harrington had been trailing Sophy without her knowledge. Why? The obvious conclusion occurred to him and his lips thinned.

To think he had nearly been caught because of another man's lust for a woman. Not that Sophy was not worthy of such lust, but the Fox, while having all the normal appetites of the flesh in abundance, never let his carnal inclinations interfere with business. Taking care of Edward and framing Sophy had been strictly business.

Hearing the sounds of the others gathering in the hall, he put the problem from him for the time being and went out to join everybody else. It was several hours later before he had time to consider the problem of Ives Harrington and the possible implications of his marriage to Sophy.

Sir John Matthews had been there and gone after pronouncing his shock at the murder of Baron Scoville and promising to notify the proper authorities. The Fox had seen to it, that while he said nothing himself, that robbery was touted as a motive for the shameful deed. Edward's body had been removed.

The ladies, of course, now knew of the murder and were frightened by the news of such a terrible event occurring while they had slept such a short distance away. Lady Allenton had been aghast. Agnes Wetherby had fainted when the news of her lover's murder had been broken to her.

But none of that bothered the Fox. Beyond his concern about Ives Harrington, the whereabouts of Edward's note had taken on paramount importance in his mind and he cursed Harrington again. If all had gone well, he had planned during the ensuing furor to nip up to Sophy's room and retrieve Edward's note, but now . . . His lips thinned into a rigid, ugly line. Now that damned note might prove dangerous to him.

A thought occurred to him and he relaxed slightly. The existence of the note, he suddenly realized, was probably not going to come to light. Because of Harrington, Sophy was safely out of it and it was highly unlikely that she would admit to having a reason to meet Edward in the library. But Sophy knew of the note. And no doubt, Harrington.

All his problems, he thought grimly, seemed to go back to Harrington. He did not trust the man; did not trust his sudden and inexplicable conversion to vice-prone pursuits; did not trust his instant friendship with Meade; and especially did not trust him since Meade seemed to have conveniently come across such interesting news, if Meade's drunken hints could be believed. In the meantime, the Fox had much to consider and plan.

* * *

Ives, too, had much to plan and consider, not the least of which were his nuptials. After Sir Matthews had given his pronouncements and departed, Ives climbed the stairs and knocked on Sophy's door.

When he entered her room, Sophy was dressed and packed, her valise resting on the bed. Her features pale and set, she asked, "May we leave?"

Ives nodded. "Yes. I have given Sir Matthews our direction and he saw no point in our remaining here. I believe that several other of the guests are going to be leaving shortly also."

Sophy glanced away. "And our marriage. You are still determined upon it?"

He approached her and taking one of her cold little hands in his, dropped a warm kiss upon it. "I was never more determined about anything in my life, sweetheart."

She flashed him a look. "You may come to regret it," she warned. "I am not a malleable creature, nor one noted for her docility."

Ives grinned, his devil-green eyes dancing. "Which should only make our life together most interesting, don't you agree?"